Artésque

Artésque

The Search of Dústiny
Books IV, V, VI

T.D. Cannon

Copyright © 2020 by T.D. Cannon.

ISBN: Softcover   978-1-9845-8370-3
          eBook   978-1-9845-8369-7

All rights reserved. No part of this book may be reproduced or transmitted in any form or by any means, electronic or mechanical, including photocopying, recording, or by any information storage and retrieval system, without permission in writing from the copyright owner.

This is a work of fiction. Names, characters, places and incidents either are the product of the author's imagination or are used fictitiously, and any resemblance to any actual persons, living or dead, events, or locales is entirely coincidental.

Any people depicted in stock imagery provided by Getty Images are models, and such images are being used for illustrative purposes only.
Certain stock imagery © Getty Images.

Print information available on the last page.

Rev. date: 06/16/2020

To order additional copies of this book, contact:
Xlibris
1-888-795-4274
www.Xlibris.com
Orders@Xlibris.com
815296

Contents

Artésque Nervál ix
Prologue xiii

Chapter 1	Lóftor Vestá..	1
Chapter 2	Jartál	8
Chapter 3	Book & Quill	18
Chapter 4	Enclosed inside	26
Chapter 5	Mightier than the quill..	36
Chapter 6	Penitence	52
Chapter 7	Conflict Card	59
Chapter 8	Blooming	66
Chapter 9	Repast	88
Chapter 10	A warming bed	113
Chapter 11	Feathering the Fur...	122
Chapter 12	By the breeze	129
Chapter 13	Turning Evermore	157
Chapter 14	HefterÁll	171
Chapter 15	Always The Know-it-all...	181
Chapter 16	Assignment..	186
Chapter 17	Of metal and Spite	200
Chapter 18	Eñchar	211
Chapter 19	Shields	227
Chapter 20	Swords	237
Chapter 21	Of Cuts & Roses	247
Chapter 22	Season's End	263

- Part Two - 269

Chapter 1	Castle Over	282
Chapter 2	Turning and Yearning	290

Chapter 3	Nightly	298
Chapter 4	First Light	303
Chapter 5	Shelved	310
Chapter 6	Stay a little	324
Chapter 7	By & By	329
Chapter 8	Of Clouds & Feathers	335
Chapter 9	Nesting For The Sun	347
Chapter 10	Once More	357
Chapter 11	Just Don't Think About	369
Chapter 12	Dirt, Rocks, and Trains	373
Chapter 13	Pains On Track	382
Chapter 14	I've Seen This Chapter Before	394
Chapter 15	Soothing Melody	406
Chapter 16	Agility	416
Chapter 17	Sword and Feather	430
Chapter 18	Home is what you make it	442
Chapter 19	Hofáfor	455
Chapter 20	A New Day	476
Chapter 21	The Irons Burn Hot	484
Chapter 22	Merely Too	495
Chapter 23	Nightly Crew	507
Chapter 24	Hop, Skip, & Jump	514
Chapter 25	The Depths	526
Chapter 26	Fly Fly Fly	539
Chapter 27	Final Acts	553

- Part Three - 563

Chapter 1	Wounds Heal Slowly	566
Chapter 2	Paranoia	572
Chapter 3	Before the Calm	578
Chapter 4	Fields of Envy	588
Chapter 5	Evanescent	595
Chapter 6	Capital Matters	605
Chapter 7	Smithy	614
Chapter 8	Lasso	631
Chapter 9	Messenger	642
Chapter 10	Medicine Man	651

Chapter 11	Resistance	660
Chapter 12	Faith	681
Chapter 13	Twilight	692
Chapter 14	Simplicity	701
Chapter 15	Homecoming	705
Chapter 16	Rounding Home base	723
Chapter 17	Capital Training	735
Chapter 18	Step One	752
Chapter 19	Can't Skip the Small Stuff	762
Chapter 20	Winding Road	768
Chapter 21	Thicket	787
Chapter 22	Bunker Down	795

7

Artésque Nervál

The following text, like the cover, entails a form of language known as Nervál. All words in the form of Nervál shall be italicized, as well as phonetically spoken/read. Taking a look at Nervál (N-er-v-all), the use of accent marks in the language is to help the readers give emphasis to a certain letter's sound.

The definition of Nervál means: the common language spoken by a certain group of people; before the use of New - Tongue. There are three types of Nervál that will appear in the following text; although different in meaning, they remain phonetically spelt. Not all words are followed by their definitions; nor are all words simply one word. For example, the Únoff (Un-off) word Frendéloft (friend-day-loft) describes a feeling followed by an action; which is common in Únoff Nervál.

Here are a few, more important words to understand:
Artésque – (Art-s-k) OR (Art-s-q)
Únoff – (Un-off)
Dẃoff – (Do-wa-off)
Flóff – (Flo-Off)
Drágeff – (Drag-F)
fróx – (Fur-ox)
Márjx – (M-are-jex)

For more information on the book's symbols, meanings, languages, or world. Please visit the author run website: Search up "The Series Artesque" hosted on wiki fandom.

The cycle is a run-on sentence, an infuriating mishap, devoid of pause, or rest, one that only those who notice, care enough to get upset about; to others, it is a mindless loop, an unavoidable repetition that is blindly glossed over without a care. Many within the town, and even Reynard have accepted the quick days, the sudden starts and stops hardly messing with their minds. For Preston however, it is the absolute loss of stability, a maddening concept to think about while lying in bed or sitting at a table.

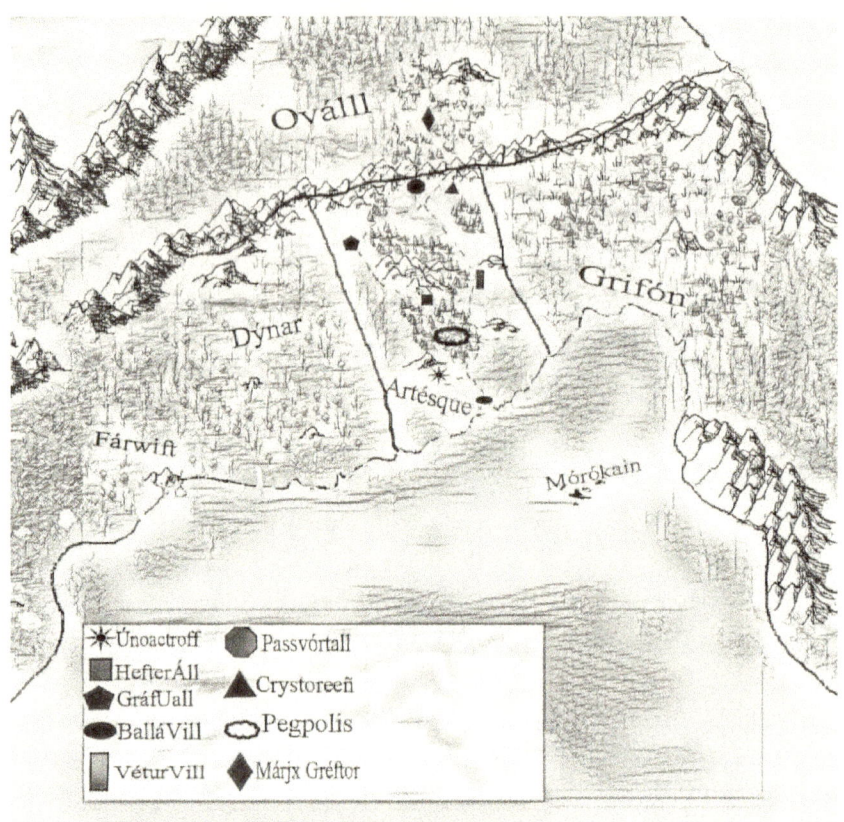

Gallery: To find more please visit the **"Artesque Series"** hosted on **fandom**.

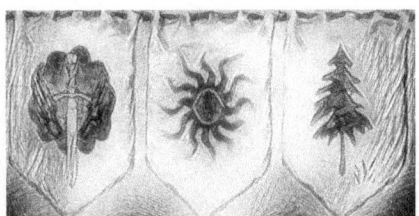

Flags of The Three

Gloftór

Flags of known holds

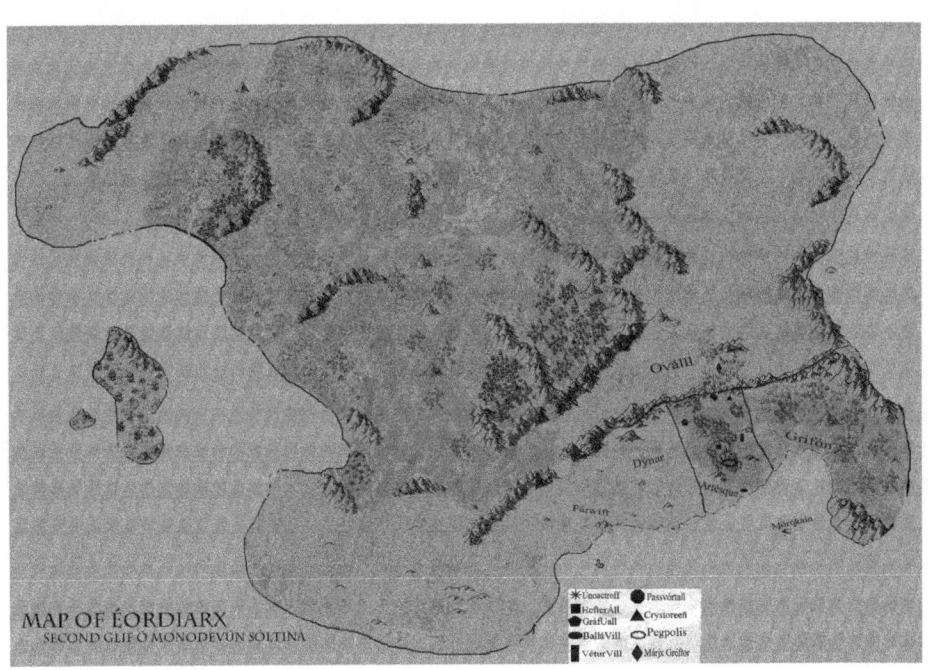

Prologue

The cool air is crisp, unlike the almost freezing seat Preston has found himself almost molded into; the blanket has served its purpose, though the sores on his back force the man to fidget uncomfortably against the hardwood of the carriage. Each movement drawing a quick gust of air under the blanket, which both irritates and frustrates Preston further.

Traveling by morning is hard but traveling in the ever-fading light of a lengthy day is far worse. Even still, a piece of Preston is happy to be leaving the Capital behind him, *VéturVill* may be boring, at least it is safe.

Despite this happy thought, Preston has found it difficult to reach some level of rest within the carriage. Reynard has curled himself up in the other blanket, though even he does not rest as he merely stares to the window.

Clover too has continued to linger in this world, no book to her hand as she continues to glance over to Reynard, an action that has drawn a bit of annoyance from the small fox-boy at times.

Emotions were high when they set out, though within the last hour or so of the chilly weather, conversations have ended, and all forced smiles or pleasant comments have also ceased. The cold does well to soothe the pain; its chill does little to welcome the trio home.

Preston has found some serenity, mainly by forcing his eyes closed, and rubbing a finger to the amulet still around his neck. The magic within the amulet is warm, and as Preston continues to coax it out with his ever-darkening mind the feeling of its smoothing nature becomes a necessity.

Even still, he continues to linger, the weight of everything proving too much to simply ignore, despite the magical amulet around his neck.

The dull, almost glazed over expression on Preston has not gone missed as Clover focus on it as she has for some time now. Yet, it is only within the last few moments that Preston truly takes notice to the stare as he shifts his hand from the amulet. Catching the woman's gaze however does not spark a conversation to the carriage, as the silence within it proves too hard to break.

Instead, Preston merely turns his head to the world outside. Sóltina's sun has continued to linger just above the horizon, though the mountains that line *VéturVill's* furthest side leave the road cold to its direct light. The fields of brown and death however do not go unseen as Preston merely stares to them, the sound and rock of the carriage being the only true sight of movement within the ocean of withered life around them.

"We should arrive in *VéturVill* quite soon."

Clover's voice yields no reply from Reynard or Preston as they merely nod to the words. Despite this, Clover persists as her attention turns to the fox-boy beside her. "Reynard are you feeling well?"

"I feel cold."

"Well..." Clover's magic sparks up as the blanket begins to wrap around the fox-boy again. "You need to use the blanket, not just lay on it."

"I know."

The simple reply draws a sigh from Clover as she moves a hand to his forehead. Though her action prompts Reynard away as he bats a little to her cold hand. "I feel okay, Clover."

"Alright, alright." Clover sighs. "When we get home, draw a warm bath. Do not worry about how long you soak, just come to me when you are done."

"Okay."

"Good." Clover passes a sweet smile though she turns away with another slight sigh as she folds her hands to her lap.

Slowly coming out of his stare outside Preston shifts an eye to the woman's hands as he holds out the blanket to her without a word. Clover simply waves it off as she speaks up. "We are almost home. Preston you should stay warm."

The words only draw Preston's hand back as he tugs the blanket to legs again, his eyes settling back to the world of winter outstretched before him. A few of the smaller buildings near the outskirts of town have come to Preston's sight, though he hardly glances to them as he just stares to the snowbanks lining the main street.

The carriage does not go silent again as Reynard speaks up, his sheepish tone coming to Preston. "Does your back hurt?"

Peeling his eyes away from the window Preston shakes his head, his tongue licking to the faint cracks in his lips as he speaks up for the first since they left. "I'm fine."

As the sights outside continue to get more and more familiar Reynard seems to find his voice as he glances to Clover. "S-sorry for not listening to you."

"It is alright." Clover holds a smile to the words as she nods, her eyes coming to the bandage on Reynard's leg as she continues. "We all should have stayed in the room."

Her words do not stop Reynard as he lowers his head. "Sorry I got you hurt, Preston."

Clover again chimes in for the quiet man as she scoots closer to the fox-boy. "It was not your fault, Reynard." She turns an eye to Preston as she continues. "And I am sure Preston has no regrets."

Looking over the fox-boy's downtrodden expression Preston nods, his right-hand brushing against the amulet as his chest as he speaks up. "I'm fine, just a few cuts, Rey, nothing to worry about."

The words do little to help return the boyish, carefree attitude to Reynard, though a voice from outside takes everyone's attention as the carriage beings to slow. "Miss Vine, we near your home."

Tilting her head towards the window near Reynard Clover calls out. "Thank you." Like usual, her comment sparks a motion as she now bends a little in her chair to pick up the two satchels at her feet. Though unlike normal, the quick pace lingers as she brushes a hand to Reynard's head. "If you wish to rest a little before a bath take the blanket with you, but I want you to get clean before you got to sleep, okay?"

Reynard simply nods as his hold to the heavy blanket loosens. "You can take it."

Clover's magic comes over the blanket as she moves it to the free seat next to Preston, her magic quickly folding it as she continues to say something to Reynard.

Preston however turns his gaze away as he brings his hand to the bag at his feet, though just as soon as he moves the blanket to bring the bag up Clover's magic takes holds. The colder air rushing in as blanket begins to bend in Clover's spell yet Preston merely sighs as he moves the satchel over his shoulder.

The carriage's speed continues to fall as the dull red door of the library comes into sight. A brief moment passes before the carriage comes to a complete stop, as it does Preston curls his legs a little more to himself, allowing Clover and Reynard to stand up first.

As the door opens to the woman's magic Clover steps out, turning back to where Reynard stands as she helps him down the stairs.

Preston rises, copying the sluggish pace of the boy as he too now starts down the stairs, Clover turning an eye to his lumbering movements.

Preston of course pays little mind to the woman's cautious stare as he instead turns his eyes to the world around him. The air outside is cool and dry, the clouds above still thick in their brilliant white color. All around the main street the various planters in front of the houses are empty, and the snowbanks before each door the only things truly yielding any color to the sleepy town. Yet the depressing colors of dull wood and snow are hardily the welcome the trio needed.

This of course does not stop Clover nor Reynard from going about their normal routine as the fox-boy dips inside the dark house, Clover now coming to Preston's side as the carriage pulls away behind her. "Coming inside?"

Glancing back to the carriage Preston nods, taking a step into the library as he tugs to the satchel on his arm.

The house, to no surprise is cold as Clover comes in behind the man, her hands sparking up to balls of magic as he moves them into the house.

The tap of Reynard's claws now echoes a little on the wood as Preston closes the door.

"I will get the heater working, but I think the stones will need a charge soon."

Turning her head to the stairs Clover nod. "Alright... be careful of the flame." A sigh rolls from Clover as no reply comes from Reynard. Though, the tap of his feet to the floor ring out as the hallway begins to glow, an orange color coming to the ceiling of it as the heater cracks up.

Spotting the color upstairs Clover again calls out. "Reynard make sure you get clean; I will have something ready to eat in little."

"Okay."

The reply draws another sigh from Clover as the woman merely moves back to the table, placing both her bag and Reynard's to the wood.

Looking them over Preston takes a step forward, his hand coming to them only to be batted away as Clover turns to him. "Do not worry about this." She gives a simple smile as she nods. "Just go upstairs and rest, I will get you both before too long."

Preston glances back to the two satchels though he nods all the same. "You um... you want help with-..."

"No." Clover shakes her head. "Thank you, but... Preston you need to rest."

The words draw a nod from Preston as he forces a smile. "Right." At the words he turns his eyes to the stairs, his left arm coming to the bag at his side as he slowly pulls the satchel from him.

The man's somewhat sedated walk holds Clover's eyes, though she nonetheless turns away as her mind kicks into gear with what needs to be done. The sound of her hooves starting towards the kitchen does bring Preston's eyes back downstairs, though only for a moment as he instead continues up. However, as he reaches the top of the stairs he does not start immediately to his room. Instead, he blinks to the fox-boy now sitting against the wall, his tiny legs curled up to his chest and his head buried to them. Sighting this, Preston drops his bag to the floor in front of his door as he begins to walk towards the fox-boy.

The sound of his approach prompts Reynard's head up, his ears remain flat as he turns a sad gaze to the man. "S-sorry about getting you hurt, Preston."

Preston merely blinks to the comment, his expression remaining dull though the lingering depression of the day only growing as he looks over Reynard's tearful expression. Unfortunately, the emotion is drained from

Preston at the behest of the amulet around his neck, he nonetheless feels the impact of the boyish guilt, even if his face does not show it.

Taking a step towards Reynard, Preston takes a seat across from the young *fróx*, his back pressing against the wall, despite the obvious discomfort it brings him. His actions draw Reynard gaze as Preston nods to him. "It wasn't your fault."

Reynard nods though his eyes just fall back to the floor between them as he curls up more, his tail wrapping to his legs. "Why did she do it?"

Preston mows the question over as he shakes his head. "I don't know."

Reynard sniffs at the words as he glances back to Preston. "D-do you think she will come back?"

Again, Preston shakes his head. "I don't know... but, I don't think so."

"Wúna... Wúna was her sister."

"Yea."

Reynard shakes his head. "Clover always said the *devún* were kind... why would she try hurt her sister like that?"

A simple shrug comes from Preston, unsure of how best to answer the question. "I don't know."

Reynard turns his eyes up again as he sniffles. "You don't know a lot, do you?"

A faint smile comes to Preston's face he draws his own legs back to him, his hands coming to his knees as he shakes his head. "Yea... you're right, I don't know a lot about this."

Reynard fixates on the floor for a moment, though he forces his gaze back to Preston as he speaks up. "Does it scare you?"

"Yea." Preston holds his smile as a faint chuckle rolls from him. "It scares me a lot."

Reynard's eyes fall again as he goes silent, though Preston continues as he nods to him. "But I... I don't know... I just trust them, Nyota, Clover. I trust that what happened is over."

"We should have listened to her, we should have stayed in the room."

"Maybe..." Preston lowers his head as he meets Reynard's gaze. "But that doesn't matter now, yea? What matters now is feeling better."

Reynard cocks a half smirk, though his expression remains bleak as he replies. "I guess."

"Yea?" Preston holds his own smile as he nods to the boy across from him. "Besides we got other things to worry about, like Clover's cooking, yea?"

The smirk to Reynard's face holds as he nods, though his melancholy tone remains as he replies. "Yea."

Preston takes a breath. "Everyone's okay, and you can't blame yourself for what someone else did, you know."

"I know." Reynard's head falls a little more to his hands as goes quiet.

Preston sits across from, his own silence coming in as he merely finds himself unable to come with something to say.

Though, Reynard brings his voice back as he glances to the man. "Sorry about your brother, Preston."

The words bring a simple nod from the man as he swallows his thoughts. "Me too."

Reynard's head lower, Preston's turning to the furnace on his left as the duo settle into their spots in the hallway, both unable to come up with something more to say. Yet, as the minutes roll on both merely sigh, their heads coming to the wall now as they drift into their thoughts. The sounds of Clover moving about downstairs echoing into the hallway above, though neither find a desire to move from the warmth on their side and the company across from them.

Chapter 1

Lóftor Vestá

The days have all but mashed together, an endless stream of mindless hours spent toiling away in the library. Conversations of the blood sky and cracked moon filling most interactions Preston has had with anyone beyond Clover and her friends. While at first it was a topic the man could at least comment on, the nonstop talking point for those visiting the library has become an inescapable nuisance. While it makes sense that so many would want to seek out Clover option, especially seeing as how she was even summoned to the town hall to speak on the Princess' behalf, the fact that so many have continued to come in days later, with the same questions has simply become maddening.

Clover however has remained upbeat about it, with Reynard seemingly none the worse given his participation. Though, with so little to talk about, and with the days seemingly cut in half Preston has found himself feeling empty, a lack of fulfilment or purpose in his day to day routine.

Since they returned from the castle Reynard has warmed up considerably to him, not that he was not already friendly beforehand. Though while their relationship has blossomed, Clover and Preston's has turned cold.

The duo's after dinner conversations have all but ended, with Clover hardly seeming to care. On the surface, they remain pleasant towards one another, sharing in laughs and basic conversations at the table, though both keeping to themselves beyond it. Preston's training in magic has also come to a fairly swift end, with Clover very rarely mentioning it. While Preston has found himself questioning it, he nonetheless lacks the nerve to truly bring it up. Lingering alone with the woman often brings a feeling of guilt, Preston's mind focusing to his current living arrangement as the main reason for this. Beyond the trivial answer Preston has presented, there lingers a simple truth. Neither have truly been open with the other since the events at the castle. But they have shared some fairly endearing conversations; most involving Matt's sudden departure which Preston, even with Clover's assertion still doubts. The fact is, Clover has remained far too removed, focusing on her various tasks each day, rather than to a lengthy exchange as she had before. What little they do talk at night, if any, is nothing like it was. Preston too is at fault for this, far too incapable of moving on from the mental image of striking Clover nearly a week ago, yet far too ashamed to bring it up to move past it.

Despite all this, breakfast has remained a pleasant event, one that at least has brought fair conversation between the trio. Today marks the seventh day since their return, the fifth sleepless night. It also marks the third day since Clover explained why the hours of the day have gone by so quickly. Of course, while the explanation of balancing the new magic within both the Célntals taking some time may have made sense for Reynard, it did nothing for Preston. If anything, it merely confused the matter more.

Truthfully though, Preston has stopped caring about time. With both Matt and Damien now gone, dead, or both, and Preston stuck until he is cured there is hardly anything left to worry about. Each day is nothing more than an endless cycle of repeated words, books, eating and, waiting to eat again. The cycle is a run-on sentence, an infuriating mishap, devoid of pause, or rest, one that only those who notice, care enough to get upset about; to others, it is a mindless loop, an unavoidable repetition that is blindly glossed over without a care. Many within the town, and even Reynard have accepted the quick days, the sudden starts and stops hardly messing with their minds. For Preston however, it is the absolute loss of stability, a maddening concept to think about while lying in bed or sitting at a table.

Yet, like the last few days, Preston sits at the table, his right hand stroking the amulet around his neck. A content, albeit dull smile situated to his face, the fresh growth in his small beard pulling attention away from the bags under his tired eyes.

As usual, the meal either Reynard, Clover, or both have made is fair enough, though it hardly is good. Even still, Preston has eaten without a comment about it, just as he has for the last few days.

Reynard sits to Preston's right, something the man noticed from his few glances over to the fox-boy this morning. On his left is Clover, though with both already exchanging their normal greeting, conversation at the table has come to its low point. The first two days back Reynard had attempted to cox the Preston's normal sarcasm out, but he has since given up.

Much like Reynard, Clover's friends have taken fairly well to the new, somewhat more banal Preston. This of course may simply be Clover's doing, as everyone did come by at some point in time, Preston himself never did hear any conversations about what really happened at the castle. At least not when it came to Preston's new amulet.

Of course, little thought has been given to this, and even less as Preston takes notice to faint yawn on his right.

"Well... that was good."

The words draw Clover's attention as she passes a simple smile. "I am glad you enjoyed it."

"Me too." A faint chuckle comes from Reynard as he shifts from his seat, his small hands coming back to his plate and cup as she continues. "But *maybe* Preston can cook something tonight? Maybe, something interesting like the wet bread... huh?"

Preston's gaze shifts to the boy, though his mouth hangs open and his gaze remains half-closed as he replies. "Uh-huh."

"Really?"

Again, Preston just stares to the fox-boy. "Huh?"

"Cook?" Reynard cocks his head. "Do you want to cook something tonight Preston?"

It takes a moment, but Preston seems to come back to reality as he closes his mouth, blinking to the boy staring back to him as he nods. "Wh-what am I doing?"

Clover chimes in at the words. "Preston is probably a bit tired.... I got you both up a little earlier."

The lie does not go unnoticed by Reynard, though the fox-boy gives a simple nod to the comment as he holds a faint smile to seated man. "Yea, hope you wake up, Preston."

"Ha-ha, yea." Preston just nods to comment as he awkwardly rubs his hands to his legs.

Again, Clover chimes in, her more upbeat tone holding. "Reynard, go ahead and get ready, I can open the library in a little."

With a nods Reynard starts away. The tapping of his claws is a bit quicker than most days, though Preston hardly takes notice to it as he just turns back to his plate, his fork pushing around the crumbs still on it.

Clover however takes a deep breath as she pushes her plate a little away from her. Despite her breath, she remains quiet for a moment, yet she eventually finds her voice as she speaks up. Her soft blue eyes now studying the man's face, the know-it-all tone absent from her as she does. "How are you feeling, Preston?"

"Huh?" Preston sits up a little. "Oh, uh... fine."

Clover nods to the comment as her eyes shift to the fork still tapping against his plate. "No soreness or pain in your back? Or your side?"

"No." Preston slowly brings the fork to rest on his plate as he focuses into the women beside him, his lazy gaze and somewhat slacked jaw coming back to him.

Clover however just straightens her posture as she nods. "Do you wish to talk anymore?"

"Yea." Preston moves his hands to his lap as he slumps a little. "What about?"

"Reynard knows what happened, Preston, though I do not think he truly understands it. Can you try and be a little more excited around him? I am still trying to get him to sleep at night."

The somewhat lengthy comment along with the question takes Preston a little off guard as he squints a little confused to the woman. "What?"

"Preston..." Clover gives a slight sigh as she nods, her words coming out a little slower. "I know it might be difficult to talk about, but it has been a few d-..."

"Whoa, whoa." Preston waves his hand to the comment as he stammers over the woman's words. "I-if I don't want to talk then saying that doesn't make me want to talk. Ha-ha, that would make no sense." He nods. "But for what it's worth I'd rather not talk right now."

Clover's ears perk up as she nods, taking notice to the man's shifty stance, his continued biting at his bottom lip, and the faint green glow within the amulet. "I am sorry Preston; I did not mean for it to sound badly. I understand you are grieving... I just thought you may wish to talk about it."

"No, no." Preston gives a simple chuckle as he shakes his head a little more. "It's only been a few days, why-why would you think you can just casually bring it up like that?"

Clover nods. "I understand you need more time Preston I was just-..."

"What's a good amount of time? Tell me what's a good amount of time to get over, it Clover? Tell me what's a good amount of time after seeing your brother just disappear right bef-..." Preston's words break as he tightly slams his jaw shut, his right hand shaking to the table as his eyes draw down to the glowing amulet around his neck.

Sighting the glow both Preston and Clover go silent, though the man's frustration has already boiled over as he merely rubs his thumb to his cheek. A faint smile coming from him as he turns away, his hand still shaking a little as he attempts to hide it by clasping his hands together.

As a sigh rolls from the man Clover speaks up. "The amulet is something to help keep your emotions in check, Preston. You cannot rely on it the-..."

"I know." Preston sighs again as he pulls his eyes away from the wall, his hands coming from the table as he nods. "Maybe later, Clover. For now, I just... I just want to forget about it." He pushes his plate away as he ends his comment.

Clover's hands spark up as she looks over the amulet, though the sight of the magic merely draws Preston's voice backup as he shakes his head. "Don't."

"I want to check Master Nyota's spell." She nods. "It will not take more than a moment."

"Tomorrow." Preston waves to the comment. "Let me... let me just get this off my mind." As his comment comes to an end Preston stands up.

"Where are you going?"

"I'm gonna lay down for a minute." Preston thumbs to the stairs as he backs away. "I feel a bit tired."

Clover's magic comes to the various items around the table as Clover follows the man's shift from the table. Despite the movement behind her

Clover's focus remains to the man as she nods. "Preston, you cannot sit upstairs all *déy*."

She cocks her head up a little as she continues. "I was invited to the Town Hall again, come with me. You need to do something if you are unhappy."

"I'm not unhappy." Preston forces a slight smile though Clover merely cocks her head to the man, drawing another quick comment from Preston as he nods. "Look I did want to talk, I just..." He sighs. "So, the Town Hall? It's not going to be crowded, right?"

"No." The satyress straightens her posture as she continues. "If you want to rest before we go, do so. But I think this might be good for you."

"Yea." Preston nods. "I just need a minute before people start coming in." He waves a hand to the woman as he starts up the stairs. "Come get me before you open the library and I'll be good." He nods again. "I think I need to get out of here anyways."

"Very well, Preston." Clover gives a simple nod, her eyes setting to the kitchen's half-wall as Preston moves towards the stairs. But even as he moves back towards his room, the promise of a warm bed for another hour or so, his pace remains sluggish.

Chapter 2

Jartál

The morning has been peaceful, with the quiet sounds of chirping birds, few shouting matches in the muddy street below, and Clover, happily enough staying out of the hallway since Preston retreated upstairs. Yet, while the time of rest since breakfast has been pleasant, Preston's quick sleep he found himself spirited away too seems to come to an end as the sound of Clover's hooves ring to the stairs.

The sound of her approach does ring to Preston's head, though he remains asleep despite the noise. Sadly, no matter how hard he attempts to hold onto his enjoyable nap, the door opens.

The room itself is a bit darker than downstairs, especially with the windows' closed off from the world outside. Clover has no problem turning her eyes to the man within the bed. For a moment she is quiet, but as Preston remains unmoving, Clover speaks up, her hand coming more to the knob she leans into as she does. Her somewhat relaxed stance however is overshadowed as a more proper tone carries her words into the room. "Preston *jé déy dóf breśton; Á yé sléfto?*"

At the strange words Preston shifts in the bed, cracking one eye open as he rises, a slightly faked yawn following his reply as he rubs his hand to his face. "What?"

"The *déy* is bright Preston, and yet you still sleep." Clover takes her hand from the door as she nods. "You agreed to accompany me, do you remember?"

Preston slowly nods to the words as he glances to the window, the days have been going fairly quick, he nonetheless takes notice to the fact that morning has passed. Sighting this, he moves from the bed, quickly pulling his shoes close to him as he does. "You didn't wake me earlier?"

Clover shakes her head. "I had attempted to earlier, though you did not come out when I knocked."

"You knocked?"

"Just a short while ago." She draws her right hand up as she brings into view a small group of stones floating in her magic. "I decided to recharge the furnace while you were sleeping." She trails on. "Get ready, I wanted to leave in a moment."

Preston merely slips back on his shoes as he stands, though Clover already moves from the doorway as he attempts to follow after her. "You could have woken me earlier, you know."

Clover's trot does not halt at Preston's words as she instead continues to the furnace at the back of the room, the stones floating behind her as she nods. "I understand, Preston. But Reynard was able to help in the library, and there was hardly a reason to wake you." She passes a friendly smile to the man as her magic takes hold of the small metal gate. The stones now quickly move into place within the furnace, Clover's blue magic sparking a small fire within it as she finishes her task. "Do you feel better?"

Looking over the small fire now starting up Preston nods. "Y-yea."

Clover holds her friendly smile though her eyes fall away from the man as she moves back towards the stairs. "Well you seem a little more rested. Shall we?" She moves past the man without a glance to him as she starts to the stairs, her tail brushing just above the step behind her as she continues down it.

Preston swiftly follows after her, his mind still slowly losing its fog from his second waking as he looks around the room downstairs. Already he feels an urge to call off this tagging along, a stiff reminder to just how quick the day will end creeping to his mind, a feeling of pointlessness to the simple trip he realizes that now draws near. Luckily, something catches his attention, at least long enough for his mind to suppress his apathetic thoughts. To his surprise a few books are still laid out on the table, along with Clover's check in and check out lists. However, Clover lapse in her normal OCD cleanliness is only noticed for a moment as Reynard speaks up from where he stands next to the door.

"You awake, Preston?"

The comment sparks a slight smirk to Preston's face as he shrugs. "I'm up, right?" He motions to his legs as she continues. "Haven't fallen down yet either."

A faint smile comes to Reynard's face as the fox-boy nods. "You missed Clover getting upset."

"Oh yea?" The smirk to his face holds as the blond man merely turns an eye to where Clover stands, her attention to the satchel she swings on over her shoulder as he speaks up. "What happened?"

"Someone was checking out a book and accidentally dropped it in the road." Reynard nods, the smile on his face hold firm as he continues. "You should have seen the look on Clover's face, it would have woken you up pretty quick."

"I would prefer not to think of it, Reynard." Clover chimes in from where she stands at the table as she nods. "Besides, Preston will wake up enough before tonight." She nods as she continues. "I have asked Preston to be my assistant for the meeting."

Preston squints to the comment though he says nothing as Clover continues to dig into her bag, pulling out a brush as she quickly runs it through her normally free flowing man. But as his eyes meet the sight of a clipboard and paper poking out from her bag Preston speaks up. "Do you want me to write stuff down?"

"Hmmm?" Clover glances to her bag as she places her brush back to it. "I have a very good memory Preston do not worry about it."

A faint laugh rings from Preston as he nods. "Alright, so what will I need to do?"

"Anything you can write will help, simple notes." Clover simply waves her hand to the comment as she moves towards the door. "Just enjoy the fresh air, Preston." She opens the door as a chilly breeze rolls into the library, one that forces Reynard away as he chuckles with a quick comment. "Stay warm."

- - -

(Later)

The sun is high in the sky, settled well above the short skyline of *VéturVill*, yet despite its position little warmth has truly graced the small town. The thick clouds have allowed the town to remain bright, though the lack of true and direct sunlight has allowed the banks of snow to remain relatively unchanged. The faint chill in the air also does little to help the situation, though the heavy cotton clothing has done their job well enough.

Yet, even with the slight nip in the air the walk has been rather relaxing; the streets have been calm and as much as Preston might hate to admit it, the fresh air has been enjoyable. Of course, after spending so much time in the stuffy library any new smells have been a welcomed change, even the thick smell of the muddy street.

The pace of the duo has followed Clover's trot, though her typically more rushed or rather focused trot has kept Clover just a little ahead of Preston. Despite this slight gap between them however, Clover has still managed to maintain a fair enough conversation.

Although, the sight of the dark wood, stone-made, two story building inching ever closer has taken hold of Clover's attention, drawing a new silence to the woman. With Clover now quiet, Preston turns his eyes to the building, soaking the sight of the medieval town hall in. The building's top layer no longer has its sandy hay-like shine, instead the hay roof has dulled from the snow to a more bistre color. Despite this, the building still stands out from the other wood creations around town, if not just from the hay the simple roundness of the building within the sea of boxed houses.

Though as the town hall's entrance draws near Preston's mind slowly comes out of his thoughts. Clover however maintains her pace, her magic sparking to the door as she continues inside. The building itself is warm, and the light pouring from the ceiling along with the torches are bright and inviting. Unlike the first time Preston ventured into the town hall there are a few others bustling about inside, in fact, the town hall itself seems rather dead, despite being midday. Of course, those few who do still wander the building quickly take notice to both Clover and Preston; one such person is a fair dressed, *Dŵoff* woman, who approaches the duo. Though just barely middle aged in appearance the slight sagging in her pig-nose has caught Preston's attention, something he finds it hard to ignore as the woman continues forward.

A friendly smile crosses the woman's face as she speaks up, her gaze focusing to Clover. "The *Jartál* was not expecting to see you so early, Miss Vines."

Clover's trot begins to slow, as she nods. "Yes, we are a bit early."

The *Dŵoff* points to the stairs as she replies, her friendly smile holding. "Well you are welcome to wait for the *Jartál* upstairs, she may be ready."

"Thank you." Clover's speed comes back to her as she starts towards the staircase at the back of the room. Though as Preston and Clover move away from the pig-nosed woman, Clover speaks up again. "There should be no problem, Preston."

Preston gives a slight smile to the comment as he just nods. The walk across the first floor only takes a few moments, although as Clover's trot comes closer to the staircase the duo is brought to a halt, their eyes turning to the guards that now straighten up from where the lean against the walls.

"Hold."

One of the two, short, hairy men steps forward as he stares to Clover. The light chainmail armor and bright yellow cuirass of the two guards may be eye catching, though it is hardly as impressive as the guards within the Capital. Yet, the large spears the guards wield does take Preston's attention as he stiffens just a little.

The guard quickly gives a little smile as he steps back. "Ah, Miss Vines." The guard wags a finger to the woman as he waves her on. "Sorry, to keep you wait'n just had to give my eyes a moment."

"No problem." Clover gives a simple nod to the comment as she starts forward, drawing Preston up behind her.

The staircase leads into a small midway platform, where a torch and banner hanging to the wall. The banner itself is nothing new, though the rarely seen sigil of the small town still draws Preston's eyes as he looks it over again. The dull, earthy browns of the banner are hardly vibrant, yet the single bright green tree that stands in the middle of the earthy canvas has always amused Preston, if only for the fancy stitching of such a simple design. Of course, Preston's sight of the banner is cut off as he turns to the second flight of stairs behind him.

Clover has naturally already started up, her tail bouncing with every step. Despite the movement however, her tail remains relatively unchanged, the loosely brushed hair already as messy as it would ever get.

"The *Jartál's* meeting hall is just to the left."

"Okay." Coming up the stairs behind the woman Preston turns his eyes to left, quickly spotting the single, closed double doors centered into the wall.

Clover of course is the first to move to it as she knocks her hand into the simple wood. "*Jartál* Caféll, it is Clover Vines."

Within seconds a reply comes from within, a cheerful, almost over rehearsed friendliness greeting Preston's ears as Clover moves her hand to the knob. "*Oh! Come in, come in!*"

Opening one of the doors Clover starts inside, Preston close behind. The scent of pine hits Preston's nose as he crosses the threshold, but the source is quickly brought into view as he looks to the long oak table spanning the room.

"Ah, Clover Vine, early as usual."

The simple pleasantries pass by Preston's attention as he stares to the two women at the end of the table just in front of the window. Caféll or at least the person who continues to talk, looks to be a fairly young, maybe early thirties *Dẃoff* women. Her skin is a creamy white, far different than the sandy tones more other have, though her fair complexion only helps to amplify her dark red, almost autumn toned hair. The heavy robe she wears is a dull red, almost tree bark-like color, though it fits well. Beside her is a younger looking *Dẃoff*, her own hair resembling that of Caféll's as well as her facial structure, including the smaller sort of pig-like nose.

Preston's stare however does not linger as Caféll's green eyes turn to him. The politician guise of friendliness now directed to him. "Well hello, I do believe I we have met before. Are you from *Únoactroff*?"

Clover merely waves to the comment as she speaks up to overly jeweled woman across from her. "This is Preston Armor, he works with me at the library, and is my assistant for the meeting."

"Oh, yes." Caféll gives a simple smile as she presses her back comfortable to the chair, she sits in. "I heard something of a *Fárwift* creature under your care." Caféll squints to Preston as she nods a little. "A relation to the *Drágeff* or some type of kin of theirs?"

Preston simply shrugs. "Kin is fine."

"Hmm." Caféll brings her smile back to Clover as she continues. "I do hope young Reynard is well."

"Reynard is fine." Clover again gestures to Preston as she pulls forth the clipboard and inkwell from her satchel. "I merely wished to give him a rest." As the items comes to Preston, he passes a look to the woman on his left, though he nonetheless moves his hands to them as Caféll speaks up.

"Well then, if you would, have a seat we can begin. It should not take long."

At the words the duo takes their seats at the long table, Preston laying the clipboard and paper down with ease as he looks over the ink pen sticking out of the bottle in his hand. Clover of course pays his slightly confused glances no mind as she speaks up, her hands folding before as she leans to the table. "If this meeting is in regards to the cloud cleanup I would suggest you call in *Pexřá* Elva, my plans from the previous *Lor-Roth* do not need changing." Clover pats her bag as she continues. "I did bring a copy if it is misplaced."

Caféll merely shakes her head, a slight chuckle coming from her to the comment as she speaks up. "Oh no, no, we still have your plans, and with their details there is no confusion." She continues. "There is actually a different reason I sent for you here." She turns her head to the woman next to her as she holds her hand out.

As the younger woman quickly brings a fair-sized stack of papers from something underneath the table Clover speaks up. "Oh? What is it?"

Caféll holds her tongue for a moment as the woman beside her moves the letter from atop of the stack to the table before her. "As I am sure you are aware, Princess Sóltina has sent out a statement of her sister's recent... departure. As well as how we are to handle questions of the bloody sky that followed it."

Clover blinks to the statement as she nods. "I am not sure I am able to answer anything beyond what the Princess has said."

"Oh, no, no." Caféll gives a simple laugh. "We both understand this. But along with the Princess's new banner, rules and um... documents." She pats the stack to her right as she continues. "It seems the Princess has entrusted our town with a new venture, one that I am eager of course to start, though still do not fully understand." Caféll straightens her posture as she passes the papers towards the center of the table until Clover's magic takes hold. "Her letter has stated that you shall be making the decision on this matter."

Clover scoots a little closer, her eyes looking over the letter as both she and Caféll begin to settle into some conversation. The back and forth begins to drag on, Preston's attention to the drab political speak now losing him as he instead turns to look over the room around him.

Around the walls hang all sorts of banners, most of which Preston has never seen, yet some of the words underneath them do catch his eyes. Though, the fancy lettering only holds his interest for a moment as he turns to long, metal axe on display in the middle of the wall. Although the blade portion seems to be smashed, the axe looks to be in fantastic condition, with its bright plaque proudly on display within the meeting room. A few carved words can be seen in the wood towards its handle, but the letters and Preston's distance keep the man from understanding them as he squints to it.

"...Did you get that Preston?"

The words quickly bring Preston's mind back to the woman next to him as he just stares to her wide eyed and confused. "Get what?"

Despite Preston's turned gaze, the annoyance to his words can still be seen in Caféll's face. Clover however does share in this as she instead repeated the words, a knowing smile coming to her face as she does.

"The newest additions to the town's *Wóvátor* near *ób vásil ó ÉverMoar* will need more *Helió* stones for its fire."

Preston cracks a slight smile to the words as he glances across the table, though he nods all the same as he clears his throat and moves his hand to the inkwell set out before him. "Yea, got it Clover."

The satyress gives a slight smirk as she turns back to Caféll's continued ramble.

Preston however begins to write as he tries to sound out the foreign words, knowing all too well there is no way to get the words right. Even still, the smirk holds to Preston's face as he looks over the words he scribbles out.

You told me to write so here you go. There needs to be more helow stones for the ~~wo wava~~ wovator near the ~~obb~~ ob vastill o Evermore. Whatever that means.

A light sigh comes from Preston as he tilts his head up to better listen into the woman across the table.

Chapter 3

Book & Quill

Despite Clover's earlier assertions, the meeting took far longer than Preston was led to believe. Naturally, Preston had a few quick comments for his companion when they stepped out of the meeting, yet Clover was quick enough to apologize for it, as well as reassure him that the notes would not be needed. The comments of course did help, but the gibberish Preston had been forced into writing down was hardly an enjoyable experience. Especially seeing as how Preston was unable to truly stop and ask if the notes were going to be needed while doing it.

Despite this, Preston has kept the clipboard and few pages of notes tucked under his arm since they left the meeting, ensuring that none have dropped. The day has passed them on, with the sun now far beyond its high point, as Preston expected.

Unlike the other days, Preston does not find his strength zapped by this knowledge, his pace even quickening as sights the dull red of the library's door just down the street.

However, just as Clover's magic starts to the door's handle, it opens, two *Dwoffs* stepping outside and into the street with a book in their hold. Clover halts for the moment as the two women continue into the street, never once stirring from their conversation with one another.

It is not at all uncommon to see someone new coming in or out of the house, after all, it is part library. Still, the idea of a house always being unlocked does spark an uneasy feeling in Preston's gut.

He merely bites his tongue as Clover trots inside, her magic holding the opened door for the man behind her. Preston follows in after, but his eyes immediately focuses to the three unknown people still perusing the library section of the house.

"There you are!"

Reynard's voice takes Preston's attention, as he turns to where the short *fróx* moves from his seat at the table. The table is messy with the library's ledger sprawled out upon, as well as several books and various lists, of course Reynard pays it little mind as he speaks up. "Anything new?"

"Actually, quite a lot." Clover's magic pulls to the bound papers within her satchel as she brings them out to show Reynard before turning an eye to the customers still in her library. "Princess Sóltina wishes me to look over something for her."

"Huh?" Reynard shrugs. "But you are not an advisor?"

Clover cocks a slight smile to the comment as she nods. "Yes, but I am Nyota's assistant, and with him so busy I have been-..."

"Excuse me, but do you have any books on *Alcrex Márjx*?"

The new voice turns Clover's attention as she looks to the dark-haired satyr standing a little from their group.

Clover however does miss a beat as she nods, tugging her satchel around her shoulder as she nods. "Of course, just over here."

To the woman's absence Reynard now turns to the clipboard in Preston's hold. "Did Caféll have you write a lot?"

"I guess you can call it that." Preston hicks up the items in his hold though Reynard quickly chimes in a faint hyena-like giggle.

He holds one of his tiny paws towards the man as he nods. "Let me see, it cannot be that bad."

Sighting the extended paw, Preston lowers the clipboard and notes to him.

"Alright..." Reynard's smile fades and his fox ears poke up. "Oh..." He cocks a slight smile as he moves the clipboard to the table. "Clover told you that she never needs the notes right?"

"Yea." Preston crosses his arms. "Yea... she said that."

Reynard holds his smile as he waves the comment off. "Caféll just wants people to write while she is talking, Clover says it makes her feel important. I just draw things when they start."

"That's funny." Preston cracks a slight smile. "I ended up doing that halfway through."

"Oh?" Reynard turns back to the clipboard as he jumps up to his seat, flipping the front page over as he stares to the simple stick figure drawings. "You did!"

The boyish excitement draws Preston's smile a little wider as he nods. "Yea, got a little bored." He shakes his head. "Wish she would have said something, I'm fine with the notes being pointless, everything else I do is... but she could have said that before I took them."

Another faint laugh escapes Reynard as he settles into the chair, his bright eyes turning to Preston as he nods. "Clover is not the best with feelings. But she thought it would help, do you feel more awake now?"

The happy face now staring up to him brings a sudden silence to Preston, luckily their conversation is cut short as Clover steps between them. Her hands move to the inkwell at the table as her magic draws forth one of the lists from the table, though her attention stays to the *Únoff* next to her as she writes something down. "Alright, Mr. Dior, that will be two *Sivý*."

The man nods as he dips his right hand into a pocket in his thick leather vest. A fair sized, and slightly stretched out pouch comes from the pocket. Yet, the pouch opens with a light gold flash of his own magic, as he draws out two, slightly misshapen silver coins to Clover.

While Preston has seen the coin money before, he has never truly handled any. Preston's job for the most part, aside from helping people get books down is mostly just restocking the shelves and ensuring no one tries to run out without paying, which luckily enough has never happened. Aside from the few times Clover has paid for something in front him, this is the first real time he has seen any coin so close. No emblem can be seen indented into the coins, yet Preston hardly gets a good look as Clover's magic draws it to her hand with quick comment. "Thank you, *plestá dêy*."

The *Únoff* nods as he starts towards the door of the library.

With him gone Clover turns her sight to the two other customers still wandering around. Though she floats the coins into the box at the far chair without batting an eye. With the payment now out of sight and no one walking towards her she turns her attention to the faces beside her. "Are you going over what Preston has written down?"

The comment draws a quick reply from the man as he nods. "You could have done better with bringing me along, you know?"

Clover merely squints to the comment as she shrugs, her simple smile holds to her face as she crosses her arms over the forest-green corset of her dress. "Oh? But it was good for you, a little bit of stress never hurt anyone. Besides, you worked your mind." Her words pause as she looks over Reynard's shoulder to the clipboard at the table. "You did quite well, Preston, I can actually make out some of the words here."

The is no sarcasm in the woman's tone, which only adds to the child-like praising of her words as Preston shakes his head. "Great."

The quick reply prompts Clover's eyes back to the man as she shrugs. "It is a complement, Preston."

Preston blows his breath just a little as he nods, shifting in his stance as he glances elsewhere in the room. "Happy to amuse you, Clover."

The comment only further holds Clover's gaze as she speaks up. "It was good for you to get out of the library."

"Yea it was fine." Preston clears his throat as he nods. "I just didn't know I would need to write."

"I do not need the notes, you knew that." Clover shrugs. "I do not care about the quality."

"Alright, I'm just saying don't-..." His words come to an end as he rocks forward, glancing to the front door that opens just behind where he stands at the table.

The sound of the door opening forces a fake smile to Clover's face as she too turns to it, though as the customer comes in, she relaxes a little. "Elva, how are you?"

Clover takes a step aside from the table as Elva speaks up, her normally stern face softening a little as she crosses her arms. "There is little to complain about."

"Oh, good." Clover glances back to the library section of the house as she continues. "Can I help you search for a book?"

"I do not find enjoyment in parchment, Clover, you know this." Elva pauses for the moment as she drifts her eyes towards the library portion of the house. "But I do find myself with a free moment, I had wondered if you wished to practice your sword."

Clover just shakes her head to the comment as she replies. "No, I still have customers and the library needs to be open, I am gone enough as it is."

Elva waves a hand to Reynard and Preston as she continues. "Have one of them earn their keep, you should take this opportunity to spar with me."

Though the comment draws an annoyed glance from Reynard and Preston, it is Clover who speaks up again. "Sorry Elva, I do not have time. Perhaps a book by *Bentró Swell* would take your interest?"

Elva cocks a smile to the words. "A *Flóff* tale of glory? Why would you carry such a book, the *Dẃoff* cannot read it and the *Únoff* have no interest for it."

Clover flashes her own smile as she nods to the words. "There are still some in town who enjoy the stories."

"Yes, *Flóff* that were too weak to enter a camp of the Emperor." Elva gives a slight laugh as she continues. "The stories probably frighten them."

"Do you wish to read it, Elva?"

Elva gives a faint sigh though she nods all the same. "I suppose." She glances back to Preston as she continues. "I would still insist on leaving the shop to one of your *incápy*. After all, I am surprised to see this one up… feeling better, Preston?"

Clover's ear flicks to the comment, but the man's voice comes out before she can speak up. "I'm fine."

The simple smirk stays to Elva's face as she notices the slightly more cocked up head and tightened gaze Preston holds to her. "Good, perhaps now you can be useful around here."

"Preston helps whenever I need it, Elva." Clover holds her hand out to the library section of the room as she continues. "Care to come find your book?"

Elva turns an eye to her friend as her arms uncross. "it should be thankful for such a gracious host. I would not allow this laziness."

"Of course." Clover nods to the words as she takes a step towards the library section. "Shall we find the book?"

Elva holds her smirk though she starts away, trailing after her friend as she leads her into the next room. Clover's trot halts as she turns back to Reynard, the papers on the clipboard taking on a faint blue glow for a moment as Clover speaks up. "Reynard, could you put that in my room please?"

"Sure." At the words Clover's magic fades from the clipboard, and Reynard takes the clipboard into hands.

The movement of the young fox-boy takes his attention for a moment, as Reynard steps towards the stairs Preston's gaze turns back to Clover and Elva.

"...I truly think you will enjoy the book." At the words, the long list floats from the table behind Preston as the quill follows after it to where Clover stands.

Elva however gives no reply as she instead looks over the bound leather book Clover had quickly found for her a moment ago.

"That will be two *Sivy*."

A faint laugh comes from Elva as she dips her hand into the hidden pocket in her armor. "Coin for a book." Despite the comment Elva pulls forth two silver coins as she drops them to her friend's hand.

Clover's magic moves the coin beside her as she quickly writes something to the paper. "You will enjoy it, Elva."

"Hardily." Elva looks over the book in her hand as she continues. "Field strategy and battle plans may help, though fights are won with action, not thoughts." She moves her hand to her side as she trails on. "A good sparing would have served us both."

"And it will." Clover sighs. "Another time."

"Hmm." Elva gives a simple nod to the words as she turns towards the door. "Fair winds, Clover."

"*Plestá déy*, Elva."

As the avian woman leaves, Clover's attention turns to Preston as rolls up the paper in her magic and then turns back to the bookshelf behind her. The light chime of magic fills the room as she moves back to where Preston stands, a book floating behind her. "Here, I thought you might want to read something."

Preston slowly takes the book from the woman's magic as he looks it over.

"It is an old story, one typically told to foals but... it is still a rather interesting tale." Clover's words end as she turns back towards the few other people still lingering in the library.

Preston looks over the book a little more as he takes a little breath. "Alright, I'll look it over."

The words draw Clover's eyes back to him as she nods. "Good, I hope you enjoy it."

Chapter 4

Enclosed inside

    The day, like the last few, has rolled on rather quickly since Preston and Clover returned home, not that Preston was surprised. Some customers took their time, but the vast majority of the time spent within the library was devoid of any real distractions from the outside world. Clover naturally had no problem with this, as she easily found a new book to read through once everyone left. But, sighting the falling sun once more Preston was unable to shake off the feelings stirring within him. Even with Clover's simple waylay, the day has come to a quick end, and just like the others before it, Preston has nothing to show for it. Another day of wasted potential stalled only by Preston's own inability and lack of caring to truly break free of his endless cycle of monotony. Even the book Clover gave him remained unexplored, a fear of boredom staying his mind from its adventure, yet one that only perpetuated his accidie.

    The world outside has grown dark, and Reynard retired upstairs soon after dinner. Though the fox-boy said nothing about it, Clover again being the one to cook even with Preston being up and about most of the day did seem to annoy the young *fróx*. Lucky, the simple dinner was one of Clover's better dishes, and Preston's still somewhat standoffish attitude kept Reynard from commenting.

    Dinner itself has been over for the past hour and a half, with Clover cleaning off the table soon after Reynard left. Strangely though, she did not bid Preston good night as she had been, yet neither did she invite the man into one of their lengthy conversations like they used to have. Instead, the duo has gone about their separate course, with Preston tidying up the library and Clover somewhere within the kitchen.

The simple, albeit tedious chores have at least given something for Preston to linger on; yet, they do little to fill the feeling of emptiness the quick days have brought on. They nonetheless are more distracting than the books Clover had given him.

Unfortunately, Preston is slowly stirred from his mindless actions of stacking and cleaning the books as he squints to one of the tombs in his hold. In truth, while Preston cannot read most of the titles within the library, he has at least learned Clover's system of book placement. Focusing on the markings or letter styles of the tiles to determine where they go. Yet, as he looks over the book a little more, he finds himself unable to distingue the lettering as something entirely *Únoff* or *Flóff*. Worst still is the lack of symbols on the book, making it harder to tell if it were a school of *Márjx* type of text.

While the fact that Preston can run through a simple checklist of the alien language in his head is fairly surprising, it nonetheless does not help as he turns his attention back to the kitchen's half-wall. Clearing his throat, he calls out. "H-hey, where does this one?"

The lighting in the house is fair, with several of Clover's balls of magic lighting up the room, though as Clover's short figure comes into view it is quickly apparent that the room is too dark for her to see the book properly. Within a few seconds Clover's form flashes with a blue light, the satyress teleporting across the room as she looks over the book. "Oh, that is a new book on *Márjx*. Third bookcase from your right, second shelf from the bottom..." She squints her eyes. "It should be the tenth book from the left."

She shoots a quick smile before turning back to the table, her eyes casting over the stack of papers *Jartál* Caféll gave her. As she moves towards them however a laugh comes from Preston. "You barely even looked at the title?"

"Mhmm..." Clover moves to the table as her magic comes over the stack of papers, quickly teleporting both herself and the stack to the small loft above the library. The sound draws Preston's attention as he looks to where the woman sits down on the couch overlooking the area, though she already nosedives into the first piece of paper in the stack as he speaks up.

"The book doesn't have one of the markings on it."

"Hm?" Clover glances up from the stack as she waves her hand. "It is a book on *Dújarx*, open it up and you will see the markings of *Eñchar* and *Héthtex Márjx*."

Despite the comment Preston simple moves the book into its place on the bookshelf, his attention next the next two books cradled in his left arm. "Alright..." He again squints to the title as he clears his throat. "Por- *Pórtavel Wéth*?"

"Fifth bookcase, anywhere in the middle shelf would be fine."

A faint smirk comes to Preston as he places the book to an open section in the bookshelf. "Alright, last one... I think it says uh..."

Clover glances to the book, quickly taking notice to the slightly redder color of the leather binding. "You can put that one here."

Following her extended finger Preston moves to the bookshelf near the loft's staircase, placing the book randomly on one of the selves. With it gone Preston sighs. "Alright, all done I guess."

Clover slowly raises her head from her papers as she passes a quick smile. "Splendid... sleep well, Preston." She holds her smile to the man for a moment before she turns her head back to the paper in her hand.

Preston merely nods to the comment as he turns to the room behind him, yet as he starts away, he pauses. Turning around again he shrugs. "You staying up?"

"Hmm?" Clover quickly nods. "Oh, yes." She pats the papers beside her. "I only glanced through these earlier, I need to give them a proper read."

"Oh?" Preston looks over the papers. "So, what's it about?"

Clover merely blinks to the question as she speaks up. "I do not know until I read, Preston."

"Yea." A simple laugh escapes the man as he nods. "Guess that was kind of a dumb question..." He shifts his weight a little. "Still surprised you don't know what it's about, seeing as how you been glancing through it all day."

"Well..." Clover moves the paper in her hand back to the stack as she nods with a sigh. "Princess Sóltina's task for me is something new." She rambles on. "I know of it, but I will need some extra time before I actually start on it."

"Yea? What is it?"

Clover pauses for a moment though she points to the table all the same as she speaks up. "Have a look."

Preston follows her motion though as he comes to the table he shrugs back to the woman. "I won't be able to help."

Clover's magic flashes quickly as she teleports herself next to the table, her hair a mess now from the quick spells as she places the stack of papers on the table. "Perhaps not but have a look."

A low blue magic comes to the stack as the papers rise, drawing forth a folded-up piece of paper from within the stack.

The paper unfolded maybe five times, leaving the seemingly heavy paper nothing but a tissue of its former self as it opens up at least three times the size of the normal papers beside it. Preston squints to the light ink on it as he takes a step closer. However, the blue light of the room quickly brings the picture to his eyes as he speaks up. "What is that a train?"

"It seems so." Clover crosses her arms as her magic fades from the paper. "It hardly matches your drawing, but some of the other sketches I was able to understand."

Preston moves to her side, his gaze locked to the drawing as he speaks up. "How'd she do this?" He moves a hand to the stack of papers as he thumbs through them. "What else did she send you?"

"Do not touch it." Clover's magic pulls Preston's hand away as she quickly continues. "Sorry, I just do not want you bending the papers." Her magic manipulates the stack again as she takes a few steps away from Preston. "But... here is something else she sent."

Again, the folded paper opens up within Clover's magic as the new pace comes neatly over the drawing of the train. Like before, the ink or pencil that was used to draw the picture is faded, yet Preston nods to it as he taps a finger to the page. "That's train tracks? How'd she get all this?"

Clover's eyes fixate to the man's poking at the paper though she maintains a friendly tone as she nods. "Magic is nothing more than thoughts and emotions. Her spell must have drawn on your thoughts, Princess Sóltina is *devún*, she must have been able to see inside your mind."

Preston rubs a hand to the side of his face as he continues to gawk at the yellow pages sprawled out before him. "That's a bit creepy, she can just read minds now?"

Clover slowly shifts the papers away from Preston as she shakes her head, her own eyes casting over the drawings as she speaks up. "It is no different than feeling another's magic, Preston. Princess Sóltina is simply able to go further."

The man stays silent as he just stares to the papers a little more. Though as Clover begins to fold them up again, she draws him back to reality as she speaks up. "Perhaps you could help me with a few things? If you feel okay."

"Yea uh... I feel okay." Preston crosses his arms again, his right hand coming to the amulet around his neck as he plays with it a little. "What did you need?" A slight laugh comes from him as he moves towards one of the chairs beside him. "I hope you don't expect me to build it, 'cuz there's no way I can do that."

"Oh, no." Clover waves her hand to the comment. "It shall not take long for an *Únoff* builder to create something with these documents. But the Princess wants me to come up with a pathway for this train to follow."

The woman's eyes come back to Preston as her confidence sparks back to her voice. "From what I have glanced through, she wishes to use the carriage trails with these tracks; but does not know where to set up one of these um... stations."

Preston shrugs. "Okay? So, like, she wants me to tell her where to put them?"

Clover slowly nods to the question as she gives a simple smile. "Well she consulted me, but I am still a bit unsure as to what this creation is."

A faint smile comes to Preston as he tilts his head up. "So, you want me to explain it again, so you look for here, huh?"

Clover remains stoic in her expression as she merely replies. "It is up to you, I have what I need to read... though if you could explain it a bit, it might help me figure out where best to place it."

Preston nods. "Well, trains, if-if she's going to make one like this it's going to be pretty loud. So, you know having it at least a decent way away from the town would be a good idea. But why here? There's like nothing out here?"

"*VéturVill* is the largest town near the castle, aside from the *Pegpolis* and *Féllcreed*." Clover squints to the man as she trails on. "Unless of course these trains fly?"

A slight laugh comes from Preston as he waves his hand. "No, no, that's not gonna happen."

"Well then that is why the town was chosen." Clover shrugs. "*HefterÁll* is closer, though with the forest construction would be slowed. The Princess wants to test how quickly this form of transportation would be before she furthers it."

"You said you didn't get to read all of it?"

Clover glances back to the stack as she shrugs. "I read through the important parts already."

"Alright." Preston sits back a little more in his chair as he takes a deep breath and looks towards the ceiling.

The sound of his movement draws Clover's gaze as she cocks a confused smile to the man's expression. "An answer does not have to be reached right away, Preston."

"I know." Preston continues to rub his thumb over the amulet around his neck as he nods. "So, she wants to follow the old roads?"

"It would be easiest. The land has been flattened near most."

"Makes sense." Preston nods. "Well then just have it end near the front of town, it's not that hard."

"I believe Jartal Caféll will want it to end near her hall, it would after all bolster the town's prestige."

The words draw a nod from Preston as he replies. "Right, but if it goes through the center of town it would be pretty loud."

"Yes." Clover nods. "And since you have brought that to my attention it is something I can hopefully sway her with. If not, another solution will need to be met."

Clover passes a smile as her magic takes hold of the papers. "If you come up with anything else let me know. I hope to have a letter sent to the Princess soon with some suggestions."

Preston squints a little to the sight of the woman's magic and her tone as he nods. "You sound like you're trying to kick me out."

Clover's right ear flicks to the words as she shakes her head. "I would not kick you out, Preston, you are my guest until-...."

"No, no." Preston waves his hand to the words. "Phrasing I know. What I meant is, it sounds like you're trying to get me to go away. You know, send upstairs or something."

Blinking to the comment a little Clover nods. "You were interested in my task; this is my task. I value your input, though I still need to read through everything..." She glances away a little. "And I do not wish to stress you out with thought."

Preston's hand slowly pulls away from the amulet he has mindlessly been playing with as he leans forward. "I'm feeling okay, and this actually kinda interesting."

"I am happy to hear."

Despite the words and Clover's own friendly, albeit somewhat faked smile the room falls silent for a moment. At the lack conversation Preston simply nods, patting his hand to the table as he stands up. "Right, well, something to think about is what happens when the town starts to grow."

Clover cocks her head to the question. "What do you mean?"

Preston sway near the table as he shrugs. "Well, trains hold a lot of people I'm sure you'll read about that. When you got a lot of people coming through the town there's gonna be a lot more people trying to make a quick buck." Preston waves his hand as he quickly nods. "You know, people trying to make some money, some coin."

The woman pauses for a moment as she just lets the words sink in. However, she gives a simple shrug as she speaks up. "A positive influence, if it works."

"Yea." Preston glances to the stairs and then back to Clover as he nods. "So, if there is nothing about that, let me know, we can brainstorm." He shrugs. "It's not magic or something crazy, so this is at least in my wheelhouse."

"Y-yes." Clover's eyes fall to the papers beside her as the sound of Preston moving to the stairs rings into the house. Yet, as the sound counties Clover finds her voice, a low comment rushing from her as she straightens up. "I am happy you accompanied me earlier, Preston. Your writing has improved with the quill."

The words draw brief pause from Preston as he simply leans into the stairs, his right foot already placed to the first step up. Despite this, he turns back to the table as he nods. "Yea... I uh, I should apologize for that, I didn't mean to be rude or anything."

Clover merely shakes her head, her light blue eyes staying turned away from the man as she replies. "There is nothing to apologize for."

"Sure." Preston wobbles against the staircase as he falls silent.

In the absence of his voice though, Clover's fills the room as she brings her gaze to his. "Do you wish to talk? It may help if you-..."

"Not tonight." Preston shakes his head. "Thanks though, I just... I don't want to talk about it."

A sigh of relief comes from Clover as she nods. "Good. I-I mean, not that you do not wish to talk but that you are able to know how your feel on the matter, that is."

"Yea."

Again, Clover's voice spikes up a little more as she now sways in her stance a bit, her hands comes to the table as she braces herself against it. "But if you do wish to talk, we are able to."

"I know." Preston clears his throat as he points to the stairs. "Well I'm uh... I'm going to turn in for the night."

The comment draws a quick reply from Clover as she nods. "Good night."

"Good night, Clover." With simple nod Preston starts up the stairs, the sound of his echoing into the house below as Clover's eyes fall to the stack of papers next to her. Though the satyress holds her ears to the noise, she does not move away from the table.

Within a few moments, the door opening and closing upstairs rings to the house, prompting Clover to take her seat as settles in for her lengthy night of reading.

Chapter 5

Mightier than the quill

The new day has rolled in rather quickly, with Clover following her trend from yesterday and waking Preston up early. Unlike yesterday Preston has yet to retreat upstairs for his morning nap. A product of Preston's relatively peaceful night of sleep which has done its part in warding off the desire. Of course, as the morning has trailed on, the lack of real excitement has brought the thought to mind several times already.

At every passing of such a thought the extent of the man's patience and friendliness has been put to the test. Since the first true light of late morning shined into the library a steady stream of customers has ventured inside.

In truth, Preston has never had a real problem talking with the would-be people he has found himself living around. Although, being expected to find a book or even understand the strange titles almost instantly has begun to take its toll on the man. While *VéturVill* may not have a true elite class of citizens, the vast majority of those who come in for a book tend to be those with money. Not wholly uppity, though not the type of people to really deal with while still learning the language.

Despite this, Preston has held himself well, finding a corner of the library where he fiddles with the books on the shelves, most unmolested.

Of course, as the sound of someone coming up behind him takes his attention, the moment of reprieve has come to an end.

"Ah, I never would have thought someone of your height would find themselves serving a library."

The comment takes Preston's attention as he turns to face the short, fur capped wearing *Dwoff* man. Meeting the short man's gaze only prompt him to continue on as he passes a smile to Preston. "I assumed you would be hauling the forest or something."

Preston just blinks to the man as he speaks up. "Yea."

The *Dwoff* merely nods to the words as he glances around the library. "Hm, well, I do not suppose you could direct me to a book on *Alcrex Márjx*, could you?"

The name sparks a slight smile to Preston's face as he nods. "Yea, but are you looking for something specific?"

"I would think not, the elixir I mean to craft is fairly common." The short man gives a simple chuckle as he nods. "Though I do not rightly remember the ingredients."

"Alright." Preston moves to the bookshelves he stocked last night as he pulls out one of books, pausing just for a moment to check the symbol of on the side of the book. "Here you go."

"Splendid." The short man looks the book over as he continues. "Now, will you be taking my name or someone else?"

"Someone else."

The words spark a slight smile to the *Dwoff* as he looks Preston over again. "Of course, should have known *Brivtó*."

Preston squints to the name, but before he can speak up the fur-capped man starts towards where Reynard sits at the table. A few people already standing near him, yet for the most part the library is relatively quiet as Preston turns away, no longer interested in the *Dẃoff*.

"You make for a decent librarian, Preston. At least when you know where the books are."

The comment draws Preston's attention as he turns to the woman a little behind him. "Now I know why librarians want people to stop talking."

Clover cocks her head to the comment as she speaks up. "Strange, a librarian should enjoy sharing knowledge."

"Mhmm." Preston glances over the crowded table as he trails on. "Still surprising to see this place crowded every day, well relatively crowded I guess." He glances back to the bookshelves around him as he continues. "Ten, err twelve bookshelves... sure they're tall, but still can't believe this counts as a library."

A slight smirk comes to Clover's face as she turns her attention back to the shelves. "It is *VéturVill*."

"Okay so you agree with me?"

Clover shrugs. "A larger library would be nice for the town, though it may not matter."

"Right." Preston nods. "So how big are-...."

"Fair winds, Clover."

It only takes a second for the deep, feminine tone to be recognized. However, before Clover and Preston can turn to greet the avian-woman, Elva has already moved to their side, the book from yesterday in her hand. "Your suggestion was adequate, Clover."

The comment immediately draws a slight chuckle Preston as he looks over the book in her hold. "Whoa, I'm surprised you could read all that."

"Are you saying I cannot read, Preston?"

Another faint laugh comes from Preston as he shakes his head. "No, not that, just surprised you read all of it so quickly."

Clover's magic takes over the book in Elva's hand as she cuts into the conversation. "Elva is a fast reader she-..."

"Yes." Elva's comes over Clover's as she continues. "While thick tomes may be a thing for the *Únoff*, all those in positions of power must learn to read. I would say I can read faster than Clover, providing a good reason too."

Clover nods as she looks over the book drawing closer to her. "It is not a competition, Elva."

"So true, Clover." Elva turns her eyes over Preston's body as she nods. "This one would be unfit for any sort of challenge." She nods to the stairs. "Should you not be asleep, the *déy* all but started, Preston. You would not wish to be tired for lunch."

"So, Elva did you enjoy the book?"

Clover's question steals away Elva's gaze, though Preston now rocks in his stance, wanting to continue their back and forth. Still, he bites his tongue as Elva answers. "As I said, it was adequate. Weather patrol has started their clean-up of the sky; there is little for me to oversee in this process."

Clover gives a simple nod as she takes the book into her hand. "Well I am happy to hear, perhaps you would like a-..."

Elva immediately shakes her head. "I will not be needing anything else." Elva glances back to the table were Reynard sits, the last customer now getting checked out as the avian-woman continues. "I wonder if you would take me up on my offer, to spar with me, Clover."

"Elva I need to stay here-..."

"*Hmpf.*" Elva shifts her attention, her noise cutting Clover off as she cocks an eye to Preston with a quick comment. "What about you?"

Preston merely squints to the question. "What about me?"

"Are you not a male, Milk-Chest?" She taps to her neck as she continues. "That amulet may help control your feelings, but there are only two ways to deal with grief Preston. Combat or coitus. Yet all you do is sleep and carry books around."

"Elva-..."

Clover's words draw the avian-woman's head as she nods and waves a hand to her. "I have a reason for my words." She shifts back to Preston. "If Clover does not wish to spare fair enough, she has proven to me before that she is capable of protecting herself. You, however, are weak, wasting your time with *Unoff* enchantments when all you need is to let out your anger. Come, spar with me, you may learn something."

Preston shakes his head. "I'm not going to fight you."

"You will not get hurt, Preston. I have control over my blade, and fret not over hurting me, you will never get close enough."

Clover looks over Preston's slight hesitation as she speaks up. "Using real swords is still too dangerous, Elva."

A chuckle rolls from Elva as she shakes her head. "Hardily, do you truly believe I would hurt him? Drawing such weak blood would be a disgrace to my blade." A cocky smirk comes to Elva as she nods. "Well, Preston?"

Preston merely blinks to the comment as he stammers a little.

Although, the mindless sentence brings Elva's voice back as she shifts to Clover a little annoyed. "Would you not agree that he needs something aside from books?"

The satyress quickly shakes her head as she speaks up. "Well of course, but this is hardly a safe choice, even with you, Elva." Clover moves her left hand to her hip as she shakes her head, her gaze slightly shifting away from Preston as she speaks up. "I forbid you from doing this."

A laugh comes from Elva as she moves her own hands to the steel colored plateskirt at her waist. "You speak as if he were a *yiftiñ*." She holds the smile as she nods to Preston. "Come, we can set out now, Preston."

Despite Elva's more jubilant tone as Preston continues to linger without an answer nor without a movement her smile begins to fade a little.

"You know what, yea." He nods as he shifts his gaze to Clover. "I think I need a little break from here."

"Good." Elva gives a simple nod. "I had hoped you might realize how lucky this opportunity might be for you, to actually get some proper training in the sword." She turns away as she moves towards the door. "Come along, I know a warm spot outside of town for our training."

"We're leaving now?"

"Of course." Elva gives a simple laugh. "Unless you need to ask permission from Clover that is."

A faint sigh rolls from the satyress as she shakes her head. "Of course not, Preston can do what he wishes."

"There you have it." Elva nods. "Now come, Preston."

At the comment, Preston follows the avian-woman, Elva making short work of the house as she moves outside and into the cold. Preston however lingers just for a moment as he passes a nod to Reynard. Though as the cool air hits his face he speaks up. "Still cold, huh?"

Elva's eyes turn to the sky as she speaks up. "The cool air will soon be replaced with the fresh heat of flower's reblooming. Besides, the brisk chill will keep you alert."

"Right."

The comment slowly brings Elva's eyes from the clouds as she stares to the path set before her. "It only takes a few flaps to reach our sparing spot, but the trek may prove to be an excellent warm-up for you Preston."

- - -

(A Fair Venture Later)

While the cloud cover has indeed loosened up a bit from the weather patrol, the same thick blanket of white can still be seen in the distance; however, their walk out of town has brought a new warmth to the man. The sun itself is bright, no longer hidden behind the clouds above; while welcoming, the light sweat clinging to Preston's brow has become an annoyance.

For the most part, Preston has kept up with the avian-warrioress, though as the incline of the dirt path they travel on continues, Preston does fall back a little. The rolling hills of the fields outside of the town, coupled with Preston own lack of real exercise quickly getting the better of him.

The man's quiet panting, which Elva has chosen to ignore for the better part of the journey has finally spurred her voice, as she turns back to her straggling follower. "You cannot be tired... this is hardly even a walk."

Preston squints to the comment as he turns back to the town of dull wood houses. "What? Have you even seen how far we are?""

Elva merely shakes her head. "Pathetic display of stamina, Preston." She turns around as she reaches the top of the hill. "The end of your journey is just below, hurry."

At the words Preston speeds up, lowering his head a little as he forces himself up the hill.

Just as he reaches the woman awaiting him, she turns and continues down the steady slope. Preston however does not move to follow her, opting instead to take notice to the bright, healthy trees that span the fields now in view. The sight of the trees takes Preston by surprise, the chill in the air is still present, yet very little snow actually covers the ground. The fields of grass too look to be relatively untouched by winter, unlike the dead grassland flanking the town behind him. Noticing this, Preston turns back to the town and then back to the health area around him.

"What is this?"

"That is one of the outer farms." Elva waves her hand to the fields around her as she continues to move away from the man. "Can you not tell?"

"How is everything so green?" Preston gives a faint laugh as he starts after the woman, all the while still looking over the world around him.

"Of course, the clouds never fall over the outer farms. At least not all at once."

Preston simply shakes his head. "Why even have it snow then? It just makes it a hassle to get through town."

"It is placed in the fields to promote new growth." Elva glances to the greener pastures around her as she continues. "The farms must lay dormant at some point, the *Jartál* decides when."

Preston simply shrugs to the comment as he speaks up. "Alright, then why is it cold in the town?"

"Because it keeps the stench of the *Dẃoff* at bay." Elva's wings flex out a little to her words as she turns from the path and towards a dirt patch in the field beside her. A few knee-high rocks jet out from the field around them, though the area is smooth and level, unlike the grassland around it.

Near the far side of this semi-circle is a small tree, with a few fair-sized red buds growing within its branches. Elva pays this little mind however as she moves towards it, stabbing her dagger into the trunk as she begins to undo the belt holding her weapons around her waist.

Preston continues forward, his plethora of questions seemingly coming to an end. Instead, he simply watches the avian-woman before him now pulling out two neatly polished, and well-kept steel blades from the belt now hanging at the tree.

His stare draws Elva's voice as she squints to him. "I do not know why Clover had told us to act warming towards you, I see no inner torment in your face."

The words halt Preston as he shrugs, his hands tightening up to his chest as he pops his knuckles and rubs his hands together. "What do you mean?"

Elva's wings flair out a little out as she starts to loosen the ties to her armor chestplate, although her words continue without a pause. "Clover has told us what happened at the Capital... She has said you have grown quiet. A much-needed change for you, I believe." The smile holds as she rolls her eyes over Preston's body. "I hear no difference in your tone. I believe you have just grown idle." She taps her hand to neck as she pulls her armored chest-plate away from her upper body, revealing her cotton undershirt. "It is the *Únoff* magic, it suppresses feelings."

Preston continues to roll his hands over one another as he nods, his head shifting away from the woman. "She told you about what happened?"

Elva balances the heavy metal armor on her right arm as she nods, hardly even acknowledging the weight. "Yes, I feel for the loss of your kin, Preston. Although, I do not condone sulking."

The words bring a quick reaction from the man as he shakes his head. "Hey! It's only been a few days! You don't even know what-..."

The dirty blonde-haired woman simply cocks a smile as the amulet around Person's neck begins to glow, his angry tone quickly fading as his rant comes to a sudden halt.

Sighting Preston's dopey face, Elva speaks up, all the while as she holds her armor to the man. "I claim no expertise on the matters of magic.

I simply know, pent up emotion is nothing to keep. Clover may be able to brighten your amulet, though to properly deal with your feelings you must let them out. Cast aside the amulet and put this on."

Preston looks over the armor held out to him as he speaks up. "I won't fit in that."

A smirk comes to Elva's face as she nods. "Your chest is nearly as large as mine, Milk-Chest, your figure will suit the armor well enough to keep it still."

With a faint sigh Preston takes hold of the armor. The armor itself is heavy, though Preston brings it over his head as he fiddles with the loose leather straps at his sides. Despite Elva's lean figure, the armor fits over the man's shoulders fairly well, though not enough to actually tie it down. "I feel like a football player."

The laugh goes unreciprocated as Elva moves to the man's side, attempting to pull the armor down a little more. After moments of fiddling with it Elva moves back to the tree, taking up one of her swords as she passes it to Preston. "Take the sword Preston, and give me your amulet."

"Wait, what?" Preston looks over the sword as he takes a step back, his hand coming up to the amulet around his neck. "Why do you need this?"

"Simple." Elva waves her hand to the man as she continues to hold her palm open for the amulet. "That magic will hold you back, you must let yourself relax. If you cry, so be it, your worth can sink no further to me."

Preston blinks to the words, his right-hand fumbling with the amulet as he speaks up. "Wait we can't fight, you're not wearing anything but a shirt?"

Elva shrugs. "I have fought with less." At the words Elva turns around, moving to the further side of the dirt area. "This will be nothing but blocking Preston, you will never get close to me. But it will allow you to work off any built-up emotion, and me a spar."

"I'm not doing this; I could hurt you."

The words seem to draw a swift reply from Elva as the woman barks back at him. "Ready your sword and your stance, Milk-Chest!"

"You're crazy, Elva."

The women's wings flair out as she tightens her hold on the short sword. "Preston, ready your stance or I will strike."

"I'm not going to-...*whoa*!"

Preston's words are cut off as he watches the short sword slash towards him after a rather sudden lunge forward from Elva.

"What are you doing?"

The woman's shoulders are hunched a little, and her sharp eyes are pinned to the man as she smiles and continues to circle him. "Your sword, Preston, bring it up. Though you may think your hands a snack they are more useful than for tempering your jitters with nail biting."

Even with Elva's snarky remark, Preston hesitates, no sharp reply coming from him as he just stares somewhat dumbfounded to the situation before him. Inevitably, he tightens his grip as he brings the sword up.

The blade wobbles a little in his hand, yet the sight of Preston's hold brings Elva's circling to halt. Elva stands straight, her sword at her side yet her confidence remaining the same as she speaks up. "Cast the amulet aside, Preston."

"No, I need to-..." His words are cut off as Elva lunges forward forcing him to jump backward.

"What are you doing?!"

Elva speaks up, her encircling of the man starting up again. "Your brother, what happened to him?"

Her raised voice, mixed with Preston's confusion to the situation sparks a quick response in the man as he shakes his head. "What does that have to do with anything?"

Once more Elva's steps forth with a powerful swipe, her blade striking against Preston's sword, which stumbles the distracted man just a bit as he calls back to her. "Stop!"

"What happened to your brother, Preston?"

Elva takes a step forward, bashing her blade to Preston's as the metal on metal clashing rings into the fields.

Preston yells out as he forces Elva back. "He's gone!"

"Why will you not say more, Preston?! Were you too weak to protect him?" Elva's words are quickly followed up by a heavy flap of her wings, kicking the dirt into a frenzy as it blows to Preston. With the distraction in place, Elva follows through with another thrust forward. This time pushing the man's blade away and then jabbing to the protection at his stomach.

The sight and feeling of the blade actually hitting the man's body brings a rapid burst of emotion as Preston pushes against Elva, causing a spark of his magic to shove her back as he looks over where the sword struck him. Naturally, the armor did its job, yet the feeling of the blade hitting him still draws a shout from Preston. "I didn't know what to do! Alright?!"

Elva halts as she listens to the man's continued rant. The sudden fear of the blade messing with Preston's mind as he finally admits to the guilt swirling within his chest. "I said I'd watch after him and I didn't, is that what you want to hear?"

No tears greet the man's eyes, and his voice does not crack despite the high in his emotions. Although Elva pauses all the same as she watches the amulet around Preston's neck now flickering.

However, this does not stop Elva's reply as she merely loosens her stance. "Doubt is what held you back, though perhaps there truly was nothing you could do. It is a pity. Of course, your failure does not surprise me."

Preston's hand on the blade tightens as he shoots his head back up, a newfound annoyance and anger to his eyes. "What did you just say?"

Elva squints to the glance as she raises her sword. "I had intended to spare your feelings, though from any *Flöff's* view, you failed because you were weak. Too scared to protect those you promised your blade to."

Without warning Preston darts forward, his emotion driven strike easily avoided as Elva jumps over him, landing with ease in the spot where Preston once stood. Her wings hardly making a sound as she calls back to him. "Very good Preston, very-..."

Elva's words are cut off as she quickly brings her sword up to block Preston's next slash. The vexing gaze set to her drawing a laugh as she pushes Preston back with her might. "Allow your frustration to pour forth, Preston."

"Shut up!" Preston steps back, only to thrust forward a moment later as he frees himself from Elva's blade. His skill along his movements are predictable, with each subsequent attack being blocked with ease as Elva merely dances around him.

"Breathe Preston, hate my words, though do not lose sight of their purpose."

Elva's comment yields little more than an angry, almost growl from Preston as he cups both hands hard to the hilt, slashing or jabbing the blade forth with nary a thought to his actions.

Just as before, Elva makes swift work of deflecting to side stepping his advances. Though, her eyes continue to linger to the bright flickering within the amulet around Preston's neck.

Their dual continues on for a few moments, Elva holding the upper hand with hardly a heavy breath in her actions. Yet, a new green glow has steadily begun to form around Preston's hands, one that Elva has failed to take true account of.

Preston of course pays it little mind, his eyes focusing into Elva's stance as he pushes forward, his sword coming forth with a quick jab.

Elva rapidly jumps back, batting the sword away, though Preston's frenzy of swipes do not halt as the sound of metal on metal starts to chime to the field.

"Preston you need to-..."

Despite the attempted comment, Preston's eyes stay latched to the avian woman, an almost animal like rage in his gaze. While the erratic swipes of the sword are hardly a thing of grace, the considerable speed coupled with the true to life anger in Preston's motions have begun to force Elva back. Prompting the woman to take a more defensive stance as she continues to ward off the man's steady approach.

No matter how skilled Elva may be, her luck finally comes to an end, her holding back proving to be her downfall as the last slash finally makes contact. No scream comes from the woman, though with a powerful flap of her wings she forces Preston away, the visible slash on her shirt waving to the power of her gust.

The power of her wings, in tandem with the wide eyes Elva has pinned to the man finally spark something within Preston as he pauses, the realization of what he did sinking in. Of course, Preston only gets a moment of gawking as the amulet around his neck spikes up, a shocking sensation similar to that of brushing up against an uncovered electrical socket now rushes through his body. The faint jolt rocks the man's hands, prompting Preston to drop the sword from as he stumbles backwards.

"*Brevet* Preston." A smile comes across Elva's face as she brings her hands to her slashed top, a finger dipping into the cut. As her finger comes out the sight of blood greets Preston's eyes.

"I cut you?! I-I didn't mean to-..."

The man's shaky voice does nothing to the woman, as she instead sheaths her sword. "Fret not Preston, it is merely a scrape-..."

"No!" Preston shakes his head. "I did that! I didn't even realize I was doing it?!"

Elva waves her hand to the comment as her wings slowly start to fall to her sides. "My flesh is thick, Preston. A simple cut is of no concern; besides you should feel proud of it."

Continuing to ignore the words Preston moves his hands to his neck, pulling to the amulet as he speaks up. "I couldn't stop myself."

"Preston it-..."

"I couldn't -..."

Elva takes a step forward as her voice raises. "Preston, stop!" Elva crosses her arms as she looks the man over, the smile that once crossed her face now faded. "This was a sparring match, you allowed your emotions to carry your attack, you did not hold back. This should be something of triumph for you, yet you stand there worrying about a simple cut. Are you not a man?"

"P-proud? How can I be proud of that? I could have hurt you."

"You give yourself too much credit. I was never in any true danger." Elva turns her attention to the sword on the ground as she moves to collect it. "I am not frail like Clover. Tell me, do you not feel better? The beat in your chest? The warmth in your muscles?"

Preston rubs his hands together as he lets the questions drift away into the fields around him. "I've felt depressed, guilty even... but not angry at you, or anyone. I just feel like time is slipping by. Even if I get better there's no reason to go back, and there's nothing here to stay for. I just feel empty."

Elva rolls her eyes as she takes another step to the man, smacking a hand to his shoulder.

"What was that for?"

"I asked you how you feel." Elva shrugs. "Yet your response is some dribble of an *Únoff* heart." A sigh rolls from Elva as she trails on. "I suppose it is all the same, I should return you to Clover before your wound acts up. After all, you have drawn blood, and I doubt I would be so laid back if we were to start again."

"Sorry about that."

"Do not apologize." Elva shakes her head. "It only lowers your worth. Now come forth, I need my armor back from your Milk-Chest."

Chapter 6

Penitence

It has been a few hours since Preston returned to the library; Clover, for the most part, asked little about the duel, and Elva said nothing of the slash under her armor. Of course, this has done little to stir Preston's mind from what happened.

While the constant feeling of the day wasting on has yet to leave Preston's mind, the fight itself has helped keep Preston's mind grounded in reality. If only for the sole purpose of figuring out how he was unable to stop himself from the aggression he showed.

Naturally, no answer has come to Preston, and the day has counted on, despite his feelings towards it. Dinner has come and gone, and the moon has come to settle over the land as it normally does. Unlike the last few nights, Preston was the first to retreat upstairs and has since remained there, even after the sound of Reynard's paws tapped their way past his door.

The bed feels like stone this night, cold from the chill of the world outside and still not broken in from the short time Preston has laid in it. In truth, tonight is actually a bit warmer than most other nights, what with the clouds above the town having been mostly broken up throughout the day. However, the furnace upstairs has only recently been cranked up, yield little time for it to warm the bed before Preston retreated into it.

Because of this, Preston's eyes have locked to the ceiling, unable to give in to the sleep he wants.

To his right is the window, the curtains closed with just the small slit in the center allowing any of the pale moonlight into the room. Unfortunately, though, the crack is just wide enough to strike against Preston's eyes whenever he turns to his side.

The silence throughout the house however does little more than allow Preston's mind to swirl. Luckily, the man's thoughts are quickly pushed aside as the faint sound of Clover's hooves starts in from the hallway. Her trot is not as loud as usual, yet Preston can still count the steps she takes down the stairs as he holds his eyes to the door.

The sound of her hooves quickly fades somewhere downstairs as Preston begins to sit up, glancing to dark shades on the window as he stands.

With a few quiet steps, Preston moves to the door, opening it into the slightly brighter hallway he now comes into. The furnace on his right maintains its glow as he shifts towards the staircase. Downstairs a blueish light has taken hold and ever form where Preston stands the sound of papers moving about can be heard.

Cocking his head down a little, Preston descends the stairs, his eyes focusing to the table that quickly comes into view.

Sure enough the sight of Clover comes into view, a loose, off white nightgown holding to her body as she continues to manipulate a few scrolls and pieces of paper to the table before her. Preston however remains silent as he instead looks over the woman from behind. As he catches himself drift to her tail he speaks up and blinks away. "You okay?"

The words prompt Clover's left ear to flick a little as she turns to face the stairs where Preston still lingers. "Oh, Preston." Her magic fades as the stack of papers comes to sit on the pulled out a chair next to her. "You adjourned rather early tonight, are you feeling well?"

Despite the friendly question Clover shifts a little uneasy, her left hand close to the top of her night gown as she awaits the man's response.

The room downstairs is hardly bright, though the position of the Clover's ball of magic does a fine job of lighting her tan, youthful face. Yet Preston does allow his eyes linger for long as he shakes his head turning his gaze to the ground as he speaks up. "Yea, just a bit tired I guess."

"You did not hurt yourself, did you?"

Preston shakes his head again. "No, no, I'm fine." He pats his side. "It was only a quick little fight, no need to worry." He motions to the table. "So, what are you doing?"

Following the gesture Clover turns around, placing a hand to the table as she steps back. "Oh, I just wanted to look over *Jartál* Caféll papers again."

"Oh yea?" Preston clears his throat as he leans into the wall on his right a little. "Was it busy today, you know the library?"

The small talk seems to catch Clover by some surprise, though she eases up a bit as she shrugs. "No more than any other *déy*."

"Well that's good."

Clover moves her right hand to one of the papers on the table, drawing it up to her. Though she hardly gives it a look as she instead glances back to Preston. "So how was the duel with Elva?"

"Eh, like I said... I didn't get hurt."

"Yes." Clover nods as she attempts to look over the paper in her hand, she again turns away as she speaks up. "She left rather quickly, Elva that is... and you hardly spoke about it at dinner."

"Yea." Preston gives a slight chuckle to nothing in particular as he continues. "I uh felt a little out of it, not like sick or anything but..." He glances to the necklace around his neck as he nods. "What's this thing supposed to do?"

The sudden questions draws a confused blink from Clover, at least for a moment. Though the normally quick satyress picks up on the nod as she replies. "It is to help with your emotions."

"Right." Preston takes a deep breath as he leans a little more into the wall. "It's to keep me from hurting people, huh?"

"Preston." Clover shakes her head. "You are not a danger to anyone."

"Yet right?" The quick reply does not end as Preston taps again to the amulet. "This thing supposed to stop that, yea?"

"I believe you are thinking too much about it... did something happen-..."

"No, no, I just..." Preston stops himself. "Actually yea, I cut Elva."

"You cut her?" Clover's ear flicks to the comment as she draws forward a little, leaving the table of paper behind her as she speaks up. "She said nothing of that, why did you wait so long?"

"I don't know I just... I feel like I'm a fog with this thing on." Preston pushes away from the wall. "It was during the duel, I didn't mean to do it, and she just seem to laugh it off afterwards."

A sigh rolls from Clover as she nods. "How did you feel?"

The question draws a laugh from Preston as he shrugs. "Horrible, how else should I feel? I didn't even feel like myself while doing it."

Clover merely folds her hands as she lets the words mow over for a moment. All the while she maintains a fairly caring disposition as she speaks up. "Would you care to talk about it further? Perhaps it would even be beneficial to practice a little magic?"

It only takes a split second for Preston to speak up as he shakes his head to offer. "No."

"Preston, the amulet was designed to help with your emotions. Even we have spoken little about your brother, let alone how you are feeling. It could help with-…"

"Not tonight." Preston shakes his head again. "I don't even know why I told you what happened, obviously it's no big deal, she didn't even say anything."

The satyress shifts her hands as she opens up a little more, her magic moving the stack of papers from the chair as she pulls it further from the table. "Preston it would not hurt to talk."

The sight of the chair being pulled out draws Preston's gaze, though he nonetheless shifts from it as he speaks up. "I can handle it." He chuckles. "I just need to get over it and get home."

Clover blinks to the words. "Get over it?"

"Yea, I just need to forget it." Preston shrugs as he chuckles. "I just need to forget about it, all of it."

"Preston, suppression is not healing."

"You know what's not healing? Having this damn thing around my neck all day." He chuckles a little more as he rubs his thumb to the amulet. "Thing itches and chokes me sometime. But if I take it off, who knows what will happen, you know?"

Clover merely close her mouth as she steps forth, her magic taking hold of the amulet around Preston's neck as quickly pull it from the man's neck. The feeling of it leaving neck however only prompts Preston to dart for it as he speaks up. "What are you crazy?!"

Opting not to break it, Clover's magic loosens as Preston tugs it back over his head. "Preston it is simply an enchantment, nothing more."

The words do little to draw Preston from the amulet he tugs to around his neck as he slowly glances back to the woman. "You don't feel it."

Clover shrugs to the words, her arms crossing over her petite chest. "Then tell me how you feel?"

"You... I can't explain it." Preston moves his hand as he stammers. "I just don't feel like myself." He glances back to the stairs. "I'm just gonna go back upstairs."

"Wait." Clover's words are followed by the quick sound of her magic she teleports in front of the stairs, a look of concern or confusion now taking hold over her face as she speaks up. "Master Nyota will need to know how you are doing, talk to me Preston."

Despite the quick spell Preston easily turns his gaze away as he shakes his head. "Look I shouldn't have come down here, I'm fine."

Clover's head falls a little as she gives in. "Very well." She takes a step aside as she nods. "Sleep well, Preston."

The words draw Preston back, as if her were a child looking for attention. Despite this however, he does speak up, though still unable to truly look at the woman in the eyes. "I'm sorry."

Clover squints to the words as she crosses her arms, a bit fed up with Preston's game. "For what, Preston?"

Though a bit uneasy, Preston forces himself onward. "I'm sorry for the castle, for doing what I-..."

"Stop."

The suddenness of Clover's response along the word brings a squeamishness to Preston's stomach, as well as a tightness in his chest. Yet he says nothing as he watches the woman's eyes drift away from his. "It would be wrong to not allow the forgiveness you seek, especially knowing that your actions where not your own. Though I hardly see this as the proper way to ask for it." Clover nods. "What happened was not your fault, if I believed you were a danger I would not have agreed to watch after you. That said, and what has frightened me is how much you have changed. It is a bit selfish to believe you would be so open with me, though like Master Nyota, I wish to help."

As her words come to an end Preston nods. "Yea, I'm sorry."

Clover nods. "I know." She takes a breath. "I suppose I should have tried more myself, even I admit I was distant from bringing it up. Perhaps you can forgive me for this."

The perfect manipulation goes unnoticed as Preston nods. "O-of course."

"Thank you." Clover flashes a simple smile as she casts her eyes to the upstairs hall. "Sleep well, Preston. We shall speak more when you feel up to it."

"Yea." At the response Clover presses against the wall, allowing Preston start up the stairs as they brush past one another, both somewhat averting their gazes. Yet, as Preston starts away Clover does not immediately turn her eyes to the table, instead she lingers her sight until the man moves from view. Only with him gone does Clover finally turn away, her attention falling to the work she set out to do earlier.

Chapter 7

Conflict Card

The morning has come rather quick for Preston, sleep proving to be no real problem despite late night conversation between himself and Clover. Interestingly though, the satyress did not stop at his door this morning, even after their fair conversation from the night before. The sound of her hooves, however, did eventually stir Preston from his slumber and into the waking world.

Luckily, the warmer air within the library has worked in Preston's favor, allowing him to more easily avoid his ever-present desire to sleep the day away. Watching Reynard's reacts to Clover's newest attempt at breakfast also had its own pleasures, helping to keep Preston's interest in the world beyond his bedroom.

The amulet around his neck is still ever present, a constant nagging to his mind and his fairly bleak emotions. Today, at least so far, has been better, the dullness replaced just a little, much like the winds of spring now beginning to stir within the fields around the town.

Of course, Clover's choice in breakfast also helped, even beyond the looks it drew from Reynard. While not a culinary wizard, Clover's attempt at making pancakes from scratch seems to have done pretty well. The side of meat is of course a bit overdone, though for the most part, the meal itself is intact, with two choices of pancakes. One which Preston has found tastes similar to blueberry and the other with a sweeter, almost strawberry flavor. The fluffy, pan sized saucers of bread may be more donut like when Clover makes them, what with the middles sometimes falling out.

Still, the pancakes are no Preston special, even if they are better. And judging from the continued glances Reynard has given throughout breakfast, Preston has found the fox-boy feeling the same. At least by the way he pokes to the somewhat more mussy center of the pancake.

"Reynard did you move the foal books?"

The suddenness of Clover's voice perks the fox-like ears straight up on Reynard's head as he turns to the woman. "No, why?"

"Well, they were moved from the other *dèy*."

With a shrug Reynard replies. "Maybe we should move them higher?"

"Hmm." Clover nods. "Perhaps we will, after breakfast."

"Oh!" Reynard jumps from his seat, quickly pulling Preston and his own plate from the table as he plops Preston's plate over his to hide food. "We finished; we can do it now."

A simple roll of the eyes comes from Preston, though he says nothing as the fox-boy begins to clear away their side of the table.

His actions are quick, Clover hardly having a moment to speak up before the fox-boy turns into the kitchen near the table. Despite Reynard disappearing behind the half-wall however, Clover's voice still rings into the house. "If we are going to change it, I will need to get my list."

Clover pauses for a moment before turning her head to the library section of the house. "But I do not want to arrive at the blooming market late..."

"Blooming market?"

The question only adds to Clover's normal know-it-all tone as she shifts her attention to the man. "It is the first market in town after the cooling-..."

Clover's voice is cut off as Reynard comes back into the room, casually rubbing something from his paw into the child-size shirt he wears. "Clover only enjoys it because new books come into the market."

"Well of course Reynard, the library could always use more books." She shrugs. "I also enjoy seeing all the flowers dressing the booths."

Reynard merely rolls his eyes to the comment. "Clover the only flowers that open this quick are the *Coréopsis* flowers."

"And they are still quite nice to see."

Preston cuts through the woman's reply with a faint laugh as he crosses his arms and leans back in his seat. "So, more books and some flowers, huh? A real festival."

The sarcasm does not go missed, a smirk even coming from Clover as she brings her trot a little more towards where she had sat this morning. The closed inkwell, satchel bag, and rolled up scrolls still linger where she left them. "Yes. Now, shall we adjust the bookshelves before we set out?"

A sigh rolls from Reynard though the fox-boy nods. "Fine."

The tap-tap of Reynard's paws click across the room as Clover floats over the inkwell and the scroll. However, she turns her head from her assistant as she gives a simple smile to Preston. "Preston, would you mind helping?"

"I guess not, what are we doing?"

"Take the books from the top shelf of this two and place them on the middle selves. I want to clear off the top for now."

The woman's pointing brings Preston forward as he nods. "Couldn't you just use magic?"

"Yes." Clover nods. "Use yours."

Preston cocks his head back to the woman as he speaks up. "Clover I don't want to do that. Besides, we'd be here all morning if I did it."

The satyress just shrugs as she brings the quill from the inkwell floating next to her. "You are right, it would take a long time. Best you start now instead of giving excuses."

A slight hyena-like chuckle comes from Reynard as he moves a chair to face the library section of the house. The sound is a little annoying, but Preston turns back to the shelves in front of him as he awkwardly brings his hands up. "I'm saying this now, I really don't feel like doing this, so if I burn anything, it's on you."

Clover shakes her head. "I trust you will contain yourself, Preston. Besides, you need to use your magic. Also, do make sure to read the title before switching the books, Preston."

"Yea, if I ever get one from the shelf." Preston gives a little sigh as he focuses on the books before him. "Shouldn't I have that glove thing on?"

Clover straightens out the scroll next to her as she shakes her head. "Not for this, the spell is quite simple."

"Mhmm." As the man's noise come down, he clears his throat, and slightly hunches his shoulders, his gaze to the books.

The flickering of his green magic is slow to come to the spine of the first book in the row. However, Clover holds her gaze to it as she just studies the low shine of the man's magic.

Her silence brings Reynard's voice up, as his boyish voice comes to the room. "It might be easier to do the motion of pulling it out, at least for the first one."

Preston nods to the words, as he pulls his hands back. His motion draws the book out, though it falls from the shelf as he tugs it out; luckily, the magic tightens around it before it hits the ground.

"Good, Preston." Clover's happy tone quickly shifts back to her dull, know-it-all voice as she glances back to her list. "The title?"

The glow to the book sparks up a little more as Preston takes a deep breath. The book slowly comes up to eye level as Preston squints to the words. "Magic for Foals."

"*Márjx* For Foals." Clover writes something to the paper as she continues. "Now, if you would, pull the first book on the second shelf out you can-..."

Clover's words are brought to an end as a sudden shrinking comes to the room, Preston's amulet sparking up as the man is forced to dart his hand to the burning sensation where the amulet lies. The sudden feeling along with Preston's own jerking motions prompts the book to fall to the ground as he tugs the amulet from his shirt. Though, with his spell coming to an end the amulet's glow as well as its sound ceases.

"Fuck!" Preston pants a little as he pulls his shirt down from his neck, mainly ensure his chest has not actually been burnt.

His shout however only brings Clover's voice up as her magic takes hold to the book now resting on the ground. "You should be more careful, Preston."

The words draw a sharp response from Preston as he watches the book casually float into its new destination with ease. "I told you I didn't want to do this!"

Reynard shrinks a little to the outburst, like a dog being yelled at as he takes a step away from Preston. Clover however simply blinks to Preston's anger as her ears perk up a little, her tone remaining unchanged. "Preston it was just a mishap it is nothing to get upset about-...."

"Mishap my ass!" Preston tugs the lip of his shirt down a little more as he continues to yell. "Look at this red mark! This thing burnt me!"

The continued yelling does little to sway Clover as the woman simply shakes her head. "Preston you are fine, you need to just take-..."

"I'm fine? Ha!" Preston continues to look over the red mark as he shakes his head. "I'm not going to-..."

"Preston, go sit down."

Clover's voice never raises, though her look draw a quick silence to the man as Preston stares her down. Yet, again Clover remains unchanged in her gaze and her stance. Though this is not what finally forces Preston to step away, instead it is the sight of Reynard's confused and rather scared face that prompts the man to back down. Doing so only brings a heavy feeling of shame and regret as Preston turns away, the amulet's normal effect now taking hold.

Both Reynard and Clover watch the man move back towards the table, Preston opting not to sit down as he instead, stands beside the table, his hands to his pockets.

With a slight sigh Clover speaks up, her more cheerful voice taking Reynard's attention. "Well no sense in waiting now."

Clover's magic starts up, her hand taking on a bright glow as a blue hue comes to the books on the shelves, within moments the magic rings out and the books jiggle as if they have been moved. The unmistakable sound of a teleportation spell bounces to the walls as Preston merely looks on.

"Why'd you want me to do this if you could just teleport them?"

Clover gives a quick glance to the man before nodding. His tone is not angry, though Clover still pauses before answering him. "Some text are of different material, so they will be jumbled. I will still have to go through the titles; but I can do so later. For now, I would rather begin heading to the market."

The cap comes to the inkwell, as she turns back to the table to set her supplies down. Reynard follows the motions as he turns his eyes to Preston, his sheepish expression still linger. "You... you did well Preston."

The innocents in Reynard's voice coupled with his boyish expression only prompts Preston to sink further into his quick regret as the man attempts to clear his throat. "T-thanks."

Clover nods to the comment, though she continues to eye the man as she speaks up. "Will you be accompanying us Preston. As I recall, we have yet to actually taste a pizza, correct? You may be able to find the ingredients in the market."

A somewhat forced smile comes to her face as she draws her satchel over her. As she adjusts the bag around the right side of her blouse, just above her medieval styled skirt she nods. "Yes?"

Before the man can speak up, Reynard chimes in. "You did say the wet bread was good, and if it will taste better than last time... it would be nice."

Preston shifts in his stance, his voice dropping as he replies. "I uh... I don't want to spend any money on it, I'm not even sure I can make it, you know?"

Clover turns her gaze to the door as she starts towards it. "You should still look Preston, it will give you something to do."

Preston gives a slight groan as he follows after the woman. "Fine, but no promises."

"Good, then come along."

Chapter 8

Blooming

The clouds above the town's main street have all but disappeared, leaving nothing but a few wispy remnants. As a result, the air is warmer, and the world is finally without its dull lighting. Preston may not have the best knowledge of the town's layout, though, he knows enough of it to guess at their close proximity to the town's center. Of course, the obvious widening of the street as well as the plethora of *Yáppy* pulled carts that have come into view are a pretty good giveaway to this fact.

Sadly, the fresh, warm air of spring is slowly chased away as they inch closer to the market. The once pleasant air of the town now filling with the thickening stench of animals and cabbage being to blow in. Worst still is the cluttered noise of the market that begins to ring in from their proximity. While lively, the racket is nevertheless a bit annoying, at least for Preston.

Clover and Reynard shift their walk, drawing Preston closer to the large roundabout leading into the marketplace. However, the crowds within these tight corridors of wooden booths take Preston by some surprise. Even still, his eyes do eventually shift away from mobs of people as he turns to the colorful banners and strings of yellow flowers that line the simple wooden booths. The chatter of children can be heard just above the rampant calls of those bartering in the market, though most of the cheerful laughs only come up from the rapidly melting piles of snow still sitting around the outer areas.

Clover's trot does not stop, her group moving further into the conglomerate of people, the joy filled sounds of children quickly being drowned out by the somewhat more prominent tones of those bickering amongst the hordes.

Despite all this, Clover's words still draw Preston's attention as she moves a hand to her bag. "Well, I shall start my browsing towards Bella's shop if you need me."

The comment takes Preston's attention as he turns to her, though before he can speak up Clover continues. "Reynard could you show Preston around for a little? The crowds can be a bit much on the first *déy* and I want Preston to have time to look around." As her words come down a tan, fairly sizeable pouch of coins comes from Clover's satchel. The coin purse is a bit different than the ones Preston has seen at the library, though Preston can see recognize the bag's purpose from the sound of the coins within. The size and puffiness of the bag's sides however are a bit odd; Preston has only ever seen Clover get money from the library, and on most days the average coin received by closing time is rarely above twenty or so. Yet, the coin purse Clover floats down to Reynard seems fairly filled, and just from the color, Preston knows this is not the only sack of coin Clover has.

Reynard takes the pouch to his paws as he brings the simple string over his shoulders to drape down his chest. Though efficient, the size of the bag makes Reynard lean a little to one side. Despite this, Reynard's light excitement goes along well with his boyish swaying as he speaks up. "Can we stop by Bella's?"

A faint smirk catches to Clover's face as she shrugs. "I suppose, but make sure you spend time in the market."

"Oh of course, of course!" The *fróx* quickly straightens his posture as he takes the lead towards one of the side streets of the marketplace. "Come on, Preston."

Lagging behind the little fox-boy, Preston shifts his gaze from where Clover now fades into the mob of the market. "Shouldn't we have just stayed together?"

"Clover only ever stays near the booksellers." A smile crosses Reynard's face as he continues. "And she can take a long time before she buys anything. We will just meet here at Bella's."

Preston blinks to the comment. "How do you know I won't waste time looking around?"

Reynard cocks his head back to the man as he nods. "You... you would not do that, right?"

The questions draws a little laugh Preston as he shakes his head, turning his attention away from the fox-boy and now towards the crowds they near. Reynard's path has brought them around the market near a line of booths far away from the entrance, still plenty of people bicker and buy around them. Not as many as the other side, though nearing the noise Preston does find the sweat beginning to grow on his neck, and his hand slowly coming up to the amulet hanging under his shirt.

"Do you like the market?"

Preston clears his throat as he tightens his arms closer to his side, the faint bit of anxiety still building as he attempts to answer. "It's fine."

Reynard gives a simple smile to the comment, his boyish voice continuing as he nods. "It is nothing special, but I always liked how they dress up the booths. Are you happy you came?"

"Happy? Why? Because I get to see some wilting flowers stuck to some wood?" Preston blows his breath, his quick comment coming down as he glances to the fading smile on Reynard's face. With another sigh Preston lowers his voice. "Look I'm happy, it's just, I don't feel right." Preston shrugs. "Helping in the library is fine, but that's all I do. Every day, it's the same routine, and when something does happen, poof, it's gone, maybe an hour or two of something different, just like today. We're not going to find anything here; we're going to walk around and then head back. This is just another distraction, and it's draining." A faint chuckle rolls from Preston, his eyes shifting away from his one fox audience as he continues his rant. "I get that I'm complaining but staying home wouldn't have made a difference. If I didn't go, I'd sit inside wasting another day and feel like shit. Don't get me wrong, I want to be here, I want to have a good time, I want to enjoy this, but I hate it already, and I don't even know why. It's bullshit, and I'm rambling I know that... It's stupid and I'm stupid for saying it I just..."

Finally, Preston takes a breath, an angsty shifting, coupled with a nervous laugh charging forth from the man; a guilt washing over him, knowing full well how much he has overshared. A fact only made worse as Reynard finally squeaks out a reply, the fox-boy's ears as well as his shoulders slumping downward. "I'm sorry we made you come out here, Preston."

"No, no." Preston forces his head up, a smile crossing his face as he nods. "I'm fine, you know maybe the flowers and the people around here is what I need, something to shake me from this funk." He chuckles. "Look I'm an idiot, I'm standing here complaining about everything passing me by and we haven't even walked around yet. I'm wasting my own time and yours, ha-ha."

The laugh does little for Reynard, though the fox-boy nods all the same as he speaks up in Preston's lonely silence. "Well should we look for the ingredients?"

"Yes." Preston's answer is far from believable, his quick enthusiasm catching Reynard off guard. Even still, he continues. "Tomatoes, cheese, dough, and probably like some sugar or salt or something." A slight laugh rings from the man as he drifts his hand to the amulet at his chest. "You'll also need to come up with a topping you two might want."

"Well." Reynard holds his eyes to the man beside him as he nods. "I know where to get cheese, and Gwendy should have the same dough Clover got last time. But tom-ate-os? Not sure about that... but we should be able to find it."

Preston continues to tighten his body as he glances around the hordes of people they begin to move into. While most remain too preoccupied with their bartering and bickering the noise itself begins to quickly overwhelm the man. Despite this, Preston again attempts to shake off his dread of the public as he focuses back to the ever-energetic fox-boy beside him. "Right... so they're small, round, red, and usually have a green steam on them, uh... does that help?"

Reynard just gives a toothy smile as he nods. "We can get the cheese first, at least we know what to look for." His words are quick to end as he lowers his head and begins to move through the crowd. His short frame yields little problem as Reynard begins to weave his way through the market's outer edges. Preston however struggles to keep pace with the short fox-boy. While the outer edges of the market are not tight, the makeshift corridors of wooden stands cause a sort of funnel effect in the flea market like set-up. Naturally, Preston bumps into a few people, leading to several awkward apologies with the hairy, pig nosed people around him as he attempts to follow after Reynard.

The contrast of Reynard's bright fur against the dull stone and dirt of the ground makes it easy for Preston to spot him, especially over the short *Dwoffs* that crowd the area. Though, as straightforward as his path appears, Preston finds himself unconsciously drifting further and further away from the market, his heart pounding and his hands fidgeting with sweat as he pulls away.

It is only after Preston plants a foot into the slush on the outer edges of the market that he finally sobers up enough to realize he wander out of the market's slow-moving line. Still, the river of people continues to flow as Preston steps further away, his right hand against one of the outer buildings surrounding the market square. The noises of the market fill the air, mixing with the smell of dirt and herd animals, yet, Preston pays the world little mind; his focus to the heat at his neck. Though the sound of footsteps behind him do stir Preston's head as he turns around.

Sure enough, a middle aged, gray haired, and droopy nosed *Dwoff* meets Preston's gaze. The hairy dwarf sized man is dressed in tattered rags, his feet without shoes, revealing his curled or broken toenails. Though what causes Preston to straighten his posture is the *Dẃoff's* eyes.

The *Dẃoff* stares towards him, yet his gaze is hardly fixed, as if he were looking past Preston and beyond the building that blocks his path. Unfortunately, the uneasy stare is not the only thing Preston must deal with as *Dẃoff* speaks up, his yellowed teeth coming into view. "No blood sky, no blood sky."

The *Dẃoff* shakes his head with a smile as he points above almost giddy. "Dat *devún* saw to dat she dids."

Preston flashes a smile as he glances back to the market beyond the dirty figure. "Y-yea."

His response only seems to draw the *Dẃoff* closer as the hairy man nods with a smile. "Dat she dids, dat she dids. One *devún* now, smiles to her, less the sky bleed once more. Saw the pieces fall I dids, too far to get, though someone, someone will. Beyond dat *Hóbbel Vásil*." The *Dẃoff* continuous forward forcing Preston to step aside as he moves to sit down in the slush of the dirty snow.

Preston just blinks to the dirty man for a moment, almost surprised to how little respect the *Dẃoff* seemed to have for personal space, especially seeing as how the *Dẃoff* now sits just beside Preston's right foot, like a deranged child captivated by the snow. However, as Preston attempts to step away with a simple nod the *Dẃoff* reaches up, planting his hand to the man's arm as he tugs him back. "You agrees did you not?!"

The nonsense now being yelled causes Preston to jerk his arm away, though the *Dẃoff* seems to have little strength as Preston pulls himself away. "Get off me!"

Preston's sharper tone causes the *Dẃoff* to pause, though within moments the dirty, pig-nosed man simply turns away and beings to murmur to himself. Realizes just how crazy the *Dẃoff* is Preston backs off, shifting his head back to the continuous flow of people circling the market.

Opting to stay away from the main four rows of booths, Preston travels along the outer edge of it, his eyes scanning for Reynard's orangey fur against the dull background.

"There you are!"

The boyish voice takes Preston's attention as he turns to the sight of Reynard squeezing his way through the crowd. It takes the fox-boy a mere moment to reach Preston's side as he looks up to him. "I thought you were right behind me?"

Preston replies rather swiftly. "No… how'd you not notice?"

Reynard shutters a bit. "S-sorry."

With a sigh Preston attempts to steady himself, his gaze turning away from the fox-boy in front of him. "Maybe we can go a little slower, yea?"

"Okay." Reynard moves to Preston's other side as he motions for him to follow. "Um, I found the cheese Clover bought before, just wanted to know if you saw a different type you liked."

"Oh?" Preston squints to where Reynard seems to be tugging him along, his eyes focusing on the more spaced out booths, with several animal pens jetting out behind them.

However, it is the smell that quickly takes Preston's attention. While the simple wood pens are nothing too perfumed, the stench of cheese quickly flairs Preston's nose as he turns away from the few animals tied to the stacks in their wooden cells.

Preston's eyes turn now to a heavier set, curly red-haired *Dwoff* woman standing behind her booth. Her brown apron covered in cheese, or some type of milky mixture. In truth, the rather unsavory conditions of the food at each booth is a bit of a turn off for Preston, especially as he notices the meat merely hanging off hooks around him. Or, the golden cheese wheels, barely safe sitting atop the wooden booth with a thin towel.

While a bit off-putting, Preston is unable to turn away, half due to the crowds of people behind him and half due to Reynard's continued push towards the booth. As the pair draws near the woman's rather deep voice comes to their attention, as she continues to talk with the other *Dẃoff* in front of her stand.

"...I said, that *Biltýs* not for sale. Now, you want somethin' or not?"

The *Dẃoff* before the booth is much smaller, although the gray hair on his face and arms would suggest his age; and from the slightly annoyed tone he takes it does appear that the man feels insulted. Though the tone he strikes is one only an annoyed father could take up.

The bickering continues, Preston shifts his gaze to the few animals behind the booth. Two, brow, goat-like creatures stand tied to a short stake. Although, the double tails and single small curling horns in their foreheads would suggest a different sort of creature, the smell and eyes tell a different tail. Especially coupled with the large teats hanging down from their stomachs, beside the two creatures are three buckets of milk, and several bugs flying around the open lids.

"You, a tall thing, *hmm, brivtó*?"

The mindless face on Preston is quickly washed away as he snaps his eyes from the buckets to the woman now staring back at him. "Y-yea."

"Hm..." With a nod the woman waves her hand to the various cheeses resting on the cloth before her. Her sales pitch coming forth with little efforts. "What you like? All flavors, fresh milk, made with my own hands, not *Únoff* magic."

Clearing his throat, and shift a bit awkwardly, Preston speak ups, his eyes washing over the various cheeses. "I think we need this one."

The woman squints to the comment as she looks around her booth. "We?" She bends forward a little as her voice heightens. "Oh." Though her expression does not change she does lose a bit of their friendly tone as she nods. "Whole wheel? Four *sivý*."

At the words Preston stutters a little, his hands gingerly tapping to his pants until a paw nudges him. He quickly takes the pouch in hand as he fishes out the coin. The pouch is surprisingly deep, far more so than the little bag would lead one to believe, though passing it off as some sort of magic Preston continues to fish out a few of the silver colored coins. The somewhat rough texture and weight of them is a bit different than Preston had expected, but the enjoyable clang of the coins does ring out as he passes them to the *Dwoff* woman before him. "Here you go."

With the coins in hand the women scoots over the wheel of cheese, prompting Preston to pass the pouch back to Reynard as he takes hold of it. The smell is mostly gone, thanks to the special wrapping, though the weight of the heavy wheel does come to Preston as he tucks it under his arm.

Moving away from the booth Preston speaks up. "The first thing I've bought here is cheese."

Hearing Preston's somewhat more cheery tone the fox-boy perks up. "What?"

Preston shakes his head. "Nothing, just thinking out loud." He gives a sigh. "What's next?"

With the simple nod Reynard motions towards something beyond the crowds. "The green vendors tend to stay near the front, they should have the other ingredients."

"Okay." The man brings his eyes up as he studies the next few booths they quickly walk past. However, again he gives a simple laugh as he turns to his short companion. "You know, I could be the first person to invent the cart here. Think of all the extra things you guys would buy."

Reynard squints to the comment as he shrugs. "We have carts?"

Preston just waves the comment off as he speaks up. "It's different-..." His sentence falls short as he catches sight of something on the booths. "Wow, look, tomatoes."

"Where?" Reynard shifts his head around the booths though Preston merely pushes forward from the fox-boy's confusion.

Coming to the booth, Preston continuing to study the fruits, surprised to actually see such a familiar thing. Like last time the vendor behind the booth speaks up. "Ah, *Plestá déy*, see something from the *Fárwift* you like?"

The farm tanned *Dẃoff* behind the booth gives a simple smile as he awaits Preston's words. "Hey yea, let me get a few tomatoes."

The friendly smile slowly drifts from the short, hairy man's face as he nods. "You what now?"

Preston clears his throat and stupidly points to the wood box filled with the red orbs. "Um, those."

"*Rojs?*"

"Ha, yea." Preston clears his throat again. "The name just slipped my mind rojs."

The *Dẃoff* smiles as he speaks up. "That be two *Sivý* for the basket."

Preston blinks to the comment as he looks over the basket. There perhaps sits maybe a dozen or so fair-sized tomatoes.

Reynard however has already tapped Preston's free arm with the pouch. Not wishing an awkward moment, Preston tightens his hold of the cheese under his arm as he begins to fish out the coin.

With the coin now coming to the booth The *Dẃoff* gives a simple smile as he takes hold of a baskets. "*Plestá déy.*"

"Yea, you to thanks... uh thank you." Quickly passing the pouch back to Reynard, Preston takes hold of the basket. A few other patrons have begun to linger around the booth, though for the most part Preston's anxiety has been kept at bay, mainly from the silly smile he holds as both he and Reynard step away, thankfully with Reynard pointing out his stuttering. "At least these things look normal, and not rainbow colored or something."

Reynard just gives a simple nod as he looks over the shiny red orbs in the basket. "So, what do they taste like?"

Preston shrugs. "Oh, they taste terrible like this; we just need them to make the sauce, I kinda remember how to make some." Preston takes a deep breath as he halts his walk. "So, where is Gwendy's booth?"

"Gwendy's bakery is near Bella's shop, near the front." A slight hop comes to the boyish fox as he begins to move through the crowd a little faster. "Follow m-..."

"Oi there!"

Reynard's path is cut off as a burly pig-nosed man steps forward, a large steel axe joyfully swaying in their grasp. "You look to be strong, eh? Got something a man's hands needs, my friend!"

Preston pauses as he looks over the medieval blacksmith before him. His clothing is thick leather, despite the weather, his beard is misshapen, and scraggly, much like his hair. His words, however, are fair, and well-rehearsed. Worst still, the blacksmith is a master of following through, cutting off Preston before he can even speak. "Strong, yea? A true stallion as the *Kloopéi* would say, aye?"

Preston's eyes drift to the booth filled with weapons just beside the *Dwoff* as he speaks up. "Yea, I guess?"

"Good!" The short man just laughs as he pats a heavy hand to his axe before holding it out to Preston. "Put your hands on this axe, let your furry companion carry the women's work.

Preston merely takes a step back from the axe as he shakes his head. "No thanks I-..."

"A tall fellow such as yourself?" The *Dẃoff* shakes his head as he moves behind the booth placing the axe to the wood. "*Fárwift ó Dýnar* my friend? My weapons will make you feel at home again. The real weight of a hammer, aye? Not some *Maná* filled *Únoff* toy or some fancy *Flóff* craft, no! Real metalwork, from real mines of *Éordiarx*."

Preston glances to Reynard for a moment as he stammers. "I'm not interested in anything."

"Nonsense!" The *Dẃoff* tugs Preston closer to the booth, his smile fading a bit as he looks over the rather squishiness of Preston's arm. "Look there, your scales are weak, you need a real weapon to grow your spine!"

Preston steps back. "You deaf? I'm not interested, buddy."

The phrase seems to tick the *Dẃoff* off as he slams his hands down on the wood booth. "You think my craft is no good eh? Think only the Gulwing's metal is fit for your hand eh?! Off with you then you *Kloopéi*, and do not come crawling back when the sky turns to blood again and you need to defend yourself! See then if the *Flóff* forge be open to you."

Reynard speaks up as he moves to the booth, though he is forced to stand on the tips of his paws as he holds a finger to the *Dẃoff*. "Stop throwing such words."

The boyish voice takes the *Dẃoff's* attention as he bends over the table and then turns back to Preston. "Your taming skills are poor, lad. Look at this beast, it barks at an honest merchant."

The burly man gives a little laugh as Reynard tries to break in. "I am a *fróx*!"

"Ah, you be a *tát* with brushed fur!" The blacksmith continues his laugh.

"Hey!"

Preston's words hardly stop the laugh of the *Dẁoff* as the blacksmith merely crosses his arms. "Oh, did I offend you? Take it up with the guards if you not be willing to buy something. Now off with you, you be scaring away my customers with your weakness!" He nods back to Reynard. "Seek no quarrel with me four-paw, you nor that border running *Fárwift*."

The sudden change in the short man's attitude only builds to Preston's as he takes a step forward, the basket of tomatoes swaying with his step as the amulet under his shirt burns a little. "You think I'm scared of you? Step out here and I'll show you how fuck'n scared I am."

"Preston..." Reynard pulls to the man's pant leg as he continues in a hushed voice. "We should just find Clover."

The tug draws Preston's gaze as he feels a quick rush of sanity pouring over him, the weight of the onlookers forcing his shoulders down as the amulet's cooling takes over.

The *Dẁoff* merely holds his smile as he watches Reynard and Preston starting away, his voice not staying silent for long as he turns and shouts into the crowd. "Weapons for sale, finest *Dẁoff* craft!"

The exchange has ended, and Preston and Reynard now move away from the row of booths, coming to the edge of the market. Though, as they draw further away Reynard speaks up. "S-should we have apologized?"

"What? Hell no!" Preston scoffs. "I should kick his ass."

"You would get hurt." Reynard's head sinks as he fiddles with the pouch around him.

"Bruises heal, Reynard. People like that need to be taken down a peg." Preston sighs as he cocks an eye to the fox-boy. "Never apologize to someone who acts like that. Who even told you to do that?"

Reynard's eyes stay to the ground. "Clover and Nyota have always said it is rude to start a squabble without reason. We did take his time."

Preston shakes his head. "I doubt Clover would apologize."

"Yea..." Reynard brings his head up. "Well, at least we are closer to Gwendy's now." Reynard's nod takes Preston's attention, as he looks over the dark wood two story building a few houses down on the left. A slight smirk comes to the man's face as he takes notice to the few simple wood carved signs hanging from the buildings. The signs, despite their medieval craftsmanship, are colorful adding to the lines of flowers and banners that crisscross the sky above the market.

The building quickly comes to arm's length, but Preston and Reynard pause as a satyress exits the building, a heavy looking covered basket in her hold. The woman does not bat an eye to Preston or Reynard as she moves back into the market. Although, her absence brings the short foxboy forward as he moves into the building.

Preston however, stops at the doorway, as he looks over the interior. To his right and even his left sits a few white wood tables and chairs, nothing special but it would mark the first sort of restaurant he has seen since he has been here. Strangely though, it is the long counter of glass containers that holds the man's interests; because behind the almost modern like arrangement are a few baked pies, simple cakes, and various other pastries or sweets. The walls are even marketing the treats, with little carvings of them etched into the wall's frames.

As the man moves a little from the door, and it closes behind him a little bell chimes to the bakery. Within a flash, the reddish-orange furred woman pops from the back room. "Oh, *plestá déy* to you Preston!"

The feline features of the woman are amplified by her smile as she comes to the counter. Although Preston is more focused to the drab cook-like apron and plain clothing the usually eccentric woman is clad in. "What brings you by without Clover?" Her nose flicks as she looks the man over with a slight shiver. "Gwendy smells frustration, this would not be a personal meeting would it because-..."

Almost immediately her smile changes and her tone lightens up as she notices Reynard, an almost embarrassed voice comes forth as she leans over the counter. "Reynard is here too!"

At the happy acknowledgement Reynard speaks up. "Preston wants to buy some dough for a dish he is making."

Gwendy cocks her head back to Preston as she repeats the word. "Just dough?" Her smile holds as she looks over the man once more. "Gwendy did not know you knew how to bake? And with such a good scent to you... are you looking for a mate?"

"W-what?"

Gwendy merely gives a laugh as she turns her eyes back to Reynard. "What is he looking for?"

Reynard merely shrugs, once again prompting Gwendy to shift her quick eyes back to Preston.

Shaking off the strangeness of Gwendy's first question, Preston speaks up before the woman can. "I want to make a pizza, but I doubt you have that kinda dough. So, do you have any thin sort of dough?"

"Oooh, what is a *pit-zah*?" Gwendy gives a slight laugh as she brings a paw to her right cheek. "Oh! That is fun to say, pit-zah! Pit-zah!"

The comment brings a slight chuckle to Preston as he nods. "Well, it's hard to explain. But, it's like a bread-..."

Reynard chimes in. "It is wet-bread. Do you have any dough?"

"Give me the lightest dough you've got." Preston cuts in. "Also, you got any salt or sugar we could use?"

Gwendy hums for a moment before she turns back to the doorway she entered through. "Gwendy knows, just a moment."

As the woman dashes out of sight Preston shifts his attention to Reynard. "How do you guys understand the word sugar but not tomatoes?"

Reynard shrugs to the comment. "You say it strange, but it is close enough."

Preston begins to reply though the sound of two feminine voices coming out coming from where Gwendy retreated to instead takes his mind. The chatter is low, and no real tone can be judged from it, but the words and faint accent shared in the other room is enough to hold Preston's ear. Yet, it takes just a moment for Gwendy to bounce back into the room, a covered basket in one hand, and a small box in another.

"Alright, here you are, best dough in all of *VéturVill*, you know."

Preston gives a little smile to the words as he speaks up. "Nice little rhyme."

Gwendy just gives a smile as she passes the basket towards Reynard. Though, as the fox-boy reaches up to exchange the coin purse with her Gwendy relents, placing the basket to the counter as she speaks up. "Do not worry about the coin, Reynard." She extends the box to him as she continues. "We actually need a few *Kélf* stones charged. With the warming air we will need more cold places to store our stuff, and the clouds are just too expensive."

Reynard nods as he gives a little smile. "Oh, alright. Clover can charge them." He looks over the box. "Are they in here?"

Gwendy nods. "Yes! Oh! And do not try to eat them, they are nowhere near as good as a *Cúffy*, it makes your mouth tingle all wrong. But Gwendy does like the way they feel when they shake, just not on these lips." A giggle ends her words as she bounces away from the table with an overexcited farewell. "Well, *plestá déy*, both of you!"

Reynard gives a simple nod as he readjusts the coin purse around himself, attempting to hold up the two new items in his hold. Preston however dips down as he slides the cheese wheel into the basket and takes hold it. "Don't worry about this, I carry these two, you okay with the box?"

"Of course, it is not too heavy." Reynard eases both hands under the box as shows off a smile, though Preston merely smirks to the fox-boy as he looks over the fair-sized item in his hold.

With another goodbye the duo set out, the bell chiming once more as they step outside. "Alright, cheese, dough, tomatoes, salt and stuff, the rest is at the house. You're okay carrying the elf stones, right?"

"*Kélf.*"

"Yea that thing." With a blow of the breath Preston shifts his eyes away from the crowds still within the marketplace. "Okay, where is Bella's again?"

"Just a little further."

Like the last few stops, Reynard's quick pace supersedes Preston's, and the man is left watching the bobbing tail of the little fox-boy as he easily wades through the market's outer edges.

Luckily, the outer rim of the market is devoid of people, and Preston finds himself reaching the other side of the market within maybe two or three minutes.

The stone made building, even if it is sorts of compact, definitely stands out from the majority of wood-based structures around it. Purple cloth window shades sit to the building, giving it a pleasant feel to it, along with several other colorful flowers hanging from the windows it is not as noticeable today.

It only takes a moment for the fox-boy to open the door as he starts inside. Preston following behind as he tries to hold the door open with his foot, all the while trying to balance everything within his hold.

"*Plestá déy* to you."

The young sounding voice strikes Preston as he comes into the stuffy, fabric smelling building. Though his eyes do not bring Bella into view, instead the man's gaze quickly fall to a satyress standing behind the counter. The girl is young, maybe sixteen or so, at least from what Preston can tell from her height compared to Reynard's. The woman's hair is a light brown and pulled into two, short, ponytails that sit to either side of her head, casually draping down to her chest. Her horse-like legs that poke from the eloquent cream-colored dress are a bit darker than her hair, but despite her color, something in her face sparks a close resemblance to that of Bella.

Preston's silent stare however draws the young woman's voice as she looks the man over, almost a little apathetic to the would-be customer. "You are tall...." A slight giggle comes from the girl as she cocks her head. "What was your mother part *Jéfar* or something?"

"Juna, do not insult the customers." The more proper, Southern Belle like voice is quickly followed by the sound of hooves as Bella comes out from the cloth covered door behind the counter. Her tone quickly changes as her eyes come to the two new faces in the room. "Oh, Reynard, Preston." A sigh of relief comes from her as she nods. *"Plestá déy."*

Reynard quickly speaks up as his ears poke up to the top of his head. "Hello Bella!"

Bella holds her smile, though her eyes now drifting to the young satyress as she speaks up. "I do hope my sister has not offended you, I am sure it was just a filly's *Fon*."

Bella's comment does not go unheeded as the younger woman merely rolls her eyes and steps away from the counter. "If I am such an embarrassment why do you not just send a letter to mother, she would happily send me off again-..."

Bella gives a little laugh as she waves her hand to her sister. "Oh Juna, ha-ha, could-could you retrieve my measuring strip for me? We do have customers."

A faint sigh rolls from Juna as she slowly trots away, Bella traces her sister's walk out of the room although, as she exits Bella shakes her head, a groan escaping her before she turns back. "Ugh, sisters.... I shall not burden you with my feelings." She clears her throat as she continues. "What can I help you with?"

Reynard quickly speaks up as he takes a step towards Bella. "I would not mind your feelings, Bella. If-if you want to talk."

Bella cocks a simple smile as she bends down a little, her chest coming more level with Reynard as the fox-boy takes a step back to maintain eye contact with the woman. "Oh, Reynard, you are such a good friend, though I do not wish to punish you with my ramblings." Bella raises up as she turns her attention to Preston. "What brings you two here?"

Reynard again chimes in. "We are just waiting for Clover. Are you sure there is nothing I can help with?"

Bella gives another simple smile as she waves her hand. "No, no." Her eyes drift up a little as she sighs. "I have my own little assistant; I just need to find time to work and not manage ha-ha..." Her thoughts are brought to a halt as she brings her hand to her chin, her eyes now focused back to Preston. "Hmm, those colors are quite fitting on you with your hair. Of course, the rough look is still something new; perhaps a shade darker for your top, hmm?"

The satyress continues to tap to her chin as she repeats herself. "Maybe..." Her gaze slowly drifts to something in the room. However, the sound of hooves trailing back in brings her far off gaze to an end.

"Here you go Bella." The young girl holds the strip of measurement paper to her sister.

Bella hesitates to take it, but she does as she gives an acted smile. "Oh, yes, thank you, dear." She looks back to Preston and Reynard as she speaks up. "Now, what is it that you needed?"

Neither Preston nor Reynard speak up as they just stare back to the woman a little confused to the question they already answered.

"Oh yes, silly me. I have already finished your orders." Bella places the tape down. "Um, I will drop them off *témont*." She gives another light laugh.

Lucky, as her words come down the door behind Preston opens, and the familiar face of Clover takes everyone's attention. The satchel around her looks a little heavier, yet the woman hardly reacts to its weight as she speaks up. "I had thought I saw you two come in here."

"Ah, hello Clover, perfect timing as always."

Bella's comment brings a slight pause to Clover as she glances to everyone else in the room. "I hope I am not disturbing you with your-..."

"Nonsense." The friendly smile holds to Bella's face as she continues. "This little distraction was actually quite welcomed. I have been struggling to get my mind back on designing." She motioned to Preston. "And well, seeing Preston's more um... hirsute face has given me a few ideas." Her trot comes up as she nods. "Do forgive my shyness darling, we must talk more *témont*."

Clover nods as she turns away a little. "Oh, of course Bella, though I may be a bit busy-..."

"Do not worry." Bella shakes her head. "We will find the time."

With faint sigh Clover nods again, her smile holding. "Yes, Bella."

"Splendid dear!" Bella rounds the counter as she moves to curtain behind it, though she pauses as he beckons her sister. "Juna, do try and be a bit more cordial with our visitors, please. Especially if I do step away *témont*."

Juna straightens up, though her expression hardly changes as she merely rolls her eyes and glances back to the three strangers still in the shop. "Are you going to buy anything or not?"

"Ha-ha." Bella cups her hands as she glances between the trio and her sister. "Perhaps a little less *psyñial*, hmm?"

Clover chimes in at the comment. "It is quite alright, Bella. We should not be lingering here anyways, we merely agreed to meet up when we were done shopping."

Bella continues to linger against the curtain as she nods. "It is no bother, dear. Juna should get use to people in the store."

"I will never get used to the smell of *Dwoff*."

Bella raises her voice with a forced laugh. "P-perhaps we should trade places for a bit, yes, Juna?"

At the exchange Clover turns her attention to Reynard and Preston. "We should get going. I shall see you *témont*, yes?"

"Yes, yes." Bella waves to Clover as she continues to focus on her sister. Preston takes hold of the cue as he turns to face Clover, ushering Reynard outside. It hardly takes a moment for the group to move back into the market, though as they do Clover speaks up.

"So how did it go, did you find everything you needed Preston?"

Reynard pries his eyes from the sight of Bella's shop as he takes hold to Clover's question. "Yea! Preston got everything he needed for this wet bread."

A faint chuckle rolls from Clover as she turns back to the man. "I cannot wait to try it, properly this time I might add."

Despite the comment, Preston is slow to turn his attention away from the crowd outside. "Oh, yea, I'm sure you'll like it."

Cocking her head to the rather bemused tone, Clover pauses in her trot. "Something wrong?"

"Huh?" With a forced smile Preston turns his eyes from the hordes at the market, his arms adjusting to the weight he holds. "No, I'm fine."

"Good." Clover's hands spark up as the items in Reynard and Preston's hold come to her magic. "Hurry up you two, I want to get back before another rush comes to the market."

Chapter 9

Repast

The long day has slowly started to come to its inevitable end, the bright world of *Artésque* calming and cooling the landscape outside as the sun fades. For Preston however, the setting sun has only brought him from the kitchen to the dinner table, as the man continues to usher in the last few dinner items he prepared.

Perhaps it was the day of fresh air, or the cheerful disruption of Reynard, or maybe just the ever present the amulet around his neck, but Preston has found a speck of joy. Nothing truly breaks the looming cloud of wasted days Preston has built up in his mind, though it has done enough to bring a real smile across his face.

Sure, cooking with the somewhat primitive tools were a bit difficult, yet the subtle help from Clover coupled with the other times he worked in the kitchen had made the task a bit easier. Of course, it was Clover's more playful side that truly motivated Preston; a bit forced for sure, even so it worked to get Preston moving.

Cordial greetings and pleasant smiles are one thing, but to actually have Clover interested in a conversation is something else entirely. At first it was a bit unnerving, given how little the duo has actually talked in the past few days. Nonetheless, it was enjoyable, a fact Preston is hard pressed to actually reveal. Even now as strutting into the room, a culinary hero.

The large, flat metal sheet resting to Preston's hold is still fairly hot, despite the layers of towels over his arms and the amount of cooling time he gave it. Either way, the proud little smirk to his face holds as he nears the table Clover and Reynard were forced to wait at.

Both of course offered to help, with Clover suggesting to use his magic as a sort of makeshift practice session. Fearing Reynard's fur or his own magic messing up the food, Preston ignored the offers.

"Alright you two." Preston slowly places the warm plate to the center of the table, all the while making sure the towel does not slip from the hot rim he holds.

Reynard sits up a little in his chair as he looks over the gold crusted rolls of bread, spilling from the rolled-up pieces is melted cheese, meat, and steam drenched, sweet smelling reddish sauce. Bleeding rolls only draw a comment from the fox-boy as he turns to Preston. "I thought you said it was flat?"

A slight chuckle comes from Preston as he throws the last towel over his shoulder. "Well, I messed up a little. The sauce is good, at first I thought we bought the wrong thing; like seriously, why the heck are the tomatoes yellowish on the inside? Bit weird, and they're kind of bitter. But!" He holds the height of his last word as he continues on. "I give you... pizza rolls. Just as good, and way easier to eat. And, well, they are better than what I made before."

Clover runs her eyes over the rough shapes bread as she talks. "I am sure it will be *délussey*."

Preston just shrugs as he claps his hands. "Oh, almost forgot the garlic knots." Another laugh rings from the man as he trails back into the kitchen. "So, the garlic is a bit different, but like everything else tasted the same, so you'll like it!"

As Preston's words echo in from the other room Clover leans over the table. "Reynard, I understand these look rather odd, but we should still be respectful, for Preston's sake." Her eyes look over the meat poking out from the pizza rolls as she sighs. "Even if we do not like them."

Reynard's nose twitches as he looks over the rounded dish at the center. "Actually, I think they smell alright."

The sounds of Preston coming back into the room prompts Clover to return to her normal posture, her hands cupped to her lap as she attempts a smile. Although, she does hold a questioning eye to the heavy scented, almost rope-knot looking creations of dough sitting to the newly placed bowl. Preston however does not allow a comment, as he gives a loud sigh and almost collapses into his seat, his hand moving to the cup of water in front of his plate. "Well, dig in, I've slaved all day for this moment."

Clover does not shift a muscle as she continues to look over the food in front of her. Reynard however, moves his paw to the sauce oozing rolls as he speaks up. "Which is mine?"

Preston gives a little hum as he sits up in his chair. "The ones on the right have that meat you wanted. The ones on the left would be what you said Clover likes."

The words prompt a slight flick in Clover's left ear as she shifts her gaze. "Oh, you did not have to make something special for me."

"Naw, trust me, making these things with different stuffing is pretty easy."

Reynard is the first to bring one of the fairly sized rolls to his plate as he quickly takes a bite. A smile quickly comes to Preston's face as he watches the fox-boy's ears perk straight up and his eyes lock to the roll.

"Yea I put some pepper on it, er... well I guess it was pepper, it's fine. You like it?" Preston moves his own hand to the rolls as he takes one into hand, and then to his plate to let it cool. "Not bad huh?" He takes a bite of his own as he nods. "Huh, yea it's really not that bad, guess those classes online actually helped."

The comment goes without recognition as Clover finally brings her own hand to a roll.

Sighting the woman, Preston holds an eye to her. Clover's face shows her skepticism, despite her facade; yet she still brings the sauce-soaked roll to her lips as she takes a bite a feeble bite. Almost instantly, like Reynard, her ears perk up and she looks over the roll in her hand.

"So, you like it?"

Clover shrugs as she forces a quick swallow to talk. "It is a simple, yet a tasteful treat. Hard to believe it is a dinner."

Preston just replies with a nod. "Wait till you're done, you'll feel full. Reynard that reminds, don't-..." The man's voice is brought to a halt as he looks over the sauce covered muzzle of the young *fróx*, as well as the hoarded garlic knots and pizza rolls, he has moved to his plate. Reynard slowly turns his gaze up as his ears flatten. "Did I take too many?"

Clover chimes in. "Perhaps you do not need that many."

"Alright." Reynard moves a few back to the bowl, Preston watching carefully to ensure he does not grab one of them later, though the boyish voice continues as he glances his way. "What else can you make?"

"Huh? Oh, well..." Preston takes a deep breath. "Uh, I can probably come up with a few more things, maybe." His eyes drift back to the table as he trails on. "Although right now I am more worried about eating before you take everything."

A faint smirk crosses Clover's face as she turns her attention back to her own plate, though she hides it as she presses her cup back to her lips.

- - -

Later

The library has grown dark since dinner came to an end. Reynard has retired upstairs per his normal bedtime, his stomach protruding a little more than a normal though, but a content smile held to his face.

The table is clear, yet Preston continues to wipe at a little spot of sauce that somehow has worked its way into the wood of the table. Behind where he sits, the low chime of magic poofing into the room, followed by its blue light takes hold. Perhaps two more times the sound is heard before Clover's hooves echo to the quiet library, her trot brings her back to the table Preston still sits at. "Do not worry about the table Preston, you did prepare the meal after all."

Preston shrugs to the comment as he stops his scrubbing. "Yea, I think I'm done." He leans back a little more as he folds the towel before placing at the edge of the table. "It's like a permanent stain, it's weird. But with how Reynard was eating I guess you should be happy that's the only thing that got splashed."

The faint jokes yields nothing from Clover as she merely nods. "He enjoyed it."

"Yea." Preston nods as he looks over the table. "Nice to feel like I did something around here."

"You help out quite enough, Preston." Clover casually shifts her attention away from the table as she pops another ball of light blue magic to the room, her motions slowly pushing it towards the ceiling.

Preston however, remains silent as he takes the moment to look over the satyress in the brighter light. Her clothing, or at least her top is a button looser, though nothing too revealing. Her hair too has lost some of its more brushed look, though it never truly looked fancy to begin with.

His silence brings Clover's eyes back to him as she speaks up. "Do you not believe it?"

Preston takes a deep breath, the odd mix of musty books and the sweet pizza sauce filling his nose. "Well I feel like I did something today. A lot better than grabbing a book for someone, I could tell you that."

Clover holds the light smile to the comment as she sets her trot to the table. Though she does not take the seat next to Preston as she instead sits at a more formal spot across from him. "What would be something worthy of mention? Wet bread?"

The man crosses his arms, the amulet pressing against his chest as he shrugs and looks away. "I'm not trying to be ungrateful; I'm just saying I'm happy I did something." A low sigh rings from the man's throat as he looks around the darker room. "Who knows, maybe I'll come up with something else, I got nothing else to do but think."

"Thinking is not a bad way to pass time, Preston. Those who do not use their minds, tend to wallow in less productive ways."

Preston quickly turns his attention back to the woman as he shakes his head. "I'm not complaining or anything."

"I did not think you were." Clover dips a hand below the table, adjusting her skirt as she relaxes a bit. "But, perhaps we can attempt Bella's solution for everything." Clover glances back to the man across from her as she nods. "Would you rather talk now?"

Preston settles into the chair a bit more, his arms easing around his chest as he nods. "Talk huh? Why not."

Clover squints to the words as she cocks her head to one side, her soft blue eyes working over the man as she speaks up. "So yes?"

A moment passes before Preston speaks up, though he carries the fledgling conversation as he fidgets in his chair. "Yea, it's a yes.... so uh, what's up with Bella's sister? First time I've seen her."

Clover nods as she too settles into her chair. "She was removed from her school of *Márjx*, some sort of unsightly behavior with a fellow student as I understand it."

"Oh, great?" Preston clears his throat. "So, did you talk to Bella before we got there?"

"No." Clover shakes her head. "I avoided Bella's shop until I saw you two go in, I did not want to get caught in her webs of twaddle."

A faint laugh comes from Preston as he nods. "You just listened to gossip?"

"I spoke no ill nor did I partake in its consumption." Clover continues. "I had merely spoken with Elva when we split, she had mentioned it. In fact, it was her who suggested I stay away from the shop, at least until we were finished."

"Ha-ha." Preston lowers his hands to the table, though they stay clenched together as he speaks up. "You and Elva were talking crap? Didn't think she was the type."

Clover shrugs. "I do not understand your-..."

"Where was she anyways?" Preston bobs a bit in his chair. "Elva that is."

"Cloud patrol." Clover cocks a slight smirk. "Did you not notice the warmth in the market?"

"I was kinda too busy avoiding people." Preston pats the table. "Gotta worry about stepping on people, you know? *Ahem*, so, anyways, why did she ignore us?"

Clover holds her smirk as she nods. "I believe it is my turn to ask a question, correct?"

The words draw a simple shrug from Preston as he replies. "I didn't know we were taking turns."

Clover backs off a little as she lowers her smile. "I enjoy a bit of structure within our conversations."

A forced chuckle rolls through Preston as he replies. "Hey, it's fine with me, I remember the old routine. What's the question?"

Clover nods, moving her chair a little closer as she slips into her more favored role of leading. "I wish to know more of your old life." Her words slow as her friendly tone keeps up. "I know we have talked about it before, but it is still a topic I know little about." She motions to the man's chest. "Might be helpful to share your feelings, the amulet only does so much."

The last comment is what holds to Preston the most as he glances down to the bump in his shirt. Though he bites his tongue to the question he wants to ask as he answers with a deep breath. "Alright, well as you know Matt and Damien are not my real brothers."

Clover nods as she attempts to prompts more from the man. "I understand that, yes."

"I was sort of taken in by their parents." Preston nods. "Because, well, because mine died. Good story, I know, probably missing out on details but I can get graphic if you need me to, not like it matters now."

The sudden change in tone of their light conversation takes Clover by some surprise. Yet the candor of Preston's words only adds to Clover's inquisitive gaze as she straightens herself.

Preston's hands shift a little from where they sit on the table, yet his words do not halt. "Sorry, not used to talking about, I guess. Um, well I was about ten or so when it happened." The man's voice stops as his gaze sets to something else in the room, his tongue now licking at his teeth for the moment. "I-I kinda don't know how to explain what happened, Clover."

Clover shrugs. "That is fine, just continue sharing."

"No, I get that you will listen and everything it's just you won't know what I'm talking about."

Clover shakes her head. "It will be fine Preston, just talk."

Preston clears his throat as he takes his arms back to his person. "Alright, whatever. So, where I'm from we've got these things called phones. It-it's pretty much just an instant way of talking with someone not in the room... you use them to you know, get ahold of someone quick."

A pause comes to the man, as a slight smirk comes to his face as he thinks over his words, the warmth of the amulet holding back any real emotion but doing nothing to block the thought about it. "I was with Damien at his house, just being a kid and wanting to stay longer." Preston laughs to himself. "So, I called my parents. They were on their way to get me and when my dad picked up the phone. *Boom.*"

Clover merely blinks to the man, unsure of what to think as she looks over the emotionless face before her. Yet, as the silence in the library continues, the expression on Preston's face changes. At first it was subtle, a slight quiver in Preston's lips, his eyes unable to lock to the woman staring him down, the look on her face only questioning or faintly judging his words. As a few seconds pass Preston's internal tears turn to outward anger, his mind conflicted to the ease at which he said what he said. He slams his hand to the table, prompting Clover's once curious gaze to turn more serious. Yet, the laugh now coming from Preston keeps her intrigue as the man shakes his head.

"So, yea, that's a good story. Happy I could remember that for you, happy I could be a piece of shit. I mean seriously." He chuckles, gesturing to his face. "I think about my parents being dead and all I can do is laugh? That's great. Good medicine." He chuckles again. "My turn for the questions, was everything today just to keep me from freaking out, huh? This a test to make sure I'm turning into a monster, right?"

Clover's smile has left her face as she speaks up. "Preston I was merely asking a question. It is good to open up, and you choose your topic."

"Fine!" Preston sniffles, his actions forced, an anxiety filled, guilt driven push to cry at the horrific bubble of emotion now bursting to his head. Yet, despite his desire, the amulet does its job, holding his emotions at bay, leaving him nothing more than a swallow facade of sorrow. "I want this damn necklace off."

"Stop, Preston." Clover's hands spark up as she binds the man to the table, though the force is gentle as she continues. "Just talk."

Preston does not struggle against the blue warmth now engulfing his hands as he instead turns to the ceiling, his right leg bouncing to the floor as he does. "I don't feel like talking. I-I don't even want to think about this."

"Just relax Preston." Clover's magic creeps up the man's arms, ending around his head as faint blue glow takes over his sight. The simple spell is hardly felt in the beginning, though as Preston stares to the woman across from him, he calms down. Within the small link between them, Preston finds himself, and takes a deep breath, his thoughts clearing just enough to resettle.

Clover however softens, her expression turning to shock as the rush of Preston's held back emotions now assail her unguarded mind. Interestingly, she takes it well enough, hardly batting an eye before finally ending her spell.

The magic ending however is like a sudden and sobbing wake up call for Preston, as he finds himself almost missing a piece of himself without her mystic warmth. Even still, he takes notices to Clover's sudden change.

Clover however is the first to speak up as she quickly brushes away the tear from her left eye. "I should not have asked you; I apologize."

Preston merely blinks to the words as he notices the woman now rubbing her hands together. "What did you do?"

"It was just a simple calming spell, Preston."

"You were in my head?" Preston blinks again to the woman as he leans forward. "You-you were in my head again?"

"No." Clover sighs as she turns away in her seat. "It was no different than the light spells we have shared."

Preston nods. "You felt it?" He shakes his head. "Right?"

"You are so guilty." Clover finally stops rubbing her hands together as she glances back. "Why do you carry it?"

"I bury it." Preston shrugs. "I-I don't think about it, but with Damien and Matt gone I-...." He pauses as he swallows hard. "It just hard to keep it down with everything that's happened. No matter what you try to say to me, it won't change it. I called them to stay longer, a childish demand, and I'm still here when they're not. Same thing with Damien and Matt, I would have to face that fact back home, and-and even if I could, I'm a monster now so-..."

"Stop." Clover sighs, her eyes coming back to Preston almost disgusted with his comments. "We all struggle Preston, it is how we deal with struggle that matters. Your footing must be on solid ground, even if it is the edge, do not sit there and worry about why you sit, simple enjoy the fact that you do. Do you truly believe such foolish things?"

Preston follows her sigh with his own defeated breath as looks her over, a faint shaking still to her despite the comment. "Well that depends, do you believe what you just said?"

Clover straightens up a little. "I do, especially when the truth is unchangeable."

The words tumble in Preston's head for a moment as he nods, prompting his head down as the moment of silence takes over the room.

Clover however does not avert her gaze, taken instead by the anticipation of his reply. Though, as the world outside continues to pass, and the room fills with nothing but the chime of her magic lights, she speaks up. "Preston?"

The name draws the man's eyes as he pats the table with a smile. "You're right." A forced smile crosses Preston's face as he stands from his seat. "Thanks for the talk Happy-Hooves, I uh, I think I just needs to lay down for a bit." He rubs a hand to his nose as he glances to the stairs. "Cheese will keep me up all night anyways, might as well turn in."

"You choose to make it a *Fon*?" Clover blinks to the man as she continues. "Is false joy all you wish to have?"

"All happiness is temporary; I'm just cutting out the bullshit in between." He points to the towel Clover pulled to her when she sat down. "Give me that and I'll put it up."

"Preston?"

A sigh comes from the man as he lowers his head, his forge persona coming to an end as he speaks up in a lower tone. "Look, I appreciate this. Deep down, I do. But sitting here talking about it is not going to help me overcome something from years ago."

"Perhaps not." Clover nods. "But it may help with what troubles you now."

"Not really, I'll deal with it the same way I always have." He taps his head as he stares the woman down. "You felt it, I'm not lying, I'll be okay."

Clover is struck mute as she watches Preston just nod back to her. In the absence of her voice Preston takes the towel from the table. "I'm going to put this up and go to sleep."

Again, without another words Preston walks off, the sound of his footsteps trailing into the kitchen as Clover merely watches him, unable to deny his comments though unwilling to agree.

It takes only a second for the man to reappear in the library, though the satyress just gives a simple nod as she continues to look over the man's face. Preston follows the nod good night as he starts up the stairs, unaware to the knot of emotions forming in Clover's stomach. The conclusion is reached, especially as Preston begins to start up the stairs.

Still, as undesirable as the conversation has ended, Clover remains seated, even as the sound of the man's footsteps fade from the library's bottom floor, leaving nothing but the low hum of the orbs. However, as the quiet settles in around the woman she stands, her hooves a little shaky to the ground but she catches her balance as she just looks around the lonely room.

Her trot slowly starts to the stairs as she carefully places each hoof gently to the wood. It takes a few moments, but she brings herself to the top of the stairs. Her walk does not continue down the hall as she instead turns her attention to the half-cracked door of Preston's room.

The low clop of her hooves echoes into the bedroom as she peers inside. Naturally, the less than stealthy satyress catches Preston's attention as he merely sits to the bed, his hands cupped at his knees and his eyes facing the hall. "You know you're not really that quite if you're trying to follow me."

"I understand." Clover glances into the hallway towards her room as she takes a small step instead, a faint sigh rolling through her voice as she closes the door behind her. The room is fairly well lit, the moon coming in through the window and unshaded by the smaller houses around them. Even still, Clover pops a small, light blue, ball of magic beside her.

With the room lightened up a bit more Preston cocks his head, a question coming front and center to his mind. "What are you doing?"

The know-it-all tone is somewhat absent from Clover, yet the always sure wording, and more formal voice Clover tends to carry has stayed. Interestingly though, her stance is a little off balance, almost as if she struggles to find her footing in the room as she shifts. "I admit I perform poorly in such casual conversations. I prefer a more straightforward approach."

She folds her hands as she nods, her eyes staying locked to Preston as she continues. "Our talk was indeed not for simple pleasantries. For that I am sorry, Bella would have suggested a conversation, so I attempted it. Though the point of it remains, I wished to ensure your amulet is helping to manage with your... predicament."

While the comment is a bit hard to take, Preston is nonetheless surprised, though not angry. But, his arms cross as he nods, letting the words sink into his head as he attempts to formulate a reply. "Maybe next time choose a better question. Hell, you could've said our conversation was nothing more than an experiment check-up, I would have been fine with it."

Clover tightens her gaze, her head slowly coming down a little as she nods. "It is not some sort of observation, Preston. You are not a subject of study." She pauses. "I merely wished to ensure you were well. The market can be stressful, truly to anyone."

"I'm fine."

Preston's quick response is followed by Clover's as the woman steps forward, the ball of light following her inching closer. "I believe you, but I still worry." The words do little to change Preston's expression, prompting Clover to continue. "Preston, I felt you. Emotion like that, it is guilt and worry you should not hold."

"It's not a big deal." Preston chuckles. "It's just the amulet."

The lack of care in the man's voice draws a stiff reply from Clover as she nod. "It is more than that."

A bit of annoyance comes to Preston's tone as he shifts back to the woman at his door. "Nyota's not going to find out, this amulet is doing its job, you've been good to me, don't worry about."

Clover shifts again as she shakes her head, a more serious tone taking hold as she replies. "I am sorry that I bought such emotion back to you."

Preston blinks to the comment. "It's okay."

A sigh rolls from Clover as she glances to the ball of light, forcing it towards Preston as it moves into orb around him, the blue glow slowly being replaced by a greenish light. Preston however shifts away from it as he leans in the bed. "I'm not lying to?"

Clover nods. "I understand that." She focuses on the light as she trails on. "You recall what you read in Master Nyota's journal, right? About our magic?"

A simple shrug comes to Preston as he nods, still attempting to shift away from the orb above him. "I guess, why?"

"While I detested your reading of it I am nonetheless happy you did." Clover's confident tone alters as the woman nods. "Our... our encounter that night in *Passvórtall* along with what I felt within you has left me rather confused." She shifts her eyes back to the man, almost upset in her thoughts. "I pride myself as a student of magic, and such thoughts are rather unwelcomed, Preston."

No message is received as Preston merely shrugs, unsure of how best to respond. "Hey, don't worry about, it's been awhile, don't think about it."

"But I will." Clover gives a slight sigh as she lowers her hand, the orb of green magic pausing above Preston's head. "I feel for you, as-as someone I am tasked with looking after and... and more importantly as a friend. I-I prefer our talks to be short and with a goal, I-..."

"Hey, you've not done anything wrong you-...." Preston's chuckles his own cut in quickly cut out as Clover speak up again.

"Preston I should not have forced you into a conversation you were not ready to have." Clover nods. "And I apologize. But I cannot simply turn to my bed knowing what I felt within you."

Preston again chuckles. "I'm not dying, I just got a lot on my mind, you doing your magic stuff was probably not the smartest thing, but it's fine, I'm fine."

"Perhaps." Clover moves her hands to her hips, a faint power pose now on display. "Preston, I want you to take the orb."

Glancing to the light above him he chuckles. "I'm not in the mood to play with your balls, Clover."

The laugh goes unreciprocated as Clover merely stares the man down. "You hide with humor Preston, I prefer not to." She nods again to the light.

With a sigh Preston reaches up, taking the orb to his hand as he looks over the faint warmth now washing over his palm. "Now what?"

Easing up a bit, Clover takes a step forth. "Now, we talk."

Shifting a little from where he sits Preston replies. "Here?"

Clover's left ear flicks to the question as she shifts away. "I would prefer not to lay on a bed."

Preston nods. "We would just sit?"

"Correct." Clover nods to the floor. "Would you care to use the floor? It... it would allow us to be closer than at the table."

"Bit strange, Clover?"

Clover shrugs. "If I were standing it would be a lecture, I do not want this to be something you find negative."

Glancing to the wood floor Preston nods. "Sure, um... want a pillow?"

"Yes." Clover steps forth as Preston spins around to retrieve the two pillows from the bed. The idea of sitting on the floor is a bit strange, but he says nothing more as he stands up and hands the pillow over to Clover.

The satyress takes hold of it as she turns around to find a spot to place it. As she plans her seat Preston merely slides off the bed, his back resting against it as he comes to the makeshift spot on the floor. His eyes do however drift to the woman's backside as she takes her seat, the fuzzier hair on her legs catching his attention the most.

Even still, as she turns back he is nonetheless surprised to see her rather normal looking leg position, despite her obvious lower body. Seated now,

Clover speaks up. "I think it would be best if we start simply. How is your wound healing?"

Preston shrugs. "Fine, it's still a little blotchy, but it's fine."

Clover nods, her overall aura suggests her mind is focused to some goal, yet it quickly becomes clear that something else seems to nag at her thoughts. Unfortunately, Preston is forced to bite his tongue as the woman continues her questions. "There were no times during our trip into the market or even after we got home that you felt... different?"

"No, I was good the whole time." Preston stretches a little, his back pressing more into the bed behind him as he glances to the ball of light above him. "You sure you'll get all this from one orb?"

Clover gives a rather quick nod as she speaks up. "Of course. Now tell me, do you feel as if anything has changed?"

"I mean we are sitting on the floor." Preston chuckles. "Kinda different."

"Preston." A brief sigh rolls from Clover as she pulls the orb of light to her, the green light quickly changing color as she gazes into it.

The smirk to Preston's face holds, though it wanes as he looks over the woman's rounded face taking shape within the brighter, blue hue of the light. Her eyes remain focused to the orb, her ears pointed at attention, her senses seemingly working on overtime to search for something in the flickering light. Though, the pure focus on her face draws a question from the man as he breaks his silence in the moment. "Sorry for the answer, it's just, you literally asked that question earlier... but look I'm not mad at you or anything."

The words prompt a slight flick in Clover's left ear as she glances up from the orb, though her gaze quickly retreats back down as she appears to shrug the comment off. "I-I would not expect you to be. I am merely attempting to help you as Nyota wished."

Preston nods. "I get it." He trails on. "But you don't have to do this just because of what you felt, I think about that stuff a lot. Just because you got a taste of it doesn't mean I need sympathy. I'll be fine."

Clover's eyes slowly shift from the orb of magic as Preston begins to look off to something in the room, his thoughts still coming out. "So much has happened, it's like I close my eyes for a second and when I opened them back up, I've moved. It's like a car ride I've fallen asleep on." He chuckles to words. "I just feel dizzy, like my head spinning while I'm sitting still. I hate sitting around doing nothing, but I can't bring myself to do something. I'm grateful I'm alive, but I feel guilty all the same. Before I could just laugh it off, stuff it down and pretend like all this is a dream. But it's not." He shifts back to the woman now locked to him. "It's crazy, this place. It's-it's too laid back, to... to almost boring to feel real, yet at the same time I think about what's happened, what I've seen. I-I've seen things I never would have seen back home, never would have dealt with, and it's like coming at me so fast, like the fucking moon turned red! That women, W-Wúna, she just comes downstairs, and boom, you know, we went from talking about going home, to that! And Matt?! Sure, he was always an ass, but what the Hell?" Preston just laughs, his hands drifting to his lap as he shakes a little. "It's fake, you know, it's all fake. Life doesn't just do something like this, magic's not real, people don't just change, things like Clamor or-or Clarity, things like that ain't real, demons, monsters, that's not real! Like if that stuff happened it should be fantastic, right? Like some five-star, movie or something, I feel like I flip a page and go from one day to the next, everything I say is just a script. I'm tired of it, I don't deserve to be here, and most of the time I don't deserve to be upset, but I can't shake it."

Preston begins to tap his hands together, physically counting out a list as he talks. "Wake up, go downstairs, eat, wait for people to come in, lunch, dinner, it feels like I'm running. I think about just a few months ago and it's like years; that was fake, being a kid, being back home, doing schoolwork, whatever! That's the fake stuff, and then I look around and see this shit, I just don't." He groans as he rocks forward, a laugh spilling out as a surge of emotions bubbles up. "I-I can't even explain it."

He laughs as he continues, his gaze setting to the wall on his right. The wood of the wall holds his attention, the craftsmanship he never noticed now suddenly having such meaning as he looks over the smoothed brown of the finish within the light blue glow.

Clover however just blinks to the man, unsure of the rant's purpose. Though, she shifts back to the ball of light near her. The spell has done its job. Without a word, she moves closer, tugging the pillow she sits on as the ball of light returns to Preston.

The light hum of the magic does not go ignored as the man glances to it.

Clover merely speaks up, despite Preston's turned gaze. "The *Ůnoff* may have been the first to develop words, though so much is lost when one speaks." She pulls the now greenish orb back to her, drawing Preston's eyes as she continues, the ball now floating to her palm as the color drains towards her hold. "Words are nothing more than commands, raw thoughts or emotions shared between one another are lost with them. It has never been the breath that carries weight, and for many, it is not the message, but rather the emotion, the thought that sways another." Clover lifts her hand, the mixture of blue and green within the ball of light holding as she focuses to Preston, a newfound sense of understanding to her face, though somewhat overshadowed by a melancholy expression. "I should not stir such feelings within you, especially if they are so hard to explain."

She reaches her hand out, a little sheepishly, but she holds it all the same as she nods. "If a string of words could so easily change one's mind magic would hardly have power, Preston."

"Yea?" Preston looks over the woman's extended hand as he eases back to his seat, his own hand reaching forward as he nods. "So, what are you going to do?"

Clover forces a slight smile as she nods. "I do not know the words for us, Preston. I know only the feelings."

At the words Preston's hand moves to Clover's, though her hands are smaller, Preston's by far are softer, less worn down by swords, or by spells. The gentleness of their hold stays as Clover reaches her other hand out, Preston quickly following suit. Their makeshift seats inch closer as Clover draws Preston's hands to rest over hers. "Let your mind rest, Preston. You should not fear yourself, nor give punishment for the past."

Clover's head bows, a faint glow coming to her hands as Preston takes in the warmth. Despite the spell and Clover's display, Preston remains skeptical, the amulet at his chest far warmer than the magic between them. Feeling it, Preston chimes in. "Clover I think you should go."

The words prompt Clover's left ear to flick, her head cocking up a little, though her confidence and the sweet expression remains the same. "Preston you fear nothing."

"I do, I just don't care right now." Preston looks over the glow between their hands as he trails on. "But I do worry about hurting you. I don't want to snap at you, or anything."

Clover nods, yet she does not halt her spell as she replies. "I am not binding you here, if you choose to end this embrace, do so."

Preston merely blinks to the words as he glances back to his hands, their fingers do not interlock, and while a faint veil of magic surrounds them it is Preston's own strength is what keeps his palm to Clover's. Realizing this, Preston eases up, coming even closer as he leans in, purely to show his appreciation for whatever Clover has attempted to do. Strangely, his mind does clear, or at least he finds himself merely focusing to low chime of the magic.

Clover however backs off, her head slinking back and her arms flinching to how closer Preston has come to her. Even still, her spell holds as the room continues to pulsate with the glow of her magic.

This carries on for a minute perhaps, no words, merely the sounds of their breathing as Preston bows his head to the woman before him. Though, as the minutes pass, Preston raises his eyes, locking them to Clover. No true thoughts to his mind, the action merely a reaction to the stiffness in his neck from the previous position. Clover, however, again shifts uneasy, her eyes darting to and from the man's gaze as she attempts to adjust herself on the pillow.

Naturally, the uneasiness in Clover's expression takes Preston's attention as he squints to her. "You alright?"

Unable to look the man in the eye Clover speaks up. "Of course. Does the spell help? It is a simple calming spell, used to help one think. Master Nyota taught it to me."

"It's fine."

Clover nods, her words rushing out a little. "Good, it uses the air around oneself. Your breathing seems easier, that is good."

Preston again squints to the words as he raises his head a little more, his hands coming over Clover's with a bit more of a tug as he eases his fingers between hers.

The spell does not break though Clover's ears fall as she turns her attention back to the man seated before her. "You should focus on the spell, Preston... not me."

"Yea." Preston looks her face over, prompting Clover to follow his eyes as she bashfully attempts to shoo him away with her gaze. Yet, Preston remains all the same as he speaks up. "You said you have a hard time telling the truth, right?"

A slight laugh comes from Clover as she quickly shakes her head. "I do not lie."

"No, but... but you ignore things, bend it to what you want, right?"

A bit annoyed Clover shakes her head again. "Preston I-..."

"I just want to know." Preston swallows. "If, things were different. What would... what would you think of me?"

Clover blinks to the words. "I would think no different of you." She takes a breath, her eyes shifting to the ground. "I have known you for a short time, though I feel as if you are kind... you have an enjoyable presence, you cook well-..."

"I cook well?"

"Yes." Clover nods. "And you should be less hard on yourself. We all have struggles, Preston. Some we care little to talk about."

"Right." Preston follows the nods. "So, friends?"

The question seems to force an uneasy twitch to Clover as she replies. "What else could we have been?"

Following the rather emotionless tone Preston shrugs. "I don't know, I guess I was just asking."

"You feel sad."

"*Pff*, no?" Preston chuckles. "I was just asking, I get that I'm an alien space wizard, Happy-Hooves."

Clover merely flicks a smirk to the words, though she hardly allows the passing joke to stay as she speaks up. "I can feel you still, Preston."

"Okay?" Preston nods, his hands still holding to Clovers. "And if you didn't want to feel it, you could pull away, right?"

Clover raises an eyebrow to the comment. "I suppose."

A light chuckle rolls from Preston. "How come I don't feel anything from you?"

"Do you feel calm?" Clover nods to their hands. "Do you feel settled?"

"Ha-ha, you gonna say that's all you?" Preston nods. "How come you can feel what's in my head but I can't."

The word forces Clover to shrug. "There are just certain things you should not feel."

"I get that, I just." Preston holds his smirk. "It's kinda unfair you know, you know everything right now, and I just stare at you, knowing nothing."

A faint smirk crosses Clover's face. "I do not know everything; I merely feel you."

"Yea? What do you feel when I look at you?"

A rush of red comes to Clover as the woman shakes her head.

No answer comes however as Preston nods, taking his hands from the woman. "Clover I thank you for doing this but I-..."

Preston's words are lost to the room as Clover leans forward, a quick and unheeded kiss stolen from the man. Despite the speed at which Clover pulls away, a faint spark of magic crackles to the room as the pair are left staring at one another.

The action of course brings only more questions to Preston as he blinks back to the woman before him. Though, he manages to work its way to his lips. "What was that?"

The confident to Clover is gone as she swallows. "I do not know." She shakes her head, the lack of direction in her own emotions and actions becoming clear even to Preston. "I apologize for the action, I cannot explain it further."

Preston simply nods. "I'm not mad, I just... I don't know."

"I understand." Clover glances back to the door. "I should not conflict you anymore, I should have better control over my emotions, and for that I apologize."

As Clover begins to shift Preston's hand darts forward, keeping her from standing.

Nothing more is said as Preston now acts, swallowing his fear and moving closer.

Much like the first, their kiss is sudden, yet as their second kiss breaks Preston looks over the woman, their hands now embracing as both sit to their knees on the floor. Still, neither truly moves to take charge, even as they stare panting towards one another.

The hesitation quickly passes however as Preston moves back in, drawing the woman closer for their third kiss. Clover gives in, the crackle of light between their lips simply becoming too powerful to fight as the buzzing, almost tickling sensation carries on.

Falling back a little, Preston draws Clover closer, his back pressing against the bed as he instead moves his hands to Clover's sides, further attempting to bring her closer. Not fight is had as Clover follows the motion, crawling forth after the man as they continued to press into one another, their feelings for one another simply bubbled over beyond return.

Preston's right hand moves to the woman's clothing as he attempts to figure how it stays on. To his surprise, it is nothing special as he begins to undo the first few buttons of her top.

Realizing this, Preston waste no time as he moves his hands to the shirt at Clover's shoulders. The feeling of his hands prompts Clover to wiggle a little, freeing her right shoulder first as she aids in the slip of her garment.

Despite the eagerness within both, Clover's hands still dart to the falling top section of her clothing as she holds it to her like a blanket, breaking their passion kiss for the moment. Pulling away little, Clover's head tightened to her body, as she sheepishly turns away to Preston's gentle, albeit encouraging hold. Even still, and despite the awkwardness for Clover, she speaks up. "Should we not lie down?"

The drastically different tone the normally know-it-all and steadfast woman squeaks brings Preston to a halt. Like the eye of the storm, Preston settles in the moment of heated passion as he looks the woman over. Truly, Clover is nothing eye catching, her tan complexion hardly sets her apart from anyone other commoner, the way she keeps her mane is nothing special, and her petite upper body is hardly something to revel at. Though her lower body is shapely, it is nothing beyond the typical proportions of her unique anatomy. Despite all this, the roundness of her face, coupled with the out of character naiveté and purity she unintentionally has on displays is simply intoxicating. Surprisingly, no animalistic nor male desire is sparked as Preston retreats a little from his more forward approach. Instead, he moves as close as he can as he begins to slowly caress the woman before him. "Just relax for a minute, there's no rush."

His hands continue to slowly move up and down her sides as he draws his lips to the woman's neck, planting a small kiss to the tender area as Clover fidgets to his light touch. This little bit of torment and tender love trails on as Clover slowly begins to ease up, her arms relaxing as her simple undergarments come into view above her stomach. Her chest heaving with the silent fighting in her more reserved sexuality.

Clover continues squirms at the slow, methodical pace Preston sets, though she does not fight it. At least, not verbally. Despite the affection, she remains tight, her hands clenched and her body tense against Preston's touch.

This display holds even as a faint shuttering rolls through her, followed by a brief moan. Sadly, and almost instantly, she speaks up. "Sorry."

The apology only draws a chuckle from Preston as he shakes his head. "Just relax."

Though hardly reassuring, Clover's eyes shut as she slowly attempts to move a hand to Preston's head, her tight fist loosening just a bit from his continued exploring of her neck.

Chapter 10

A warming bed

The sun has already begun to peek over the town of *VéturVill*. Yet, the call of the morning's light holds no power to the two bodies still wrapped within the bed's warmth.

The air in the room is thick, with a slight musky scent hovering just above the normal smell of the wood. Clover's small frame is pressed to Preston's, her tail weaved between the man's legs, her fuzzier lower body is mashed into the man's thigh, though the natural heat of her body is hardly something to complain about.

No birds chirp beyond the room and only faint whispers of those passing by outside manage to break the calm of the room. Yet, as peaceful as the morning is, the ever-present weight on the man's arm slowly begins to stir Preston from his slumber.

Steadily waking up now, Preston takes in the morning air as he shifts his face from the tangled mass of light brown mane directly before him. The movements bring a low, morning groan from the satyress, but the almost inaudible noise does little to bring her from the rest.

With his hand now free Preston looks over the woman beside him. Clover's fur covered ears poke out a little from her mane, although the color of them hide well within the brown of her mane. Even the more skin like portions of the rounded ears is tanned, further blending in with the mass of mane they poke from.

Despite the enjoyable sight, A faint yawn rings from Preston as he continues to just lay in the bed's warm embrace. Hardly a thought curing in the man's head as he remains. Instead, the blank void of his mind is consumed, the image of the woman beside him taking his full gaze.

Unfortunately, Preston's gentle stare nears its end, as Clover herself begins to stir beside him. A faint yawn greeting Preston's ears tail woven to his lower body is pulled away. As the satyress' tail comes back to her, she moves a little quicker. First her left ear twitching a little as she glances behind her, almost as if she is surprised to see her surroundings.

Clover seems to settle however as she turns more to face the man, her head falling back to the pillow as her soft, blue gaze washes over him. For a moment neither speak a word, merely blink to one another as each attempt to hold out for the other. Naturally, Clover's patience runs out first, as she speaks up, her morning grogginess showing through. "Good morning."

The tone is surprising, the softness of it, mixed with the faint shyness of her words. A faint smirk crosses Preston's face as he speaks up. "Good morning." Not wanting to fall back into the pit of silence, he continues, pressing his head up as he clears his throat. "H-how'd you sleep?"

"Well, you?"

Nothing changes in Clover's face as Preston attempts to carry on from the sort reply. "Good, good. Nothing to complain about."

"Good." Clover forces a slight smile as she begins to take better stock of their surroundings. "Morning came fairly quick."

Still hold the smirk, Preston replies. "Yea, it did." He clears his throat again, glancing back to the window Clover has a view of.

Clover however does not stir further, a welcomed treat as Preston turns back to her. "So, I guess I got you to sleep in, huh?"

"I suppose you did."

A quick laugh escapes Preston as he nods. "Should we um... should we get up before Reynard wonders where you are?"

"We should." Clover tugs a bit to the covers, drawing them to her chin as she continues. "He tends to sleep well until I wake him, though it would be best for him not to question my absences."

"Oh yea, I get it." Preston nods again. "Don't need him asking anything."

Despite the words the conversation suddenly dies, both left staring at one another for a moment before Clover breaks it. "I should put something on."

Though Preston clearly saw the simple undergarments of the woman before she tugged the blanket over her, he nonetheless follows her subtle request. "Yea, I can grab my stuff and change in the bathroom or something."

"No. I suppose that would not be necessary, and I would not want your feet to wake up Reynard." Clover slowly pulls herself from the bed, the covers still tight to her form as she turns her attention to the clothing she neatly folded sometime during the night. "I can teleport to the bathroom."

Preston nods to the words, following the woman's hard-set gaze as he does. Though he inches closer as he speaks up. "You're okay, right?"

The words prompt the satyress' left ear to flick as she immediately turns to him with an answer. "Of course. I have no ill will to our... our talk last night."

Backing off Preston nods. "Yea, yea, okay, just asking."

Clover blinks to the man. "You do not believe me?"

"What? No, no! It's just early, my brain is just not working yet, you know." Preston passes his comment off with a laugh as he turns away, forcing another clear of the throat as he looks over the wall pass the foot of the bed.

A simple nod comes from Preston as he speaks up. "Of course."

"Good." Clover takes a breath. "I need to get up now."

"Yea." Preston turns away as he waves his hand. "Go for it, I'm not looking."

At the words Clover crawls away, the sound of her hooves quickly coming to the wood of the house as she collects her stuff. Within a moment, the sound of her magic rings to the room as she teleports away.

With Clover now gone Preston turns towards the closed door in the room, a sigh rolling through him as he moves out of the bed and sets his sights to the dresser near the bed. The air is cool, but nowhere near as cold as previous days. This of course does little to make the chilly amulet still resting around his neck feel any better. Running a hand along the metal in an attempt to warm it up, Preston bends down and begins to fish out his clothing for the day. The more winter colors suit him well, though with such a similar color scheme Preston hardly has a favorite outfit.

It takes merely two minutes from Preston to put on his stuff, the heavier cloth proving difficult to tug at in the early morning. Of course, Preston pays it no mind, instead enjoying the day's start without his normal apathy.

The quiet morning seems to come to an end as a boyish voice rings in from the hallway. "Clover are you in the bathroom?"

Hearing the voice Preston moves to the door, opening it to see the fox-boy just outside it. Judging by the unbrushed fur and half-lidded gaze Reynard has not been up long. Spotting this, Preston chimes in. "Yea I heard her go in about a minute ago."

Reynard yawns. "But it is so late? She just got up?"

Clover's voice comes out from behind the door. "Sorry Reynard, I must have slept in. D-do you think you could put the stones Gwendy wishes me to charge on the table downstairs?"

Reynard shrugs as he steps towards the stairs. "Okay."

The tap-tap of Reynard's paws on the wood holds the man's attention, a faint smirk to the sound, though in his silent stare another noise catches his ears behind the bathroom door. The faint sound of grunting and spitting, followed by a quick run of the sink. A bit strange, but before Preston can speak up Reynard calls up from downstairs.

"Clover, I put the stones on the table!"

The comment quickly brings the woman to the door as she opens it and moves into the hallway. "Thank you, Reynard." A towel presses to her mouth, though as she spots Preston, she lowers it and squints to him. "Something wrong?"

"No." Preston shakes his head. "Nothing."

The comment sparks Reynard to come back to the bottom of the stairs as he looks up to the duo above him. "How do you feel Preston?"

The boyish voice draws Preston's gaze as he waves a hand. "Oh, I'm find buddy. How'd you sleep?"

Reynard nods. "I slept great, I even slept through Clover getting up."

"I am not that loud, Reynard." Clover rolls her eyes as she starts down the stairs, a smile coming to her face as she notices Reynard stare. Clover's eye shifts however to the table as her trot picks up some speed, her lower morning tone changing a bit as she looks over the stones on the table. "When did Gwendy say she needed these by?"

Reynard shrugs. "Soon?"

Clover moves to the table, magic coming to the box as the four or five colorless white stones sitting within them shift to the tug. Yet, before her trot can reach the table a knock at the door takes her attention.

Preston glances around the room, instinctively looking for a clock despite there not being one. "It's not time to open is it?"

Clover says nothing but Reynard moves to open, and as he does a smile crosses his face. "Oh, Bella!"

The welcoming voice is followed by a panicked attempt to brush his fur down as Reynard steps aside for the satyress.

Bella merely smiles to the fox-boy as she turns her gaze to the other two faces in the room. "Good morning everyone, I hope I am not interrupting you all." She squints to Clover as a faint chuckle rolls through. "I had always thought you got an early start to your mornings, Clover?"

A faint sigh rolls through Clover. "I do." She moves from the table as she attempts to hold a friendly smile. "What brings you by?"

Bella adjust the satchel around her as her curled mane bounces to her movement. "Well I was dropping off a few items up the road and was on my way back to the shop. We agreed to talk so I thought I would stop by." A little laugh comes from Bella as she continues. "I can always come back, it does my sister good to learn how to manage a shop without me."

"O-oh yes, of course." Clover just nods to the comment as she folds her hands. "Well it is always nice to see you."

Bella cocks a smile as she waves her hand. "I know that look Clover. Do not worry, I shall not be staying long. While I trust my sister, I would prefer to keep my business."

Clover blinks to the comment. "I-I have no problem with your visit."

Bella holds her smile as she glances to Reynard. "Of course not dear." The fox-boy happily shares in the woman's light chuckle, though he does not interrupt as Bella steps forward to the table. "Oh, are you charging *Kélf* stones?"

"Yes, Gwendy ask for them." Clover nods. "I should have had them done before last night, actually."

Bella again gives a friendly laugh, her hand coming to her chest as he attempts to fake some surprise. "Clover Vines, I am impressed by your ability to act so normally in the morning." Bella places her satchel to the chair she stands by as she closes her eyes, arches her back a little and begins to almost monologue.

The dramatic scene only draws a smirk from Preston as he crosses his arms to the woman.

"A cup or two of *Léle*, a long rest at the table or somewhere more comfortable and then I work my mane." Bella shakes her head, her eyes opening as she waves to her friend. "I just cannot be seen with my morning beauty, it is simply... too shocking." Bella's words quickly come to an end as she looks her friend over. "Oh but... but sometimes I enjoy an easy start. After all everything from the night before is so warm, I understand."

Reynard glances back to Clover, Bella's comment slowly sinking in as he blurts out. "Hey Clover, you wore that last night?"

Despite being fully aware of what she has on, Clover still looks herself over as she speaks up. "Well yes but-..."

"No, no." Bella shakes her head. "I need no explanation." Bella chuckles as she nods to Reynard. "Clover has simply moved past such matters." Bella nods, her thoughts taking hold as she taps a finger to her mouth. "Though I would still worry about my mane."

Reynard chimes in after Bella's lower comment. "Can I get you anything, Bella?"

"Hm? Oh, no, I am quite alright, thank you." Bella clears her throat as she passes a smile to Clover. "So, any news Clover, something exciting from the Capital maybe?"

Clover turns her gaze to the table as she moves back to it. "Nothing of any real interest. Just a few gems that need to be filled."

Reynard again chimes in as he nods happily. "Clover also has a new task from the Princess."

A mixture of fear and intrigue cross Bella's face as she tugs to the collar of her dress. "O-oh, something harmless, I hope? I would hate to worry about the sky again ha-ha."

The words flick Clover's ear as she gives a little laugh. "Just a simple paper to write."

Bella gives a quick laugh almost sigh to the comment. "Interesting."

Clover nods as she turns her attention to the stones in the box. Her hand comes up and over the stones as a bright almost cyan glow shines to them, the spell ends quickly as the stones visibly shake a bit to the fresh charge.

Bella playful claps her hands to the display as she nods. "Such power and yet the Princess has you work on a paper?" She flicks her hair. "Such a loss of potential I do so apologize."

Despite the praise Clover merely brushes it off. "It is just a simple spell. You will be returning soon correct, Bella? Would you mind dropping this off for Gwendy?"

Bella blinks to the comment as she looks over the box. "You finished? Just one spell?"

A little laugh comes up from Reynard as he takes a seat to the table. "I know, it still surprises me."

Clover waves a hand to the comment as she speaks up. "It is just practice."

"Practice, ha." Bella nods as she closes their distance and takes the box into hand. "Gwendy is on the way for me." Her eyes still stay to the object as she continues. "Perhaps I might take you up on training, it would be nice not to bother you so often."

"It is no bother." Clover nods. "But thank you for taking the box."

Bella gives a little nod as she straightens her posture. "Of course... I suppose I should be on my way." She turns to Reynard and then to Preston as she gives the same nod. "Next time I shall stay longer, such a quick visit is hardly enough."

Reynard happily nods to the comment. "You can come by any time!"

"Oh of course dear." With a faint laugh Bella collects her things and moves towards the door. It only takes a few moments for the woman to leave the house, and as she does Clover closes the door and turns her attention towards the stairs. "Preston you would not mind me using the bathroom first, would you?"

The man shakes his head as he speaks up. "It's fine with me, I can wait a minute."

"Good." Clover gives a little nod to the comment as she moves back to the stairs. "Perhaps we may practice a little magic when the sun is high, Preston."

"Fine by me." The man gives a simple nod to the question, as he watches the woman heading up the stairs.

With Clover gone Reynard speaks up. "So, do you want to make breakfast?"

Chapter 11

Feathering the Fur

"Very good, Preston."

The words hold no weight to the man's focus as he continues to just hold his keen eyes to the extra books Clover floats into his magical juggling act.

"Just keep in mind that magic is both the thought, and emotion of the user." Another book floats past her as she continues. "That is ten now, Preston."

The man gives a simple laugh as he holds his hands steady. The time for customers to pick-up or drop-off books has already came and went, so no real distractions have occurred. Of course, the nagging thought at how trusting Clover is with her books, especially seeing as how renting them out nets the house their coin. Lucky, Clover speaks up as the thought begins to settle in Preston's head.

"I suppose that is enough."

A sigh comes from Preston as he drops his heavy hands to his sides. Just as he does this the magic around the books vanishes, quickly forcing the man to shoot his arms back-up to catch the books in a bubble of his magic now forming. A laugh rolls through him as he turns his smile to the woman on his side.

Clover however shakes her head, hardly amused as her magic easily overcomes his, taking the books and neatly stacking them to the table. "You should have remembered that your spell ends when you do, Preston."

"Yea, yea, yea." He chuckles a little, his eyes falling to the glove around his hand as he begins to undo the straps on. "I like this thing, it's a lot better than just using my hands."

Clover glances to the glove as she shrugs the comment off. "A *Gloftór* should be used with prolonged practice; it is hardly needed now."

"Oh yea?" Preston continues to undo the leather straps as the glove slips off. "Then why did you tell me to use it?"

"Simple. Pent up magic can be hard to control. *Devún* know you have been slacking on your practice, Preston." Her magic sparks up to something else on the table. A tomato, or at least what *Artésque* has as a tomato floats to Clover's side as she nods. "Use your magic to overcome mine, and then bring it to you."

Blinking to the rounded fruit the man sighs again, tugging the glove back over his hand as he speaks up. "You should've said we weren't done, Clover."

Clover's typical know-it-all tone is quick to bring a reply as she speaks up. "I never said we finished, you assumed."

"And you didn't correct me." With the glove back on Preston flexes his fingers out. "So just take it from you?"

"You will need to overcome my magic, but yes."

"Piece of cake." Preston raises his hand to the fruit as his magic slowly comes over Clover's blue glow. The sight of his building spell draws a smile to Clover's face as she begins to speak up. "Perfect, now take it to you."

"Uh-huh." Preston pulls his hands back, a motion Clover focuses in on as her smirk widens. Though the woman does not correct his posture as the tomato begins to pull away from her magic, now fully coming under Preston's control.

"Just bring it to your hand and-..."

Clover's words are brought to a halt as Preston brings the tomato up to his mouth for a quick bite.

The juice pools to the bottom of the magical bubble holding it up, though despite his giddy smile Clover rolls her eyes. "I did not say for you to eat it."

Preston shrugs as he looks over the floating fruit. "Oh well." He shakes his head. "You know, these things are a little bitter, and smaller than I remember... maybe I'm losing my mind."

Preston again pushes through his thoughts as he continues to control the rounded orb. "So how dumb do I look trying to do something so easy?"

Ignoring the comment, a little Clover trots towards the table, her eyes casting over the various items she laid out before they started. "I do not expect mastery, Preston, I except effort."

Preston nods his head to the words as swallows. "That bad huh? Alright, new question, why is it green?" The man looks over the tomato in his hold as he gives a little laugh. "When I learn a fireball, thing is it going to be green?"

A slight giggle rolls from Clover as she brings her hand to the small clear stone on the table. "I will never teach you a spell like that."

"What?" Preston cocks his head. "Why not? I need to protect myself."

Clover merely raises her eyebrows as she shakes her head again. "*Diśtro Márjx* is not for *étrometáy*, it requires deference, Preston."

"Okay?" Preston remains unchanged to the words. "So, teach me a small one."

Clover again chuckles. "I am not teaching you such a spell, not even a small one as you say."

"Oh yea?" Preston nods, his bottom lip poking out as he eases his left hand to his hip. "You afraid I'll do better than you?"

"Yes." Clover giggles again. "I fear most for your skill." Her posture straightens as she floats the bitten fruit from Preston's hand, and instead replaces it with the small, clear stone. "Moving on, you are to charge this stone."

Preston gives a little laugh as he holds the stone back to Clover. "You think I can charge one of these things? Here give me a piece of paper to fold or something."

Clover pushes the hand back as she nods. "This is a *Helió* stone. Simply perform any spell and it will absorb it for the light."

The words take Preston's attention as he speaks up. "Okay, so is it going to hurt?"

Clover shakes her head. "No, it will just take in your magic."

Preston looks over the stone. "Alright?"

As Preston continues to stall a noise takes his attention. A quick smile breaks to his face as he places the stone down to the table and turns to the knocking at the door. "Guess we got a customer, huh?"

Clover blinks to the sound as she teleports to the door, her hand swiftly coming to it as she attempts to greet whoever is on the other side. "Oh, hello Elva."

The once proud smile has fallen a little from Preston's face, though the distraction is still welcomed as the man steps away from the stone at the table, his arms crossing. He watches the tall, warrioresque women striding inside, her head held high and her wings tucked to her back. The warming weather has altered the avian woman's attire, as she now wears her open stomach steel and wool trimmed top, a form fitting metal skirt coming down to her shin guards and boots. Still, the same bright colored feathers sit woven into the woman's hair, just above her pointed right ear. They bounce to her words as she speaks up. "You may wish to know *Flóff* letter carriers are now permitted to carry *Únoff* mail again."

Elva brings a closed letter up from her right hand as she continues. "Your name was top of the list at camp."

"Oh?" Clover takes the letter in hand as she opens it. "Master Nyota has sent an update of his events within Únoactroff."

As the satyress slowly sinks into the text Elva's eyes shift to Preston. "You seem to have a glow, Preston. Have your winds grown calm?"

Preston gives a little smirk to the comment, though his eyes drift to the almost perfectly healed cut on her. "Something like that."

"Hm." Elva turns away. "I offer no congratulations for how long you sulked." She glances back. "Why do you wield a *Gloftór*?"

Preston glances down to the glove as he nods. "I'm uh... learning stuff."

A laugh rolls from Elva as she nods. "Clover is teaching you how to light the oven with magic, hm?"

"No, I already know that."

"Pathetic."

"Elva." Clover's call does not turn the woman's head, but it does alter her words as the avian woman nods.

"I am merely happy to hear you do something." Elva's eyes come to her friend as she continues. "What does Nyota write, Clover?"

A faint glare comes from the satyress, though she nevertheless speaks up. "Well, I am not sure. This letter seems a little scattered. It is his handwriting, though it appears as if he had to stop several times while writing. His thoughts must have slipped him each time, but from what it seems he is well."

Elva nods to the words as she speaks up. "I hear he attends every meeting with the Princess, does he make mention of it?"

Clover slowly lowers the letter in her hand as she smiles. "He does. Though it is his wisdom she requires. Master Nyota has always said he would rather be hated for honesty, then hailed for lies. Soon enough though his tongue will have him removed from the court, something I am sure he hopes for."

A slight smirk comes to Elva's face as she nods. "The feathers of my kin would have fit him well." The avian woman turns her attention back to Preston as she moves her hands to her hips. "Preston, a snout of the *Dẇoff* would better fit you."

Spotting the annoyance in Preston's face Elva quickly rushes another comment. "Though perhaps if you wish to sway my opinion you could accept another sparring match?"

Preston waves his gloved hand. "Sorry, I'm a bit busy, Feathers."

Elva nods to the comment. "Perhaps another time then." her eyes turn to Clover as she speaks up. "Good to see the stubbornness of your *Courtásoff* has returned. He would be dull without it."

Clover's ear flicks to the comment as she speaks up. "Goodbye, Elva."

With a slight nod Elva and her smug smile move to the door, and quickly back outside.

Preston however just blinks to the wood as he cocks an eye to Clover. "What did she call me?"

"Nothing." Clover takes a breath as she turns to the man. "Shall we continue with the training before I retrieve Reynard?"

"I guess." Preston cracks his knuckles as he rubs his hands together. "But to be honest, I'm not really feeling up to it."

"Oh?" Clover cocks her head. "Is something wrong?"

Preston shakes his head. "No, no, just you know, never done this."

Clover gives a little laugh as she speaks up. "You shall be fine. Pick up the stone, Preston."

Hesitating a little more Preston glances back to the stone, his left hand reaching up towards the amulet at his chest. However, he pauses again as he instead reaches for the stone. "So, any spell right?"

"Any spell."

With a blow of his breath Preston's right hand sparks up, his green magic coming forth from the *Gloftór's* center with ease as he focuses into the stone now beginning to hover above the table. Such enough, the dormant stone begins to fill with his green glow as Preston lets out a faint chuckle.

Clover follows suit in the man's happiness as the stone continues to shine ever brighter. "Do not doubt yourself, Preston. Given enough time, I am sure you would be a fair beginner."

The comment draws Preston's smile as he nods. "Oh, that's the goal right there, let me tell you."

The sarcasm only bolsters Clover's expression as she nods, her eyes focusing on the stone at the table.

Chapter 12

By the breeze

The last three weeks have brought many changes to *VéturVill*. The snowbanks that littered the sides of the streets have been replaced with fresh wildflowers. Mimicking this brighter landscape is the weather, which too has quickly returned back to comfortable springtime feel. The city of dull wood and rare stone houses has also been flanked on all sides by the new sprouts of flowers that once laid dormant. Even the *ÉverMoar* to the southwestern bank of the city has altered, its trees bright green to the warmth.

Preston too has changed, shedding his once dismal mind set for his normal sarcastic sense of humor. And much like the growing color in the world around him, Preston's beard has filled, the reddish-blonde color adding a bit of roughness to his more pale, white face. The reactions of course have been enjoyable. Clover nor Reynard seem to mind much. Though Gwendy's somewhat more frequent hugs and squeezes have become a bit strange, especially with the faint nuzzling she attempts to do. Bella however, has clearly stated how much she hates it, with Elva merely commenting that it hides nothing about his weaker body. However, with Clover saying nothing against it, and even somewhat enjoy it Preston has continued to let it grow, along with his hair.

The scarring to his side has also faded in the past few weeks, thanks of course to Clover's help. The blotchy skin has remained and even seems to flare up at time, Preston has managed to keep this to himself. His newfound understanding of magic and his acceptance of the amulet around his neck has also allowed the man to approach things a little more calmly.

Clover's training has still yet to go past simple levitation, light, and teleportation spells.

Preston however, is not the only one in the house to have changed in the short weeks. Both Reynard and Clover have found a liking for Preston's cooking, even when the meals come out a bit different than he expected. Though, for all their encouragement, there have been a few minor problems with Clover's change in pallet, at least from what Preston can tell.

"Alright, I get it, Cordon bleu was a bad idea." No response comes from the bathroom as Preston holds his laugh down and knocks again. "You alright in there?"

The door slowly opens as Clover comes out. The sight of the woman's tired and slightly sickly face bringing a slight chuckle to Preston as he speaks up. "I didn't even know you could throw up. Y-you know being half uh-..."

Clover's annoyed stare brings Preston to a rambling stop as he clears his throat and glances away. "S-so next time I won't mix cheeses."

Despite Clover's appearance the woman nods, her faintly weak voice coming out. "Actually, it was rather enjoyable; just perhaps a little filling."

"Oh." The man moves into the bathroom just as he continues. "Okay, I'll keep that in mind." He swings the door a little as he glances back to the toilet. "You don't need to use the bathroom, again do you?"

Clover shakes her head, a hand moving to her stomach as she speaks up. "I do not think there is anything left."

"Cool 'cuz I really gotta pee." He tugs the door behind him, though Preston stops it with his foot as he cocks an eye to the woman. "You're alright, yea?"

"Yes."

"Okay, I'll just be a minute."

The door closes as Preston's comment just barely makes it out, though Clover hardly cares as she trots towards the stairs with a slight groan. Despite her slow pace, the satyress comes to the first floor fairly quickly and her attention now turns to the table Reynard sits at.

The clap of her hooves turns the fox-boy's head as he speaks up. "Do you want something to eat?"

Clover waves her hand to the comment as she speaks up. "Just some water."

"Oh." Reynard moves from his seat as he starts towards the kitchen. "Be right back."

The tap-tap of Reynard's paws fall silent as the fox-boy glances to the stairs. Preston's bare flop against the wood as the sound echoes into the quiet library. "Would you like anything, Preston?"

"Uh... yea, just a little something, I'm not really all that hungry."

Preston's eyes turn back to Clover as he trails on. "You know, if your stomach is upset you should drink some tea or-..."

Clover's ear flicks to the words as she speaks over him. "My stomach is fine, Preston."

"Okay, just saying. Some bread might help too if-..."

The know it all voice chimes up a little more as Clover shakes her head. "I know what I need."

Preston moves to a seat as he gives a little laugh. "Alright, point taken."

Reynard starts to the kitchen, his own smirk to the annoyance in Clover's tone. Her look however keeps Preston from any jokes though as the man merely sighs and settles into his seat. The chairs have never really been comfortable, though the thicker clothing Preston sleeps intend to give some added cushion.

Clover too remains quiet, one hand to the table and the other clenched to her stomach, a rather irritated expression holding strong to her face.

Within a few moments the sound of Reynard's return greets the duo's attention. The fox-boy's swift pace brings him to the table rather quickly as he passes the mug to Clover. "Thank you, Reynard."

A bowl of assorted, though tiny, fruits is moved in front of Preston as the man gives a little nod. "Thanks." Looking over the colorful little appetizer Preston speaks up. "So, Clover, what is our agenda today?"

Slowly moving the cup from her mouth, Clover speaks up. "Well I intend to find a spell to help settle my head after the morning's rush. Princess Sóltina's letter should also be arriving before too long, and I will need to be focused for that."

Reynard chimes at the words. "I can help Bella search for gems around *Tróven Ravine*, right?"

"No." Clover shakes her head. "You will not be going near the forest."

Reynard blinks to the comment. "But I will be with Bella and a few others?"

"Reynard, I do not want you near the forest."

"Well..." Reynard nods. "What if I only stay for a little?"

Clover again shakes her head. "Reynard if you want to help why do you not stay with Juna? Bella has already said she does not feel comfortable leaving her sister alone."

"Juna does not like me."

Clover squints to the comment. "She said something to you?"

Reynard shrugs. "Well no, but she does not smile like Bella does when I help."

"Then do not go." Clover wags a finger to the fox-boy. "I see no reason why you would want to linger in Bella's store anyways."

Reynard's ears fall a little as he nods. "Well I want to help Bella."

Clover remains firm as she speaks up. "I do not want you near the forest."

"Alright." Reynard sighs. "I could still go to Bella's and maybe Gwendy will let me help bake something."

Clover cocks an eye to the comment. "If you want something to do you could always stay and help here?"

Reynard's ears poke up as he glances between Preston and Clover. "I would.... but... but I already helped sort the books, and we went through the list last night. I want to do something else."

A faint laugh comes from Preston. "That or you just want to walk behind Bella."

"No." Reynard nods. "I just enjoy helping, like a good *fróx*."

Clover rolls her eyes a little though she still wags a finger to the fox-boy. "Do not say stuff like that, you do not always have to help someone."

"I know, I would really only help Gwendy or Bella." Reynard shakes his head. "Elva's stuff is a bit much."

"We could always go back to the market, Reynard." Clover shrugs. "There may be some new books."

Reynard nods. "Yes… or I could help Gwendy and eat stuff."

Preston chimes in with a faint laugh. "Not bad. Hey, does she have any more of those things." Preston taps his hands together. "Those um, like cannolis or you know the wrapped-up bread with that berry crap in the center?"

"Burri-Ties?"

"Yea sure." Preston nods. "You should pick me up one."

Clover slowly eases her other hand from her stomach as she leans more to the table, her left hand coming to her chin. "Or a *villtý cúffy*."

"Dude, I just want some ice cream."

Clover slowly blinks out of her gaze as she pushes the simple cup of water away from her. "Iced cream?"

"Yea, it's good." Preston shakes his head. "No idea how to make some. I think it's like milk, ice, and salt? I can't remember it."

Clover rolls her eyes. "More cheese stuff."

"It's not cheese." Preston crosses his arms. "Just because it has milk doesn't make it cheese."

Reynard chimes in, his boyish tone raising a bit. "Is it melted cheese?"

"What?" Preston shakes his head. "No, it's not cheese."

Reynard props himself up a little on the chair. "Why not?"

Preston shakes his head. "B-because it's not cheese, I said ice cream, how can you think it's melted?"

Reynard blinks to the comment. "You say a lot of strange things."

"You said that a nut can be made into butter."

Clover nods to the words. "You did say that Preston."

"Yea." A chuckle rolls through the man. "And it's true, it's peanut butter, it's nothing special."

A hyena-like laugh comes from Reynard as he nods. "You made such a mess smashing those."

Clover groans. "And you mixed it with milk."

"I don't know how to make peanut butter, and it wasn't milk, it was cream." Preston sinks in his chair. "You guys wouldn't be saying anything if I made it. Just wait I'll figure it out and-..."

Preston's words are brought to a halt as a knock on the door takes his attention. However, he glances to the window behind Clover as he spots the sun just barely shining into the tight street outside the house. "What the Hell? It's too early for people to want in, think it's Elva? I bet it's Elva."

Reynard blinks to the comment. "Maybe Bella?"

Clover glances back to the door as she stands. "It would be a letter this early." Again, Clover moves her hand back to her stomach, though this time it is to tighten the robe like bottom of her clothing as she moves to open the door.

Preston merely leans back in the chair to catch a glimpse of the satchel toting *Flóff* standing just at the door. "Clover Vine?"

"Yes."

The *Flóff* dips his hand into his bag. "Got a letter for you, your eyes only."

At the comment Preston merely rolls his eyes, an action that draws a faint smirk from Reynard.

"Thank you." With a nod she steps away, her magic closing the door behind her, the letter in hand.

Reynard looks back to the door before glancing to Clover. "Who is it from Clover?"

The satyress is silent for the moment as her eyes make quick work of the paper. Although, as she turns her eyes back to the table she starts to take a few steps to the stairs. "It seems we have been summoned to the Capital by the Princess."

Preston mindlessly smirk to himself as he pops a berry into his mouth. "Huh... wait are we leaving now?"

"A carriage is to follow this letter." Clover pauses halfway up the stairs as she looks over the letter. "It does not say for how long, so I suppose we should bring a few things."

The suddenness of the request prompts a bit of anxiety within Preston as he finds himself unable to sit still in the chair, turning himself fully to face Clover. "Wait, wait, they can't just make us leave?"

Clover blinks to the comment. "I am a student of Master Nyota, I will not ignore a summons." She shrugs. "You both can stay if you wish to."

"What? No?" Preston waves his hand to get the ever-impatient woman's attention as he trails on. "What's it for, what are you doing?"

Clover shrugs rather nonchalantly as she replies. "I shall find out when I arrive."

Reynard moves from his chair as he follows after the woman. "I can get ready soon, you will not leave without me, right?"

The look in Reynard's face mixed with Preston's persistent questioning finally clicks for Clover as she blinks to them. "It is just a letter? B-but if you both with to come with me, I will need you packed soon."

"Okay!" Reynard charges up the stairs after Clover, the sight of him prompting the woman to turn around towards the upstairs hallway.

The noise of their exit from the room however does not stir Preston from his seat as his right-hand creeps up to the amulet under his shirt, his hands and legs becoming stiff to the idea of leaving so quickly. Though, he does his best to push the thoughts from his mind as he turns back to the bowl of fruit.

"You do not have to come, Preston." Clover cocks her head to the man as she stops at the stairs.

"It's fine." Preston flashes a smile, his hand still stroking the amulet under his shirt. Clover merely nods to the comment as she continues upstairs. Preston however remains seated, a magical glow coming to his hand.

- - -

(Later in The Day)

"...How long did the letter say we would be away?"

The boyish comment slowly draws the woman's eyes from the book in her hold as she speaks up in a slight huff. "The letter did not specify a time."

Reynard just nods to the comment as he turns to look out of the carriage's window, following the same routine he did earlier when he asked.

Clover stays her gaze, simply to ensure the answer satisfies the fox-boy, though with no further questioning Clover turns back to her book.

The suddenness of the conversation, even as short as it was prompted Preston's own sight from the quickly changing landscape outside. Yet, with Clover's head back to her book and Reynard mindlessly staring out the window Preston chooses to stay his tongue, his head turning back to the window. His left arm is settled on the side of the carriage, his right gently tugging to the amulet under his shirt, an action neither he nor anyone else really pays much attention to.

The trip from *VéturVill* to the capital is nothing new, and surprisingly the man is able to tell how close they are to the city even with the minimal landmarks around the rural roads. Of course, the caravan that usually stream in and out of the city has always been a good tell.

The road has gotten a little less bumpy, a sign of the frequent traffic; the truth, of course is that after a four-hour trip the rock of the carriage becomes normal.

Looking over the road a little more, Preston speaks up, his throat clearing as he cocks his head to the woman beside him. "So, the train is going to be coming through Venturn-Vill right?"

Clover moves her eyes from the book as she nods. "Yes, a train is to come through *VéturVill*."

"Good." A little chuckle comes from Preston as he sighs. "A train ride would be better than this."

Clover just gives a simple nod as she turns back to the book. "I am sure it will be."

The rock of the carriage continues as Preston looks over the book in the woman's hands. "What are you reading?"

The satyress continues to look over the page she is turned to as she speaks up. "A simple spell book."

"Hmm, so Happy-Hooves doesn't know everything."

The words prompt a quiet, hyena like giggle from Reynard as he looks over Clover's cocked eyebrow.

Preston however continues to poke his fun to the stupid comment as he bends a little to see the title. "What's it about? Anything I should read?"

Clover folds the top of her page as she speaks up. "I do not think you would like it." Clover flashes a smile as she continues. "The words a bit more complex for your liking."

A smirk crosses Preston's face as he shakes his head. "Was that supposed to be a joke? Come on, you gotta do better than that." Preston nods. "You know, yea, tell me a joke, give me your best one."

The question quickly causes Clover to lose interest in the conversation as she glances away. "No, Preston."

Reynard perks up a little as he nods. "Clover do you have a *Fon*?"

"No." Clover tugs to her skirt bottom as she shakes her head. "I do not wish to be your *étrometáy*."

"*Pff*, that means she doesn't know any."

"Preston, do you have one?"

The boyish excitement quickly prompts Preston to clear his throat as he sinks a little in his seat. "Well I mean yea, but... but you guys don't normally get my humor."

Clover chimes in as she glances to Reynard. "That means he does not know any."

"No, no I got some jokes." Preston wags a finger to the woman. "Just got to think of one that's appropriate for... oh okay here me out." Preston chuckles as he rubs his hands together. "What do you call a dog with no legs?"

Clover and Reynard just blink to the man as Preston continues. "It doesn't matter because he won't come..." Preston clears his throat. "So, yea, I don't really tell jokes but um, you do get it right?"

Reynard merely forces a smile as he nods. "It was okay."

Preston snaps his fingers. "Same things I hear after sex."

Reynard cocks his head. "What?"

"Preston, perhaps you should save your wit for later."

"Yea." Preston nods to the woman's comment as he attempts to wave off Reynard's question. "Just another dumb joke." He claps his hands. "Oh, here's one."

Clover shoots a look to the words though Preston maintains his smile as he nods. "No seriously, here try this one. Would you rather be lost in a cave or in a forest?"

"Preston that-..."

"Forest." Reynard happily chimes in. "At least you can find stuff to eat."

"Alright not bad. I mean, that's kinda an easy one. Clover?"

Though she pauses Clover eventually speaks up. "Forest."

"Cool." Preston nods. "Would you rather live alone or surrounded by annoying people?"

Reynard blinks to the statement. "If I live alone can I still talk to someone?"

"Good question, no, think about it as if you live in a forest or something."

"Alone." Clover shrugs as he glances between Reynard and Preston. "Next?"

Reynard rushes his answer. "People!"

"Okay." Preston nods, another question forming to his tongue. "Would you rather know how you die or when?"

Reynard's ears fall a little as he mows the question over. Clover however chimes in fairly quickly. "When. You cannot stop it so why not know."

Preston puffs his bottom lip out to the comment as he nods to Reynard. "Rey?"

"Um, how?" Reynard nods. "So that I could try and stop it."

"Alright, not bad." Preston continues. "Would you rather be married to a ten with like bad personality or a five you get along with?"

Both Reynard and Clover glance to one another as the fox-boy speaks up. "What do the numbers mean?"

"Oh, so like um, a ten is a person who is really uh... good looking and like a five is someone who is just average." Preston waves his hand. "But keep in mind like the ten is like really hot, like your dream person." He gives a light chuckle as he glances to Clover. "Just for the sake of the game."

Reynard taps his hand to his mouth, Clover however chimes in with a confident answer. "Neither."

"Well no you have to pick one." Preston chuckles. "that's the point of the game."

Clover's ear flicks to the words as she replies. "Why? I choose neither."

"The ten." Reynard flashes a smile. "Is that wrong?"

"Naw." Preston chuckles as he nods to Reynard. "There's no right or wrong." Preston glances to the window as he nods. "Continue?"

"Yea!" Reynard's happy tone prompts Preston on as the man nods.

"So, would you rather be feared by your parents and loved by your friends or hated by everyone but totally powerful?"

Reynard shrugs. "I pick from the four?"

A little laugh comes from Preston as he shakes his head. "No, you pick one or the other. Clover what about you?"

The satyress has returned to her book as she waves to the comment.

However, as Preston begins to speak up the carriage bounces a little, the clapping of the horses' pulling the carriage forward now ringing to the stone road beneath them.

The rock of the carriage draws Clover's eyes to the window as she speaks up. "We will be at the castle soon." Her hands to the small satchel beside her as she continue. "We shall talk with the Princess and then find Master Nyota."

Preston and Reynard both just nod to the comment. Though in truth, Preston's attention has turned to the two bags he agreed to carry, one for himself and Reynard's. He brings the first bag to his lap as he just fiddled a little with the strap.

The noise of the carriage continues to play into the cabin as the ever-growing city rolls past the windows. The white stoned portion of the upper part of the city now comes into view, the always colorful *Únoff* district happily greeting Preston's sight.

"Clover, why do you think she wants to see you?"

"I am sure it is nothing serious." Clover waves her hand to the comment. "There will be no talk of the Grifón, no tales of *Drágeff* fighting. I am sure it is just a simple meeting, perhaps to inform us of events since Wúna's departure." The woman gives a quick little giggle to the boyish voice as she continues. "Besides, if it is anything within my bailiwick, I will not keep you two from wondering."

"Bale of what now?"

Reynard chimes in. "Clover will not trammel us with her pedantry, Preston." A hyena-like laugh quickly rolls from the fox-boy as he looks over Preston's cocked eyebrow.

Preston shrugs. "D-did I miss something, is there a thesaurus behind me or something." Playfully Preston turns to the wall behind him as he pats the wood. "What the heck are you guys saying?"

A faint sigh rolls from Clover as she nods. "Sorry Preston, I believe Reynard is having a *Fon* at my wording."

Reynard holds his smile as he nods. "Clover hates not knowing what she is summoned for. She forgets *miñutortˊ*."

"Do you even know what you are saying at this?" Preston cups his hands over the bag in his lap. "Like 'cuz I've never heard you two talk like this before."

Clover holds her gaze to Reynard as she speaks up. "*Miñutortˊ* is an *Únoff* idea that one should alter the words used within another's presence, to help avoid anger, sorrow, or bickering... and I am hardly anxious, Reynard, I simply prefer knowing a bit more when summoned here."

Ignoring the latter part of Clover's comment Preston speaks over Reynard, despite the fox-boy's breath. "Hang on, so you guys don't say everything you want around me? It's not going to offend me or whatever. I don't care, words are meaningless."

Reynard's childish smile holds as he nods. "*Yé, ẏallven óff baẏẏo béh neóftó vál?*"

Clover lowers her head as she gives an almost motherly scolding to Reynard. "*Dólt néat maló, ó dólt-sús vál-Ner?*"

"*Métier, métier. Til whoa fon, til whoa fon.*" Reynard nods, a laugh still following his comment as he turns to Preston's confusion. "*Samény maló, Preston?*"

"Well I know you're talking to me." Preston clears his throat. "What are you two arguing about?"

Clover pulls to her skirt bottom as she glances out the window. "There is no argument, Reynard has heard me."

"*Yéat*"

"Reynard."

Preston waves his hand. "No, no, it's funny." He continues as he clears his throat and deepens his voice to a more serious tone. "A yeet, back to you Reynard, whatever that means."

"It means yes, Preston." Clover gives another glare to Reynard, which finally draws some sense to the fox-boy as the smile quickly runs from his face.

"Sorry, Preston."

"No, no." The man laughs. "I'm not mad or anything, just this uh… it's not in my wheelhouse."

"Wheelhouse?" Clover squints to the word. "What is this?"

Preston smirks. "So, what that means is-…"

"We have entered the castle grounds, Miss Vines." The carriages steadily slowly down as the hill up to the castle comes under the wheels. Though Clover still pops her head to the window as she calls back.

The incline brings Preston's hands down to the next bag as he slings it over his shoulder; like Preston's, Reynard's bag is light and most likely nothing more than a toothbrush and a few other items.

The wheels of the carriage continue to slow as the castle outside grows near. Just as the cabin stops its rocking, the driver's voice chimes in. "We have arrived, Miss Vines."

Clover straightens her posture as she calls back to the window. "Thank you." Her eyes however stay to the outside world as she speaks up. "I wonder what is being added?"

Preston and Reynard both shift their eyes to Clover's window as they take notice to the cleared-out field. The once lavish, green field stretching towards Nyota's tower has been cleared; of course, not in its entirety, though a large section is now barren, with nothing but dirt to greet their gaze. A few *Unoffs* can be seen in the clearing, though none seem interested to the carriage as they go about their work, either by moving boulders or placing a white, almost marble stone to the ground.

Preston shifts his attention to the other side of the carriage, his eyes greeting the meeting hall, as well as the new additions of decorations or flowers around the fountain and waiting area outside. Of course, the group's collective stares come to an end as speaks up. "I shall ask Master Nyota about it later, we should get inside."

Clover's hands spark up in a blue glow as the carriage door opens up. As normal, Preston waits for the shorter satyress to move out first. Yet, his paused motion only draws Reynard forward as the fox-boy hops down the simple steps of the carriage, his tail bobbing from the slit in his clothing.

As Preston finally moves from the carriage, a deep voice calls out from the castle. "Ah Clover Vine, and her retinue, how I feel safer already."

Preston squints to the fair sized and more heavily armored *Unoff* as he looks the man's half-lidded almost apathetic gaze over. Clover, however, speaks up without a pause as she cocks a little smirk. "Stone Hooves, your respite from the sword was rather short."

Stone Hooves just nods as he crosses his arms. "Mar your smile mage, your brother and the Princess know my worth. Neither hoof nor claw enter this castle unvetted, a feat I believe we all can applaud after the situation here."

Clover glances behind the stallion before her, though her eyes dart back to Stone Hooves as she nods. "Where is Elden?"

A faint sigh rolls from Stone Hooves as he takes a step aside as he speaks up. "The Guard Master is well. Now, the Princess desires your company, best not to keep her waiting."

With slight nod Clover start forward, drawing Reynard and Preston in behind her as Stone Hooves leads the way. Though even with Stone Hooves back turned to them, his remarks do not cease. "With Mage Nyota's increasing input I suppose you wish to be referred to as advisor?"

"I would not want such a title."

A slight laugh rolls from Stone Hooves as he raises his right hand, which prompts the castle's doors to open with the glow of his magic. "Unwilling to accept new graces... I see you still remain as stubborn as the old Mage. Though I must admit I prefer not having to call you advisor. At least your unpresuming nature yields that..." A slight groan comes from Stone Hooves, followed by a low comment, though his mumbling is hardly recognizable as he starts inside the foyer.

Preston follows in after the woman's trot, however his eyes quickly turn to the newly placed windows and polished stone flooring. The man's stomach tightens a little, and his gaze is set to a distant stare as he just looks to the room, his right-hand fidgeting with the amulet under his shirt. Yet, his pace is unaltered, even as the group turns into the hallway. His legs becoming stiffer and his breathing growing harsh as he glances towards the tower's entrance across from the doorway.

Stone Hooves and Reynard continue forward, though Clover pauses, shooting a glance to the man. The feeling of her gaze draws Preston's as he forces a smile and quickly moves to meet up with the group.

Clover however holds her gaze, even as they enter the dull coloring of the hall. While the dim lighting is calming, the sound of the armored hooves echoing into the hallway is a bit annoying.

"The Princess is in the throne room." Stone Hooves halts at the large, closed doors as he continues. "I leave you now, Clover..." His eyes turn to Preston and Reynard as he just sighs, nods and trots away.

Clover brings her hand to the door as she opens it and proceeds inside. The lighting of the room is far brighter than that of the hallway, two brilliant, and bright golden orbs of magic hoovering to the ceiling.

However, despite the welcoming hue within the room the small group still pauses, their collective gaze holding to the angelic woman seated at her throne. Sóltina's eyes are closed, her hands folded to her lap, and her chest moving with a calm, steady breath as if she were in a trance.

Yet, the sound of Clover's slowed trot brings Princess Sóltina's eyes. The woman does not flick her gaze, nor does she seem startled by the group before her. Instead, the typical warm smile appears to her face as she speaks up. "*Plestá déy* to you, all of you. I trust that your trip was fair?"

Clover and Reynard both instinctually give a little bow, with Preston quickly attempting to copy them after their motions. Clover however speaks up without skipping a beat as she raises her head back up. "We set out as soon as the carriage arrived."

Princess Sóltina nods to the comment as she stands from the throne. "As I assumed you would. Now than, I suppose we should get to the reasons I summoned you." The women's wings fold a little more to her back as she continues. "I know you will forgive me for my brisker tone, though as you three know, Clamor's statue still remains within the castle's grounds. Safe of course, though this fact has not kept the court nor the Lords of Trade from more obstreperous comments."

Clover glances to Reynard, quickly noticing the fox-boy's downed ears and step closer to her, Clover speaks up. "F-forgive me Princess, I had thought this summons was regarding my reports. Perhaps of the train project or something else."

The avian woman gives a little nod as she smiles. "My letter was vague for a reason, rest assured not everything I have to say is so unappealing."

Clover straightens herself as she nods. "My apologies, Princess."

"No apology is necessary, Clover. I have a task for you, Clamor's statue is to be taken to *HefterÁll*, I would have you and your company see it there as Nyota is unable." Sóltina continues. "With Svle Nyota unable to do this, I thought I would seek out his acolyte before turning elsewhere."

Clover's ear flicks to the words, but she stays silent as the Princess trails on. "Clamor's statue is to be moved through the *ÉverMoar* forest. It is imperative that it reaches the safety of its new keep before nightfall. I and Svle Nyota, both agree a mage must be present for its settling." Her words lower as she drifts her eyes a little between Preston and Reynard. "I fear Clamor's influence may still pose a threat, miniscule as it may be, no chances can be taken."

"Agreed." Clover nods without batting an eye. "I am more than capable of seeing your work through, Princess."

Preston swallows hard to the statement as he struggles to not turn an eye to Clover.

"This is not just my work, it is the work of Artésque." Princess Sóltina straightens up a little more as she continues. "If you do wish to help, the second part of your venture involves the delivery of a parcel for me." A slight smile comes to her face as she nods. "My top advisor shall be awaiting your arrival at *HefterÁll's* castle."

Clover nods to the comment as she gives a little bow. "I thank you for this trust, Princess."

Princess Sóltina returns the simple bow as she speaks up. "And I as well. Fair travels."

The words bring Clover's trot up as she turns back to the throne room's doors; Reynard immediately follows after her though Preston remains, his gaze flicking to and from the angelic woman standing before him.

Sóltina says nothing, her smile, the same friendly, warm, and all to welcoming expression molded to her face, etched to her with the same confidence that her words had. Yet, despite the facade, Preston remains fearful, skeptical of the smile now brighten the room. Though, he nonetheless bows his head and turns to the doors the duo passed through.

Clover and Reynard await him, yet Preston is the first to speak. "So how far is this place?"

Preston's comment slows the newly determined spring in Clover's hooves as she speaks up. "Sóltina has stated our travel is to cut through the forest, we shall arrive at the castle well before nightfall. Providing the more narrow trails are cleared."

A quick laugh escapes Preston. "So, we just wander the forest with an evil statue at dusk huh? No objections Clover? You said yes pretty fast in there."

Clover's left ear flicks to the laugh, though she bats an eye to Reynard beside her before replying with a rather clam tone. "It is purely for safety; a mage is required." A rather chilly gaze settles to Preston as she follows her last breath. "We have nothing more to discuss."

Preston nods, his right-hand dancing to the strap of his bag, though more importantly his thumb rubbing to the amulet just under his shirt. "Yep."

The group's pace has quickly brought them back to the foyer of the castle, which does little to wane Clover's determined steps as she passes outside. The warm light of the sun greets Preston's face, though his attention much like Clover now turns to the new group of armored satyrs standing near a gray, marble like statue.

Stone Hooves takes a step forward as he speaks up. "Ah, good we shall have the statue ready with the *Moofs* soon. Unless you said no?"

The words turn Preston's attention as the man now stares to the two large, bison like animals hooked to the flat-bed chariot just off to the side. The raggy furred creatures have two, long, curled horns poking out from the sides of their heads, a stench too permeates from them, something rather apparent even given how far Preston is away from them.

Preston's eyes are brought from the bison though as Clover speaks up. "We shall set out in a moment; I wish to speak with Master Nyota first."

"I would prefer to leave soon, Miss Vines." Stone Hooves nods to the cart. "Best we not keep our company long."

"And we shall not." Clover nods, turning away from the group of armored guards as she starts into the field adjacent to the castle.

A sigh rolls from Stone Hooves as he simply watches. "*Hofáfor* then, the mage only comes from his tower when dragged by the Princess."

Both Reynard and Preston quickly follow after Clover, though Preston speaks up as he glances back to the entourage they soon will accompany.

"Don't you think it's a bit strange they knew you were coming along? We just talked to her."

Clover glances back to the castle though she merely shrugs the comment off as she speaks up. "It is such a simple task, I would not refuse it, the Princess simply knew this."

Preston's right hand comes to fidget with the amulet under his shirt as he shakes his head. "I don't like that; I don't like that she expected you to say yes."

"It was still my choice, Preston." Clover focuses back to the tower across the field. "Now keep up, we should not keep Stone Hooves waiting, I prefer his silence when traveling with him."

- - -

The walk across the mostly barren field to the tall, stone made tower was not long. Yet, the workers' irritated eye which stayed pinned to the small group's tread did make for a rather uneasy walk.

Luckily, the constant gaze of them is left behind as Clover moves to the tower's closed door with quick knock.

For a moment, no voice calls back, and the door remains closed, this draws Clover back in as she again knocks. "Master Nyota, it is Clover."

Another moment passes, although this time the door opens. The long, wispy, white bearded man pokes his head out from the tower. His eyebrows furled in curiosity to the small group outside of his home. The dark olive and gold trimmed robe seem to be the only coloring to the old satyr, aside from his amber eyes. "Ah, Clover. I had feared the knocking was another summons to a meeting." Nyota shifts his eyes to Reynard as he nods, the beard wiggling in the process. "Reynard too, *Plestá Déy*."

Once more Nyota's eyes shift, although the friendly smile is dropped from his face as he looks over the taller man standing a little off to Clover's right side. "Oh, hello? Who might this be?"

Clover gives a simple laugh to the old satyr's confusion as she gestures to the man beside her. "Master, it is Preston."

"Preston?" The name does little to Nyota's stare, although the smile does come back to his face as he steps aside. "Well, pleasantries to any friend of my assistant." He gives a simple old man smiles as he shuffles back into the tower, all the while giving a little slack to his right leg.

Clover blinks to the slowed pace as she steps in, her head lowering. "Master? Are you well?"

"Hmm? Oh yes of course, why do you ask?"

Preston comes into the room, Reynard to his side as he looks over the house. For once, no scrolls litter the floor, although a few stacks of books have seemed to sprung up since their last visit. Of course, the room does not hold priority to Preston's mind as he speaks up. "Well for one you don't remember me. Getting old there Gandalf."

The words perk Nyota's ears up as a wider smile breaks through his white beard. "Ah! Preston!" The smile is short lived as a boney finger comes to wag at the man. "Now I see why my mind has deceived me, my assistant has allowed you to turn into a beast." Nyota rubs to his beard as he nods. "Yes, you should not change your face, especially for an old stallion with so much on his mind."

The old voice just brings a smirk to Preston's face, even as the old man's wrath turns to Clover. "Of course, one can only imagine why my assistant has allowed you to grow so unruly."

Clover blinks to the comment as she shifts her eyes between the old satyr and Preston. "I do not hold power over another's decisions Master."

"Bah." Nyota shakes his head as he starts towards one of the larger stacks of books in his makeshift library. "I have never known you not to voice your opinion."

Preston gives a little chuckle as he crosses his arms. "So, you don't like the beard? I'm just trying to be like you."

The old satyr pauses next to the books as he looks over Preston. "Oh, well, do not let it get to you. Some things are just out of our reach, yes?"

Preston cocks his head to the words as a boyish little giggle rings up from beside him.

Reynard's laugh is cut from the room as Nyota's lengthy tone comes back. "Now Clover, as much as I would loath sending you on a tedious errand, the Princess insist that a mage escort Clamor's statue... um the destination escape me, but I am sure Princess-..."

"We have already met with the Princess, Master. We shall be leaving soon. I had just wished to see you."

"Oh?" Nyota blinks to the comment. "Yes, well I should have known my faithful student would attend to the greater good. I of course suggested myself to go; but the Princess bid me not to, for my leg's health that is." A little cough comes from the stallion as he continues. "Of course, I also suggested the statue would be better served in hole somewhere." He looks back to the stacks of books he stands near as he brings his hand to his beard.

Clover glances to Nyota's leg, though she breaks the silence in room as she takes her eyes from it. "What is to become of the clearing, Master?"

Nyota raises a finger as he moves from the books. "The clearing? Oh yes, the noise outside." He sighs. "It seems the Princess is trying to reward me for my deeds, as miniscule as they were. There is to be a new *Márjx Gréftor* erected in the field. From what we have discussed, it shall be free to all, not just those of higher stock. A place of learning, and a place where this collection can be properly stored. Now, do not distract me a moment, I have misplaced something."

The old *Únoff* begins to circle a little as he looks around the various book stacks. However, after a few moments he sighs. "I suppose I can transcribe it from my journal later."

Clover looks around the room as she speaks up. "What are you searching for Master?"

Nyota waves his hand as he takes a step back towards the group. "Oh, do not worry now, your minds are filled enough. If you can, stop at the castle before you head back to *VéturVill*, I will have something for you." He gives a little nod as he takes in a deep breath. "Now, I understand you must be going soon, but since you have stopped in, I must ask a few things."

Nyota shifts a little to Preston as he gives a little nod. "I can see a slight spark in your eyes Preston, one that was absent when you last left. I trust you are recovering?"

Preston hesitates for a moment, but he gives a little nod as he speaks up. "Well last time I got on a chair no one offered me a rope, so I'd say pretty good."

Nyota nods, his eyes darting away. "Good... good... I had wondered how the loss might affect your condition. May I see your amulet, Preston?"

The man moves a little closer as he pulls the amulet from where it lays on his chest.

The sight of if however, brings a quick and happy laugh to Nyota as he pats the man's shoulder. "Ah, good. A bright shine to it." He turns to Clover as he continues. "It is a good thing you have been helping to manage his magic, Clover."

Nyota quickly turns back to Preston as he waves his hand. "Not that it would have been dangerous, it is just far safer to not have pent up magic within one's self." A little chuckle rings from the stallion as he turns back to Clover. "Now, I do hope you have not skimped on your work my student. As I recall, you turned my final test down. Which means you still need to have one. Must stay ready, you may never know when the time comes."

Clover's posture straightens as she moves a hand to her bag. "Actually Master, it is one of the reasons I wished to see you."

The woman dips her hand into the bag as she continues. "I have been practicing my charging spells." Her hand comes back as five clear crystal stones float in front of her.

"Oh?" Nyota looks over the floating stones, however the enthusiasm to the old face is hardly real.

Luckily, Reynard stirs the group's attention as he speaks up. "Just wait Nyota, you will be surprised with what Clover can do."

A smile comes to Nyota's face as he nods. "I am sure I will."

The words prompt Clover's magic a little more as she forces her eyes to the stones. The ring of her magic bounces and echoes to the spiral stone-made room, as it continues to glow with an ever-deepening blue hue. Nyota's smile holds the same as he just stares to the spell before him.

Perhaps half a minute passes before Clover sighs, and the stones drop a little lower in her hold. "The most I have done is ten, and I am hardly tired after."

Nyota merely nods. "Quite a show of your skill, though I hardly would expect something less. Now drain them."

Clover blinks to the request as she speaks up. "To what?"

"To yourself of course." Nyota chuckles. "Let me see how well you manage."

"But Master, a spell like that is not within our teachings."

A little laugh comes from Nyota as he nods. "I am sure you have studied a little outside of your schooling. Now please, demonstrate it."

Though Preston understands hardly nothing of their conversation, he nonetheless takes notice to Clover's expression. The woman's ears have dropped a little, yet her confidence does not seem to alter as she turns her eyes back to the stones.

The spell takes about the same amount of time, though nothing changes in Clover execution. Her hands remain steady and her control seems perfect, despite the spell supposedly not being something she has practiced. The stones glow, though their color is drained away as Clover's hands now shine brighter towards the end of her display.

The stones sits dormant now, their color gone as Clover shifts her eyes to Nyota. "There, Master."

Nyota merely nods. "I could ask you to perform such a spell well into the night, and you would hardly need a break, would you?"

Clover says nothing as Nyota nods again, a somewhat bittersweet smile crossing his face. "I appreciate your training Clover, but we both know you have moved beyond what I can give you."

"That is not true Master, I still learn-..."

A faint laugh and cough escapes Nyota as he nods. "And I am sure you do, but we must soon face the reality of our arrangement. There is far too little I truly have left to teach you, you do not require my eye for everything, you must accept this."

Nyota's magic takes hold of the stones as he eases them into Clover's bag. He takes a step towards the woman as he smiles, though he casts his eyes to Preston and Reynard as he nods. "We shall talk another time, for now, return to Stone Hooves. I have kept you all long enough."

Clover takes a deep breath as she gives a shifty smile. "Of course, Master."

A slight laugh comes from the old satyr as he waves on the group. "Go on now, I shall be here when you return."

Clover moves back towards the door, adjusting the bag around her as she does. "We shall return soon, Master."

Reynard gives his own little goodbye to Nyota, however Preston turns his attention to the woman now stepping outside as he moves to her side. "You alright?"

The question is quickly brushed off as Clover instead focuses to the field before them. "Come on Reynard, we should set out."

The comment prompts Reynard after the duo, leaving Nyota alone as he watches the group move through the door for a moment until his sight is lost. With the door closed he turns from it. "Well, I suppose I must tend to my journal." The old stallion shifts his eyes to the stairs as his old voice continues. "Oh Wispy, you have missed our guests." A slight chuckle rolls with his cough as he moves his first hoof to the stairs.

Chapter 13

Turning Evermore

The rock of the carriage, despite the more overgrown, dirt roads of the forest has not been unruly or even very uncomfortable. Then again, both Reynard and Preston have found something else to focus on. The forest itself was interesting, though the copy and paste like nature of the old forest quickly grew old.

Instead, Clover has been the focus of the duo. Sadly, as another slightly more jarring bump to the road hits the carriage the coach wobbles, forcing Clover's eyes open as she takes a deep breath and turns to the window.

A simple chuckle rolls from Preston as he speaks up. "I thought the whole idea of having you sent along was to be awake in case something happened?"

"I was not sleeping."

"Ha!" Preston waves his hand to the comment. "You had your eyes closed and your head against the wall. Been like that for a while actually, what's your excuse?"

A light laugh rings from the fox-boy though Clover still speaks up as she shakes her head. "I was merely thinking for a moment."

"Yea?" Preston shrugs. "What are you thinking about?"

A sigh rolls from Clover as she nods. "Nothing for you to concern yourself over."

"You sick?"

Clover squints to the question. "What? No."

Preston shifts forward, his hand extending as he waves the woman to lean towards him. "You were sick this morning, maybe that spell messed with you."

Clover waves the man's hand away as she replies. "I am not sick, and I have never felt ill after a spell."

"Mhm, let me feel your head."

Clover rolls her eyes. "You are no healer, Preston."

"Nope, just an alien space wizard, now let me feel your head.

With a slight blow of the breath Clover leans forward, though she glances to Reynard before finally giving into Preston's request.

Preston moves his hand a little under her bangs as he speaks up. "Well, you're not warm." He gives a little chuckle as he moves his hand back. "Maybe you should take it easy, this is just a quick ride, right?"

A slight smirk comes to Clover as she nods. "Not all of us can sleep as long as you do."

"Funny." Preston clears his throat as he glances out the window. "But I think I've done a good job getting up. Better breakfasts, right Rey?"

Reynard says nothing, though his hyena like chuckle says enough. Of course, Preston's laugh is brought down a little as he catches the woman's somewhat annoyed gaze. Even still, he nods to her with a smile. "It's okay Clover, it takes a very select bit of skills to do what you do in the kitchen."

"You know Preston." Clover nods. "Perhaps Nyota was right about your beard. I have noticed you scratching yourself like a common forest creature."

"That's so Happy-Hooves?" Preston crosses his arms. "So, you don't like the bread?"

Clover pauses for a moment, though as she draws a breath in she speaks up. "It was merely a *Fon* that perhaps-*Cheerrrkkk*..."

The quick sound of snapping wood precedes an uproar of voices outside. The cabin comes to a sharp halt as a familiar voice rings out above the noise. "Do not touch it, do not touch it!"

Everyone inside the carriage gives their own unique reactions to the sudden stop, somewhere between confusion and fear. The boyish voice of Reynard's is the first to ring to the cabin however. "What happened?"

Clover stands from her seat as her left hand begins to glows. The door to the carriage flings open just as the windows of the carriage close to Clover's magic. The woman's take-charge tone comes forth as she turns an eye Reynard. "Do not leave the carriage."

Preston just blinks to the woman's words as he watches her jump from the doorway, the door closing behind her with a hard slam of her magic. Thought hardly a second passes before Preston moves to follow after the satyress.

"W-where are you going? Clover said to stay here?"

"Yea, yea, and do that, I'm just going to make sure she's alright." Preston moves a hand to the door as he opens it, turning his head to the commotion outside. He quickly jumps from the simple steps as he closes the door behind him. Reynard however opens up the back window as he brings his eyes to the world.

The flat-bed that once held the stone statue now leans to one side, its back right wheel broken. The large bison-like creatures have been unhooked and now flail about, their hind legs kicking wildly towards the sky as the driver and a few guards attempt to steady them. Of course, the irritation of the large creatures seems to annoy the other animals within the convoy, as even the unicorns that pull Stone Hooves' carriage begin to grow unruly.

"Calm those brutes! Sergeant lend a hoof over their! To arms all of you, we must be ready!"

The metal sound of swords being drawn brings Clover's voice up as she takes a few steps forward. "What happened?"

Stone Hooves's ear flicks to the voice as he turns to the approaching satyress. "Have you no eyes?" The man holds his hand to the upright standing statue as he continues. "It seems the wheel has fallen away. Yet the beast landed perfectly. Did you not enchant the wheels?"

Clover squints to the comment as she speaks up. "The spell was fine-..."

"What? You had not thought to enhance the wheels further? For cargo such as this?!"

The satyr's voice brings a quick response from Clover as she straightens her posture. "Do not rush your words, my spell is not to blame."

"*Hmpf*, look at your effort and tell me it is not your fault." Stone Hooves tightens his gaze as he swings his head back to the two armored guards near the statue. "Scout the tree line, we must ensure this is no ambush. Move! We must have a secure perimeter if a messenger *swóóp* is needed."

The guards quickly react to the words, sparking a slight bit of magic to their *Gloftórs* as they rush to the road's edge. Stone Hooves's eyes come back to Clover as his orders still bark to the guards. "I do not wish to have any problems in this exertion! Use your eyes, keep your words simple!"

Preston gives a slight chuckle to the words as he looks over the armored satyr's heated face.

The laugh of course takes Stone Hooves's attention as he speaks up. "Do I amuse you *Drágeff*?"

Clover takes a step in front of Stone Hooves as her voice rings out. "No one has touched the statue?"

Stone Hooves holds a hard stare to the woman, but he turns back to chariot as he trots towards it. "The statue fell like this."

"Then step aside." Clover follows Stone Hooves' trot, her eyes curiously looking over the statue as she does.

"Miss Vines, I suggest we get a move on. The forest in this area is deep-..."

Clover holds a hand to Stone Hooves, causing the satyr's face to glow red with frustration, yet he bites his tongue as Clover stares to the ground. The area around Clamor's stone has begun to stir, a sight that quickly prompts Preston to take a step forward as he moves a hand to Clover's arm to pull her back. Clover merely pulls against the hand, as she speaks up. "Bring me the wheel."

The ground under the statute continues to move, though as a moment passes a mass of worms or worm-like creatures begin to show themselves. Though their purpose is unclear, Clover speaks up again. "The wheel, now."

Stone Hooves extends his gloved hand as the broken wheel floats to him. "We have spares, this is a waste of time."

"As long as the damage is recent to stone or wood it can be repaired." The wheel comes under her magic as she takes a knee near the broken piece of wood.

Stone Hooves however shakes his head as he calls to one of his guards. "Where is the replacement I called for!?"

A guard steps forward from behind one of the carriages. "Sir, the wheels are gone!"

"What?" Stone Hooves shakes his head. "What do you mean?"

The guard floats out several wheels, a few bugs dropping from them as the guard simply shakes his head in confusion. "Look, the wheels seem to have been chewed! The beast did it!"

Clover chimes in. "No, look at the ground, we need to remove the stone from the forest."

The base of the statue has sunk further into the dirt, the once solid ground now turning to mush with the worms beneath it.

Stone Hooves however just shakes his head. "Help me move this."

"Do not touch it!"

Preston holds his eyes to the magic surrounding the downed chariot as it begins to rise a little from the ground. The wheel is pushed up under the chariot as the sound of Clover's magic rings out a bit more.

The sight of her spell however is cut from Preston's eyes as the man instead looks to thrashing animals around him.

Stone Hooves barks another order. "Settle them, sergeant, settle those animals!"

The chime of Clover's magic is quick to die down as the woman pants a little. "T-there, all done." Clover sighs. "The wheel should hold."

Stone Hooves gets a wide smile as he looks over the chariot. "Splendid, we can move the sta-..."

"Captain Stone Hooves! Captain Stone Hooves!"

The satyr quickly turns to the running guards as he speaks up. "What? What is it?"

Before the guards can speak up a flock of birds pour out from the tree line. Acting quick however, Stone Hooves forms a bubble of magic around the area as the birds bat against the magic. As intense and abrupt as the sudden flock is, Preston does little more than jump a little as the noise of the birds quickly pass over them.

Stone Hooves scrolls the guards as he shakes his head. "You are frightened over a flock?!"

"No sir, listen!"

One of the guards points to the tree line they ran from, the mass of birds has passed by, though Stone Hooves is reluctant to lower the barrier. Even still, as he lowers it an unmistakable growl rings through the area, further spooking the bucking animals around them.

The sudden sound of the growl prompts a shout from a few guards. "*Néftors!*"

Stone Hooves brings his hand to the hilt of his sword as he darts his eyes to the outer brush around the road. The sound however comes back up, this time closer and sending the two unicorn-like horses into a fit as they buck against their harnesses.

"Quiet them!"

Preston moves to Clover's side, as she stands from the ground. "That cannot be, Sóltina's barrier is strong in the light."

"Well it must not be!" Stone Hooves shakes his head. "A noise such as this must be a *néftors*, unless the trees have become ravenous."

Just as Stone Hooves words leave his mouth the underbrush of the forest begins to sway, mossy bodies coming into sight as they dart around the road. The shape is unmistakable, and the smell of wet dog is undeniable as Stone Hooves chimes in once more. "Stand your ground!" Stone Hooves' glove glows bright as a barrier of magic forms around them.

However, just as the magic grows around them, one of the beasts quickly makes a mad dash towards it. A loud chime of magic rings to the road as the wall pulses, forcing the wolf back.

A howl rings out as the forest begins to stir further. The chatter is unsettling, though Stone Hooves's deep voice calls over the noises. "Help me load the statute, we leave now!"

The two guards are hesitant to drop their hold on their weapons, but they do as they move to the statue.

Yet Clover quickly jumps before them as she speaks up. "No, do not touch it."

"How else would we move it?" Stone Hooves shakes his head, his barking trailing on. "Magic would awaken the beast further, you said it yourself, this corrupt must be removed from the forest!"

"We cannot move it by hand."

"And we cannot let it sit." Stone Hooves points to the ground, the worms still working the stone into the dirt as he turns away from Clover. "Madness may consume us, though this stone must be moved."

Clover's hands spark up as she holds Stone Hooves back. "A sword under his control is not what we want."

A sigh rolls from Stone Hooves as he speaks up. "How else do we move it?"

Preston points to it. "Tip it over, and then slide it up with ropes."

Stone Hooves simply shakes his head as he points to the carriage. "Return to your seat, your ignorance suits silences best."

"Do we have rope?"

Stone Hooves squints to Clover's question, though he nods. "We are not going to place this beast closer to the ground."

"No, but get rope, and bring the cart around." Clover turns to the driver of her own carriage as she nods. "Move forward."

The driver cocks a slight smile as he darts his eyes back to the ever wolf filling area outside of the barrier. "With respect Miss Vines, I do not think they will let us."

Stone Hooves snaps his fingers as he points further down the road. "Guards, secure the path before us, barricade it with a spell large enough for the convey."

Without a word several guards move forward, though many continue to quell the pack animals still going wild.

Stone Hooves returns to his own carriage, prompting both his and the driver behind his carriage to come forth. Rope now comes under his control as he drags it beside him in his magic. "What now?"

"Throw the rope around the stone, ensure it comes under his arms." Clover motions to the chariot off to her side. "I can push the ground up and we can pull it on top."

Stone Hooves shakes his head. "The other rope was enchanted yet it still broke, what will stop this from breaking away?"

Clover nods. "What has stopped Clamor from summoning something stronger than *wýrms* to dig him away? He is weak, this will work."

At Clover's comment the wolves outside of the barrier stir up in a frenzy, barking and howling as many charge into the barrier. The sound of them brings Preston's eyes back to them as he watches them slamming into the barrier. The barrier hardly moves to them, yet the mossy bodies of the wolves show something else, each time they bash into the light they burn, the unpleasant smells mixing to the forest around him.

Preston's right hand comes to his amulet as he watches them further, the creatures slamming into the barrier with a sizzling sound following their yelps as spell forces them back.

"Preston, take hold of the rope and help if you insist on standing."

"What?"

Clover repeats herself as she holds the rope to him. "The rope, take it."

Stone Hooves chimes in as he tosses the rope over the statue. "You merely need to pull weakling, nothing more." The rope slides off the statute as he collects it and begins to tie it tighter.

Passing the rope to Preston Clover moves her attention to the unmoved cart, her magic taking hold as she drags it to where she wants. The bison continue to ignore their master's coxing, though their efforts are not needed as Clover settles the cart where she wants it.

The sound of the wolves continuing to assault the barrier rings through the forest, though Preston holds his eyes to the statute as Stone Hooves finally manages to bring the rope around it. "The rope is set." he glances to the forest floor as the worms continue to stir under it. "What now?"

Clover takes a knee beside the cart, her eyes looking over the flatbed portion of it as she places a hand to the ground. "Get ready to pull." She takes a breath as her hand sparks up in blue glow.

The area around the statue quickly takes on her magic, the soil itself looking to harden as the worms beneath the stone squirm to the tightening ground. "Keep it steady!"

The sound of roots snapping ring under the statue as the ground itself begins to rise steadily to Clover's magic. Though the struggle now begins as the worms attempt to tip the stone over, forcing Stone Hooves, the drivers, and Preston to tighten their hold to the rope. Of course, as Preston begins to slip a nearby guard attempting to settle the horses darts over to help.

The ground continues to rise as statue is slowly, but surely pulled towards the cart, Clover magic ensure the dirt remains smooth, as if the stone were being pulled across ice.

Yet, as the statue draws closer, a sound greets Preston's ears. A voice, though not loud, calls out from somewhere in the forest.

The wolves have stopped their assault, the call to Preston seemingly prompting them to halt. Stone Hooves, as well as the others turn to the human like voice as they turn to where the wolves stand beyond the barrier.

Though, while many cast their eyes and ears with confusion, Preston does so in fear as his hold over the rope slacks. "Matt?!" Preston quickly turns his head around the road as he calls back again. "Matt!?"

The sound of Preston's voice brings Stone Hooves's deep tone back as he struggles to hold the statue up. "Are you mad? We need to get out of the forest, hold fast to your-..."

Once more a voice calls out, this time more easily understood. *"Preston! Where are you?"*

Clover blinks to the voice, though it is faint, it is unmistakably Matt's. Her eyes dart to Preston as she speaks up. "Preston it is a trick, do not listen to it."

Despite the words Preston calls out. "I'm here! I'm here!" His hands dropping from the rope as the guards that moved to help him is now left alone.

Clover's eyes widen as she notices Preston taking a few steps towards the barrier. "Preston stop!"

With Clover's attention pulled away from her spell the dirt ramp that has slowly pushed Clamor up begins to fall.

"What are you doing, stay your spell mare!"

Stone Hooves' words quickly draw Clover back to her magic as she corrects it. Unfazed by the commotion behind him Preston moves towards the barrier as he calls out. "Matt! Come to my voice!"

Just beyond the road the bushes are parted, a tired and dirty faced Matt stepping out from the underbrush. A feeling of joy rushes over Preston as his eyes settle over the boy, his clothing is the same as he recalled it from the castle, yet a bit dirty as if he had rolled in dirt. Though, Preston's joy turns to terror as the wolves between them now turn to where Matt stand, their snarls now ringing out.

Preston now presses himself to the barrier as he attempts to draw the wolves' attention. "Hey, hey! Look at me, look at me! Matt run, I'll find you."

Clover continues to watch the scene unfolding before her as she struggles to hold her spell. "Preston, it is a lie, step away from the barrier!"

Stone Hooves chimes in as the group continues to tug the statute up. "Help us you fool, we are nearly there!"

Their words are meaningless as Preston continues to beckon Matt forward. "Run to the light, what are you doing?!"

Matt's eyes fill with tears as he shakes his head, a look of bewilderment taking his voice as he speaks up. "What's happening? I-I woke up in the forest, Preston what's happening? Where are we?"

The wolves take a step towards Matt, prompting Preston to move towards the barrier, yet just as he steps out a sharp force tugs to the man's shirt. Throwing him to the ground as the pack of wolves charge Matt.

A horrifying scream rolls through the forest, yet Matt is seemingly tackled out of sight as the wolves dart back into the underbrush, their apparent prey dragged along.

"Matt!!"

Stone Hooves brings his heavy hoof to Preston's back as his magic pushes him down. "It is a *fántress* you fool!"

Despite his words the screams and howls continue to echo into the world. The lingering sound of the boy being torn apart dwells, far longer than any illusion should as Stone Hooves continues to press the man into the ground.

For perhaps a minute or two nothing else is heard beyond Matt's cries for help; yet, what is worse is the silence that quickly follows it.

Stone Hooves' magic drops over the man, and he steps back, though his eyes continues to scan the forest as he nods. "Get back to your seat."

Clover moves to Preston's side as she helps him up, her own eyes darting back and forth from the forest. "I-it was a trick, Preston. Nothing more."

Preston shakes, the amulet under his shirt glowing bright as he attempts to nod to the woman's words. Yet, as he slowly gives into Clover's gentle tugging, his eyes turn to Clamor's statue and where it sits on the cart. The stone face smiles, an expression that only further plunges Preston into his depression as he falls back to his knees.

Stone Hooves however holds a stern face to Preston's weeping as he shakes his head and calls out. "We must get moving, hitch the animals and let them run off any frustration they have."

The various bison and horses are walked back to their posts, though they settle there is still an unmistakable attitude to them.

Stone Hooves continues to bark orders, arming his guards with bows as he directs their eyes to the forest, yet they all return to their seats on the coaches.

"Preston."

The gentle words draw the man's gaze as Clover helps the man to his feet again. "It was a trick, yes?"

Preston's right hand fiddles with the amulet under his shirt as he forces a nod. "Y-yea, I know."

"We need to get going." Clover looks the man over as she tugs him along. "You need to come along."

"Yea."

Stone Hooves watches Clover guiding the man along, her hand resting on his back with a faint blue hue of magic. Though, despite the obvious spell, he bites his tongue as he instead gestures for his men to prepare for departure.

Chapter 14

HefterÁll

The sun has lingered just above the tree line, its angled light casting over the forest road. Of course, the ever-lowering orb in the sky has continued to hold everyone on edge, especially as the thicket of trees outside stays firm to the path before them.

Luckily, the genuine fear of the wolves following after the convoy has kept Preston's mind at bay, allowing him something else to focus on as he plays with his amulet. Though in his heart he believes Matt was a trick, his feelings still bubble just under the thin veil of fear that everyone else shares.

Though, as another few moments pass, Preston's eyes drift back to the window as he starts to take notice of the trees. Their spacing begins to grow, and the trees themselves begin to look young. It is of course no surprise, being that they have been on the road for well over an hour and a half, yet the sight of the forest ever so slowly beginning to clear is still a welcoming sight.

Clover however does not take notice to the world outside, seemingly in some sort of trance or meditation neither Preston nor Reynard have attempted to stir her from.

Although, as the tree line continues to space out, Preston moves a little closer to the window, now just trying to get a better look of the world outside. The trees have started to give way to a quick incline, with dark forest grass filling the area they now roll into.

The incline of the hill is quickly felt as the coach begins to lean back. The simple motion brings Clover's eyes open as she turns to her window. "We should be near the city now."

Preston just nods to the comment as he continues to watch the thick dark fields of grass moving past the window.

Just as sudden as the incline had started, it begins to end, the ground growing more level. The driver's voice takes Preston's attention as he glances towards the front of the carriage. "We near the checkpoint."

Clover nods despite not moving to the window. "Good, we are ready."

As she quiets down, she moves to collect her bag, drawing it around her as she gives a simple sigh.

The noise draws a response from Preston as he nods. "You alright?"

A simple smile crosses Clover's face as she nods. "Of course, are you?"

Preston's reply is halted as another voice from outside starts up. *"Halt, papers."*

The voice takes Preston and Reynard's attention as they both turn towards the window. The carriage comes to a stop as the driver's voice starts up. *"We are transporting a statute to the castle. Same as those before us."*

"Papers?"

A small booth like building can be seen on the right of the road, but the faces to these voices remain unseen. Of course, the carriage starts to move as the stranger's voice comes up. "Alright, *move along.*"

As the wheels begin to move the faces of two silver, armored clad *Dwoffs* comes to Preston and Reynard's gaze. Though neither guard meets their eyes, and the carriage moves too fast for Preston to really get a good look at the two guards.

Just past this small checkpoint is another quick incline. However, Preston's eyes stay to the large area of what looks like bushes; for what seems like miles up the road these bushes grow in rows.

"What's with the bushes?"

Clover gives a quick glance to the window as she speaks up. "They are vines."

"Vines?" Preston nods. "Grapes? Like for wine and stuff right? Shouldn't that be you know, protected or something?"

Clover shrugs to the comment as if uninterested. "I am sure there is a barrier spell around them; the city is home to the school of *Eñchar Márjx*, their spells would be less obvious than mine."

Preston just blinks to the words as he nods, his eyes turning back to the fields of grapevines. "Okay."

The rows of grapevines are full, and bright with the colored berries, something clear even from Preston's distance. For perhaps the next ten or so minutes nothing but the bushes are seen, although, as another incline in the road comes to the wheels the fields are cut from sight. Leaving nothing but the forest in the far-off distance. A new sound also rings to the man's ears, the sound of wheels rolling to stone.

Before long, the first few buildings are seen. Nothing special though, just simple gray stone, two story creations. Within a few moments more, more buildings come into sight, and the sound of the horses pulling the carriage now claps a little louder to the solid ground. The sun has started to turn orange as it falls closer and closer to the edge of the world. The sight the ending day has likely kept many of the city's inhabitants inside, as how few people are seen walking the streets.

"We should arrive at the castle shortly. According to the Princess, an advisor should be waiting." Clover straightens her dress as she speaks up. "It will be nice to rest once this is over."

A slight chuckle comes from Preston, but he does not turn from the window. Instead, he just continues to look over the new city. Unlike *Passvórtall,* the air is not thick with the smell of wet stone, but this city does have its own unique smell, somewhere between flowers and fresh grass. The buildings have continued to grow with every moment, and with it the city's color has begun to show with the dark green banners strung up around some side streets which mix well with the fresh flowers hanging about.

A few torch or orb streetlights stand around the roads, but no flame or light shine to them yet. "So, is this castle across a river like the other one?"

"No, like I said, this is the *Eñchar Márjx's* city, a barrier protects it." Clover pokes her head out of the window as she continues. "You can see it just up the road."

Preston moves his own head out of the window a little more, as he looks down the road. The houses come to a halt on this street perhaps a mile or two from the large three tower structure at the end of the road. The castle is made of dark grey almost basalt colored stones. All roads seem to lead to the structure, as it sits seemingly at the center of the city. Interestingly, the stone looks perfectly carved, a trademark of *Únoff* work, despite the abundance of *Dẃoffs* Preston has seen. The structure is perhaps three or four stories tall, with the tower on the right and left extending a little higher, a silver cone capping each one like a lighthouse.

The third tower extends from the center of the castle and is much larger from the other two. Still with the same silver cone at the top. However, in the open area under the cone sits a large silvery-blue orb. Shining bright, despite the golden light bathing it from the setting sun.

Preston shakes his head as he speaks up. "Why does every other castle have some sort of defense when the Capital doesn't?"

"The Capital must appear welcoming." Clover's ear flicks as she looks back to the window. "Do not get scared, Preston."

Preston squints to the comment. "What would I be afraid of..."-*fffsshhhaaaa*.

The chiming sound of magic that rings to Preston's ear is quickly over as the man looks around the cabin a little confused.

Reynard gives a little laugh at the man's stare as he speaks up. "That was the barrier."

"Yea, got that."

Clover moves her head out of the window as she speaks up. "Stop the carriage in front of the castle, we need to speak with someone before we continue."

"*Yes, Miss. Vines.*"

The carriage rolls for another few moments before it slows to a stop. As it does Clover stands, and Preston shifts his legs. The woman quickly moves to the door as she takes a step outside, Reynard following after. Preston however remains behind, his eyes turning to the door as a sudden fear overcomes him.

Both Clover and Reynard stand without care outside, yet the boyish fox takes notice to Preston's pausing as he turns an eye to the man. "Preston?"

The name stirs Preston as he quickly clears his throat, ducking his hands to both his bag and Reynard's as he nods. "Yea, yea, I'm right behind you." He quickly brings the bags around him, though his shuddering breath forces him to take an extra moment.

Even still, Preston starts outside as he moves to stand near Reynard. The fox-boy lingers rather closely, his paws rubbing against one another with a bit of angst.

The sight of the stopping carriages bring a few *Dẃoff* guards forward from around the castle's courtyard. While they all seem calm enough, their tones still call for a quick reply. "State your business here."

The silver armored, and hairy faced guards hardly look any different from one another, all hosting the same sort of pig-nose and pinkish skin. Though small differences in height and their beards do distinguish them a little from their fellow armored comrades.

With Stone Hooves still exiting his carriage Clover speaks up, a rather proper tone coming from her. "Princess Sóltina has sent us to-…"

With a quick sound of a spell, Stone Hooves teleports beside Clover. "I can handle this, mage." A quick clear of the throat precedes Stone Hooves as he continues. "We have been sent by the Princess to escort Clamor's statue. Summon your lord and your best movers, the animals will not follow us in."

The much shorter *Dẃoff* just blinks to the words as he speaks up. "*Vón Dorñ* himself?"

"Yes." Stone Hooves holds his hand to the stone statue for a moment, but his voice comes back up as he turns to Clover. "The Princess sent an aid some time ago, please take my associate to them."

One of the guards nods as he turns to Clover. "I shall escort them, follow me."

Preston and Reynard both follow after the satyress' trot, as the guard directs them towards the few stairs leading to the castle's doors. Preston turns his head to the carved ceiling as he gives a slight laugh to the almost Italian like architecture surrounding him. Although, his sightseeing is quickly stopped as the guard speaks up. "How long is *Vón Dorñ* to remain in the city?"

Clover nods to the words. "It is not our place to say."

"R-right." The guard just nods as he turns to the hall on his right. The walls of the castle, unlike outside are lightly colored with an almost alabaster look to them. A few banners are hung to the walls with a few various vases or other decorations in every corner of the halls. All in all, giving the castle a more regal feel then the Capital's simple look. It also looks far more modern than *Passvórtall's* carved out walls.

The hall pours out into a large room, two closed white wood doors to the end and four large spiral staircases to the room's edges, a few potted plants sit as decoration to the stairs, though, Preston's attention is to the pacing satyress in the middle of the room.

"Cherisa!" Clover's slightly excited voice rings up before the guard's introduction. Which forces him to go silent as the two *Unoffs* trot towards each other with open arms.

As the two women embrace Preston looks the unknown satyress over a little closer. She perhaps is a foot taller than Clover, with light red hair and two chestnut colored legs coming down from her layered, regal pink, almost gold like dress. A small gold band wraps her head, but it looks to be merely keeping the mane from her eyes rather than something of importance.

Their embrace is quick to end as the sweet regal tone rings from the red woman. "It is so great to see you, I had grown fearful when your carriage did not arrive on time. Was all well?"

Clover nods as she speaks up. "There was a small mishap, but nothing to fear."

Cherisa's eyes widen a little as she shakes her head. "How horrible!" She sighs. "But you are here now... that is all that matters." Her eyes turn to the short fox-boy as she speaks up. "And I see you brought Reynard along." A playful laugh comes from Cherisa as she trails on. "But it seems his manners are elsewhere. No greeting Reynard?"

The comment brings a nod from the *fróx* as he smiles. "S-sorry... Cherisa I am still setting from before."

While Clover's lie took root without question, Reynard's face instantly sparks a bit of candor compassion in Cherisa. "Do not apologize, dear." The older mare turns an eye back to Clover as she steps to properly greet the fox-boy. "I would assume it is Clover who should apologize."

With a quick shake of the head Clover laughs. "Merely a small mishap, Cherisa."

"Yes." Cherisa continues to rub Reynard's back until the fox-boy seems to brighten up, as he does Cherisa straightens. "Well we will have to discuss this Reynard. It is unwise to settle alone, despite what little Clover might say."

Reynard nods. "It-... it was nothing, Clover is right. Sorry."

A faint sigh rolls from Cherisa, though to Preston's surprise she does not press the issue, instead merely turning back to Clover. Her eyes drifting pass Preston, however she merely glances to him before returning her full attention. "I suppose duty should take importance over our pleasantries. The *Jartál* has already been informed of his new assignment of protector, and since has arranged a holding area beneath the castle. Head Mage Duscle has even been tapped in finalizing the area. All that is needed of you is to present yourself to the *Jartál*."

The woman turns her eyes to the guard as she nods. "Inform our guest outside to proceed to the back of the castle, the *Jartál's* guards are waiting near the cavern."

"I believe they make for it now."

"Stone Hooves must be with them." Cherisa shakes her head as she waves to the guard. "That is all, thank you."

"Of course." With a simple bow the guard turns away and begins to exit.

Cherisa turns to Preston as she nods. "You are excused as well."

"What?"

Clover waves her hand to the comment as she speaks up. "This is Preston, I have been tasked with-...looking after him, for Master Nyota."

"Oh." Cherisa nods as she takes a small step back. "Yes, Elden has mentioned that name." Her smile holds, but her voice quiets as she continues. "We shall have to talk Clover, it has been far too long since we have had the chance."

"Of course, Cherisa."

The red-haired woman gives a little sigh as she straightens her posture. "I do mean it."

"As do I, Cherisa."

"Hmmm." Cherisa nods. "Well, I suppose we should get you better acquainted with the *Jartál*, just through here, we have been waiting." Her trot starts towards the closed doors, which prompts Clover to follow after her.

The doors come open as Cherisa announces to the room. "*Jartál* Dauth, allow me to introduce Clover Vine, Svle Nyota the bearded's assistant."

Sitting in a red, velvet-like throne at the end of the short hall is a heavier set *Dẃoff* man, with a large graying beard hanging to his face. Preston holds his smile at bay to the short rendition of Santa Claus in gold and silver robes. The weight does not actually meet the standards of Santa, but the soft face and light smile to the *Dẃoff* does bring the thought to mind.

"Well met Clover, the Princess has stated you come highly decorated."

Clover blinks to the comment as she gives a little bow, further attempting to come into the room she so quickly was ushered to. "I would not consider myself decorated, I merely aid Master Nyota."

The man just gives a little smile to the comment as he stands from the throne. "You are modest, good. Though I trust you understand that the Princess would not send just anyone to escort Artésque's greatest threat. I do hope however, the presence of mage Duscle will not be a problem."

"No, not at all."

"Splendid." The man takes a deep breath as he nods. "I thank you for getting the statue to me. Mage Duscle will ensure its safety. The Princess and I have been planning for sometime now, so you will excuse this brief meeting. Cherisa has instructions to take you to your rooms. *Témont*, we shall finish up, too many hands so quickly only breed problems. And for this matter we do not want problems."

Clover pauses for a moment, but she nods as she finds her voice. "As you wish."

The *Jartál* gives a simple nod as he sits back to his throne. "Good, Cherisa, if you would."

With a nod Cherisa prompts Clover and the small group out, her magic closing the doors behind her. With them closed she speaks up, her voice a little lower. "I know that was a bit abrupt, though *Jartál* Dauth believes in quick meetings, he also is a bit fearful of pre-planned meetings." She nods. "Though after many visits I agree with the Princess's choice, and I am sure you will too."

Clover nods. "I am sure I will. Lead on, Cherisa, a bit of rest will serve us well."

Chapter 15

Always The Know-it-all

Perhaps an hour or two has passed since Preston and the others arrived at the castle, and it has been a considerable amount of time since Cherisa lead them from the throne room. The castle's guest rooms are just about the same as all the others Preston has seen; stone made, lit with magic, and hosting no windows, hosting a bed and some knickknacks. Of course, with a guest needing little more than a bed and a place to store their things Preston can hardly complain. Furthermore, the bed is soft a rather simple comfort after today's journey.

Unfortunately, the time spent in the rooms were short lived, as before long Cherisa returned. Naturally though, the mention of food snatched up Preston without much effort. The after-dinner conversations always were fair to keep the man's attention will into the early evening. Even with the majority of topics being rather unfamiliar to the man.

Instead of a dining hall, Cherisa choose a different place to eat, which came as some surprise to Preston, given her more regal tone and appearance. The loft somewhere on the second floor however has been a rather enjoyable setting, almost homely. A few simple bookshelves sit around the wooden table, and while the table itself is hardly large enough for all of them, it served its purpose throughout the meal. The most impressive feature to the room, however, is the large window to the far side of it that looks out into the city. While not spectacular in its view, it gives a nice change of scenery from the stone walls of the building.

"...I do hope this was okay, Clover." Cherisa's pinkish magic floats a napkin towards the woman as she continues. "I have simply grown tired of dining in castles, I prefer a bit of solitude."

Clover shakes her head as she takes the napkin from the magic. "Of course, this was nice." She turns towards the window as she smiles. "The room is quiet, I enjoy it."

A light giggle rolls from Cherisa as she nods and turns to Reynard. "Did you enjoy your meal Reynard?"

The *fróx* passes a quick smile as he speaks up. "It was good, but it does not replace Preston's night to cook. I wanted another pizza."

The comment draws a smirk from Preston though as he has for most of the dinner, he remains silent.

Despite the foreign word Cherisa smiles and nods her head in agreement. Clover however does not answer the woman's confusion as she speaks up. "How have you enjoyed your role as the Princess' new advisor?"

Cherisa gives a simple sigh as she leans back in her chair. "It has been fair; I enjoy being able to help. Though, I do wish I had more time with Elden." Another sigh rolls from the woman. "The duty of advisor often conflicts with my duties as a wife."

Clover passes a quick nod "Your work with the Princess is important, I am sure Elden does not mind."

A giggle rolls from Cherisa as she waves her hand. "You sound like Elden. Still, with how long we have been wed, I often feel guilty for not bearing him a foal yet."

Clover again gives a quick as she reaches for her cup. "Your worth is more than a foal."

"So you would say." A groan rolls from Cherisa as she continues. "With all that has happened I find more of my nights filled with conversation, few with Elden. And they are so dull, what a *Jartál* or advisor has to say is hardly enjoyable. There is no real training for what we do. I often feel as though my role is little more than a way to keep the Princess' ears from ringing. Why most of my talents have simply been put to use quelling the fears of Wúna. It has grown difficult to say a new keeper will soon join the Capital when Sóltina hardly looks for one."

"When will there be a new Célntal keeper?"

The boyish voice takes Cherisa's attention as she turns to Reynard. "Hopefully soon, but one must be elected by not only the princess but by the head mages as well. There was hope of locating one of those who served with Clarity, though nothing as of yet. It is almost as if they have vanished."

The *fróx* gives a little smile as he speaks up. "Will it be Clover?"

"Oh no, no." Clover shakes her head as she waves the comment off with a laugh. "I would not be interested in that."

Cherisa cocks a smile at the woman's quick response. "Well of course not. As I understand it, you are but one task away from completing your schooling." Cherisa gestures towards Preston as she trails on. "Once you have finished you will finally have your life back."

Clover takes notice to the gesture as she speaks up. "Oh, Preston is not my final assignment."

"Is that so?" Cherisa shakes her head. "Then what is your final assignment?"

"I do not know." Clover's nonchalantly shrugs as she puts her drink back to the table.

Cherisa blinks to the comment as she speaks up again. "You do not know?"

"We have not had a formal conversation." Clover flashes a simple smile. "We will eventually."

Preston focuses in a little more to the comment as Clover trails on. "I understand it must seem strange; but I have simply not finished learning all that I need to."

Cherisa nods. "Of course, and from the looks of your eyes I dare to say you have been trying to learn every school, not just your own." She smiles. "As an advisor I am permitted to suggest something to you, though as an older mare I understand you may not care to heed it."

Clover smirks to the comment, though she says nothing as Cherisa continues. "My advice is this, Clover. Studying, and indeed helping with Master Nyota's escapades are wonderful. Though you must accept conclusions once you arrive at them. There is more for you to accomplish beyond a quill and beyond your schooling."

"Of course, Cherisa."

Clover's response is quick, something Cherisa seemed to expect as she leans forward a bit. "You look tired Clover. You should get some rest, the morning will come far quicker than we all think." Cherisa stretches a little. "I also have been instructed to give you something from the Princess, though I fear if I do so now you would head out."

Clover nods to the comment as she stands. "It always seems our conversations are short, Cherisa."

A giggle comes from Cherisa as she nods, her right eyebrow raising a bit. "I am surprised you do not need any further convincing." She motions to the plates. "Feel free to leave your things, I shall be here a moment longer."

Reynard stands from his chair at Cherisa's words with a faint yawn. The sight of them both now standing draws Preston, though Reynard once more takes everyone's attention as he speaks up. "What time are we getting up?"

Clover turns to the comment as she moves a little from the table. "Most likely at first light. Preston, do you remember the way to your room?"

"Yeah."

"Oh." Clover nods. "Good night than."

Cherisa settles into the emptying room as she just watches the small group now walking away.

Chapter 16

Assignment

The castle's guest room has a fair, orange hue to it, thanks to the various lamps Preston has lit around the room. In truth, lighting the fires was a bit of a pain, though not being able to prompt his magic kept him from any other source of light.

Even still the added warmth has been enjoyable, especially as Preston sits to the edge of the bed, his focus turning to tying on his shoes. While Preston may not be sure it is morning, a feeling in his gut suggests that it is close enough.

Waking up early has not been something uncommon for Preston, sleep comes and goes, but the early mornings have become a pattern. Even if Clover is not in the bed next to him, Preston has found himself waking up all the same.

A sigh rolls through Preston as he brings his hands up and leans to the bed. The amulet rests comfortably on his chest, though the weight of it slowly draws his attention as he moves a hand to collect it.

Though as he does, a hand knocking at the door takes his attention.

"Preston, are you awake?"

Staring to the door for a moment Preston calls back. "Yea, I'm up."

The man's voice prompts the door to open, as Clover takes a step inside. However, the satyress gives a surprised look to the man as she speaks up. "Oh, you even have your shoes on."

"Surprised?"

Clover waves a hand to the comment as she speaks up. "Somewhat..." She squints to the man as she speaks up. "Did you sleep well? Your eyes look tired."

Rubbing his hand to his face quickly Preston replies with a laugh. "I'm fine. Though I went to sleep with that dang light above my head, you know magic and whatever. When I woke up to use the bathroom, it was gone, stubbed my toe before I made it into the hallway, but other than that I slept good." Preston looks the woman's slightly more flipped up bangs and nicer clothing over as he chuckles. "You wake up better?"

Clover continues to study the man's face for a moment though she relents as she takes notice of Preston's eyes. "Yes, even with the slightly cooler air." She glances to herself for a moment before hiking her eyes back to the man. "We set out soon."

"Oh? What's the rush, castle on fire or something?"

Clover's ear flicks to the comment as she speaks up. "Preston, that is not something to laugh about, castle fires are a tragedy."

Preston just shrugs the comment off. "Alright, well are we gonna pour cement over Clamor and lock him underground or something?"

"We are to meet the *Jartál* behind the castle, Reynard is already up. Once we are done we shall have breakfast and continue with anything else the Princess wants."

The man nods to the comment as he watches the satyress starting back to the door; he follows after her with a light laugh. "So, I've tagged along, think if I keep doing this she'll make me a knight? I think I-..."

Preston's words fall dead as he comes out into the hall and catches eyes with the few guards standing near Reynard.

Stone Hooves cocks a smirk as he moves from his leaning against the wall. "A knight? At least your goals are not as unhinged as your brother's. Perhaps a bar wench would be more suited for your physique and pale tone."

A slight chuckle rolls through the three other guards near Stone Hooves as the comment hits them.

Clover however brings her voice up quick as she trots down the hall. "Foul winded comments to your comrades will not alight you the title of general, Stone Hooves."

The satyr's hard face comes back to him, as he straightens his posture to a more military stance. "You sound like a *Flöff*. My mission to ensure your safe travel has been completed; my comments reflect nothing on my abilities."

"Of course, Captain Stone Hooves."

The words holds the satyr's mouth closed, as he instead just focuses on the woman's trot through the castle.

- - -

(A brisk walk later)

The trek through the castle only took a few short minutes, with surprisingly no wrong turns. Though the journey outside felt rushed, stepping into the morning sun was a welcomed wake up for Preston. The continued breezes carrying in the scent of the forest beyond the city has also been a pleasant addition.

"Ah, finally." Stone Hooves takes a few steps forward as he watches the carriage slowing coming to a stop, its ornate flags of the Capital still swaying to its motion.

The two unicorn-like animals hitched to the front remain prim and proper, even as their reigns are pulled back; a far cry from the animals of yesterday.

"Setting off now, sir?"

Stone Hooves nods to the comment as he continues on. "Yes, I look forward to returning home." He turns back to Clover as he continues. "I shall give the Princess an update on your progress, mage."

Clover just gives a little nod to the as she speaks up. "Clear skies, Stone Hooves."

The comment brings a slight smirk to the satyr as he nods. "I do not need the sky, hoof and wheel serve me better."

"Of course." Clover gives a little sigh as she turns back to Reynard and Preston. "We should see the *Jartál*, come along."

Stone Hooves holds his eyes to the small group's walk as he calls to them. "You should find no problems, I personally helped the security as you slept."

Clover quickly passes a nod back to Stone Hooves. "I do not question it." She motions to the castle grounds around them. "Our carriage has not arrived yet."

A chuckle rings from Stone Hooves as he nods. "Then eat, you do not need to concern yourself with my work."

Clover replies with a simple bow. "Enjoy your trip back, you have done what was asked Stone Hooves."

Though a visible sigh escapes Stone Hooves, he nevertheless turns back to his carriage.

His gaze averted; Clover sets out to the open hallway towards the right of the castle. The heat already absorbed from the dark castle's walls can be felt in the cloister, but the open stone pillars to Preston's side keep the walkway to a cool temperature.

A few guards patrol the castle's outer walls, but none really give Clover's group a second look. The thought that the man's height may have intimidated them has even brought a slight smirk to Preston's face, even with it unconfirmed.

Though despite this idea, Preston still bats a wavering eye to the sight of the guards' weapons. Especially as Clover's trot down the cloister turns to a more open area somewhere behind the castle. Coming into view are two guards, each standing to either side of the opening; they are of course a little shorter than Preston, although the armor they wear is much more lavish with what looks like gold plating in the trim.

Clover's trot slows as they near the spear wielding *Dwoffs*, though a voice quickly stirs the group's gaze. "Ah, Mage Clover."

The familiar bearded, gold and silver robe wearing man gives a quick step towards the group as he holds his smile. The few guards standing around him however, do not hold the same friendly disposition. "Your other companion and his men saw to the statue. Or did you wish to see it for yourself?"

Clover nods to the comment, yet as they begin to talk Preston's attention drifts away. Instead, as he exits the stone floor of the cloister, finding himself staring into a completely walled in area behind the stone castle. The sky above is open, and clear, the ground around him is made of gravel and thick blue-green blades of grass. In the center of this garden stands a large, bright pink cherry tree; although unlike a normal tree, it is immense, looking more like an oak tree with moss of pink flowered branches hanging down from it.

The tree's size is amazing, though the cooler air underneath it is a bit unwelcoming. Yet, the continued conversation keeps Preston's mind from this as he instead focuses back to the words now directed towards him.

"...I am not sure however if your companions can venture with you into the castle's sanctuary."

Clover blinks to the comment as she turns to Preston and Reynard. "O-oh? Well, these are my assistants."

Dauth slowly nods to the words as he speaks up. "Yes, well this decision will stay up to Sagitta Duscle." He holds his hand out. "I suppose they follow until he suggests otherwise, if you would please, I feel as though it is time to put Vón Dorñ finally out of our minds."

As his voice comes down, he turns and begins to walk around the length of the tree. After a few feet however, the back-most part of this enclosure comes into view. A large, dark metal, almost bunker like door sits embedded into the castle's outer wall. No decorations sit to it, and the metal door has no visible handles, as far as Preston can tell.

Dauth waves his hand to the guard as he speaks up. "Open the door."

At his command one of the guards comes to the *Jartál's* side, just as Dauth brings a skinny, blue glowing stone, and cloth chain from his neck. The guard takes the stone as he moves towards the door, stopping only at a small slit near the far-right side of it.

Preston watches the stone glowing as he speaks up. "So, is that like a key or something?"

The question brings an uneasy shift to Clover, but she keeps her eyes from Preston as Dauth nods. "Of sorts, yes." He turns back to the door. "But it is not a normal key as you can see,"

The door continues to glow, though after a few moments however, it cracks open, sliding to right of its own power. As it opens a man steps into the light, a deep red and black robe wearing satyr filling the doorway.

The stranger has dark brown hair, with a few sprinkles of gray mixed throughout. His face shows some age, though like his hair, his beard is only peppered with gray, the smile he wears is also proud, almost youthful. "You have the look of a mage, Clover Vine I presume? Svle's student?"

As Clover begins to bow with respect, Dauth cuts in before she can speak up. "I do not intend to be rude, but perhaps pleasantries can be held after, yes?"

A quick nod overcomes Duscle as he takes a step aside. "Of course, follow me into the chamber."

Dauth hesitates for a moment as he glances to Preston and Reynard. "Is it wise to allow so many?"

A smile chuckle rolls from Duscle as he answers. "What good would my work be if it is not tested?"

Dauth gives a reluctant nod as he starts forward, prompt Clover and the group to follow.

The inside of this bunker like creation is well lit, with bright, orange flame torches. Yet, as the *Jartál* comes to Duscle's side the *Únoff* still poofs a bright dark blue ball of magic next to him.

The two guards are next to file in, followed by Clover, Reynard and finally Preston. However, the tight hallway of stairs down gets a little tighter as the door behind the man starts to close by itself.

The sound of it, and the absence of the sky brings Preston's voice to a whisper as he taps Clover. "So uh, how do we get out?"

Clover simply waves her hand to the question as she continues to hold her ears to the conversation at the front of the group.

"Stone Hooves and his company were able to move the statue once we found a suitable area for its storage." Duscle gives a little laugh as the steps down come to an end. Before the group is now a labyrinth of tunnels, though their presents does not shake Duscle's smile. "I am quite fond of this part, even if it is simple." He motions to the split paths before them. "These tunnels are illusions, something for all would-be intruder to stay occupied with if they made it through the castle's grounds."

Dauth swings his head around the entrances as he speaks up. "Then how do you remember the correct one?"

"Simple, if you hold any doubt in your mind about which way is correct the hallway expands, leading you in a circle and back to this spot. Do stay close though, it will pick up on your confusion if you take your eyes from me." Duscle holds his amused smirk as he starts confidently into the middle most tunnel.

The confidence of Duscle's lead brings Preston's voice up as he taps to Clover. "So is every head mage crazy?'

Though Clover responds with a silent glare, the look on her face is not one of anger or annoyance, and the faint smirk to her draws a smile from Preston. Even still, the man turns his gaze back to the satyr at the helm of the group, his mind settling into their walk down the tunnel's length.

The air is fair, the smell of stone filling the tunnel; yet as stuffy as it is, Preston keeps his mind occupied to the faint sound of magic from somewhere further on.

Preston's time for guessing is short-lived, as perhaps five or so minutes of walking later the source comes into view. A bend in the tunnel leads the group to a bright, almost violet wall of light, its glow twisting and turning as if its color were a reflection of light upon a clear waterfall. The sight of it causes Preston to do a slight double take, his time with Clover has allowed him countless exposures to barrier spells, though none as brightly hued as the one before him.

"This is the outer part of the holding area." A chuckle comes from Duscle as he comes to a stop. "Triple powered with some of the relic *Kélf* stones of *Márjx Gréftor*, and enchanted with my own personal collection.

The spell is designed to break with only the uses of the key... If you would *Jartál* Dauth."

At the words Dauth steps forward, holding the stone key towards the light. "How long do I hold it out?"

Duscle gestures to the wall as he nods. "Simply touch the key to the wall, *Jartál*."

For a moment Dauth hesitates, though he inches forward all the same, drawing the stone ever closer to the light. A loud, echoing chime begins to resonate from the wall as the shimmering light throughout it begins to twist and turn even more than before.

However, within a few moments the veil of magic slowly starts to drop; beyond it a familiar statue takes shape. The sickening features of the goat face stares to the group; bathed in a white light that shines down from the ceiling.

Duscle trots in, no fear in his steps as he speaks up. "The *Helió* stones you see above Clamor have been enchanted to negate any residual power left within him. I would rather like to keep the spell I used to craft it secret, if that is fine *Jartál* Dauth."

The *Dŵoff* shakes his head, still in awe of the beast before him. "I would prefer not to know." He regains his wits as he straightens up, his eyes falling to Clover. "Well, does this meet the princess's requirements?"

Clover turns her eyes to the room and then back to the hallway they came in from as she speaks up. "How many guards are to be placed outside?"

Duscle gives a faint laugh as he nods. "This is a castle; it is always guarded."

"But would there be permanent guards here?"

"Yes, of course." Dauth continues. "Aside from those who roam the courtyard, four of my best will always be placed within this sanctum.

Though only at the front, I do not wish for their eyes to see the horror of Vón Dorñ."

Holding his smirk Duscle speaks up. "I would believe my spells are quite suitable to contain this stone, spears and swords would do little more than clutter this room. Though I suppose I support guards at the entrance."

Clover nods, her gaze focusing back to the mage. "I do not doubt your spells, the security here is far beyond anything I have seen." She shifts a little as she continues. "I see no problems with this arrangement. Perhaps Cherisa could lend an eye, I was only to help escort the statue."

Duscle quickly speaks up with a smile as he nods to *Jartál* Dauth. "Well if Nyota's student finds no faults, I for one am content."

"Yes." Dauth takes a deep breath as he straightens his posture yet again. "I wish to put this behind me. Be sure to put these spells up upon our exit."

"Of course." Duscle waves to the hallway as he turns his gaze to the statue. "If you wish to leave now simply walk back through the tunnels. I made sure to halt my enchantments as we passed them."

"Good, I would prefer air not tainted." Dauth turns towards the tunnel starting out with his guard.

Sighting their exit Preston takes a step towards Clover. "S-shouldn't we leave if they have the key?"

The concern in Preston's voice draws a slight laugh from Duscle as he looks back to admire his work. "The *Jartál* wishes to bury his concerns, so let him leave. I have the other key, do not worry." He takes a breath as he looks over Clover's companions. "I know of Nyota's student, but not of you two-..."

Reynard quickly takes the opportunity to speak up as he nods. "We are Clover's assistants."

"Ah." Duscle turns his light brown eyes to Clover as he continues. "A rather energetic little *fróx* ha-ha. And you would be?"

Preston waves his hand. "Oh um I'm-..."

"Preston hails from the *Fárwift*." Clover shrugs. "Hardly recall his tribe's name."

"Oh, very well." Duscle nods. "I hope it is not too bold, I understand you have another errand to run according to Cherisa. Though I had hoped we might sit down and speak as mages. Nyota would not entrust just anyone to a task like this, perhaps we should have a more formal conversation and introduction later."

"Of course, Mage Duscle."

A laugh rolls from the older satyr as he waves his hand. "Please, just Duscle is fine, no need for titles amongst peers."

"Of course." Clover nods. "I shall make a point of stopping by." Clover's eyes flick to the statue as she trails on. "You shall be here?"

"No, no." Duscle glances to the statue as he shakes his head. "My work here will be done soon enough. No need to watch the stone." Duscle cocks an eye to Clover's unturning gaze. "I understand there was an incident on your venture here. Care to elaborate?"

Clover shakes her head. "A wheel was broken away from the cart."

"The stone is rather heavy."

Duscle's comment does little to deter Clover's set gaze as she continues. "The ground also began to churn with the forest's help, and there were voices."

Duscle nods as he gives a light chuckle. "Is it believed to be the work of Clamor?"

Clover hesitates for a moment, but her voice finds its way as she shifts a little. "I would not wish to say."

"Wise choice, I suppose, no need to cause a fuss when the statue is safely kept." Another slight laugh rings up from the satyr as he turns back towards the statue. "It shall be rather interesting to battle your abilities, Clamor." He holds his little smirk as he turns back to Clover's group. "Well I suppose I should erect the spells again; come I shall let you out first."

The satyr's trot sparks Preston to step aside, as Duscle starts to lead the group back through the maze of tunnels, all the while as he talks. "You know, the school is not too far from the castle. If you do find the time you all can stop by. I understand Nyota does not bother with *Eñchar* spells, but there is no reason I cannot offer a few things to his pupil."

The conversation starts to trail into the hallway, Preston however does not follow it. Instead, he pauses in the chamber, his eyes caught to the strange smile carved into Clamor's stone. The smile itself is not what holds his attention though, but rather his attempting to remember if it existed before or not.

Stranger still, is Preston's right hand, that has slowly creeped up to the amulet tucked under his shirt. His eyes never leave the stone's smile, and the voices around him are silent, until, at least until Clover tugs to his sleeve. "Preston?"

Preston blinks to the furry eared woman beside him for a moment. But he quickly nods as he lowers his hand. "Huh? We leaving?"

Clover nods as she starts back to where Reynard and Duscle wait. "Come along Preston, Cherisa should be waiting for us."

"Right waiting, everyone seems to be doing that…" Preston clears his throat, glancing away from the stone as he turns to group.

The twist and turns in the tunnel surprisingly feel a lot shorter hardly taking a few minutes to navigate. Still, the end of the tunnel could not come quick enough as Preston's eyes finally set to it. The long staircase may be foreboding, but a certain spring comes to Preston's step as he pushes forward in the group a little bit.

Again, like the tunnel, the end of the staircase comes rather quickly, though. Duscle does not immediately open the door as he instead speaks up. "Well I do hope to see you again, Miss Vines."

The glowing stone key comes into Duscle's hand as Clover nods. "If our next task is simple, you shall."

A faint laugh rolls from the older man as he turns back to the door. The chime of magic starts up, the echo of which causes Preston's head to shrink as he waits. Yet, the sight of the heavy door sliding to its side negates the excessive magic's squeal.

The outside air quickly rushing to Preston's face, with a pleasant cooling breeze as he inches ever forward.

"Well, off you go." Duscle steps aside as Clover starts out of the bunker's door.

Preston moves a little in front of Reynard as he takes in a deep breath of fresh air. His eyes lock to the large tree as he speaks up. "Finally..."

"You did not have to go in."

Preston blows his breath as he shakes his head. "And what if something happened? No, no, let's just be happy it's done."

A sigh rolls from Preston as his eyes drift to the red-haired woman trotting out towards the little group. A satchel hangs to her right side, just under the package in her grasp.

Clover turns back to the entrance of the garden area as she smiles. "Cherisa, good to see you again."

The slightly taller satyress just gives a little smile as she replies. "You knew I would not leave without seeing you once more." She taps the large package in her right hand as she continues. "I also have the Princess's second task, and assumed you would check up on Stone Hooves' work." She glances to the bunker's door. "No issue?"

"None." Clover blinks to the package as she takes a step towards Cherisa. "What is it?"

"I had hoped you would know. The Princess asked me not to look in it." Cherisa gives a light laugh. Cherisa waves her hand to Clover's slow reply as she trails on. "I was however allowed to open the map portion of your burden." Cherisa dips her hand into her satchel as she brings out a rather large folded up paper. "You are to see a merchant on the far side of the city, a Lyon Dif, the castle's Stewards says he is just an old metal smith. I do not know anything beyond this."

Clover nods to the comment as she takes the map and package into hand. "I am sure she has a good reason."

Cherisa gives a simple smile as she straightens her posture. "The *Jartál* seems eager to put this behind him, and I do look forward to seeing Elden before too long."

"Oh but of course, I can see to the Princess' request. Head home."

"I may." With another nod goodbye Cherisa starts out of the garden. As she leaves Reynard and Preston come to Clover's side, Preston's voice coming out first as he looks over the map. "So how far is this place?"

Clover unfold the map as she studies it. "...Not too far, shall we start off?"

"Really? Like now?" Preston glances to the castle, his feet already hurting from their simple trip. "Why not, it's not like this place has a pool or anything."

Clover cocks an eye to the comment though neither she nor Reynard question the word as they instead focus on the map.

Chapter 17

Of metal and Spite

"Ugh..."

The annoyed sigh, that continues to ring to the woman's ear finally brings Clover's voice up, as she turns to the blonde man a little beside her. "Is something wrong Preston?"

"No, not at all."

Clover rolls her eyes to the comment as she turns back to the path before her. "Then why do you insist on sounding like a wounded animal?"

Preston gives another sigh as he rubs the upper-most parts of his leg, making for an awkward hopping-walking as he does, which naturally draws some eyes from those passing by. "How much further is this place?"

"It should be at the next street." Clover shakes her head. "You do realize you did not have to come, correct?"

"But we want to be with you." Reynard chimes in, struggling all he while to keep up with Clover's trot. "We just want to know if you are sure this time."

Clover's left ear flicks a little to the words, but she keeps her voice in check as she unfolds the map again. "We are close, I just had not noticed the side street before."

Preston continues to rub at his legs as he speaks up. "You know, when you said we were leaving I thought you meant that we were getting into a carriage or something. The body is not made to walk around all day."

"The body is made for far more than a trek through a city, Preston. Besides, this is far shorter than our trip through the *Oválll*."

"Yea?" Preston brings his hands up as he replies. "That was also before I was *stabbed*, Clover."

The satyress cocks her head to the words as she turns back to the man. "Does your side hurt?"

"W-well no, but come on." He pats to his side. "This can't be good for it."

Any compassion that once graced Clover's face quickly runs off as she rolls her eyes. "Mhmm..." Clover's attention falls back to the map as she speaks up. "Walking is good for you, Preston."

Preston cracks a slight smile to the words as he nods. "The body is fine, let's just hope this is the right corner for a change."

A little snicker comes from Reynard as he quickly averts his eyes to the cobblestone ground of the side streets. The road may be narrow, but the houses are sparse, and many face away from this side street, while it makes for an easy trip it does add to the slight bickering of the group.

Though, unlike before no quick wit greets Preston's ears, instead, Clover rolls the map up as she proudly points to the bend just before them. "We have arrived."

Preston turns his attention to the two-story building Clover continues to hold her hand to. The building in no way is nice, but compared to the few other houses around it, it does not stand out as a wreck. What does make the building stand out however, is the sign hanging out from the second-floor window. The wood is dull and weathered, but the emblem of a lamp can be seen on it.

"What is this guy again?"

Clover is silent as she adjusts her hold of the package in her grasp. The group quickly comes to the front door, which much like the sign is a dull, dark wood. Clover brings her hand to it as she knocks.

After a few moments the door opens, revealing a young girl standing in the doorway. The girl looks perhaps ten years old, light brown hair pinned up into a ponytail. Her skin is pale but healthy, with a smaller than usual pig nose sitting to the *Dwoff* girls face.

Clover blinks to the girl as she speaks up. "H-hello, is Lyon Dif home?" The sweet tone is a little shocking, especially seeing as how the whole trip has been filled with Clover's typical know-it-all tone.

The girl in the doorway hesitates for a moment as she looks over the three strangers before her. "Yes?"

Clover gives a little smile as she speaks up. "Could you get him?"

"Grandpa does not like his first name."

Clover nods to the comment as she speaks up. "Sorry, could you have Dif come to the door?"

With a moment of hesitation, the girl nods as she starts away from the door. However, no kid like hop comes to her step, instead Clover, like her companions beside her watch a much different stride. The girl's right leg limps along the simple wood flooring, almost being dragged without the sound. As the girl gets further into the room however, the reason comes into view. The portion of her right leg is nothing more than wood, although hidden by her girly dress it can still be seen.

Clover is the first to start in as she speaks over the sound of her hooves. "Dif is not too far, yes?"

The girl's walk through the house comes to an end as she points to the downward staircase sitting next to the second-floor stairs. "No."

Clover gives a little nod as she takes another step forward. "Thank you, we can go from here you do not have to get him."

"Grandpa will not let strangers into his workshop." Just as the girl's words come to an end, she starts down the stairs, her hand firmly to the added railing.

The slow descent down the staircase only prompts Clover and the others to come in, their eyes fixed to the girl going down the stairs with worry.

The descent finally comes to an end after a few moments as the girl's head disappears from sight. The girl's voice rings up from the room downstairs, though not a moment later a deep raspy voice calls out in response. "Beth, you know you are not supposed to come downstairs without help!"

The girl gives a response though her words are brought to an end as the sound of stomps coming up the stairs now ring into the house.

Within seconds an old *Dwoff* comes into view, his pig-nose sagging to his wrinkled and scruffy face, his head mostly bald with only a few dark spots of skin acting as hair. However, the thing that stands out most is the fierce look in his eyes as he sets the girl down beside him.

"Hello mister Dif I am-..."

"Intruders, that is what you are!"

The raised voice quickly cut Clover's pleasantries from the room as Dif trails on, his granddaughter watching from behind the old man's right leg. Preston and Reynard still linger in the doorway, but the old man's eyes have only locked to Clover. "How dare you allow my granddaughter to go down these stairs, and what right do the *Únoffs* have in my home?"

"W-well I-..."

The old *Dŵoff* waves his hand to Clover as he attempts to push her out. "Out! Out! Or else I will call the guard for stepping into my house!"

Clover is pushed out despite her protest, the door slamming to her face.

The group says nothing as Clover pounds her hand to the door, her shock quickly fades. "Open back up, please, this was a misunderstanding!"

"Be gone with you!"

The response only prompts Clover to again knock at the door. "Mister Dif I am Clover Vines, her with a package from Princess Sóltina of the *Únoff* crown."

The sound of a lock clicking comes to the group as Clover moves her hand to the knob only to find it locked. "Did you not hear me?!"

"Be gone! We do not know this Princess nor any Princess of the Únoff!"

Clove's face tightens as her hand starts to glow, the lock clicking open as she forces the door.

The old *Dŵoff* looks up stunned from where he kneels down next to his granddaughter, his observation of the girl's peg leg ceasing as he stands. "How dare you open the-...!"

Clover holds the package out, a firm voice coming from her as Reynard and Preston awkwardly shift still in the doorway. "I am here to deliver something to you."

Dif simply blinks to the package extended to him as he shakes his head. "I closed my door and myself to you, what right do you have to open it? What power does your crown have over us? You did and have continued to intrude upon and disrupt my home. I say what right do you have?!"

Clover stares blank, unable to answer as she holds the package out, her hand lowering.

The old man shakes his head. "Well? I am waiting for your excuse mare?"

Clover's posture tightens as she scoffs to the word. "I have been sent here to deliver a package from *Princess* Sóltina."

"Once more with this title." A slight smile comes to the man's face as he crosses his arms. "I am ruled by Chancellor Clay alone."

Clover nods as she once more flexes the official seal on the package. "This is important."

"Very well, tell Princess Sóltina to send it to Chancellor Clay; I will not deal with one of the Princess's advisors." Dif rolls his hand. "Off with you!"

Clover shakes her head as she quickly speaks up. "I am not one of the Princess's advisors, I am Svle Nyota's assistant."

"Oooh, what a wonderful title, do they give it to all who deliver mail?" Dif holds his hand out as his voice raises. "Do not answer. Merely tell whomever you like that I am not accepting your package."

Clover's voice quickly starts up as she shakes her head. "But you have to take your package."

A low grumbling comes from Dif as he steps forth. "Must I escort you-..."

Clover's expression has now altered as she presses the package to the man's chest, forcing him to take hold of it with her magic. "I do not see why the Princess wishes you to have this, but I will be sure to tell her of your gracious acceptance."

Without another word Clover turns around and walks from the house, Reynard and Preston stepping aside to let her pass.

Reynard follows after the fuming woman, though Preston lingers as he watches Dif opening the package.

"Wait... what is this?"

Preston holds the door open as Dif calls out once more. "...what are these drawings?"

Dif steps towards the door as he yells to Clover who has yet to stop. "You! How does the Princess know of my work, spies?!"

Finally, Clover stops, turning back to the open doorway as she shakes her head. "You have your package, take up as many questions with Chancellor Clay as you wish."

Preston glances to one of the papers in Dif's hold as he speaks up. "What is that, a mini water-wheel or something?"

The comment brings an annoyed glare from Dif's as he shakes his head. "This is no water-wheel... it is moved by steam!"

Preston shrugs as he speaks up. "Steam engine."

The frustration in Dif's voice holds Clover's attention as the old *Dwoff* speaks up. "Now the *Únoff* wish to name my invention as well? With a foolish nonsense!"

Preston just shrugs to the man not knowing what to say. "Clover?"

The sound of the satyress' hooves comes back to the stairs as Clover's more typical tone takes hold. "Would you like to talk now?"

Dif hesitates for a moment, but he nods as he turns back to the room behind him. "A moment, Beth." He steps out, forcing Preston to move back onto the street. "What is this about?"

Clover looks over the envelope as she nods. "May I see everything?"

Dif squints to the questions, but he nods all the same.

The man's gesture quickly springs Clover's magic, as the envelope and its numerous papers float to her. The low chime of the blue glowing light surrounds Clover as the satyress' eyes scan through the papers orbiting around her.

Preston holds a slight smile to the floating papers, but he quickly takes notice to Dif's stare as he drops his smile into a more serious expression.

The chime of magic slowly comes to a halt as the papers come back to a neat stack floating next to Clover. "Princess Sóltina has asked for your help in a new project known as, the Artésque Train System."

"I decline then." Dif moves a hand back to the door, though Clover's magic stops the old man from leaving as she speaks up.

"The train would allow for faster travel across areas of Artésque, and you must have seen the first paper, it is a fairly sized payment for your help."

"Oh, I saw it, payment does not sway my thoughts, why does the Princess know of my work, hmm? Spying! Something I intend to report, same as you, Clover Vines! Intruder!"

Clover quickly shakes her head as she speaks up. "We shall not have a *Mot* in the street."

"Yes, less the city sees how easily a temper can flair. Student to the famed Nyota you said, yes? Was trapping an old *Dẁoff* against his door part of that training?"

Clover forces the package and its papers back to Dif as she speaks up. "We are done speaking."

"Really?" Dif slams the package to Preston, who quickly fumbles with keeping hold of its contents. Dif however does not back down as he draws Clover's attention again. "I have lived through two Princesses and Lowdwin; just because Sóltina is *devún* does not mean she deserves my respect! You stand her as her representation, and yet you wish to turn away at my questions because I do not bow to her name. But by all means, trot away mare, and tell them of your failure."

Clover visibly grinds her teeth, a sight that has both Preston and Reynard stunned in silence as they await her response. As before though, she speaks up, unable to leave. "What is your question?"

Cocky now, the old man speaks up. "The hauteur of the *Únoff*... ha-ha, tell me, how does the Princess know of my work?"

The response is quick as Clover speaks up. "I do not know."

"Typical." Dif pats to the package in Preston hold, cocking an eye to the taller fellow though ignoring his curiosity as he speaks up again. "What is a train? And why would I wish to help?"

"It is a means of transport, faster than a carriage."

"A new way for coin to move for the *Únoff*." Dif shakes his head. "I care not for this, take it away."

"It would help your lot as well." Clover shakes her head. "The Princess has begun changing things for the betterment of all of the Three."

"Oh I believe there is change, look at the *Únoff* power, no sister to compete with." Dif waves a hand to the comment as he continues. "Tell me, are these...these trains going to travel between outer regions?"

Clover nods as she speaks up. "Of course."

"But not in the beginning, they will be for the Capital, correct?"

The comment takes Clover a little off guard as she nods. "Yes, why would they not?"

A low sigh runs from Dif's cracked lips as he speaks up, surprisingly in a slow slightly lower tone. "The outskirt settlements need more help than any city." Dif points to the package as he speaks up. "I want the Princess to extend this means of transport to the outer settlements early, not last."

Clover blinks to the request as she shakes her head. "I-I would not be able to guarantee anything until I have informed the Princess."

"Then see to it that you do." Dif holds his hand out for the envelope as his words come to an end.

Spotting the gesture Preston hands over the envelope, again drawing an eye from Dif as the old man attempts to figure him out.

"I will inform the Princess of your suggestion."

Dif nods as he opens his door. "I shall not lose sleep, now leave, I have your papers you so kindly delivered."

Clover raises a hand to the comment but the door closes before she can speak up. A huff comes from Clover as she previously pulls out the map and begins to trot away.

Preston and Reynard give one another a glance before trailing after her. Yet it takes Preston merely a moment before speaking up. "Mad?"

Clover pace only grows as she answers. "I do not see why the Princess has interest in that *Dwoff*."

"Well, it makes sense if he's invented the steam engine." Preston shrugs. "Or whatever he wants it called, he's smart."

The comment does nothing to Clover's tone as she continues to look over the map. "I doubt he has created anything."

Preston squints to the comment. "Because he's a *Dwoff*?"

Clover's ear flicks to the comment as she turns around, her eyes now tight and her voice in a rush. *"Méi néat Nóff, yé breston mane baften!"*

Preston blinks to the words as he holds a slight smile.

Of course, the smirk to the man's face only adds to Clover's annoyance as she takes another step towards him. *"Dóf samény fon?!"*

Reynard waves his paw between the two taller people next to him as he speaks up. "Clover, he will not understand."

Clover quickly takes herself from Preston as she mumbles something. "Hurry up." As her words come to an end the satyress starts down the road, her tail slightly flicking behind her.

Sighting her walk Preston turns his attention towards the direction they originally come from. "Wait, were are we going?"

Reynard taps Preston's leg as he shakes his head. "Maybe we should just fol-..."

"We are going to visit the *Eñchar Márjx* school, I wish to have an intelligent conversation. I wish to see true inventions of the mind, not some wet-wheel described on parchment." Clover's eyes continue to hold to the map as she trots down the road.

Preston just blinks to the comment as he picks up his pace, his head cocking a little to one side. "Are you mad?"

Clover does not move her gaze as she replies. "We agreed to meet Sagitta Duscle, and I do not wish to stay in this city for long." Clover's tone and straight-shot trot halts Preston's comments, as he like Reynard just follow after the satyress.

Chapter 18

Eñchar

The continued trek through town has begun to take its toll on Preston's already worn shoes; his normal huffs and puffs come out a little louder with each step now. The added chafing has also not been made any easier, thanks to Clover's continued yet silent walk.

It became clear after the first block that the satyress is still vexing or perhaps annoyed; though neither Reynard nor Preston have dared to speak. Mainly just out of fear of her rants.

Interestingly though, Reynard has also chosen to remain quiet, although he has occasionally broken his silence to ask Preston a food related question.

Once more a sigh rolls from Preston's mouth, as he moves to dodge another passerby. The city, at least around this area is nice, with all sorts of decorations and bright flowers lining the houses. Sadly, the people do not seem to reflect the world around them, as most of the short, hairy *Dwoffs* seem to be just rushing about.

The city does not seem to be as diverse as *VéturVill*, but the man has been able to spot a few *Únoffs* trotting along the streets. And as strange as it might seem to Preston's own thoughts, he knows there has to be a few

Flóffs in the city to keep the clouds from the sky, especially seeing how clear the air above truly is.

"How are your feet Preston?"

The unexpected voice actually takes Preston off guard for a moment as he replies. "Huh?"

Clover slows her trot a little as she speaks up. "Your feet, do they hurt?"

"Well yea? We've been walking all day." Preston shrugs. "But it's fine. Fresh air."

Clover brings her trot next to Preston as her tone shifts a little with a sigh. "I mean your shoes, are they well?"

"Uh..." Preston glances to his feet. "They aren't crying?"

The satyress waves a hand towards the ground as she continues over Preston's pause. "I do not wear shoes, so I would not know their quality."

Preston gives a simple shrug as he speaks up. "They're fine."

Clover blinks to the comment as she turns her eyes to Preston's shoes. "They look rather loose; I cannot believe they feel fine." She brings her head back up as she nods. "I suppose Bella can decide when we get back... and do not worry, this will be our last stop here."

"I don't need shoes, Clover." Preston chuckles. "I'm fine."

With a nod Clover replies. "Bella will decide that."

"But I-..." Preston's words are cut off as Reynard gives a gentle nudge to the man beside him. Turning to the fox-boy Preston shrugs, though Reynard merely nods to the woman in front of them, tapping his paw to his mouth for Preston to shush.

With a roll of the eyes Preston nods, following after the woman into the side street with little more than a sigh. But as he does his eyes lock to the large tower like building at the end of the road. The squared shape of the tower and its building beneath it are a mixture of sandy colors with orange stone, coming to a point at the top of the tower, were a bright orb hovers. The school, or at least what Preston believed to be the school is three or so stories tall, the same stone and coloring as the tower. "So, is there a force field around this thing too?"

Clover shakes her head as she speaks up. "There are no barrier spells around a place of learning."

Preston holds his eyes to the building as he nods. "Alright... you sure we're just allowed to walk in?"

Clover gives a simple laugh as she continues on. "Of course, Sagitta Duscle asked us to."

The walk to what Preston suspects to be the front entrance only takes a few moments. Everyone that has come out from the building and those who lingers around it are *Únoff*, though this aura of sophistication does not stop them from gawking to Preston.

Most everyone who walks past them has a satchel or bag over their shoulder, heavy books or scrolls poking out from within. The sight of all them brings a comment from Preston as he looks around. "This place reminds me of my college." He looks to the building they now start up the simple stairs to. "But it looks like a church... guess that means selling your soul would get you a class but no books, huh?"

Neither of his companions reply, forcing Preston to brush off the awkwardness of his comment alone as he merely glances about.

Clover is the first to the double doors, she opens one as she speaks up. To Preston's surprise, her eyes turning to him. "College? It is the same as our *Unvérnitys*, yes?"

Reynard starts inside as Clover follows after him, her voice still directed to the man behind her. "You should feel comfortable then."

Preston is silent as he starts into the school's doors. The room's ceiling is surprisingly high for a three-story building, of course it really is no surprise, especially as the unmistakable feeling of magic beings to weigh on Preston's shoulders. The room is also well lit, with the various balls of light floating halfway to the ceiling. The interior is open, with a few tables and chairs scattered around the room, most are filled however with what Preston would assume are the students.

Most of these students in the room keep their eyes from the group, but Preston has caught a few of their curious glances. Sadly, the time to take in the room comes to an end, as a man comes in front of Clover's lead.

"Excuse me, may I help you?"

The man's hair is dark brown and short, his face is young, and his voice is even younger, despite his attempt at authority. However, the bright blue and gold robes he wears would suggest some sort of power beyond his questioning.

Clover gives a little nod as she speaks up. "We are here to see Sagitta Duscle."

"Master Duscle?" The satyr runs his eyes to Clover as he speaks up. "You must be mistaken, no one walks in and simply asks for the Head Mage, especially not with their pets."

Reynard cocks his head to the comment, the fur on his neck perking up a bit as he stares up to the man. Clover however steps forward her head coming up high. "My name is Clover Vines, and we were invited."

The satyr just blinks to the woman as he speaks up, remarkably unchanged in his expression. "Did you believe a name would mean something? I see no paper with you. Now leash your-..."

Before Clover can even speak up another's voice rings to the room. "Do you not know the name?!"

The unknown voice quickly gets a face, as a light skinned, dark haired satyress comes in front of the group. The woman fiddles with the satchel around her as she continues. "How do you not know the name, Clover Vines?"

The satyress turns back to Clover as she gives a little bow. "It is an honor to meet Nyota The Bearded's assistant."

Clover gives a little smile as she waves her hand. "There is no reason to bow, I am merely a student the same as you."

The blue robed satyr's eyes now widen a little as he speaks up. "O-oh I am sorry, I had not connected the name Vines to Lord Eadric."

Clover's smile slowly fades as she gives a simple nod. "Yes, well is Master Duscle back?"

The satyr quickly speaks up as he starts down the hall. "Yes, yes, I will-..."

Before his words could come to an end the woman next to him speaks up. "Perhaps I should take them, you may have forgotten where Master Duscle is with your poor perception." His path is cut off as the dark haired satyress now takes the lead, all the while never moving her eyes from Clover. "My name is Lyla Gran, and you are far from a student Miss Vines, you are what any with a true passion for adventure and magic wish to be."

Clover simply blinks to the comment as she nods. "N-nice to meet you. Though you do not need to honor me."

Lyla nods. "Of course, my mistake." She holds her hand out as she starts her trot up. "Please follow me."

As the hallways in the back of the room come closer Clover speaks up again. "We will not be bothering Master Duscle will we?"

Lyla shakes her head as she starts into the hall to her right. "Oh no, if he asked for you he must be expecting you."

The walk through the school's first floor is fairly straightforward, thanks in part by the simple box design of it. Every few feet there is a closed off door, which Preston could only guess would be a classroom of some sort. Despite how tightly fit they must be. Though he pays it little mind as he turns to the fox-boy next to him, Reynard's fur still stands up, and his brow has yet to unfurl. As Preston attempts to comfort the fox-boy he merely speeds up, wishing to get a bit closer to Clover.

Sighting this Preston merely shakes his head, his eyes turning back to the walls around them.

"I believe Master Duscle will be in the library, he tends to stop there before returning to his chambers." Just as the woman's words come to an end the group turns left in the next bend in the hallway. This time sighting the large open double doors to the room at the end of it. To Preston's surprise they have somehow gone upstairs, as evident by the window behind him. Of course, his eyes turn as his nose tingles, a familiar scent hitting him.

Clover and Lyla continue to trail on with a simple conversation, which prompts the man to nudge Reynard as he speaks up. "Well at least it smells like home."

Reynard passes a small, but friendly smile, mostly not catching on or perhaps too nose blind for the joke.

Lyla stops at the library's doors, turning to Clover and her group as she speaks up. "Master Duscle should be in the back section, have a nice visit Miss Vines." Lyla holds the smile as she moves from Clover's gaze and back into the hall.

With a simple nod goodbye Clover starts into the bright, albeit musty smelling room. Reynard follows in after her, with Preston close behind.

The library has a few people standing around the shelves; although no one really moves their eyes from the books in front of them. The layout of the library is a little awkward, with a few pillar shaped shelves sticking out in the pathways. Yet, the group makes it to the back portion of the area fairly quickly. As they do, Clover's eyes lock to the dark red and black robe wearing satyr, standing with his back to them.

"Master Duscle?"

"Hmm, yes, just put the books on the table." Duscle does not turn around as he just waves to the table beside him.

"It is Clover."

"Clover! Oh yes, yes." Duscle quickly turns around as he pulls two books from the shelves, the books now float next to him as he smiles. "Ah so glad you could stop by." He glances to the window. "And with such timing, I see why Svle likes you, it is almost as if we were just together."

Clover gives a little smile as she speaks up. "We are not a bother, are we? We simply had time and thought-..."

"Oh no, no, I have only one more person that requires my help later, and that is far off, you are no bother, please." He holds his hand out to something on the other wall. "Follow me, I have something for you in my study."

Clover takes a step aside as she watches the satyr trotting towards a dead-end corner of the library. "Your study?"

Duscle gives a little laugh as he nods. "Yes, I have an enchanted shelf to act as a portal to my study." He gestures to the torch with the bright glowing stone as he continues. "The *Kélf* stone is enchanted to act upon any of my magic, here allow me. Oh um... do take a few steps closer everyone, would not want to be only partially teleported."

Preston's eyes widen as he speaks up. "Wait, what?"

"Just a moment." As Duscle turns his attention to the torch.

Preston however, continues now whispering to Clover. "You never said I could get split in two when I was doing that stuff."

Clover lowers her head as she whispers back. "It is almost impossible to do it."

"Alright, just take a hoof forward." Duscle's voice takes Preston and Clover's attention as they take a step forward, Reynard quickly following.

Duscle gives a little smile as he snaps his fingers, causing a small purple pop of magic to appear at his fingertips. The room around Preston however quickly flashes into a bright purple light, followed by a sharp rush of air past his ears. The man snaps his eyes shut as he just listens to the magic chiming in his ears.

However, the flash of dark blue magic is quick to come to an end, as the new room comes into view. Preston is a little wobbly, and instead just leans his back to the wall, all the while as he scans the circular like room around him.

Around the room stands a few bookshelves and cabinets, with a few various knick-knacks Preston cannot rightly identify. In the middle of the room sits a dark green and red rug, with a large dark wood circular table sitting on it. There are a few carvings in the wood, but Preston cannot make them out from where he stands. Across the room is the start of a spiral staircase, leading to an upper level.

Duscle moves into the room, Reynard and Clover following behind. "Like I said earlier, I can spare a few *Eñchar* spell books I think you may find interesting." The glow of Duscle's purple magic starts up again, as the few books he had in the library float to the table.

As they settle he turns towards the bookshelf on his right. "They should be right here…"

Clover watches the man's trot to the bookshelves as she speaks up. "How will I be returning the books?"

Duscle takes two books from the shelf as he gives a little laugh. "Oh do not worry Clover, all my books come with a return spell; I will summon them back in due time." The laugh continues as he holds the books to Clover. "My study is free to everyone in the school, I have my securities on everything, a perk of this *Márjx*."

Clover just gives a simple nod as she takes the two books into hand. "Thank you Master Duscle."

"Oh, I am not your teacher, we are both colleagues in the study of magic." Duscle holds his smile for the moment. "How is Svle, faring well?"

Clover nods. "He is fine."

"Good to hear, good, good." Duscle chuckles. "Capital Mage is a rather precocious position, one that takes its toll on many. Why Svle must be busy too if the Princess tapped me for her project." Duscle squints a bit to Clover. "He is well though?"

Again, Clover nods. "Yes, of course."

"Good." Duscle taps his desk a bit, his eyes drifting around the room. "Oh my manners, perhaps you would like a drink? Home favorite I would assume?"

"Oh no, I am quite alright." Clover waves her hand. "Even for *Vé-Vény*."

"A shame, I am often reminded I am more enjoyable with a drink." Duscle smiles as he moves to a bottle of wine, though as he places a hand to it he squints past Clover. His eyes coming to the tall, blond haired man still leaning on the wall. "My, are you alright?"

The question turns Clover's head as she now takes notice to Preston's stance.

Preston's right hand rest against his chest, and his face seems a little flustered. "Yea, I'm fine."

Duscle gives a light chuckle as he waves his hand. "Nonsense, come here, you may be feeling a little disoriented from the spell." He turns to Clover as he continues. "Enchantment teleporters are much different than normal spells you see, a bit more power on the senses."

Clover just nods as she continues to watch Preston's slow walk.

As Preston comes closer to Duscle the satyr moves Preston's hand. "Does your chest hurt?"

Preston shakes his head as he moves a little from the older man's hand. "No, just need to catch my breath."

The comment does little to alter Duscle's eyes, and once more his voice comes up as he notices the chain around Preston's neck. "May I ask what you have around your neck?"

Preston just blinks to the question as he glances to Clover.

The woman quickly speaks up as she gives a little smile to Duscle. "Nyota fastened an amulet for Preston, it is really nothing."

"It is not enchanted is it? No *déstrot* to Nyota, but he is not a master of *Eñchar Márjx*."

Clover nods to the comment as she turns to Preston. "Perhaps you should let Duscle examine it for a moment."

Preston hesitates, but he brings his hands to the amulet's chain, as he moves it from his neck. Just as the amulet moves from his chest however, his breath comes back to him.

Duscle takes the amulet to his hand as he looks the dim, magically glowing amulet over. "Ah, well I can see it is enchanted." He squints to it as he takes it from Preston, turning and trotting away from the group, an action that draws a stare from Clover. "The enchantment is quite potent... though it needs a charge."

Preston wobbles, his once steady breathing now becoming heavy as he feels his skin crawl, and a palpable heat overtaking him.

Clover takes notice to the man's sudden change as she casually pulls a seat from the table. Preston sits as the woman starts to pace after Duscle. "Is something wrong with it?"

"Well, no, not really. It has been a little altered, although I doubt the teleportation spell could have done anything to such a well-crafted spell." He continues to study it for a moment before turning to Clover. "Where did Svle find this? Did it have a flaw within it?"

The satyress just shrugs as she speaks up. "I would not be able to say."

"Hmm, it is quite interesting." Duscle's attention turns to Preston as he smiles. "Just give me a moment, I believe I can recharge it." Just as his words come to an end, Duscle starts towards the staircase at the back of the room.

The sound of his hooves however brings Preston's voice up. "Clover, how long can I have that thing off?"

Clover blinks to the comment as she shakes her head, her voice coming back in a whisper. "Do you feel okay?"

Preston rubs his hands together as he speaks up. "I just don't really feel right."

"I am sure Duscle will have the amulet back in no time Preston." Reynard's confident voice brings a slight smile to Preston's face, as the man just moves his arms to the table and his head to his hands.

The strange heat building to his body continues to burn just under his skin. Though not painful, an unscratchable itch has begun to form all over his body, a maddening feeling as he fidgets at the table.

Clover and Reynard both now take a seat at the circular table, however they both keep an eye to the slight twitches in Preston's face.

For the next few moments the study is quiet, until Preston again speaks up. "What's taking so long?"

Just as the words leave Preston's mouth, the sound of hooves coming down the stairs perks his head up.

Duscle comes back into view, the amulet now glowing with a purple shine around it. However, a more serious look has been etched into his face. "Clover, Reynard, could you move away from your friend please..."

Clover blinks to the comment as she stands from the table. "Is something wrong?"

Duscle's eyes do not turn from Preston as his free hand sparks up in magical glow, something that prompts Clover to straighten up at. "This amulet had another magic under Nyota's, and it is the same as those found on the amulets Princess Sóltina had me examine before... the enchantment has been linked with the *Atémor*."

Preston slowly moves his hands back to his lap, as his heart skips a beat from Duscle's hard stare.

Clover quickly holds her hands up as she steps in front of Duscle's sight. "You cannot know this for sure."

"I can!" Duscle's magic stays steady. "Now move aside, we must secure him before he turns and seeks out his master beneath the castle!"

Once more Clover attempts to quell the frantic mage. "Calm yourself, hear your words, why would we travel with an *Atémor*."

"You did not know obviously. You are but a student." Duscle nods. "The amulet has concealed the creature, *Passvórtall's Héthtex* will help your friend's affliction."

Clover shakes her head. "That is not a place for the sick, it is a storehouse for experiments, give me the amulet."

"Miss Vines listen, this amulet carries a hex, you cannot touch it or you will-..."

Clover shakes her head. "Yes, yes I understand what it is, but that is why Nyota picked it."

The low glow to Duscle's free hand falters as the older satyr shakes his head to the comment. "What? Nyota knows this? Why has he not removed the magic then?"

"That enchantment must stay in the amulet... it-it keeps Preston safe."

There is a brief moment of silence in the room, as the satyr just stares between Clover and Preston. "Y-you admit to his affliction?! Does the Princess know of-..."

Clover's voice quickly comes over the stallion's as she straightens her posture. "Yes, she was present when Nyota performed the spell, search the amulet you can feel his magic." Clover holds her hand to Preston. "Preston was injured aiding Nyota's quest into the *Márjx Gréftor*."

Duscle's eyes widen even more as he takes a step back. "W-what? But-but all head mages must be contacted before a trip into the *Márjx Gréftor* is commenced. There is no telling what creatures could have followed Nyota through the *Márjx Gréftor's* safety barriers, the mages there could be in peril if something had gotten through-..."

Clover's demeanor does not alter as she cuts the rambling voice off. "The *Gréftor* was already overrun, taken by Princess Clarity. Extend your hand." Clover's hand takes on a blue glow. "Test if I lie."

The satyr is struck silent as he just stares to the woman before him, yet he extends his hand, taking on Clover's magic as his eyes widen.

Their silent communication however does not last long as Preston struggles to stay quiet, as a pain shoots through his chest; forcing him to bend a little in his chair as he wraps his arms to his body.

Clover's ear flicks to the sound as she takes her hand from Duscle. "I must have the amulet."

"What you have shown me..." Duscle steps away. "It is true? Yet... yet none know this?"

Clover steps after the now pacing satyr. "Master Duscle, the amulet."

Duscle turns back to the trio within his study, his expression clearing. "Y-you have shown me something you were not supposed to. I am sure the Princess would be displeased if she found out."

At the comment Clover draws her hand back. "I do not see why that matters in this conversation."

"Yes." Duscle chuckles. "My manners, we are all friends here." He extends his hand, Clover however hesitates for a moment to take the amulet. Though as Preston continues to moan from the chair behind her, she takes it.

As she turns her back to Duscle the old mage settles a bit, his attention to Preston. The blond man cares little though as he moves his left arm from his chest as he eases the simple piece of jewelry around his neck. The pain does not immediately subside, but the strange weight has been added to his body once more, and the itching seems to clear.

"Are you okay?"

"Y-yea..."

The words turn Clover's attention back to Duscle as she speaks up. "Send a letter to the Princess, I am sure she will explain anything you wish now that you know."

"Now that I know?" Duscle shakes his head, his arms folding as he speaks up. "Does-does the Princess have no respect for tradition? All Head Mages must be contacted! If the old powers are gone the caverns lie unprotected, how dare she allow you to know of such things, you are no Head Mage!"

Clover nods. "I am sorry you feel this way, though if she has not told you, it is not your place to know. I am sure the Princess will understand... but you must keep this information to yourself, surely you understand we do not want a panic."

"Panic?" Duscle blinks to the word, his senses coming to him as he slowly nods. "Y-yes... I will be sending a letter, asking for a full report on-on what has happened. I feel blinded, something I do not appreciate, not after I have rendered aid for her."

"Again, I understand your frustration." Clover nods. "But the Princess will need your support in this, just as she has entrusted you with keeping your project secret from the city, you must as well, keep this, at least until she directs you to break such a story."

Duscle merely takes a seat at the table as he folds his hands. "Yes." Slowly he nods his head as a shifty smile appears. "Y-yes, of course." His eyes continue to dart between Clover and Preston as he nods again. "If you forgive me, this is a lot to take in, I wish to clear my thoughts before I send a letter."

Clover gives a simple bow as she floats the two books from the table. "Thank you for your assistance Master Duscle." She turns back to Preston as she places her hand to his shoulder. "Can you walk?"

"Yea." Preston pushes himself from the chair as he stands. Reynard, despite his shorter size comes to the man's side as he rests a hand to his leg, for what little support it gives.

As the small group moves back towards the wall, they teleported in front of Duscle's voice comes back up. "The amulet has been properly recharged; enchantment spells should not affect it." His gaze sets to Clover as he continues. "Though if any outbreak of the *desatá* is to be found in your wake once you leave, I shall not hold my tongue of your companion."

"Understood." Clover's hand glows with a light blue magic as she gives another smile. "Thank you." The sight of her however is quickly zapped from the room, as the chime of magic rings to Duscle's ears.

The three absent visitors however do not immediately start the satyr trot however as he instead sighs, his eyes falling to the table before him.

Outside of the study Preston glances to the stone wall as he speaks up. "Was telling him a problem?"

Clover sighs. "He is an old *Únoff*, he will stay loyal to the crown's wishes... especially now that he knows of Nyota."

Catching Preston's confused stare Clover nods. "He surely felt Master Nyota's magic, even I know he grows old. Duscle will bid for the Capital Mages' tower, mark my words. It would also not surprise me if he called on my support."

"Sorry, I guess I should have stayed at the castle."

"No." Clover shakes her head. "It is not your fault. At least now your amulet is charged, it is up to Duscle now." She waves her hand. "Let us just forget about this and return."

Chapter 19

Shields

It has been a few hours since Preston and the group left Duscle's company and returned to the castle. Despite the time, the man has yet to leave the bed he flopped down to once arriving back; this lack of motivation is not spurred on because of its comfort, but of another reason.

Preston's room is dark, aside from the light green ball of magic he positioned above the bed. Although, the green light does little to the stone room besides from giving it an eerie feel. The hue of it does not affect the man's sight of the amulet he fiddles with. The woven wool chain has started to lose its white coloring and has also begun to fray on its length.

The amulet still has the light purple glow of Duscle's magic, but it is too faint to really light anything other than his hand.

Preston's heavy stare is brought to an end, as the sound of a hand knocking on the door rings through the room.

Clearing his throat, he speaks up, hiding the amulet within his shirt as he does. "Come in."

The door opens as the light brown haired, tan skinned satyress starts in, her eyes immediately knowing to fall upon the bed. "Will you be eating something?"

Preston moves to sit up in his bed as he speaks up, a faint laugh in his voice. "Is it already that late?"

"You have known it was.... I wish to get home before too long *Témont*, so we will be starting out early; it would be smart to eat something now, it will also allow us to make a quick stop for Nyota."

Preston gives a little nod to the comment as he stretches his arms a bit. "Alright, then I guess I'll eat something."

A slight smile comes to Clover's face as she watches the man stand from the bed. However, it does not last as she brings her voice back up. "How are you feeling?"

With a simple shrug he answers. "Never better, always good to know at any moment I could turn into some werewolf thing and kill everyone, really helps me sleep at night you know?"

A sigh rolls from Clover as she leans into the doorway, her arms crossing as she glances away. "Should I ask again, or will I be met with another *Fon*?"

"Don't like the cruel reality of it?" Preston laughs again. "Maybe we should tell that Dauth dude, sure he'd love to know he has a monster running around."

Clover's eyes widen a little as she quickly tugs the door closed behind her. "*Lóvo baften*, do you wish to be taken away?" Before Preston can answer Clover continues. "Stay your tongue, Preston, talk like that will get you the dungeon."

"Maybe that's where I should be."

"Enough!" The frustration in Clover's voice draws Preston's head up as the woman continues, a true scolding in her tone. "If you wish to huff or sulk in your worry do so without me. Life does not care if you are happy Preston, it continues despite your smile."

With a bit of hesitation Preston nods. "Okay."

Clover cocks her head as she nods again. "Okay?"

"Yea, okay." Preston shrugs. "So... what's on the menu?"

With a roll of the eyes Clover pushes the door open behind her and takes a step out.

"What's wrong with that?"

Clover simply sighs. "You should work on your emotions."

A laugh comes from Preston as he near the doorway. "Yea, sorry I'm still not sure how to deal with my problem-..."

Clover rolls her eyes, quickly drawing a more rushed comment from Preston as he squints to her. "That bothers you? How'd you think I feel, huh?"

"It is just the amulet attempting to steady your thoughts Preston, you were scared earlier is all."

"The amulet?" Preston laughs as he tugs to the necklace under his shirt. "I hate this thing, it itches, it's hot, and it reminds me I'm not human anymore!"

"Lower your voice." Clover glances down the hallway, though her comment falls on deaf ears as Preston chimes up again.

"No, you're acting like this is no big deal, Hell this is the first time I've seen you since we got back here, this is the first time we've talked, don't you think you should have said something earlier?"

Clover blinks to the question, her arms crossing again as she looks up to the man. "You are not the only one I travel with, Preston... and what should I say? You locked yourself away, if you wished to talk you should have stayed with us." She shakes her head. "Why am I defending myself?"

She pokes to the amulet under Preston's shirt. "You will feel find in a moment."

The action forces a heat up Preston's neck as he glares down to the shorter woman before him, the cockiness of her stance and her words drawing a bit of anger. "In a moment? Are you se-...."

Despite his display, a coolness begins to overtake him, his jaw almost locking to his words as within an instance of his anger his mind has cleared. The amulet's slight pulsing of light takes Clover's attention, though she merely looks away as she waits for Preston to choke down his next comment. A feeling of emptiness creeps in, not forced joy or some sense of relief, but rather an ever-growing feeling of pointlessness, teetering on the edge of depression and madness.

Clover speaks up in Preston's silence, her voice lowering as she attempts to broker a peace, despite the lack of eye contact. "Perhaps I should have come earlier, I had believed time with your thoughts is what you wished."

"It's okay." Preston nods. "You were right, I'm still adjusting to the amulet."

"Of course." Clover starts down the hallway, Preston slowly following behind. "We were invited to dine with Dauth, although I assured him, we would be too tired to be proper guest. I do hope where we ate yesterday is fine, I enjoyed Cherisa's hideaway."

"That's fine."

The comment does not spark Clover's voice again, as she instead just focuses on the castle's pathway laid out before her.

Despite the slight pain in Preston's feet each time he plants his foot to the stone flooring the man trails after the satyress with a fair pace. Within perhaps five minutes the duo comes into the familiar area from last night. It is at this point Preston takes notice to the darkening world outside.

The sky is a dark red, with the sun almost nowhere in sight. However, Preston's eyes move to the orange furred fox sitting at the table in front of the large windows.

As Clover and Preston come a little closer to the table Reynard's ears perk up, and his voice comes out. "Ah there you are, I am starving."

Clover gives a simple smile to the comment as she moves to take a seat across from him. "You shall live."

Preston plops down to his seat as he gives a relieved sigh. "You'll just be thinner."

A slight smile comes to Clover's face as she turns to Reynard. "Did you tell the cooks we are here?"

"Yes."

"Alright, I just hope that-..."

"Miss Vine?"

The male voice takes the group's attention, as they now turn to see an armored *Dwoff* guard coming into the room. However, it is the man following after the guard that takes Clover's immediate attention as she stands from her seat. "Eadric?"

Preston's eyes hold to the man as he looks him over. His clothing is a regal purple, with a gold emblem of what looks like grapes on the right side of his chest. His hair is a dark, salt and pepper like color, unlike the brown furred legs poking from his clothing. However, Preston's eyes have locked to the man's clean-shaven face and his slightly smaller ears, a trait he has only seen in Elden.

Strangely, this *Unoff* never once glances to Preston, instead too focused to Clover as he draws near. Clover however stands from her seat, folding her hands as she takes a step towards him. "H-hello."

No smile crosses the satyr's face as he speaks up. "Hello? After *moros* of your absence in both sight and writing? And what is this, you address your father by name, not with respect?" He holds his arms out as he continues. "I believe a more proper welcome is in order."

Clover nods, almost as if following an order as she comes to embrace the man.

Preston merely sits slack jawed as he glances to Reynard for some confirmation of the *Únoff's* words, yet Reynard sits as if he were guilty of something, silent and with his ears folded to his head.

Clover's slow reaction to yielding his embrace does not halt the satyr's light laugh as he pats his hand to Clover's back. His eyes however now drift to the table as he releases her. "Ah, and a good evening to you as well Reynard. I hope you are keeping Clover from trouble."

Reynard gives a simple smile as he nods. "Of course, Eadric."

The name quickly rings to Preston's ear as he watches Eadric's gaze come to him. However, it is quick to leave as his voice comes back to Clover. "My daughter, I do hope you will allow me to talk with you for a moment."

Clover blinks to the comment as she nods. "Of course."

Eadric turns to the guard next to him as he nods. "Thank you for bringing me here, but I no longer require your lead." The guard nods as he turns back to the hallway, he came in.

As the guard starts away, Eadric starts his trot, Clover following beside him. The sight of the two satyrs leaving however is followed by Reynard and Preston, at least until they round one of the castle's corners.

"As I am sure you know Clover, the second-floor wraps around the castle. Though I would not force my position as your father… I do hope you will give me at least half of the walk?" Eadric holds his head to the satyress as he continues. "Yes?"

The hall Clover enters is bright with the light of the moon shining in from the windows on her left, and the few lit torches on her right. However, an almost cold shiver comes to her voice as she speaks up. "I have no problem speaking with you father."

Eadric cracks a slight smile. "So, I am to believe you would have visited your mother and I before you return to the old *Lóvo*?"

"Master Nyota is a brilliant mage, father." Clover holds her gaze to the hall before her, despite her quicker response.

"Was a brilliant mage. Now, he seems relatively inclined to advisory work I hear, something he seems to have pushed onto you."

Clover's ear flicks to the comment, as she speaks up. "Father, I have traveled with Master Nyota for his last few quests-..."

"And how many of these endeavors were magic related?" He shakes his head. "Bringing along a foal such as you into the *Ovállll* suggest his level of thought has slipped. Do not deny it, I have ears in the Capital."

"I joined him. He did not seek me for it." Clover lowers her head again. "I was not forced."

"All the more reason why you need to forget this pursuit!" Eadric's trot halts, just before the next turn in the hall, his posture turning to Clover as he continues. "We have stood by and even supported your venture into *Márjx*, though even you must realize it is no longer schooling that you commit yourself to."

Clover says nothing, her hands remaining folded and her eyes staying to the ground.

Eadric gives a sigh as he places a hand to Clover's shoulder. "Do you know how I was informed of your whereabouts?"

Clover pauses as she focuses on the stone flooring. "Am I to assume Cherisa told you?"

Eadric studies her turned gaze for a moment but continues all the same. "Surprisingly, no. I was told by Sagitta Duscle and he-..." Eadric brings his hand to Clover's chin as he turns her gaze. "Look at me. Because Sagitta has told me horrible things, things that I once disregarded as falsehoods from the Capital, yet now I know them as truths, Clover."

Clover moves from her father's hand as she nods, her head coming up. "What do you wish to know?"

Eadric blinks to the more confident display as he nods. "I wish to know what my daughter is doing in her studies?" He raises his hand as he points to her. "You rarely write, and when you do, I can hardly believe it. Only your brother speaks the truth, and what little he tells us keeps us up for nights!"

"What stories has he spun, father? You seem to have known about my travels with Master Nyota."

The simple tone of Clover's voice brings an annoyed stare to Eadric's face as he speaks up. "You are to be studying magic, not bolstering an old mage's faltering grandeur."

"I was taken under Master Nyota's tutelage, and as such I am committed to his way of teaching-..."

"Teaching?!" Eadric blinks to the comment as he speaks up. "You are a student of *Álter Márjx*; you are not in training to take over for Svle Nyota, Capital Mage or not, your time spent away from home has been far longer than any peer. Do not lie, from what Elden has told me you are the one postponing your completion."

"Father I-..."

"I have not finished, Clover." Eadric's voice halts for a moment before he points to the other end of the hallway. "Tell me, is what Sagitta said true? Is that strange *Dẃoff* you dine with truly an *Atémor*? And what of the wounds on your face? Do they come under Nyota's ever watchful eye?!"

Clover pauses at the comment as she stutters out a response. "I have no wound."

"A father knows the splendor of his child, and I see upon you marks." Eadric pulls Clover's arm, poking to the mostly healed scraps on her. "Is this your way of admission without words?"

Clover pulls away from his hand as she speaks up. "He is not an *Atémor*, Master Nyota has stopped the process-…"

"Then why would Sagitta speak otherwise, as well as your own brother? Why I had not believed it when he had sent the letter, but hearing it again… Clover, this is a dangerous beast and your actions together with your lies have shown me that you-…"

A slight laugh comes to Clover's voice as she shakes her head. "He is no danger, what Sagitta saw was nothing Master Nyota had not warned about-…"

"No. I will not hear that my daughter knew about this." Eadric holds his hands to the walls around him as he speaks up, his voice a little lower though. "You are in a *Dẃoff* castle, Clover. With a creature; if it were not for starting a panic I would have it seized now and you taken home."

"Father, I have been tasked with-…"

"Thus is just more proof that Nyota is not fit t-…" Eadric halts his words as he brings his hands to Clover's shoulders. He sighs as he looks the younger satyress over. "I do not wish to argue this anymore, Clover…"

Clover is silent as she just stares to the man before her.

"I did not come here to bicker; you know that I and your mother supported this decision to pursue magic. I just think about how long we have waited for you to finish, and it worries me. We wish you safe and for your life to move on."

Clover slowly nods as she shifts her eyes. "I know this."

"Good." Eadric's hands fall from her shoulders as he sighs. "Then you will come by the manor before you set off. It would mean everything to your mother. Although, I will not be telling her you were in town, just in case-..."

"We will visit." Clover gives a simple smile as she nods. "Reynard would enjoy that."

A wide smile comes to Eadric's hard face as his eyes almost sparkle. "Splendid. I had hoped you would make the correct decision... now, shall we finish our walk with peace?"

"Of course." Clover holds the simple smile as the satyr's arm comes around her shoulders, and he turns her to the direction they originally set out to, though in the darker light Clover's smile fades.

Chapter 20

Swords

The loft area Clover brought Preston to has further been taken into the night since the two satyrs trotted off. Although, the smell and warmth of the food that was brought to them, has kept his mind at ease.

Yet, as Preston puts the plate back to the table in front of him he speaks up. "So, what's Clover's dad like?"

Reynard continues to stab at the last few morsels of food in his bowl as he turns to the man. "I was only a hatchling when Clover still lived with her parents. I do not really remember much." A slight laugh comes to his words however, as he continues. "But, I do remember Clematis, Clover's mother. She was nice."

Preston cocks his head to the comment. "Hatched, right... how old is Clover?"

The fox-boy taps his paw to his chin as he shrugs. "It changes with the Célntals' Keepers."

Preston nods. "So, you don't know?"

Reynard just shrugs as he puts the bowl back to the table. "No, but I wonder how much-..." His comment breaks with a yawn as he continues. "...longer Clover will be gone."

The yawn brings a slight response to Preston's own tired mind, but he pushes through as he speaks up. "Did you see the way Clover acted when she saw him?"

"Well, her parents have been a little mad at how long Nyota's teachings have taken... I cannot remember why."

The words bring a slight smirk to Preston's face as he shakes his head. "You're forgetful right now, you tired or got a food coma?"

"Yeah, d-do you think you could walk me to my room?"

Preston squints to the boyish comment as he cocks his head. "Uh... why, do I have to check for monsters under the bed or something?"

Reynard's ear flicks to the words as he speaks up. "You really think something could have got inside the castle?"

"No, no, it's just a figure of speech."

The *fróx* just blinks to the man for a moment before he continues. "Well, Clover normally makes an orb spell for me. I cannot sleep if it is too dark."

"You want me to do a spell?"

Reynard nods his head.

The nod brings Preston's voice up with a slight hesitation, but he pushes past it as he shrugs. "Y-yea, I can do that. It's simple right?" A slight laugh rolls from his lips as he stands from his seat. "Come on."

Reynard follows the man's walk as they leave the loft area. Preston however, gives one more glance to the other hall Clover went through before drifting into the hall he believes leads back to the bed chambers.

The walk takes a few moments, but the familiar area comes to Preston's view. The torches in front of the door are lit with the stones in them glowing ever so lightly. The man's eyes drift to the other doors past his own as he speaks up. "Which one?"

Reynard now starts in front of the man as he moves to the door near the end of the hall. "This one."

Preston trails after the short *fróx*'s walk in half the steps, and as the door opens he looks around. "Okay, so just a simple light thingy right?"

Reynard nods.

"Alright." Preston takes a deep breath as he shakes his hands a little. "Alright..."

With another quick breath he awkwardly brings his hands up as he stares into the darker room.

"Should I just wait for Clover?"

A slight laugh comes to Preston's voice as he shakes his head. "Naw, I got this." The tingling to his hands quickly takes his attention as he now tries to refocus to the room. A slight green shine comes to his fingers, and as the strange pin-needle feeling builds he clenches his fist.

He holds for a moment, his breathing almost stopped, until he jets his hands forward. The motion quickly causes two slightly brighter then wanted green orbs to poof in front of him.

Reynard squints his eyes to the light as Preston's almost out of breath voice comes up. "Alright, uh, I meant to have two... but... where do you want this?"

Reynard starts into the room as he points to the ceiling. "Just place it there, it should hopefully die down."

Preston nods as he turns his eyes to one of the balls of light. His hand moves towards it from beneath, and just before his fingertips touch it, it floats upwards. "Alright, well there you go."

"Thank you, Preston."

"No problem." Preston chuckles. "All the stuff you guys have done for me, it's the least I can do."

Reynard moves to his bed as he nods, though he sheepishly turns his head from the floor as he kicks his legs slowly. "I still appreciate it... and I would appreciate it if you do not tell anyone I am afraid of the dark."

"Don't worry about it." Preston shrugs. "I hate the dark too."

"You do?" Reynard's ears perk up, his boyish tone holding true as he beams to the man still in his doorway.

"Yea." Again, the man shrugs. "Just because I'm older doesn't mean I'm not afraid of things, you just get used to being afraid."

"That..." Reynard shakes his head. "That is not very comforting."

"Guess not..." Preston takes a deep breath. "I'm just saying you don't have to thank me. I'm always free to help, makes me feel like I have a purpose, you know, ha-ha. Preston, conquer of the dark, ha-ha."

"Okay." Reynard nods, his sheepish nature coming back to him a bit as he glances around the green hued room. "Clover says you still feel like a burden, you are not. I think she likes having you around just like I do."

Preston simply blinks to the comment, his own eyes flicking to the empty hallway on his right as he nods. "Yea, well thanks for that."

"Sleep well, Preston."

"Yea." With a quick breath Preston perks his shoulders up. "Goodnight, Rey, don't let the bedbugs bite."

The comment quickly washes Reynard's smile from his face, however, Preston turns and moves into the hall before the *fröx* can speak up. All the while as he pops another orb of light to follow him.

His own room comes next to his path, stopping him as he glances back into the hallway, contemplating a trip back to the loft to wait for Clover. After a brief debate, his hand comes to the door, as he opens it and moves inside. The bed made, though a bit different than he would have left it, he hardly pays it much attention as he instead kicks his shoes off and moves towards it.

He pulls the door close as he sighs, a hand brushing against his hair as he looks around green washed room. With another sigh he takes his shirt off and tosses it, as neatly as he can to the dresser where his bag sits. Naturally it falls to the ground after a short battle to stay gripped, though Preston shrugs it off as he shuffles forward.

He lazily pulls his worn-out socks from his feet, a hop to his step each time he does so.

Eventually his right hand comes to the bed's covers as he pulls them back, which causes the three neat purple and brown stitched pillows to tumble about the bed. Though his trousers are a bit hot, the fully stone walls give off a fair enough chill to keep them on.

Without a thought more, he rolls into the bed, the room falling silent around him, albeit with the low, steady chime of his magic above.

A deep breath rolls to Preston's chest, causing the amulet to shift a little. However, Preston ignores its movement as he brings his right hand just under the floating orb. "Any chance you could be a T.V.?"

The low chime continues as Preston pushes his fingertip to it, causing it to float ever further from his pursuit much like a bubble would.

Preston stares to it for a moment before he closes his eyes.

However, the man's mind is not allowed to cut off for the night. As the sound of the door opening rings to his ears. The noise quickly springs Preston up as he stares to the unmistakable figure in the doorway. Though the familiar face still draws a questioning stare. "What's up?"

The satyress slowly comes into the room, closing the door behind her. However, the woman does not speak up, her expression lost in thought.

"Clover?"

"Yes?"

The low voice brings a slight smile to Preston's face as he nods. "You uh, you good Captain Happy-Hooves? Kinda got a stare going on."

No response comes from the woman, as she instead just continues her observation of the floor in front of her. Her rounded ears are down a little and her expression still seems wrapped with thought, despite her answering.

The rather abnormal behavior brings Preston up further as his voice takes on a more serious tone. "Hey, are you alright?"

Clover raises her head at the words as she speaks up. "I should not be here, Preston."

Preston merely blinks to the comment as he nods. "Alright? Why's that?"

No answer comes and the continued pauses only draw Preston's curiosity as he speaks up again. "You want to talk about something?"

The woman moves from the door as she drifts her arms to the center of her earthy toned dress. Her hands fold however, and her eyes remain uncertain, a clear feeling of doubt or uneasiness pouring out in her stance and in gaze.

"May, I lay with you?"

Preston stares blankly, his eyes wide as he blinks back with a simple answer. "Uh I mean-..."

"Just lay?" Clover quickly adds.

Preston shrugs as he moves over in the bed. "Sure?"

Despite the offer, Clover hesitates, only stepping forward as the awkward pause draws on for too long.

Without a word and nearly zero eye contact Clover comes into the bed, her heavy garments of the day still wrapped around her. The smell of the world beyond the room is thick on Clover, yet Preston ignores it as he lays back down, his mind more awake now than at any other point throughout the day.

The green light of the room remains unchanged, bobbing where Preston had last attempted to grasp it. Yet, as the steady chime of magic cheers into the room, Preston finds himself speak over it. "So?" He turns an eye to the woman who lies to her side, her gaze set to the wall away from him. "You want to talk?"

No answer comes from the woman as Preston instead inches closer, attempting to move an arm around her. To his surprise Clover does not forfeit her defensive curling, instead brushing his arm away as she speaks up. "I do not wish to be a cosseted."

Preston again attempts to move his arm around the woman as he shakes his head. "I have no idea what that word means, but I'm here if you want to talk."

Clover's arms do not part to the man's touch, nor does she turn as she replies. "I said I wished to lay, I did not ask for conversation."

Preston merely widens his eyes to the comment as he scoots back towards his side, his hands folding over his chest as he nods to the ceiling. "Okay, point taken."

Clover falls silent again, not even a sigh rolling from her as she remains curled to the edge of the bed.

The silence in the room holds for a moment, until Preston gives a simple laugh. "Not even going to compliment me on my magical abilities, hmm?" He clears his throat as he squints to the wobbly orb above him. "That's like my fifth one today you know."

"*Brevet.*"

Preston merely licks his lips to the single word answer, attempting to place the woman's tone. After a moment of thought however Preston pushes on with his words. "Yea, better watch out, I might get better than you."

Clover remains still, though she replies all the same. "Your shaping needs work."

"Shaping?" Looking over the orb a little more Preston shakes his head. "I kinda like the pear shape, gives it character."

No response comes from the woman as Preston shifts his gaze towards her. "How should I get it rounder?"

"Concentrate."

"Mhmm... riveting wisdom there, no really." Preston chuckles a bit. "The power is within me and all that, right?"

"No." Clover continues. "Somethings will just be beyond your skill."

Preston folds his hands, his eyebrows furling as he replies. "Well what can I do, I got stuck training with you."

"Will all of your comforting words end with taunt?"

A faint chuckle rolls from Preston. "Didn't know I was supposed to comfort you, I thought you just wanted a silent bed warmer."

Clover's head shifts a little to the comment as she speaks up. "And you wonder why you fail if you cannot achieve such a simple task."

"Do you hear yourself?" Preston shakes his head. "That's like a lot of words to say *shut up*." He chuckles as he turns his head to the woman. "Just say shut up next time, it's a lot easier."

Once more Clover falls silent prompting Preston's smile to slowly fade as he turns his head back to the ceiling, though not before one last quick comment. "At least I got you to admit it."

"Admit what?"

A smirk comes to the man's face as he takes notice to his baiting. "That you just wanted a bed warmer."

Without a pause Clover replies. "If I had wanted one, I would ensure it stayed quiet."

"See..." Preston blows his breath as he loosens his folded hands for a dramatic gesture that goes unseen. "...just say shut up, it rolls off the tongue better."

"Quiet, Preston."

"Ha!" Preston inches towards Clover's shoulder as he places an arm to her. "That's the closest I'll get huh?"

At his tugging Clover glances an eye to him. "I said I did not want to talk."

"Fair enough." Preston nods. "Turn around and I won't say anything else."

Despite a quick huff Clover follows the request, turning around as she holds her hands under head, propping her up to where Preston comfortably lays just an inch away. The expression on Clover's face that she entered with has washed away, though no smile greets Preston's dopey grin. Instead Preston's eyes meet an expression of curiosity, as if she awaits some grand gesture or comment.

Yet, as nagging as the urge is to speak up Preston's smirk falters as his gaze lingers to Clover's light blue eyes. With one last smirk Preston gives in, opting instead to go against his nature, and remain quiet. The green hue of the light above washes over the bed, no noise disturbing its song into the night as Preston and Clover merely soften their gazes, a subtle, yet undeniable feeling of comfort overtaking them. Moments turn to minutes, yet neither break the agreement as they instead just lie against one another.

Chapter 21

Of Cuts & Roses

Preston's mind is at ease this morning. In truth, there is nothing in the room to suggest morning has come, seeing as how the room is still fairly dark and no window to the world beyond greets his eyes. However, the sight of the almost nonexistent orb of magic above the bed would suggest a considerable amount of time has passed.

For the moment however the idea of starting the day is far from the man's mind, his attention too wrapped up in the warm embrace of the bed. There were no strange dreams last night, and no cold sweats, despite the events of yesterday, instead, the night was filled with bliss. A hard to imagine feeling for, especially with how scarcely it actually graces him, yet in this moment he is filled with it and nothing more.

His right arm is asleep, stuck under the woman who stays to his side, though he does not attempt to draw it back even as he realizes this.

Clover did finally shed her daytime clothing later into the night, leaving nothing but her normal nighttime undergarments to tease Preston's mind. Though even as he gets another good look at her, Preston remains still, his mind far too slow in the morning's wake.

Clover's back is on full display, a canvas of light sandy colored skin for Preston to stare into. She remains motionless, even as Preston's gaze continues to linger on her and his free hand begins to caress her frame. As per normal, Clover's tail has found its way around Preston's legs, her thicker horse mane mixing in with the fur of her lower body, a pleasant heat, though one that leaves Preston a bit clammy.

The room holds its silence for the next few moments, allowing Preston to find himself lost in the woman beside him. Sadly, it comes to an end as the fizzing sound of the orb above the bed rings out. Turning his eyes up to the orb Preston watches as it begins to lower, wobbling more than before as it begins to lose its glow even more.

In the ever-fading light Preston lets out a sigh, knowing all too well that this morning will soon come to its end. Sure enough, his light fidgeting begins to stir the satyress against him.

As she moves Preston frees his arm, the slight feeling of pins and needles stinging into his hand as he watches.

With a yawn Clover begins to roll, her tail pulling through the man's legs as she adjusts herself to the warm body beside her.

The sleepy gaze sparks a smirk to Preston as he speaks up. "Good morning."

The words twitch Clover's nose as she cracks her left eye just a little. "Good morning…"

The groggy voice draws a response from Preston as he casually stretches his arm out. "Still sleepy? Thought you were a morning person?"

"I am… I just do not feel well." Clover closes her eyes as she shifts, her gaze now turned to the ceiling.

"You don't feel good?" Preston squints to his own comment as he continues. "Did you eat anything before you came in here?"

"No."

Preston shrugs as he speaks up. "You're hungry."

"Mhmm…"

The mindless response brings a light chuckle to Preston. "Good answer." He glances to the door as he trails on. "What time do we have to leave?"

Clover however, remains silent for a moment as she instead just tries to hold onto her sleep.

The smirk on Preston's face however holds as he pulls the woman closer to him, drawing a bit of annoyance from Clover as he continues to disrupt her slow waking. "Your feet are ice by the way, do you know that?"

A slight grin cracks to Clover's face, but she stays silent.

However, and like normal, the silence in the room does not hold for long, as the sound of something knocking at the door rings out. "Preston, have you seen Clover? She is not in her room?"

Clover's right ear flicks to the boyish voice as she sits up and turns to Preston. The man follows the motions as he calls back to the door. "Uh, yeah, she woke up a few minutes ago. She probably went to get breakfast."

"Oh, okay."

Clover blinks to the door for a moment before she moves from the bed. "I should go change before I see him."

Preston watches the satyress floating her clothing from yesterday to her. It takes a moment for Clover to catch his eyes, but as she does she waves her hand to him. "Get up, we cannot have Reynard waiting too long."

With a sigh Preston stretches out his arms. "Is it really that big of a deal if he knew we slept in the same bed?"

Clover does not answer the question as she instead just straightens her posture. "I shall meet you in a few moments, do make sure you pack... and brush your teeth."

"Alright I-..."

Before his words can come to an end, Clover disappears in a flash of blue magic; leaving nothing but the low sound of the spell's chime.

With a yawn Preston moves his feet to the cold, stone ground, his eyes turning to the satchel bag across the room.

- - -

Clover wasted no time getting Preston and Reynard through breakfast, encouraging them to quickly scarfed it down for some previously unplanned stop before heading back home. Of course, the slight uneasiness in his stomach has left the man wishing he had not followed along so willingly in his eating.

The morning sun has claimed the world outside, its warmth almost beckoning Preston to return to his slower start of the day. This calling is taken to heart as Preston passes through the castle's doors, pausing, to stretch his arms out with a yawn.

Clover continues down the few steps, Reynard not too far beyond as he attempts to keep pace. Preston continues to hold his stretch as he moves his eyes to the carriage sitting in front of the castle. "We're leaving now?"

The words halt Clover, as she fidgets a little with the strap of her satchel. "We were asked to stop by my parent's home before we left, it is on the way."

"Oh, I didn't know that." Preston cocks his head to the comment, Clover says nothing, seemingly focused on her trot to the carriage.

Reynard is quick to follow after, with Preston trailing close behind. It only takes a few moments for the small group to settle inside the carriage, and as they do Clover pokes her head out of the window. "We will be returning to the Capital after a short stop at Villa Vines."

"Yes, Miss Vines."

"Villa, sounds fancy." Preston gives a simple laugh which Clover meets with a faint smile. Preston takes a deep breath as he moves his bag to the ground. "So, how far is this place?"

"Not far." Clover's answer has no emotion to it, and her eyes stay to the window as the castle begins rolls past the window. With Clover's quick answer Preston falls quiet, settling in for their ride.

- - -

Near fifteen minutes have passed since the carriage pulled away from the castle and surprisingly it took just under ten minutes to leave the built-up medieval city. Though, the more rural roads of the city's outskirts have slowed the group's progress, despite their being few others on the road. Even still, the fields of grapevines have come to replace the two-story buildings Preston has known as the backdrop since they left the castle.

The ever-growing forest lingers just up the road, though Preston finds himself fixated on the rows upon rows of vines as a thought begins to form in his head. "Hey Clover, does uh... does your family own all of this?"

Clover looks up from her bag as she nods. "Yes."

A light laugh comes to Preston as he continues to look out over the fields laid out before him. "So, what stops animals from eating everything?"

"Master Duscle I would assume, as a friend of my father I am sure his spells surround the area." Clover glances once more to the window, though she says nothing further.

The carriage slowly turns into a more rural path through the grapevines, a low chime rings to the cabin but Preston's voice does not halt at the magic. "So how come you didn't study under him?"

Clover gives a little sigh as she places her bag to the ground. "Master Nyota knew what I wanted to achieve, and allowed me to be his student."

The comment does not truthfully answer Preston's question, but he stays silent all the same as he nods. "Alright."

The simple reply draws a quick comment from Clover as she speaks up. "We will be arriving at the villa in a few moments. You may wish to stay in the carriage, we will not be here long."

"Oh?" A slight chuckle comes to Preston as he crosses his arms. "Don't want me to meet your parents or something?"

The light-hearted smile on Preston's face does little to alter Clover's stoic expression. This lack of emotion to the joke slowly chases away Preston's smile as he clears his throat. "You really want me to stay in the carriage?"

Reynard cocks his head to the words. "They would not mind Clover, especially if you say he is Nyota's friend."

Clover blinks to the comment, though she turns away with a slight huff as she nods. "I suppose." Her posture straightens up however as she continues. "We are getting close."

The words spark Preston's curiosity, but from his position in the carriage he can only see the fields outside his window.

The ever-slowing speed of the carriage's approach however seems to confirm Clover's comment though; and as the carriage turns a little Preston's view changes. Just down the road sits the villa. The building itself is made of an off-white stone, somewhat similar to that of marble. The roof has a crimson hue to it, the tile folding over one another in a barrel like style. Set out before the house is a large courtyard, with two extending cloisters coming out towards the entrance of the courtyard. Like most structures Preston has seen, nothing otherworldly stands out, yet the craftsmanship of building itself still holds his attention.

As the carriage comes to a halt, Clover is the first to stand, her eyes turning to the door as she inches towards it. Reynard and Preston follow after her, though Preston struggles with turning his eyes from the lavish courtyard that seems to wrap around the house. A garden of yellows, reds, and oranges, surrounded by a labyrinth of green pokes out from behind the house, mixing well with the courtyard in the front.

The size of the house finally draws a faint chuckle from Preston as he cocks an eye to Clover. "So why did you choose to live in a library?"

No response comes from Clover, as she instead just moves to the closed gate of the house's front yard; she calls back to the driver as she continues. "We will not be long."

The driver just gives a simple nod as his reply.

With the nod, Clover turns back to the gate, her hand taking on a light blue color.

Preston squints to the action as he speaks up. "You got a key or something?"

"The lock is a simple family spell." As Clover's voice comes down the sound of metal clicking rings from the gate. At the noise the satyress pushes into the courtyard.

Yet, just as Preston and Reynard start after Clover, a voice rings up.

"Halt, who are you?"

The stern voice quickly takes Preston's attention, as he now stares to a leather-bound guard. While the armor is not as extensive or as becoming as those of the castle's guard, it nonetheless is surprising that the villa has its own guard.

Clover is the first to speak up. "I am Clover Vin-..."

The guard's eyes widen as he nods. "Oh yes, yes, sorry, please go on. Your father said you would be coming."

Clover just nods as she starts her trot further into the courtyard.

Preston however, keeps an eye to the guard as he watches the guard returning to the out of sight chair under one the cloisters. However, as Preston continues on the building before him takes his attention once more.

It takes a few moments for the small group to come to the two large wooden doors of the house, though as they do Clover brings her hand to one of the brass colored knockers.

The heavy sound rings to the closed in courtyard as the group now waits. Within seconds the right door opens to a dark-haired and light caramel furred *Únoff* woman. Her hair is wrapped in two ponytails that lay over her medieval maid like outfit.

The woman is young, perhaps a few years younger than Clover. Although, her voice does not hold the same confidence that Clover's does. "May I help you?"

"Could you please take us to Eadric." Clover nods. "My name is Clover Vines, he is expecting me."

The women quickly nods to the comment as she takes a step back. "Lord Eadric and Lady Clematis are-..."

Her words are quickly brought to an end, her mouth slamming shut as a voice from behind her calls out. "Clover? Do my ears deceive me?"

A face to the regal sounding voice is quick to come into view behind the young maid at the door. The maid lowers her head as she steps aside even further, allowing this new *Únoff* to come into view. The smile the satyr wears is friendly, albeit, far too perfect to be real emotion. Even still, the warming disposition of the man now in view draws a smile in reply from Preston.

The satyr's clothing is covered in jewels and clearly has a much more distinguished appearance than most others Preston has seen. His hair too is well kept, short and with a fairly unique dirty-blond hue, with the fur of his legs an off white. Thought what is more interesting is the strange scent that follows him, while Clover herself has scented soaps at home the smell that lingers around the man is thick as if it were cologne. Interestingly, while the smell is thick, it remains pleasant, almost drawing Preston closer despite how unfamiliar this new face is. Nothing about the man is rather eye catching, he is neither too lean, nor to muscular, yet he remains far more handsome than most.

Preston's slight gawking however is brought to an end as the unnamed man continues. "I was wondering why Eadric was so giddy this morning. I feared it was due to my departure." The satyr holds a flashy smile as he continues to work his eyes over Clover.

Clover's ears have slightly fallen a little, her voice too being replaced with her rarely heard more proper and slow tone. "He was not to inform anyone."

"As he did not." A chuckle rolls from the satyr. "Though if he had I would have appeared far less rushed." He gives a slight bow to Clover as he nods. "I apologize, I had plans to leave this morning."

Clover quickly speaks up. "I carry no ill feelings; we are both busy."

"Nonsense." He motions for the maid to run along as he continues. "I know just where your parents rest, I shall take you. It will be good to speak for what little time we both can spare."

The maid gives a simple nod as she starts away. With her gone, the satyr extends his hand, which Clover reluctantly takes. "Come, they will be pleased to see you." As his words end, he plants a kiss to Clover's hand.

The action sparks a look of confusion to Preston's face, though he says nothing as he merely recalls how poorly Clover had at first introduced him to Elden. Though, as they move inside Clover still does not properly introduce the group.

Instead, Clover merely follows after the satyr still holding her hand. However, they hardly take two steps in before the stallion speaks up once more. "Your guard should wear a weapon." He glances to Preston as he continues. "Would not want rumors *méi Fiándya*."

"Preston is accompanying me and Reynard for Master Nyota."

Clover's response sparks a smile to the satyr's face as he nods. "Of course, and how goes your keeping of Clover, Reynard?"

"Good." Reynard's response is quick, and Preston takes notice to it, yet he continues to say nothing as he merely tries to understand his companions' sudden change in demeanor.

Yet with a lack of conversation, Preston elects to keep the silence as they move more into the house. At the middle of the large central room beyond the small foyer there is a grand staircase, lavished in gold colored railing splitting at the top into two upstairs hallways. The floor of the room is a sandy colored tile, perfectly polished to reflect the light of the large chandelier above the room.

The lights of the chandelier are nothing more than bright light spells, but the positions of the orbs look almost like light bulbs.

"The lord and lady are resting in the upstairs loft." A chuckle comes from the man as he continues to talk with Clover.

The closeness of their walk finally breaks Preston's silence as he bends down a little to Reynard. "So, this guy, is he like an uncle or something?"

Reynard slowly speaks up with a quick reply. "No."

Preston is silent for a moment as he continues to follow after Clover and the stranger, though as he starts up the staircase, he speaks up again. "Okay... who is he?"

"Lothario Faróuk, he is a Lord of Trade."

A simple shrug comes from Preston as he lets the worthless explanation sink in, all the while as his eyes stay pinned to Clover's tense shoulders and her hand still wrapped to the stranger's.

The man's eyes however turn elsewhere in the room, as he instead begins to focus on the house around him. The decorations around the rooms do well enough to keep his attention as the group continues somewhere upstairs. The long rugs spanning the halls, decorated *Helió* stone torches and carved windows give the villa a homey feel, though far beyond the simplicity of *VéturVill*.

Sadly, the sandy walls of the house give way, as a room comes into view just down the hall on the right. Which, judging from the turns and steps Preston has counted, this area must be near the back side of the house, overlooking the garden he saw outside.

The group's pace starts up a little more, Faróuk takes the lead, his hand finally falling from Clover's as he steps down into the loft area. "I do hope I am not intruding your lounging, but it seems we have a stranger amongst us."

Clover now starts in, Reynard following behind; Preston lingers at the doorway, a bit of stage fright overcoming him as he merely watches the scene before him. The room does indeed overlook the garden, the sweet smell of flowers just barely overtaking the smell of wine that fills this semi-outdoor lounging area. Of course, the man's attention falls to the woman now rising from where she lazes.

"Clover! You should have sent a letter!"

The feminine voice that rings to Preston's ear has an unmistakable tone of kindness to it. Which naturally, brings Preston a little more into the room. The room is nothing more than a sunroom, two windows to the front of it, a few bookshelves and decorative objects around the walls. Preston's eyes however, immediately latch to the two *Únoffs* moving near.

A slight smile comes to Preston's face as he watches the slightly rounder, light brown maned and brown furred satyress, her arms open towards Clover and Reynard. Her coloring is not as tan as Clover, but her eyes have the same calm, blue shine as Clover's. Her clothing's color also seems to mimic Clover's earthy tones.

Despite the warm welcome for the group, Preston cannot shake Eadric's gaze. Luckily, Faróuk Seems keen on calling attention back to himself as he speaks up. "I agree, Clematis, A letter of her arrival would have been appreciated."

He holds a smirk to Clover as he trails on. "My eyes have hardly grace my *Fiándya* twice within the last few *mořo*."

Eadric gives a simple laugh as he shakes his head. "You are far too modest; we both know Clover has eluded her duty far longer."

Faróuk waves his hand to the comment as he responds with his own chuckle. "Merely a consequence of Clover's study, we cannot be blamed for our passing encounters."

"Either way." Eadric turns his gaze to Clover as he continues. "These consequences are soon to reach their end."

Clematis turns back to the two men as she speaks up. "Conversation for another time, let us sit for a while, we have far more interesting things to discuss."

"Ah, how I wish I could." Faróuk glances to the window as he speaks up. "I have business in the city, truth is, I should have set out a little while ago. I had not wanted to interrupt your time together."

"Nonsense, you are always welcome to us.... must you really set out?"

Faróuk nods. "I am afraid I must. Though I shall return later." He turns back to Clover, giving her a quick squeeze of the hand before once more nodding to Eadric. Despite his talk, he moves away from the group rather easily, his well-equipped smile fading with ease as he steps past Preston and into the hallway.

With Faróuk gone all eyes turn to Clover, though Clematis speaks up first as he draws her daughter towards the couch. "If you had sent a letter, we would have informed Lothario of your arrival."

Clover nods as she speaks up. "Clearly he had other engagements."

"Watch your tone, Clover." Eadric continues. "Why I cannot even recall the last time the two of you sat down for a real meeting, we should be thankful Lothario is so understanding of your magical *fántress*."

Clover blinks to the comment, though she raises her head a little as she replies. "I have done good by crown and by Master Nyota."

"So too has Lothario; wealthiest landowner in *BalláVill* and second only to the *Jartál* in *GráfUall*. I only guess what wonders you would bring to this family if you all but stayed out of danger."

Clematis quickly rolls her hand to the comment as she shakes her head, her smile holding to her face though a bit of nervousness taking hold as she speaks. "Our daughter did not travel out here to hear us bicker over Faróuk." The satyress takes Clover by the arm as she continues. "Come, sit, sit, sit." She turns an eye to Eadric. "Clover will do right by your namesake; we have raised her properly."

With Clover seated the woman's attention now comes to Reynard as she pinches his cheeks for a second. "Oh, and you too my little *ro'ha cúffy*."

Reynard's tail sways a little, as he starts to the chair next to Clover. Clematis's voice, however, does not halt as she turns towards Preston. "You are dismissed, thank you."

"Not that one dear... the tall thing is a companion."

Eadric's words perk up Clematis's ears up, as the woman just nods with a slight laugh. "Terribly sorry dear." She turns back to Clover as she continues her light chuckle. "A rather large fellow, yes? Where did my daughter find you?"

Clover chimes in at the question. "Preston is a friend of Master Nyota's, he travels with me now."

A faint chuckle comes from Eadric as he shakes his head and pours a cup of wine. "You should keep familiar company, not stallions of any breed." Eadric sighs as he glances back to where Preston continues to linger in silence. "Well, have a seat."

Preston slowly begins to walk into the room, yet Clover again speaks up. "Actually, we had not planned to stay too long."

"What? Why dear?" Clematis shakes her head. "You have only just arrived?"

Eadric merely smirks to the comment as he turns away, taking a sip of his drink.

"We were sent to the city by the Princess to deliver a package. We... I just wanted to stop in. But we must return to the Capital before night."

Clematis's happy smile fades a little, but she nods all the same as she replies. "Oh, yes of course." She pauses for a moment before she turns back to Preston. "Well, I suppose I cannot make you stay."

"We have time to talk, mother."

Clematis nods to the words, yet she does not perk up to face her daughter. Instead, she turns her face to Preston as she speaks up. "Where are my manners, what is your name, dear?"

Quickly reacting to the woman's stare, Preston speaks up. "My name is Preston, Preston Armor."

"A guard for Mage Nyota? Yes? I suppose it makes sense for the Princess to have another look after him in his age."

The blond-haired man gives a little chuckle as he shakes his head. "I'm not a guard."

Clematis squints to the comment as she cocks her head, and continues to stare up at the taller man. "You are traveling from the *Fárwift* then?"

"Uh..." Preston turns his eyes to Clover as he holds his pause. The satyress quickly speaks up. "Preston is just a friend of Nyota, he is from the *Dýnar*."

Clematis gives a little smile as she nods. "Oh the *Dýnar*-..."

Eadric now chimes in as he places his glass down. "Dear, perhaps you should come sit down. Clover has said, she must be going soon, no need for you to probe."

As Clematis starts towards her seat, Preston just moves back to the wall, as he just stretches his legs a little. Clematis's cheerful voice, however, is not lost for long as she takes her seat. "Well it was pleasant to meet you Preston." A slight laugh comes to her voice as she continues. "And I do feel for you, a friend of Mage Nyota's asked to accompany my little Clover, I apologize for how early you must have woken today."

Preston gives a simple chuckle as he nods. "I've gotten used to it."

Clematis cocks her head to the comment as she speaks up. "O-oh, I was not aware you two were so acquainted. Does Nyota usually send you along with Clover?"

The confusion in her mother's face brings Clover's voice up as she smiles. "Preston is visiting Master Nyota, but the last few *mořos* have kept Nyota very busy. So Preston has stayed at the library."

Eadric sets his glass to the table as his slightly deeper voice comes to the room. "*Mořos*, you say?"

"Only while Nyota is occupied."

Clematis gives a simple laugh as she nods. "Well, I must have forgotten how big the library was. Tell me, have you thought any more on a purchase of a small home in the Capital, you would be closer." The satyress rolls her hand as she continues. "The house would be done hopefully in no more than three *moŕos*. Which should be about the time you have finally completed Nyota's rigorous finals."

The words bring a slow nod from Clover, as she speaks up. "It would seem as such."

Eadric gives a light chuckle as he nods to Clover. "More of Nyota's overstepping of action, something I know will be laid to rest once you are wed. Lothario will see to that, he has assured me."

Preston squints to the comment, as he now swings his head to Clover. However, the light brown haired satyress just nods as she stands from the table. "Of course, this is why we must be going."

The sight of Clover standing brings a faint sight to Clematis, but she holds her own as she speaks up. "You will be writing more, yes?"

Clover's hooves work almost as springs, as she moves to the door with only a few steps. "Yes."

Reynard now follows after the woman, as she starts quickly out of the room. Preston, stays halted, until he finally is able to snap himself from the room and back into the hallways.

Clover's trot however has kicked into an almost spring as she moves down the hall. The sound of her hooves echoing to the area does little to calm Preston's thoughts. Sadly, the man just follows after the spaced-out group in silence.

Chapter 22

Season's End

The rock of the carriage has been steady but not sickening; and as the last turn out of the vineyard is executed, the main road levels the wheels out.

However, the smoother ride does not draw forth anyone's voice. Instead, Preston just continues to stare out into the forest; its maze of green inevitably set before them to overcome. Preston's mind however has stayed heavy, a question burning to his head, though one he struggles to ask in mixed company.

The silence has had little effect on Clover however, as the satyress just holds her face to the book in her lap. Strangely, her normal, peaceful expression when buried to a book is not present, and her rounded ears almost twinge with some sort of annoyance. Despite the ease at which she holds her tongue.

Perhaps fifteen minutes of silence pass before finally it breaks, Preston now speaking up. "So yea... how long have you had a fiancé?"

It takes a moment for Clover to realize the comment was directed to her, and as she does finally look up from her book she only shrugs. "What did you say?"

"Your fiancé."

Clover blinks to the word for a second, before her head falls back to her book. "I do not understand the word."

Preston's voice quickly shoots back into the tight cabin as he sighs. "The guy you're going to marry, Clover."

The satyress pauses her hand on the book's page before she flips it. "Lothario Faróuk, he is a friend of my father, yes."

"So? Just yes?"

Clover brings her head from the book once more, as she cocks her head. "What?"

"Never mind..." Preston rolls his hand as he adjusted himself in the seat. "How long have you known the guy?"

The satyress pauses for a moment. "Mhmm... since I was young."

A slight laugh comes to Preston as he shrugs. "You don't talk about him?"

Clover sighs as she flips another page, which draws her eyes back down. "It was not important."

"Not important?" Preston shakes his head, his hands feverishly rubbing to his knees. "How is something like that not important, Clover?"

Preston's quick responses have continued to split Reynard's attention between the two other people in the carriage.

Clover's tone does not rise, but the way she closes the book shows her shortening temper. "Because it was not your concern, and I did not feel like discussing it; just as I do not wish to discuss this now."

Another slight laugh comes from Preston as he speaks up. "Why, afraid your fiancé might find out about me?"

Clover's ears stand up as she leans to her window. "Driver, could you please pull the carriage to the side of the road for a moment?"

"...Yes, Miss Vines."

As the carriage begins to shift directions a little, Clover's blue eyes come back to Reynard. Her tone taking on a barely heard soft chime. "Reynard, when the carriage stops could you please step outside and tell the driver it will be a moment?"

The fox-boy gives a quick nod as he speaks up. "Okay, Clover."

It only takes a few seconds for the carriage to pull off to the side, and as it does Reynard moves to the door. As he steps aside Clover's magic quickly sparks to her hands, closing the door and creating a wall of magic around the windows of the carriage. Lastly, the window shades close, leaving nothing but the glow of Clover's magic to light the inside.

"This will be quick, Preston... so what do you wish to know?"

The satyress' annoyed and slightly angry tone only adds to Preston's guard as he speaks up. "All I want to know is why you haven't told me."

Clover sighs as she moves her book to the seat beside her. "I did not tell you, because it was not important for you to know."

"Clover, how the Hell is it not important?" Preston's eyes drift a little to the door as he lowers his voice. "We've slept together and you're getting married, Clover?! That's something I should know."

The woman just blinks to the comment as she shakes her head. "I do not see how sleeping with you would-..."

"Dammit Clover don't play word games; you know what I'm saying." The slight awkwardness of the woman's naive comments, and his own irritation have built to the man's body. A low green glow has formed to his hands, despite his calm tone.

Sighting this Clover rolls her eyes, a faint laugh coming from her as she speaks up. "Calm yourself, Preston. It was merely a mistake twice over, you let emotions fuel your magic like a common colt."

The words do little to draw a resting breath from Preston as he merely stares to the woman. "What?"

Clover's ear flicks as her voice sparks up a little more. Her soft eyes now also tighten as she stares to Preston. "I have agreed to nothing. My espousal has been set for me since I was old enough to be wed. This is why I left to study magic with the only mage that would take me in."

Preston quickly snaps back as he throws his hands up. "Then why don't you tell your parents! They can't force you to-..."

The satyress' expression quickly faults as she turns from Preston. "I-I cannot... it is my duty as a daughter to strengthen ties with another family." Her voice continues as Preston takes notice to the woman's quick loss of fire in her eyes. "*Unoff* marriage is for benefit only. This is why my parents have allowed me to stay with Nyota's teachings, because my status shall benefit Lothario once my final test is given..."

Preston's voice is a little lower as he speaks up. "B-but that doesn't make any sense. You can't say no at all?"

Clover brings her eyes back to Preston as she shakes her head. "I have no reason to. Lothario is wealthy, prestigious, our families will be happy, and he is a suitable mate. That is all marriage is."

The man hesitates for a moment, before continuing. "Not always." As his comment rings into the magic lit carriage he trails on. "Th-then why did you not stop what we have done?"

The man's words take hold in the satyress as she turns her eyes from Preston's. "It appears I should have. For if you do not understand how it was a mistake than I apologize."

Preston pauses for a moment, shocked at the rather coarse words.

Clover however continues as she speaks up. "Your mating must be viewed differently than how the *Únoff* view it. Yes, it is reserved for foaling, but as a mage, it has been known to better one's own magic. A catharsis that all strive for in times of stress, I merely took advantage of something far weaker than I."

"You-you just used me?" Preston's head falls, his hands finally losing their green glow as he does.

There is a moment of silence in the carriage, as Clover turns her gaze back to the blond-haired man across from her. However, her soft gaze is hidden as she straightens her shoulders and speaks up. "Magic is thoughts and emotions, Preston. How could I deny such an experience as a student of magic?"

The comment leaves a sick and used feeling to Preston's stomach, but he nods, sadly able to understand what the furred, half horse creature before him is saying. The glow to his hands has now halted, and a slight pain comes to his chest. However, the thought that it may just be from the amulet rest to his chest holds off his emotions. "Alright..."

Clover relents, the sadness in Preston's face backing her off as she nods. "I-I am sure Master Nyota will assist you. You should be home, and far from me soon anyways, it is what you want."

"Of course."

"Well it is." Clover gives a quick laugh. "What reason would you have to stay." The satyress holds her eyes to the man for a moment before giving a sigh. "Are you satisfied?"

Preston swallows hard. "I heard what I needed."

"What you needed?" Clover scoffs. "As you have said to me, it was nothing, a simple time of fun. What reason do you have for being upset?"

"I guess I don't."

Clover squints her eyes. "You guess? Buck up Preston, be a stallion not some silly colt."

Preston says nothing, his head hanging as he merely stares to the woman across from him, his hands cupped to his lap. "It was meaningless, I get that."

"Preston you must understand it... after you..." With a sudden shake of her head Clover stops, the near emotionless words from Preston chasing away Clover's eyes and her reply. "We are done talking. Sulk if you must, I have done nothing to you." Her hands take on a blue glow. Releasing the magic around the carriage and opening the door for Reynard.

The short fox-boy now starts back to his seat, however his eyes dart between the two emotionless face in the carriage.

Clover does toss a light smile to him, before turning towards the window. "You may continue."

The wheels start to turn, and the carriage now begins to rock like before; and Clover even takes her book up, like before. Yet, the silence that again takes hold in the cabin is a little different. Not that Preston takes much notice of it, as he instead just stares up to the wood above him, just wondering how much longer the ride will be. Reynard says nothing, Clover's head buried to her book and Preston's amulet a wash with color under his shirt, both more than subtle clues for him to remain quiet, despite his boyish yearning to talk.

- Part Two -

The late morning air has been thick and humid, despite the fact every window but Clover's is open to the carriage. Preston's head still hangs against the end of the simple cushion of his seat, as it always does. Yet, his mind has not been allowed to slow into a dull rest, and with his fingers chewed and picked to the skin, Preston finds himself sitting in silence. Familiar faces to his sides yet left wanting as the man simply listens and feels to carriage's continued journey.

From the amount of time that has past, it would be hard to guess that they are perhaps halfway through the forest. Although, the slightly bumpy ride suggests that the forest floor they ride to is out of reach from the normal flattened roads.

A slight sigh comes from Preston as he brings his head up a little. A twinge in his neck shoots his hand to it, and as he massages the pain, he scans the two other bodies in the cabin.

Reynard's shorter frame and animalistic features have allowed the young fox boy to curl up a little. Much like how a dog would, his tail is wrapped around his body and his paws are on the seat.

Truthfully, the fox-boy lays a little up against Preston, but it is not like the man is going to wake him and ask him to move. Mostly because the fox boy looks so peaceful, but also because of how silent the ride has been thus far.

Preston's eyes now slowly drift to the half horse woman across from him. Clover's own attention has been held by the book in her hand, not that it is surprising. Still, the light blue eyes usually tire from the off-white paper.

However, it does not come as a surprise that they have stayed. Despite the fact that their conversation happened merely hours ago; the feelings of it, at least for Preston seems to linger. Almost like waking from a bad dream, real though hardly wanting to understand what conjured it.

The rumble of the carriage's wheels are cut a little from Preston's mind, as he now just stares and listens to the satyress turning to the next page.

Clover's eyes may not move, but the slight movements in her face would suggest she is at least, aware of the man's stare.

Yet, Preston's stare moves from her as he now instead wanders his gaze to the world outside.

The lush green forest scene outside is not unfamiliar. However, this does not make the sight of it pleasing by any means. The thick tree line, and shrubs only bring a dismal feeling to Preston's already dampened mind, a dismal road through the forest, because no other path has been found.

The sickening feeling of the forest is not the only feeling assaulting Preston's senses. Seeing as how every few feet there is a part in the canopy, and the warm sun's light shines to his face. Quickly burning off the cold shadows he inevitably welcomes back.

For perhaps the next couple of minutes Preston holds his head to the window, before giving into his own laziness and resting his back to the seat.

As the man settles, he stares back up to the ceiling. His hands resting on his lap, the satchel bags he was asked to bring laying against his legs on the floor.

With one more sigh, Preston tugs a little to the wool made shirt, just to allow a bit of air to run across his body. Yet, it only adds the need to scratch at himself as the clothing falls back to place.

Strangely though, the only spot that itches is where the necklace lays against. Noticing this, Preston resettles his hands in his lap, and just continues to look over the dark wood of the cabin.

Yet, the silence of the carriage is broken, as a voice rings in. *"The capital's purlieu grows near Miss Vine."*

The words stir the satyress across from Preston, as she now sets the book aside and calls back to the driver. "Thank you."

As her own words ring around the cabin the young fox boy now begins to awake next to Preston. He slightly digs his back paws into Preston's side, but the claws do not stab into the man for him to speak up.

Preston however, does turn his attention to Reynard, as the *fróx* starts to yawn. "Are we there?"

The words spark a slight smile to Preston's face, but Clover is the first to speak up. "We are arriving in the outskirts." Clover holds her hand to the window.

The scene outside almost immediately starts to change, as the wheels of the carriage continue to turn.

Replacing the green forest wall of trees, there now rolls past the window a few simple wood houses. Not as neat as *VéturVill*, although the familiar outer town does allow Preston to pinpoint how far he is from the castle.

Although, for the moment, the man just focuses in on the tree line behind the simple settlement. The area is still nothing more than a main road leading out of the forest and into the capital's foothills. Yet, the trees look to be a little more cleared out, or at least the forest line looks to be pushed back a little more.

Preston now brings his own eyes to his window for a better view. Sure enough, the people outside are guiding the strange bison like creatures and six legged gazelles Preston has now come to know as *Yáppys*. The animals and handles may be different, but what they haul in their carts are the same. Cut logs, still with the bark wrapped around them, but devoid of any leaves are being pulled through this little town.

There is no sound of trees falling, but the sight of how many log filled carts are being pulled along the carriage it would suggest there is some logging going on somewhere.

"That's a lot of logs."

Clover resettles to her seat as she nods to Preston's words. "The Princess must be starting her advancement projects. I do hope it does not disturb any *Mostrér*."

The words take Preston's attention. Half because it marks the first time Clover has spoken to him since they left the villa, but also because of his own intrigue. "You think she's starting the train tracks? Even without uh... that one guy's engine?"

The satyress continues to just stare at her bag, as she places the book to it, yet she does speak up. "Perhaps, it would make sense to begin early."

Preston nods as he speaks up. "You think the Princess will change his mind?"

An almost annoyed sigh rolls from Clover as she replies. "I shall see once I inform her of my failure."

Before Preston can even suck in a breath to speak, Reynard chimes in. "But Clover it is not your fault Dif refused the project."

Clover nods as she moves the satchel's strap around her body. "The Princess instructed me to deliver her package. Now, I must tell her Dif refuses to help unless these trains are allowed to enter outer regions before the Princess wishes them."

Preston now breaks in as he laughs. "Well I'm sure she will not blame you, it's not like you had a choice in his answer."

The words flick Clover's right ear, and her posture now straightens. "Oh? So, fault cannot be placed on someone that does not control a decision, Preston?"

A cold moment off settles into the carriage as Preston just blinks to the woman across from him, not wanting to speak up.

Reynard's own fox ears stick up, as he looks between the two other passengers. "Are we also seeing Nyota?"

Clover's eyes slowly drift to the question as she nods. "Yes, we shall be seeing him first."

Reynard nods as he turns towards his closed window. "We must be close to the outer parts of the Capital by now." He brings his paw to the shade as he moves it and looks outside. "C-Clover, look at this."

The tone takes Preston and Clover's attention as they now move to look out the other side of the window.

The outer settlement they passed through a few minutes ago has reached its end; the extent of the forest clearing they saw when they first came to the Capital a few days ago can now be seen in full.

In truth, Preston has no idea how far the forest has been pushed back from before. But, the castle sitting far off on the hill can now be easily seen from the cleared out area. Although, it is not the only thing Preston's eyes turn to.

Instead, he now stares to the large almost rectangle like area, with an arch standing almost as tall as how Preston remembers pictures of Grand Central Station. The structure is by no means complete, in fact the only thing that truly shows its height is the large arch like opening, that faces them. However, the form of the rectangular building can be seen by the way the ground is cleared.

Honestly nothing suggests any similarities to Preston's first thoughts about the station. Yet, strangely, sighting the large arch opening that has been started for some reason did bring the image to mind.

Preston's eyes now turn to the other clearing set out in front of the would-be station. At first glance it looks to be nothing more than another carriage path. However, the more built up road would suggest something will be laid to it.

Noticing the path, Preston quickly moves to the other side of the carriage. Sure enough, the built-up path, and a few workers can be seen a little way out the window. Preston cannot really see the tools they are using, but he can tell there are some glowing lights, which would suggest magic or some magic tool he is unaware off. To his surprise though not all workers are *Unoff* or *Dwoff*, some beings even look to be more furred like Reynard. Although, the workers are too far and moving too quickly to tell.

As the carriage starts to turn a little more toward the hill up to the Capital, Reynard speaks up. "Is that the train Preston?"

The question even holds Clover's interest, as she turns an eye to the man. Preston however, just laughs as he speaks up. "No, no, that's just where people will go to get on; and it will also be where the train is like serviced and stuff." Preston's smile slowly fades as he turns to Clover. "D-do you guys even have the tools for that?"

Clover cocks her head as she gives a quick response. "I am sure the Princess is aware of what she may need. After all, she looked over your thoughts."

Preston gives a little smile. "Yea..."

"Besides, I am sure the Princess will call you back to the castle if need be."

The woman's quickly added comment just forces Preston to nod his head, as he takes a moment for it to sink in. "Well... she'd better do it before I'm gone, huh?"

Clover squints to the remark, though Reynard chimes in before she can. "You are leaving?"

The man shrugs as he crosses his arms. "Well I mean that's always been the plan, right?"

"Reacting a bit hasty, Preston. Master Nyota will only send you off when it is safe." Clover's almost lower tone just brings a laugh to Preston as he nods.

"But if you choose to stay close to Master Nyota I am sure the Princess will repay you."

Preston holds his smirk as he nods. "Right, praise the Sun-God."

The comment changes Clover's expression a little, yet she stays silent as she instead just looks outside the window. "We have entered the Capital."

The blond-haired man once again turns his head to the window, although the simple wood houses of the outskirt settlement, has been replaced with a few more stone made houses or more elegantly made wood homes. Still, not as further up the hill as *Passvórtall*. Yet, the buildings and people outside do seem completely different than the farm like area just down the road.

The man moves back to the seat as he points to the bags at his feet. "Do I need to bring these?"

Clover shakes her head as she speaks up. "No. Unless directed by the Princess, I hope to get back home before night fall."

Preston just nods as he moves to cross his arms again. The weather, even in the cabin is rather warm, but the feeling of his arms so close to his body is more comforting, despite the heat.

The rock of the carriage continues for the next perhaps ten or fifteen minutes. At least until the incline of the hill gets a little more prominent;

once it does Preston stretches his legs a little, and readies himself to step outside.

The carriage's wheels turn for just another moment before the driver's voice chimes in. *"We have arrived Miss Vine."*

Clover is the first to move towards the door, as she opens it and steps outside. "Thank you."

The driver's voice continues. *"I hope you will not mind, but I shall switch horses at the stable before we continue to VéturVill."*

"Of course."

The words bring a slight annoyance to Preston as he follows Reynard out of the cabin. "Another four hours... fun."

As Preston takes his stance outside, his eyes drift to the doors of the castle opening up to the light brown furred, tanned-skinned *Únoff* coming outside. His hand rest on the hilt of his sword, that pokes just above his bronze kilt like armor. "Ah, I miss the *déys* where the walls were in place around the Capital. It is not safe to have carriages this close to the castle."

Clover responds. "Walls are unwelcoming."

Stone Hooves gives a little smile as he crosses his arms and trails on. "You sound more and more like the mage everyday... I suppose I should inform your brother of your arrival; the *guard master* will be pleased."

Clover gives a little smirk to the comment as she moves around to the front of the carriage. "That may be, but I must visit with Master Nyota before I venture into the castle."

"Ah, so you are coming into the castle. I take it the Princess's task went well than?"

Clover halts her trot for a moment, but Stone Hooves just smiles as he turns back to the castle doors. "Luckily for you the Princess has not had court, she should be forgiving as always."

As the satyr moves back into the elegant stone building Clover's trot starts back up. Preston and Reynard follow after the woman, moving in front of the slightly tired out horse in the front of the carriage. However, their eyes quickly meet the field between the castle and Nyota's tower.

Despite it only being a few days since they left the capital, the field looks even more cleared away than the two of them can remember. Although, clearing the boulders is still only step one, a few builders can be seen ripping away some of the wild grass. The white stone ground, like the fountain area always to the right of the carriage, has come a considerable way. Yet, the structure is nowhere near guessable, at least in regard to how long or tall the building will be.

Preston just gives a little chuckle as he and Reynard match Clover's speed. "You guys really know how to build fast."

"Planning Preston, it is an *Unoff* value."

The fact that she just said this without removing her eyes from the tower across the field brings a slight smile to Preston's face, as the man just nods.

- - -

The trek across the field only takes a few minutes, thanks to the more leveled walkways and cleared away obstructions. As the small group comes to the door Clover knocks to it.

Almost instantly the sound of someone's voice echoes through the door. Yet, no guessing is needed as the dark blue and gold trimmed robe wearing satyr opens the door, his voice however holds to the conversation he was still having. "...I am not saying no to your question, I am merely suggesting you alter it Erta. Now, who is at my door..."

Nyota's auburn eyes turn to the three people at the door as he smiles. "Ah, Clo-..." His words are quickly cut off as a heavy cough rolls through him.

The sound of his cough brings another voice up, this time from behind him as a dark gray and white coated *fróx* steps forward. "I implore you Mage Nyota, listen to what I have to say."

The feminine voice has a strong, unidentifiable accent to it; yet Preston is still too busy looking over the new face to really pay much mind. The *fróx* looks maybe a few inches taller than Reynard, but her almost racoon like coloring is completely different than the young fox-boy's. Which of course has led Preston to wonder if she is indeed a *fróx* or not. That and the dark green sash this would be animal wears over her chest.

Nyota's voice comes back up as the old *Únoff* waves his hand to the comment. "No, no, Erta, I do not wish for any more potions. Now, I have guests, we can continue this conversation later."

Erta's eyes tighten, but she nods as she moves out of the door, just after the new small group of visitors comes inside.

Judging from Clover's confused stare and Reynard almost gawking gaze it would be safe for Preston to assume neither have met this *woman* before. However, as she leaves the tower Clover speaks up. "What is wrong Master?"

"Bah." Nyota wags his hand to the satyress as he speaks up. "Why does something always have to be wrong with me in your eyes Clover? And- and... what is that thing?"

Clover blinks to the satyr's quick stop; Preston has no problem locking eyes with the confused old man before him.

"Did you forget me again Gandalf?"

Nyota quickly snaps out of his confusion as he speaks up. "Oh, Preston..." He snaps to Clover as he continues. "How can you say there is something wrong with me, when Preston looks to be turning into beast."

Before Clover can speak up Nyota turns back to Preston with one last comment. "Of course, this is not to suggest you look unpleasant with the beard, Preston."

Preston just nods as he sighs. "You know me, always looking for your approval."

Nyota smiles as he rubs to his own white beard. "As well you should. Perhaps Clover will learn how to respect her elder's private matters with you around hmm?"

The light brown haired satyress just rolls her eyes as she now looks around the messy and cluttered house. "Well someone should worry about you Master, it looks like Wispy has stopped."

"Bah, Wispy eats too much. Now, have you come to take your final test my faithful assistant?"

The room goes quiet for a moment as Clover's eyes widen. "N-no Master... you told us to return to the Capital once we have Clamor settled."

"Clamor-... Oh yes!" Nyota's pale and sickly face almost brightens immediately as he starts to trot towards the stairs. "I have a gift for Preston, something he may use, unlike the *Gloftór* he ungrateful neglects."

Preston holds his hand to Clover as he calls back to the ascending satyr. "Blame Clover, she's supposed to teach me."

The comment does not bring the playful response the man hoped to see in the woman's face. Luckily, Nyota chimes in as he pauses at his study's entrance. "Hm... I see you have still yet to learn to not make a mare angry. Perhaps Clover needs to be a little more firm on you. No matter, where was I-.."

The low sounds of Nyota's voice can be heard echoing down from the stairs, but the words are meaningless chatter to the group downstairs.

Clover holds her eyes to the study for a moment before she turns back to Reynard and Preston. "I need to inform the Princess of our trip." She gives a simple smile to Preston as she nods. "It seems Nyota only wished to see you, so there is no need for me to take more time. I shall return and then we shall leave."

Reynard and Preston both just nod to the woman, as she moves and leaves through the door. Just as she does this Nyota returns, with some sort of stone clenched in his right hand.

The old satyr halts down the stairs as he speaks up. "Where did Clover gallop off too?"

Reynard speaks up as he points to the door. "She went to inform the Princess of our trip."

Nyota nods as he starts back down the stairs. "I suppose she does not need to be here for this." He looks over the stone as he comes to the bottom of the stairs. "Truthfully though, I had wanted her to see one of *Álter Márjx's* more elaborate creations. No matter."

He turns his attention back to Preston as he gives an old man smirk. "Here you go, Preston."

Preston looks over the small, light cream-colored crystal in Nyota's hand as he speaks up. "What's that, a *Helió* stone or something?"

Nyota gives a simple chuckle as he speaks up. "Oh no, this is a *Kélf* stone, bathed in the light of the *Márjx Gréftor* for *a* lifetime, many call it an *Ord'-quartz*. A very imprintable little stone that I have infused with a powerful spell for you."

Preston draws his hand back as he shakes his head. "Yea I'm not touching that."

"Bah, the stone is perfectly safe, Preston."

A slightly nervous chuckle rolls from Preston as he glances around the messing tower. "Well I'll wait a little, besides I'd rather not touch anything that can zap me until I use the bathroom."

Nyota tucks the stone back into his robe as he trails on. "Wait for Clover if you must."

"No, no, I don't need her to check it, I trust you. Just gotta use the bathroom, and stretch my legs before I do some magic." He nods. "Do it all the time right Reynard?"

The fox-boy simply shrugs to the comment though Nyota still speaks up. "Very well, top floor, near my quarters." The old satyr moves towards the stairs as he continues. "Come, Reynard, we shall wait in my study, I need your help cleaning."

Chapter 1

Castle Over

The day's sun has continued to hold its place high in the sky, the light baking the field of grass around Clover as she trots through it. Though a bit hotter than Clover normally likes she takes it well, brushing just a few strands of hair from her face as she nears the castle.

Clover's eyes come to the lightly armored guard in front of the door as she speaks up. "I am here to speak with Princess Sóltina."

The guard gives a simple nod as his hands start up in a low glow of magic. "Welcome back, Mage Clover."

The cooler air of the castle quickly draws Clover in as she gives a simple nod to the guard she passes. However, just as Clover trots into the castle's foyer a voice calls to her.

"Clover!"

It only takes a moment for Clover's eyes and ears to recognize her older brother, as Elden makes his way down the foyer. A wide smile stretch to his face is warm, though Clover merely replies with a weak smirk.

Elden's arms extend as he nears his sister. "Cherisa said you would be coming back to the castle."

Clover gives into the quick embrace, which halts Elden's voice for the moment. "...I trust your assignment went on without issue?"

The words slightly alter Clover's smile, as she sighs. "No, Lyon Dif, a *Dwoff* inventor would not listen to the Princess's wishes."

Elden blinks to the comment, but his voice is quick to start back up. "The statue, Clamor is safely kept correct?"

"Oh, yes, of course." Clover gives a little nod as she continues. "There were no further problems after the forest."

"Yes, Stone Hooves told me." A slight sigh comes to Elden as he places a hand to Clover's shoulder. "This was Nyota's last task for you. What the Princess asked of you beyond that does not matter."

Clover moves a little from her brother's hand. "I was given this task by the Princess, not Master Nyota."

Elden follows after Clover's trot as he speaks up with a slight laugh. "Of course, but surely Nyota recognizes the importance of what you did. The Princess herself even gave you the honors of-..."

"The honor of aiding my Master, when he is unfit. That is what the Princess gave me." Clover halts at the outlet of the hallway as she turns to her brother. "I will be sure to tell you when my last task is upon me. Once I do, you can tell mother and father as you are so eager to."

Elden shakes his head to the comment as he moves to block Clover's path. "I am not father, Clover, I just do not want to see you hurt again."

Clover's mouth quivers with her next words, but before she can speak up a voice calls from the castle's doorway. "Captain! There has been reports of *Mostrér*s near the outer *Dwoff* settlements. Chancellor Clay has already been sent to evaluate the reports."

The leather armored satyr at the doorway looks out of breath, but he stands straight backed as he awaits Elden's respond. "Send word of my impending arrival."

"Yes, sir."

The sound of the castle's doors closing rings to the foyer. Which quickly prompts Clover's voice up. "I will not keep you, Captain Elden." As her words end, her trot starts back up. Leaving Elden to watch from where he stands.

Yet, Clover's pace and the castle's own simplistic layout allows the satyress to near the throne room in mere moments. The sound of voices starts to echo into the hall as Clover turns to face the open throne room.

Clover is silent as her eyes move to meet the regal dressed and white winged woman, towering over the shorter satyress beside her. Princess Sóltina quickly takes notice to the new body in the room, as she turns her eyes from her adviser with a raised hand to halt her. "Clover, you have returned."

The pleasant smile brings Clover forward as she nods. "Yes, Princess."

Princess Sóltina turns her eyes back to her adviser as she speaks up. "Would you kindly give us a moment."

Without hesitation the woman gives a little bow of the head as she encases the papers in her hands with magic and walks past Clover.

As the woman clears the doors they close to Sóltina's magic. "How was your trip, Clover?"

"Everything went well, Princess. Clamor is safely kept and *Jartál* Dauth understands his position. But..."

Clover's quick words falter for a moment as she straightens her posture. "...Lyon Dif, would not agree to your proposal, Princess."

Princess Sóltina's demeanor is almost unfazed as she cocks her head. "Oh, and why is this?"

"He refuses to listen to *Únoff* ruling, unless directed by Chancellor Clay, Princess." Clover studies the angelic woman's unchanged face, almost with a slight confusion as she awaits a response.

However, Sóltina's tone comes back to the bright room without a hitch. "Well, I suppose it makes sense. I have a court with Chancellor Clay before the day is out, I will address it then. I trust there were no problems?"

Clover blinks to the comment as she speaks up. "You are not upset?"

Sóltina shoots a slight grin as she shakes her head. "I instructed you to deliver the parcel, not to persuade. How could I be? Give my regards to Svle Nyota, and Preston."

"Y-yes, Princess." Clover gives a little bow of the head, as she turns back towards the door.

"Oh, and Clover, I have sent word to the *Jartál* of *VéturVill* regarding the train's path. I have placed you in charge of the project there."

Clover's ear flicks to the words as she turns back to the Princess. "You have nothing to worry about."

Sóltina gives a simple nod to the comment as she continues. "I assumed as much, I could not think of a better person to act as my eyes there."

"Thank you, Princess." Clover continues to bow. "I will not fail you."

- - -

(Elsewhere in the Capital)

"Will it be easy to use?"

The cream-colored crystal gives off a little chime in Preston's hand as the man continues to study it. He rolls the stone to his hand, much as he has done for the last ten minutes or so since he came into Nyota's study. Reynard sits beside him, eyes fixed to the same crystal in the man's hand, but with a much more disparaging look.

However, Preston's dull tone brings Nyota's voice up, as he moves from where he stands in the doorway. "I must say, Preston, you are not as enthusiastic as I had hoped."

Preston turns his gaze from the stone as he looks to the old satyr. "I just... I never thought I would get to make this decision again."

Nyota nods to the words as he quickly speaks up. "Well, after last time I thought a more durable means of magic would be needed. Sóltina and myself did not want any residual items from to travel with you... but, I suppose this is the best way."

"Yea..." Preston looks over the hand sized stone again as he gives a slight smile. "Nothing for me here... and you're sure I won't need the necklaces?"

The words lower Reynard's head, but the *frók* keeps his mouth shut as Nyota start up again. "No, no. Your exposure to magic should fade, and with it, your condition. But the stone will need to charge, so place it in direct light for the next *wek*. Clover will know when it is ready, and she will help with the last step."

Preston quickly snaps his head towards the old stallion as he speaks up. "Can I just do this today?"

Nyota crosses his arms as he clears his throat. "I-I seemed to have forgotten to properly charge the stone myself. I am sorry my friend." He chuckles. "Though I am happy to see you eager."

The blond man gives a simple nod as he looks to the crystal in his hold. "Yea, me too."

"Well a few-..." Nyota's words are cut off as the sound of a teleportation spell pops downstairs. The old satyr is quick to turn to the sound, as he rushes from the room. Reynard and Preston do not move, until the raspy words of Nyota hit their ears. "Clover! How far were you when you performed such spell?!"

Immediately Preston and the short *fróx* start after Nyota. However, as the tan skinned and light brown haired satyress comes into view, she has already started her reply. "Not far, just beyond the castle. I was not going to trot its length four times, Master."

Nyota shakes his head as he moves to Clover's side, his arms extend a little concern to her shoulder. "Rest! Rest! You must be tired, even I seldom teleport the field."

Clover gives a simple smile as she moves from the satyr's hands. "I am fine, Master."

The words halt Nyota, as he squints to her. "How? Such spell requires so much magic?" The stallion quickly continues as he wags his bony finger to her. "You have not been skimping on your studies to perform this as *Étrometáy*, have you?"

"Of course not, Master. Ask Reynard."

Nyota falls silent, as he just looks over the youthful satyress before him. His lacking voice however sparks a comment to Clover, as she looks to the stone in Preston's hold. "Have you shown Preston what you wished to?"

"Y-yes." Nyota snaps from his stare with a faint cough as he continues. "I have given him a spell, locked inside an *Ord'-quartz* it should help him home."

Clover's ear flicks to the words as she gives an almost annoyed glare to the bearded satyr before her. "A *Ord'-quartz*? You mean the only *Ord'-quartz* you have left?"

Nyota waves his hand to the words as he speaks up. "What purpose does it serve if not to be used?"

"Master, that stone is far too important to be used as a-..."

"It is already done, Clover." A laugh comes from Nyota. "A stone is simply a stone, no matter how long it sits."

Clover's eyes turn back to the stone in Preston's hold. Her glare holding as her eyes meet to the man's. "Very well, Master. It seems you have made your mind up. Was this all you needed Preston for?"

The old satyr blinks to the woman's tone. "Well I had hoped to explain the spell to you Clover. After all, it is unique to *Álter Márjx*."

The satyress just nods, her tone however never shifting from her annoyance. "I look forward to hearing it. Although, I feel as though my trip has left me a little drained. Perhaps another time, Master."

Nyota slowly nods as he pulls to his beard. "Y-yes, yes. Of course." He gives a simple smile as he continues. "Another time."

Clover bows a little as she turns to Reynard and Preston. "Shall we be off?"

Reynard moves at the words, with Preston following behind. Yet, before the man can come to Clover's side Nyota speaks up. "I shall only hold Preston a moment longer."

The words slowly nod Clover's head as she moves to the door. "We shall be outside..." Her eyes slowly turn to Preston as she continues. "...when you are ready."

Her tone, despite her facial expressions cannot be hidden. Yet Preston is unable to speak up as Reynard and Clover move from the tower and out the front door.

With it closed Nyota turns to Preston. "Has my assistant been good to you?"

Preston shakes his head to the comment, as his own question bubbles to his mind. "How important is this stone?"

"Bah, it is merely a stone. Nothing more." A slight cough halts his words for a moment, but he trails on nonetheless. "Has Clover been tired? Has she been pushing herself more?"

Preston shrugs to the comment as he shakes his head. "She's been the same."

Nyota pulls to his beard as he nods. "What of her magic, has it changed? Color, sound, power perhaps?"

Preston shrugs. "It's a little lighter sometimes, why is that bad?"

"No, no, there are many reasons it can change…" Nyota continues to roll his hand across his beard as he stares to the ground. "I-I suppose I am just confused, I have never seen my assistant so disinterested in a new spell."

Nyota turns his eyes to the stone in the man's hand as he nods. "Though I suppose I hardly have much left to teach." A deep breath comes to the satyr as he pats Preston's arm. The stallion's mouth quivers for a moment, almost as if he is about to speak. But he shakes his head before straightening up. "You have a lot to think about. Take care, my friend."

Preston nods as he turns towards the door. "Thank you."

As the words come to an end, Preston moves out of the room. Just as the sound of the door closing rings to the tower, Nyota begins to cough. His legs buckle a little, but he plants his arm to the wall as the sickly cough rolls through him for a moment. It comes to an end after a few seconds, but the satyr is left panting as he turns back towards the stairs in the tower.

His voice is low as he clears his throat. "No, no, buck up, you have more to do." The words echo to the tower as the stallion starts to the first step.

Chapter 2

Turning and Yearning

The last two hours in the continuously rocking carriage has finally started to break everyone down. The ride itself has not been the problem, seeing as how it has been the same normal path as always. However, the amount of riding has definitely posed a problem. Clover even has abandoned her book, opting instead to rub at her neck out of obvious discomfort.

Reynard continues to toss and turn from where he has curled up beside Preston. Most likely unable to sleep in the heat. And Preston now wiggles to the lightly cushioned seat, no longer wanting to feel the wood he sits on.

The sight of Clover, however, does draw a comment from Preston as his own annoying body aches tingle to him. "You alright?"

The quick break of the silence that has lingered in the carriage since they left the Capital takes Clover off guard. Her right ear flicking to the voice as she turns her eyes to Preston. "Yes, everything is fine."

A deep sigh rings from Preston as he just nods. "Then why do you keep rubbing your neck?"

Clover's hand comes to rest in her lap as she shakes her head. "It was nothing."

"Really? Because it looks like you hurt your neck."

Preston's continued voice brings a quick reply from Clover as she speaks up. "Stop, Preston; I am fine."

"Mhmm..." Preston crosses his arms as he trails on. "Got a spell for it?"

Clover blinks to the comment for a moment, but her voice comes back all the same. "I would not want to wake Reynard with the sound of my magic."

Preston gives a simple chuckle as he nods. "Makes sense."

A slight groan and yawn is followed by Reynard's voice. "Who can sleep like this?" A quick shift in his position puts Reynard upright as he continues. "Are we close?"

Clover quickly takes the change in conversation as she nods. "We should be home soon. The driver's speed has been steady." Her hand slowly comes back to her neck as she mindlessly starts to rub it again.

Preston quickly takes notice to it as he laughs. "Gonna try that spell now?"

The words bring a quick and dirty stare to Preston, as Clover's hands take on a blue glow. Within seconds a spell pops to the cabin, however a light wall of magic now sits between Preston's side and Clover's.

Preston blinks to the spell his legs sit through as he speaks up. "What's this?"

Clover taps a finger to her lips as she mouths a word. "Shh..."

Her actions quickly bring a response from Preston as he nods. "Funny."

Despite the comment Preston turns towards the window, a heavy sigh drawing from him as he stares out into the world.

Reynard however glances between the wall of magic and the man near him as he speaks up. "Why are you and Clover feuding?"

Preston simply takes his eyes from the window as he stares to the bag at his feet. His thoughts slowly drift to the stone Nyota gave him as he answers. "It's nothing."

The comment draws a bit of annoyance from Reynard as he nods. "How long will you be feuding over this nothing?"

Preston slowly rubs his hand to his hairy chin as he speaks up. "I'll be going soon, it won't matter."

Reynard blinks to the comment as he quickly chimes in. "B-but why?"

Preston turns to the fróx as he shrugs. "Home, I'm going home."

The words linger in the carriage for a moment, but Reynard nods as he turns his head to the floor. "Right."

The boyish pouting does not go unnoticed, yet as Preston looks over the fox-boy's saddened expression he finds his thoughts loosening. Unfortunately, he glances to where Clover sits behind her wall, sighting Preston turns away, his eyes focusing on the world outside.

Reynard remains quiet, his stare to the dull floor as the carriage continues on.

The rolling fields that sit to the outskirts of *VéturVill* have now come into view. The lavish grasslands beginning to get colored with the new growth of flowers poking up from within. Still not fully grown from winter, but much more prominent than before. For the next, perhaps ten minutes Preston watches the wide fields moving past his eyes. However, the sound of Clover's spell fading rings to the carriage and takes his attention.

"Well I take it that you are done, Preston."

The satyress' voice brings a little reply from the man as he glances towards her. "Yep."

His quick answer prompts a change in Clover's expression, her ears lower a little and she slightly cocks her head, a bit perturbed. However, she is unable to speak up as the driver's voice from outside rings in. "We have arrived in *VéturVill*, Miss Vines."

Clover snaps from her set gaze as she calls back to the window. "Thank you."

She moves to scoop her belongs from the ground. "It will be nice to be home again." A slight smile comes to Clover's face as she continues. "I look forward to a bit of normal."

Preston just nods to the comment as he looks out the window, just watching the simple wood homes now darting pass him.

No response comes from the carriage, but the satyress bites her tongue for the rest of the ride through the sleepy town. Hardly passing a look to Reynard or Preston.

The carriage continues on, for perhaps the next five minutes, the dreadful silence looping forever it seems. Slowly, the carriage begins to stop, its ever-nearing halt drawing Clover's anxious hand to the door.

"We have arrived, Miss Vines."

Clover springs from the carriage, her words following her first step out. "Thank you, driver." Her hands move to the pouch of gold coins on her side as she steps from Preston's sight. However, as he and Reynard step outside a familiar voice hits them.

"So, Elva was correct."

Preston and Reynard both turn to their right, the young fróx's voice taking the lead. "Bella!"

The curvy and always well-dressed satyress gives a little smile as she trots closer towards where they stand. All the while making sure never to drift too close to the dirt covered wheels of the carriage. "What luck do I have? Elva had just swooped down to tell me she saw a carriage coming into town." She gives a sheepish smile as she pats to the small white and gold stitched pouch on her side. "My *Kélf* stones just ran out and I was heading to the town hall to have them charged."

Quickly moving her hand she nods, her eyes casting over the group as she continues. "Now, neither of you got hurt on this latest venture, correct?"

Preston shakes his head. "No we-…"

His words are cut off as Reynard hops a little, his boyish tone coming over the man's. "Of course not, it was a simple trip to the Capital, nothing else."

The carriage to Bella's left slowly starts to move from the front of the house; as it does, Clover's voice now chimes in from where she unlocks the front door. "Bella, it is good to see you."

Bella's attention turns from Reynard's happy face as she gives a light laugh. "Oh to you as well, though I had hope my welcoming still counts if I ask a small favor. Would you would charge a few *Kélf* stone… if of course you are not too tired I can look elsewhere."

The door to the library opens as Clover shakes her head with a smile. "No problem at all, come in."

Reynard quickly steps aside for Bella to walk in front of him. Not that Bella notices. The fox-boy following swiftly behind her, Preston coming in last.

Bella and Clover's light chatter continues, though their voices still ring to his ears, his attention comes to the thick smell of books that now greets him.

Despite it only being a few days since they left the house, the strong scent sparks a slight feeling of sadness within Preston.

Preston continues to stand in the open doorway as his hand slowly drifts to the necklace hanging just under his shirt.

He stands lost to his thoughts as his fingers swirl the amulet. Of course, his absent mind does halt the world around him as a voice calls out.

"Preston, could you close the door?"

The request snaps Preston from his absent-minded stare as he turns to where Clover and Bella stand. "What?"

Clover nods to the door as she set her satchel to the table in front of her. "The door."

"Yea." Preston turns back to the door and moves his hand from the amulet. As he closes the door he turns back to where the two satyress stand.

Clover's earth toned dress hardly compares to Bella's purple cloak and gold lined gown. In truth, Bella's clothing may not be the most elegant thing Preston has seen her in, but the simple bright stitching complements the women's filled out body rather well. Casting a rather bland shadow to Clover's frame.

"...I understand you must be tired Clover, perhaps just one stone will be fine."

The words do nothing to deter Clover's smirk as she floats out the hand full of stones from Bella's pouch. "Nonsense, we merely sat in a carriage."

Clover's blue magic takes the stones into the air above the table and begins to darken in color. The chime of her magic rings through the house as the stones start to glow where they float.

The house that was once only lit with the window at the front now glows with Clover's aura. However, as the spell nears its end, the blue glow takes on a slightly greener tint.

Of course, Clover's spell ends quickly as she shudders a little, her voice never losing its confidence. "There you go, fully charged."

Bella stares, almost amazed to the stones that float back to her pouch. "My word! That was quick, have you been practicing?"

Clover holds her smile as she shakes her head. "No more than normal."

"Well..." Bella gives a simple laugh as she rolls her hand. "I must say, I am still impressed." Her eyes drift back to the satchel in front of Clover as she collects her things. "Oh, I feel so rude. I should have waited for you to settle. I was simply swooned by my luck."

Preston cocks a simple smile to the comment. "Don't feel bad, quick meetings seems to be our specialty lately."

Clover again waves the comment off as she speaks up. "It is fine, Bella."

"Hardly, I always seem to interrupt you after a trip, and you are always so kind. No, *témont* I want you to stop by the store. I think it is time we re-enhance some of your clothing. After all, you have not come in with them since your trip with Nyota."

"Bella, it-..."

"It is the least I can do, Clover. No excuses."

Clover slowly gives into Bella's words as she nods with a sigh. "Alright."

"Splendid." The satyress looks to Reynard and then back to Preston as she continues "Well, I should get out of your mane. Everyone will be happy to hear of your return."

The sight of Bella nearing the door forces Preston to move aside a little. However, Bella does not immediately leave as she turns back to where Clover stands. "I shall see you *témont*, Clover."

"*Plestá déy*, Bella."

"To you all as well, dear."

As the words come to an end, Bella starts outside. Just as the door closes However Clover reaches for her neck, and her sweet tone changing to a lower and more tired voice. "We should unpack, we can eat after."

Reynard nods to the comment as he starts up the stairs. His satchel slightly dragging to each step as he continues up them.

Preston however, does not start out of the room as he continues to look over the tan faced and light brown haired satyress in front of the table.

His stare is quickly picked up, as Clover glances to him. But, she turns back to her bag as she floats it up to her. "You should unpack as well, Preston."

The blond-haired man watches a few books float from Clover's bag before finally starting towards the stairs.

Getting about halfway up he turns back to where the woman still lingers. "I can help cook."

Clover glances up to the man thought she turns her gaze as she shrugs. "Do as you wish."

Chapter 3

Nightly

It has been a few hours since Preston has gotten unpacked and settled into the library house. Outside the sky is dark, the moon just now barely coming over the horizon. Its pale light casting over the world with a peaceful hue, the cracks still visible on it, sitting as a reminder to just how foreign this world is to Preston.

The library, however, is bright with the light blue orbs Clover usually pops into the house. Yet, the bright room stands in contrast to the cold shoulder Clover has continued to wield towards Preston since Reynard finished eating and headed up stairs.

Despite the long trip, Preston is neither tired nor ready to sit in his room for the night. Unfortunately, Clover's silence holds him from speaking.

Clover on the other hand has shown a few signs of her exhaustion, her ears are down a little, a yawn escaping her from time to time, and she blinks often to refocus her eyes. Even still, she continues to read through the two books Sagitta Duscle gave her yesterday; the journal of notes she has compiled throughout the duration of this forced endeavor beside her, growing as her interest does.

She does this half out of curiosity and half, as Preston sees it, as a way to ignore the man across from her.

The work is tedious at best, and above all else a false display. Both people at the table can feel the tension in the room, yet neither has aimed to break the silence that holds it back. Though, as the satyress again starts to write something down, Preston finally speaks up, his arms tightening in their crossed position as he clears his throat. "Clover?"

The voice draws Clover's hand to a stop as she looks over the paper before her. The pen in her hand coming back to its inkwell as she glances to the scruffy faced man. "Mhm?"

Preston leans a little more forward in his chair as he clears his throat. "I had a few questions-..."

Clover is quick to cut him off. "What about?"

Preston nods. "About the stone Nyota gave me and-...."

Before his words can come to an end, Clover's know-it-all tone comes back to her. "The *Ord'-quartz*? The gift Nyota was given when he became the castle's mage? You want to know about that now, huh?" Clover gives a slight laugh as she just looks back to her book. "Master Nyota has wasted its potential by-..."

"Clover, I want to know if it can really get me home."

The satyress brings her head back to Preston's gaze. "Yes... I believe it would." Her tone halts a little as she just nods. "Perhaps I am a little jealous. It is for a good reason he enchanted the stone."

Preston is silent for a moment, but the questions burning in his mind quickly spark his tongue again. "What about this?" Preston pats a hand to the amulet under his shirt as he continues. "Will I need this?"

The satyress stares to where the man's hand rest as she shakes her head. "From what we know of the *Atémor* they live off their host's magic. You have said there is no magic in your world, thus the... spell on you would not hold."

"Alright, but what about that Hercinia's guy when you and Nyota made the crown. They don't have magic?"

Clover nods to the comment, but she speaks up all the same. "A *Flóff* does have magic, same as the *Dẃoff*. It simply holds to each person differently; the magic you feel now will not follow you."

"Right." Preston sighs, his arms crossing again as he just falls quiet again.

Clover looks the man over for a moment more before turning her eyes back to her book. "You have no reason to worry." Clover's smile slowly fades. "You will be gone from this world soon enough, Preston."

Preston gives a light chuckle to the comment as he lets the comment tumble in his head. "Yea. I've been gone for... what, a few months?" His laugh continues as he shakes his head. "Life back home is gone, especially with all that's happened."

Clover squints to the words as she speaks up. "A bit excessive?"

"Hardly." A light chuckle rolls through the man as he trials on. "I either lie and live with it or tell the truth and end up in a psych-ward."

Clover cocks her head to the comment. "You are referring to your brothers?"

Preston rolls his eyes. "Astute, aren't you?"

Clover's ears perk up a bit. "Excuse me?"

The amulet under Preston's shirt glows, causing Clover to glance at it, though Preston takes no notice of her eyes as he replies. "Just a comment, it means nothing, words mean nothing."

"Words mean everything, they are what make your uninvolved and crass form of communication, Preston." Clover shakes her head.

"Crass?" A laugh rolls through Preston, as a faint uneasiness in his chest starts to crawl under his skin. "Please, like you can get insulted." Preston rolls his hand to the women's increasingly more agitated expression.

"Hey look, I'm just thinking out loud." He rubs his hands together as he laughs. "Yep, just trying to get my thoughts in place, you know? Just trying to fucking think with this damn necklace on!" His raised voice prompts Clover's ears up though spotting her look of surprise Preston continues to laugh. "Sorry, didn't mean to scare you, I guess I should be happy we're talking, Hell I might even find out who else you've slept with, got anyone else you're going to marry soon?"

Clover glares back to the man, a commanding tone overtaking her. "Preston, I think you should go to sleep, let your mind rest."

Despite the seriousness in Clover's tone Preston is unable to stop, a chuckle escaping him as he bites his bottom lip and glances away. An anger bubbling up out of nowhere that he just instead attempts to quell. Though he finds it hard to fight as he glances every so often to where Clover sits, practically unfazed to the comment.

Despite the fiddling Preston displays, he shows no real signs of heeding Clover's suggestion. Realizing this, Clover speaks up, her voice as sure as ever. "Give the stone to me in the morning. I shall find a place for it to charge." She slowly draws her books closer to her as she trails on. "After it is charged, I will see to it that you are home safely."

Preston just nods to the comment as he looks over the woman's soft blue eyes, despite the furling in her brow the look past her irritation is soothing, and something Preston quickly takes hold on. "Okay."

"Good." Clover nods. "You should lay down now."

"Yea." Preston sighs as he pushes himself from the table, his eyes unable to connect back to Clover's as he speaks up. "Sorry for-..."

"Sleep, Preston." Clover's gaze falls to the books, with not a glance back to the man.

Sucking to his bottom lip a little, Preston nods, his legs quickly carrying him to the stairs. Most of the hall is dark, with only the light of the heater at the back and the orb usually floating somewhere in the bathroom to his left.

However, Preston finds his way to the first door on his right with ease. The moon has come into the world a little more, but its abnormal path across the sky has not brought its view to his window. The darker room however does not stop Preston, as he instead just clenches his right hand.

A faint green glow of magic begins to zap between his fingers, and as it does, he slightly throws his hands into the air. The motion quickly pops a small green orb in front of him, that the man casually pushes towards the ceiling of the room.

It only takes a moment for Preston to pull the simple covers of the bed back, and within another moment he has settled into the bed. The night air is still a bit nippy in *VéturVill*, which is a little strange, seeing as how all weather in Artésque is controlled from what Preston knows. However, it holds no effect to the man's already cumbersome mind.

Preston for a moment just stares to the ceiling above him, his heated words replying over and over to his mind. Though he finds some solace in just admiring the orb of green he poofed from just a thought in his head. His hand drifts to the amulet at his neck, his clouded mind clearing just for a moment, at least until he hears the unmistakable sound of Clover's hooves starting into the hallway.

Like normal, Preston closed his door, but the crack at the bottom allows the shadows of those outside to be rather visible from the bathroom's light.

The sound of Clover's hooves stops for a moment, just as her shadow nears the door. Preston's mind agonizingly mistakes the chime of the orb above him with the sound of the door's metal knob turning. Yet, after a few moments Clover's shadow moves from the door and the sound of her hooves disappears in the other room.

As the sound of hooves subsides, Preston's mind drifts back to its questions and doubts. Leaving the man to stare mindlessly at the bobbing orb above the bed.

Chapter 4

First Light

The morning's first light, for Preston at least, came slower than normal. Half because of the house's heavy book scents he has yet to accept and half because of the man's inability to shut his mind off late last night. Of course, no matter how hard Preston forced his head into the pillow, the ever-creeping sun outside did not slow, and no matter how hard he wished to stay in bed the inevitable sounds of morning drew him outside.

A faint sigh rolls from Preston as he continues to occupy the middle seat at the table. The sun pours in from the window behind Preston, warming his back as if a light blanket were atop him.

The man's thoughts this morning are cold and as he continues to idly sit downstairs alone they grow colder.

Reynard is most likely up by now, but Preston has yet to see the little fox-boy.

Another sigh rolls through the blond-haired man as he brings his right hand a little more to his lap. His head tilts as he stares to the hand sized stone Nyota gave him. As he has before, his arm raises a little as he lets the sun strike against the stone. Just as before, the cream-colored crystal changes hues, a dazzling display of movement taking hold within it.

While it remains the same in his hold, the lava-lamp like movements begin to speed up, even with this short brush against the light. The new orangey color forming holds the man's attention, at least until a knocking at the door behind him calls him.

The sound at the front door almost freezes Preston. His eyes dart to the window, but from its view the visitor remains unseen. For a moment Preston questions whether or not to open it, but he pushes himself from the simple wooden chair as he places the stone back to the table.

Again, the sound of someone's fist knocking to the wood rings into the house. It only takes a moment for Preston to open the door and only seconds to recognize the two women at its threshold.

A simple smile comes to Preston's face as he steps aside. "Early don't you think Bella?"

The satyress holds her proper sounding tone as she waves the comment off. "Well I had suggested to come later, but Elva wished to accompany me." She trots inside, though her friendly greeting is dropped as she looks over the bags under Preston's eyes. "Are you well?"

Preston is unable to answer as the taller, tan skinned, avian women steps in, forcing Bella to one side as she surveys the room. Luckily, Bella's attention turns to Elva as the shorter woman holds a nasty eye to being forced aside so quickly. Elva of course does not notice or does not care as she merely looks for Clover.

For Preston however, he takes the moment to truly size up the two women's differences. Naturally, Bella's mane is neat and curled, unlike Elva's windblown and slightly uncared for hair. Their clothing however is what sets them apart the most, even beyond Elva's wings and Bella's fur. Bella is sporting some sort of medieval dress, that magically conforms to every curve of her body, undoubtedly a model of beauty for the *Unoff*. The dark and light blues that make up its coloring putting to shame Elva's dull shades of iron and steel.

The warrioress, as usual, wears her armored top and wool undershirt that cuts in the middle to reveal her toned midriff. Her long steel skirt is the same dull coloring as her top. In fact, the only real color to the outfit is the hilt of the two swords that are held to her waist by the weathered red belt wrapping around her.

Despite the lack of color to her outfit, the three bright feathers still sit nestled over her right ear.

Elva's sharp eyes meet to Preston's gaze as she squints to him. "Sick, Milk-Chest, or is your constitution low again as normal?"

Before he can speak up Bella chimes in. "Oh, he is fine dear. No run-ins with the blade this venture."

The comment only brings a smile to Elva's face as she turns more to Preston, her hands resting to her hips. "Pity, what little skill you did gain has surely been casted to the wind now."

Preston gives a simple chuckle as he crosses his arms. "Still as warming as ever I see."

Elva gives a slight smirk as she replies. "Do not cross your arms, it makes you appear weak and fat."

Preston shrugs. "Why hide what I am?"

"Ha-ha, yes." Bella waves her hand to the comment as she speaks up. "You are hardly corpulent, Preston. You merely need to tighten your clothing." She squints to the man's attire. "Is that not what you wore before?"

Elva chimes in as she holds her gaze to the stairs. "Smells as such."

A friendly laugh escapes Bella as she blinks away from Preston. "Y-yes, well is Clover well? She is normally up by now."

"She's fine, always a bit slow in the morning."

"She is not feeling well?"

Bella's concern is overshadowed by Elva quick chuckle as she speaks up. "You're cooking, Milk-Chest?"

"Funny." Preston sighs for a moment as he runs his hand to his beard. The action makes Bella twinge a little as she watches him messes with it. "I think it was the riding this time. Even I don't feel good."

Bella clears her throat, prompt Preston to stop his tugging at his beard. "Should we come back?"

The avian women glances to the door as she nods. "I would, Preston's cooking seems to linger for some time."

Preston shrugs to the comment, slowly giving into the banter as he smirks. "It's not my cooking, I'm good at it."

Elva cocks an eye as she nods. "Oh, I can see you enjoy your craft."

"Yea?" Preston nods. "Every try duck? A turkey, chicken wings, Elva?"

His self-inflicted laugh is met with Bella and Elva's confusion, which immediately ends the conversation as Preston clears his throat. Luckily, the awkwardness is sidetracked as a new voice rings to the house.

"What brings you two by?"

The sweet sounding and pleasant voice is unmistakable. However, as everyone turns towards where Clover stands at the stairs, they meet something much different than what the voice suggests.

Clover's light brown mane is brushed, and her normal drab coloring is on display, but the earthy tone mixed with the exhaustion in her face, makes her look a little too green.

Bella moves a little more to the stairs as she speaks up. "Do you recall our plans?" As Bella moves towards the stairs her tone drops. "Although... I understand if you wish to rest or-..."

"Oh, no, I am fine Bella." Clover straightened her posture as she speaks up. "The Princess has asked me to oversee a project in *VéturVill*. I can see the *Jartál* once you and I have finished." Clover slowly starts to tap a hand to her chin however as her confidence fades. "Although, I need to stay in the library for those who need to return their books."

Bella waves her hand to the comment as she speaks up. "I am sure Reynard will tend to the books, Clover."

"No, he is still asleep. I must have kept him up." Clover's ears drop a little as she gives a simple smile. "I shall meet you at your shop later Bella."

Bella shifts a little as she speaks up. "Well, my sister is gone till *apřtor-déy*. I had planned to be busy. N-not that I cannot tend to your dress needs, but I had hoped to focus on my friends first."

"Perhaps I-..."

The seemingly never-ending banter of plans changing and talk of dresses continues to echo through the library as Preston moves to take his seat at the table. As he does, he looks back to Clover, who still stands at the top of the stairs.

As the conversation continues Preston notices the chatter becomes meaningless. Clover is usually planned, and seeing her trying to just now create an agenda for the day is actually quite amusing. But the tennis match between the women comes to its inevitable conclusion as Bella relents, Clover's never-ending stream of excuses winning the day. Both women now just head upstairs, though Preston cannot recall why, despite just hearing them.

Elva stands near the door now, and as the sound of Bella and Clover's voices rings from upstairs she speaks up. "Well, I see Clover is busy." She turns to Preston as she nods. "Perhaps another time we can test your skills with the sword?"

"Sure, why not." Preston nods. "Thrill of death always gets me motivated."

"*Hmpf*, killing you would be a waste of time." Elva glances to the door. "Even still, going against you is like going against a feral animal, your lack of skills means your actions are unpredictable, it is useful."

A smirk comes to Preston's face at the words, but before he can remark the woman leaves, no goodbye catching the man's ears, simply the sound of the door closing.

For a moment the library is quiet again, however that changes quickly to the tap-tap of claws ringing from the staircase. As the fox-boy comes into view Preston speaks up. "Good morning, Reynard."

"Mmhhmmm..."

The reply sparks a little smile to Preston, as he watches the sleepy-eyed fox walking over towards a seat at the table.

"...Clover would not stop moving last night." Reynard pulls himself onto the chair as he slumps his head to the table's wood. "And I thought I was in a *fántress* when I saw Bella. Ugh... why did she have to see my fur before I could brush it."

The words just hold Preston's smile as he looks over Reynard. "Oh don't worry, she probably liked it."

Reynard's right ear flicks as he turns his half-closed eyes towards the man. "You think?"

"Yea, she probably wants to brush you."

A faint smile starts to crack through Reynard's lips, which reveal his fairly sized canine teeth. Of course, as he moves his head to the table his eyes close, the smile lingering as he does. Preston just watches as the *fróx* next to him starts to literally fall asleep, his body in the chair and his head to the simple wooden table. The noise from upstairs is too far off to understand, which leaves Preston to his thoughts as he shifts his gaze back to the stone on the table before him.

However, Reynard's peace and quiet does not last long as the sound of Clover and Bella's hooves start down the stairs draws him back up. Naturally, Reynard and Preston both turn to the commotion.

Bella and Clover's hands glow with their chiming magic, however no fantastic spell is on display; instead, a few neatly folded dresses are simply floating after them.

Bella is the first to speak up as her flashy, but sincere smile pops to her face. "It is good to see you up still, Reynard." Her trot comes to where Clover has halted as she continues to talk. "Clover has a few errands to gallop, but she also needs help in the library. I am sure you will help. Right, dear?"

Clover quickly speaks up as she rolls her eyes to Bella's sweet Southern Belle tone. "Reynard, I am sure you would rather get your re-..."

"I feel fine, Clover, really." Reynard straightens his posture as he nods. "I can look after the books. Ha, they do not run too far!"

Clover gives a simple nod as she sighs. "Of course. Shall we, Bella?"

The curl maned satyress immediately snaps back to the door as her magic opens it. "Oh yes, we should be off. After all, these dresses definitely need some fittings."

As the two women disappear outside and the door closes Reynard's head comes back to lay on the table. However, his eyes do not close as he just sighs. "I should get the check-in book."

Reynard slowly peels himself from the table as he starts away from the table. Preston watches his walk for a moment, but eventually just looks back to the morning sun hitting against the window in front of him.

Chapter 5

Shelved

It has been perhaps five hours since Clover and Bella left the library; and while that amount of time is not abnormal, the uncharacteristically hecticness has been. Reynard had said early on that there may be a few extra books to return and catalog however Preston did not really expect the young *fróx* to continuously fall asleep at the table.

Eventually, Preston ended up taking over. While he is of course no stranger to taking control of the library, he nevertheless would not have made it throughout the day without Clover's seemingly fool proof system. Preston may not be able to pronounce half the books, but connecting the spelling and or the name of the patron was fairly easy. Combining this with the numerous times the man has helped restock the library and a rather straightforward cycle of check off book, place book, repeat made for a quick turnaround time. Though, the number of customers coupled with Preston's own distaste for generic social interaction has made for a less than desirable day.

Understanding how to count coins and actually check a book were also two things Reynard failed to properly explain. Though, with a few snap decisions, and a plethora of misspelled names on a list, Preston has managed.

In truth, and aside from the poor penmanship Preston feels pretty proud of himself, and at the very least focused his mind on something more than yesterday. Especially seeing as how today was the first real day he has written anything for a considerable amount.

It also has allowed Preston to meet a few more of the always unique townsfolk. Despite the strange beings, staying around Clover and her friends for the past few months has allowed Preston to grow used to the sight of tails, claws or even wings.

"...Uh, that'll be five *or-did*." Like always, Preston's shaky sentence ends with a faint laugh as he awaits a response from the black and white-furred *frόx* in front of him.

A slight smirk comes to the skunk colored *frόx* as the interesting toned feminine voice rolls out. "Your words funny, no? From the *Fárwift*, yes?"

"Yep, farswift or whatever."

The *frόx* just nods as she brings her paw to the dark purple satchel around her. "You are interesting, yes." The five normal looking gold coins are placed on the table in front of Preston as the *frόx* takes her book from the table.

Preston clears his throat as he dips the quill back into the inkwell next to the paper. Which, like before gets a few drops onto the table as he pulls it out. "And your name?"

"Azara, yes."

Preston nods as he starts to write the name next to the book's title.

Are-ze-da, checked out JibDél Tai.

"*Plestá déy*"

The words take Preston's attention as he looks down again. "Yep, yea, uh, pleasant day."

As the *fróx* starts towards the door Preston shifts his eyes back to the main part of the library. A few people still peruse the shelves, a sight that brings a slight sigh from Preston as he fidgets on the hard seat.

However, the small group slowly starts to drift back to where Preston sits, all with books in their hands or paws. Preston's eyes come to the *Cáfty* closest to the table as he speaks up. "Hello."

The whole process takes perhaps eight or so minutes, but eventually the library is cleared once more. Sadly, the home may not stay empty as Preston's eyes continue to drift to each passerby outside.

Standing from his seat he stretches for a moment; his slow walk however starts towards the sign Reynard put in the window. Preston may not know exactly what time it is, but his stomach is telling him it is close to lunch.

The blonde-haired man quickly takes the sign from the window as he calls to the empty house. "Hey, Reynard you hungry?" As he awaits a response, he looks over what he thought was an open sign. To his surprise, there are no words, just a strange squiggly line.

Before he can study the simple wood sign further the front door opens with a deep male voice following in.

"Oh no, you are not closing. You shall not be adding fees to my books."

Preston just blinks to the slightly shorter than normal *Dwoff* man that has stepped into the house. Though he cannot bring his voice out as the man continues to wave the leather-bound book at him. "You shall be taking these..."

The fur clothed *Dwoff* slowly looks around the room as he pauses. The heavy clothing catches Preston off guard, especially the brown fur cap that sits atop his head. Sure the weather is always a pleasant temperature when it is not snowing, however it is far too hot for a fur cap.

The short man finds his voice as his eyes come back to Preston. "Oh, I see, the *brivtó* is the keeper."

Preston squints to the word as he shakes his head. "What does that mean?"

The short man just sighs as he waves his hand. "*Oi Brivtó, offtú Neýphot.*"

Preston cocks his head as he speaks up. "Wh-what?"

"Hm, I see Clover has not told you to remember regular customers. It is good for *Ord'*. No matter *Brivtó*, here are my books."

Preston takes the small stack as he nods. "Right, um, thank you."

The *Dẃoff* blinks to Preston's slow movements as he waves his hands. "Well go on, the books are not too heavy, and they do not bite."

A slight smile comes to Preston's face as he walks back to the list at the table. "Ha-ha, yep... and your name is?"

"Look for Stony."

"Okay, you're all set."

The *Dẃoff* man just nods as he turns back to the door. "Good, no pain."

As the man leaves and the library becomes quiet again Preston looks to the new books in his hand. "Alright... *ób ó Mÿtheñ.*"

Preston sighs as he thinks over the words. "What is that... myth, so stories, right?"

No answer comes from the empty room, although Preston continues to look over the gold colored lettering as he slowly drifts back to the chair. His fingers start to drift into the book's pages as he sets the would-be open sign to the table.

He quickly puts a check next to the book's name on the list, which just so happens to be the last book on the list. A smile comes to his face as he realizes he took the sign down at least after every book was collected.

However, he continues to study the book in his hold as he opens it a little more.

In New Tongue

Although our home of Oválll has become too hostile to occupy, this does not suggest the land of Artésque is without perils. Take for instance the native Mostrér, these fierce woodland beasts claim dominion over the ÉverMoar. Although unstudied, the Unvérnity ó Coñjro Márjx states that these creatures of the forest may have been created of a natural magic.

Yet, if these creatures were created by Éordiarx as some sort of protector why are they so easy to avoid? Their strong stench and constant growls leaves one mind with questions of their mÿtheñ. The Koá-Koé however, are not so simply circumvented, yet have since been proven not to be mÿtheñ.

The Flóff bird of Mÿtheñ possess a hard Drágo skin, two long taloned feet, spiked tail and a beak molded for ripping armor. Although most Flóffs deny fear of this winged beast the name still will stiffen their wings. Once thought by Únoff mages to be the work of Grifón sorcerers these creatures were nonetheless prized for their eggs. Their value only rivaled by the wings of a powinxe. However, the Koá-Koé is not of Mÿtheñ and no longer believed to be of magic, instead it has joined the halls of other formidable beasts of the sky and land once thought to be a gértdestá. From Rárk-Tor to Mostrér these beasts are perhaps nothing more than animals imbued just enough with natural magic to set them apart from a common Yáppy. Fersome, yes, though hardly...

Preston's hand flips through the thick pages as he continues to randomly search through the book. Like most books he has seen, there are no pictures just text and the odd hand drawn sketch.

Despite the less than flashy font style however he does halt on another page.

> *...The Bastlikist, or lord of the fang, as some Cáftys refer to it is said to be a prodigious Slynar with the head of a tát. Although still never seen, the Bastlikist is said to pry on the unruly litters of Cáftys.*
>
> *Told to live under large grassy fields; as mÿtheñ says, only the nose of the beast would sit above the dirt, where its sweet-smelling whiskers could tantalize any unlucky wanderer.*
>
> *Still, this beast of the plains pales in comparison to the Spínder of Sviý-...*

Preston's focus on the book is dropped as the door to the library opens.

Luckily, the familiar face is quickly recognized, and the man's relaxed posture is allowed to linger. However, he does not immediately greet the light brown maned and tan skinned satyress.

Instead, Preston just looks over the layered dress. Unlike Clover's normal dull colors, the dress is a shiny silk white coloring, a long dark green band and vine like embroidery wrapping her body.

The sound of the door closing brings Preston's gaze to the women's soft blue eyes as he finally talks. "You look nice."

Clover halts at the words and even takes on a look of confusion. At least, until she looks herself over. "Oh." The sound of her magic quickly takes to the silence as two unseen objects come beside her. One is nothing more than a stack of papers, but the other is a large and slightly overstuffed satchel.

Preston gives a simple laugh as he crosses his arms to the women's confusion and response. "A normal response would be thank you."

Clover brings her eyes back to the man as she straightens her posture. "I had no desire to wear this out, Bella simply insisted it needed to *breath*."

The sound of Clover's hooves begin to echo from beneath the dress as the round eared women moves a little more into the room. Her expression taking on her know-it-all persona. "The shelves are a bit disorganized..."

Preston squints to the satyress as he taps his thumb to his lips. "How come you don't like compliments?"

"I beg your pardon?" Clover's ears poke up a little more as she pauses her trot through the room.

Preston waves his hand to the dress as he speaks up. "You look nice, Clover."

Clover blinks to the comment as she shifts a little where she stands. "Thank you." She quickly trails on. "I see Reynard closed the library a little early."

Preston adjust his spot in the chair as he shrugs. "Uh, no, I did that. He was barely keeping his eyes open, so I let him go to sleep."

"Did you record the books?"

A slight laugh comes from the man as he pats to the scroll in front of him and then points to the chest by his feet. "All the books, names of people, and coins, all accounted for Captain."

The laugh goes unshared by Clover as she merely replies. "Well than I suppose I have no problem with the early end..." She waves her hand to the stack of papers that now float over to the table. "I am to review these plans for the *VéturVill* train, it can now take my attention."

The papers' blue shell of magic is quickly lost as they settle to the table. However, the satchel floating next to Clover wobbles a little as the chime and color alter. Of course, Clover quickly takes control as she brings a glowing left hand to her head with a sigh.

The slight change of her blue magic to a light blue-green sparks Preston's voice as he sits up a little from the chair. "You alright?"

"Hm? Oh, yes, yes." Clover moves her hand back to her side as she starts towards the stairs. "Bella's bag has an enchantment to make it larger. I should set this down."

Before Preston can comment back, the woman has started up the stairs, her voice once more coming into the room. "Hello, Reynard."

The sight of the *fróx* moving past Clover alters Preston's gaze, as he now just gives a little smirk. "Nice nap?"

Reynard's snout wiggles a little as he turns to Preston. "It was a rest. I do not take naps."

Clover has now moved from Preston's view, but the man does not even take notice to it as he continues his smirk to the young fox-boy. "So, a cat-nap?"

Reynard cocks his head as he shrugs. "Cat?"

Preston shakes his head as he waves his hand. "Never mind. You hungry?"

The fox-boy nods as he moves a little more to the table. "Sure, but can we really eat?"

"Huh?" Preston squints to the comment. "Why wouldn't we?"

"Clover is dressed like a Princess, are we not going somewhere?"

A simple yet friendly chuckle rolls from Preston as he nods. "Not bad." He turns his eyes to the stack of papers Clover let down before she left. "But we might have to find a different place to eat once she starts all this."

"What is all this?"

Preston shrugs. "I don't know, ask your girlfriend, she went with Clover."

Reynard shakes his head. "Ask who?"

The fox-boy comes to sit across from where Preston is, his ears up and his stare holding a bit of confusion etched into his furry face.

"You're serious?" Preston gives a little laugh as he looks around the room. "Come on, I've been here long enough to know things aren't that different."

Reynard just blinks to him as he awaits for the man to continue.

A mixture of awkwardness and amazement settling into Preston's mind and stomach as he speaks up. "Uh, okay. You know how you like Bella right?"

The fox-boy's eyes widen a little as he stays silent.

"...Well, where I come from two people that like each other sometimes call each other boyfriend or girlfriend, kind of a title you give one another. It's a little childish but that's what it's called. So uh, I was making a joke about you and Bella." Preston squints as he pauses. "But... I mean that's if you two could even bec-..."

Reynard's tooth smile starts to show as a hyena like laugh rolls from him. "Bella has said she likes me?"

Preston waves his hand as he quickly chimes in. "Well-uh, yea, I mean I've not heard her. But... wait, love is not even a word to you guys, how can you use like and mean it the same?"

The fox-boy's smile starts to fade as his childish voice comes out almost as a squeak. "I do not understand."

Preston gives a simple laugh as he nods. "Clover said it's not even a word."

"What is?"

"Love."

Reynard's posture has continued to shrink into the chair, but he now holds a courtesy eye to the man as he repeats him. "Love? What is that?"

Although this is only the second time Preston has faced this particular conversation, it does not feel as strange as before. And as a result, his words pour out a little easier. "It's something that means you like something or someone a lot. Pretty much to where you would do things for someone or something that you normally wouldn't do for others. Make sense?"

Reynard nods slowly as he speaks up. "So, like watching the library for Clover? I do not enjoy it, but I do it because she hatched me."

Preston bites his lip as he shakes his head. "No, no, that's just like... uh love for family?"

Reynard just blinks to the words as he stutters into the conversation. "Is that why you watched over the library for me?"

"Well, I did that 'cuz you were tired." Preston slowly shrugs as he rubs the back of his neck. "And we're not family, you know."

"But..." Reynard looks to the table as he trails on. "...Clover took you in like me. So that makes us family, right?"

"You and Clover? Yea, you're like an adopted brother..." The smile Preston had at the start of this awkward but nevertheless interesting conversation now fades as these words leave his mouth. However, he trails on. "So, like an adoptive brother you have responsibilities and are part of a... family."

Reynard pauses as he looks over Preston's change in face. Yet, his childish mind allows him to push past the man's obvious pause of thought. "Let Clover adopt you."

A faint laugh rolls from Preston as he shakes his head. "That's not really how it works."

Reynard's ears fall as he speaks up. "Is it because you would not be hatched?"

The boyish voice halts Preston for a moment, as he just looks over the orange and light red furred fox-boy across from him. "Family's just a word, right? I may not know what every word means like Clover, but it just means a group. We're a group, so we're a family. There you go."

A slight smile comes to Reynard's face. However, before he can speak up, the sound of a teleportation spell popping near the stairs takes their eyes.

As the brighter blue light quickly subsides their gaze meets to Clover. Yet, the elegant white and green dress has been replaced with her normal brown leathery bodice, dark green undershirt and earthy toned skirt that hangs just above her hooves. Clover's mane is a little ruffled, most likely from the shirt she pulled on. Though, she has never really been known to wear it too fancy.

As the spell comes to an end and her magic subsides she gives Reynard and Preston a glance. "Was the *déy* fair?"

Preston just nods as he moves his hands from the stack of papers in front of him. "Nice entrance."

Clover just shrugs as she waves her hand. "It was a simple teleportation spell. You could do the same if you tried." Her own words flick her ear.

"Which reminds me. Too much laziness with magic can be harmful. We practice *témont*."

"Alright, and what about this?" Preston brings his hand to the stone that has sat atop the table for most of the day. "Didn't Nyota say this should charge or something?"

Clover's pleasant smile fades as she looks the stone over. "Have you had that out this whole time?"

Preston is a little taken aback by the sudden change in tone, but he cannot speak up before the woman has darted to the table and taken the stone to her own hand. "J-just sitting on the table? What if it had been taken, Preston?"

Reynard's ears slowly fall as he watches Preston sitting up a bit more in the chair. The normal sarcastic smile set to his face whenever the man is challenged. "Well, it's not like I knew where to put it Clover. After all, you said you know what to do with it. Why didn't you do something with it?"

The satyress is silent for a moment as she looks the stone over. "Y-yes, of course." She hands it back to him as she sighs. "But please, do not leave this stone out like that."

Preston nods as he blinks to the woman. "Yea, alright…" He glances over to where Reynard sits as he continues. "Sure thing Princess."

The comment quickly brings a slight smile to the fox-boy. Clover on the other hand just blinks to the words as she speaks up. "Did all your writing harm your head?"

Preston gives a simple chuckle to the ever-changing tone of the day as he nods to the stack of papers in front of him. "Hardly, have you seen my handwriting? Besides, I'd like to see you after reading all this."

Clover gives a little smirk to the comment as she turns back to the library. "I have read more for Master Nyota; now, could you please bring me the check-in list. I am sure somethings must be reshelved."

With a groan Preston stands up, scroll in hand as he moves to where Clover seems to be going. "So much for lunch."

Reynard hops from his chair as he moves towards the kitchen. "Do you want something before dinner?"

His comment, although not fully directed to Clover still gets the satyress' attention as she continues to look over the bookshelves. "Bella and I stopped by Gwendy's, I am fine."

Preston stands next to where Clover sits as he calls to the fox-boy, never moving his eyes from the list in his grasp. "Surprise me, Reynard."

As the tap-tap of Reynard's claws to the wood floor leave the room Preston turns back to Clover. "Think he'll get his fur in it?"

The comment does not alter Clover's stare, but she does float the list from Preston's hand as she just nods. "Mhmm."

The low chime of her blue glowing magic now rings to the room as the satyress looks over her hoard of books. However, Preston does not follow her gaze as he instead takes interest to her tired eyes.

"You still feeling tired?"

Clover's right ear flicks to the man's voice as she turns to him. "No." Her eyes shift from Preston's as she clears her throat. "You can sit down if you want. I would not ask you to do this."

Preston just gives a little laugh as he looks back to the seat, he has occupied all day with a little disdain. "I'm actually more interested in why you didn't sleep well."

The satyress turns her attention back to the books as she speaks up, a sigh rolling through her. "Just thinking."

Noticing the woman's blasé expression Preston chooses not to egg her on, he just nods and starts back towards the table. "Maybe you should hold off on the reading tonight, huh? It's not going anywhere."

Clover's posture straightens as she turns to the man. "Yes, but it is the plans for the train. It may not be going anywhere but you are. It is best to have everything in order before we lose you, correct?"

The words tumble in Preston's mind for a moment. But, he nods as he speaks up. "Didn't know you wanted me gone that bad, Clover."

A sigh rolls from Clover. "Preston, I do not wish to argue with you, please."

"What?" Preston chuckles as he holds his hands up. "I didn't say anything."

"Just..." Another sigh escapes Clover as she nods. "The goal is to not need you, but to use you while we have you."

Preston shrugs. "I'm here to be used."

Without a word Clover picks up her stuff and begins to head to the stairs.

Seeing this, Preston speaks up. "Going somewhere?"

"Yes." The women gestures to the stairs. "I think it best if we wait to talk, I need to focus." She nods. "Help Reynard, he would appreciate it."

With another shrug Preston replies. "Fine."

Chapter 6

Stay a little

Like most nights, Preston has lingered downstairs well past dinner. However, like last night Clover and Preston's normal conversations do not echo in the library. In fact, Preston does not even reside at the table, instead the man has found himself laying across the soft in the library's rarely used loft.

Preston's size does not allow for a very comfortable arraignment, but his legs do not hurt enough to move, even as they drape over the side of the couch. The light in the library is a low blue-green thanks to Clover and Preston's balls of light that met in the middle of the house. Aside from the low chime of magic, the crickets outside and the sound of Clover turning pages, the library is rather tranquil. Strangely though, Preston has yet to even yawn, not that he would be able to follow through on the sleep it would spell.

Instead, Preston's mind has been running with a few questions. As the sound of Clover turning another page rings through the house, Preston brings himself up from the couch. While Clover is content to ignore the world around her, Preston is not. The house is not small, though with little to distract Preston other than his amulet, and hardly nowhere to comfortably lounge around, the duo has inevitably come back together. With neither properly ceasing this aura of passive aggressiveness that fogs the room.

With a sigh and a lick of his lips, Preston calls out. "Hey, Clover."

The satyress looks up from the table as she speaks in a fairly loud whisper. "*Shhh*, your voice echoes."

Preston slowly gets down from the loft as he lowers his voice and closes his distance. "So, when I head home will the-..."

"Preston, the *Atémor* feeds off the host's magic. Once you return, it will die." She shakes her head. "You must find something else to focus on."

"Okay..." Preston nods as he sits down in the chair across from her. "Since I'm not allowed to vent, and you seem to be omnipotent suddenly, let me ask you something else. What makes you so sure I won't die with it?"

For a moment, the know-it-all look to Clover's face is lost, but she holds her confident voice all the same. "You will not."

"Yea you said that; I'm asking why?"

Clover again blinks to the comment as she tries to continue. "Because it would not make sense."

A slight laugh comes from Preston as he nods. "Nothing that's happened to me makes sense, Clover. Why would this be different?"

"Preston, you are just worried I do not see why you-..."

"Yes, I am. I am worried." Preston's slightly raised voice falls almost immediately as he nods to the woman next to him. "Clover, the fact that I'm even here is something too crazy for me to wrap my head around. I just need to know if going back is the right thing to do."

Clover is silent for a moment as she just studies the man's face. "Preston, your thoughts are hardly founded in logic they are found in fear."

"Well no shit, what else should I be thinking about?" Preston shakes his head. "I just wanted to hear your opinion."

Clover's eyes shift from Preston as she nods. "My opinion has not changed, it is a fact, everything that is known about the *Atémor* suggests you will be fine. Accept that." Clover trails on. "You have an opportunity to return to your own life, you should be happy."

"Yea, sure, I'll get right into happiness once I find it." Preston sighs. "If I remember, its eight bottles in and under a cheeseburger." He sucks to his bottom lip. "And some fries."

A melancholy laugh follows Preston's words, though Clover's voice comes up all the same as she looks the man over. "Happiness is a state of mind, why must you sulk like this, why are you not simply accepting it?"

Preston moves his hand to where the amulet hangs as he clears his throat. "Because I'm held back by a wool chain, what don't you get about that?"

"Preston, that charm only helps to calm you, you control who you are, not the spell." Clover's magic sparks to the necklaces around Preston's neck, within seconds it floats from him as she continues. "You hide behind it, simply say what you wish already."

Preston's heart quickly begins to race as he stares to the amulet dangling in front of him. "Clover! What are you-..."

Clover shakes her head as she lays the amulet back to the table. "*Shhh*, Reynard is asleep, now breathe and focus."

Preston rubs his hand to his chest as he starts to sweat. "W-what are you talking about? I need that thing."

Clover squints to the comment. "No, you do not, it restricts your magic and tempers your feelings. Truly, I grow tired of your attitude."

"C-Clover, stop playing around. Nyota said I needed it." Preston reaches for the necklace, but just as he does it disappears in a flash of blue light.

With a shake of the head Clover crosses her arms. "You have to control your own emotions Preston you must-..."

Preston's eyes widen as he begins to pant. "Where is it, Clover? Where is it?!"

"It is my room; you can sleep without it tonight-..."

"Are you crazy?! I can't go a whole night without it! I-I already feel sick and my heart is racing."

Clover nods as she speaks up. "Good, now harness your emotions, control them, think through them."

"I don't care." Preston pants, his hand holding to his chest as he shakes his head and stutters, a display that only draws a roll of the eyes from Clover as he continues. "I know what the amulet is, and I know what it does, I hate it, I hate it so much but-..."

"Preston control your-..."

"Don't tell me to get control!" Preston shakes his head. "Positive thoughts, mind over matter, fuck that, at least with that thing I don't have to feel, and when I do!" He pats to the table with a hard hand. "Boom! Nothing, so give it back!"

Clover shakes her head, her voice unchanged even as she looks over Preston's flustered face. "Give me your hands."

Preston squints to the woman in front of him as he continues to rock in his chair.

"Your hands, Preston." The impatient satyress moves her hand to the man's as she interlocks their fingers. A low blue-green light begins to shine around their hands, Clover stammers a little to their feel, but her voice stays solid as she speaks up. "You just need to relax, Preston."

The words are meaningless as the time for talk ends for Preston, instead the only sound he hears is the increased drumming of his heart within his ears. His anxiety has reached its limit and his vision begins to blur as he feels his body going limp. However, his eyes never leave the light surrounding his and Clover's hands. At least, until he slumps out of the chair and hits the ground.

- - -

Preston's eyes open as his ears ring, the huffed sound of his breathing drawing his mind back to the world. Though, as he gets his bearings, he finds himself standing in the bathroom, his arms hard pressed into the counter as he stares at his reflection. Unfortunately, the longer he stares the more disordered his image becomes, no dark skin and no bug-eyes greet his gaze, nor any other *Atémor* features yet Preston still feels inhuman.

The mirror becomes nothing more than a swirl of colors as Preston steps away, though as the colors twist and turn Preston finds himself unable to turn away. Instead, he lingers, at least until a sound catches his attention.

While the tapping of claws at first seems to be Reynard's the savage breathing is far beyond what the small fox-boy is capable of. Furthermore, as Preston stares to the door the breathing draws closer, the wood visibly shaking to the breath of the beast beyond it.

Preston knows what lies behind it, though this does bring forth the courage he needs to face it, instead he slinks away, opting instead for the corner opposite of the door. Powerless, he settles into the nightmare as a long scrape at the door rings to the tiled floor.

Chapter 7

By & By

Preston's eyes open with a slight laziness, the room around him following suit as he takes a moment to place it. Yet, the warmth of the blanket and the sun pouring in from the window are felt, even in the slowness of the morning.

The man's eyes quickly latch onto the body next to him; which brings a response from the tan faced and light blue eyed satyress. "*Plestá déy*, Preston."

Studying the women's slightly tensed eyes brings Preston's voice out, as he clears his throat. "What happened last night?"

Clover's gaze slowly softens as her head relaxes to the pillow. "You had an unexpected reaction to me removing the amulet." Her confidence is gone as she continues. "You... do not remember anything?"

Preston shakes his head as he pushes himself up in the bed. The sight of the covers shifting from the man however quickly sparks a reaction from Clover; as she begins placing a hand to his shoulder and speaking up. "Perhaps you should rest a little more?"

The words go unnoticed as Preston instead looks over the ripped wool shirt he has on. The necklace dangles in the center of his chest, which is the only reason his voice is not rushed. "W-what happened to me?"

With a faint sigh Clover follows Preston's up-right position in the bed. Clover is dressed in her everyday get up, which of course only begs the question as to why she even choose to lay down next to the man. Though he bites his tongue to the question as he instead just listens.

"When I removed the amulet, you began to-... well."

Preston moves his right hand under the amulet as he speaks up. "Change?"

Clover nods. "Yes, but it was-..."

"I thought you said that wouldn't happen?"

"I said that-..."

Preston's voice carries over the woman's as his face gets a little flustered. "You see! That's why I told you not to take it off. So-so what does this mean? Is the necklace still going to stop the-..."

The man's rushed words are quickly halted as Clover's hands start up with a light blue glow. Her magic has formed over Preston's mouth, yet he does not struggle, due to the strangely calming warmth that now comes over his body.

Clover's voice is smooth as she nods. "The enchantment is fine, Preston. You have nothing to-..." Her comment is cut short as Preston brings his hands slowly to her wrist. However, it is not the feeling of the man's hands that drop the spell, but rather where his hands are placed.

Clover shudders, prompting Preston to look down. Three jagged marks are etched into the woman's wrist and lower arm. No blood is visible, but the wounds are fresh, bright red and hardly healed.

Noticing the cuts Preston drops his grasp, but his words still roll out. "I did that."

"It is nothing, merely a scrape, Preston." Clover gives a simple smile as she continues. "It was my fault."

The satyress' words fall on deaf ears as Preston stares to the marks. "No.

Clover shakes her head as she speaks up. "You did not mean it."

"To Hell with meaning it, I can see it." Preston moves to the edge of the bed, planting his feet to the cold floor as he brings his hands to his head. "I feel sick."

The comment brings Clover forward in the bed, but she stays a fair distance from him as she talks. "I induced your sleep last night, you should feel a little weak, especially after sleeping for so long."

Preston shakes his head as he continues to rub at the headache now beginning to form in his mind. "Ugh..."

Clover just studies the man's back as she nods. "I will give you time."

Within moments the bed behind Preston starts to shift. Clover's hooves plant to the wood as she gives one last look to Preston. "Come downstairs soon."

Preston says nothing, but the door closed behind the sound of Clover's hooves all the same, leaving Preston alone to his thoughts. The silence however is not welcomed as the man continues to stew, a drowning weight overtaking him. The fatigue he feels in his muscles does little to help the sensation, the cooling feeling at his feet seems to be the only thing tethering Preston's mind to the waking world as his body calls to lay down again.

The sounds elsewhere in the library slowly begin to funnel upstairs. Judging from the voices the library is most likely open, unfortunately, at the moment Preston cannot tell if the voices are in his head or not.

Suddenly, however, a new noise takes Preston's attention as he glances to the door opening, halfheartedly expecting it to be Clover, which only prompts a quick gaze.

"You linger like a stubborn cloud up here. Get up!"

The forceful tone does not carry its full weight as Preston just shrugs the comment off. "Hey."

Elva's wings stand at end and twitch a little as she glares to the man still clinging to the bed. Her eyes have their own unique look to them, which seems to demand a level of respect, and a degree of fear. The sharp drill sergeant like stare draws Preston's attention as she trails on.

"Stand up."

Preston quickly stands from the side of the bed. Aside from the light shirt Preston normally sleeps in he is technically dressed, which quickly prompts a response from Elva as she barks another order. "You lack the proper wear, and it is well past first light. I had not expected such *slothéñ* foibles in Clover's home."

For a moment the avian woman halts her words, and her wings slowly lower. Which allows Preston to notice Clover standing in the hallway, however Elva's voice is quick to come back. "Prepare yourself, Preston. Clover's *incápy* is my loose talon for the *déy*, and I intended to pull you until you break."

Preston squints to the question as he speaks up. "What does-..."

Elva's eyes tighten and her crossed arms loosen as her deep voice rings out. "Did I say speak?"

The man quickly goes silent, but rather from the sight of her sharper than normal gaze, not her words.

Elva again settles, and her almost talon like hands begin to shift back hips. "Now, get re-..."

"Okay Elva. You got him up." Clover pushes past her friend, which brings a slight surprise to Elva's face, but she stays silent as Clover continues. "...But Preston should just rest." A smile comes to the satyress' face as her right hand takes on a blue glow.

Within seconds the unmistakable sound that always seems to follow a teleportation spell rings to the room. Clover is the first to speak as she looks to the new objects in her right hand. "Here, I had Bella fashion you new shoes. I did not know your size, but Bella seems confident they will fit with her spell."

Preston looks over the brown leather boots, they are not the fanciest of things but it is not like Preston would reject the gift. Preston slowly takes the shoes as he gives a little smile. "You didn't need to do that."

Clover shrugs. "You needed new footwear it was-..."

Elva rolls her eyes. "Clover, you have a task to attend to." Her hand gestures to Preston as she continues. "The creature needs to be active."

Preston cocks his to the winged woman. "Creature?"

Elva's head turns slowly towards him, a look of contempt coming over him. "You are not to speak."

Clover quickly chimes in as she waves her hand. "I merely have to check on the Princess's project."

Elva shakes her head. "Milk-Chest, hallway, now." As her words end, Elva moves into the hall without a second glance.

"Elva was just wondering why you slept so long; I do not know why she insists on you accompanying her"

"No, I think it makes sense." Preston nods as he brings to slip his new shoes on. "I think I should leave, give me time to clear my head and give you time to focus."

Clover blinks to the comment as she nods. "Well, yes, but-…"

"See, it's a good idea." As Preston bends down to tie the shoes he takes notice to how loose they are. "You said these are magic right?"

"Hmm? Oh, yes." Clover's hands take on a blue glow, which quickly takes hold to the shoes. Preston watches in amazement as the leather of the shoes begins to mold to his feet. The texture surprisingly is like satin, but not as slick as it grips to him.

"Wow…"

Clover gives a little laugh as she nods. "I must say, Bella does have her spells to perfection."

Preston shifts his feet a little, no tug from the leather pulls against his skin and the shoes feel without the normal new-shoe hardness. "I'll say."

Clover's ear flicks as she cocks her head. "Hmm?"

A faint laugh comes to Preston as he looks the satyress' confused face over. "It's just a saying. It means-…"

"Preston, I do not wish to linger in the hall." Elva trails on. "Words are pointless, actions are all and yet you both simply stand, move!"

Elva's voice quickly breaks Clover and Preston's conversation; which prompts Preston to stand as he nods to Clover. "Alright, Elva."

With a simple nod goodbye from Clover, Preston and Elva start down the stairs and into the slightly crowded library.

"Where are we going?"

Elva does not stop her speed as she speaks up. "Stay silent and follow Milk-Chest."

Chapter 8

Of Clouds & Feathers

The air is warm, and the skies are clear with only a few large clouds painted to it, acting as buffers to the wisps of white beyond the town. The wind stirs the scent of flowers from the distance, despite how far off they must be. Of course, flowers coming back so quickly after a winter spell cannot be something out of the ordinary; especially for a world with winged women and house legged men. A strange, and awkward thought that only beats to Preston's head as he continues to follow after the silent avian-warrioress before him.

It has been perhaps twenty minutes since Preston and Elva left the library. The small town took merely ten minutes to walk through, especially with Elva's speed and path that seems to steer clear of the main street's clutter.

However, the speed at which Preston has been forced to keep has brought forth a few things. First, how hungry the man is at missing breakfast and secondly, that he missed out on his early morning bathroom stop.

Though of course, basic needs of normal daily life seem not to apply for Elva. Especially as she unfazed by the early morning walk, even as Preston struggles to keep up. "So… how far are we going?"

No answer comes from Elva, in fact, she seems completely unfazed by question as Preston speaks up again. "Oh, yeah... forgot you were doing that whole drill instructor thing."

"Is that supposed to mean something?"

Elva's pace in front of Preston begins to slow a little as she drifts back to where he walks.

"It's a military thing, someone who whips people into shape. I never joined so that's the best de-..."

"Whipping has proven ineffective. The point of training is to learn something, not harm your cadet." Elva cocks her head to Preston as she continues. "Your form hardly speaks to the performance of such service, so I do doubt you know."

A slight chuckle runs from Preston as he speaks up. "Yea, I'm fat, but don't forget who still saved your ass before."

Elva's wings tense a little as she turns her gaze back to the rural path before her. "You did not save me. You were stabbed due to poor combat skills, providing that wretch Clarity a moment to relish."

"That's right, I took a dagger and saved your life." Preston nods. "So, there you go."

"You have a scar, a reminder to how you failed in fight, do you wish me to thank you still?" Despite the question, Elva does not turn her head to the man, her focus staying to the path.

Even still, Preston replies. "Nothing would make me happier."

"Shame. For I remember nothing I owe thanks for."

Preston shifts his eyes to the hiller path before him, though as he adjusts his eyes to the muscular woman leading, he laughs. "Really? Because I remember you knocked out on the floor, Elva."

"Yes, and as I said, I remember you bleeding on the ground. Why? Because your mind is fogged with the clouds of arrogance." Just as Elva's words end, the woman pulls her sword from its sheath on her right hip.

The sight of the blade pauses Preston for a moment. Sure, he has been living in this world for some time now, but the sight of a sword is still something that takes a moment to register.

Preston's lack of words or motions does not halt Elva however. She points to the scene. "You remember our sparring match near the farms, yes?"

For a moment, Preston looks around the lower hills in front of him. The trees he saw before have now begun to grow tiny red and green apples that can be seen despite the distance. However, the fact that Preston can even see the bright fruits from where he stands actually surprises him.

"Is there magic in the farm or something? Why can I see everything so clear?"

Elva turns her head just briefly, all the while as she pulls another, slightly smaller sword from her other hip. "The *Dẃoff* know how to grow. Of course, there would be nothing without *Flóff* rain."

Preston pumps his fist. "Glory to the clouds!" A laugh follows him as he shakes his head. "You don't own the rain."

The words spark an annoyed look to Elva's face as she straightens her posture, the two swords hard in her grasp. "Mind your words, Preston, while we do not own them, we guide the clouds that do."

Her comment does not force Preston to adjust his tone, but the blades in Elva's hold do catch his eye again. "I mean, the water was already here, right? So, it's not like you brought that with you."

"We attempted to move some water from the *Oválll*, but the winds would not allow us. I suppose it is for the best, the rain here is smooth and fresh." Elva's posture begins to lax as she continues. "The water here also does not need as much purification… I forgot how much I missed the songs of clean water."

"I think we've gotten off topic." Preston shakes his head with a little laugh. "Wwater doesn't sing."

"And a *Yiftiñ* should not turn clouds, Preston!"

"Whoa, whoa, I don't even know what you're saying." Preston clears his throat as he finds his eyes quickly fading from Elva's piercing gaze. "O-or I can just be quiet."

The avian woman nods as she begins to roll her left arm. "Good, now prepare yourself."

Preston blinks to the comment as he awkwardly shifts in his stance. "Well as much as I love getting put on my ass, I need a bathroom break first."

Elva shakes her head to the comment as she extends the longer sword's hilt to Preston. "No, I shall bring a cloud for you to wash later."

Preston sighs as he lowers his voice. "Not that kinda bathroom break." He clears his throat. "Why don't you wait just a little over there."

Elva turns her gaze to a wider area in the path. "Near the tree? I suppose the shade would be good."

"Yeah, sounds good." Preston does not move down the path as he instead starts to walk into the field and towards the higher blades of mostly dead grass.

Elva squints to the man's walk as she speaks up. "Preston?"

"I'll meet you down there…" He pauses. "By the way, is there anything I should worry about in the grass?"

The woman gives a little smirk as she shakes her head. "Just *wéveanś*. They enjoy the softer flesh of most creatures."

Preston pauses at the comment as he looks to the dirt at his feet. "What do they look like?"

Elva holds her smirk as she begins to walk down the hill. "Be quick, Preston."

A sigh rolls from Preston as he watches Elva starting away. With her gone he relaxes, a slight breeze running through the fields around him, the sound of the grass crashing against one another is smoothing and similar to a wave breaching the shore.

The colorful feathers nestled over Elva's ear begin to waver in the breeze, but the woman stops their movements with a brush of her hand. As she moves her hand from her head her eyes focus in on the short blade she holds. Her left hand clenches the longer sword's hilt as she begins to expertly twist the blade in her hand.

The sides of the blade are finely shaped, just like all her weapons; although the grip is a little worn down from its excessive use, not that Elva has a problem mastering the feel of the faded helve.

Within moments, the short trek down the hill comes to an end as the tree's branches begin to block a little bit of the sun. Elva's eyes shift to the single tree in front of her. This is not the first time she has seen this tree, especially being that the road is on her patrolling path. Strangely, it is just now that she realizes this is an apple tree, despite how often she has flown by it.

The leaves shift with every breath of the world around her; unfortunately, the silence of the field is broken as Preston's voice rings up. "Well it's a good thing it's not that hot out, huh?"

Elva's response is quick, as she watches the man draws near. "Why do you speak so much now, when before a dark cloud hung in your throat?"

"You're talking about why I was quiet earlier?" Preston cocks his head. "Thought talking was pointless?"

Elva nods her head as she replies. "It very much is, yet your attitude towards Clover bothers me nonetheless." She squints to the man. "I do not like to be bothered, Preston."

Preston shifts to the comment as he rubs his neck. "I don't like it either." He shakes his head. "It's not the same anymore, I mean not that I knew what it was before... Nyota just wanted Clover to watch after me, and now she-..."

"Guards you as a helpless *yiftiñ* in a nest?" Elva smirks.

Preston shakes his head. "Took the words right out of my mouth, Feathers."

Elva nods. "Good, now take a sword, Milk-Chest."

"You know." Preston looks over the extended hilt, though he does not take it as he furls his brow. "I wasn't trying to be an ass to Clover, I just..." He gestures to his shoes as he continues. "I have no way to repay her for anything, I sit around doing shit in the library, that's hardly a-..."

"You repay Clover's generosity with dismal behavior, yet, you fly away from her with darkened clouds?" Elva shakes her head. "Take a sword, forget your ramblings."

"What? No." Preston shakes his head. "Why did you ask me how I felt if you didn't care?"

Elva slowly begins to sheath the two swords in her hold as she answers. "I do not care, and I did not ask, I merely stated I do not accept your treatment of my friend, Preston."

"Whoa, you're a great person to talk to, no really, how much do I owe you?" Preston shrugs. "What was the point of this?"

Elva's crossed arms do not loosen as she continues to study Preston's flustered face. "The *Flóff* do not hold value in our emotions. In truth, I find even the voicing of your feelings about Clover's kindness petty. *Flóff* males are prized for their stable flight and strong mind, one cannot be swayed by soft winds less wings tighten."

Preston shrugs. "And the point of this is?"

Without hardly a hint of emotion Elva replies. "Perhaps some *Únoff* ideals swirl to one's mind after leaving the clouds for fifty *yúrf*."

Preston squints to the comment. "Fifty? Like Fifty years?" Preston takes a fresh look at the tan and muscle toned woman in front of him. Her hair is bright and deeply colored, and no wrinkles sit to her face, like his first thoughts she looks no older than mid-twenties. "How old are you?"

"Do not let *Únoff* measurements clouding our sparing, Preston. It has been sixty-three *yúrf* since I was a hatchling."

"Whoa." Preston gives a little laugh as he nods. "Well, you should know you look really good for your age."

The hawk-like glare does not shift as Elva speaks up. "Flattery will not stay my hand, but I am pleased you can so easily set your thoughts aside."

"Years of practice." Preston chuckles.

"Time spent on the mastery of a worthless skill." Elva shakes her head. "I am hardly surprised at how well it fits you."

"Worthless skill for a worthless person." Again, Preston chuckles.

"And yet you master it." Elva nods. "*Brevet*."

"Mhm." Preston continues. "So, when I lean in can you just got for the neck? It would save me a lot of time in a warm bath."

Elva pulls her blades out again. "Enough of your strange words, take a sword."

A sight rolls through Preston as he nods. "Yea, just don't break your hip, old lady."

"Age is nothing to the *Flóff*." She spins the sword in her left hand.

"Even still, I thought you were Clover's age, knowing how old you are is kinda disturbing." Preston trails on. "How old do you think I am?"

Elva stretches her wings and rolls her neck as she replies. "I have no care for your age... and Clover is but a child. A foal of *Únoff* scrolls, not yet ready for marehood. I have forged my name with the tips of my nails, not clawing at another's cloak."

Preston's eyes slowly drift to the wings now sprawled behind Elva. "Are you jealous of Clover?"

"Not at all." Elva's wings lower as the woman shakes her head. "Clover's name carries the same weight as mine within our fiefs. She is no different than Gráf Mane the fourth. I however, like every other *Flóff*, find the *Únoff* to be a farce. One should be able to challenge another's title, but none can challenge *Únoff* rights based on words alone."

"Not following." Preston chuckles.

"Because you are a *bafte*ñ, Preston." She again holds the hilt of her sword back to Preston. "Ready?"

The longer sword's hilt dangles in front of Preston, however, the man does not grab it as he rubs his right hand to where the necklace hangs under his shirt. "You know, I really don't think I'm feeling too good. Maybe we can try and kill each other tomorrow, heck might even beat you to it."

Elva shoves the sword into Preston's grasp as she smirks. "Do not fret, Preston. I have already assumed you would act skittish." The woman's hands come to the straps on her armor chestplate.

Preston watches the avian-warrioress shed her armor. However, the feminine shape of the armor still brings a laugh as he speaks up. "Really? This again?"

The comment goes unresolved as Elva instead holds the armor toward him. "You shall not get hurt this way."

"To be honest, I really don't care. It would be nice to see some blood, remind me I'm human still." Preston's snide tone prompts a response in Elva as she shoves the armor to Preston's chest. "Enough stalling Milk-Chest!"

The command ends Preston's sarcasm. However, his thoughts do not shift as he speaks up once more; this time a little quieter. "Hey, listen, I really don't want what happened last time to-…"

"You shall not be tempted by the *Atémor*, Preston. This will be good for you."

Preston stares a little shocked at the woman's unchanged face as he stutters. "How do you know about that?"

Elva's stance relaxes, and with an unpleasant sigh she speaks up. "Clover is not above trivial talks. Especially when pursued by Bella."

Preston blinks to the comment as he shakes his head. "Aren't you worried?"

"Of course not, I have killed mindless creatures before… *Atémor* are hardly a threat."

The words immediately strike a cord in Preston as he speaks up. "What if I turned?"

Elva shrugs. "I slay you."

Preston shakes his head. "And what if you hesitate?"

Elva tightens her gaze. "I shall not hesitate." She nods. "Besides, is that not the point of your amulet, to keep your senses?"

"I don't know anymore." As Preston's comment passes from him a groan rolls from the woman across him.

The warrioress squints to the man before her as she holds her anger. "Why must you cyclone, Preston? Do mere words cause such a moue, or is it simply your weakness?"

"Hey! You don't know what I have to deal with, what I have dealt with!"

"Yes of course." Elva nods, her impatient stance shifting as she continues. "I hear books carry a sharp edge, though I am sure Clover would tend to your wailing."

"Fuck you." Preston quickly trails on, his hot temper fast outrunning the ever-present soothing spell around his neck. "Do you even realize what I've been through? Matt was killed right in front of me, and you know what you've said about that? You've said that I should just move on. Who the fuck says that?" Preston claps his hands together. "Did you not understand what I say when I said he was vaporized in front of me? Do you not understand how insane that even sounds for me? And-and that's just one person, what about Damien, what about being fucking stabbed, what about everything else that I've seen, what about what's inside me right now!"

"What about it, Preston?" Despite Preston's shouting Elva speaks over him without so much as a change in tone. "Death is final Preston, you do not honor the fallen with sorrow, you honor them with life. You have seen things, *brevét*, but your breath is meaningless if it merely repeats troubles to no end." She shrugs. "Those who must voice their concerns rather than deal with them are normally attempting to convince themselves of their strife. Do something else if you cared."

"Let's fight, huh? That's gonna make it better? Fine!" Preston tosses the armor to the ground as he pounds his chest. "Well come on! Let's fight!"

Elva holds her gaze to armor that now sits to the dirt, though she holds her tongue as she extends a sword to Preston.

Without a thought Preston takes hold of the sword. "Well come on! You wanted to-...*oof!*"

Before Preston's words can come to an end Elva lunges forward, knocking Preston to the ground in one swift motion. She stands over him, proud and angelic as her wings flare out. A newfound look of disdain coming to Elva's face as she speaks up. "Your anger has left you open. Now stand or polish my boots."

Elva begins to circle him, a lion waiting to strike as she calls out again. "Stand!" A smile now shines bright like the feathers in her hair as she continues to await Preston's response.

Preston grinds his teeth as he attempts to get up, yet as he does Elva merely sends a stiff kick to his side. "That is how you stand! Be prepared *bafteñ!*"

Her kick sends Preston rolling away, though he does not stay down for long as he springs up with new vigor, his sword clenched hard with both hands.

Elva smirks to the display, though she simply side steps Preston's would-be charge as she slaps him in the back of the head. Like a bull chasing the muleta Preston turns back and charges again. This time Elva merely bounds over him, a quick blast of her powerful wings bringing her up. Though she does not miss the opportunity to kick the man in the back as she jumps his length.

Landing behind him, Elva's eyes lock to the man's. "Take your time, Preston, allow your mind to clear before you act."

Despite the ominous sword in Elva's hand and the embarrassment of his last couple of attacks fueling his frustration, Preston listens to the words. His mind slowly coming clear as the amulet burns against his chest. In this moment of clarity, he copies Elva's profile stance, but with both hands staying glued to the sword, much to Elva's amusement

Chapter 9

Nesting For The Sun

The sky has grown cloudy since Preston and Elva stopped their last sparring match. It is no secret that Elva would inevitably win. However, the fact that she even acknowledged some of Preston's deflections says something.

For the moment, Preston could careless about accolades. Instead, he continues to lean against the shade tree as he fights to lower the loud and tired gasps for air that bellow from him.

Despite what Elva thinks, some freshly collected cloud water, and a few apples does not make for a hearty brunch after the hour-long training regimen fit for a knight.

Of course, she on the other hand may disagree. Elva sits almost opposite of Preston to the tree, her wings sprawled to her sides, but limp. Both swords are in her lap, as she continues to sharpen them with the strange pearl colored stone she pulled out during the break.

Aside from the sounds of stone on metal the newly returning chatter of the fields has made for a relaxing break. In truth, Preston has never really liked the outdoors; yet, watching fields bow and bob to the swaying winds is rather enjoyable. It would perhaps be a bit more pleasant without the ever-building layer of dark clouds in the distance threatening to come down. Even still, the aches in Preston's body have kept his mind clear and off the amulet around his neck.

Elva's head does not shift as her deep, though feminine tone comes out. "Shall we go once more, Preston?"

A slight laugh rolls from the man as he quickly tries to regain his voice. "You're never satisfied, are you?"

"Nothing is more satisfying than *céla,* even a small triumphs carries some joy." The sound of the blade being sharpened does not stall as she trails on. "And while you are not a worthy partner, I enjoy having a spare away from camp."

Preston squints to the comment as he rubs his hands to the few scraps on his arms. "This is how you spend a day off from work?"

Elva simply nods to the comment as she stands in one quick movement thanks to the gust of air she flaps behind her. The dust kicked up prompts Preston to brush away at the dirt, though as he coughs he stills listens into Elva' words. "Yes, now, rise."

"What? No, you've won every time." The man's comment sparks a slight smile to Elva's face, as the avian woman sheaths the two swords.

"I do not require another conquest; now rise, I shall not get caught in a storm due to laziness. You are not capable of finding your own way home, *incápy.*"

Preston slowly pushes himself from the tree as he speaks up. "I think I could find my way back if I needed to." He squints as he continues. "What's that mean anyway?"

"I suppose that was an attempt to impress me. *Brevét* on thinking you know your way to Clover's home." Elva cocks a smile.

"What?" Preston shakes his head to the woman. "No, the word?"

"*Incápy?* To the *Únoff* it is a title given to things that cannot care for themselves. Animals, foals, and such." Elva continues. "It suits you."

With a sigh Preston rubs his brow. "Okay... whatever, I'm too tired to ruffle your feathers."

Elva squints to the words. "I would never allow you to touch my wings, such things are disrespectful."

Preston just nods as he looks over the woman's large hawk like wings. "Then why not wear armor?"

"I do not require protection on them, none ever get so close." Elva's confidence only draws an eye from Preston, yet the man just nods.

"I may not be fast, but I got stamina and magic boots."

"If you grab for my wings, I will snap your hand." Elva turns an eye to Preston as she awaits his response.

Preston shrugs. "I'm quicker."

Elva's arms loosen to her sides and a confused look comes to her face as her pace slows to Preston's. "Is this a challenge you offer?"

"Ha, sure, why not. If I lose you snap my hand." Preston rolls his right shoulder a bit as he continues. "Then you can move to my neck."

Elva smiles as she nods. "Be forewarned, Preston. I have not lost a challenge since I was bested in *Thráw* by Tair."

The name resonates in Preston's mind for a moment. But he passes it off with a simple nod. "You remember all your losses?"

"Every *Flóff* remembers a loss." She nods. "We use them to grow, I believe you will be able to do the same after more training."

Preston again nods as he gives a faint laugh and focus to the downward slope in the road before him. Though as they continue Preston speaks up. "Thanks for this by the way."

A sigh rolls from Elva as she takes notice to Preston's tone. "Do not cyclone, Preston."

"I'm not." Preston nods. "I just…" He finds his hand coming to his necklace, though in his silence Elva stops.

Her once somewhat happy expression has fallen, her normal, uncaring and sure face now greeting the man as she speaks up. "Death is inevitable, all those around you will die, and it will hurt. It is best to not care."

Preston fiddles with the amulet under his shirt as he forces a smile. "Yea… I agree with that, but I've spent a lot of my life pretending I don't."

Elva turns her sharp gaze with a shake of the head. "Lies bind the strong and damper the flame of will. Pain may slow you, though it does not kill, bite your tongue to complaints. You had said you wished to repay Clover for her kindness, do so by giving her less to worry about."

The words bounce around in Preston's head for a moment, though he nods all the same as his hand tightens to the amulet around his neck. "I didn't mean to-…"

In a huff Elva remarks. "Then choose not to."

Preston's hand sparks to the amulet, forcing its spell as a smile crosses his face, a false sense of calming coming to his mind as his dopey smile turns to Elva. A burst of confidence and joy swirls within him as he takes notice to the woman's wings. "So, how about a race? No magic, no wings, deal?"

Elva merely shrugs to the comment as her speed takes hold to the dirt path again. "I hardly have a reason to accept your challenge, Preston."

"You want out?"

A smirk comes to Elva as she shakes her head. "You cannot best me, not even with what little magic you know."

The cocky tone only prompts the man further as he nods. "We'll see about that."

"We shall."

- - -

(A little later)

Like the journey out of town, Elva's pace has made short work of *VéturVill's* primitive streets. Of course, Preston has lagged behind a little, the amulet's jolt of joy fading just as the pasted the market square. Though Preston knew their trip was close to its end, not that Elva acknowledged it. But as their trek draws near to the library Preston speaks up. "About time."

Elva nods. "Get inside, the rain should start soon."

"Okay and what about-..." Preston's reply just barely rolls from his lips as he suddenly is forced to halt it, his hands waving off the dirt now kicked up. Without a goodbye or even a warning Elva has sprung into the air, her swift wings dashing her towards the sky. He moves into the house to avoid the dust and to Preston's surprise the library is empty of people.

Yet, before Preston can speculate as to how long he was actually gone his eyes catch on to something truly disturbing. The table and surrounding areas of the table are covered in unraveled scrolls, opened books and what looks like broken quills and inkwells.

The man's words now direct to the orange furred fox-boy attempting to clean a puddle of spilled ink from where he sits on the ground. "Did we get robbed?!"

Reynard's ear flicks to the voice, almost as if he was unaware someone new was in the room. "What?"

Preston again calls out as he moves a little closer to the table. "Robbed! Did someone steal stuff, Rey?"

The fox-boy stops his dabbing at the floor as he takes a look around the cluttered floor. "Um, no. Why?"

The relaxed tone slowly brings Preston's adrenaline down as he shakes his head. "W-what happened?"

"Oh, Clover has been teleporting back and forth from the Princess's project. It seems to be a big project." Reynard gives a little smile as he lifts his ink covered paw up to Preston. "You should move, Clover has been teleporting somewhere around there."

Preston takes a few steps back, and from his new position he sees a few strange marks written to the floor in what looks like white chalk. However, before he can question it a flash of blue-green light pops in front of him, quickly followed with a low, thunderous sound and a voice.

"...Okay, Reynard, I think I have it done this time. I teleported across the field before, but this should..." The satyress continues to rack off a few things to the poor fox-boy but Preston's attention has turned to Clover's overall figure now. Her clothing is normally earth toned, however, there actually looks to be dirt on her lower body and her hooves too look to be caked in mud. Her hair also looks far more wild than normal, only adding to her overall disheveled look.

Clover has yet to turn around since she teleported, nor has she stopped talking, even as she collects a few colorful stones and opened scrolls. "...I shall be back in a moment."

The words quickly spark Preston's arms forward as he places his hands to her shoulder. "Hey don't you-...*DAHHH*!!"

Preston's words are quickly cut from the room as a jolt runs through his body and he falls to his butt.

"Oh, Preston! I am so, sorry!" Clover holds a handout to the man on the ground as she continues. "You startled me."

Preston's mouth quivers but he is unable to talk as he just looks up to the woman.

Clover gives a little smile as she speaks up. "Oh, the spell... do not worry, you are just stunned, it should pass in a moment."

With a gasp Preston speaks up. "Ow! *W-what wazzz d-dat?*"

Clover holds the items in her other hand a little close to her body as she speaks up. "I was not expecting someone to grab hold of me, it was a quick reaction."

"W-well..."

Preston's stuttering words continue for a moment, but Clover's friendly smile is slowly lost as she holds her hand out. "One moment, Preston."

In the blink of an eye Clover vanishes in a cloak of blue-green magic. As the satryress's leaves Reynard's sight, the fox-boy moves to Preston with a slight laugh. "You okay?"

"*Gr-Gr-Great.*"

Reynard just smiles as he pokes his ear up to listen to Preston's continued voice. "...W-what is she d-doing?"

"I told you, the Princess' project. Clover went to inform the *Jartál* of the plans... but, the Princess had already sent a few things for the *Jartál* to give Clover. She is working on setting a *télpréith* for future supplies."

Preston squints to the comment as he slowly starts to stand on his shaky legs. "A what?"

No reply comes from Reynard as the same burst of blue and green pops back into the room. However, unlike before when Clover exits this spell makes her sigh and grab for her stomach, not a scroll from the table.

Reynard quickly moves a chair for the satyress, which Clover aptly takes. "Uh... thank you, Reynard."

As the woman sits Preston speaks up. "What are you even doing?"

"Please, do not talk so loud." Clover holds a hand to the man as she just closes her eyes and leans forward.

The lower tone and the absent atmosphere of Clover's know-it-all self takes Preston by surprise. He looks to Reynard, but the fox-boy just shrugs. "You okay?"

Clover gives a little groan as she speaks up. "The Princess wanted a *télpréith* setup for here and the Capital. That way the workers can move material easier." Another groan comes from Clover as she speaks up. "Nyota sent plans with the Princess's orders... but I did not know how to do the spell. So I had to learn it first. Then I realized I needed more *Kélf* stones, so I had to speak with *Jartál* Caféll, and of course I had to explain myself to someone who could not understand the complexities of my task. Did you need to know that?"

The woman halts her words as she tightens her hands to her stomach. "Ugh..."

Preston shakes a little, attempting to work off the spell, though he follows through with his thoughts all the same. "You overdid it, you should just rest."

"Mhmm... I cannot rest. I will not know if the spell worked until *témont*." She points to the marks on the floor as she continues. "This may work now but I need to work on an alternative."

"You should go upstairs and rest." Preston shrugs. "You already said this works, what's the issue?"

Clover slowly brings her head up as she rolls her eyes. "Preston do not comment on things you cannot understand. Just because this works now does not mean I can rest, I have too much to do."

Preston shakes his head, his gaze locked to the tired face staring back to him. "Clover you look like crap, go rest."

"Preston go wash up, the sweet scent of *borétef* you carry is simply too pleasant." Clover pushes herself from the table as she motions to the mess around the house. "I can focus better with you gone-...." Clover stumbles a little as she plants a hand to the table.

Reynard and Preston both steps forward, yet only the fox-boy comes to Clover's side as Preston stops in his approach, his eyes clinging to the scratches on Clover's arm now on display.

"Are you okay, Clover?" Reynard continues to help steady the woman, though Clover merely takes her seat again as she fakes a smile.

"Of course, just.... just a bit tired." Clover sighs as she slowly turns to Preston, the surprisingly pleading gaze however makes Preston straighten up as she talks. "Could you help me up to my room?"

Reynard blinks to the comment as he speaks up. "You are not mad at Preston anymore?"

"No, no." Clover waves her hand. "I never was, I was merely... thinking."

"It's not an issue." Preston moves a little closer to Clover as he continues. "Hey, Reynard, I'll be back in a minute to help you clean up. Okay?"

Though confused, Reynard steps aside as he sheepishly just watches.

Preston bends down to Clover's level as he slowly moves his hand around her frame. Clover stands, all the while leaning against the man as they begin to walk toward the stairs.

While it seems strange for Clover to be so weak after a spell it nonetheless does not draw a comment from Preston. Half out of his lack of knowledge with magic and half out of his desire to avoid an argument with the woman. Luckily, Preston is able to chase the thoughts away with ease as he instead focuses on helping the shorter satyress up the stairs.

Clover's steps are slow, but with Preston's support they make it up the stairs with hardly a moment beyond normal. With the final step now past them Clover's arm comes to Preston's as she pushes away, her pride too hurt to make eye contact as she speaks. "I will rest for a moment, thank you."

"Yea." Preston licks his lips, his voice poised to carry on, yet he finds himself falling silent as Clover merely turns away from him. In a moment Clover moves into her room and closes the door behind her, finally prompting Preston drift away, his eyes falling to the floor as he clears his throat. "Alright, Reynard." He turns back to the stairs. "Let's get this tornado cleaned up."

Chapter 10

Once More

...although under the category of Coñjro Márjx; teleporting is still widely used among all fields of Márjx. As such, all young foals should start with such training, simple spells for foals are located in the following chapter; with more advanced spells following, to continue with Coñjro Márjx teleportation, see chapter three.

Spell one: Ensure that the caster is of six mořo old before attempting this spell. The caster should have a well fitted Gloftór and an Únoff of at least novice mastery in basic Márjx present.

Step one: Instruct the foal to focus on a desired location. Typically, foals respond strongly towards their mare provider; calling of the name and hand gestures are suggested as well. Vivid description of desired location has also been proven to be beneficial in the accurate completion of such spells.

Step two: As most foals under one yúrf are prone to emotionally triggered spells, a simple teleportation should occur within moments. If no magic is prompted after a few moments step one must be repeated, with continued prompting and more suitable sensory stimulation.

Basic Márjx should be learned within the first six mořo. If an acceptable amount of Márjx is not shown within the allotted time the foal should be deemed

Noston and training should be stopped. Consultation with Passvórtall Héthtex should be considered.

As Preston's eyes glance to the end of the page he gives a silent laugh and shakes his head. Yet, the man does not halt his hand as he turns to the next page. Preston started this hefty book perhaps an hour or two ago; it was one of the last few books that needed to be accounted for and reshelved after he and Reynard had dinner.

Truthfully, Preston did not intend to read it. But, after noticing that the book was about teleporting it piqued his interest. The text is a little dry for his taste and some pages are beyond his understanding thanks to the strange language, however, with most of the pages being New Tongue at least it allows Preston to it read.

One of the dim, green balls of light Preston set into the house once the sun began to fall still hovers over the man's shoulders. The sky outside is dark, but not yet completely taken by the night. Still though, the green glow of Preston's magic makes the inky text of the book a little harder to read.

The man adjust himself in the hard wooden chair as he plants his elbows on the table in front of him. The leather-bound book wobbling in his hold as he sighs.

If simple teleportation spells have been learned the foal should attempt the same spell but with its eyes covered. Typically, a foal will cry during this portion of the learning, making their magic more unpredictable. This is to be expected and encouraged. As with any magic training, the more spells learned the higher one's ability to manipulate magic grows. Without the proper amount of emotional output higher spells may cause mental and physical damage within the caster. For further reading on the effects of magical profusion seek chapter five.

After a foal has learned both sighted and unsighted teleportation stronger tel...

Preston's thumbs begin to creep through the pages as he whispers to himself. "Chapter five... chapter five..."

The weird marks that signal the chapters are not the normal numbers Preston knows, but it does not take a genius to figure out what symbol equals five.

The effects of magical profusion on the caster. Magic is everywhere and is within everything, such is the decree of the Únoff. However, magic is merely allowed to enter a being for manipulation, too much and the caster may become corrupted and sickly, too little and the caster will fall ill within their mind. Balance is essential in understanding magic; each Unvérnity ó Márjx believes in different balance. Through all, thoughts and emotions must be tamed, but allowed to gallop freely.

Signs of magical profusion: Failing spells, sickness, mental pain, anger, and psyñial vé ston tendences. Both external and internal profusions hold this list, however, external profusion may also change the color of one's magic. Although not always a concern, the change in coloration of one's magic must be determined to ensure one's safety.

Most colors are attributed by the color of the caster's ocúlús, although some may be determined by factors not yet fully understood. Some notice color variations as a result of Shéo with numerous participants. Which is easily altered with a steady regimen of higher spells to use the excess emotional magic. Elder Álter Márjx masters suggest that Shéo be used to increase one's own magical output.

However, it should be noted that steady regimens of higher spells may cause magical profusion as the caster's ability to perform spells may be hindered; causing sickness and in some instant death. One must understand profusion is both beneficial and dangerous; as it promotes growth but strains those unprepared.

This is why...

"Oh, you are still up?"

The voice quickly takes Preston's attention as he looks to the satyress now at the bottom of the staircase. "Yeah, it's a little early to go to bed for me."

Clover simply nods as she trots into the room; her speed however slows as she notices the book in Preston's hands. Her mane is a little messy from where she has been laying down and her clothing is a bit looser than she typically wears it, however, her inquisitive eyes keep their glow as she studies the man. "Reading something, Preston?"

Preston just smirks to the comment as he looks back to the book. "Well I need something to pass the time."

Clover just nods as she moves a little closer to the table. "Books are used for more than just passing time, Preston."

"Eh." Preston shrugs. "It definitely helps me sleep."

"Of course." Clover cocks her eye to the book as she speaks up. "And what tome of arcane knowledge is helping to dull your sense right now?"

Flipping the book over Preston struggles with the glossy title in the dull green light. "Uh... something about basic magic and-..."

"Oh! You are reading Borton *Márjx*!" Clover happily nods as she holds a finger to Preston. "One moment and we shall discuss it." Before the man can even reply the satyress has already moved from the table and pass the kitchen's half-wall. The sound of plates or cups moving can be heard, but Preston keeps his voice down as he instead just closes the book and waits for Clover's return.

It only takes a few minutes for the woman to come back into the room. However, she is not alone as she floats two empty mugs, a plate with some sort of pastry and a half-filled bottle. The bottle is what Preston quickly recognizes as he watches Clover coming back to the table. "Thought you didn't like to drink that stuff?"

Clover takes her seat across from Preston as she floats her items to the table in her light blue magic. "I am not fond of *Humé*... but it is filling, and Reynard will not be coming down while he sleeps..."

Preston just nods as he watches Clover's magic quickly starting to pour into one of the two tin colored mugs. "So, what prompted your interest in the book?" The smile holds to Clover's face as she continues. "How far have you made it?"

The mug closes to Preston begins to float towards him, stopping in front of him as Clover awaits his grasp. Noticing this Preston gives a simple chuckle, though he sighs as he takes the cup to the table. "Well, it said teleportation, figured I should brush up on that since, you know."

Clover nods as she tears off a little piece of the yellow pastry next to her mug. "Oh?"

The sweet smell of the drink near Preston mixed with the scent of Clover's food is welcomed as the stuffy smell of the books and ink are quickly chased from Preston's senses. And sighting Clover's chewing the man speaks up in her silence. "Yep, figured I shouldn't waste a day, what with you not feeling too well earlier."

Clover nods as she quickly swallows the little piece of bread. "Of course." Her tone shifts as she shrugs. "But I would have helped you. Master Nyota's stone has been charged since you left with Elva, so we can begin if you wish."

Preston is silent as he lets the words sink. However, his stillness is broken as he nods. "Not tonight, the book was enough."

The satyress' ears perk up as she responds. "Oh? Are you not eager to leave?"

Preston shrugs. "It comes and goes."

Clover takes a sip of her drink before she answers the question. "What of *témont*? Would you wish to practice then?" Clover rolls her hand as she reaches for another piece of bread. "We could start after my visit to the worksite, if the *télpréith* is working properly we will have plenty of time."

Another simple shrug comes from Preston as he glances away from the table. "Sure thing." He glances to nowhere in particular as he trails on, merely working his eyes around the dark room as he comes back to Clover's face. "Anything I could do to help?"

"Hmm..." Clover taps a finger to her mouth as she continues to chew. "I suppose you could look at the Princess's plans. She has sent them for the *Jartál* to review."

"Okay."

"But that should not take long." Clover takes another sip of her drink. "Did you learn anything from the book?"

Preston follows her lead as he takes a sip of his drink, his throat clearing to the thick, and warming slosh of liquid now rushing past his lips. "Nothing much, just some stuff about magic." He turns an eye to his drink as he slowly brings it to rest at the table. "Think I could ask you something?"

"Of course." Clover leans into the table, a hand coming to her cheek as she props herself up. She rocks her head a little as she begins to talk, though Preston's eyes simply focus to the scratches on display now. "I have read the book numerous times, what chapter would you like to talk about?"

Preston nods as he sparks a smile to his face, his eyes turning to the cup near Clover as he speaks up. "Well, since you're a lightweight, and we're drinking, I figured I should ask this now, you know, before you get all loopy."

Clover cocks her head to the shaky sentence as she playful chimes in. "I believe your word loopy is akin to *lóva*, which I assure you will not be happening, not even with Gwendy's *Hópdo* bread."

"Mhm, well bread or no bread." Preston clears his throat as his right hand draws his drink closer to him. "Are you sure you're feeling well?"

A faint chuckle rolls from Clover as she pulls herself from her more relaxed posturing, quickly returning to her typical, back firmly planted to the chair, style of lounging. "I am fine, why?"

The man gestures vaguely to the book as he responds. "I read some stuff before you came down that talks about being sick because of having too much magic or whatever. And, well look, you've not really been the same for a little and I've noticed your magic changing colors; I just want to make sure you're at least noticing it too."

Clover is silent for a moment, and merely just stares back to Preston, her ears a little lower than when they first started talking. Yet, something in her silent stare suggests some type of surprise, Preston cannot tell why.

Interestingly, and despite Clover's pause, she speaks up with a rather typical tone. "There is no reason for your worry, it is merely..." Clover shrugs, her eyes shifting away from the man as she chuckles. "...the amount on my mind."

Preston squints to the comment. "Stress?"

Clover chuckles to the comment, the drink shooting to her mouth as she shakes her head, her words muffled by the cup as she drinks. "Hardly, Preston."

Preston thinks over the comment as he taps his fingers to the mug. "And the change in magic? I mean, is that normal?"

Clover eases her hand as she replies. "A change in magic can occur for many reasons, as I am sure you read."

"Well, yea." Preston chuckles. "But it's not like I understood it."

A simple smile crosses Clover's face as she nods. "Then do not trouble yourself with something beyond your understanding, Preston."

Though a smile graces Clover's lips, the words sliding past it carry a slight jab, one that Preston finds difficult to ignore as he laughs. "Guess

I should apologize for caring about yea Happy Hooves." He takes a quick drink as he shrugs. "Sorry."

Clover merely sucks to her bottom lip, her smile fading as she nods a little. "Yes, well how was your time with Elva? The nicks on your hands suggest she talked you into a spar?"

Preston glances to his knuckles and the faint scraps on them from the times he fell earlier, hardly something he even noticed himself. Another laugh rolls from the man as he crosses his arms. "It's not like she gives you much of a choice." His hands brush up against his amulet, the faint warmth of it starting up as he holds his smile. "But yeah, we did a few things like that." Preston continues to bob his head as he trails on. "It was... nice."

"Nice?" Clover shrugs.

Preston puffs his bottom lip out, his right hand rubbing to the amulet under his shirt as he glances away, lost to the words he attempts to choose. "Didn't sleep well yesterday, it was nice not to think for a bit."

Clover's ears perk back up as she leans a little over the table. "Do you wish to discuss any dreams?"

Pausing to lick his lips for a moment Preston shakes his head, a hand quickly coming to his chin as he rubs his bread. "No, it was nothing special."

"Preston." Clover moves her drink aside for a moment as she nods. "I would like to hear."

While Preston does not uncross his arms the woman's soft gaze begins to work on him, and sure enough after a moment Preston relents. A sigh rolls from him as he nods. "I heard it, Clover."

Clover merely blinks to the vague comment as she shakes her head, asking the obvious question as she speaks up. "Heard what?"

A faint laugh comes from Preston as he loosens his arms, tapping to the amulet beneath his shirt as he speaks up. "What do you think? We took this thing off, you think I heard my-..."

"I hear you, Preston." Clover attempts a smile as she speaks up. "What happen? What did you see?"

Sighing again at Clover's sudden cut-in, Preston reluctantly continues. "I saw myself in the bathroom, staring into the mirror." He shrugs, a faint laugh drawing from him as he feels the amulet growing hotter under his shirt, his skin beginning to itch as he fidgets in the seat. "I knew what it was, I knew I was going to see that face, one of those damn things. But no, I saw nothing, I didn't see my face or even one of theirs staring back to me, instead it was just a mix of colors, mindless splatters on a canvas." He nods. "And that's when I heard the thing, claws dragging on the floor, some grade-a horror movie type cliché." He chuckles again, glancing away from Clover's intently listening stare, knowing full well the words held no meaning to her.

Even still, he stays heated as he chuckles. "And that's it, I stayed, and listened to it."

Clover blinks to the quick end of the story, her head slightly tilting as her ears fall just a bit. "That is all?"

Preston shrugs. "Yep." He cocks a smile to the stare across from him. "What you thought there'd be more? Well so do I." He pats to the amulet under his shirt as he trails on. "I'm terrified, not because of some nightmare, no, but because I only remember a second of it. I only remember a second, Clover. The mirror, me staring at it, and then the claws. I'm not an idiot Clover, I saw how late it was when I woke up, I slept all night and I can only remember a second of what happen to me."

Clover shakes her head. "It was a dream Preston, they are fleeting, hardly something to remember great details of?"

"Right." Preston chuckles again, not knowing how to process the sudden mixture of emotions now starting to bubble in his gut, however not having to worry about them as the tug of war begins to play in his mind, the amulet quickly pulling ahead. "But I don't remember anything else, just that room, and just the sounds. I blacked out, and when I woke up, I get to see you, look at your arms Clover, I don't remember that, I don't remember any of it."

Clover moves her hands under the table as she leans forward. "You did not hurt me Preston you-..."

"Yea?" Preston chuckles as he pounds his hands softly into the wood of the table, his voice coming to a hushed yell as he rambles on, his face now brushed with his frustration. "Clover I don't remember. Look, answer this, h-how'd I scratch you huh? How'd I scratch you with my nails?" He turns his hands to the woman as he stares to the chewed off parts of his nails. "How'd I scratch you like this?" His chuckle continues, a maddening sound playing forth as he finds himself unable to stop. "I bite my nails because I'm jittery, I'm jittery because I can't think straight. I'm numb, all my thoughts are scattered, I feel like I'm only saying and feeling half of everything, I'm watching each day, not living them! But I can't take this damn thing off because I'm scared, I'm terrified of what would happen, what I'd feel. I'm tired all the time, Clover... I'm tired of being lonely, tired of fear, tired of what I might have to do, and-and above all else I can't stand the guilt."

"Guilt?" Clover merely blinks to the comment as she speaks up. "What are you guilty of?"

Preston merely chuckles, his eyes tearing up as he rocks in his seat, unable to reply.

The man's howling only prompts Clover on, her inquisitive and somewhat controlling nature egging on her questioning. "Preston, Preston?"

"W-what am I guilty of?" Preston continues to revel in his crazed giggles as he drifts a hand to his amulet. "Why don't you ask Damien, or-or Matt? Better yet, why don't you just take a look in the mirror, see what you get to see. Because I don't see myself anymore, do you?" He turns his head to the ceiling as he continues to just smile. "Oh that's funny." He continues to laugh. "Y-you know, I hate this thing, but I can't do this, I can't think about this right now." His hand sparks up in a green glow as the amulet's subtle spell sparks up. A rushing wave of euphoria now taking hold over the man's smile, though as he pants the smile merely folds, leaving a gasping husk of stillness where Preston once sat, emptied of the emotions which once began to surge.

Clover springs to her hooves at the sight of the spell, a look of surprise and concern taking hold as she moves a hand to his shoulder. "Preston?"

The name prompts Preston to close his mouth as he resettles in his chair, his hands drifting to his lap as he speaks up, a low and broken tone calling forth. "I'm here."

Immediately Clover's voice spikes up, calm though evident sound of her temper. "The spell was designed to help your emotions, Preston. When did you start doing this?"

Preston just shrugs, his eyes half-lidded as he does. "I always touched it, I could feel it scratching against my chest, so... I started helping it."

Clover blinks to the words as she pulls the amulet to her hand, never once attempting to pull it from the man. "You will drain it."

"So." Preston cocks a smile as he looks away. "It drained before without me using it, so what if I make it faster. It's doing its job."

"Job?" Clover tugs to the man's shirt as she draws his gaze back to her. Despite her tone, Preston stays, his eyes pinned to the soft look Clover has on display. "You are no *Atémor*." Clover shakes her head. "How can I make you believe that?"

Slowly tilting his head, as if he were just waking from a dream, Preston moves his right hand to Clover's arm, the snail's pace drawing Clover's attention as he rubs to the marks on her arm. "I don't think you can." He clenches his hand as he swallows hard. "Sorry."

He takes his hand back as he slumps into the seat, the amulet now falling to his chest as he drops from Clover. "I think I'm gonna go sleep."

Neither say anything, and neither move, despite Preston's words. Instead, Clover remains standing at the table, with Preston merely focusing into the drink he hardly sipped at.

Yet, as the moments drag on Preston finally begins to shift, his legs bringing him up as Clover steps aside, her arms crossing as she turns her gaze to the ground.

Though as Preston moves past the woman, Clover speaks up, her know-it-all tone gone, and her aggravation now replaced. "Preston... just." She sighs as her arms uncross and plant to her hips, her head coming up as she stares the man down. "Just let me see the amulet more often."

Preston nods, tucking the piece of jewelry back into his shirt as he glances to the stairs. "Okay."

Clover sighs quietly as she too glances to the stairs and then back to the man, though she longs to say more she finds herself unable as she merely lingers in silence.

Inevitably, Preston again speaks up as he nods his head. "Sorry.... I'll uh... I'll see you in the morning."

Clover nods, her trot bring her back to the table as she replies. "Of course, sleep well, Preston."

As the man starts towards the stairs Clover's eyes turn to the book still at the table. Though as Preston's steps begin to echo into the house her attention instead turns to the work Preston and Reynard so neatly set aside from the table.

Chapter 11

Just Don't Think About

"...Ugh, he's at it again."

The obsessive thumping of music coupled with the all too frequent shouts of anger finally snap Preston as he tosses his pencil into the anatomy book. His unfinished notes pushed aside as he simply runs his hands against his scalp, an annoyed sigh bellowing from him.

The morning is still young, and the weather right now is cold. The sounds of the city have been relatively tame today, which at first led Preston to believe he could actually do some studying for his upcoming exam. Yet, this thought was quickly dashed upon learning of his newly acquired responsibility of the day. Perhaps the most annoying part of the arrangement was the fact that the younger teen Preston was tasked with looking after was supposed to be sick. Hardly something that would call for blaring music from down the hallway.

With one more sigh Preston stands up and turns towards the door of the room. The floor is a minefield of game controllers, wires, overturned shoes, and clothing, though Preston masterfully navigates the mess as he moves to the door.

The man's speed quickly brings him into the hall as he now sets his eyes to the closed door near the end of its length. The sound of Preston's knocks are barely heard over the music however as he instead opts to call over it. "Hey! Hey, dumbass!"

With no reply or sign of the door opening Preston bangs to it one more time before opening it "Hey, I can't hear myself think-..."

Preston's voice comes to a halt as he looks the younger kid over. The room is a bit dark and the shades are shut, but the glow of Matt's compute lights his face up well enough for the older man to notice something. Matt's eyes are red and he looks upset sighting this, Preston speaks up.

"What's wrong with you, lose a game or something?"

"Get out, Preston! Why don't you ever knock?!" The sharp reply breaks

Preston's lower tone as he walks over to the blaring speakers on his right. As he turns the music down, he replies with a sarcastic laugh. "Don't yell at me, shrimp, you're the one trying to wake the dead

Despite the lack of noise now holding their conversation off Matt's voice still carries some boyish height to it as he yells. "Get out! Leave me alone!"

A stern finger comes up from Preston as stare the younger teen down. "I'm just turning the music down!"

Matt waves the comment off as he speaks up. "Congratulations, you did what you came in here to do, so fuck off."

Preston crosses his arms. "Watch your mouth, Matt."

A slight laugh comes from the kid as he sniffles a little. "*Oooh*, yea, I'm so scared. Get out of my room."

The annoyance of the conversation builds a little more as Preston takes a step forward. "Okay, first off you're supposed to be sick, and second off when everyone's gone, I'm in charge of babysitting your ass. Show some respect."

"I don't need babysitting!"

Preston just chuckles to the comment as he speaks up. "Yea, right. Just keep the music down and we won't have a problem."

A flash of anger comes to Matt's face, but he never stands from his chair as he speaks up. "Go to Hell."

Preston blinks to the comment. "Matt watch your mouth."

Matt chuckles at the comment as he leans back in his chair, his eyes coming back to his game. "Fuck you, hit me, see if I don't tell my parents how you act, see if they don't toss you onto the streets. Shit I'll even tell them to drop you off where your parents got hit; think I'm scared of you, you fucking dumb-..."

"Enough-..."

"No!" Matt pauses his game, again never raising from his chair as he speaks up. "You wanna do something hit me, if not fuck off."

Preston rolls his tongue to his cheek as he attempts to stare the kid down, though Matt merely laughs as he turns away, his ranting continuing. "That's what I thought stupid ass bitch, go cry to your therapist.".

"You know what..." Preston's words break as he laughs a little, though he trudges on as he nods. "You can sit here and cry over a video game or whatever you're doing. Because you have nothing in your life to complain about, Matt, fucking nothing. You're an upper middle class, white little prick, trying to act out for no reason. You don't need any medicine, you're just a self-centered, manic-depressive piece of shit."

Matt just laughs to the comment, though Preston continues, a stiff finger pointing to him as he does. "Don't fuck'n laugh, because everyone's patient with you, poor Matt he's depressed. Everyone's depressed, welcome to the world." Preston throws his hands up as he pretends to cry. "Boo-hoo, mom, mom I don't feel so good, I'm sick, I can't go to school and get beaten up because I'm a fuck'n psychopath and I can't stop staring at Trenton's girlfriend, ma! Keep me home, oh fuck'n buy me a skateboard, that'll make me cool or-or buy me some computer so I can jerk off to-..."

"Get out, Preston!" Without a moment of hesitation Matt tosses his keyboard across the room, though it misses Preston entirely as it slams into the wall, its pieces scattering around the floor as Matt begins to incoherently scream obscenities.

Matt turns his rage towards his computer as he slams his fist into the computer, causing the screen to bend around the teen's hand. As Matt continues to thrash wildly, Preston's eyes turn to the dresser on his right, his mind quickly snapping from his own anger as he rushes towards it.

Matt continues his assault of his own desk as Preston all but tosses out the top drawer, taking hold of the pills as he lunges back to Matt. "Stop, stop! Put this in your mouth."

The words do nothing to Matt as he bats to Preston's hands. "Don't touch me!"

Preston grows furious as he looks over the trashed computer Matt sits in front of. "You're going to hurt yourself, just take the damn pill!"

Matt throws himself to the ground as he attempts to hide his face to the man, though Preston merely follows after him as he tries to roll him over, the bottle rattling to his movements. "Stop! Just stop moving, Matt!"

"Get off me! I don't want it!" Matt continues to force himself away though Preston hangs on as he replies.

"Stop, stop! You're gonna be fine, just take the damn medicine!"

Chapter 12

Dirt, Rocks, and Trains

The low sound of the wood door cracking in the morning's unique air brings Preston from his dream. His eyes darting open as he stares to the window just beyond his bed. His face takes on the warmth of the sun outside as he looks out to the clear blue-bird sky now taking over the world. Yet his admiration to the world before him is quickly pushed aside as he turns to the woman standing at the door.

"Ugh..." Preston gives a quick sigh as he rubs his hands to his face. "Sorry, did I sleep in?"

Clover gives a simple shake of the head as she pushes the door open a little more. She is dressed in her normal everyday attire, but her slightly unbrushed hair suggest that Preston is not too far behind the rest of the house.

"Not at all, though I am glad to see you awake." She taps a finger to the doorknob as she continues. "You slept well? Nothing you wish to talk about?"

Preston shakes his head, slowly pushing the memory his dream brought up further from his thoughts. "Nothing special, why?"

"No reason." Clover tugs a bit more to the knob, but she releases her hold on it as she steps into the room a bit more. "You will be accompanying me; I will be seeing the *Jartál* again."

"Okay, uh... alright." With a rather noisy stretch, Preston moves from the bed. Yet, as he stands he takes notice to Clover's sudden change in gaze, her slight look of surprise quickly reminds Preston of something as the he cooler air now hitting his chest. He swiftly moves to collect one of his few shirts as he plays off Clover's lack of attention. "Got a little hot last night."

Clover shrugs as she speaks up, her chanced glance back to the man confirming that he has put a shirt on. She folds her hands as she continues to fumble where best for her eyes to go. "I suppose it is my fault, I should not wake you like foal." She perks up a little as she cocks an eye to the man. "Do you feel well, nothing happened last night?"

Preston blinks to the comment as he shakes his head. "No? Did-did I do something?"

A laugh comes from Clover as she shifts in her stance. "No, no, nothing... it has been rather warm,

"I know right?" Preston's cheerful smile holds as he remains unaware of Clover's skeptical gaze. Though his pleasant voice continues with a slight tug the waistband of his pants. "I've never really worked out or anything. I mean I'm not fat." He chuckles. "But I think this forced diet and consistent walking around has definitely made a difference."

A light-hearted chuckle rolls from Preston as he moves his hands from his pants and to the amulet dangling at his neck. The stone within it is dull, though he nonetheless drops it into his shirt as he trails on. "Now, don't get me wrong, I still want a big, greasy cheeseburger. Ahhh, yea, that-that would be solid."

With the amulet now out of view Clover merely stares to the bump at Preston's chest, awaiting to see any change, though she forces a friendly smile all the same as she replies. "As I have heard."

"Ha-ha, I don't think you'd like it but…" He shrugs as he turns back to the dresser, pulling out a fresh pair of pants. "Reynard would."

"Perhaps." Clover gives a simple nod as she loosens her hands from where she has them folded. "Breakfast is ready, come down soon."

"Yep, just gotta change and brush my fangs." Preston glances around the room for his boots thought he cocks a bright smile to Clover as he nods. "Hey what's my official title by the way? Am I like ambassador of Earth or Consultant of New Technology, I doubt you're bringing me along to write for you again?"

"Official titles are not simply given out, Preston." Clover pastures as she nods, Preston's more cheerful expression slowly pulling back her know-it-all tone. "Though I suppose you would be a consultant if any questions arise that I cannot answer."

"*Pff,* so basically I'm going to stand next to you the whole time." Preston chuckles. "Whatever's fair, let's just hope I don't scare anyone."

Clover squints to the comment as she speaks up. "You hardly look menacing Preston, though the fur on your face could scare a few." The words spark a shared laugh between the duo, only helping to spur Preston on as he nods. "So, you gonna just stand and watch? Not like you haven't seen this aliens naked before."

The simple smile on Clover's face fades as she nods, a sudden silent taking hold to the room as Clover's posture drops. "No, Preston, and it is a gaffe that we have known one another."

The word goes unregistered to Preston, though the polite yet cold tone of the woman ends Preston's joking as he shakes his head. "You know I was just kidding Right? Clover I don't-…"

"I know." Clover's hand comes to the doorknob as she fiddles with it, her body almost leaning towards the hallway behind her as she trails on. "It is not a bad thing… just a mistake."

Preston's neck tingles, mostly from the confusion and slight embarrassment of the woman's eyes, though he scratches his nose as he replies. "Wh-what was the mistake, Clover ha-ha?"

The satyress' gaze shifts to the bulge at Preston's chest, though she does not let it linger as she nods. "I do not wish to have this conversation again Preston... I... understand your thoughts and I apologize but."

Preston gives a little laugh as he again scratches to his nose. "No, no, you're fine; you were just using me for some magic ritual, I saw the book."

Clover remains calm as she replies. "So, you recall last night?"

The man shrugs as he begins to unfold the pants on the bed. "I remember enough."

"Very well." Clover looks around the room as she continues. "Then I do not wish to talk, the amulet is to help temper normal emotions, nothing beyond it."

"Well it works good both ways." A cocky smile pops to Preston's face as he awaits a response.

Sighting it, Clover's ears perk up. "You will not be using the amulet whenever you please, you can talk through your feelings and-..."

"Talk through-..." Preston laughs, though the cynical chuckle is not one of crazed emotions like last night, and the man quickly follows through his broken sentence as he nods. "And-and how do we talk ha-ha, I really don't think you know a spell for this." Preston trails on. "In fact, I bet if there was one, you would have done it already, I really, really doubt you want to have this conversation."

For a moment Clover is silent as she continues to shift between Preston's eyes and bulge of the necklace under his shirt. However, Clover finally brings her voice up as she settles to the man's ever sheepish leer. "I cannot have feelings for you Preston." Clover shrugs, her gaze fixed, her back tight, and with nary a hint of emotion to her tone. "It is that simple."

The stillness in Clover's voice is harder to hear than a scream, and it cuts far deeper than the sting of a blade as Preston is left speechless for a moment. Clover staring staying unflinching even as the man finds his voice. "But did you?"

The satryress's stance is stern and her expression remains the same, though she pauses just for a second before she answers. "Preston, I-..."

"Clover?"

The boyish voice from the hallway breaks the conversation as both Preston and Clover turns to hall, Clover now pushing the door open as she speaks up. "Yes, Reynard?"

"Is everything okay?" His eyes drift towards Preston but they never linger as he continues. "...you two were talking kind of loud."

Clover flashes a little smile as she takes a step into the hall and next to the young fox-boy. "Oh yes, everything is fine. Preston just had a bad dream."

Reynard just nods to the comment as he turns to Preston for some sort of confirmation. Naturally, Preston smiles to the innocent face now turned to him. "Y-yeah, yeah, I'm fine, just a little thing, nothing major."

Clover's voice quickly takes Reynard's attention as she speaks up. "Yes, well, I am heading out a little early. If you two wish to join later I will be near the Town Hall, there will be a gathering." The satyress gives a simple nod to Preston as she moves from the doorway and towards the direction of the stairs.

Her voice calls back to the hall as she begins to descend. "Make sure you eat something, Reynard."

Reynard moves from the doorway as he replies. The absent sight of him however sparks a motion in Preston, as he now moves his boots back to where they sat before, he picked them up.

The quiet in the room does not last too long however, as the tap-tap of Reynard's feet comes back to the door. "Are you hungry Preston? Clover does not seem to be stopping for breakfast."

Blinking to the comment he glances to where he just tossed his shoes, though he fakes a smile all the same. "Uh, yeah buddy, uh, I'll be down in a little bit. You can eat without me if I take too long."

"Okay." Reynard once again moves from the doorway; this time however he waits a moment until the sound of Reynard's claws against the stairs greet his ears. As they do, he sits back to the unmade bed and begins to look out the window, his mind merely trying to process Clover's easy escape.

The sky has grown brighter, still with no clouds in sight; beyond the roof of the house across the road Preston can see the rolling fields that encase the sleepy little town. The fields are an ocean of green, their growth swaying to the winds, even from what little Preston can see of them. The motion itself is calming, allowing Preston the time he needs to collect his thoughts before he finally stands again. The man continues to stare out the window as the sound of the door downstairs closing rings through the house.

(Later)

It has been about thirty or forty minutes since Clover and Preston's little chat, and since then Preston has taken his sweet time avoiding anyone by staying upstairs. However, with little left to do but brush his teeth again Preston finds his thoughts drifting more to the world beneath him. Soon enough his better half wins, half out its desire for food and half to ensure Reynard is well.

"*Plestá déy*, Preston..." Reynard's voice takes the man by surprise. He stands but halfway down as Reynard calls to him, though before Preston can reply the fox-boy trails on, his big eyes turning towards him as he does. "Are you feeling well?"

Preston shoots back a simple smile as he nods. "Yeah, I'm fine."

"Okay, did you want something to eat? I can make-..."

Before Reynard can finish the sentence, Preston waves him off. "It's alright, I can do it." The man looks over where Reynard sits again as he takes notice to the open book in front of him. "You just enjoy your story."

Reynard gives a little smirk as he turns back to the book on the table. "Have you ever read this?"

The man's eyes turn now to the extra pile of scrolls that now occupy a once unused cubbyhole near the stairs. "Clover do these?"

Reynard glances to the scrolls as he answers. "She was up early, she must have."

"Right." Preston clears his throat as he drifts towards the table. "Sorry about that, what'cha reading?" He studies the title for a moment though as the gibberish begins to form on his tongue he speaks. "What is that... *Jé mořo ó Lóva?* Nope, never seen that one."

The man's slight chuckle is followed by Reynard's own light giggle as the boyish voice now rushes back. "It is about *Gráf the first,* and how he stopped the *Jéfars* from overrunning a city with his magical sword *Nifty.*"

Another slight laugh comes from Preston as he cocks his head. "Wow, magic sword huh? Nifty? That's uh... that's a good name."

"Yes?" Reynard looks back to the book as his confusion holds. "It is one of the most powerful swords given by the old *devún.*"

"I guess you caught that sarcasm." Preston shrugs as he begins to explain himself. "Sorry, I just, that word already kinda has a meaning to me."

"Really?" Reynard cocks his head. "What does the word mean in your tongue?"

Preston shrugs again. "Like uh, cool, you know neat but like in the badass way, not the oh it's really clean or cold sort of thing." Preston rubs his neck. "Did that help at all?"

Reynard slowly nods his head as he speaks up. "Ass is a flank right? So, it means an ugly rear?"

A simple laugh comes from Preston as he shakes his head. "No, no, badass means like..." He looks over the innocent face as he clears his throat. "You know what forget that word. Nifty means like something is good, yeah that's better."

Reynard flashes a toothy smile as he nods. "Yeah! Then the sword is badass!"

"Ha-ha." Preston gives an awkward finger gun to the fox-boy as he smiles. "Maybe don't say that around Clover." He blinks to his words. "Come to think of it, you don't repeat things I say when it's just you and me right?"

Reynard shrugs as he pulls the book closer to him. "I am not a foal, I know what is not appropriate around a mare, Preston."

Preston just rolls his eyes as he nods to the comment. "Great we just invented guy-talk, not really something to be proud of but... it's kinda badass."

Reynard copies the man's sly smirk, though he loses it as his more inquisitive mind takes hold. "Preston, how are you not from *Artésque* but you know New-Tongue? You even know words Clover does not know and she studies the tongues of Éordiarx?"

Again, Preston just shrugs as he speaks up. "You know, I think about that sometimes, but I don't really have an answer for you. Where I'm from it just... it's not like this."

"Hm." The Reynard merely nods, his face suggests some sort of disappointment though he remains far too polite to pursue an answer.

Instead, he points a paw to something else on the table. "Do you think about going home a lot? Because Clover left this for you."

Preston turns his attention to the glowing, light cream crystal sitting in the middle of the wood table. "She left it huh?"

Reynard nods. "Yes. Clover charged it."

Preston gives a sarcastic laugh as he shakes his head. "Thought she said never to leave it out?"

"She did. But I do not think Clover was thinking too much, she also forgot her book on *télpréith*... are we going to see her later?"

Preston pauses for a moment as he straightens his posture. "She needs the book?"

Reynard nods to the question.

With a faint sigh Preston shrugs. "Then yeah, I guess we can bring it to her. Just let me get something to eat and we can go."

"Alright. Oh, could we also see Bella? I think Clover wanted to talk to her." Reynard's snout almost transforms into a full-on smile as the fox-boy's obvious lie awaits Preston's answer.

"Well we are supposed to keep the library open, don't you think?" Preston chuckles a little. "Kinda hard to do that if we stay gone all day."

The comment breaks Reynard's smile, but the fox-boy nods as he speaks up. "Yes... knowing Clover she will not leave until her task is completely finished."

"But... if we get the book to Clover quick, I guess we could stop by Bella's, it's just the other side of town." Preston does not wait for Reynard's comment as he turns back to the kitchen. "We'll get the book to Clover in a minute."

Chapter 13

Pains On Track

The venture through *VéturVill* has trailed on for perhaps ten or so minutes now, however, unlike yesterday heading to the Town Hall does seem as tedious. Sure, the houses are nothing special, being that all of them are normally two story, wooden homes, but the sight of them lining the one main street Preston and Reynard travel is nice. Unlike other larger towns or cities that Preston has seen *VéturVill's* main street is rather roomy, of course the lack of carriages could explain that. Still, a few six-legged *Yáppys* and their various carts are passed by on their way to the market, a welcome sight that sadly was avoided yesterday with Elva's knowledge of the side streets.

The air is fairly warm, and the sky is clear, which have helped to form a few beads of sweat on Preston's forehead, though his perspiration is hardly enough to take his attention. Instead, the man finds himself focusing in on the anxious feeling tumbling in his head at the sight of so many new faces. Luckily this strange bit of anxiety is slowly, yet surely being worked off by the amulet Preston toys with at his chest. Preston also finds some solace in the fox-boy's cheerful demeanor, which helps to keep Preston talking, no matter how foolish or unimportant his comments are. "You know, I use to avoid books all the time. Now, I can't seem to get away from them."

Reynard turns his head to the taller man beside him as he speaks up. "Really? Is that why you are slow at reading?"

A slight laugh comes to Preston as he shakes his head. "No, I just get caught on some words." Preston squints to the road in front of him as a thought comes to mind. "You know, come to think of it, there are a lot of books with New-Tongue. How is that? You guys still have to be using old printing presses, right?"

As expected, Reynard blinks a little confused to the comment. But, the fox-boy answers it as best he can. "Most books are formed by the *Únoffs*, there are a few spells that duplicate writing. Clover knows some, but she says they are too hard to focus on."

"Hm, how come the almighty Clover can't do them?"

Reynard gives a slight smirk to the comment as he answers. "She is not a student of *Alcrex̄ Márjx*."

"Ah." Preston just shrugs. "Silly question… what are the schools again?"

As Reynard readies himself to reply Preston takes notice to his straightened posture and almost joy filled expression. Undoubtedly, Clover's enjoyment of being smarter than everyone has rubbed off on Reynard, and at least for this, it shows. With a smirk, Preston listens in. "There is *Eñchar Márjx, Alcrex̄ Márjx, Coñjro Márjx, Diśtro Márjx, Álter Márjx* and *Héthtex̄ Márjx*. Although, most call those who study *Héthtex̄* healers. While each school brings prestige to a family, most consider *Héthtex̄* and *Alcrex̄* to be less than desirable."

"Why?"

Reynard shrugs to the comment. "I do not know, I just have heard Clematis say it a few times."

"Hm." Preston gives a simple laugh. "You could probably tell me a little about each one huh?"

Reynard nods. "Of course."

"Not bad, that's pretty neat."

A smirk comes to Reynard's face at the comment, though he merely rolls his hand to the man. "Every *Únoff* knows it." His smile fades a little. "Even me."

Preston brushes a hand to the fox-boy's head as he shakes his head. "Hey, you're more of an *Únoff* than me." He turns his attention to something down the road as he pauses. Reynard too takes notice to the echoing sounds, as his ears poke up a little more.

The dark wood and stone made building layered with the hay-like roofing that Preston knows as the Town Hall looks to be under siege. A mass of people gathering at its doors, most are short and even from this distance Preston can tell that the crowd is predominantly *Dẃoff* with a few *Flóff* poking up throughout the mob. Though no pitchforks, torches, or even picket signs, grace Preston's sight. Yet, the horde of yells that emanate from the Town Hall are loud, and the mass of shaking fist could potentially start a tornado as far as Preston is concerned. Sight this and realizing that neither's pace forward has stopped Preston takes a step forward, ensuring that the fox-boy stays behind him.

Preston's voice deepens a little as he scans the crowd that takes up most of the road in front of the Town Hall. "Reynard, I want you to stay close, got it?"

The fox-boy slowly nods as he speaks up. "It looks like half the town is out here... I have not seen everyone this angry since Princess Clarity put a new tax on *Dẃoff* drink."

Preston and Reynard's pace slows as they near the mass of short dwarf-pig people. The mob's yells are now more audible as Preston and Reynard stand at the back simply soaking it all in.

"What be this new Únoff project?!"

"It be a tax!"

"We did not warrant this!"

"Why does the Princess act as Chancellor Clay?!"

"This is our town, not them Únoffs!"

"This is our home, not an Únoff hold!"

The angry mob continues to erupt as Preston looks past the bobbing heads and shaking fist. Luckily for Preston his height allows him to see over the crowd, where as Reynard continues to try and jump to see over the hairy, pig-nosed people in front of him.

Preston's eyes quickly get ahold of the mob's directed comments. The autumn haired *Jartál* Preston met once before stands at the front of the crowd. Surprisingly, Preston can see her, meaning there must be some platform in the front. However, the look of bewilderment on her face and slow hand gestures to try and quell the mob before her only suggest that she has no control over the situation, and the mob knows it. To her sides stands a few *Dẃoff* guards and undoubtedly her cabinet of advisors. Sadly, no one really looks to have any suggestions as they all just stand in the same dumbfounded way as Caféll.

However, to the left of the hardly audible *Jartál* stands another familiar face, Clover. And judging by her facial expressions, the lack of control Caféll is demonstrating has started to affect her.

The rage filled and confused comments continue for only a moment more as Preston watches Clover's hands take on a fairly bright blue glow that can even be spotted from his position in the crowd. Within moments a loud explosion of magic comes over the crowd, most, including Preston jumping to the noisy display.

However, the silent shock only lasts a moment as a commanding feminine voice starts up in the front. The slightly know-it-all and higher pitched yell is immediately recognized by Preston and Reynard as they listen in.

"**Enough**! You all have questions allow the *Jartál* to answer them!"

A voice next to Preston calls out at the end of Clover's statement. "Oi, and why should we listen to the Princess' saddled mare?"

The short man next to Preston uncups his hands as the crowd again erupts.

"*Aye!*"

A laugh comes from the *Dẃoff* next to Preston as he nudges him. "Oi, you be tall, start yelling, let the *Kloopéi* hear your anger."

Preston waves his hand to the comment as he speaks up. "Actually, I kinda wanna know what's going on."

"Oh I can says what is go'n on." The pig-man nods. "What be go'n on is be the *Únoff* stealing our jobs!"

Preston merely nods to the comment as he speaks up. "And how's that? What project are they talking about?"

The *Dẃoffs* blinks to the man though his anger does not subside to the question as he speaks up. "What it matter? It be an *Únoff* project, it be no good for our lot."

Once more, the crowd is silenced as Clover's voice manages to come over the crowd. Even bringing Preston's eyes back to the front.

"Listen!"

The *Dẃoffs* that were looking to Preston now turn back to the stage, he and everyone else watching as the *Jartál* waves a paper about. Her low voice barely a whisper in the wind from where Preston stands, unlike Clover's, but he makes out the words as he listens. "...here is the letter from the Princess. This project, known as the Artésque train system was developed by a *Dẃoff* inventor by the name of Lyon Dif and is backed by the *Únoff* leadership to prompt faster travels amongst the provinces of Artésque."

A voice rings out from the crowd as the *Jartál's* slightly rushed voice pauses for just a quick breath. *"Oi, what does it mean faster travels? We have carriages!"*

"Aye!"

"Aye, we have carriages!"

"I say the Únoffs pull the carriages!"

The *Jartál* again waves the paper as her voice comes over the crowd. "There is more, there is more... VéturVill has been chosen for the first test of the train system. Which when completed will make the trip to and from the Capital much faster."

"Maná!"

"No new Maná!"   *"It be more Únoff Maná!"*

"How does it work?!"   *"Explain it!?"*

The comments halt the *Jartál* as she studies the paper. "It-it says it would be too complex to explain."

The mob erupts again as fists begin to fly. *"Tis a lie!"*

"What be complex?"   *"AYE!?"*

"More Únoff lies!"

As the commotion of the crowd continues to grow Clover's eyes lock to the man towering over the mob towards the back. No words need to be said, as her gaze says it all.

Tapping to Reynard Preston bends down. "Run the journal up to Clover."

Reynard at first just blinks a little confused to Preston, but as he gives him another pat on the head he begins to move towards the outskirts of the crowd. With Reynard now moving towards the front Preston nods, prompting Clover to take notice to bobbing orange-red furred head moving around the mod.

With Reynard moving Preston speaks up, his eyes falling to the *Dẃoff* around. "Can you guys move, I wanna get closer."

Almost immediately the two *Dẃoffs* before him turn around. "Oi? What for, you be tall enough?"

"Well I want to hear." Preston nods. "I wanna know what these new taxes are, I wanna know how much these *Únoff* are gonna make me pay."

The two *Dẃoffs* slowly step aside, allowing Preston to step forward, he copies this explanation, and this slowly trek towards the front several times. Each time prompting the other *Dẃoffs* to nod in agreement.

As Preston begins his push through the thick mob Clover's voice starts to simmer the yells around him. "If you wish an explanation you will get it. Just please allow it."

Though Preston has helped, his efforts along with Clover's more commanding presence only lowers the shouts, not stops them. Nevertheless, Clover starts. "The train system is a means of faster travel that will hopefully, in time connect all of Artésque-..."

"You already said this!"

The comment is quickly silenced as Clover pushes forward. "The train is not run by magic..." The words settle the crowd a little more as Clover continues. "...Lyon Dif, a *Dẃoff* has created a steam engine that will-..."

"You what?"

The question pauses Clover as she refocuses to the confused and more annoyed crowd before her. "A steam engine is a device that promotes movement through the use of heated water to move pistons and gears that rotate the wheels."

It is obvious that Clover has listened to Preston's various explanations of how the train works, however, the crowd and even the *Jartál* have an expression of doubt and laughter.

"How can heated water do this?"

"Aye!?"

A few more questions ring out behind and beside Preston, but Clover again begins to corral them as explains further. "Water is not turning the wheels; steam is operating pistons that turn them."

"Aye? And how can water be used to travel fast? There be no rivers from here to the Únoff Capital?"

Clover replies. "The water is carried on the train."

Another laugh rings through the crowd as more comments spring forward.

"The Únoffs are mud-kickers!"

"This will never work!"

"No Dẃoff would create something like this!"

"Tis more Únoff ambition, let it fail!"

As the mob that was once so filled with angry now begins to collapse in on itself in laughter Caféll makes her move. She steps in front of Clover as she shows her own smile. "Dẃoffs of *VéturVill* it has become clear to me that this plan is flawed. Yet the Princess of the *Únoffs* is paying for our participation, I suggest allowing this project for the *Ord*!"

"Aye!"   *"For the Ord'!"*

"For the Ord'!"   *"For the Ord'!"*

"For the Ord'!"   *"For the Ord'!"*

Caféll just nods at the comments as she speaks up. "Yes, yes for the *Ord'*!"

The laughter of the crowd continues as some members begin to turn away, their laughter ringing to the town. Sight this, Preston begins to fight his way to the front, something Clover takes notice to as she begins to move from the stage. It takes a few minutes for Preston to move past those still lingering, though as he does, he comes to the edge of the stage, where he finds Clover and Reynard.

Looking over the book in Clover's hand he speaks up. "Guess you didn't need our help."

Clover taps a finger to the book as she looks over the more cheerful crowd. "They laughed."

Reynard chimes in, his boyish smile turned to Clover as he speaks up. "Well at least they are not upset."

Clover's left ear flicks to the comment as she shakes her head. "Yes but-..."

"Miss Vines! Miss Vines!" Caféll steps down from the stage as she holds her shyster's smile. "Although I would not have suggested making the Princess' project a *Joás* I must say having the town laugh it off was brilliant. I am sure we will have plenty of workers here willing to make *Únoff* coin."

Clover does not share in the *Jartál's* enthusiasm as she replies. "It was not a *Fon, Jartál* Caféll, the train does run with the use of water, not magic."

The comment slowly drains the woman's bright smile as she lowers her voice to the satyress. "Clover, I have always regarded you with the utmost respect when it comes to advising for the *Únoffs* of this town. However, I must say, if this truly is the project, it makes a mockery of what the *Únoff* stand for. I mean really, steam as a means of travel? It is a bit strange."

"It will work." Clover motions to the book Reynard gave her as she continues. "I have an example of its mechanics."

"Hm…" Caféll just nods as she speaks up. "If you insist on it I shall look it over. But if you excuse me, we still must sway the workers."

Clover rolls her eyes to the comment. "Simply place banners around town, *Únoff Ord*, they will flock to it, no matter their understanding of it, this meeting shows that."

Caféll straightens her posture a little as she nods. "Yes well, unless I am mistaken, you must finish your work on the *télpréith*." Caféll gives a simple nod. "So, until next time Clo-…"

"It is finished. I have even begun a secondary path if the material fails to come through." Clover crosses her arms. "I think it best if everyone in your company understands this project."

"Excuse me *Jartál* Caféll, what about us?!"

The familiar voice quickly brings Preston's head to the smaller group of five *Flóffs* still standing where the mob of hairy pig nosed people were. Preston had seen some of them scattered throughout the crowd, but their joining together is something far more noticeable. Not just because of their height, but because of their polished, and well-kept armor and armament.

Caféll quickly changes her expression as she notices the group, taking the summons as a means to escape Clover as she moves towards them. "Oh, yes *Pexřá* Elva? What is it?"

Judging from Elva's crossed arms and annoyed expression the normally outspoken avian woman has been kept silent by the yells of the mob. Yet, despite her wait to talk her tone still carries her normal dominant spirit.

"You have cleared the air for the *Dẃoffs* now please explain to us why *Flóff* weather schedules have been changed?"

Caféll gives a simple smile as she waves the comment off a little. "Oh it is merely to help with the construction. It hardly changes the schedules."

Elva's expressions to the smile Caféll gives her does not change as she replies. "The changing of *Flóff* weather schedules with as little notice as you have commanded is strictly forbidden unless by *Flóff* decree. *Jartál*, I would have to report this."

The *Jartál's* smile falls from her face at the words, but before she can speak up Clover steps in. "Elva, you are being ridiculous-...."

Elva's wings flare out as she drops her laid back stance and takes a step towards the makeshift stage. "Do not overestimate our amity when it comes to matters of the *Flóffs*, Miss Vines."

The comment prompts a wide-eyed stare from Preston as he looks over Elva's serious and slightly vexed face. However, the simple and low "okay" that Clover replies with is really what takes Preston's attention as he now turns to the satryress's locked jaw, her teeth surely latched to her tongue.

The surly expression is dropped as Elva regains her posture and turns to the well-dressed *Dẃoff* once more. "*Jartál*, we expect a written and signed document from you explaining why our schedule has been shifted by *témont*." Elva's wings lower as she continues. "If we do not have a letter to send to *Pegpolis* your command is null." At the end of her sentence Elva and the other *Flóffs* spread their wings and takes to the sky.

The various speeds and strengths of their wings kick up a little dirt, which forces everyone on the stage to turn their heads for the moment. However, as the sound of the wings leave everyone's ears Caféll turns to the people behind her and near the entrance to the town hall. "Alright, we all have much to do! Come now, come now!"

As the sounds of a plan coming together begins to ring out in front of the Town Hall Caféll turns to where Clover and Reynard stand. "Miss Vines, I am not familiar with *Flóff* law, could you-..."

"Write the letter for Elva, of course." Clover's expression is almost blank as she nods. "I shall do this after I am finished here."

"Splendid, I am off." Caféll turns to Preston for the moment as she nods. "Thank you for your help, as always you are a shining example of civic duty and *Únoff* skill."

As the *Jartál* starts towards the hall's entrance Clover's voice comes up. "I will be home later. Thank you for bringing the book, I must have forgotten about it."

Reynard gives a little smile as he speaks up. "It was nothing, can we help here, Clover?"

Clover gives a little smile as she speaks up. "No, just go home and manage the library while I am away."

Preston now chimes in as he looks over Clover's dull face. "Come on, there's gotta be something we can do?"

For a moment Clover is silent, but she slowly nods her head as she speaks up. "Reynard, could you find my old journal. Master Nyota had me study The Three's Laws before, it would help with my letter. This one helps, but the others under my bed would have a bit more on their laws."

Reynard happily nods as he moves to Preston's side. "You can count on us Clover!"

Clover forces a smile. "Thank you."

Chapter 14

I've Seen This Chapter Before

The walk back to the library has sparked very different thoughts to both Preston and Reynard's minds than when they left earlier. Mainly the idea that the walk seems to be shorter, perhaps a result of watching the crowds get riled up.

"...so that's just how things are decided in town? No real meetings just a bunch of screaming?" A faint laugh comes from Preston, however he keeps his voice down as he and Reynard continue down the mostly *Dẃoff* populated street.

Reynard just nods to the comment as he holds his smile to the man. "Well, this is the first time any new project has been started in town. Most just use the inns as a place for rest until they continue to *Passvórtall*, so it must have been strange to hear."

Preston just shrugs. "But they don't even know what they agreed to?"

The fox-boy shrugs as he speaks up. "I do not know much about *polis̀* or *pliht*. But, I have heard Nyota explain it to Clover, he says that *polis̀* only works because none challenge its reason, none challenge their reason because there is none. Especially when coin is offered."

For a moment Preston is silent as he thinks over what Reynard has just said, however, the more the man thinks over the fox's comment the more Preston gets confused. With another laugh he speaks up. "So, *poliś* is government?"

Reynard cocks his head to the man as he slowly repeats the word. "They are the *Únoff* and *Dẃoff* words of how life is run."

Preston just nods as he takes in a deep breath. "Yep, government... still, the words of wisdom don't mean much." His words slowly drift away into the chatter of the passersby as he now focuses in on the library's front door.

The fox-boy next to Preston begins to slow his own pace as he takes notice to the same conglomerate of people Preston spotted in front of the library. "Oh, looks like the rush is early..."

"Yep."

As Preston and Reynard draw closer to the building a voice rings out from somewhere in the group of fifteen or twenty people.

"Oi! It be the tall one!"

Just as the voice rings out the group starts up in a laugh as both men and women alike turn to gawk at the taller blond-haired man.

A few members of the group continue their heckling as Preston and Reynard draw closer. "That Clover be no so smart now, huh? Steam wheels!"

A laugh rolls through the crowd as they somewhat block the door to the library, their jokes continuing. "Explains her choice in housemates, a tailless *Drágeff* and a *ro'ha tát*!"

Reynard chimes into the comment as both Preston and Reynard stop a few steps from the group. "I am *fróx*!"

"More like talk'n *nurín*!"

A member at the front of the group laughs as the short, hairy man points to Reynard, calling back to the voice that just rang up from somewhere behind him. "Nothing to eat there, just fur, like all dogs."

The fur on Reynard's neck stands up a little, though Preston chimes in as he looks down to the *Dŵoff* man before him. "So, you guys here for some books or not?"

The *Dŵoff* merely chuckles to the deeper voice Preston choose to use as he thumbs to the man standing over him. "Look 'ear, the *bafteñ* be upset! You seen it writing?"

Preston copies the laugh as he moves his hands to his hips. "That's funny, because I'm not kept around for writing, I'm kept around to keep the library quiet."

The words slowly wash away the *Dŵoff's* smile as the hairy, pig-dwarf nods. "Aye?"

Preston nods. "Aye."

The *Dŵoff* chuckles a little, thumbing to Preston again as he looks back to the group behind him. "Well there we have it." The *Dŵoff* turns back to Preston as he trails on with a laugh. "And 'ear we thought you was just a bed warmer for that *Kloopéi*."

Preston speaks up. "You buying something or not?"

"Aye, but your master be away." The *Dŵoff* shrugs, his hands coming to his pudgy sides as he postures. "So go on, tell us a *joás* about water, huh? Can it make me fly now too?"

Preston shakes his head. "No, but if you'd stopped being afraid of it, you'd smell better."

The *Dŵoff* lets out a laugh as he nods. "Aye? Would I smell like a mare as you do? What is that, soap? Women's water!" He takes a deep breath as he continues. "I smell like a man! Someone who knows their way around hard work."

From the behind the *Dŵoff* a feminine voice chimes in. "It would make stand'n behind ya better!"

A laugh rolls through the group including the *Dŵoff* at the front, though the hairy man just turns his attention to hose behind him as he calls out. "Who was that? Mary? Mary that you? You bet steam fix that jagged tooth Mary?" He chuckles as he prompts Preston, his pig-nose flaring as his laughs. "Come on tailless, would some steam fix that razor? After all, it be faster than a carriage, it can do anything!"

Preston merely blinks to the comment, the laughter rolling through the group once more only helping Preston to realize how truly ignorant this gathering is. Though, Preston moves his hands from his hips as he nods. "No, it can't do that. But, I'd bet if you showed the Princess a boiling pot you could persuade her to buy a new set of teeth, probably shinier ones too."

The *Dŵoff* at the front chuckles. "They hardly last, not with how she be using her mouth!"

Preston shrugs. "Told ya, you gotta bathe more often."

"Ha-ha! There be a *joás*!" The *Dŵoff* nods. "What else you think that Princess would do for a boiling pot?"

Reynard chimes in. "You should not speak ill of the *devún*."

"Quiet dog, the smarter folk are talk'n!"

"Hey, hey." Preston holds a smile as he leans in front of the *Dŵoff*. "We can stand here and make jokes all day about the Princess, but don't yell at my friend again."

The *Dŵoff* blinks to the man as he shrugs. "*Hmpf*, and what if I do?"

"Bite your tongue, Kalub." A shorter, fuzzy capped *Dẃoff* steps forth from the crowd as he pats the thicker, pig-nosed man. "It is obvious Clover does not keep the *brivtó* for it mind, think of his writing. So stop these *joás* before I have to make a wide enough *cáskte* for you."

A laugh comes from the group though Kalub merely shifts in his stance as he replies, nodding to Preston. "Ya think this soap user could hurt me Tiberius?"

"No, but in case he does, think of my poor back, you would need to be deep to cover your stench."

Again, the crowd chuckles to the comment, though Kalub shouts back to them as he nods. "Alright, alright, get your *dah-gah* books and shut your gobs!" The *Dẃoff* takes a step aside as he posts up against the wall.

Reynard steps forward as he speaks to Preston. "Find Clover's journal, I will handle this horde." His boyish voice calls over the chatter as he moves to the door and unlocks it. "If everyone returning a book could follow me, please, everyone else is welcome to browse."

Preston lingers, his eyes pinned to the crowd now moving into the library. Every *Dẃoff* carries a smile or smirk to their face, obviously enjoying the banter that was on display, though as Preston scans the crowd he turns to the *Dẃoff* still leaning against the house.

As a moment passes and the line of hairy, somewhat smelly pig-dwarfs pass by him Preston starts inside, yet not before a voice takes his attention.

"*Brivtó*, you will help Stony get out of this library quick, yes?"

Preston pauses at the door as he nods to the short, fur cap *Dẃoff*. "What do you need?"

"Good." The *Dẃoff* dips his hand into his satchel as he pulls forth a book. "Mark my name from your list, Stony, do not forget."

Preston takes the book as the *Dŵoff* continues. *"Plestá déy, brivtó."* Without a comment more the *Dŵoff* starts back into the street. Book in hand, Preston comes into the house.

Reynard has already been swarmed at the table, though Preston moves past the line as he plops the book down. "Stony's book drop off."

With a quick nod Reynard takes the book. "Okay."

A woman at the table turns a smile to Preston as she chuckles. "Care to give us some of your writing, dear?"

Preston just forces a smirk to the woman, his eyes somewhat pinned to the jagged smile. Of course, he steps away, nodding to the stairs as he steps away.

It only takes a moment for Preston to reach the upstairs hallway, the noise down below echoing throughout the house, much like the dreaded smell of the books and their binding. Loud as it is, Preston ignores it as he holds his eyes to the door at the end of the hall.

Sure, he has looked inside Clover and Reynard's room before, but the man has never truly been in it for any amount of time. The voices downstairs slowly begin to drift from Preston's mind as he opens the door and sets his eyes to the room.

The room is much larger than Preston's; the floor like the rest of the house is made of wood, but under each bed and in the middle of the room sits a large circular rug. The color scheme is an earth toned, brown and dark green, no real pattern is visible, but the layout of the color does bring a forest to mind. Preston's eyes slowly drift to the larger bed at the left side of the room. A fair sized, oak colored dresser sits beside it. Although two beds occupy the room, Reynard's side of the room does not really take up much space. The bed is much smaller for the fox-boy, and the chest at the foot of his bed suffices for the few items Preston has seen the *fróx* wear.

A simple desk and chair sits up against the window at the far side of the room with a few brass or silver items atop it desk. However, Preston's inability to identify the items quickly snaps the man's attention back to the bed he now stands in front of.

"Okay... under the bed."

Preston sits to his knees as he moves his hand under the bed. The motion quickly stops as he feels a fair-sized box.

It only takes a moment to pull the light-wood case from beneath the bed. There is no lock visible, but Preston still hesitates to open it, for fear of a magical safeguard. Setting this aside however, he opens it with ease as he stares to the box's contents.

To no surprise, the contents of this hidden box are nothing surprise, as nothing more than loose papers and a few journals greet Preston's eyes. Not that he had expected anything else. Preston looks over the journals as he laughs a little. "What is this a cheat-sheet on magic?"

As Preston thumbs through the pages he quickly notices something. All the words or at least what he thinks are words are in a completely different language, though a few detailed sketches catch Preston's eye. Not being able to read anything turns Preston's attention to the other journals as he sets it down.

Like the first, the next two, dull, leather bound books are filled with the same impossible to read language. The pages are dry to the touch, but Preston continues to thumb through them out of curiosity.

However, as Preston continues through the last journal something changes. Towards the middle of the book the text begins to change. The words, although English now resemble that of an elementary school student's handwriting. The spelling is fine although the words themselves look a little stressed or sloppy in spots.

For the first few pages Preston just glances at the text, reading only short parts. This of course sits fine with the man as he quickly realizes this journal is little more than a collection of notes for Clover's magic lessons, something she must have learned over her years.

With a sigh Preston begins to slump against the bed as he readies himself to get up and help Reynard. However, as he flips another page, he stops. Unlike the other books or even the start of this one, the next two pages are short, no writing in the margins, and no detailed pictures gracing them.

Preston's eyes move to the top of the page as he begins to read.

Half Harvest, second Évex

My respect for Master Nyota's waivers this night. This suggestion to keep a journal of my thoughts is Lóva, so too is this request to better my New-Tongue spelling. There is no point to this and writing it as such yields no better emotions.

I place no blame for my boredom to the devún; they have done so much in such a short time to aid in the learning of this strange tongue. I understand the reasons of únoteñ of The Three, especially with the Crystoreeñ now gone. I simply believe it will take many more cycles to get to the point the eldest devún desires.

Even now my thoughts stray. Master Nyota ensured that writing would clarify my feelings. Jéf dóf fon, as nothing is clear, and my mind only seeks answers.

I suppose this is my own doing, Master Nyota knows of my feelings towards home, perhaps this is a test to challenge my magic after such emotionally draining time.

As all trottor Únoffs I honor my mother and father, I wish to fulfil what is expected of me. As I promised when I left to study I would étrome their desire for me and Lord Faróuk to stay in touch at any possible time. However, I now find my trips home a burdin. I miss the home I knew in the Ouálll, although HefterÁll has allowed for expansion I see no point in it. Wealth is the power to do something worthwhile, land for only one yields nothing.

> *Yet, I still return home. Not for my inescapable fiándyo or even to please my father's demand, but simply because I know it is my responsibility. My prestige with Master Nyota and within the school of Álter Márjx is merely an inn for my journey's path. Like all stays, no matter how restful, I must leave soon.*

Preston squints to the next few words as he attempts to read past the ink blots in the paper. The spot of ink actually takes Preston off guard as he has never known Clover to leave any mess on a page.

> *... I am still yet to see Master Nyota's purpose. Reading my last entry only further sinks my heart as I know full well they are my own words, my own log to further feed these fires of frustrations. I have assisted in so much in the new land of Artésque and I am the only Vines to ever reach this level in any school of Márjx. Why must I settle? Jéf dóf fon, I now ask myself questions just as Nyota. I know my answers, I simply choose not to heed them. I must thank Lothario for this, of course, not to his face but in some way.*

> *For yúrfs I have searched for the answer to my unfortunate dústiny; only to now understand it has nothing to do with it. I have thought the noises in the other room a fántress for many of my visits. Lothario always wishes a room close to mine so that, as he calls it: may be closer to his little Clover. However, the low cries and moans of the house servant that night has always led me to believe otherwise. I am no prize to be waited for, nor am I a tempting mare for my future mate. I am no more than a promise of power. My repute furthering only aids in the spread of my name, a name soon to be bound, hoisted up upon another's house.*

> *Lothario has shown me night after night that I am simply his future pelf, legitimized with a bonding of names. Worse still, I allow this. I could discredit my name as well as my fiándyo by allowing myself to be no longer trogerloft. Though I am foolish, I am promised to the house of Faróuk my acts*

would not discourage a stallion of such grandeur, if anything a practiced mare would only satisfy him more.

My inkwell has begun to run dry despite the fact that the walls still groan with vigor. I dare not exit my chambers, but neither do I desire my cold bed. The fire at my desk has also begun to dim and with its fading light I find my thoughts of anger and sorrow now drifting to feelings of jealousy.

Nyota has suggested ending any journal with a question to be answered in the next. So, my question, why continue this?

As the last line on the paper comes to an end Preston quickly flips the page. However, it is not words that catch his eyes, instead, it is the finely ripped pages in the book's spine that take Preston's attention. There is no way of knowing how many pages have been torn out, but judging by the return of Clover's messy notes it would suggest a few.

Unable to read the rest, Preston's mind slowly begins to tumble with the question of why Clover ripped the other pages from the journal. Blinking back to the book Preston continues through it, skipping the nonsense Clover would call notes.

He thumbs through each page though nothing more comes of it. He closes the book as the rest of the pages appear blank. Though as he sets it down his eyes catch to the torn-out pages still safely kept in the box before him.

He hesitates, though his own curiosity gets the better of him as he fishes them out. One by one he unfolds them, only to find more of the *Unoff* gibberish, each appearing to be nothing more than notes on magic. Though as he continues his rummaging, he finds a half-ripped page. Picking it up he takes notice to typical handwriting he has seen Clover use, yet even this page is but a fraction of what it used to be.

Even still, Preston reads through it, a sense of wonder overcoming him as he finds Clover's more personal thoughts something far too interesting to put down.

...I am the daughter of the Vine's house, despite what Nyota's sickness could mean I would never be the next head mage for Álter Márjx. Nor would I be the Princess's next advisor. I am destined to be a figurehead, my alignment with Lothario will seal this fate. Not only have I fooled myself into happiness, but now I have torn myself away from the only person who has cared for me because of it. Nyota's time grows near, I only hope he lasts until the deed is done.

Comfort in the words of those untouchable is venom, their touch more of poison that dulls the sense of loss. I trouble knowing how relieving it can be.

Despite what Nyota suggested so long ago, I shall not be ending this with a new question to answer. Instead, I leave this note: the warmth in the bed only grows cold, so never leave a candle lit for someone to find it.

As Preston's eyes run the course of the line he pauses. Questions swirl in the man's mind, sadly, before the man can dwell on them the tap-tap of small claws nearing the door takes his attention. Preston quickly jumps to his feet, tossing the book and page back to the others.

Just as Reynard turns to the door's entrance Preston speaks up. "Yeah I got the box, but I don't know what one she wants."

Reynard nods. "No problem, I know it, can you take over downstairs?"

"Sure thing." Preston moves to the door though he pauses as he glances downstairs. "They calming down a bit?"

Reynard shrugs. "I think they care more for Clover's speech than the books they rent."

Preston nods. "Did someone say something to you?"

Reynard shakes his head. "No, but a few wished to make a *Fon* at your writing. They find it amusing that someone who works here has the writing of a foal."

With a roll of the eyes Preston starts downstairs, drawing a few glances from the audience beneath him as he descended.

Chapter 15

Soothing Melody

The night's air is crisp, and the chill is felt even through the magic filled furnace that runs in the hallway. The moon has yet to fully come out, but the world has a unique glow to it; of course, this is expected with the number of stars in Artésque's night sky.

While the balls of light that stud the sky are warming, the sight of them have always carried another feeling for Preston. A feeling of intense, and sometimes overwhelming loneliness.

Most days allow for easy distractions to sweep Preston's mind from his thoughts. Sure the world Preston resides in is medieval and the people are alien; but the same rules apply. Life is life, and it continues all the same, and despite Preston's feelings towards it. In a way, this has helped in Preston's efforts to soldier on, at least on the surface.

Still, for every shared laugh comes with it two bizarre events, or worse still some moment of true terror. For all of Clover's smiles or Reynard's charm there has never been a lasting feeling of belonging, which of course may be for the best, especially with the choice Preston now gets to make soon.

For the moment however, the night's silence as well as his own thoughts come to an end. Preston's ears latching to a sound downstairs, like a predator to their prey Preston stands, his focus to the sounds of hooves against the wood.

Moving to the door Preston stalls in the hallway, the low blue glow coming from downstairs drawing him closer, though ever slowing his approach.

The low chime of Clover's magic is strangely lower than normal, and as Preston reaches the bottom of the stairs, he notices only one ball of light has been placed in the room. Stranger still is the light wobble it possesses.

The man's eyes quickly turn to the satyress at the table. Already the inkwell Reynard set out is opened and the quill left on the table is now wet with ink as Clover continues to write.

Preston stops his approach as he clears his throat and begins to talk in a low voice. "You're home late, everything okay?"

Clover's right ear flicks and her head shifts from the paper in front of her as she gives a tired sigh. However, she does not reject the conversation as she simply puts the quill in the inkwell. Stretching a bit in her chair as she replies. "*Jartál* Caféll proved a bit difficult to talk with, and the example of the spell took some time."

The comment brings Preston closer as he nods with a faint laugh. "Yeah? All mighty Clover struggled with a spell?" Preston sets his eyes to the chair across from the woman as he laughs.

Clover replies in part with a light chuckle to the words, a yawn preceding her next comment. "No, it simply took a bit longer to make it perfect."

Preston scratches to his beard as he takes his seat. "It had to be perfect?"

The words straighten Clover's posture as she nods. "But of course, the *télpréith* allows materials for the project to travel with ease."

"You know, I was wondering about that. Why do you need a train if you can just teleport?" Preston's eyes turn to the wobbling ball of magic above him as he clenches his right hand. The warm feeling of magic bubbling just below his skin, unfortunately, his concentration stays to the voice across from him.

"A *télpréith* gets its power from the *Coñjro Márjx*, too much exposure has been proven to make its users um... a bit abnormal, though it works perfect for-..." Clover's voice continues but for the moment her words are halted as Preston sends his own ball of light green magic to better light the room.

The sight of his magic draws a further smile from Clover as she nods. "A *télpréith* is best served for those without a mind, thus it helps move certain material." She nods to the ball of magic. "You seem to have no trouble with that spell."

Preston watches the ball of light slowly ascending to the ceiling as he shrugs. "Yea it got easier." He takes a breath as he folds his hands. "So you've used that chalk circle, you gonna grow tentacles or something?"

"I only used it for a moment." A faint laugh rolls through Clover, but she turns to the paper laying before her as she quickly covers her laugh with a louder clear of the throat. "Perhaps we will use your *Gloftór* soon, it will be useful when you practice higher spells."

Preston shrugs, giving into Clover's choice in conversation. "I just need to practice my teleporting stuff a bit."

Clover nods to the words as she brings her eyes back to Preston, although the man still continues to stare at the balls of light above him as she begins. "Yes, your skills have improved, in no time, Master Nyota's stone should carry you home." Clover's voice quickly spikes up as she looks around the table. "Y-you did place it somewhere safe, yes?"

A quick laugh rolls through Preston as he crosses his arms and looks over the satyress' expression. "Ah a question of my reliability, good thing too, can't let all those complaints go to my head."

Clover gives a little smirk to the comment as she cocks her head. "I should not have to treat you as a foal. But if you wish, I can."

Before Preston can speak up the satyress continues, however Clover's voice takes on a slightly higher pitched tone as she reaches over the table towards Preston. "Preston, I am very proud of your improvements. This is a sign that you may yet be able to properly learn as an adult."

The smile to Preston's face stays wide throughout Clovers playful antics. However, it is not the tone that brought the smile but simply the fact that Preston got Clover to play along. "Wow, not bad, I almost believed you." Preston wags a finger to her. "You must be tired from doing everyone's work today, it's affecting your judgment."

"I did not do everyone's work... just most of it."

"Ha." Preston shakes his head as he speaks up. "At least you know how important you are. Helps the ego."

Clover simply sighs as she looks back to the paper in front of her. "Importance has a strange way of showing itself."

Preston's eyes drift to the paper in front of her as he speaks up. "Well it's Elva, she's got a strange way showing friendship... probably just got her feathers ruffled."

"Preston." A light giggle escapes Clover's mouth as she shakes her head.

"What? Come on, she's complaining about moving the clouds. Heck even if I understand that complaint, I would still call her crazy." Preston just shrugs as he gives his own light snicker. "You looked like you had a few choice words for her earlier, did you write it all done?"

Clover nods as she moves her hand to the journal Reynard and Preston put out earlier. "No. Elva enjoys structure. This is not the first time I have written a formal letter regarding the town's actions, and it will not be the last." A light sigh breaks her breath as she continues. "But, I do not understand why she demands it. It would make more sense to just ask me instead of waiting in town meetings." Once more the satyress' words halt as she looks over the work still needing to be done before her. "Well, I have kept you too long. I am sure you do not wish to watch me write."

Preston waves the comment off as he speaks up. "Watching you is better than staring at the ceiling."

A light smile comes to Clover's face as she squints to the man. "I am pleased to know I am more interesting than the ceiling."

Noticing the upbeat tone Preston quickly trails on with a grin. "What can I say. You got a certain appeal."

A laugh escapes Clover's smile as she looks herself over. "I believe what you see would be dirt and sweat, neither of which, I am sure Bella would suggest wearing."

Preston just nods to the comment as he looks the woman over. Clover's mane is a bit worse for wear than normal, though even that observation has become routine. Even still, a certain shy, cuteness comes from how she brushes it to one side. The rounded features of her face force a steep drop to her hair as it hangs from her.

The glow of the magic above the table makes her normally tan colored skin a bit lighter, and her already soft blue eyes are made even more gentle in the hue. The luster and calming affect her gaze has always held still shine, albeit a bit more dull from her obvious fatigue. Though some dirt and dust layer her clothing it is hardly noticeable in her attire's earthy tones. The laces of her tunic near her chest are loosened more than normal, a peasantry for her of course, though it reveals her seldom seen undershirt. Clover's figure does not boast any grand sight of cleavage, but even the slight dip of her undershirt is enough to keep Preston from truly noticing any blemishes of her outfit.

However, Preston's eyes do meet back to the woman's face. For a second or two Preston is silent his eyes simply drinking in Clover's body. Though Preston has noticed it before he has never truly dwelled on it, but as he looks her smooth skin over, he does now. No blemishes, unwanted bumps, or unsightly skin irritations have ever been noticed on Clover, or on any *Unoff* for that matter. A strange thing to accept in such a medieval world, but Clover is simply beautiful, a fact that none could deny, or at least as far as Preston is concerned.

Clover catches Preston's slightly lengthy stare, but before she can question it the man speaks up. "Bella can't suggest anything to you because she can't make someone amazing even more baffling."

The comment, as with most of Preston's intended complements does not receive a typical reaction from the woman. Instead of a light giggle as Preston thought, Clover merely nods with an almost apathetic tone. "That was quite nice, Preston. Even your words were more advanced."

The tone quickly brings Preston's voice up as he shakes his head, his gawking to the woman's perfection dashed as he finds himself pulled back to the reality of who he stares. "Why do you do that, Clover?"

The question comes as a slight surprise to Clover as the satyress now shrugs. "What do mean?"

Preston sighs as he fidgets in his chair a little. "Just take the compliment, it's true, so why fight that?"

A slight laugh comes to Clover, but the woman brushes Preston's tone off as she simply pulls the journal closer to her and takes her well inked quill to her hand. "They are directed to me, so I decide how I am to accept them. It was quite nice. Do you wish me to act more of a filly?"

"Well no. But, come on, Clover." Preston's shoulders and head lower a little as he slumps towards the wood table. "I meant it."

Clover squints to the comment, almost with a hint of confusion as she speaks up. "Dirt makes me appear more pleasing?"

Preston again sighs as he shakes his head. "Come on, you're too smart for me to spell it out."

The satyress once more places the quill back to the inkwell as she shakes her head. "Was this a complement, Preston? I honestly do not see how insulting my intelligence could be."

"No. I'm not insulting you, I-I just don't understand why you reject any comment about how amazing you are." Preston stammers on though says nothing more.

Clover's left ear flicks to the words, her tone however stays low as she continues to hold a slightly skeptical and confused eye to the man. "My skills with magic and *polis* are gained through practice and exposure. Any can achieve-..."

"No, see you're not understanding it again. I mean you're amazing, I see you how Nyota sees you, how Reynard see you." Preston's words quickly break through to Clover, her eyes blink away as she folds her hands closer together. Sighting her reaction Preston rapidly begins to add more to the passion in his voice. However, his thoughts are too quick to check.

"I know you don't like compliments, but I don't want you thinking you're worthless or just some prize to be won. You can do anything you set your mind to Clover; I've only known you for a short time and I can say that and mean that." A bittersweet smile comes to the man's face as his words start to get a little hard to push out, yet, despite the feelings Preston pushes through. "When I saw your journal today, I couldn't believe what I read. You're so much more... extraordinary, amazing, uh breathtaking, any word you want to use! You're so much more than what you think. Y-you make me feel like everything that has happened in my life has happened for a reason. You make this place so much better for me, and yet you act like you're helpless, like you can't do something if you want to."

Preston quickly notices Clover's silence as he begins to bring himself down. "Do you not know that? Because if you don't you need to listen and if you do you need to stop waiting."

A moment of quiet reflection fills the library with only the sounds of Preston slightly catching his breath bouncing from the wood.

The silence is quick to break as Clover speaks up. Her face is blank, and her tone is low and clear. "You read through my personal journal?"

The words and tone feel like a cold splash of water over Preston however, he answers plainly. "A few pages."

Clover does not nod or even shift in her chair as she speaks up. "Why?"

Preston blinks to the comment as his hands begin to get a little more animated. "W-well you asked me and Reynard to get the journal for you, yeah?"

"I asked for Reynard to get the journal-..."

"He was busy with the library, so he asked me." Preston's comment does little to stop Clover's thoughts as she continues.

"Even so, he did not ask you to read them."

The man shakes his head as a warmth begins to build to his chest. "So what you're mad that I saw it? I'm not, not if that's how you feel about yourself."

Clover just smirks to the comment as she nods to the table. "You read what, three pages? And now you wish for me to believe you know some profound truth about me?" Clover stays calm as she continues. "I asked to have my journal containing the Three's laws set out so that I could finish the letter and go to sleep quickly. Obviously if I am sitting here talking to you about what is right or wrong I am not finishing the letter. So I fail to see how you are helping."

Preston is speechless for the moment as he just stares to the woman across from him.

With a sigh Clover speaks up. "I am not mad that you looked through my belongings, I thought Reynard may leave them about. But what makes me upset is that you feel it is your place to judge me because of what you have read." Clover leans forward a little as she continues. "I tore out many pages from that journal, they yield nothing for me, an experiment Master Nyota suggested."

"But-..."

Clover shakes her head. "...you only bring this up because of what you feel. My thoughts are my own and I do not appreciate the insight on matters you know nothing about, Preston."

Preston shakes his head. "Yea, and what don't I understand?"

"You do not know me." Clover trails on, her hand rolling as if to paint some clearer picture for the man. "The only reason you wish to know me is because of our mating, it was as I have said, and as you have agreed to, a mistake. I do not understand your interest in me Preston, you speak as if I am the only thing important to you." Clover shifts her eyes from the man as she swallows hard. "It frightens me, Preston. It frightens me to know how much a stranger could influence you, but more than that I feel terrible being that person."

The end of the satyress' sentence adds the final nail to secure Preston's thoughts. "I-is that really how you feel?"

Clover slowly brings her eyes back to the man, but she does not look him in the eye as she speaks up. Her low voice says more than her words as Preston listens. "I am not afraid of what you are, Preston. You are no monster, and I will not further that notion. I fear the feelings you stir." A slight shake in her words at the end of her breath take Preston back. The thought of seeing Clover upset quickly takes Preston's mind as he speaks up.

"Alright, I get it."

The satyress' voice is low and her eyes continue to hang to the table as she speaks out once more. "Will you please leave me, Preston?"

Preston says nothing as he stands. His throat is tight and his eyes heavy with feeling, but he simply turns and walks towards the stairs with only the light chime of the two balls of magic behind him sending him off.

Clover sits at the table for a moment, merely listening to the man's steps. Though as he continues away she brushes a hand to her nose and swallows hard, her years of training over her emotions and thoughts kicking in as she opts to pop another ball of magic to the room as she focus back to her work, nay a thought more.

Chapter 16

Agility

It has felt like days since Preston came back upstairs, despite the fact it has only been a few hours. This fact of course does not find its way into Preston's mind. Instead, the only thoughts held are cold and bitter. The mixture of sadness and shock from the situation has not lifted, and now as the man continues to dwell on Clover's words it only worsens his state of mind.

Even the calm night and silent room around him does not quell his mind. This in part is from the amulet around the man's neck however. The low green glow of its stone and slight burning feeling of the metal has persisted despite how Preston prompts it spell. Worst still, the thought about simply removing the itchy amulet has begun to win in Preston's mind.

With a sigh Preston turns his eyes to the door. The hallway is of course not visible because of the door being closed, but it is the sounds in the house he pays more attention to. Nothing can be heard from the hallway and it has been an hour or two since Preston heard Clover walk to her room.

Still, Preston moves slowly from the bed as he plants his feet to the floor. However, something strange meets Preston's mind, the feeling of standing on carpet. Preston's eyes quickly dart to the floor, only the man's feet are not what greet his eyes. Instead, two clawed, furred covered appendages sticking out from where his feet should be.

"What?!"

Preston sits to the side of the bed as he pulls his shirt up and stares to the amulet. The skin where the amulet lays against has become darker and now burns with the cooler air brushing up against it. However, the man does not scream. Instead no fear fills his mind as anger now replaces it.

As Preston stares to the changes on his body he slowly begins to accept them. Almost instantly, the sensation of heat pressing against his body halts and as it does a low noise starts to chime in Preston's ear.

"Embrace me."

The green glow of the amulet continues into the room as Preston's hand slowly comes around it. Yet, just before he snaps it from around his neck the sound of a hand knocking on the door breaks his concentration.

The voice cannot be recognized but the words can be. "Preston, are you in there?"

For a moment the man just stares to the door as the low chime of magic begins to grow louder.

- - -

The call of Preston's name begins to draw the man's eyes open. The dark wood room is lit from the window, the cloth shade is closed but the room still glows with the morning light now shining.

The voice at first resembles Clover's, however, this quickly is proved untrue as the name and a stern knock at the door rings in once more. "Do you forfeit your challenge already, Preston?"

With a fast clear of the throat, Preston calls back and begins to sit at the edge of the bed. "Don't lose your feathers, Elva. I'll be out in a sec."

As Preston stands to put on his new wardrobe for the day he pauses, and looks to the amulet hanging in his shirt. Aside from the ever-thickening hair on his chest nothing looks out of the ordinary. He squints, unsure as to why he even checks, though he pushes the strange action aside as he attempts to recall his dream.

Unfortunately, the distant memory is brought to an end as Elva calls out again "You best not insult me, Preston. It will only lead to a more embarrassing defeat."

Preston just nods to the comment, not even truthfully giving the words much thought. "It's just a bet." As his breath ends he pulls a new shirt on and tosses his old one to the unmade bed. His trousers are quick to be replaced as he once more tosses the garment behind him.

He pauses to slip his boots on before opening the door.

Elva stands in the hallway, her toned and muscular arms are crossed in front of her polished steel top, the few colorful feathers sit above her right ear. If not for these her expression would be as plain as the polished armor she wears. "Clover will not be extending your challenge again."

Preston shakes his head as he rubs his hands through his fairly lengthy blond hair. "What are you talking about?"

"Your challenge, I shall not wait another *déy*."

Preston shakes his head, though the bet he recalls he does not remember a set day, something states plainly. "I didn't even know we had a day."

A slight smirk comes to Elva's face as she replies. "Your confidence is arrogance than?"

Preston just shrugs. "That's me." A light sigh comes from Preston as he pushes past Elva and turns to the bathroom's open door. "But I still expect to get my ass handed."

"I would not have the time to cut it all." Her smirk draws to an end as she watches the wood door close to the hall with Preston behind it. She moves towards the bathroom as she uncrosses her arms. "What are you doing? We are late already."

Preston's voice calls back through the door as Elva continues to stare to the wood. "What all normal people do when they wake up. I'll be out in a minute, unless you want to watch."

"Nascent, male." As Elva turns her gaze to the stairs as she makes quick work of them.

An orange furred figure moves into view from the kitchen as she graces the final step. "Is he awake?"

Elva nods as she looks over the plate and cup in Reynard's grasp. "Hardly."

The fox-boy just smiles as he speaks up. "You want a bite? He calls it an *oh-mit biscut*!"

Elva squints to the small, round bread on the plate with a little disgust, mainly because of the yellow and white oozes that seems to be spilling out from inside it. "Was it alive?"

Reynard looks back to the plate balancing on his left paw as he speaks up. "Well, no. Why do you ask?"

The avian woman just waves the comment off as she turns back to the stairs.

Reynard follows her gaze though he moves to the table as he places the plate and cup down.

In a minute Preston exits the bathroom and starts down the stairs with a sigh. "Yea, yea, yea, I know. We need to get going."

Before Elva can speak up Reynard's boyish voice chimes in. "Good morning Preston, I made you an *oh-mit biscut* to eat quickly."

Preston gives a little smile to the fox-boy as he takes the biscuit and cup from Reynard. "It's an omelet biscuit, but close enough." The man takes a bite of the bread as he continues to smile to the young eyes watching him.

However, the crunch sound in his mouth and the taste of burnt meat and fine pieces of fur makes it a little difficult to hold the smile. Luckily, the man takes a quick sip of water as he turns to Elva with a cough. "So I suppose you won't let me sit and eat right?"

"I have a strict schedule, even when not on-..."

Preston quickly cuts the avian women off as he scarfs down the last few bites of his breakfast. "I get it, I get it." As he chokes the food down with a gulp of water he places the cup to the table and starts towards the door. "Alright, let's go Feathers."

Elva says nothing as she exits the house, hardly pausing in her step for Preston.

With a low sigh Preston nods to Reynard. "I'll be back in a little."

The young *fróx* steps forward as he waves a paw to the man. "Wait, Clover wishes me to tell you something."

The pause for a moment as he listens to the boyish words. "...Uh, she said that you are to continue your teleporting training later; and you are not to be too tired. She said it is important that you have the proper time to learn since you took a break."

"Since I took a break?" The laugh quickly falls from Preston's breath as he nods. "Yeah, alright. I'm sure I'll be back before she is. Bye, Reynard."

"Yes, *Hofáfor*, Preston!"

With one final nod to the boyish fox Preston closes the door and continues into the dirt road to where Elva stands. However, as the man looks around the medieval surroundings a thought comes to his head. "Is it really safe for Reynard to be left alone?"

Elva squints to the question almost confused as she shrugs. "He is no cub. Besides, I have seen him show a fang when he does not get his way." The woman pauses for a moment as she looks the man over again. "Do you worry for him?"

Preston gives a little chuckle as he nods. "Well yeah, he's not really the tallest thing in the world."

"Hm, but neither is he the smallest. Now, come, I do not have all *déy*." Elva's wings stretch a little as she begins to walk down the road. "You do not fly and I know your speed."

Preston rolls his neck still trying to work off his morning stiffness as he speaks up. "Yea, yea."

The road is bustling a little more than normal this morning. Of course, the direction Elva seems to be taking is towards the marketplace, which always has a bit more traffic. Strangely though, the vast majority of *Yáppy* pulled carts hale long cuts of tree. Which of course makes moving in and out of the traffic a bit harder.

"What's with the trees?"

Elva does not take her sights from the road before her as she replies. "Clover's project seems to have started. Perhaps *VéturVill* will no longer be known solely for its fields."

The words roll in Preston's head as he continues to watch the seemingly never-ending carts of logs streaming in from the town hall's direction.

(A bit later)

The trek through the town ended perhaps six or seven minutes ago; leaving the grasslands that surround the sleepy town as the only sight to behold. Although the outskirts of the town look similar all around, Preston knows Elva is not heading towards their normal training spot under the tree.

Noticing this Preston speaks up. "So, I take it we are not going to the normal spot, huh?"

"Astute..." Elva nods. "Clover has yet to deliver our letter so I must be present when she arrives in our camp."

Preston squints to the comment as he picks his speed up to meet Elva's side. "You're not going to give her a hard time for not delivering your letter first thing in the morning, are you?"

Elva raises an eyebrow to Preston as she continues to hold her pace. "Will you attempt to sway me from this?"

"I'm not sure I can say anything to change your mind. I'm just saying it's wrong."

"Wrong?" Elva looks the man over for a moment before she continues. "Was it not wrong that we were kept from the town's plans? And just expected to shift rain schedules on a whim? We do not control the weather we simply manipulate its path, Preston." Elva shifts her eyes back to the upward sloping path before her as she trails on. "Of course, I would not expect you to know that. All *Únoff* misunderstand our powers."

Preston shakes his head as he gives a little laugh. "I'm not an *Únoff.*"

"No, but you act as one." Elva trails on. "You feel, you vent, and you prattle as such."

A defeated sigh comes from Preston as he just rubs to his eyes. "Look can we skip the banter today? I'm happy you get to kick my ass and I get to pretend fight you for a little, but I'm not in the mood for talking."

"That would be a first." Elva nods, yet even she continues. "Do you admit fighting is better suited to help your feelings?"

Preston again just sighs. "I don't know Feathers, maybe I just like holding a sword."

"Combat or coitus, there are no other ways to deal with pain, and you are hardly a creature for one to boast mating with."

Preston just laughs, a true to life chuckle as he shakes his head. "You always know what to say."

Elva nods. "I speak plainly, not hidden behind some fog of *Ûnoff* meanings. You should embrace that; it would help discipline your rage."

"I don't have rage, I'm just tired." Preston scans the fields around him, hoping that Elva will stop her chatter.

Elva however replies, her tone unchanged as she does. "We all do, and those closest to us unfit to tame it feel its wrath, just as Clover has come to find."

"What?" Preston picks ups his speed as he comes to Elva's side. "What did you say?"

Elva nods. "You are too beaten down to admit, and we are hardly familiar enough to speak it plainly, but I saw the marks on Clover's arms, and I listened to her explanation. Hardly truthful, though I have learned to see through Clover's words."

Preston follows beside the woman with shame on his face and regret in his heart, both feelings that pour forth as he weakly responds. "She told you?"

"Do not fret, Preston, my buffeting of you will not be in some attempt at revenge, Clover, in her own words, took fault." Elva cocks an eye to the man as she shakes her head. "Though the look on your face suggest your conversations with Clover have been less adequate."

"I-I can't seem to talk to her." Preston licks his lips. "And I don't know how to bring it up."

"Good." Elva takes a breath. "Do you wish to know something of Clover?"

Preston nods, unable to find the words to properly answer.

"She is two things, perfidious and profound." Elva nods. "Did you know her choice in words changes upon her company, what might that suggest?"

"I don't-..."

"Do not answer." Elva nods again. "While I accept your *Únoff* ways I do not wish to further them. Breath deep, her wounds will heal and so too will your mind, given time and ample distraction, Clover knows this too."

Preston swallows. "I don't want to stay."

"Leave than."

Preston chuckles. "I don't know where to go."

Elva takes a breath. "You seem keen on staying helpless, stay in your thoughts all you wish, but know once a sword is in your hand, I shall not show mercy, you did after all challenge me."

Pushing his thoughts aside Preston glances to the ground and then to Elva as he takes a deep breath. "You know Feathers, I think you're taking that challenge a bit too seriously."

"Hardly." Elva cocks an eye to the man. "And stop calling me Feather, Milk-Chest."

Ignoring the comment Preston looks to the grasslands around him. "What did you mean by camp earlier?"

"It means you are among the lucky few. Normally only officials or tradesmen are allowed into *VéturVill's* patrol. Of course, you will be the first to enter without formal news or anything of importance to offer." Elva turns to the man as the slope of the hill ends and they reach the top. "It is not much to look at, though."

Elva's words slowly melt into the breeze around the man as he stares to a clearing in the field just down the road. A few decent sized and colorful tents poking up from the mainly gold and green colored field. The smoke of campfires lifting into the air, despite the hidden nature offered by the wall of spiked wood poles that protrude from the encampment. A large watchtower with a glowing fire sits to the middle of the camp. The most distinctive feature of the wood structure aside from the colorful *Flóff* banner is the fact that there is no ladder. Of course, with every creature in the camp having wings it would make one useless.

Preston continues to look over the camp as he follows Elva down the road. "You live in a tent?"

A faint laugh comes from the avian woman as she nods. "Another one of your *Únoff* tendencies. Yes, I live in a tent. Most *Flóff* find hard materials as a cage."

Preston nods as he speaks up. "What about rain?"

Another light laugh comes from Elva as she shakes her head. "Why would we allow rain in our camp?"

The sound of the woman's quick laugh now transfers to Preston as he joins in. "Well, I think I'll stop asking questions. I wouldn't want to sound more stupid."

"On the contrary Preston, your questions are interesting. You bring thoughts to my mind that I normally would not question." Elva turns to the man, but her smile fades more to just a smirk as she nods. "But cease your chatter."

Before Preston can speak up another voice breaks through the wind. However, the young almost tomboyish tone almost catches the man off guard. *"Pexřá Elva!"*

A quick glance around the field adjacent to the road reveals no one, yet the voice seems so near. Luckily, before the man can question it further a bit of dust and the rapid sound of wings flapping takes Preston's attention.

Again, before the man can react something pokes to his chest.

"What is this?"

As Preston's wits slowly come back to him and as the dust clears the man notices something. A short, dirty blonde haired, tan skinned and pointy eared *Flóff* girl standing in front of him. The girl appears to be maybe seventeen or eighteen. However, the light leather top and bottom leggings with steel studs mixed in suggest that she must at least be old enough to fight. The sword also poking at Preston's stomach would seem to confirm this.

The man's smile fades as he looks over the green eyed and brown winged girl before him. The happy and slightly curious smile however does hold Preston from attempting to fight off the sword.

Luckily, the girl's blade is quickly batted away as Elva's pushes it from Preston's chest. "He has challenged me, Ellette."

Elva's sword is batted away now as the girl brings herself into the air with a giddy laugh, her sword holding to Elva's as she talks. "What?! *Pexřá* Elva has accepted a challenge?"

Preston halts his walk as he watches Elva swing the blade back to the girl. He knows the force at which the avian woman can swing, and knowing this he can tell this little sword fight is nothing more than a game to the two *Flóffs*. Yet, the clanging of their metal swords does deter the man's steps as he tries to listen in.

Elva takes a step closer to the girl, all the while as their swords stay clashed together. "Even a powerful *swóóp* allows a *tát* to run, Ellette."

Ellette simply laughs as she takes herself more into the air as she bashes Elva's blade away. "But the *swóóp* does this only for fun?"

Despite the fact that Preston is now lost in the conversation, he cannot take his attention off the two's banter as Elva responses. "And fun it is to watch it run."

As the girl hovers above Elva's drawn sword her eyes come to Preston's figure. Within the second Ellette brings herself over Preston. She sheaths her sword as she cocks her head to the man. "You sure it is safe to bring him into the camp?"

Elva puts her own sword away as she nods. "Preston is nothing more than Clover Vines' *Étrometáy*, he will serve the same purpose."

A happy squawk like sound comes from the girl as she quickly lands next to Preston. "Oh! He is from the library!" The girl's joy filled expression is contagious as Preston now smiles and nods.

Yet, before the man can speak up the girl turns back to Elva. "Next *mořo* I am allowed to enter the town. Will you show me how to reach it?!"

Elva smirks to the comment as she cocks her head. "Oh? Do not let your mind wander early. I still make all the decisions for the *yiftiñs* at camp."

Ellette's posture straightened as she speaks up. "I do not forget." The girl's posture quickly changes as her wings sprawl out, which makes Preston have to take a step back. "However, I believe I will prove myself worthy of leave."

Just as her words end the girl lunges forward, sword drawn. Her surprise attack is of course quickly thwarted as Elva steps aside and slams her own blade against Ellette's.

A happy laugh comes from the girl as Elva taps the tip of her sword to the girl's neck. "You should plan your attacks better. I could see your excitement before you sprung." Elva lowers her blade as she awaits Ellette's words.

The girl however just laughs as she too puts her blade back to its sheath. "I try *Pexřá*. But I get excited when I have my hand on a blade."

Elva just nods as she pats the girl on the shoulder. "We all do. Now I am sure you have an assignment. Do not stall on it because of me."

The girl groans as she takes herself into the air. "It is merely scouting. The other *wóvátor* gets all the fun from the forest. I merely stir the grass and chase off *wéveanś*."

"I did the same, Ellette."

With another groan Ellette nods. "Yes, *Pexřá*." As her words end the girl takes herself into the air and then into the clouds.

As the girl leaves Preston's sight the man looks over Elva's smile. "So… was that your sister?"

Elva's smile ends as she cocks an eyebrow to the man. "No."

Preston shrugs as he speaks up. "She likes to pull blades on people."

The smile comes back as Elva starts her walk again. "She is smart to."

"Right. Also what is pet-ra mean?"

"It is *Pexřá*, Preston. It means second in charge."

Preston's eyes widen a little as he nods. "Oh, so Elva the great is not number one?"

Elva gives an unamused look to the man as she nods. "Elva the great, as you say, understands her limits."

"Whoa." Preston nods as he thinks the words over for a moment.

Elva squints to the man's tone as she pauses her walk. "You are surprised?"

Preston shakes his head as he looks over the log walls inching ever closer to their walk. "Just surprised that you have limits."

"Only when it comes to position, Preston." Elva straightens her posture as the closed wood gate of the camp comes within throwing distance. "Now, go to the gate. I will open it."

Before Preston can answer Elva takes herself into the air and quickly dashes towards the camp. The man squints his eyes and brushes against the dust, though he continues forward all the same.

Chapter 17

Sword and Feather

The late morning sun has continued to pound against Preston's back, despite the clouds in the sky. Truthfully, the comfortable climate of Artésque never really changes during the day. But, the constant direct sunlight Preston has received since he's been told to wait outside of the closed wood gate has begun to warm his thick wool clothing a bit too much.

Luckily, after another few minutes the gate finally begins to open. Elva quickly comes into view and as she does Preston speaks up. "Did you forget I was out here?"

Her annoyed expression rapidly halts Preston's words, but the damage is done as she shoves something into the man's hold. "As I said Preston, it is a rarity for an outsider to venture in. I also had to borrow some armor for you, would not want Clover yelling about a scratch."

Preston looks over the hard leather top Elva has handed him, though it is at this point Preston notices Elva's normal steel like armor has been replaced with a light green, scaly looking top. "Wait, I thought we were racing?"

Elva gives a simple laugh as she hands a curved, but dull sword to the man. "This is for the camp's amusement. Now, put on the armor and wield this sword, it is considered arrogant and rude to come in unprotected."

Preston pulls the leather top over his head and down his body as he begins to fasten it as best he knows how. "What are you wearing?"

Elva raises her eyebrow to the man as she taps to the green scales. "This is armor mixed with *Koá-Koé* skin. As light as leather but strong nonetheless. I made this myself from the beast."

"You killed the *Flóff* bird of myth?"

For a moment Elva is surprised, but she quickly regains her wits as she smirks. "The *mÿtheñ* says that if you leave the eggs that the hatchlings will find you. Of course, it has been a long while since I crafted this armor. Now, come, the camp is awaiting a show. And... be silent." As Elva opens the door more Preston peers into the camp. Sadly, his scanning of the area is brought to a swift end as he takes notice to the other people.

Near the watchtower's base perhaps ten or so *Flóffs* stand, most are men, but a few women's breastplates can be seen, the others are too hard to discern with the helmets and armor they wear. There is no silent exchange between Preston and the warrior fit *Flóffs*, instead a laugh erupts in the camp.

"Elva, what is this? You accept pity challenges of the *Dẅoff*?" The tall, fit, though slender, dark red haired and brown winged man that stands a little to the center of the group continues to roll with laughter as he waves a hand towards Preston. "What is your name outsider?"

Before Preston can speak up another voice rings up from the group. "Actually, Stysen he looks more *Fárwift*."

Elva brings her own voice up as she stops in front of the crowd. "His name is Preston."

The laughter subsides for a moment as Preston speaks from behind Elva. "Uh, Preston Armor."

With a nod from Elva the laughter comes back with a roar, but this time the group slowly finds a spot to sit or lean against the watchtower as Stysen and a few other wave to Elva.

Holding her own smirk Elva turns to Preston. "As you all see this is who has challenged me. Although unfit to wield a sword he still thought it wise nonetheless."

As the chuckle continue Preston speaks over Elva. "To be fair I challenged her to a run not a sword fight." The comment only adds to the *Flóffs'* joy, their laughter even sparking a slight snicker from Elva as she slowly pulls a dull blade from her waist.

"Preston, the challenge is set. Knocking the other's sword from their hand helps, though only pinning your opponent to the ground yields a point."

The red haired *Flóff* now sitting on a wooden crate beneath the tower speaks up as he nods to Preston. "Do not go for the legs, Elva is far too grounded. It takes an unexpected gust to sweep this warrior from her feet."

Elva cocks an eye to the voice as she calls back. "Something your wings are unable to muster, Stysen."

The laugh now turns from Preston's ears as Stysen attempts to wave it off with a smile. "Yes, yes. Now will you two start before *Alphé* Kassie commands us to our stations, *Pexřá*?"

Elva raises her blade towards Preston as she nods to the man before her. It takes a moment for Preston to notice Elva's gesture, but as he does he raises the curved sword she gave him.

As Preston's sword even remotely taps to the avian woman's she springs into action, batting the curved blade away and lunging for Preston's chest.

Preston narrowly dodges the blade's tip as he screams back. "Whoa, Whoa, calm down, Feathers!"

The onlookers begin to cheer and laugh at Preston's expense, this of course only prompts Elva to continue as she holds her joy filled smile to the fight now underway. Preston continues to escape her slashes and stabs by simply backing up. However, with a powerful strike from Elva, Preston's hands wobble and the sword is almost sent flying from his hand.

Seeing this Elva wraps both her hands to the hilt of the sword. "Do not hold back Preston. For I shall not."

Preston's grip quickly is regained, and the moment of reprieve has allowed a thought to come to the man. There is no way Preston can hope to wear Elva down, and judging by her attacks she is only holding back for the sport of it. Yet, another thought has come to Preston's head and as it does he focuses his eyes to the hilt of Elva's sword as he begins to remember what Clover taught him.

Elva's smile falls from her face as she notices the sword in her grasp starting to glow green. "Your magic will not knock the blade from my hand Preston, my armor blocks it."

The words do not halt Preston's spell over the woman's blade. "I wasn't trying to knock it from your hand." Just as the man's words end he lunges forward and slams his sword to her's.

His inexperience and raw power clashing into her tightly held blade forces Preston to drop the sword. The magic around Elva's blade does halt her from swinging as fast; this however, was not the magic's only intent. The impact of Preston's sword slamming into Elva's has caused a ripple reaction that vibrates the blade from Elva's grasp. Though Preston is surprised his half-baked planned worked he nonetheless holds a shit-eating grin to the woman.

A silent moment of shock over comes the camp, from Elva to the group of onlookers none say anything. Preston merely brings his sword up as he kicks Elva's away. He holds the sword to Elva as he pants with excitement. "I win!"

The onlookers begin to laugh as Preston holds his sword to Elva. At first the noise goes unheeded, but as the woman before him begins to smile Preston starts to notice it.

In the blink of an eye Elva pulls forth a dagger from her belt and bats away Preston's blade, within another moment she has knocked it from his hand completely. Though her movements do not stop as she swipes Preston's feet from underneath him.

She topples the man with ease as she holds the sharpened dagger to his throat.

Preston now lays flat on his back, his mind just now catching up to the flurry of motions that just transpired.

The group begins to speak up as Elva holds her position over the man. "*Nev!*"

The words are meaningless to Preston, though the smile on Elva's face says it all as she stands. "Rise, Preston."

Preston nods. "Yea, yea." He brushes the dirt from his pants as he points to her dagger. "So you can just get another sword now, huh?"

Elva nods. "This is a dagger." She moves it back to waist as she moves to collect the two fallen swords. As she does she tosses one back to Preston.

Though he catches the slight raising of his leg and terrified expression draws a laugh from the group behind.

Once more, the louder Stysen calls out from where he sits. "Be faster, Outsider."

The comment draws a sigh from the man, his once happy smile now faded as he adjusts himself.

Elva stands proud as she awaits Preston's first move, though noticing her waiting Preston speaks up. "What, you can't make the first move?"

A smirk comes to Elva as she begins to move, which quickly prompts Preston to take a scared jump back, expecting the woman to charge him.

Naturally the onlookers let out a chuckle, though unlike a mass of *Dwoff* their chatter is held to a minimum as the duel continues.

"Are you ready, Preston?"

The man just nods.

Sighting the nod, Elva's wings flar a little, with a quick flap of the wings she charges. A telegraphed attack, though one that Preston cannot deflect, nonetheless. Elva once more knocks Preston's sword from his hold, yet she does not capitalize as Preston staggers away.

Elva circles where his sword was tossed, her own blade coming to point at the man as she talks. "Come, reclaim your sword."

Preston hunches down, his body jittery as he attempts to plan his rush. With an audible yell, he charges. Elva, side steps the unarmed assault altogether, taking herself in the air and bashing her blunt sword to Preston's back. Perhaps the only saving grace was Preston's baseball slide he used to collect his sword, while hardly flashy it did help to block Elva's attack.

Even still, Preston groans as he reaches a hand to the swell of his back where Elva's sword struck him.

Noticing Preston's pause Elva charges, her attack proving far better as the force of her tackle sends Preston hurling to the ground with a thud.

The dust kicked up coupled with the "oh" sound ringing in from the group of onlookers says it all. Though Elva is not done as she plans a hard foot to Preston's chest.

The man wheezes a little as he feels his breath being forced out, and although he knows he needs to get up, he lacks the strength.

The group chimes on. "*Bev!*"

Stepping away Elva speaks up. "One more, Preston."

A cough rolls from Preston as he plans his sword to the ground, his rising a bit shaky as he leans to the curved blade. "Y-yep, one more." He blows his breath as he slowly comes up. "Alright, alright, let's go."

Elva gives a slight bow, her action somewhat taking Preston off guard, though as her wings twitch Preston clenches his hands. Inevitably, Elva charges forward, another gust of dirt filling the area as she does. Preston teleports behind her, fumbling as he does he bashes his sword to the back of Elva's knee, prompting the woman to let out a somewhat pained or perhaps surprised yelp.

She stumbles forward, her right leg shaky, although Preston does not follow through. Instead, he freezes, Elva's intense gaze coming to him as she turns and lands a stiff left hand to his chin.

Another oohing sound rings from the group as Preston spins to the punch. Elva stomps her leg, getting the feeling back as she starts towards Preston.

The world around him means nothing as he spits to the ground, his eyes catching to the blood beneath him. He touches his lip as he attempts to loosen his jaw. Sure enough more blood greets his gaze. He squints to it as he speaks up. "I-I'm bleeding!"

He stares wide-eyed to the sight of red as he glances to Elva striding towards him, sword still in hand. Despite the familiar face Preston's mind kicks into survival mode, a frenzy of emotions banging to his mind as he cocks his head.

Time seems to slow as Preston watches Elva raise her sword, though instead of blocking it he charges her, his own sword being tossed to the ground as he does. Elva is quick, and though she brings her blade down to Preston's back the man's charge does not halt, and she finds herself being tugged to ground as Preston's hands yanks to the soft feathers on her back.

Though surprised, the group calls out. *"Nev!"*

Elva merely blinks to the man on top of her, though her own shock lasts merely a second as Elva brings her hands down hard to Preston's arms, forcing him to collapse onto her chest as Elva rolls the man over, her arm pressed into his neck. "We are done!"

Despite the words and the clapping from the onlookers Preston thrashes, and even forces Elva to tighten her hold. Even with Preston's raw and untamed burst of primal strengthen Elva is able to keep the man subdued.

Preston's breathing is hard as Elva shakes him, his head banging against the ground as he begins to cool off.

The group of *Flóffs* now stand, some starting towards Elva as they cock their heads to the continued fight.

Stysen, like some other smirk to the man's panting.

"*Pexřá*, Elva, is everything well?"

Elva slowly comes off the man as she nods, though her gaze stays to Preston as she speaks up. "Of course."

Stysen just nods as he turns back to the group around him. "Well… I-I suppose we should get back to our post."

The group slowly begins to dissolve as a few inaudible murmurs raise up.

As the onlookers' eyes begin to shift Preston blinks to Elva. "What?"

Elva is silent as moves to collect the swords, though she comes back to Preston as she pulls him from the ground. Elva holds the curved blade to Preston as she nods. "This is yours now."

"I thought this stuff was just for the fight?" Preston brushes some dirt from himself, though Elva is quick to push the sword back to Preston.

"The sword is a gift, the armor I shall return later." Elva turns her eyes from Preston as she places her sword to her sheath. Elva points to one of the colorful tents near the edge of the camp. "Would you follow me, Preston?"

Preston glances to the row of tents as he nods. "Sure." He brings a hand to his lips as he wipes off a few drops of blood. As he does this he takes notice to the feathers scattered around his feet. "Hey sorry about the-..."

"You fought well, but it was not honorable, you did what you had to." Elva pauses. "Though if you had used the sword I would have broken your hands."

Preston swallows, the lack of cockiness in Elva quickly sobering the man up. "Sorry."

At the words Elva starts her walk towards the tent with Preston following behind. It only takes a few moments for Preston and Elva to make it across the camp and as they reach the tent Preston halts.

"S-so is this how you celebrate a win?"

Elva shakes her head as she holds the tent open. "No."

The quick response pauses Preston as the man just stands in front of the tent. Elva however does not skip a beat as she moves inside the tent. "You may follow Preston."

It takes a moment, but Preston nods and moves into the tent. To his surprise it is not magical like the ones Clover and Nyota have used. Granted it is not tiny, but hardly nothing is inside except a small bed, an armor stand, and, a chest sitting on the floor.

Preston looks around the tight tent as he speaks up. "Roomy..."

Elva stands to the middle of her tent, her eyes looking over the armor stand which hosts her typical polished steel. However, her gaze shifts to Preston as she begins to undo her armor a little. "How do you feel?"

Preston gives a slight chuckle as he watches the woman continuing to undo her armor. "Good... what are you doing?"

"Changing my armor." Elva nods as she pauses. "You lost your challenge, Preston."

"Yea." Preston rubs his neck. "It don't matter."

Elva turns to the chest on the floor, her hands quickly coming to it as she pulls out a small, white and gem encrusted box. The sight of it is surprising as it appears to be something Bellla would have rather than Elva. Though before Preston can joke about it, Elva opens it and pulls forth a bright feather. Similar to those above her ear.

Preston squints to it as he shrugs. "What's that?"

"It is a *Quétzal* feather. *Flóff* woman gives these to their male victor as a promise to fulfil any demand." Elva's words prompt Preston to turn his eyes to the other feathers on her ear.

He shrugs, still not understanding the gesture. "So... what makes it special?"

Elva blinks to the man's question as she slowly lowers her hand and the feather. "A *Quétzal* can only lose its feathers if it chooses to pluck them. In our way of life every young girl is given a *Quétzal* that they care for. It is said that the *Quétzal* will pick only the correct number of feathers to fit the girl. I was given five. Five great challenges to accept."

Preston looks over the three feathers already in Elva's hair as he speaks up. "Well I'm not number four, so why show me this?"

Elva nods as she gives a little smirk. "You failed your challenge, and as such I am allotted the request." She places the feather back into the box. "You lack control of your emotions, you need discipline. I offer you a chance for this, here in the camp."

Preston chuckles as he shifts in his stance. "What?"

"It is uncommon for an outsider to stay in the camp, but there can be arraignments for you to be brought in, purely to work where no other wishes." Elva nods as she crosses her arms. "The work would be hard, but you would not regret it."

Preston gives a little laugh as he waves the comment off. "I don't think I can just-..."

"It would allow the fog in Clover's mind to settle, it would allow you time to control yourself. The benefits of a *Flóff* routine would be good for you." Elva slowly begins to straighten her posture as she looks the man over. "Would you not want this?"

Preston shakes his head as he tries to think her suggestion over. "How would I continue to learn magic?"

"Clover is welcome to the camp, and as long as you follow the rules you are permitted to leave, you are old enough." Elva awaits Preston's response, her stern expression suggestion nothing beyond her words.

Preston squints to the woman. "You're serious?"

Elva nods. "You were never going to best me in combat, but I had hoped you would show your skills to the camp, you have, and they will accept you. Perhaps as a fool, but nonetheless you will find a home here, far more than what you have found with Clover."

Preston just chuckles again, his eyes drifting to the sword in his hand, though he tightens his grip as he nods. "Okay, yea, alright." He looks up. "I can do this... but why?" He cocks a smile. "You're not just trying to keep me for yourself, right?"

"Preston..." Elva uncrosses her arms as she moves them to her hips. "Your chance at mating with me was lost when you failed your challenge."

The man's eyes widen as he nods. "Do what?"

Without so much as a smirk Elva shakes her head. "I was never going to lose."

Preston shakes his head with laugh. "But you accepted it? What for?"

"Never mind that. You shall find your way around the camp once you are fully taken in. First you must retrieve your items from Clover as I arrange your stay." Elva nods to the armor still around Preston. "Remove that as well."

"Right." Preston begins to fumble with the leather armor, though he gets it off all the same as he holds it towards Elva. "You uh... you just wanted to see me take this off, huh?"

Elva takes a breath as she nods. "As *Pexřá*, Preston I have accepted many challenges, the feathers at my ear are only those who I lost to." She takes the armor in hand as she nods. "Many more live with the idea of what they could have had. You among them."

Preston just chuckles to the comment. "Whatever you say, Feathers." Preston continues his chuckle as he brushes his hair and starts out of the tent. His bread, much like his hair is messy with dirt and sweat, though he pays it little mind. The camp is bustling with the sound of heavy wings flapping and the sight of its few occupants walking about the camp. Preston cannot shake the feeling that everyone's eyes stare to him as he leaves, despite how tries.

Chapter 18

Home is what you make it

"...For how long?"

With another sigh Preston reluctantly halts his descent of the stairs as he turns back to the boyish voice behind him. Of course, the decent sized chest Preston now carries does not allow the man to stare down at the fox-boy. "I told you, I'll come see you."

Reynard just shakes his head as he slips past the man and stops at the bottom of the stairs. "But-but I do not understand why you are leaving?"

Preston finally makes it down the stairs as he sets his sights to the table near the door. The man's movements are quick as he sets the chest to rest and begins to talk. "Well, you knew I would be leaving eventually... think of this as a steppingstone, yea?"

The comment sinks Reynard's little ears as he shakes his head. "I thought you changed your mind?"

"I-... It's better this way." Preston holds a smile as he squats down to Reynard's level. "I'll come visit."

"But..." Reynard's words quickly begin to turn to nonsense as the young *fróx* attempts to voice his emotions. "...but why do you need to leave? You and Clover can train here like before."

Preston gives a little smile as he looks the fox-boy over. "I think this makes sense, and like I said, I'll stop by."

Reynard just nods as he looks to the ground, his defeated voice chiming out as he nods. "Promise?"

The tone forces Preston's smile from his face as he cocks his head, bringing a hand to Reynard's chin as he pushes his eyes up to his. "Hey, why are you so upset? You still got Clover?"

The *fróx* nods as he speaks up. "I know. I just, I liked having someone around when Clover is gone... she leaves so often, I do not know anyone beside you and Clover's friends."

Preston pauses at the words, though he stands up as he brushes a hand to Reynard's head. "I don't know that many people either, Rey, and I'm not about to abandon the friends I have here. I just need to leave for a little."

Reynard slowly nods as he speaks up. "Was it the biscuit?"

A light laugh comes from Preston as he moves back towards the table. "No, it was not the biscuit." The laugh goes unshared as Preston again turns to Reynard. "Rey, you know that right? This has nothing to do with you."

Reynard nods, his eyes still sheepish at the man's gaze. "Okay."

The man gives another slight laugh to the fox-boy's stare as he moves his hands to the chest. "I'll stop by as soon as I get a chance." As he brings the slightly heavy box up with a grunt, he rushes a comment. "Alright, I should get going."

Reynard moves to get the door as he tries his best to give a smile. "D-did you really beat Elva?"

Preston nods to the hilt and bottom part of the sword poking out from the chest. "Yep, one whole round, she even gave me that sword."

A true to life smile comes to Reynard's snout as he looks the blade over. "Did you name your sword?"

Preston cocks his head to the comment. "Name it?"

Reynard nods. "All the bad-ass swords have names."

A chuckle rolls from Preston as he nods. "Okay, name it then."

"Really?" Reynard's nose twitches to the comment. "I can name it?"

"Of course." Preston pushes the trunk up a little with his leg as he nods. "I told you Rey, we're still friends, just because I'm leaving doesn't mean I stop caring about you."

Reynard rubs his paws together as he nods. "But we are not a group anymore... so we are not family."

Preston blinks to the comment as he forces a chuckle. "Nah, we-we are whatever we wanna be." He nods to the sword as he sets the chest down again, pulling forth the dull, curved blade. "So go on, name it for me."

A smile holds to Reynard's face as he nods. "Fang."

"Fang?" Preston laughs.

"Yea, because it curves like a fang!"

"Oh yea!" Preston holds his laugh back as he nods and pets his hand once more to Reynard's head. "It's... it's great." He chuckles. "Very original, and very scary sounding."

Despite Preston's somewhat sarcastic tone, Reynard nonetheless focuses in on the smile as he nods. "Thanks, I came up with it myself."

Preston nods. "And I won't forget it, I'll tell everyone about it when I get to the camp." The word brings a little chuckle from Preston as he nods. "Very cool."

He picks the truck up once more as he moves into the street. Now standing at the threshold Preston speaks up the little *fróx*. "Oh, and if Clover asks about that stone tell her it's where she left it."

Reynard rolls his paws over one another as he nods. "Okay... uh, goodbye Preston."

Preston gives a little smile as he attempts to adjust his handling on the chest. "It's not goodbye. It's see you soon."

(A bit later)

The trek back through the town's outer fields has not gone according to plan. Surprisingly, not because Preston got lost without Elva but because of the weight Preston has carried and the uneven path he carries it through.

The sun is now close to noon and the lack of shade mixed with the weight in Preston's arms has already begun to work down the man's muscles. However, before Preston can begin to complain a voice takes his attention.

"Ah, the *tát* returns!"

The familiar tomboyish voice brings Preston's eyes to the sky as the man watches the *Flóff* coming down from the clouds. "What brings you back?" Ellette's gaze drifts to the box as she smiles. "Oooh, Elva's strikes must have been quicker than the cloud's lights. This is her prize I suppose?"

As Ellette pulls out the curved sword Preston speaks up, his voice is a little strained from the box in his grasp but he continues nevertheless. "Actually, I've been invited into the camp."

Ellette stands stunned to the comment as Preston puts the box to the ground and takes the sword from her.

However as Preston fixes the contents of his chest Ellette speaks up. "You lie."

"No." With a grunt Preston lifts the chest and continues down the road. However, Ellette follows after him as she comes to his side.

"Halt, there are no trespassers in the field!"

Preston stops as he turns back to the girl. "What?"

Ellette brings her hand to her sword as she speaks up again. "None but the invited few are allowed to venture into the camp."

Preston shakes his head to the girl's serious expression with a laugh. "I'm not lying to you."

Ellette's hand slowly comes from the sword as she looks the man over. "You-you are truly not lying?"

"No?" Preston squints the girl. "How come you weren't told? Aren't you a sentry? Shouldn't you know this by now?"

Ellette's expression sours as she looks the man over. "But-but look at you! You can barely hold that chest up? How could you defeat Elva?"

Preston rolls his eyes. "Funny, and since it matters so much, I didn't win."

Ellette blinks to the comment as she squints to the man with an even more confused look. "Then why have you returned?"

"Ask Elva. Can I go now?" Preston's annoyance only translates into laughter for the young *Flöff* as she begins to circle Preston, poking his sides at every turn.

The man attempts to follow the girl's laughter as he turns to her, however his continued words only make her laugh more. "Will you stop poking me?!"

"You are soft! Like-like a newly hatched *pófy*!" Ellette shakes her head. "Did you bed Elva so well that she claimed you?"

"What the? No, she just-... OW!" Preston takes a step away from the girl as her sharp fingers poke into his side again. "Stop!"

Ellette just laughs as she shows her hand to the man. "*Flóff* fingers." Her words do not stop as she moves her hands to her hips. "I still do not believe you. But, you have a certain look to you that suggest you are telling the truth. Hm... I shall allow you to pass."

Preston just nods as he watches the girl quickly spreading her wings and jumping back into the air. He continues to watch her for a moment before he shakes his head and continues down the road. "Bird brain."

The path, despite Preston's fatigue has become a bit shorter and as the closed wood gate comes within a stone's throw, a sigh of relief rolls through the man. With a slight clear of the throat Preston speaks up. "Uh... hello?"

"You!"

The voice comes from above the gate which quickly takes Person's attention to the *Flóff* woman hovering above. The woman wears a dark, bronze like chest plate and shin length skirt with a dark blue cloth visible between the metal and around her extremities. Her hair is a light brown and her wings are the same with a few darker spots mixed in. However, like Elva and every other armored *Flóff* Preston has met her tone is strict and demanding. "State your business?"

"Uh... I was here a little bit ago? and I-..."

The woman's face slowly lightens as she looks the man over. "Wait..." She quickly darts back behind the gate, however, before Preston can speak up again the gate opens with the woman in the center.

"You were the *Dẃoff* that fought *Pexřá* Elva, yes?" She smiles. "You squall as a *yiftiñ* when hit."

Preston nods as he speaks up. "Yeah, that was me."

The woman's smile fades as she straightens up. "I was told to bring you to *Alphé* Kassie. Follow me."

As the woman begins to walk away Preston follows after her. "Is there a way I can put this somewhere?"

The woman does not even turn her head as she continues to lead the man. "Your belongings are yours to guard."

Preston just sighs as he continues to trail behind the woman. "How far are we going?"

"The *Pexřá* said you would complain... she also said to allow your words to the wind."

"Right..." Preston looks around the camp as he again takes it all in. Nothing has changed but the sound of a hammer striking metal rings out from somewhere in the camp. Most of the tents are positioned near the back part of the walls and most are open. Preston's eyes do lock to the larger tent the woman seems to be leading him to. Despite the fact that the camp is fairly open this tent seems to be at the opposite side of all other tents, making for a somewhat lengthier walk.

"This is *Alphé* Kassie's tent. You are to enter and speak to her. I shall wait out here." Just as the woman's voice stops her walk halts.

Preston stumbles a little as he tries to understand her instructions. "Uh... could I leave this here with you then?"

The woman looks over the chest as she nods. "I suppose."

"Great!" Preston nods as he places the chest next to her. "So, what's your name?"

The woman squints to the question as she shakes her head. "What?"

Preston gives a little laugh as he straightens his posture. "Your name? I'm Preston."

"I remember." The avian woman shifts a little as she looks his smile over with a confused expression.

Preston quickly notices the expression as he speaks up. "Right, so, just go into the tent there yeah?"

"Elwine of Wyndsweep, is my name." The woman nods as she brushes some hair from her face, revealing a set of seven colorful feathers above her ear. "Proceed in."

"Nice to meet you Elwine." Preston gives another light smile as he turns from the woman and whispers to himself. *"Another E to remember..."*

The tent's opening allows Preston to notice that the tent although big is almost doubled inside. In fact, the room's flooring is even covered in a colorful blue rug instead of the simple dirty covering every other tent sits over. However, Preston's gawking of the extravagant camping lifestyle is brought to an end as a voice takes his attention.

"It is merely an *Únoff* tent. You may close your mouth."

The surroundings have left Preston blind to the old, dull grey haired and winged *Flóff* woman sitting at the table almost directly in front of him.

Feeling like a fool Preston attempts to speak up. "Oh, I've uh been in a magic tent before I just-..."

"*Shh.*" The woman looks up from the unrolled scroll in front of her as she takes the man in. Her face, despite the age in her voice or her weak frame has surprisingly no wrinkles to it, though her eyes bend up a little more than any other *Flóff* Preston has seen. Aside from her light gray eyes and the two red feathers above her left ear no other color is really to her. Even her skin is a paler yellowish tone. "You speak to much. I heard you speaking with Elwine."

Preston nods as he shrugs. "I was just saying hello."

The woman sits up a little more in the wooden chair as she folds her hands to the table. "You understand it is strange for any being aside from a *Flóff* to reside in a *Flóff* camp, yes?"

"I could see that."

The woman clears her throat in a way only the old can as she continues. "So, you understand my confusion to my *Pexřá*?"

Preston gives a little smile as he shakes his head. "Well it's a long story. Did Elva not say-..."

"I am not hearing an answer." The woman gets a little smile as she awaits the man's response.

Preston just laughs to the woman as he nods. "Okay, okay I get it I'll uh... I'll leave."

As Preston starts to turn the woman speaks up. "I did not permit you to leave."

The words halt Preston's exit, although they do add to the man's confusion. "What?"

"You abide by my rules, not the Princess' or Elva's, mine. You leave when I say you can leave, are we clear?"

Preston nods. "Yes."

"Now answer my question. Do you understand my confusion to *Pexřá* Elva's request?"

Preston sighs confused to the comment as he shakes his head. "No?"

The gray woman nods. "Then listen. While both Elva and I understand teachings beyond the normal *Flóff*, that does not mean all other in the camp do." The woman's calm voice ends as she turns a strict stare to the man. "Most here are too young to share our knowledge, or at least too young to heed it. The breeze outside is foreign and ground even more so to many, you will be tested here. There will be anger to this arrangement, though I, just as Elva does, sees value in this introduction to the world beyond the camp. Act poorly and you shall not stay long."

Preston nods as her piercing gaze stabs into his very mind. "Okay."

"Good, first rule, there is no facial hair allowed. See to it that you have it removed. Second, you are not to wander the premise without armor; what you do in your tent is your business, but on these grounds, you are a guest, and as such you must wear armor. You will also be responsible for creating your own, and for sharpening your weapons. Thirdly, though you are of age to leave and I understand you have arrangements within town, you are only to leave the camp when cleared by the gate's guard. Finally, I am in charge of all rules. Do not expect all of them to be listed. Is your mind without fog?"

Preston stares almost dumbfounded to the woman as he nods. "Y-yes."

The woman smiles as she nods. "Then as *Alphé* I welcome you. The guard outside will escort you to your tent."

"T-thank you."

Once more before Preston can exit the tent's opening the woman's voice comes to his ears. "Oh, and Preston." He again turns to the woman as he watches her turning back to her scroll. "Although I do not ask questions of my advisor I do have to say, your actions will reflect on Elva while you are her initiate."

Preston nods as he walks out of the tent and back into the day's unfiltered light.

Elwine quickly notices the man as she speaks up. "I am to show you to your tent."

Preston holds his hand to the camp as he laughs. "Lead on... wait, where's my chest?"

"I have already placed it." Elwine nods as she starts her walk towards the other side of the tent.

Preston squints to the comment as he moves to her side. "You didn't need to take it for me."

Elwine does not turn to the man beside her as she continues. "Yes, well you looked to be struggling. It is a rule to help our comrades."

"Okay, I'll be sure to remember that." He glances back to the big tent they leave, his voice coming down a bit. "Any other rule I should know? I kinda froze there, ha-ha."

Preston's words are cut off as Elwine stops and holds her hand to the tent on her left. "This is yours. If you need any further assistance, please talk to Lutin the quartermaster."

"O-oh, okay, where is um... she?"

Elwine points across the courtyard to the front left side of the camp. "He is near the forge."

Preston quickly notices the large black furnace and anvils sitting around it. This also explains the sounds of hammers hitting metal as Preston notices the brawny *Flöff* striking something on one of the anvils. "Alright, thank you."

Elwine simply nods as she begins to walk away.

With one more look around the camp Preston pushes open the tent's flap and starts inside. There are only two things in the room, the chest Reynard said he could borrow and a bed.

Seeing this, Preston drags the chest towards the bed as he sits down and opens it. Despite the fact that Preston packed this merely an hour or so ago the contents still surprise him. A few wool shirts in various sizes, some pants, a toothbrush with paste, and, the so-called magic glove. All of his worldly positions, yet hardly none of the weight to the heavy box. Preston puts everything on the bed except the glove as he looks it over.

Although the man rarely uses it the glove still brings a few thoughts to the front of his mind. And as he looks it over another moment, he runs a hand to his beard. "Ugh... what am I doing?" A slight laugh comes from the man as he looks the glove over again, however he jumps a little to the hard bed as he sighs. "What is this hay?" He bends down, taking a sniff of the simple covers as he nods. "Yep."

A sigh rolls through the man as he rubs his hands to pants. Looking around the tent he speaks up once more. "Well at least everything I own fits in one chest." Another light chuckle rings out from the man as he sighs. "As if I owned any of it."

"Do you always talk to yourself?"

The voice quickly startles Preston and he jumps to his feet, which sends the heavy wood chest slamming down to his feet. Luckily, the boots take most of the impact and Preston merely jumps again at the chest' impact.

Elva just stares unamused to the man as she speaks up. "Hm, a fool now resides in the camp."

"H-how long have you been there?"

"Just as you started talking." Elva looks around the tent as she trails on. "Are you content?"

"Yeah, yeah, I'm fine." Preston gives a little smile and nod as he awaits Elva's next inevitable question.

"Good. If you have any concerns speak with the quartermaster. I am leaving for *Pegpolis* so you will need to find your way around the camp for the next few *déys*."

"Wait, you're leaving?"

Elva nods as she smiles to Preston's quick tone. "For a few mornings, if the winds are fast. I hope you did not expect me to act as Clover. You are now part of the *VéturVill* weather patrol... or at least a guest. Which reminds me, your beard is to be removed and you are to work on your armor."

Preston shakes his head as he laughs. "Okay so what, should I shave with the sword?"

"No" Elva pulls her dagger from her belt as she spins it towards Preston. "You use a dagger."

Preston takes hold of the gem encrusted, and well forged dagger as he shrugs. "Right?"

"I will arrange an extra cloud for you if you must bathe. See Lutin about the armor. Oh, and Preston, do not lose my dagger."

Preston nods as he blinks to Elva's serious tone "Alright, I won't."

"Good." As Elva turns away Preston speaks up one last time.

"Hey." Preston nods. "Thanks."

The avian woman halts for a moment but she does not stop her exit as she leaves Preston without another word.

Chapter 19

Hofáfor

The day has rolled on rather well for Preston, no one has stopped by the tent since Elva left and the new surroundings have kept the man from getting too bored. Plus, the lengthy stroll around the camp's premises has allowed the man to familiarize himself with the other tents and facilities. Sure the few looks Preston received were a bit off putting but at least they were just looks.

Still, it is abundantly clear that Preston is different here, even more so than when he lived with Clover in the town. Luckily, the tent provides an oasis from the camp's ever watching eyes.

"Preston are you there?"

The familiar female voice quickly takes Preston's attention, pulling the man from his studying of the curved sword as he stands. Though the voice draws a sour feeling to his stomach as he shifts a little. "Yeah?"

Without a moment of hesitation, the flap opens to the orange and red light of the setting sun; but it is not atmosphere that Preston looks too. Instead, it is the tan skinned, light brown haired satyress now occupying the tent with him. Clover's expression is a mixture of emotions, though nothing gives them away as she speaks in a semi-formal tone. "I see you have shaved."

Preston's hands quickly begin to feel a little clammy as he rubs them to his pants. "Uh, yep... I kinda cut myself but I'm fine." The man casually points to the fine cuts on his neck as he chuckles.

Clover's eyes hold to the cuts as she swallows a little. "Why is it that Reynard tells me that you are leaving?"

Preston lowers his voice as he realizes he cannot look the woman in the eyes. "I thought it would be the best thing. Now we can just focus on magic with no distractions."

Clover continues to glare at the man despite her increased confusion. "What?" As her words end her hands start up a bright blue glow as the inside of the tent quickly becomes encased by her magic. As it does her voice holds to a fair, but shaky height. "Master Nyota has tasked me with teaching and protecting you. Which means I need to have you somewhere safe."

Preston just smirks to the comment as he holds his hands to the tent. "I'm in a *Flóff* camp surrounded by warriors. I doubt this place will get attacked."

"That is not the point, Preston. I am responsible for your safety and..." Clover shakes her head again as she stutters a little. "How could you leave, Preston?"

The man shrugs as he continues to hold his voice down, despite the spell Clover placed around them. "I didn't want to bother you while you were out; and I know you've had a lot of extra things come up. Worrying about me should not be on your mind."

Clover comes a little closer to Preston as she gives a fake laugh. "So, leaving means I will worry less?"

The satyress' quick words do nothing to sway the man as Preston simply stares to Clover's stern gave. "Oh come on, Clover, I'll be fine, and you know that. Besides you only care because Nyota asked you, but don't you think we've been around each other long enough?" He smirks. "It's better this way."

Clover's expression changes to a bit of shock at the comment as she stutters. "I do not worry for your safety merely because I am told to, Preston."

Preston smiles as he just shrugs. "Well thank you, but now you have plenty of time to focus on other things."

Clover's voice is not a yell, but her ears perk up as she rolls her tongue to her mouth. "Last night? Is this your attempt to prove something? It is foalish, hardly something-..."

"Last night?" Preston's eyes lock to the satyress as he continues with a deep tone. "I don't care about last night. Look, you want me gone anyways. What's wrong with me leaving early?"

For a moment Clover is silent, however, her voice comes back to her as her hands begin to flicker with a little magic. "You believe this smart? Hmm? And how are we to practice magic now, Preston? It is barred in *Flöff* territory."

"Then I'll come to the library! Look, look, why are you upset about this, it's fine?" Preston taps his hands to his chest as he continues. "I'm fine here and you get me out of your hair early what's the problem?"

Clover moves a little closer to the man, which forces Preston to press himself a little more to his bed as Clover jabs a finger to his chest. "Because I do not appreciate decisions being made for me, Preston. Especially if they not only affect me but others I care about."

"What of Reynard?" Clover's breath is heavy, and she pants as she awaits Preston's words. The moment of silence however does allow Preston's mind to clear a little as he looks the woman's tired, blue eyes over. "Caring about someone goes a little further than just doing what you think is right. Sometimes you have to do things that people won't ask you to do."

The satyress arrogantly chuckles as she steps back. "You hold no ground over me, Preston."

Preston just nods as he clears his throat. "What do you think the amulet is for, huh?"

Clover nods annoyed at the question. "To help you."

"It's to help me stay sane. I can't do that around you." Preston moves a hand to Clover's though she pulls away as Preston speaks up, a sigh following her action. "I'm sorry, but I'm afraid I'll hurt you, I'll hurt Reynard, or whatever. I can't stay in the library."

Clover gives a sigh to the words as she speaks up. "You understand you will have to return to the library for us to continue our training, yes? Burden on both our houses now?"

Preston nods, realizing his words held no meaning to the woman as he nods. "I will as soon as I can. I promised Reynard and I intend to keep that promise."

A light smile comes to Clover's face as she agrees. "Yes, he has grown fond of you."

"Yea." Preston crosses his arms tightly. "I mean that..."

"Of course." Clover's voice fades a little as she looks to the light blue covered sides of the tent. "Fine. I suppose I should be heading back before it is dark. Your mind is made up it seems." As her words end the magic to the tent fades. "Be safe, Preston."

"Get some rest, Clover." Preston continues. "You look tired"

The man's comment just holds Clover's smile as she brings her hand to the tent's flap. "Stop worrying about me, Preston."

As the satyress moves from Preston's sight the tent grows quiet again. The world outside has become a little darker but day still clings to its last hour. Preston slowly slumps his back to the bed as he stares through the tent's fabric and into the sky. Seeing Clover has stirred a few questions again; however, he merely moves his hand under his shirt as he prompts the spell within his amulet.

He shivers to the feeling of warmth now rushing through his body, a sigh escaping him as he feels his mind go blank, his worries chased away.

A dopey smile rolls to Preston's face, his mind taken to another plane. However, with all the moments of doubt Preston seems to face, a stroke of luck presents itself. This time with the sound of a voice calling from outside.

"*Mealtime!*"

The words spark a quick and undeniable reaction to the man's stomach. Which aptly take the man's attention for the moment as he moves from the bed and towards the tent's opening.

It barely takes a second for Preston to spot the gathering group of winged *Flöffs* now starting to form around the watch tower's base. A few extra crates and boxes have been pulled around the large fire now shining in the middle of the camp.

Truthfully, Preston does not know how his stay in the camp transfers over into meals and other services. But, his stomach has convinced him there is no harm in asking.

The gathered group does not notice Preston's approach as the chatter of laughter ring through the camp. No real smells of food have hit Preston's nose yet, but the lack of a breeze in the camp may have something to do with it.

However, as Preston continues to near the group a few glances come his way. And before too long someone steps forward. "Ah, the interloper. What current has brought you here?"

The *Flóff* before Preston has caught the man quickly off guard. Not because of any unexpected comment but rather with a strange accent somewhere between Australian and surfer dude. Even more unusual is this *Flóff's* wings, unlike the more typical colors of brown, white or somewhere in-between this avian warrior has a dull, blue almost ocean like hue to his feathers. Of course, being part bird, Preston does not take the coloring as too much of a shock. Still, even the *Flóff's* sandy colored hair and skin suggest something different about this sharp chinned and pointed eared man.

The length of Preston's gawking does not deter the *Flóff*, in fact the warrior clad avian simply dips his wooden spoon to the bowl in his grasp. This action quickly shakes Preston from his stare as he speaks up. "Hey."

The *Flóff* just smirks as Preston notices his wings flinching a little. "Your eyes shift less than logs against the bank. Do you have strife with the *Flóffs* of the coast?"

Preston quickly picks up on the man's tone as he watches the *Flóff* take another slurping sip from his spoon. "What? No, no! I just never met one." Truthfully the *Flóff* before Preston is not very tall or even buff to warrant any real intimidation. Yet, Preston still backs down mainly to avoid any actual conflict.

"*Hmpf*." The *Flóff* looks Preston over again as he dips his spoon back into what looks like a soup filled bowl.

However, the slightly awkward stare match Preston has found himself in comes to a quick end, as the familiar dark, red haired avian steps in. "Ah, Umiko, I see you have met our guest..."

Umiko's eyes widen a little, but his tone does not suggest anything as he replies. "*Hmpf*, teach it not to stare, Stysen." As his words end the *Flóff* moves past Preston and continues into the camp's courtyard.

Preston's eyes now turn to Stysen as he speaks up. "Yeah thanks with that staring match, it was kinda getting-..."

Before Preston's breath can run its course Stysen speaks up. "Why are you out here?"

The smile to Stysen's face is friendly, though something in his eyes halts Preston from speaking up immediately. "Uh... I thought it was like dinner or something?"

The comment brings a chuckle from Stysen as the avian moves a little closer to Preston. The avian's height is a little above average but his slenderer frame is nothing compared to some of the guards Preston has seen. Though, unlike Umiko, Stysen does bring a slight reaction to Preston as he finds himself listening to the avian's words a little more clearly. "All are expected to eat together as it allows for a stronger bound to form. In the turbulent winds of a fight the most important things are your comrades." Stysen squints to the man. "You are neither warrior, nor artisan, but your presence will still be warmly welcomed by the fires."

Stysen nods as he glances back to the fire and the group around it, he moves a hand to Preston as he walks him away. "I had assumed the *Pexřá* would have explained this... of course, I never thought I would see the great *Pexřá* invite a Walker into our camp." He shakes Preston a little as he laughs.

Preston for a moment does not know how to react to the comment, but the man still listens as Stysen continues. "Find yourself a seat beyond the watchtower, I shall bring you something this night. You must prove to this camp you deserve to eat amongst them."

"Okay, how would I do that?"

Stysen just smirks as he pats his heavy hand to Preston's shoulder. "That is for you to decide. Now find your seat."

The smile and the tone make the comment sincere, however Preston cannot shake the feeling that the sentence has not yet ended; despite the fact Stysen now walks back towards the fire and the group.

Preston does manage to shift his eyes as he looks around the camp for something to sit on. It only takes a moment for the man to spot a box a little ways away. It may not be very big, but it is large enough for the man to rest as he waits for Stysen's return.

Yet, from Preston's position which faces the watchtower and the group, Preston can tell there is no urgency in Stysen's movements. In fact, it looks as if the avian warrior has begun telling a story, at least from the way he slowly swings his blade. Further suggesting this is the laughter ringing up from the group.

With a sigh Preston begins to look around the camp. The watchtower is lit, with a simple bowl like fire sitting to one side, primitive but effective from what Preston guesses. However, before the man can think over his next move a voice takes his attention.

"Whoa, you really told the truth?"

It takes a moment for Preston to react to the young girl now sitting next to him. Not because of her words but rather what she sits on. "Is that a cloud?"

Ellette shifts her eyes from the bowl she blows into as she looks to the thick white almost ball of cotton she sits to. "Yes?" Her words are almost unamused as she goes back to blowing into the hot bowl.

Preston just laughs as he looks over the girl's crossed legged posture in her makeshift seat. Each time she blows her braided hair jiggles a little, though it seems to not bother her as she continues. If Preston did not know any better, he would make the argument that the cloud was nothing more than a transparent bean bag chair. Seeing as how Ellette slumps into it, though Preston knows far too well of its authenticity, despite the logic.

Accepting this, Preston laughs.

Ellette cocks an eye to the comment as she begins to loudly and obnoxiously slurp her soup from the bowl. "Why you laugh?"

Preston just waves the comment off as he continues to laugh. "Nothing, we're just two normal people sitting around…"

Ellette squints to the man as she begins to slurp a little slower. "Yea?"

The girl's hawk like gaze slowly starts to put Preston off as the man speaks back up. "I thought it was like rude to stare at someone?"

With another loud sip Ellette shakes her head. "You are not a *Flóff*." She slurps, a bit of soup, some of it hanging onto her chin as she talks. "What are you?"

"I'm from the uh *Fárwift* thing"

"No." Ellette takes another slurp as she watches Preston shake his head.

"Oh?" Preston chuckles as he rubs his hands together. "And how would you know that?"

Ellette shrugs as she speaks up. "I just know. So, what are you?"

A light laugh comes from Preston as he shrugs. "I'm a human."

"*Ugh.*"

The reaction takes Preston by surprise as he quickly speaks up again. "Wait, you know what that is?"

Ellette simply shakes her head as she takes another sip from her bowl. "No, but it does not sound fun to mate with." Ellette cocks an eye to Preston as she puts her bowl down a little. "So, did you spear her?"

The comment brings a quick and awkward feeling to Preston as he looks around the camp and then back to the teenage looking girl beside him. "Hey, shouldn't you be with everyone over there?"

Ellette takes her last sip from the bowl as she shakes her head. "I have my own *Quétzal* feathers... well feather. Besides, every *Flóff* knows what a male wants after a challenge. It is like rain from a dark cloud."

"Great, so, you heading over there now, right?" Preston gives an anxious laugh as he rubs his hands to his legs.

Ellette set the bowl to the ground as she wipes her mouth with her hand. "I am not to brush feathers with any of a higher rank. Besides, most do not want me sitting near them."

Preston nods. "Why's that?"

Ellette shrugs. "Spear a *yiftiñ* get the tip end." Ellette makes a stabbing motion as she nods. "Stysen has a thing about hunting what would bleed, so no one talks with me out of fear." She trails on. "Not that I care, males are *múck'di bafte*ñ."

Preston squints to the comment as he laughs. "So, what you just sit around?"

"No, *Pexřá* Elva and a few others do not enjoy Stysen's stories." Ellette shrugs. "But the *Pexřá* is set to the wind, so just us low ranks."

"What... I'm the only low ranks?" Preston chuckles.

Ellette sighs as her wings fall a little more into the cloud she sits on. "You ask too many questions." Ellette continues to rub her forehead as she trails on. "There was another *yiftiñ* perhaps a *moř̌o* ago. But she was assigned somewhere else, nice color too, not that I care."

Preston cocks his head a little to the girl as he speaks up. "So, you don't talk with anyone your age? Where's your mom or dad at least?"

"Hmm..." Ellette taps her pointy fingers to her chin as she shrugs. "*Féllcreed*?"

Preston just laughs to the comment as he crosses his arms and looks back to the group. "That's wrong."

Ellette squints to the man's reaction as she follows in with her own question. "The winds just blow in different paths. What is wrong with this?"

"I... uh never mind, this is like boarding school I guess." Preston gives a fake little smile as he nods to the girl beside him.

The comment however seems to have worked as Ellette nods back. "I do hope to meet another y*iftiñ* when I am allowed into town."

Preston sighs. "Well I would help but the only kid I know is Bella's sister."

A low, almost cooing sound comes from Ellette as she perks back up. "*Pexřá* has mentioned that name before?"

The bird noise has brought a slight smirk to Preston's face as he turns back to the girl. "She's one of Elva's friends."

"No, she is an *Únoff*. They cannot be friends, the *Pexřá* is using her for another purpose. Maybe information!"

Preston just shrugs to the avian girl's watchful eyes as he continues. "I think they're friends."

Ellette holds a bit of skepticism in her voice as she speaks up. "And what is this Bella's sister's name?"

A light laugh comes from Preston as he shakes his head. "I don't remember, and I was kinda being sarcastic."

Ellette rolls her eyes as she sinks back to her cloud. "Human minds must be very cloudy."

Another light laugh comes from Preston as he nods. "Yeah I guess I could agree with that."

A faint smirk comes to Ellette's face but Preston does not notice it as he instead focuses back to Stysen, who has continued to be the center of attention.

The silent moment however is brought to an end as a loud belching noise rings up from Preston's right. The sound quickly brings a chuckle from the man as he nods. "Nice one."

Ellette pays the comment almost no mind as she speaks up. "That is what happens with *Broffáll* stew. Fills the gut but rumbles the butt. You have any?"

"Uh..." Preston points to the group as he continues. "Stysen said it would not be a good idea to go near the group."

A slight smirk comes to Ellette's mouth as she nods. "He also said he would bring you a bowl, yea?"

"Yeah?"

Ellette just nods as she speaks up. "The winds only carry you so far. It may be time to flap, Human."

The man just shakes his head. "Yeah, I have no idea what that means."

"Shame." With a quick jump Ellette springs to her feet as she stretches, her hands slowly falling to the sword on her side as she nods. "Enjoy your empty night, the *Pexřá* has asked me to bring another cloud down for. See you *témont* if you live!"

Preston just nods as he watches the girl move from the cloud she sat on. As she moves however the cloud begins to rise from the ground, not too fast but with a slight push from Ellette it begins to raise a little more.

As the cloud begins to ascend back to the sky the young *Flöff* girl begins to walk away without even the slightest goodbye; not that Preston expected one. Still, Ellette's words slowly begin to make something clear to the man as he stares to the group a little ways from where he sits. "How did she get her food?"

With the thought in mind Preston stands, and begins his short trek to the group surrounding the fire. It only takes perhaps three or four steps however for a few sets of eyes to turn to Preston's approach. And before long, the whole group has Preston's attention.

A slightly cocky smile comes to Stysen's face as he places his hands to his sides. "What brings you back, Walker?"

The smell of the stew is thick in the air, and the memories of Nyota cooking it once before now begin to flood back into Preston's mind. "That." Preston points to the large, military sized, deep coal colored pot hanging from the spit above the fire.

Stysen holds the smirk as he speaks up. "Why were you waiting? Fleet-Fra, fix our companion a bowl!"

A slight laugh rolls through the sitting *Flöffs* as one of them near the pot begins to stir to the liquid with a wooden ladle.

Preston stands stupid as he slowly brings his voice out. "W-why did you tell me to wait?"

Stysen's eyes widen as he holds his hand to the bowl of freshly poured stew. "Ah, so you have submitted to my words?"

A chuckle rings up from the *Flöffs* as they continue to listen to the banter.

The bowl is passed to Stysen without hesitation as the avian warrior mockingly continues. "I see you enjoy the waves of others knocking you back. I say you prove that you deserve to eat with us, yes?"

Just as Stysen's words end the other avians around Preston begin to chime in. "Fine by me."

"Well, we are waiting?" The smug smile to Stysen's face only adds to Preston's annoyance at being put on the spot.

Luckily, Preston just laughs it off as he shrugs. "What do you want me to do?"

A voice rings up from the onlookers as Preston's comment drifts into the air. "Let the Walker fly, Stysen!"

"Ah, yes!" Stysen takes to the sky, fueling the fire as his winds bat ever slowly to his climbing. "A *Flóff* must fly!" He places the bowl to the top of the watch tower as he moves aside from it, his arms crossing as his wings fan the flame beneath him. "Fly! You are in a *Flóff* camp after all. What use would we have of you if you could not fly?!"

The group around him merely chuckles to Stysen's display, however Preston holds a smirk as his hands start up in a flash of green light. Within seconds the bowl is teleported to his hand, and a smile crosses Preston's face as he holds out his other hand. "How's about a spoon now?"

A look of disdain greets Preston's gaze as a few of the more brawny soldiers now stand, their hands coming to their swords. Preston merely blinks to them as one finally speaks up. "*Únoff* spy!"

"Hardly." Stysen lowers himself back to the fire as he motions for his friends to sit down. His flashy smile holds as he bends down to the bucket near the soup, pulling forth a wooden spoon. "Full of tricks, creature of the *Fárwift*."

Stysen nods. "There is a rule about magic, while it is not punishable by the *Alphé* I stand by it, as I do with all *Flóff* code." He nods. "It is not fair to discipline someone who knows not what they have done. Heed me, magic is forbidden in this camp, do it again and you will answer to me."

Preston takes hold of the spoon as he raises his bowl to Stysen. "I thought we answer to Kassie alone."

Stysen takes a step forward as his smile drops. "*Alphé* Kassie to you, outsider."

Despite the stare Preston merely smirks to Stysen's serious face as he nods. "My mistake, I didn't know."

"Ha." Stysen nods as he holds his hand out. "Have a seat, you clearly found your gull."

The other *Flóffs* that are standing regain their seats slowly as Stysen too returns to the box he sat to. The crackle of the fire rings into the night for a moment, all eyes focused to Preston as he takes the soup in.

Though as he continues Stysen speaks up. "Well, does it not appease your pallet?"

Preston nods. "It's fine."

"Good." Stysen nods. "Then slurp, let us hear your excitement to it."

Following the comment Preston begins to slurp.

A smile comes to Stysen as a few others look to relax. Though even as their faces begin to soften and their eyes begin to turn, Stysen's voice continues. "Outsider, you walk without armor and without sword, do you feel safe amongst us?"

Preston takes a sip of his soup as he nods. "Yea, I do."

"Good, good." Stysen flashes a smile. "You should, we are all one here."

Preston smirks. "Want me to start calling you brother or something?"

"Hardly, I think we come from different yolk, Preston."

The man shrugs as he glances to the other *Flóff* around the fire. "I don't Stysen, you talk a lot, you sure you're not part *Ünoff*?"

A laugh comes up from one *Flóff* at the fire, and although Stysen does not lose his temper, he does call out to the chuckle. "Something amuse you Lutin? Perhaps this outsider has stirred your chest; would you care to share stories from your time serving the *Flúry Fasá*?"

Preston tips the bowl to his lips as he watches the dark skinned and bald headed *Flóff* shakes his head as he rises from his seat at the fire. "No." He glances to the others around him as he nods. "And might I suggest you use this time for food, not talk."

Stysen licks his lips to the comment as he nods. "Of course, my *Thrće*."

Without a word the dark-avian turns and walks away, his bowl left at his seat until someone next to it moves to collect it. Yet, as he leaves Stysen's voice chimes up, his showman like charm calling attention back to him as he settles a hand to his knee and leaves forward. "Well I suppose he is right, shall we not ask what we all wish to know." Stysen smiles. "Did the *Pexřá* ask you to stay before or after you speared her guts?"

A laugh rolls from the group as Preston merely sighs to the question. Though he plays the conversation off as he loosens up. "I would call it more of a daggering." He clears his throat as he continues as he rolls a hand to Stysen. "I'm sure you get it, all talk but a dull blade?"

Despite Preston's light-hearted laugh none reciprocate as they wait for Stysen's response. Instead, the sound of the fire takes hold as Stysen merely stares to Preston, yet just as it grows too awkward a laugh rolls from the red haired avian as he gestures to the man. "A *jáff*, though I should have expected such, what with your *Étrometáy* during the fight, such sounds I rarely believe any but Fleet-fra have heard in the bed."

The group burst into laughter, Preston following suit as Stysen eggs it on. Though Preston keeps his eyes to the red haired avian as the moment begins to pass. "But no, truly." Stysen nods, his laughter gone. "How did you come to grace us?"

Preston blinks to the comment before standing, a surprising action as Stysen leans back a little. With a clear of the throat Preston nods. "Well, I guess that's something you'll find out tomorrow, huh?"

Stysen cocks a smirk to the words as he nods. "You will impress then?"

With a nod Preston moves away from the group, his mind replaying the short pissing match over in his head as he looks to the other members around him. Though as he does he takes notice to how most care little for his exit. Sighting this, a smile comes to his face as he starts back to his tent.

The sounds of the men behind comes back into the night, though Preston cares little for it as he presses into his tent and gives a simple sigh. His eyes turn to his clothing as he runs a hand across it, still feeling to the dirt that was collected during his and Elva's fight.

Realizing this he turns his gaze to the chest on the ground as he moves to open it. As he does, he pulls forth one of his simpler shirts, tossing it to the bed as he moves to remove his old one. Not knowing the cleaning schedule or if he would be cleaning it himself, he opts to fold it in a separate way, laying down to the other clothing in the chest as he makes a mental note to clean it later.

A faint chuckle rolls through him as he continues his replay of his conversation, he knows it was a game, a matching of cocks that Preston, at least for the moment, feels good about.

For the next five or so minutes Preston merely relaxes, his new clothing a breath of fresh air to his once sweaty body. The tent itself has a soothing effect, the wind blows through it with ease and the stars above shine through without a care. Though the constant chatter from outside helps to remind Preston he is not alone.

The library may yield more comforts, though rarely does it provide worthwhile distractions for Preston. Of course, as the sound of footsteps draws near to his tent the man finds himself second guessing that thought.

Even still, he rises as he takes notice to the sight of the tent opening. "Hello?"

Stepping in is Elwine, though her name escapes Preston as he instead forces a friendly smile to the unexpected guest. "Oh, hey, uh…" He shrugs. "How's it going?"

The woman's hands are folded together before her, and her tone is quiet as she replies. "I am well." Without a word her hands come to her armor as she begins to undo it.

Preston squints to the action, though before he can say anything he watches as the avian-warrioress strips off her armor, her hands continue to the simple wool shirt now covering her.

Sighting this Preston stands. "Woah, woah what are you…"

Elwine steps back, her hands pausing for a moment as she looks almost confused to Preston's rising. "No, no, we will not be touching, only mating."

The comment yields little to clear Preston's dumbfounded expression as he merely watches the woman remove her top, bringing to view her chest. Of course, just like Elva's, the breasts on display are alien to Preston, even as he looks away the lack of a nipple still sits strangely in the man's mind. Though he only caught a glimpse he fumbles with his words as he attempts to laugh off the sudden and hardly believable events now transpiring. "Ah…. um."

Elwine merely grins to Preston's shyness as her wings spread out a little, the lack of attention even prompting her forward as she squints to him. "Do you wish to lie down?"

"No, no, hey um." Preston turns back around, his eyes focusing on her face as he notices her left hand lazily held to her trousers. Even from Preston's gaze he can tell how muscular the woman is, perhaps not as toned as Elva though definitely boosting a more fit physique than his own. "Woah uh." Preston struggles to find his words as Elwin stands still, her nakedness on display without shame. "I didn't mean to do something I-I just wanted to know your name. Was I not supposed to ask that?"

Preston's blushed face along with his stammer slowly draws Elwine's hand from her pants, though she does not move to cover herself as she instead shifts her hands to her hips, a power pose as she squints to the man. "This merely a gesture of comrades, Stysen suggested our meeting."

A laugh comes from Preston as he picks up her shirt and her armor, holding it to her as he shakes his head to the crazy situations. "W-what just now? No, y-you look great, but no."

Elwine's eyes widen a bit as she looks over her garments now being held out to her, the muscular woman taking both the armor and shirt into one hand. "You are refusing me?"

Preston rubs a hand to his mouth as he again sneaks a peek to the woman's flawless, and Amazonian like features; his words come out with a sure tone as he nods. "Yes, yea, I just met you."

Despite the words Elwine merely blinks to the man before her, no hint of anger, no hint of sadness etched into her auburn eyed gaze. Instead, a look of amazement, and an all out flabbergasting stare pinned to Preston.

Still though as her body stays on display Preston grows hot. "Can you get dressed?"

At the words Elwine beings to ease herself into her shirt, though while it appears easy enough to get off, Preston realizes she is unable to merely slip it on as she begins to button it down. The rock of her chest prompts Preston to speak up as he crosses his arms. "C-can you turn around."

Elwine again obliges to the command, turning around as her wings now face Preston, of course the man's eyes turn to the crest of her rounded buttocks that poke from her loosened trousers, a sight far worse for him.

He swallows hard as he forces himself to look away. Several antagonizing and tantalizing minutes pass before Elwine is dressed again, and throughout she has remained silent, a clear look of bewilderment sits to her face.

With her dressed Preston clears his throat as he nods. "S-sorry, you look great but um... yea sorry."

Elwine merely nods to the comment as she moves her hand to the tent's flap, her look of confusion never once leaving her face as she leaves.

With her gone Preston paces, though he runs a hand down his face as he turns to the tent's opening and starts out. He pants as he glances away from Elwine and towards the mass of men still gathered at the fire.

Without hardly glance of approval he starts towards, his voice coming up as he nears where Stysen still sits on his box. "Hey! What was that about?"

Sighting the man Stysen speaks up, his gestures drawing everyone's attention as he replies. "Ah, so you finished, hardly a beast of stamina."

Preston speaks over the laughter as he points a finger to Stysen. "I don't know what game that was, but don't do it again!"

Stysen merely smirks to the fat finger pointed at him as he moves his hands to his hips. "It was a welcoming, you made us laugh, it was a gesture of good winds."

"I don't want your gesture so don't-..."

Stysen laughs. "Come now, she said you asked her name."

"So what?" Preston glances to the eyes now pinning to him as he continues. "Are you all so bestial that asking a name is something so insane?!"

"Elwine is an easy conquest, I merely save you the sweat." Stysen nods. "Of course an outsider, let alone one of *Unoff* ilk would not understand that. There is honor in a clear head, all those in camp aid one another."

He chuckles as he nods. "Besides, was it not better to feel a spear within her, rather than a dagger in a mare. I hear they are quite accompanying to anything smaller than a lance."

A laugh rolls through the group again though Preston does not follow it as he speaks up, the intensity of his tone cutting through the air of jubilant. "I rejected your gift, and I'll reject another."

Stysen's smile fades, though another's voice chimes in as he rises. "You rejected Elwine?" The *Flóff* gives a simple laugh as he nods to the group. "If you excuse me, I believe she will need some tending to."

A half smile cocks as Stysen waves his friend off. "Be gone, Fleet-fra." Stysen leans forward as he nods to Preston. "I do believe you misunderstand my-..."

"No, I think that you-..."

Preston's words are cut off as a dagger flies past his face, Stysen's movements far too quick for him to even realize as the warrior rises. "You had best return to your tent, less words grow meaningless, Walker."

The dagger continues to rock in the wood of the watchtower as Preston glances to the other avian-men now reaching to their own belts. With a nod Preston starts away, though as he turns his back Stysen cocks a smile.

"Welcome to camp, Walker!"

Preston merely ignores the comment, his mind reassuring him at how long the night will be.

Chapter 20

A New Day

"WAKE! THE NIGHT HAS PARTED!"

The shouts from outside quickly forces Preston to jump from his bed as his heart pounds to his chest. Preston grabs to the curved sword sitting on his chest of items as he charges outside. However, it is only just now that the man actually thinks over the yell that woke him.

The sky is a dull orange from the sun that has just barely begun to rise. In fact, the fire of the watchtower is the only real light shining into the camp as Preston blinks to it.

Realizing how foolish he must look wielding a sword without a shirt and his pants rolled up to above his knees, Preston aptly darts back to his tent. Yet, the man is not allowed to forget what he has just done as he quickly begins to feel lightheaded from the rush of blood in his veins.

This of course is only one more thing now compounding to Preston's mind, seeing as how last night's sleep was still filled with horrid nightmares of changing into the beast. Perhaps the only saving grace was the target of the dreams, which was Stysen rather than Clover. An earned bit of anger, albeit concerning, nonetheless.

With a faint groan Preston rubs to his head and his back as he looks to the uncomfortable bed he sprung from. Preston sets the sword, hilt first to the ground next to the chest as he opens it and retrieves a shirt. Normally Preston would change his whole attire, however not really knowing where to clean his clothing, nor knowing what spell Clover would use to clean hers, Preston aims to adjust his routine.

The camp outside has begun to stir and the noises of the world outside his tent are loud, loud enough to cause Preston's ears to ring as he groans. Even still, he works through the chatter of people as he moves outside, this time more adjusted.

The sky is still dull and the air crisp with the distinctive scent of the fields around the camp. Of course, Preston has his eyes focused on the smaller sized group of *Flöffs* gathered near the watchtower, just as they were last night.

However, before he can start his trek to the group a voice stops him. "Oh, so you did live?"

The young, tomboyish tone is quickly recognized as Preston turns to the young *Flöff* girl. "Whatcha mean? I just heard the wakeup call."

Ellette gives a little smirk as she shakes her head. "That call was to report to the watchtower. You should have been up long before the clouds glow." She cocks her head. "I had thought Stysen cut you in your sleep, since you refuse his gift."

Preston sighs, he shakes his head as he looks around the camp. "What... how do you know?"

Ellette stretches a little as she nods. "Fleet-fra likes to talk during his comforting." Ellette glances to her flat chest armor as she continues. "How could you reject her? I hear she is quite sought after."

A defeated laugh comes to Preston as he moves hand to his eyes. "I'm not talking about this with you." He rubs his eyes for a moment before taking a breath. "Where's the bathroom?"

Ellette ignores the comment. "Do you not like a woman's form? Do you like swords not sheathes? Most of the camp bathes in the clouds together so they will find out if you-..."

Preston claps his hands as he looks back to the group near the watchtower. "So how come you're not over there?"

Ellette squints to the tower as she shrugs. "I was on watch last, *Alphé* Kassie says it is best to not tire one's eyes. I am on break, also I am allowed into town now." Ellette's excitement fades a little as she continues. "Of course, if *Pexřá* returns late I shall have to wait until my next leave."

Preston nods as he attempts to lengthen the conversation. "Still going to the library first chance you get?"

Ellette quickly nods to the comment as she speaks up. "Neither gust nor storm could knock me from that path." The *Flóff* girl shrugs as she crosses her arms. "I may not know how to read that well, but I can speak it and I am sure a few *Flóff Nervál* tomes are among the walls."

"Well I hope you are allowed out today. I might see you at the library today."

A low cooing sound rings from Ellette as her thoughts continue to stir. "I also wish to meet the *Cáfty* Elva says works the bakery. I have always wanted to try sweets."

Noticing that the girl is lost in her thoughts Preston follows along. "I actually know Gwendy."

Ellette's face lightens as her wings puff out from her back. "Really? Are sweets good? Or were you just another one of her humps? I hear they hump more than we do, even have a whole pack of *Cáfty* just to-..." The girl's eyes dart to something behind Preston, her posture straightens and her voice lowers as she talks. "The clouds glisten, *Alphé* Kassie!"

The old voice comes up beside Preston, as Kassie stands a little to his side. "And a warm morning to you, Ellette." Kassie's eyes turn to the girl's slowly lowering wings. "I hope you enjoy your break."

A faint and slightly forced smile comes to Ellette as she nods. "Yes, *Alphé*."

Kassie holds her hand to the courtyard as she smiles. "I shall alert you when Elva comes back, my *yiftiñ*."

"Of course." Ellette lowers her head as she moves from Kassie's watch. As she does this the old *Flóff* now focuses on Preston. Although a smile sits to her face it does not bring any welcoming feelings to Preston, instead the smile is more of a show of power.

In fact, the look to the woman's face sparks a quick feeling to the man that he has done something wrong. A mother catching her child's hand in the cookie jar.

Yet, something in the woman's eyes keeps Preston's thoughts at bay. "As I understand it there was an incident last night? Magic used in the camp."

Preston cocks a smile to the comment as he nods. "That's what was reported?"

"I have heard mixed reports." The older woman clears her throat as she continues. "Do not make petty squabbles my business. Magic is left at the gate, I am sure Miss Vines has arranged for you to meet her elsewhere for your... practice, as she put it." Kassie's words halt for a moment as she just stares to the man before her. "Do make sure you speak with *Thrĉe* Lutin at the smith. It is unsettling to have an occupant without armor."

Preston nods to the woman. "Yes."

Kassie raises an eyebrow as she replies. "Respect is how you will last in our camp, Preston."

The man straightens his posture as he speaks up. "Yes, *A-Alphé* Kassie."

"Carry on." As her words end the old *Flóff* begins to stroll through the courtyard, her hands behind her back and her wings neatly settled as she looks to be inspecting the tents near her.

Noticing this, Preston turns tail before she peeks in at his unmade bed. With a shrug Preston turns and focuses beyond the watchtower as he starts to the forge and anvils.

It takes just a minute or two to get across the courtyard, but as Preston begins to near the forge, he slows his speed. Not because Lutin is nowhere to be found, but instead simply out of a lack of social norms. Preston has no idea how to approach the *Flóff* hammering away at anvil; judging by Lutin's attention the avian seems far too focused on his task, though Preston is too close to merely walk away.

A minute passes with Preston still unable to find the words to greet the smith. Luckily, the dark *Flóff* gives a low sigh as he stops his hammering. "Why do you linger like an unwanted fog, Walker. Speak."

Not the most welcoming comment Preston could have hoped for but the man takes the opportunity nonetheless. "Yea, hi. I need to get some armor?"

Lutin's eyes are half closed as he looks the man over. "It be fifty *Ord'* for my metal, sixty for me to shape. Twenty for hardened *lehtó* and ten for me to shape. Of course, if you have the metal it is fifteen to use the forge yourself."

"Uh..."

The *Flóff* places the hammer to the coal black apron's pocket as he crosses his arms. "No *Ord'* I presume?"

Preston gives a little laugh as he speaks up. "Would you trade?"

Lutin squints to the man. "Depends."

"A sword?"

A slight smirk comes to Lutin as he shakes his head. "If you refer to the sword you received before, the answer is no. It is nothing but a training sword."

"I beat Elva with it."

The *Flóff* sighs as he looks to the clouds for a moment before returning his eyes to Preston. "*Pexřá* Elva is a skilled scout, and an accomplished killer. One round is meaningless."

Preston's slightly cocky smile to his previous comment falters as he cocks his head to the deep voiced *Flóff* with a laugh. "Still not bad."

Lutin does not even widen his gaze as he rolls through his words without a hitch. "You are thicker than rain clouds, and I would bite that tongue before it gets too far."

"Ah, well..." Preston shrugs as he sighs. "After a few months you just kinda get used to awkward stares, didn't notice everyone wanted to kill me."

"No. Killing you would bring no glory; they wish to humiliate you." Lutin smiles as he nods. "And judging from your actions last night you can expect more. You have been labeled as the camp's *Preiśty*."

Lutin leans forward a little as he laughs. "Do you enjoy that name, *Preiśty*?"

Preston just smiles to the fact he has no idea what the man is saying. "Pressy? I've been called Press before."

Lutin just nods as he smiles. "Hm, how do you propose my payment? Can you work a forge"

A faint chuckle rolls through Preston as he looks around the forge. "No."

"What were you before, *Preiśty*?" Lutin looks the man over as he continues to smirk.

Preston shrugs as he speaks up. "A librarian, and before that a student and known bar-fly."

"Got no use for books, boy." Lutin shrugs. "What else?"

"Well I can't forge, but I could help you around it?"

Lutin just shakes his head. "You are untrained, we do not make *Dẃoff* armor here. But you could clean. Labor and I will give you the *lehtó*, good y*iftiñ* armor."

Preston just shrugs. "Alright, when do you want me to start."

Lutin points to the work bench near the camp's wood walls as he speaks up. "Put the apron on and begin cleaning the forge."

"Now?"

The *Flóff* holds his hand to the unlit furnace as he nods. "The furnace must be cleaned before I add more wood, and yes, now."

Preston slowly moves pass the avian smith and towards the apron folded on the workbench. As the man takes the dark brown and soot covered apron from the bench, he ties it and looks back to the *Flóff*.

Lutin takes the small tongs he was working on from the anival as he points to the various bins, boxes, barrels, and racks around the open forge. "After the furnace you are to clean all the tools with the brush on the rack, a barrel of water is over there. I keep my tools clean so it should not take long. Then you are to fill the bottom of the furnace with the wood in this box..."

Preston continues to follow the Lutin's hand, however with every new box or bin introduced Preston forgets what is in the last three. After about fifteen minutes of orientation Lutin sighs. "...You should be done at least with the furnace when I get back."

"What? You're leaving me here?"

For the first time Preston has seen the *Flóff* widened his eyes, albeit only to look at Preston as if he were a child. "Yes, the air carries the promise of breakfast. I must follow it. Now, clean *Preiśty*."

As the *Flóff* walks away Preston's stomach began to rumble. "Note to self, don't miss lunch." Preston's eyes turn to the bottom of the furnace as he looks to the slit he was told to pull out and clean. If it were not for the open grate that most likely acts as the flue Preston would not even see the drawer's opening as it blends in with the rest of the furnace. The man lightly touches the metal as he half-heartedly expects it to be hot, luckily it is not, and he pulls the heavy metal drawer out.

A plume of black quickly rushes to Preston's face. Coughing a bit, Preston drops it to the ground. His eyes watering a little as he looks over the holder. "Ugh…" Preston brings his hands to the metal box as he attempts to lift it, however he quickly finds it best to just drag it the two or three feet to the fair-sized pile of waste next to the large pile of wood. As he reaches the pile he takes the small shovel Lutin told him to use until he could properly dump it.

To the man's surprise the cleaning process for the drawer does not take too long and he quickly finds himself ready to place it back to the furnace. However, as he does this he gets a look at the round bowl like inners of the top of the furnace. the grates and stops that would keep the ore from falling into the fuel drawer are sturdy, but like Lutin said a few bits of metal have slipped through and will need to be hammered out to allow the heat to rise better.

Truthfully, the whole design of this furnace is a little off to Preston, but then again he has never seen one in real life. Still, the absence of the large accordion like blower to make the fire bigger as well as the use of wood for fuel makes no sense.

Naturally, Preston ignores the thoughts of logic as he looks to the tool rack for the items he was told he would need, though with such a quick introduction he pauses as he merely formulates his guess.

Chapter 21

The Irons Burn Hot

The weather in Artésque is as always a wonderful norm, just above cold and well below warm, yet the heat the man feels coursing through his body would suggest otherwise. Cleaning the furnace proved to be a bit more strenuous than first thought, on top of this Lutin has not returned since he left an hour or two ago.

The cloudless sky above has not yielded protection from the sun's constant rays, even his break to a heavy crate filled with small dark grey and slightly shiny rocks is almost pointless. The hard surface provides no comfort but the position beside the furnace has allowed some shade.

Preston's hands, much like the apron have turned a charcoal black and judging from the tickle on his face there is most likely some soot scraped across his brow.

"*Preiśty!* Remove yourself from the ore box! I shall not be collecting it if the wood breaks."

The deep voice springs Preston from the crate as he focuses to the burly, dark skinned *Flóff* now starting towards the forge's area. As Lutin comes closer, his face lightens a little. "Well, nothing seems to be out of place..."

Preston rolls his left arm a little as he speaks up. "You left me long enough. Where were you?"

Lutin shoots Preston a look that quickly silences the man. "Did any come to have weapons sharpened or armor fastened?"

"No."

"Then you have your answer." Lutin moves to the stake of wood as he points to it. "Why is the wood untouched? I told you to fill the furnace."

Preston nods as he waves his hand. "I filled it with coal, should be better than wood anyways."

"What?" Lutin quickly shifts his attention to the grated drawer beneath the furnace as he looks in. "You put these worthless rocks in the wood bin?" As the words ring through the forge the *Flóff* pulls the drawer out. "Remove this!"

Preston looks over the coal in the bin as he gives a little laugh. "Won't coal burn better than wood?"

The words followed by no action from Preston bring a response from Lutin as the *Flóff* strengthens his posture and stares down the blonde-haired man before him. "Do my words sail past your ears like wind?"

"It's going to burn the same if not better?" Preston shrugs as he continues. "Do you not know what coal is? It's the only thing in some of these boxes?"

Preston's tone delivers the words with a slight bit of laughter to Lutin, who now reaches in and plucks a piece of coal from the bin. "This is scrap. *Dwoff* are paid by weight of craft, they fill it with this." The *Flóff* points to the bins near the side of the furnace. "It is all used for roads and stone making. This is nothing more than dirt."

Preston looks over the coal piece in the *Flóff's* claw like hand as he nods. "Well yea some of it, but light it."

Lutin's wings lower a little as his sharp eyes quickly change to a squint. "You cannot light stone fool."

"Humor me, besides I left some wood in there to get it started."

Lutin wags a finger to Preston as he tosses the coal piece back to the bin. "If it fails to light you leave my forge."

Preston just laughs as he nods. "It's going to burn; I've been to a barbecue."

The words only bring another confused look from Lutin as the avian man speaks up a little annoyed. "Start the fire, *Preisty*."

The confidence Preston felt quickly fades as the man raises his eyebrows. "Uh... you got a match?"

Lutin sighs as he sucks to his bottom lip and looks away. "Enough talk!"

Preston throws his hands in the air as he speaks up. "Well how do you light fire?"

"I used wood, not stone." Lutin turns back to Preston with his head held high as he continues. "I think your small *Únoff* brain has this stone confused with *Kélf*."

A thought pops to Preston's mind at the word as the man holds his hands to Lutin. "Wait, wait. I'll be right back."

"Back? Where are you going boy?" Preston ignores the comment as he starts his run from the forge. Lutin watches the man's less than graceful jog as he shakes his head. With a sigh Lutin starts towards the wood pile and begins to pick up a few pieces.

Lutin continues to shake his head as he looks down to the half-full bin of black rock, and as the *Flóff* sets the wood to the ground to pull the bin out a voice calls out to him.

"Okay! Okay! Watch!"

Preston runs up to the *Flóff's* side as he huffs a little through his words. "Just a second..."

The sight of the man so out of breath sparks a reaction to Lutin as he looks to the tents across the courtyard. "You are winded from such a short-..."

"Okay, here I go." Preston raises his arm as he focuses his eyes to the coals. However, the action is not what takes Lutin's attention, instead it is the *Gloftór* on Preston's hand that now begins to glow.

The avian man watches glowing with a heavy look of dismay, but he allows Preston to continues. After a few moments of nothing but the low hum of magic Lutin speaks up. "What are you doing?"

A smile comes to Preston's face as he notices the coals wrapped in his green magic now begin to spark a little. "Making fire."

Lutin does a slight double take as he watches the smoke now starting to puff up from the bin. It only takes a few moments for the thick black smoke to turn into a fire as Preston's magical grip over it halts to the coals and instead turns to the bin itself. As it is pushed back to the furnace Preston turns to Lutin with a cocky smirk. "See, it burns."

The *Flóff* just stares at the fire now glowing from the hole in the middle of the furnace's bowl shape as he shakes his head. "What is this?"

Preston loosens the strap on the glove as he shrugs. "What? It's coal, don't breathe it, but it should burn better." A slight smirk comes from Preston as he continues. "How could you not know about it?"

Lutin is silent as he continues to look at the furnace. "Mind your words boy..." He sighs as he looks over the fire. "Even the *Dwoff* that sell these crates know nothing of their craft..."

The *Flóff*'s eyes say more than his words and noticing the slight anger in them Preston raises his hands. "Well you don't have to use it."

Lutin shakes his head. "Why would I not? This is no Sky-Forge, I burn enough wood to warm a town..." He straightens his posture as he eyes the man. "You make a mockery of our ways, dirt and stone is not us, boy."

Preston blinks to the comment. "I never said that it-...."

Lutin nods. "You loaded my furnaces without asking."

"W-well I would have said something when you came back."

Preston's words do little for Lutin as the *Flóff* just nods. "You are going to stay with me for the rest of my work. If no problem arise I will count this towards your first payment. However, if my forge breaks, I break your hands, *Mŕad'sci*."

Preston squints to the avian as he repeats his last word. "*M-rad-sigh?*"

Lutin speaks up. "Quiet! Give me ore, let us test this flame of stone."

- - -

(Late Afternoon)

Preston dips his hands to the barrel of water as he splashes some to his face. The day has rolled on, despite the heat of the furnace and the burn of the sun, it is a little afternoon from what Preston can tell. Of course, the only real reason Preston thinks this is because of the call to lunch he had a few minutes ago.

The man pulls his hands from the barrel as he looks back to where Lutin stands. The burly *Flóff* continues to fan the flames with his own wings, embers striking against him as he carries on with his process that has crafted the last ten or so bars of iron or steel that sit to the box beside him.

Preston's muscles ache as he watches and waits for the never tiring *Flóff* to call him over. However, as the man continues to listen for his name to roar through the avian man's mouth it never comes; and as Lutin pulls his heavy gloves from his hands and places his metal tools to the racks Preston speaks up. "We done?"

Lutin shakes his head as he looks to the fire. "The fire grows dull again."

The words sink Preston's spirit as he nods. According to Lutin only having to clean the bin three times so far is actually an improvement, not that Preston agrees. Though as he moves to follow the comment, Lutin speaks up.

"...I only need a few bars for the orders. I may let the winds carry you."

Preston just blinks to the comment as he speaks up. "So I can go?"

Lutin nods as he turns to the man. "Yes, after I ask you something."

Again Preston's heart sinks, but the man does pull the apron from his body as he nods. "Yeah?"

"Your body is weak."

Preston smirks a little as he speaks up. "Thanks?"

"Quiet!" Lutin sighs as he shakes his head. "I have watched your gaze, you think this work is foolish. While you are a poor excuse for a comrade, your mind may have uses."

"I don't think this is foolish." Preston shrugs. "Who else makes the weapons?"

Lutin nods. "Many want *Flóff* forged steel, yet a ground forge is hardly fit. If the clouds were thicker, I would not need this *Dwoff* craft. You think, give me a suggestion, boy."

Preston just chuckles. "Get a blower, stop fanning the fire with your wings."

"No, it helps the metal." Lutin seems to take some offence to the comment as he quickly continues. "Give another."

Preston shakes his head. "I don't know, get a bunch of hot air balloons, tie them together." Preston simply chuckles. "Make a floating platform of clouds, that's crazy enough to work."

Lutin squints to the words. "What is this?"

"Um... what?"

Lutin raises his voice a little. "The word boy! What is this hot air balloon?"

"It's a..." Preston sighs. "Look I don't know how to explain it, it's a thing, it's a canvas that takes the heat of a flame and goes up, I don't know how it works." He snaps his fingers. "Get me a candle, I can make a flying lantern, it's kinda the same."

Lutin nods. "Just a candle?"

Preston shakes his head. "Well you put a candle under something that catches the heat, like a funnel. If you use wax paper it's strong enough to hold it and it won't burn up."

"Hm." Lutin takes a breath. "Leave your apron."

The words bring a smile to the man's face as he hands the apron to Lutin, though with no further comment from the dark *Flóff* Preston pauses. Of course, as Lutin begins to go about his business hardly with a glance more to his once so diligent worker.

Seeing this, Preston starts to walk away.

His clothing feels heavy and his hands are ashy, but Preston tries to brush off any remaining soot or coal dust all the same. A light cough rings from the man as he spits to the ground. His slightly excited speed quickly bringing him to his tent as he ducks inside.

Now inside the man's eyes quickly turn to the box on the floor as he pulls out a clean shirt, pants, toothbrush and the makeshift paste. As the man collects the items he tightens the *Gloftór* he has worn all day. However, before he can exit the tent a voice calls in.

"You have finally finished with Lutin?"

At the sound of someone outside of his tent Preston jumps, a sudden flashback of last night playing to his mind. Though the familiar tomboyish voice settles these thoughts as the man begins to exit the tent. He squints to the girl as he looks around the mostly empty camp. "Are you checking up on me?"

Ellette shrugs to the comment. "I watched you at the forge for a bit. Your arms jiggle when you move, a sign of your weakness."

Preston gives a simple bow as he nods. "Thanks, anything else?"

Ellette crosses her arms, her eyes falling away from the man as she talks. "Elwine said she saw *Pexřá* Elva come in from the light's path, I assumed she would find you once she was done with *Alphé* Kassie."

Preston squints to the girl as he nods. "You still need her for permission to leave?"

"Yes." Ellette kicks to the ground, though her eyes come to Preston's clothing as she continues. "Are you a smith now?"

"No, I'm a janitor." Preston glances around the camp. "Where's Elva?"

"She arrived a little bit ago. No one likes forging, they say a *Flóff* should be fighting, not making. But no one would say that to Lutin, he fought in the *Flúry Fasá.*" Ellette trials on, her comments almost as wild as her hair. "Are you still going to the library?"

"Yea." Preston nods to the clothing in his hold as he speaks up. "After I wash up... which reminds me, where is the bath house. Like for getting clean, not the other stuff."

Ellette laughs as she shakes her head. "We are *Flóffs*, the waters are better natural."

Preston just blinks to the comment as he speaks up. "So, what you have a lake or something?"

"It is in the Aster Fields." Ellette's words almost have a laughy tone as she continues. "Do you like lake water?"

Preston waves his hand to the girl as he speaks up. "It's fine, I'm sure Clover will tell me to get clean before I sit anywhere."

Ellette slowly releases her arms as she looks over the glove on Preston's hand. "What is that?"

"Oh." Preston cocks a smile to the question, quickly taking hold of the opportunity to be smarter than someone else. "It's a *Gloftór*. Magic is nothing more than thoughts and emotions, this thing helps focus that."

Ellette brings her wrist up to her nose as she wipes to it. "I would not trust a glowing thing."

Preston shrugs to the comment as he speaks up. "I trust a lot of myself to glowing things."

The man's words seem to have confused the girl, noticing this brings a slight smile to the man but before he can speak up another voice takes hold to the conversation. "Tormenting the *yiftiñ*, Preston?"

Ellette quickly replies to the voice as she moves in front of Preston. "*Pexřá* Elva! You have returned!"

A smile comes to Preston's face as he watches the *Flóff* girl's excitement to something she already knew. Though Preston has to step away as Ellette's twitching wings flare out to her call. The excitement seems to have carried over to Elva as well, however not in her face but her eyes as she looks over the smiling girl. "I have spoken with *Alphé* Kassie, you have demonstrated the maturity needed to exit the camp."

To Preston's surprise Ellette jumps a little with a slight fist pump. The quickness of her actions mixed with how human the gesture was brings a true to life laugh from the man as he watches.

Elva reacts a little differently as she lowers her voice. "Do make sure you are, Ellette."

The girl quickly snaps her posture into a more proper one as she nods. "Yes, *Pexřá*, I am fully grown!"

Elva now turns to Preston as she speaks up. "I have also been informed that half of the camp wishes to fight you."

Preston simply shrugs as he replies. "What can I say, I'm well liked."

Elva smirks to the comment, however her eyes drift to the items in Preston's hands as she continues. "What is this?"

"Oh, well I have to go and do the magic stuff with Clover, and if you've not noticed I am covered in soot." Preston gestures to his clothing as he lets Elva look him over.

Ellette follow's Preston's voice as she continues. "He has been working in Lutin's forge since the clouds broke light."

A faint smile comes to Elva's face as she nods. "No doubt working a debt for the armor you require?"

Preston gives a slight chuckle as he adjusts the items in his hold. "You know I'm starting to think this is all a game."

Elva does not acknowledge the comment as she instead turns to Ellette. "You should accompany Preston, he will be going to the library until nightfall." Her gaze shifts to Preston as she continues. "Do return by nightfall, Preston."

Preston straightens his posture as he speaks up. "Yes, *per-rax* Elva."

The avian women just looks over the man before she gives a little nod to Ellette. "Find what you seek in town Ellette, my flight from *Pegpolis* has left my wings a little sore."

Ellette nods. "I understand."

With a nods Elva turns her gaze back to Preston. "I trust my dagger is safe, yes?"

Preston nods as he replies. "Of course." He nods to the tent. "It's in the chest if you want it."

"Enough talk!" Ellette quickly tugs to Preston as she speaks up. "Lead the way!"

The tug is surprisingly forceful despite her size, of course it does kick-start the man as he now leads the trek back into town.

Elva smirks to the duo, though her smile quickly and expertly fades from her face as she looks around to the other members of the camp, all scattered around.

Chapter 22

Merely Too

"...What about there?"

A low and almost silent groan echoes from Preston as he shifts his head to another countless side street. "Uh... yeah I don't know what's down there either."

Ellette gives an annoyed sigh as she rolls her eyes to the man beside her. "Are you sure you lived in the town? You know none of these streets?"

A laugh comes from Preston as he shrugs. "Look I know what the market has most days and I know where the Town Hall is. I didn't really want to explore."

"You have a *Dẃoff's* heart." Ellette pounds a hand to her chest. "I shall traverse all the roads!"

The comment tumbles in Preston's mind for a few moments as he takes a few quick glances to the girl beside him before speaking up. "W-well don't you think that is a bit dangerous?"

Ellette reacts almost confused to the statement as she chuckles. "Dangerous? To be allowed in the *Skréét* I had to track a band of *Grifón* alone in the forest of *Trávrs*. I do not believe danger exists in these streets. But if it does, I shall face it, and break its hands!"

Preston holds his gaze to the girl in silence, not out of surprise but instead out of pity. Sure, Preston may not know how old this girl truly is; but her appearance and naiveté to the world outside of the camp makes her merely a child in Preston's mind. Because of this thought the man cannot shake the strong feelings that scream to him to be an adult.

Ellette, of course is oblivious to the thoughts and feelings now buzzing in Preston's mind, and continues to look around, a glee filled smile pressed to her face. "Would I be allowed in the *Dẃoff* Town Hall?"

The question slightly breaks Preston's whirlwind of thoughts as he speaks up. "Uh... yeah, I mean they let me in."

Ellette simply nods to the comment as she continues to look around the mostly two-story wood houses. "Why live in wood? Wood burns." A slight laugh comes from the girl as she clicks her tongue. "*Mŕad'*."

Preston cocks an eyebrow to the girl as he speaks up. "It's only a problem if someone tries to burn the town down."

The girl nods but slowly catches on to Preston's gaze as she takes a slight step away from the man. "What? It is not like I would do it. Fire is so... primitive."

A slight chuckle rings through the man as he replies. "You would just send a tornado, yeah?"

Ellette shrugs almost as if the comment were just a simple question. "This town has no value for the *Flóff*."

Preston shakes his head as he speaks ups. "So it's not that the town shouldn't be destroyed it's just there is no reason to destroy it?"

Ellette gives a little smile as she continues. "You are no warrior, not even a scout, you would not understand."

"That's fine, I never planned to be."

Half expecting their banter to continue Ellette cocks her head, her excitement lowering as she nods. "What did you plan to be?"

Preston is silent as he just looks down the road before him, the library has come into sight but Preston knows he cannot just end the conversation this far away. "Let's just say I left a lot when I came here."

Despite Preston's low and melancholy tone Ellette repeats herself. "But what were you training for?"

"I was trying to become a veterinarian. It's like a doctor *err* healer for pets and stuff."

The words spark a grin to Ellette's face as she nods. "You should live in the *Únoff* Capital, I am sure there is enough animals there to tend to."

Preston's face does not change as he shifts his eyes from the girl's grin. However, as he does this Ellette brings her voice back. "S-so a healer? I could see this."

The slight stuttering in the bird girl's words surprise Preston a little as he looks back to her. "Yeah I could have been." Preston halts his words as he points to the library. "Well, we're here."

Ellette's wings flare a little but as she looks around the wood structures her excitement begins to fade. "It is not very big."

Preston gives a little nod as he moves to the closed front door and knocks.

It takes a moment for the door to open but as it does a familiar voice and face grace Preston's senses. "Preston!"

A warm smile comes to Preston's face as he looks over the orange and red coated *fróx* in the doorway. Reynard of course moves quick as he beckons Preston in. "Clover is still out but I am sure she will be back soon, you can stay a little, yes?"

Preston nods as he nods to the clothing he has carried. "Of course... do you think Clover would mind if I get cleaned up a little?"

As Preston comes inside Reynard begins to close the door with a slight laugh. "Why are-..."

"Do not close the door beast!"

Reynard jumps back a little at the voice as he watches the angry *Flóff* girl come in. "Is this how you treat those who seek books?" Ellette puffs her cheeks out as she stares to Reynard. "Must I beat you done for them?"

Despite the girl's words, Reynard merely blinks to her, a look of confusion crossing his face rather than fear.

Preston quickly speaks up as he comes to Reynard's side. "Reynard, Ellette, Ellette, Reynard. It's her first time in town."

Ellette stands maybe a foot taller than Reynard, and the fact that she finally stands taller than something else seems to have quickly gotten to her head as she now glares to the young fox-boy. "Yes, and I have chosen the library as my first conquest!"

Reynard's ears fall a little to the shout as he nods. "Okay?"

Ellette continues to bare down on as she now puts her hands to her hips. "What books to enjoy?"

Reynard just blinks to the girl as he shakes his head. "Um... what do you like to-..."

"Is this not a library?" Ellette moves her hands to her hips. "I wish to read something enjoyable-..."

Preston speaks over the girl as he shakes his head. "Hey, you're supposed to find the books you like Ellette." Preston shrugs. "Rey can help you look, but you can't just scream about books."

The *Flóff* gives a smile as she nods, her wings now flare a little as she laughs. "I am aware of this. But look at this creature... it is enjoyable."

Preston shakes his head as he gestures to Reynard. "You call people by their names, you're not in camp."

Ellette gives a slight smirk to Preston's suggestion as she looks away. Her giddy pace quickly sparks up as she moves to the library side of the house. Her wings continue to raise as she stares to the bookshelves. "There are so many..."

Reynard's ears slowly start to perk back up as he moves to Preston's side and whisper up to him. "How long is she staying?"

Preston gives a glance back to where Ellette stands as he bends down a little and whispers back. "She just wanted to see the library. She won't tag along every time, okay?"

A sigh rolls from Reynard as he nods. "Okay." He moves to close the door as his eyes settle back to the girl, his paws rubbing over one another as he just waits to get her attention.

Preston removes the *Gloftór* and places it to the nearby table. "I'll take a quick bath; Clover still have the towels in the same spot?"

Reynard nods as he continues to stand away from the library side's threshold.

Preston turns his gaze to Ellette as he moves to the stairs. "Why don't you have Rey help you find a book. He's way more help than I could be."

The comment draws a slight smile from Reynard, though the fox-boy remains silent as he now catches the girl's sharp glance.

"Very well, find me a story of death and swordsmanship!" Ellette waves her hand. "Something fit for a *Flóff*."

For a moment Reynard does not move but with a slight glance to Preston he starts towards the *Flóff*. "Okay, I think I know something."

For a moment Preston watches the two of them now scanning the bookshelves, mainly just to make sure Ellette does not pull her sword on Reynard. But, after a few moments pass the man starts upstairs.

- - -

Later

It has been about an hour since Preston and Ellette arrived at the library, and aside from Preston's very quick clean most of the time has been spent downstairs and amongst the books. Reynard and Ellette have found their spots in the small loft above the library; a pile of unread books sitting to the side of the couch that Ellette occupies. Reynard sits to the stairs with a book of his own, but the more peculiar sight is how Ellette actually sits. Her legs are crossed and run up the back part of the couch, her wings are flat and her head hangs down towards the ground with the book held so that she can read it.

Truthfully, Preston thought about asking why she was sitting this way, but one thing the man has learned living in a world like this is that some things are just too strange to ask.

Preston himself sits to the table, but not his normal spot. Instead, the man sits across from it for a better view of the two younger would-be people in the library; but also, so that he has full view of the window on his left.

The sky is still bright and all sorts of people travel the main road outside, but Preston can still tell the day is drawing close to dusk. And one thing Preston does not want to do is be late back to the camp.

"Preston, are you sure you would not want a book on forging?"

The boyish voice draws Preston's eyes as he looks to the *fróx*. "You know what, sure, might as well try to impress someone."

Reynard nods as he pulls a book from the pile, which suggests he had been planning to win the conversation all along. As the *fróx* starts towards the table Ellette speaks up. "What does this word mean? Das-tard-ly?"

Preston's voice goes quiet as he just shrugs. "Uh...."

Reynard, like the countless other times Ellette has asked about words holds his head up high as he replies without even shooting her a glance. "It is a word that means evil."

The *Flóff* girl's face scrunches up as she replies. "I do not enjoy this book..." She tosses it to the couch as she crosses her arms and stares to where Preston and Reynard are. "...why do books not just say these words, why do they find other words to mean what they are saying?"

Reynard squints a little annoyed to the quick toss of the book, though he remains calm as he speaks up. "Some words are just better." The fox-boy passes Preston his own book as he continues. "You want to feel something, not just hear someone say it."

"Ha! These words do nothing but bore me."

Reynard taps his paw to his mouth as he slowly starts back to the library. "Most *Flóff* writers have to learn new-tongue from the *Únoff*. All books are like this."

Ellette rolls her eyes as she squawks back. "I wish to read a *Flóff* tale!"

Reynard shrugs as he speaks up. "Perhaps you would enjoy Commander Til-Flit, he led a battle against the Jéfar in the *Ovâlll*. But... the story is dry as it only recounts the battles."

"I shall read it!" Ellette uncrosses her arms as she pushes herself back to the couch, this time sitting in it correctly. "May I not bring in a cloud?"

Reynard shakes his head as he speaks up. "It would damage the book."

Preston continues to watch the banter between the two of them as he places the book he was given on his folded clothing near his right hand. However, something out of the corner of his eye makes him look to the window.

It was only a flash, but the sound of the door opening makes Preston perk up, yet the thought of seeing Clover after last night quickly seizes his tongue and stops him from speaking.

Reynard and Ellette are oblivious to the door as they continue their debate. However the sound of voices quickly brings Clover in as she looks into the library side of the room with a little bit of confusion. "Reynard?"

Clover's quick movements have stopped her from spotting Preston, as the man just sits to his chair with a strange urge to just leave. Still though, he watches the earthy dressed satyress from behind as she speaks up. "Oh, hello, who is this?"

Ellette quickly speaks up before Reynard gets the chance as she jumps from the loft, yet unlike a normal person her wings gently allow her to land with grace as she bows. "Clover of the library. *Pexřá* Elva speaks highly of you."

Despite the fact that Preston cannot see Clover's face he feels her confusion.

The man's thoughts are proven correct as Clover's voice starts up a little slower. "Y-you are from the camp?"

Ellette nods as she points to Preston. "I was allowed to accompany the Walker, as I have always wished to see the library... although I must say the books do not float atop my cloud."

Clover just nods to the girl as she turns to see where Preston is sitting. As their eyes lock Preston gives a little smile. Clover's reply however is a bit more formal as she simply nods to him. "*Plestá déy.*"

The greeting was not cold, but the formalness of it has left Preston even more quiet. Clover turns back to the *Flóff* girl as she smiles. "Have you tried any of Commander Til-Flit's recounts?"

Reynard chimes in as he holds a book to Ellette. "She will."

Ellette takes the book as she turns and starts back towards the stairs up to the loft. Reynard turns to Clover as he speaks up. "Do I need to get anything for your practice?"

Clover shakes her head as she removes her satchel from her shoulder. "No thank you, we shall just be practicing the basics." She looks to Preston as she beckons him to stand. "I would not want to move too quickly; you have been away from your spells."

Preston nods as he clears his throat. "Well I still do the little things, bit of levitation and oh I lit a few fires today."

Clover squints to the comment as she nods. "Lit fires?"

Ellette calls from her spot in the loft as she opens her book. "He is smith Lutin's assistant. His *Dẃoff maná* was useful for fires... not that I saw."

The satyress gets a slight smirk as she cocks her head to the man. "You worked a forge?"

Despite Clover's slightly proper tone the man takes notice to her smirk as he shrugs. "What can I say, I have lots of ideas."

Clover again nods as she places her satchel to the table. "Well... shall we begin?"

Preston takes his *Gloftór* from the table as he nods. "Yep."

"Oh, Preston you will not need the *Gloftór*, we are merely going to try simple things."

Preston nods as he straps the glove on. "I know, but I have been using it all day. I know it's for harder stuff but I kinda like using it."

"Very well, I suppose we can start with a simple teleportation spell."

Reynard moves to the loft's stairs as he holds his eyes to Clover and Preston, to no surprise Ellette too begins to watch.

Clover points to the center of the library as she speaks up. "Try to teleport there."

Preston nods as he looks to the spot he quickly chooses; however, Clover's words have not stopped as she continues. "Just remember, magic is thoughts and emotions; all you must do is focus on what-..."

The sound of Preston's spell takes Clover's attention as her know-it-all tone drops and she looks to where Preston now stands. "Good."

A laugh rings from the *Flóff* girl in the loft as she speaks up. "This is *Únoff* practice? You learn nothing unless you have some reason to perform, where is the danger?"

Clover cocks her head to the girl's words as Preston replies. "You sure you're not related to Elva?"

Ellette blinks to the comment. "Yes?"

"Actually Preston, you performed that quite well." Clover cocks her head. "And you say that you have been performing magic without me, yes?"

Preston nods as he shrugs a little to Clover. "Well yeah."

Clover looks over Preston for a moment before she continues. "I suppose I could use a simple shock spell. It will not hurt much if it hits you."

A moment of silence fills the library as Ellette sits up a little bit more. "That is more like training."

Preston and Reynard give each other a look as the *fróx* speaks up. "Clover, are you not tired?"

Clover simply smiles as she shakes her head. "Not for this." Clover holds her smile to Preston, however the man can see right through the smile as he thinks over her comment.

Preston nods as he speaks up. "Clover I don't want you to do anything if you're tired."

The satyress shakes her head as she brings her hands up a little, they quickly start to glow a light blue as she shakes her head. "Let your mind follow your thoughts, allow the magic to bend at your will."

"Okay so what am I-... ow!!"

Preston jumps a little as Clover gives a quick jab towards his arm. The magic does not scream towards Preston, nor does it burn, though the jolt of it is still unpleasant. "What was that?"

Reynard and Ellette begin to snicker as they watch Clover's cocky stance over the man who continues to rub at his arm.

"Come now Preston, you are with the *Flóff*, you must have begun forming thick skin." Clover again sparks her hands, this time walking forward as she lightly punches her hand forward, which sends a short but quick zap of magic towards the man. Preston dodges this one as he jumps back a little. His actions however only roll Clover's eyes as she cocks her head to one side, her light brown hair following her sway. "You are to teleport Preston."

"Wait how do I-..." The man stops his words as he notices Clover's muscle tense for her next jab. Like before he avoids the shock punch, however, a new pain in his back rings to his mind as he realizes Clover has just teleported behind him.

Preston jumps again as he rubs to the center of his lower back. "Ahhhh, it's like a bee sting! Stop!"

His voice brings another laugh from Reynard and Ellette as they continue to watch in enjoyment.

Clover straightens her posture as she speaks up. "I warned you Preston. Teleport or it will hurt."

Preston rolls his shoulders as he just laughs. "Yea, yea, yea, it's so easy."

The satyress just smirks as she lunges forward with her hands glowing. Knowing what to expect Preston's mind runs a mile a minute, but one thought does stick as he finds his body grow warm for a second. Of course, the feeling of dizziness quickly overtakes him as he notices his successful spell. Though it is hardly worthwhile as he finds he merely switched places with Clover

The satyress turns to face the man as she nods. "Good, now do this a few more times and we shall move onto something else." Clover's smile holds as she trails on. "I am sure you can continue."

Preston just gives a little smile as he nods. "And then we can do some normal levitation right?"

Clover's smirk falls a little as her hands glow a little brighter. "We must focus on what we desire. I am sure you wish to finish your training as soon as possible." She teleports, forcing Preston to do the same, though Clover still jabs into him as Preston lets out a yelp.

Again, the duo on the stairs let out a laugh as Preston readies himself to continue.

Chapter 23

Nightly Crew

Preston continues to rub to his side as he has since they left the library. Clover may have said the training was successful, though by spells she used on him Preston sees it more as a venting session. Even still, it was nice and it has helped to ease Preston's thoughts over his decision to leave. While Clover's more formal nature was different, it nonetheless was a welcomed change from their passive arguing. Better still was the time spent with Reynard, and of course the bath Preston was able to sneak in before Clover's arrival.

Of course, with the sun now setting behind them, only helping to bake Preston's back throughout the long trek Preston merely wishes he had waited to take his bath. Of course, he also wishes there to be a normal bath house within the camp, something Ellette seems to scoff at with every suggestion of it.

Even still, Preston turns an eye back to the bird-girl as he draws her eyes from the continued studying of her books' covers. "Well, did you enjoy that?"

Ellette raises her head from the books as she cocks an eye to the man beside her. "*Únoff* training is weak, you will never learn."

Preston shrugs to the comment as he attempts to adjust the items in his hold. "It's not too bad."

"Magic is boring, you need a sword to really have fun!" Ellette shrugs. "But at least I know where the library is."

A chuckle rolls from Preston as he nods. "Yea and now you can-..."

"Hold on." Ellette's wings flare out as she focuses on the wooden gate of the camp now coming into view. "I do not feel like waiting, I will have the gate open for you."

"What?"

Ellette spreads her wings out further as he tightens her hold to the book. "You are slow, and we have walked since the library, I need to fly." She takes herself into the air as she nods. "You will not be too much longer, find me in camp!"

Without another word she darts off, leaving Preston along on the trail. A sigh rolls through Preston as he stares to the camp still fifteen or so minutes from where he walks. Though with Ellette now gone Preston again turns his thoughts to Clover and Reynard.

The continued trek down the hilly roads of *VéturVill*'s outskirts are smooth, albeit a bit tiring to Preston's legs. So far, life within the camp seems to be about routine, and if Preston keeps his head down and away from most of his fellow campmates, it seems feasible. Strain in his arms after merely one day of work is a bit surprising, and rather unwelcomed.

Even still, the fresh air and mindless work has been nice, even for it being just one day. Holding on to this thought, Preston perks up as he continues down the road.

Within a few minutes, Preston's speed has brought him to the wooden gate as he calls out. "Hello!" He glances towards the sky as he continues. "I'm back before sun-down!"

At the words the gate begins to open, prompting Preston to once more adjusts the items in his hold.

Unfortunately, it is not Ellette that greets him on the other side. No, instead of the young girl, a muscle and very adult Elwine graces Preston's sight. Immediately, Preston shrinks in his skin, his throat clearing as he looks the woman over. "Hello."

Elwine merely blinks to the man's awkwardness as she speaks up. "Welcome back fellow campmate, please come inside."

"Yea, totally." Preston clears his throat again as he moves past the woman, her completely normal stance and expression only fueling Preston's strangeness as he nods to her. "Well uh, have a good night."

With a smile forced to his face Preston speedily walks away, his eyes pinned to his oasis within the camp as he does. He stays to the far side of camp his eyes inevitably drift to the watchtower and those who have already begun to gather at its base. Luckily, Preston seems not to draw their attention as he makes his way to his tent. It takes moment thought as Preston passes inside, he sighs, a weight quickly coming from his chest as he begins to relax.

Of course, his respite is for a moment as he places his belongs back to his trunk and then turns back to the tent's opening. Again outside, Preston turns to the campfire, his eyes looking over the various colors and sizes of the *Flóff* warriors.

Though after merely a second of thought, Preston shifts his eyes to the lonely *Flóff* girl seated well away from the fire, her cloud already beneath her.

Preston cocks a smile as he moves to greet her, though he has to speak up a little as he realizes Ellette's head is buried to her book. "You know Rey said not to read in the clouds right?"

Ellette brings her ruffled nose from the book as she nods. "It is one cloud, hardly a storm." She titles the book as she sighs. "Next time I will find sweets, these words are hard."

Preston merely chuckles to the comment as he pushes a barrel closer to Ellette's makeshift table of crates. His actions however draw Ellette's eyes once more as she looks to where the man now begins to sit. "What are you doing?"

"Sitting down." Preston shrugs. "Wonderful seats by the way."

Ellette cocks her head. "Why would you not sit by the fire? You worked with *Thrće* Lutin."

A slight chuckle rolls from Preston as he shrugs. "I doubt they will want me over there." He scratches at his neck. "Besides, I wanted to wait for them to get fat and happy before I tried." Turning back to the bird-girl Preston trails on. "Doesn't Elva sit with you?"

A shrug comes from Ellette as she speaks up. "Some nights, but she is *Pexřá*. Sometimes she is busy, other times she is gone." Ellette pokes her chin up as she brushes her own comments off. "I am a lowly *yiftiñ*, I am merely happy to have her glance at me."

Preston merely nods to the comment as he attempts to figure out the girl's expression. Though he takes a breath as he gestures to the book. "You like the story?"

"Well..." Ellette picks it up, spine first as she lazily tilts it back to her. "It is better than the others, though the words still upset me."

"Which ones?"

The comment draws a laugh from Ellette as she turns her sharp, hawk-like gaze to Preston. "Why? For *jáff*?"

"No, so I can help you read it." Preston cocks a smile. "What's the point of getting the books if you don't read them?"

"Mhmm." Ellette again tosses the book to the crate, her arms crossing as she looks away, the sight of a stubborn child greeting Preston's gaze. "Books are for the *Únoff,* and the library did nothing."

Preston turns the book over, placing it as how it should be read as he leans more towards the girl. "And what did you expect the library to do?"

Ellette shrugs. "Help me read of course, what else are they used for?"

A laugh escapes Preston, quickly prompting Ellette's wings to flare as she speaks up. "Why you laugh now?"

"No, nothing." Preston taps the book as he leans back. "You have to read to get better, you don't just walk into a library and know everything."

Ellette's cheeks puff out a bit as she crosses her arms, her eyes closing as she shakes her head. "I cannot understand the words."

Preston shakes his head. "Alright, then tell me where you get stuck and I'll help you."

The words bring Ellette's eyes open again as she raises an eyebrow. "Why? You looking to bed me?"

Preston's eyes widen as he stands. "Alright, we're done."

"Wait." Ellette uncrosses her arms as she continues. "You said you would help?"

"I will." Preston wags a finger to the girl. "But you gotta stop making comments like that, that's my one rule."

Ellette blinks to the man, though she cocks her head as she speaks up. "You are not a higher rank than me, you cannot give an order."

"It's not an order, it's an agreement." Preston nods. "Deal?"

Ellette crosses her arms again, though she nods. "Okay."

"Good." Preston takes his seat as he leans to the book. "So, where'd you get stuck?"

"Hmmm, somewhere around-..."

A deep voice comes over Ellette's, quickly taking the bird-girl's attention as Preston too turns to it.

"Girl, your food."

Ellette happily holds her hands up from where her cloud hoovers, no so much as a thank you coming from her as she turns to Stysen.

Stysen passes the bowl to her as turns an eye to Preston. "You are well *yiftiñ*?"

Ellette begins to blow to her soup though she answers through puffs. "Yes, Stysen."

The fiery haired avian merely stares down to Preston as he continues. "Good." Without a word Stysen extends his other hand, the second bowl of soup now coming down to Preston.

Not once yet has he seen Stysen blink, while unnerving, Preston takes the bowl as he speaks up. "Thank you."

"It is kindness." Stysen moves his hands to his heavily armored waist as he speaks. "An unfed comrade is an unfit one."

Preston raises the spoon to him as he glances away. "Of course."

Stysen continues to linger over the blond hair man, his words trailing on. "When you finish bring it to the pot, we will not collect your waste."

Again, Preston merely nods. "Sure thing."

With a low breath Stysen turns away, his unending swagger carrying him back to the warmth of his friend and the fire. With his back turned however Preston cocks a smile through his sigh. "I think he's beginning to like me."

Ellette brushes her braided hair to the side as she slurps to her soup. "You did not look him in the eye, Stysen does not like that."

"Sort of a power move." Preston dips his spoon into his bowl as he trails on. "Don't let the other guys on the team know you care, did it all the time."

Ellette shrugs to the comment. "I saw him stab Tra'vers for bumping into his wings once."

Preston chokes a little to the soup as he coughs. "You saw him do what now?"

Ellette brushes the man's rushed question aside as she continues to slurp. "You worked with *Thŕce* Lutin, Stysen respects the *Flóff* rules too much to fight you." She takes a sip. "For now."

Preston clears his throat, the quick burn of the hot soup cooling as he nods. "Well I'll remember that. Good thing I'm friends with Elva."

A laugh rolls from Ellette as she glances to the man. "*Pexřá* Elva has her own respect for Stysen's ways." She nods. "Though she might spare you some pain if you two fight."

Preston replies with his own chuckle as he stirs the mostly empty broth in his bowl. "Thing she could spare me the pain of this meal, there's hardly anything in it."

Again Ellette just shrugs. "*Flóff* cooking is about being full, not taste." She rolls her tongue to the spoon before placing back to the half empty bowl. "How do sweets taste?"

"I'm sure you'll find out." Preston sets his bowl aside as he rubs his hands together. "Alright, book time?"

Chapter 24

Hop, Skip, & Jump

The days have moved more swiftly than a *swóóp* riding the northern winds, at least according to Elva. Today, as all others, has continued on with a smooth, military like efficiency. An early rise followed by a cold, cloud shower, a breakfast of something strange but filling, and the rest of the day being told what to do by Lutin. Nights, though always carrying a similar routine as the days, at least bring a different sense of purpose for the man. Ellette's reading has continued, with little progress, but the nightly sessions are enjoyable, and at the very least, keep Stysen and his cronies at bay.

Still, life now is not all bad. With Preston's monitoring of his beard and hair length a more mature look has begun to take hold, albeit with a few nicks to his skin. The food too, mixed with the exhausting work throughout the day has prompted the man to lose a bit of weight; not that Preston intended to.

A fact he realizes every day as he further tightens the straps to the finely made, hard, tan and steel studded leather Preston pulls over his chest. Despite the fact that he was told to always wear armor Preston normally places a shirt over the leather hide.

Most of the others in the camp do find it strange but none can say anything as Preston still follows the rules, just in an unorthodox way. Lutin however has been a bit more vocal, frequently telling Preston how upset he is at the decision to hide his work under a stretched out wool shirt.

With a slow roll of the neck and a slight rub to his right shoulder Preston stands from his bed, as he does this he stretches his back a little. One of the major things he does miss about the library is the beds. However, after the first week away every thought about returning was quickly shot down. Clover seems happy, Reynard has adjusted, and the lack of arguments has allowed Preston to ignore the amulet at his chest. Better still, is the absence of his nightmares. Even if the amulet's spell broke, the knowledge that those in the camp would have no problem killing him before he could harm someone, as strange as it is, it is comforting.

A low sigh comes from the man as he runs his hands to his hair to make sure it at least stays down. Today is a bit different, Lutin, though he still requires Preston in the forge has also declared a task for the man later in the day, thus Preston has been allowed into town earlier rather than later. Lucky, Preston was given a day's notice, at least allowing him and Clover to move their normal session, though it remains to be seen if there is anything more to be taught.

While the morning was made somewhat easier, it nevertheless means Preston's day will be long, now with his normal break at Clover's happening earlier.

Clover has mellowed a little since Preston first went to visit again and her formal tone has changed back to her normal, somewhat friendlier tendencies. Still, being around each other has begun to feel strange, especially when she talks of her parent's wishes for her to return to *HefterÄll* once Nyota's test is completed, which for all intents and purposes seems to now be sending Preston home.

The thoughts are quickly chased away as Preston steps out and into the camp's courtyard. Of course, a smile comes to the man's face as he notices something floating just below the watchtower's skyline.

Lutin enjoyed Preston's description of hot air balloons, and continued to ask for some time, however there was no way Preston could actually come up with a real one. But, the floating lanterns that hang in the camp's air are a nice starting project. Preston never would have guessed a candle, paper and a small cloud to hold it in place would have been so inspiring for the camp.

But then again with every *Flóff* obsessed with the sky and a lack of cloudstone to make a real floating city the thought of creating a floating structure with fire seems to have at least improved Preston's standing with most in the camp. With the exception of Stysen and some others.

Preston nods as he looks around the small clouds that bob with the candle lanterns beneath them. Magic is strange, but the fact that clouds can actually hold things when manipulated is almost mind boggling.

Luckily, before Preston's mind can melt the gate comes before the man with a familiar voice. "To town?"

The man does not even look up as he instead looks to the cool gust of air that follows Elwine's decent.

Preston just nods as he speaks up. "Yep, I'll be back in a bit."

Elwine gives a slight smile as she moves to the roller on the right side of the gate. Though the two have never directly spoken about, from what Preston gathers, the situation between them is only as awkward as the man makes it. For Elwine, their brief interactions are nothing more than that of another campmate, and as such, Preston has learned to understand that. "Accompanying *Pexřá* Elva into the *VéturVill*?"

Preston shrugs to the comment. "Later yea. Lutin seems to think it's my responsibility to see that shipment in, but I'm happy for the company."

Elwine just nods as she moves her hands to the wooden roller, her strength making quick work of the gate as she brings it open. "Fair winds, Walker."

Preston nods as she starts through the gate. "Fair winds."

- - -

(A Quick Walk)

The trek into town has become easier in the last few weeks, even the light hills on the outskirts of town do not slow Preston down. However, the influx of *Dẃoff* and *Únoff* workers that have come to lay the tracks for the nearly completed train station has caused a bit of traffic on *VéturVill's* only main road. Of course, it is only to get worse as they expand out from the town.

It was surprising to Preston that work could be so near completion in under a month. But Preston has visited the Town Hall a few times with Ellette, even making a slight detour towards the train station just down the hill. From these trips Preston gathered that most of the supplies and equipment are coming through teleportation, with the larger stuff traveling four or so hours from the Capital. With such a quick supply system, it is not surprising that the work has come along so swiftly.

Preston's thoughts slowly begin to drift back to the area around him as he now focuses in on the library. The door is closed but like Clover has told him the last few weeks, the library is always open to him.

With this in mind Preston opens the door without a knock. This quickly proves to be the right decision as his ears pick up to the slight debate going on inside.

The slightly more girly but still Southern Belle like tone is promptly recognized as Preston looks to the well-dressed Bella, who stands with her back to the door a few scrolls tucked under her right arm. "But Clover, I do *not* see why I am to bring the tapestries. The ground there is-is... well filthy!"

Clover's eyes have drifted to Preston as she watches the man close the door, but her tone and words hold to Bella as she continues. "Bella, it is a simple task, you will be fine."

The curly maned satyress throws her head to the ceiling as she speaks up. "Physically, yes, but why do I have to make and deliver it. Have you even seen these plans? It calls for all sorts of craft. Not merely one item, Clover. I am already overworked."

Clover simply rolls her eyes as she starts towards the scroll and paper cluttered table as she begins to levitate everything into a few neat piles. "You just have this one task, Bella."

"I have no problem with adding my expertise... I have a problem however, when it involves me sweating."

The comment draws a raised eye from Clover as she looks her friend over. "Bella you will survive a bit of sweat."

"Of course, I will." Bella sighs, her arms crossing. "But such a thing is so dreadful, it dries your mane and wrinkles your skin, who would pursue such work." Her slight rant comes to a sudden end as she looks her friend over again. "N-not that it is wrong for a mare to do such work." Bella clears her throat with a laugh as she continues. "Besides, how do you know I am not too busy to leave the shop?"

Preston gets a slight smile as he continues to watch the two women continuing their back and forth.

Clover shakes her head as she smirks. "You have time Bella, you said you did."

Bella shakes her head right back to Clover as she speaks up. "I have time for quick conversations with friends, I receive plenty of orders to keep me and my sister busy." Bella straightens her posture as she continues. "Did you forget you even asked for some alterations?"

Clover's eyes widen a little as she replies. "I merely asked for you to loosen a few things?"

Bella nods as she continues. "And whom do you think does this? And with what time is it done?" Bella sighs. "Why can Reynard not simply take my items?"

Clover gives a light laugh as she shakes her head. "It is too busy for Reynard to go on the streets." Clover nods. "Go home now and begin working, you will have plenty of time."

"Are you casting me of your home?" Bella rolls her hand. "How unladylike, Miss Vines."

Clover rolls her eyes to the comment as she points to where Preston stands.

It takes a moment for Bella to pick up on her gesture as she turns to where the man stands at the door. "Preston?" Her eyes widen as she repeats the name. "Oh, Preston." She glances back to Clover as she gives a simple laugh. "You could have said you had company, our banter is hardly fit for ears, dear."

Clover shrugs. "It is only Preston."

"O-only?" Bella turns an eye back to the man as she gives a slight bow. "*Plestá déy*, I hope you fare well."

The man gives a friendly smile as he nods. "Been a little bit huh, Bella?"

The shapely satyress gives a slight smile as she nears the man, all the while attempting to fix her hair. "Longer than that." She squints to the man. "You seem different? Clover says you reside with Elva now, is that still true?"

Preston watches as Bella begins to look him over. "Yeah?"

Bella gives a little giggle as she waves her hand. "I am gawking." The satyress places her hand to Preston's right sleeve as she tugs to it, her smile fading a little. "Oh, look what you have done to this fabric... no enchantment can fade these stretches, Preston." She moves her eyes to Preston's more toned arms as she continues. "Though perhaps it is time you have new clothing all together?"

The man gives a little laugh as he shakes his head. "No, it's alright I like breathing, it helps when I work in the forge."

Bella cocks her head to the word. "Forge?" She sighs. "Hard work no doubt, though it has yielded a few results, yes?"

Preston squints to the woman's scanning eyes as he replies. "I'm sure the food has something to do with it too."

Bella moves her hand to the man's upper arm as she gives a little squeeze. "Hmm, yes it does seem that-..."

"Bella." Clover finally speaks up as she watches her friend continuing to walk her hands over Preston. "Preston is not going to help you deliver the tapestries."

The satyress drops her hand from Preston as she rolls her eyes. "Oh Clover, why would I *ever* ask Preston to do such a thing? I have given you my word that I shall do it." Bella nods back to Clover as she continues to smile to Preston. "But if Preston were to offer I would-..."

Preston shakes his head. "I'd rather not get yelled at."

A smirk comes to Clover's face. "Thank you, Preston."

The comment merely rolls Bella's eyes as she eases a hand to her hip. "Very well, I shall commit." Bella shakes her head. "Preston, perhaps you should return to the library, Clover has grown fussy in your absence."

With hardly a pause in Bella's voice, Clover speaks up in reply. "Thank you for your charm, Bella."

The elegant satyress nods as she sighs. "Yes, yes, I must get home. Do visit though, Preston." She rolls her hand. "I am not sure what is allowed in Elva's camp but I am sure I could find something worth wearing."

Preston just nods as he moves from the door. With him now out of the way Bella leaves, closing the door behind her as Clover brings a hand to her head. "Ugh... I do enjoy Bella's company, but I do not enjoy her whine."

The man just smiles to the comment as he moves a little closer to the table. "So, the construction is almost done, huh?"

Clover continues to rub at her head as she speaks up. "Yes, they now move to lay these tracks... a mess of webbing it seems, though it follows the plan." Clover gestures to the door as she trails on. "Bella asked to decorate the station, I accepted. Now, I must help her and look over the Princess' plans, all while still overseeing construction."

Preston just gives a little laugh as he shrugs. "Why can't Nyota do it?"

Clover slowly moves her hand as she sighs. "His sickness has grown worse."

"What?" Preston squints to the woman as he shakes his head to the information. "He said that?"

"Elden's last letter did. We write as much as we can but never about things like this. He says Nyota seldom leaves the tower and has begun refusing court with the Three. He also writes of Nyota's strange behavior."

Preston is silent for a moment as he shakes his head. "W-well can't someone do something for him?"

Clover shakes her head as she speaks up. "No, I do not believe there to be any herbs for this sickness." The satyress sighs again as she brings her hand to her head. "Nor is there anything for these head pains."

The comment quickly sparks a response in Preston as he points to the chair. "Well sit down for a little. You're probably overdoing it, heck you don't have me to bother you all the time."

For a second Clover hesitates but she does sit as she replies with a slight smirk. "No, Reynard has begun to fill that role. It seems you had an impact on him." She cocks an eye to the man. "I still have yet to decide my feelings on that."

Preston gives a light chuckle as he nods. "That's good. Where is he?"

"He helped Bella carry a few items." Clover continues. "Your friend, Ellette went along."

Preston crosses his arms. "Yea? Well at least Bella's sister will leave her alone, that should help her work."

"Yes." Clover nods. "In truth, Bella asked Reynard to start off before her because she does not like to leave them alone."

Preston nods as he speaks up. "You get use to her." Preston thinks the comment over again as he trails on. "Ellette's not causing a problem though, right?"

"No." Clover lowers her hands to the table, but she pauses her words as she looks the man over, a faint smile coming to her face. "You look rested."

Preston shrugs as he speaks up with a laugh. "Yea? Well, thanks for the lie, but that rock they call a bed still sucks." He nods. "You look good, sleeping well?"

Clover chuckles to comment, though she pauses in her reply as she instead focuses to the clutter on the table before her. She pushes a stack of scrolls a little out of her way as she nods "My mind has cleared for some things, but I have begun thinking of others."

Preston nods. "Such as?"

"Mostly what is fast approaching." Clover nods. "Your departure, Master Nyota, returning home."

Preston takes a deep breath as he speaks up. "I think I'm good for one spell, yeah? Plus, I think I'm kinda owed one stroke of good luck."

Clover nods as she trails on. "I am not worried about your spell. You have learned much in your time with me, Preston."

The man's smile grows as he squints to the woman. "Was that a compliment Happy-Hooves?"

The words slow Clover's tone as she nods. "I was angry at the beginning."

Preston merely smirks to the comment, not yet following the woman's thoughts as he speaks up. "For what?"

Clover looks to struggle with her words as she continues. "I was angry that you left. But, after a while that anger turned to regret."

"Regret?" Preston squints to the comment as he shrugs. "What do you mean?"

"I should have appreciated my time with you, Preston." Clover sighs as she forces a smile, a faint hint of sadness in her expression.

Preston remains silent as his mouth hangs slightly agape. His silence quickly changes Clover's demeanor as the typical self-confident and ever sure toned woman begins to falter. The rarely seen, though always present shyness to Clover comes forth as she speaks up. "I should not have said that... it-..." Clover stands as she gives another nod. "I am sorry I asked you to stop by, there is nothing more I can really teach you-..."

"I'm not upset." Preston shrugs. "I'm happy."

Clover blinks to the man's expression as she shakes her head. "You do not look it?"

Preston takes a seat as he attempts to form his thoughts to words. "I left because I didn't want to hurt anyone."

Clover blinks to the comment, her hand coming towards Preston as speaks up, a low tone to her words. "Preston you would never-..."

At her motion Preston moves his arm, his words quickly coming Clover's. "I didn't know that... I hurt you before and... and I'd be lying if I told you I wasn't upset." He gives a stern though expressionless nod to the woman beside him as he continues. "We never even talked about it, we couldn't, and I don't think we really can."

The satyress halts her approach, her hand that once was set to Preston's arm now retreats, folding into her other hand as she replies. "I understand."

Preston takes a deep breath as he lets his thoughts settle. "You were right though." Preston nods. "It just took me a while to understand it. We were brought together out of chance, nothing else, no reason. I get it, with all that happened and with how quick it did, it's like you said, it was a mistake."

Clover's lips seal and her face grows hard, but her eyes stay soft as she nods.

The room now feels heavy as Preston swallows and looks to the door, no desire in his mind nor his heart to continue. "I suppose I should leave."

Clover straightens her posture as she nods, a smirk coming to her face as a deep seeded though cleverly hidden sadness holds. "I shall miss you Preston, you have been... a good friend."

Preston nods as he waits for the woman's words to finish. Though as they do, he finds himself cocking a smile. "Still got a few days left, a few more practice rounds."

"It's alright Clover." Preston gives a light chuckle as he shrugs. "We have a few more days, yeah?"

Clover nods as she smiles. "Yes."

To the words Preston takes a deep breath as he moves towards the door. "Well Lutin will be happy to have me back, I'll tell you how it went tomorrow."

Clover holds her low almost forced smile as she nods. "I look forward to."

Preston nods as he opens the door into the relatively still early morning sun. "Alright, see you around, Clover."

"Fare well." The door closes without a word, and as it does Clover turns back to the work laid out before her. With a sigh, she moves her hands to the scrolls on her right.

Chapter 25

The Depths

The metallic and mindless sounds of the hammer striking against the rapidly cooling piece of metal atop the avail rings through the camp completely unnoticed. This of course is normal as most of the inhabitants of this town away from town are always busying themselves with something or staring into the open sky above the camp with a wishful yearning to simply fly around.

Preston's own daydreaming on the contrary has nothing to do with the sky, or with any real thoughts for that matter. Instead, the man's blank stare is without meaning.

The man's dull expression although does bring a reaction to the ever-watchful hawk-like Lutin. "*Mŕad'sci*! Preston?!"

"Huh?" Preston's quick turn of the head prompts the hammer he uses to slip off the anvil, which makes for a rather foolish looking turnaround. Despite this though Lutin continues.

"Look at what you are doing! Have you only been working one side?"

Preston is pushed a little from the anvil as Lutin takes the hammer from him. "Clear the fog from your mind, Preston. You could have ruined this piece!"

Preston just stares to the only slightly stamped down bar of metal as he nods. "Alright, alright I'm sorry."

Lutin just sighs as he takes the tongs and scoops up the bar, his words lower a little as he starts back to the furnace. As the burly *Flóff* places the bar back to the fire he speaks up again. "Are you well?"

For a moment Preston hesitates but he nods as he wipes his hands to the apron he wears. "Yea I'm fine just... just thinking about home."

Lutin's lack of attention to the man's words has prompted the typical response from the dark avian as he continues to shift the bar over the flame. "Stop thinking."

Preston just nods as he takes a deep breath. "Yeah."

"*Hmph.*" Lutin turns back to Preston, his hands to his hips as his deep voice chimes out. "Since you cannot focus on work perhaps you should go and retrieve my shipment. Or you could repair the *Frólents*."

Preston just smirks to the comment as he slowly begins to remove the apron. His tone matches his unenthused motions as he speaks up. "You know I can't reach them, and someone always gets mad when I ask them to get the lanterns down."

Lutin turns back to his furnace as he looks the metal over. "I collected a few earlier, I can form the cloudstone later."

Preston just nods as he places the apron to the workbench. "I'll do it when I come back, you know how Elva is, we'll be back quickly."

"Do not agree to any further payment until the *Dẃoff* explain this late shipment. A *déy* overdo is not what *Flóff* coin should pay for." Lutin flips the metal in the furnace as he nods. "And I expect my ore unspoiled and these fire-rock well maintained, not dusted."

"I won't break anything, and I'll make sure you got what you ordered." Preston cocks an eye to the dark avian as he continues. "Still trust me to do this?"

Lutin cocks a smile. "No, that is why *Pexřá* Elva will accompany you on this first task." He rubs his arm to his nose as he nods. "Impress me with this and I will send you alone."

A chuckle comes from Preston as he gives a little bow. "I aim to please."

The *Flóff* just nods as he turns back to the bar of heated metal he now draws from the furnace. Preston of course does not watch the back-straining work as he instead starts into the courtyard and towards the tents.

The camp sits empty as it does during most afternoons, this coupled with the always uncluttered courtyard makes for an easy venture across it, as Preston sets his eyes to Elva's tent.

It hardly takes two minutes to move through the camp, and as Elva's tent comes within arm's length Preston speaks up. "Hey, we're leaving early. Like everything else I seem to do here."

"I am dressed, I merely am adjusting my armor." To the comment Preston pushes aside the tent's flap, his eyes coming to the dirty blonde haired avian as he nods.

"See? That's how easy it is." Preston trails on. "You can just stand outside and say something."

Elva squints to the comment as she now moves her hands to tighten the belt her sword and various daggers hang to. "You were merely changing clothing, Preston. You were not outside of your tent there was no problem in me seeing you without armor."

"All I'm saying is you don't have to barge in on someone." Preston wiggles the flap of the tent as he continues. "It's not see through for a reason you know."

The avian woman clicks her belt into place as she moves her hands to her hips. "You act as if your body is different than any other male's."

Preston waves the comment off. "Just saying, you'll get an eye full one day if you keep waking me up."

"At first light you should be up. A *Flöff* must be prepared for-..." Elva's words are cut as Preston quickly waves his hand to the woman.

"Whoa, whoa." Preston continues. "I'm never late, Lutin has never complained about-..."

"You are never early either." Elva nods, taking a step towards the man as she does. "And you shall not interrupt me, Milk-Chest."

Preston gives a dramatic bow to the comment. "Yea, yea, next time I won't give you a heads up to leaving early either."

"I do not need warning." Elva gestures to herself as she trails on. "I am prepared whereas you still lack your sword and even from here I can see your armor needs to be tightened."

"I just left Lutin, I don't carry Fang with me everywhere, he's curved." Just as his breath ends Elva chimes in.

"Do not say its name." Elva shakes her head. "That sword has done nothing but rest in your tent, it has hardly earned a title."

Preston ignores the comment as he looks the woman over again. "Why were you even ready? I got back early?"

"Yes, you did." Elva takes a breath. "And so I knew you would finish early." She moves past the man, her gaze setting to the bright sky as she trails on. "Now collect your sword, I wish to polish my armor in the light."

"We need to stop by Bella's if you still want to bring Elly." Preston slowly begins to inch away from the woman, his eyes setting to his own tent. "She won't know we left."

Elva's reply is quick as she glances to the man. "Ellette is to meet us at the forest's edge, with your pace we shall arrive just a little before our agreed upon time."

The comment brings Preston's walk to halt as he turns his full attention back to the woman. "What? She doesn't know the roads."

"Perhaps not in town, though I personally flew her to the forest on her first hunting assignment. She knows the roads leading in and out." A sense of pride flashes to Elva's face for a moment, though her expression changes as she lets her eyes fall back to Preston. "I suppose I cannot leave you out there for a night as I did her, Clover would be upset."

Preston gives a slight chuckle as he shakes his head. "I've had my fill of forest around here." His tone dips a little as he trails on. "Speaking of which, how far into the forest is this place?"

"Not far, just beyond the Princess' project." Elva cocks an eye to the man. "How does Clover fair with that?"

"Fine." Preston shrugs. "She looked busy and we don't have much to practice... I'm surprised you cared enough to ask?"

"I do not. Sword, Preston."

"Yea, yea." Preston waves his hand to the comment as he starts back to his tent, Elva following behind as she crosses her arms a little impatient, despite her own contribution to their previous conversation.

Luckily, Preston is quick as he comes back outside, the belt snapping around his waist as the curved sword hangs down his left leg. "Alright, Fang and I are ready to go."

Elva takes a deep breath though she turns away as she nods. "Come, and pace yourself. It shall be a lengthy walk to the outskirts of the *ÉverMoar*."

- - -

(The Edge of the *ÉverMoar*)

The sun hangs just past midday, its warmth happily hidden behind the thick forest Preston has found himself returning to. While the *ÉverMoar* does not hold fond memories for the man, he nevertheless does not shy away from it. Whether it be a venture with Clover, the amulet around his neck, or simply the fact that the forest spans most of central Artésque, Preston has learned to accept the ever-present thicket of woods just beyond the town. This of course does not help to alleviate any such fears he has of it however, a simple truth that has continued to grow ever real to the man's mind as the minutes tick by.

The duo arrived at the forest's edge a little over an hour ago, and although they were early according to Elva, the time for Ellette's arrive has far come and gone. If it were anyone else Elva might have continued on with the task, no doubt reporting the tardiness to Kassie or even dealing with the unreliable campmate herself at a later time. However, because it is Ellette, Elva has yet to move, her arms firmly crossed, her wings tight to her back, and her sharp eyes ever watchful to the skies.

Preston too has found his own means of passing the time, though with little to look at on the simple dirt road outside of *VéturVill* his attention has been to the dirt. More correctly, the now slashed at and prodded patch of ground just at his reach from where he sits on one of the many side rocks littering the path. His sword is sharp, easily churning the dirt earth with even the slightest of movements from Preston's hand. A remarkable thing, seeing as how just a month ago the sword was nothing more than a blunt tool for practice, though Lutin has since made it a weapon fit for any.

Still, even this fine craftsmanship begins to lose its luster as Preston glances more to the forest laid out before them. "You sure you don't want to head in?"

"No."

Elva's quick answer draws a breath from Preston as the man again drags his sword to the ground. Though this only satisfies his boredom for a moment. "Look she obviously forgot, it's fine we can-..."

"I see here." Elva's arms uncross as they come to her hips.

Though Preston merely squints to blue sky as he shrugs. "I don't see anything."

"Your eyes are poor compared to mine." Elva nods. "It is her."

Preston again just stares into the sky, though he stands all the same, his sword coming back to his side. "Well if it is, don't be harsh."

The comment draws an eye from Elva as she speaks up. "Our comrade is late for an assignment she will-…"

"It's her day off, and this is not her assignment it's mine you don't have to-…"

"She gave her word." Elva shakes her head. "As such she is to follow it."

Preston chuckles to Elva's more serious tone, though he quickly finds his jaw tightening as Elva turns another eye to him. For another four or so minutes the pair stands in silence, at least until a voice calls out from the sky.

"*Pexřá* Elva!" The call is quickly followed by Ellette's smiling face as the *Flóff* girl lands without a care. Elva however stands over her with a sudden and stiff tone.

"Where have you been?"

The words draw silence from the more pettie *Flóff* as Ellette immediately straightens up, her hands struggling to find a fit place to rest as she replies. "I-in town my *Pexřá*."

Elva's stance is unmoved, yet her tone seems to shift, a more sincere sound to her words coming forth as she speaks. "Are you well, Ellette?"

Ellette swiftly nods to the question. "My deepest apologies, *Pexřá*, I left later, and I had not expected the wind to be against me."

Elva squints to the comment. "How far were you into town?"

"I was with Juna, at Bella Gem's workshop." Ellette nods.

The faint hint of compassion is siphoned from Elva as she replies. "Your focus should be on learning the town. You are not to see Bella's sister again until I say."

Preston stays silent, though he takes a step forward as he stares to Ellette. Though the *Flóff* girl's shoulder slump, her reply is without question. "Yes, *Pexřá*."

Elva nods. "Good." She turns back to Preston as she speaks up. "Our destination is two flaps from here, come."

As the avian woman passes by Preston lingers until Ellette draws near, as she does the normally outspoken *Flóff* girl squeaks out a greeting. "I apologize for the delay, I lost the time with my company."

Preston cocks a smile as he nods. "Oh, don't worry about it Elly, where I'm from it is called having a friend."

Though the comment draws Ellette's head up, her eyes drift to Elva as she replies. "Juna is an *Únoff*. I would never call an *Únoff* a friend."

Elva is silent, her walk seemingly the only thing she focuses on, despite the girl's obviously heard comment.

Preston speaks up in the silence however as he chuckles. "Elva has plenty of friends not from camp, that doesn't matter."

Ellette's wings twitch a little as she sheepishly replies. "I-I know, I just-..."

Elva chimes in, though she does not turn her head. "Your choice in company is you own." Elva pauses. "Though I might suggest keeping such comments out of camp."

The bird girl quickly nods as she lowers her wings. "I shall not stir the air."

A chuckle rolls from Preston as he speaks up. "Not sure why you'd need to, I'm not one of you and the camp is still fine."

Ellette nods to the comment. "You are also not an *Únoff*."

"Ellette, there should be an encampment at the end of the road, inform the residents of our arrival, we do not wish to scare the workers with our swords."

Without question Ellette takes to the air, her hand resting on her sword as she darts up and out of the forest.

With her gone Elva speaks up. "Refocus your mind, Preston. You have a task, *Flóff* or not you have been welcomed into the camp, it is important you take that seriously."

"What?" Preston gives a slight laugh to comment. "I'm not sure how I can be more serious? We're just picking up an ore shipment?"

"Yes, we are. We are not discussing what is and is not appropriate in camp." Elva turns an eye to the man. "Understood?"

"Yea." Preston gives a thumbs up. "I get it."

A sigh rolls from the man, though he says nothing more as he merely begins to look around the forest. The path has gotten a bit narrower, though the simple dirt road is still wide enough for carriage. The underbrush of the forest is also fairly tamed, but Preston still minds his footing all the same.

Their trek continues for another moment or so, but the silence comes to an end as Ellette returns, prompting Elva to speak up. "What are you doing?"

The *Flóff* girl shrugs as she begins to land. "The camp was empty?"

"Empty?" Elva glances to the sky for a moment. "Hmm."

Ellette follows her glance as she nods. "The light is still young, could they not be at work?"

"Perhaps." Elva sets her gaze back to the path before them. "The promise of the *Jartál*'s coin may have pulled more than a few workers from the *Únoff* Lord of Mines."

Preston squints to the comment as he speaks up. "Wait, so what do we do if they can't fill the order?"

Elva shrugs. "*Alphé* Kassie will request the *Jartál* send a letter."

"That's it?"

"*Únoff* holdings, Preston. We will be lucky to find a worker." Elva's words do little for Preston as the man simply shakes his head.

His confusion prompts Ellette's voice as the bird girl merely stretches her wings, her words seemingly carrying the same nonchalant tone as Elva's. "The *Dẃoff* in *VéturVill* may be slow, but they work harder than any labor a Lord of Trade would bring."

A simple laugh comes from Preston as he replies. "Great, so who wants to tell Lutin?"

Neither of Preston's companions speak up, prompting Preston to sigh as he trails on. "Alright, I guess I get too. What a waste of a trip."

The slight hill in the road comes to an end without a care for the group, Preston now dreading the waste of a journey. Though he brings himself from his thoughts long enough to look over the sizable clearing now just a little below him. A few simple tents, some small cooking areas, and several empty hand pulled carts litter the area. A cave sits to the far end, though nothing spectacular greets Preston's vision as he speaks up. "Is this it?"

Elva's head shifts a little to where the man looks as she responds. "Yes."

Ellette gives a little laugh as she bumps into Preston's arm. "Shame you cannot fly back, huh?"

A sigh escapes the man as he looks around the clearing. "Well who do we talk to?"

Elva's wings spread out as she quickly darts to one of the campsites, Ellette follows after her leaving Preston to work his way down the slight decline of the road by himself.

Near the two avian-warrioresses however Preston speaks up. "What are you looking at?"

"Hm..." Elva pulls her hand from the empty campfire as she nods. "I shall head into the mine, clearly they are not here." As Elva starts towards the trampled pathway leading through the camp she calls out. "Stay here, it shall only take a moment."

While the comment stalls Ellette for a moment, seeing Elva starting towards the mine's entrance quickly spurs on the younger girl's curiosity as she follows after.

Sighting this, Preston starts up. "Where are you going?"

Ellette turns on one foot with a slight hoop as she replies. "Well I have never seen a mine before, I wish to see the entrance up close."

"It's just dirt?" Preston shrugs. "There's nothing special about-..."

"Quiet!"

Elva's comment quickly brings a halt to Preston and Ellette's banter as they now stare to the avian woman. The bird girl beside Preston however does not stay silent for long as she cocks her head. "Is something wrong my *Pexřá*?"

"The outer lamps are unlit..." Elva gestures to the mine's door. "The door too barely hangs to its hinges"

Elva crosses her arms as she continues to study the mine's entrance.

"So, what does that mean?" Preston glances to the door as he continues. "To be fair, that door doesn't look all to sturdy anyways, you know?"

"It is not the door that concerns me." Elva shakes her head as she speaks up. "*Dẃoff* mines are extensive, why would you not light the exit?"

Preston is silent as Elva uncrosses her arms. "A cave-in could have blown the lamps out... although the door is far too removed." Elva pulls her short sword from her waist as she nods. "Preston you are to accompany me, Ellette fly to the Town Hall, speak with *Jartál* Caféll, tell her the mine may have collapsed. Say that *Pexřá* Elva is investigating and will confirm soon."

Ellette nods. "Okay."

"*Jartál* Caféll is *slothéñ* in matters not concern coin, remind her dead miners yield little." Elva rolls her shoulder. "If there has been a collapse, they may have been stuck for a *déy*, do not leave without speaking to her. Seek Clover if you must."

Preston shakes his head. "What are we doing?"

"Ellette will fly with my words and you will hold my torch." Elva nods. "Now come along."

With the last comment Ellette darts into the sky above the mine, with her gone Preston moves closer to the woman before him. "So, what if you're wrong? There could be a panic?"

Elva's expression does not change as she speaks up. "Light the mine Preston, if this is not a collapse something may be in the mine."

Preston hesitates as he looks over the fair-sized entrance to the. "Such as?"

"Perhaps *Mostrérs*, they inhabit these parts of the forest and a pack could have overtaken the mine." She motions to the door. "Something pulled the door off, if not a creature than the miners could be attempting to seize the ore within it."

A slight smirk comes to Preston's face but his confidence fades as Elva tucks her wings behind her and starts into the mine.

"Wait, you sure you want me with you? Shouldn't we wait for help?"

"You are coming, if there is a problem you can teleport us." Elva cocks an eye to the man. "Is that not your training?"

Preston shrugs. "Well yea? But I've never tried it during a real fight."

"Then the sight of your magic will scare them off! Now stop talking." Elva sighs as she starts in without another word.

Preston hesitates but follows behind as he struggles to spark the simple light spell to his hand. However, after a few attempts he manages a fair size ball of green magic that he manipulates to his palm. In his other hand he pulls out his curved sword.

The mine is cold, despite the constant and temperate nature of Artésque, the walls are to Preston's surprise mostly dirt held up by wooden beams. Hardly a reassuring sight for Preston. He swallows as he whispers to the woman in front of him. "So, this is an efficient mine, huh?"

The light joke goes unheeded by Elva as she continues to study the green tinted path before them. "This mine goes under the forest, where the roots have pressed down the rock into ore."

Although Preston wishes to argue the logic, he stays his tongue as he looks back to the fading entrance behind them.

Chapter 26

Fly Fly Fly

The sound of wind quickly rushing past Ellette's ears does not break the young *Flöff's* attention to her path, as the hay covered roof of the Town Hall comes into view. Her speed only increases as she takes notice to a spot near the door suitable for her swift landing.

The nimble bird girl took just under six minutes to reach the town, and merely seconds more to sight her target. Despite this obviously display of speed, she remains cool, her breathing stable and her nerves calm to her task.

A few looks from those passing her by do nothing to her as Ellette darts into the building's double doors. Her determined spirit however is lost as Ellette now looks around the two-story building, a bit wary to the lay out.

Luckily, her overwhelmed stare is brought to an end with the sound of a voice. "Oi, need help, lass?"

Ellette turns her attention to the middle aged *Dwoff* that now stands a little to her right. Despite the pig-man's obvious age the *Dwoff* stands only a few inches taller than her. However, the *Flöff* stands silent with pride, unable to speak her mind as she looks over the lesser creature.

The man notices the stare as he squints his bushy eyebrows. "Did you need something?"

Ellette straightens her posture as she attempts to clear her throat and speak up. "I-I am Ellette of the *VéturVill*, and I have a message for the *Jartál*."

"Oh?" The *Dẃoff* nods as he looks the young *Flóff* over. "And what is the message, is it important?"

"But of course."

"Hmm." The man continues to hold his eyes to the girl as he continues. "Well the *Jartál* has grown busy, what is your message so that I can relay it?"

Ellette hesitates though she nods all the same. "The mine near the *ÉverMoar* forest may have collapsed, *Pexřá* Elva investigates now." She trails on, her wings folding to her back as she does. "I shall not be leaving until this news reaches the *Jartál*, a rescue may be needed."

"May have collapsed?" The *Dẃoff's* expression has not swayed as he holds his hand to the open area of the round building. "If you would wait here, I shall inform the *Jartál* of this news."

Ellette squints to the comment as her more tomboyish tone leaks out in her words. "Why not act now?"

The short man just smirks to the girl's assertion as he replies. "One does not act on mayhap, there must be vindication."

Ellette merely blinks to the foreign comments, her cheeks puffing a little as she shakes her head. "You do not act; I shall talk to your *Alphé*."

The *Dẃoff* steps in front of the girl as he shakes his head. "Workers would need to be pulled from the Princess' project to deal with this problem. We shall wait until this matter has been confirmed." The *Dẃoff* motions to a few benches near the far side of the room. "You may stay if you wish to hear the *Jartál's* inchoate response to this potential matter."

"*Múck'di Dẃoff pliht.*" Her huffed breath only draws a cocked eye from the *Dẃoff* though he is unable to say anything as Ellette turns away, her wings spreading as she nods to her words. "Clover..."

- - -

(Outskirts of Town)

"...Elva, we've been walking for a long time and we still haven't heard any screaming. You still think this is a cave-in?"

The whisper of the man's voice turns Elva's head as she talks in her normal tone. "It must still hold to your mind; otherwise why do you hush your voice?"

Preston gives a little groan as he adjusts the arm he has held up for the duration of their trip, the ball of light holding firm to where he summoned it. "Well you also said there could be something in the cave."

Elva nods to the path as she speaks up. "As we may soon see."

Preston notices her nod as he squints to the path before them. The man's eyes have adjusted a little more to the dark and green light of the cave since they started in, though he struggles to make sense of what he sees. "What's that a split?"

"Yes, and again no lit lantern." Elva slows her walk as she raises her sword a little more. "This is no cave-in, something else has happened."

Just as her words hit Preston's ears a scent assaults his nose. "Ugh... what is that?"

"What, what do you hear?"

Preston shakes his head as he continues, a hand and a hurried look coming to his face. "No, do you not smell that?" Preston's face scrunches as he trails on. "It's terrible... it's a dead body ain't it?"

Elva has paused her advance as she looks the man over. "Your sense of smell seems to outweigh your eyes and ears... good."

The lack of emotion in Elva's response does little to calm the man as he replies. "Do you not smell that?"

Elva shakes her head. "We are trained to ignore the smell of blood, it breeds fear during a fight." Elva holds her head up as she takes a deep breath. "Very faintly, I believe I smell it."

"I-I don't want to see a dead body, Elva." Preston quickly beings to coughs, his throat closing despite there being no change in the stretch. "I think we should leave."

"You shall not run from this, Preston." Elva holds a forceful gaze to the man as she continues. "If there is death here the fallen must be avenged, we do not shy from this."

"You might not but I'm-..."

Elva takes a step towards Preston, a hand coming to the lip of his armor as she pulls the man closer. "There is honor in a fight, turn back now and I shall remember this, Preston." She pushes her hand from the man, her pace coming back to her as she starts towards the split.

Sighting this Preston speaks up. "You can't see without me, Elva."

"Then I fight in the dark, recreant." Elva does not pause, her walk continuing as Preston is forced to step forward.

His voice coming to him in a whispered yell. "Elva!" He grinds his teeth as he follows after the woman, his hand clenching to his sword. "Damn it."

Elva turns an eye her companion, though Preston does not back off as her merely covers his nose and follows forth. The three-way split that has started to come into view only makes Preston more anxious as the smell grows. Preston has never smelled death like this before, though he knows he will never forget it.

The small opening between the three paths is only feet away now as Elva cautiously swings her head to each of the path's openings. Much like the cave itself, these paths are fairly sized, perhaps nine feet tall, and eight or so feet wide, an impressive feat for the wood supports, though Preston hardly takes notice to it as he watches the woman before him. "Do you see anything?"

Elva's posture lightens as she speaks up. "No, there is nothing."

Preston's eyes open a little more as he comes closer. "Well?"

Elva brings her sword to rest a little towards the ground as she holds her hand to her chin in thought.

Preston however continues to squint down each path as he raises the ball of light glowing in his hand. The pin like needle that once pricked into his wrist have subsided for the moment, his thoughts placed elsewhere other than this nuisance. He steps forward, his head on a swivel as he glances down each path. "Well what about this smell- ***crunch***."

A potato chip like crunch takes the man's attention as he turns to something on the ground. Preston lowers himself as he notices a dull, gray almost snake like shedding covering one opening of the path. The skin trails down for maybe seven feet before stopping. Realizing this, Preston swallows hard. "That's a big snake…"

Elva's silence brings Preston's head to her as he speaks up. "Evla?"

The woman remains emotionless as she plants a foot to the skin, her eyes watching as the skin flakes to her boot. "…*Koá-Koé* scales."

Preston looks to the grey skin. "What? No, your armor was green?"

"The one I fell was of Grifón lands, those that survived in the *Ováll* have turned gray..." She bends down as she runs a hand to the skin. "The beast must be migrating... I have yet to see one cross the *Hóbbel Vásil.*"

Preston nods as he speaks up. "Okay, so we need to definitely tell the town, yeah?"

Elva sheaths her sword as she swiftly moves to the path the skin lays in. Her eyes look over the ceiling as she shakes her head. "I have not noticed the scraps on the soft dirt..." Her attention moves to a wooden pillar a little ways down the path, however she pulls Preston forward to better see it. "Yes, look the wood is chipped, the beast must have claimed this as its home."

"Great, let's get out of it."

"No, no." Elva shakes her head almost with an almost glee filled smile as she speaks up. "Look at the scales, it is a small one. Perhaps only a few *yúrfs*. It is best to deal with it after a shedding, it most certainly will be too full to properly fight."

Preston's stomach turns at the comment as he speaks up. "Full?"

Elva turns an almost surprised stare to him as she nods. "Well yes, do you see any miners? The *Koá-Koé* swallows whole and regurgitates later. This must be what you smell, it must be close but not close enough, I have yet to whiff its bile."

Her wings flare a little as she pulls a dagger from her belt and hands it to Preston. "Come, we must attack now. The pit of the mine should be down this center path. It will be open there, the *Koá-Koé* is sure to have nested."

Preston just blinks to the dagger as he whispers. "Wait, Elva, this is stupid. You are going to just charge in?"

"Yes, now take the dagger, your curved blade will not pierce its hide, not even after a shedding." Preston does not take the dagger, sighting this

Elva speaks up. "What would you rather do? Head back into town and allow the beast to become more alert? The petty *Jartál* will task the *Flóff* with killing it anyways." A slight smirk comes to her face as she looks the man over. "Show me courage, Preston."

Preston forces his sword to his belt as he shakes his head. "This is crazy!" He glances to the dagger still held out to him as he snatches it. "We're gonna get killed down here, you know that right?"

Elva laughs. "And yet you stay." The smile holds to her face. "Confidence and courage are not given, it is something that you are, now come, we or it shall die."

Preston's palms are sweaty as he moves past the woman, his heart on fire as it beats against his armor. "That's a terrible speech, now come on before I realize what I'm doing."

Elva takes the lead as she pulls to the man's shoulder. "There is no honor in rushing to our death, Preston. Stay behind me, if my skills fail you remove us from danger." The path continues its normal winding like before, however the stench grows more with each step. Elva has become silent and the only sound Preston can hear is the thump of his heart in his ears. Though he passes it off with every cooling breath.

Unfortunately, the silent movement and determination in Elva has brought the two to a large open cavern in the cave. The slight claustrophobia, now in the back part of Preston's mind quickly relieved as he looks around the dark, gray-black stalagmites and stalactites covering the mine. The top of the cavern is high above, which only shows how far down they have gone. The ceiling is littered with little holes that the light of day now pours from, the sight of this and the fairly lit room around him finally allows Preston to drop his magic as he rolls his arm. A few pickaxes, mining tools, boxes and typical mining equipment aside from mine carts are present. So too, and more prominently is the thick stench of what Preston now knowns as bile.

"Look, the beast sleeps."

The words force Preston to the ground as his knees weaken, his eyes widening to the direction Elva confidently points.

The cavern is a fair size, but not enormous and to one side of the cavern where the light pours in a bit more lays a large, red and putrid mass of yellow. No feather, nor gray skin of the beast is on display, instead, a cocoon of what Preston now realizes is vomited up miners holds to Preston's gaze. Poking from it, is a spiked, and sharply pointed tail.

Preston's heart skips a beat as he just stares in sorrow to the mass. No true figures greet Preston's sight, yet the unmistakable forms of mangled hands and arms poke out from where the beast slumbers. Each breath pushing up and out the cocoon of death around it, something the book Preston read never described.

"Its scales have yet to form, this shall be easy." Elva's wings flare to her words and she starts to the edge of the ramp of rock leading down into the cavern. Her smile seems to fade a bit as she glances to where Preston still kneels. "While this may not be a clean hunt, it is still your first. You have accompanied me thus far, and despite your hesitations, I accept it. But if you were to attempt an attack you would die. Wait here."

Preston merely closes his mouth, his lengthy stare finally breaking as he nods. "Y-yea."

Elva nods as she gracefully floats herself to the bottom floor.

The simple act which only Elva's wings could have achieved cut the distance between her and the beast still slumbering in half. Realizing this Preston's body trembles, his mind now attempting to process the ever-quickening events as the amulet under his armor merely tries to calm him.

The absence of noise in the cavern has only added to the ominous feeling of the room, a low and deep breathing echoing to it as Elva stealthily and expertly draws near to the beast.

While the sight of Elva's approach is masterful, Preston nevertheless turns his gaze back to the horrid mass. However, as the man stares from his overwatch position he notices something, a second, somewhat smaller tail moving just to the opposite side of the cocoon. A pit forms in Preston's stomach, a cyclone of fear physically tugging him down as he finds his jaw unable to move, his eyes wide to Elva's continued and totally oblivious stride forward.

Elva's winds flatten out, her stance lowers to the ground, a spring coiling as she holds firm to the sword in her hand with both hands.

Quickly cupping his hands Preston attempts to whispered call. *"Elva... oh come on, Elva!"*

The distance between them is simply too much as Preston begins to panic, his mind taking hold of only one thought. His hands spark with his magic as he attempts to draw Elva's attention.

Despite the woman's focus, she does cock an eye to the man now waving erratically. Sighting her gaze he throws up two fingers up, his mouth attempting to form the words slowly for her. *"Two, there are two."*

The words seem to take Elva's attention as she uncoils herself, quickly darting to a rocky outcropping as she begins to survey the mass once more. An overwhelming sense of relief and panic quickly overcome Preston as the man throws his hands, his whispered yell still attempting to draw the woman's attention. *"Get out! Get out!"* His continued gestures, coupled with his intense emotions however prove to be a mistake, as a ball of magic spawns to the man's fingertips, its loud chiming now echoing into the cavern as Preston's excessive emotions now fuel the brighter than normal light.

Elva's eyes, even from this distance grow wide to Preston's spell, though neither have much time to exchange glances as the outermost creature begins to gently stir. The mass of red and vomit shaking from its side as the true size of it comes on display now.

The beast is long, perhaps twelve feet, slender like a snake, though a chicken like beak and feathered arms begin to show themselves as more of its nest beings to fall away.

The man quickly closes his eyes as he tries to picture the spot next to Elva, his mind racing to come next to her. Within moments the man's magic rushes around his body and with the feeling of wind now passing his ears he finds himself teleported next to the *Flóff.* However, the signature sound does not alter and as it echoes around the cavern only furthers Elva's wide-eyed stare as she now turns, enraged to the man next to her.

Before a word could be spoken the sound of the waking beast rings to the room.

Elva's wings flare as she darts into the air and positions her sword in front of her.

The first *Koá-Koé* brings its head up as its orange, chicken-like eyes attempting to focus in on what it sees.

Without warning Elva dashes forward, a bullet fired from a gun and aimed squarely to the monster's sleepy gaze. Elva meets her mark, in an amazing spectacle of bravery and strength Elva pins her sword into the *Koá-Koé's* neck, her right hand coming to another dagger on her belt as she stabs it to the beast's eye for good measure.

Though now critically wounded and pouring forth a torrent of blood the *Koá-Koé* jumps to its taloned feet and charges forward, a blood-soaked squawk of agony shaking the very walls as it collapses with Elva still riding it.

Hardly a second passes before the nest of bodies cracks open once more, the second, and slightly smaller creature now screeching to the death of its mate. Elva swings her head back to as pulls her weapons from the first, wasting no time as she launches towards it.

The *Koá-Koé*, though hardly a graceful beast manages to dodge Elva's approach by tumbling to the ground in a fit of squawks. Elva however does not miss a beat as he pushes off the wall and dashes into the creature's right wing, severing several of its heavy feathers as she passes it.

The piercing sound forces Preston to cover his ears, though he stays pinned to the action as Elva is forced to roll from the pained beast, its spiked tail flailing about the cave.

While Elva stays several clear steps ahead of the monster's wild attacks, she is left unable to fight back, her focus to the uneven terrain and hanging stones cluttering the air. Though as Preston slowly begins to adjust to the situation around him he feels the dagger in his hand against his head, a thought gracing him as he lowers his hands. He quickly wraps the dagger in a green glow, the magic now causing it to float beside him as he attempts to take aim at the thrashing beast. Knowing all too well that he cannot aim a shot at its head Preston instead focus to its chest, his mind running on overdrive as he attempts to locate a good spot to loose the dagger in his hold.

Sighting his moment, Preston sends the dagger forward, a burst of green magic taking the creature's attention just long enough for the dagger to make its mark. A loud yelp erupts from the *Koá-Koé*, spinning a bit more as it pecks to the dagger now dug into its underbelly.

While Elva takes the opportunity to rush into the air, her eyes focusing on her next strike, the moment never comes. Instead, the wild thrashes finally land a hit on something, the steel like barbs to its tail pulling forth a wooden support beam. Toppling over, it pulls forth a piece of the rock wall, the commotion in the cavern now dropping a few stalactites. Elva doges them with ease, though her sword is knocked from her hand as she does.

"Distract it!"

Preston merely freezes as he watches the creatures now eyeing him, its erratic trails coming to an end as it charges.

In hindsight he should have teleported, but Preston found himself unable to move, his hands shaking as he stood merely eyeing the beast down. Elva, ever watchful was able to throw her extra dagger into the *Koá-Koé's* side and further drawing its aggression towards her. "My sword, Preston!"

Elva continues to draw the beast, kicking down what rocks she can as she awaits Preston to move. "My sword!"

Finally, Preston snaps from his stare, his eyes falling to where Elva's blade was knocked from her hand as he rushes to collect it.

Elva's speed and flight above the cavern floor has forced Preston to backtrack a little, though he makes steady progress over the rocky flooring. Unfortunately, Elva's luck seems to wane as a pained squawk rings to the cave. The noise draws Preston's eyes though he merely watches as Elva recovers from knocking into one of the many rocks hanging on the ceiling.

The *Koá-Koé* too struggles with the surroundings as it longer wings bat against the rocky outcroppings with every hop towards Elva.

While the sword may be near Preston, he nonetheless cannot take his eyes from Elva as he notices her increasingly more pinned in position the *Koá-Koé* forces her too. Without a moment of hesitation, Preston's magic draws forth a few rocks from the ground, casting them forth as he attempts to draw the beast away.

By a stroke of luck, he hits a spot where the scales have not yet grown in. The squawk is ear wrenching, and the bird-dragon now turns its attention to Preston. It piercing gaze only prompting a hard swallow to gulp in Preston as he realizes just how poor the idea was.

Yet, as the *Koá-Koé* brings its head down to snap, Preston disappears with a quick and almost useless teleportation spell. He now stands behind the beast and is quickly brought back to reality as Elva yells to him. "Look out for the tail!"

Preston's head swings to his left as he throws himself to the ground before him to miss the swaying spikes.

Elva darts to collect her sword, Preston now toying with the beast as he teleported simply inches from where he last stood.

Though just barely effective the larger creature stumbles around the sharp flooring, its talons unable to hold itself up and its wings unable to bring it from the ground without merely knocking to the ceiling.

Its trashing brings it crashing into several more pillars as an opening to the ceiling finally gives way, several trees falling in. Both Preston and Elva shield themselves to the blast of dirt, though the *Koá-Koé* merely claws its way to freedom, the daggers in its tender flesh leaving a pool of blood as it escapes.

Despite the *Koá-Koé's* retreat Elva lands next to Preston with the same commanding voice. "Ready yourself, Preston."

The falling rocks have kicked up a bit of dirt to the man's face as he shakes his head. "For what?"

"It is fleeing, if it goes into town it will rampage. We must chase after it!"

Preston looks to the woman's twitching and bloody right wing as he shakes his head. "You're hurt-..."

"So is the beast." Elva looks over the hole in the ceiling as she nods. "It will crash over *VéturVill* if it is not chased."

Preston shakes his head as he places his hands to Elva's shoulders. "I can teleport out of here; I can also get into town faster if I do that. You can't fight it back to the forest, I'll warn the town. Head to the camp and get them."

Elva blinks to the comment as she speaks up. "Teleport us to camp."

"It's too far, best I can do for two is the mine's entrance."

Elva takes the words with a little surprise as she speaks up. "Good, I can give chase once-..."

"You can't fly like that!" Preston shakes his head. "I can probably teleport just outside of town, I can't do us both."

"I have dealt with worse." Elva's tone raises as she speaks up. "Enough talk!"

"You're right, head to camp." Preston steps back as he nods. "Don't argue." Before the woman can speak up Preston's building spell takes hold and the man vanishes from the room in a flash of green light.

Chapter 27

Final Acts

The world around Preston quickly becomes bright, as the man finds himself standing in the work camp outside of the mine. However, Preston does not really get the chance to take in the sights around him as he falls to his knees in pain.

The chime of magic that always follows the completed spell has reverberated in his ears and a sharp sting has made his whole body shake as he kneels to the hard dirt ground.

Yet, the moment of reprieve never comes as he notices a loud, familiar squawking to his left. Despite the man's constant ring in his ears and the queasiness in his stomach, Preston picks himself up and runs to a nearby wooden crate, to which he hides behind.

Just as he does the creature from the mine burst through the low trees line, it's chicken like legs hurrying it like a rabid animal as it continues its squawking calls. For a moment it looks as though the beast is simply wandering about aimlessly. But, its long scaled wings begin to flare and its tail straightens out as a few powerful flaps bring it into the air.

The *Koá-Koé*, at first is a bit wobbly, but it soon finds its bearings as it starts to glide into the fields outside of the forest.

Preston's hopes drop as he watches this. His right index finger pokes to his right ear as he attempts to stop the ringing, however watching the now flying beast starting to veer to one side has gotten Preston's attention. The *Koá-Koé* now turns towards town.

Noticing this and knowing how close the town truly, Preston is forced to his feet as he attempts to run down the path he traveled before. However, within a few short strides his legs tire and his body feels weak. Preston slows, his feet feeling like weights with every shuffled step he muscles out.

The *Koá-Koé* only gains distance as it continues closer and closer to the town.

Preston pants hard as he shuts his eyes. "Oh come on, come on..." As the man tries to steady his breathing his thoughts drift to the Town Hall itself. The image of the hay covered roof, and circular exterior of the building; however, slowly Preston feels the warmth of his magic creeping around his body.

It takes a bit of determination, but the spell Preston now attempts to fulfill begins to start up. In a flash the world around him is a blinding green and the sound of rushing air passes by his ears as he holds the spell. It lasts a few more seconds than normal and the feeling of being pulled on all sides is unsettling, but with a loud chime of magic popping to his head he opens his eyes.

To his surprise however he does not stand in front of the Town Hall instead, his thoughts have led him somewhere else.

"Preston?"

The fog in Preston's mind begins to clear as he notices where he stands. Preston's spell not only brought him into town, but actually into the Town Hall itself, not just outside. Even more surprising is the fact that he has found seemingly the only safe spot to teleport as he looks around the busy room. The ringing in his ears keep him from speaking and the daze in his eyes holds him from thinking as he looks around to the predominantly *Dŵoff* group holding pickaxes, rope, shovels.

"Preston?"

The voice snaps Preston from his daze as he quickly turns to the worry-faced satyress before him. "*Koá-Koé*!" His words falter as he falls towards the ground. However, Clover's magic takes hold just before his limp body slams to the flooring.

His comment has sparked a little muttering amongst the group as Clover comes a little closer. "What happened? You look filthy, did the mine collapses once mo-..."

The young *Flóff* girl that stood behind Clover now comes front and center as she speaks up. "Where is Elva, is she stuck inside?!"

The ringing in Preston's ear only grows worse as he forces his voice. "No."

"What?"

"N-no cave in."

A familiar feminine voice somewhere out of sight speaks up at the words. "You see, there is no collapse. Now, back to the train site, yes?"

Preston's throat closes a little as he feels his skin become hot. His breaths become gasps as Clover sets him to the ground and now kneels next to him. "Preston? Preston are you well?"

The man's face turns red and his eyes water and bulge for a moment as he blinks hard to the satyress now beside him.

The sight proves too interesting to leave as the group around him hold their attention now to the convulsing man. Clover however is at the brink of a panic as she meets the man's eyes. "Preston!"

Her hands clench to the man's arms as she shakes him a little. "Preston?! Say something?"

The group begins to chatter as thousands of unhelpful suggestions and comments begin to ring out.

Ellette takes a step back as she begins to shift her eyes from Preston's gasping. "W-what's wrong?"

Jartál Caféll cringes in disgust as she waves her hand. "Clover, take him outside! We cannot have him die in here."

Clover ignores the comment as her eyes dip to the man's chest. Her magic sparks up as she pulls the amulet from his shirt and indeed his armor with ease.

The amulet is dull but around Preston's neck a rash has formed, swelling as if some allergic reaction is taking place.

Preston's continues to pant as he scratches to his neck, the rash only growing worse.

Clover darts her hands to the amulet but a quick magical shock forces her to draw them back. Her eyes now are more determined as her hands now glow with her own magic and she again pulls to the necklace. With a little help from her magic she manages to free the necklace from the man, tearing his shirt and a bit of the armor however as her spell pulls it from him.

Finally, Preston is allowed to take a breath as he watches the simple wool of the necklace snap closed, as if it were metal buckling to a sudden cooling.

"Y-you fool!" She shakes her head. "How far did you teleport!?"

Preston shakes his head as he coughs, he points to Ellette as he struggles to speak. "*Koá-Koé.*"

The *Flóff* girl merely blinks at the name as she repeated it. "*Koá-Koé?*"

Clover's ear flicks to the more correct pronunciation as she studies the man's face.

However she is unable to speak up as a loud squawking almost roar rings through the hall. The noise is low but everyone now looks to the ceiling and doors as Clover slowly stands from Preston. *"Koá-Koé!"*

Jartál Caféll turns pale and her hair almost loses its orange tint as she speaks almost in a whisper. "By the Princess…"

The room quickly starts in a panic with a single call. *"Sound the bell!"*

Ellette draws her sword as she looks between the door and Preston. "Elva?"

Preston swallows as he pushes his voice forward. "Wing is hurt, but she's fine.

Ellette nods as she puts her sword back. "I can get to camp before her then, I will go."

The *Jartál* speaks up again as she shakes her head. "You must hurry! Without them we have no means to fight this beast!"

Clover starts towards the door as she leads Ellette. *"Koá-Koé* look for large targets, if you fly fast enough you can avoid it as it will come here."

Her comment only turns the *Jartál* more ghost white as she shakes her head and turns to her silent aid that stands beside her. "Ready any town guards still in the halls to defend." The *Dẃoff* man slowly nods as he starts away.

Preston however turns his attention back to Clover as he pushes himself up from the ground, clearing his throat he calls out. "What are you doing, Clover?"

The satyress hurries Ellette out the door as she turns back to answer the question. "I can keep it at bay. Its scales keep it from absorbing magic but I can distract it."

Preston moves closer to the door as he holds his side that now spasms from his movements. "I'll help."

"You are too weak Pres-..."

Her words are cut off as another, this time louder roar rings through the town. The bell from somewhere in the town hall now chimes as the panic from outside pours in through the threshold Clover stands in.

Without a word Clover darts from the doorway. Preston follows close behind as they both now stare to the long tail of the somewhat scaly beast soaring over the hall's roof.

Clover's hands start up in a bright blue glow as she leans to Preston. "It did not look to have scales?"

"It didn't earlier." Preston's functions have quickly started to come back but he is simply too weak as he leans to the hall's outer wall.

Clover nods as she looks the man over with a little concern. "Preston... please go back inside."

The man shakes his head as he continues to scan the sky. "If you're crazy enough to fight it, I'm crazy enough to stay by you."

With another roar the *Koá-Koé* flies back over the Town Hall, this time in Clover and Preston's sight.

"There!"

Clover jets her hands forward as a bolt of bright magic is sent toward the creature. It slams into its left wing as it turns to avoid it. A pained yell escapes its beak as it now turns its attention to Clover and Preston.

The satyress is quick to follow up as she gallops a little more from the doorway, her tail flicks behind her as she spins a little and sends another, this time much faster bolt of magic toward the beast.

Like before it strikes the *Koá-Koé's* wing, this time bringing it down right in the middle of the road. It's tail, however, crashes into the side of the Town Hall. The small indent in the building is enough to stir the bee's nest as a few lightly armored *Dwoff* guards now burst from the doors and into the street where Preston and Clover stand.

The guards bring their bows up as one speaks up. "Now!"

The volley of arrows is sent flying to the beast that just now attempts to stand. Most of the arrows seem to bounce off, but some stick the *Koá-Koé* in its soft skin. But this only sends a mighty roar from the beast as it flexes it wings to its side and lowers it head. Despite the fact that the *Koá-Koé* has not actually changed in size, the display does make it look much larger.

"Again!"

As the bow men ready their arrows Clover sends two smaller bolts of magic down the road. Though the beast merely shrugs them off as it begins to charge.

To no surprise the simple guards aptly break moral at the sight, scattering either back into the Town Hall or down the street. A pig-like squeals following their run.

Their panicked sound draws the same thought to Preston's mind as he watches the *Koá-Koé's* wobbly charge bouncing off the buildings around it but nevertheless it still charges forward.

Clover however seems to focus on her next spell as she continues to clench her hands and study the ever nearing *Koá-Koé*. However, her lack of action forces Preston to grab her shoulder as he teleports them behind the charge.

The sudden rush of magic and change of position has caused Clover to drop her spell, Preston falls to a knee in pain. But Clover quickly swings her head back to the *Koá-Koé* that now targets the guards still on the road. Without a word she begins to near the beast, each step being followed by a small bolt of magic.

The *Koá-Koé* takes a moment to notice the bolts, but as one strikes a tender spot it lets out a roar and turns. Clover matches the beast's display as she extends her hands, which now glows with intensity.

For show or not Preston is mesmerized as he watches the women's figure almost glow with her magic's radiance. Just as the creature begins another charge Clover lets loose.

Two bolts burst from her hands with a curve right toward *Koá-Koé's* head, and as the bolt crashes into it with a slight difference in speed the sound of bones popping ring through the street. The beast falls dead, its neck a little askew.

The thump of it hitting the ground sends a cheer to the maybe five or six *Dŵoffs* still on the street. However, the celebration, at least for Preston is cut short as he watches Clover fall to her side with a rather hard thump.

The man jumps to his wobbly feet as he quickly baseball slides to her side, taking her arm in hand as he shakes her now. "Hey, hey? You alright?!"

A light smile sits to her face as she looks to the man. Her voice is weak, but her know-it-all spirit stays strong in her tone. "I wonder what Master Nyota would think."

The man just chuckles as he puts his forehead to her arm. "His beard would fall off."

Clover joins the light laugh as she nods. "Elva should be here soon. She should have the strength."

Preston shakes his head to the words as he looks to her face. "For what?"

For a moment the satyress is silent, but as she turns her head a little to the right, she closes her eyes. "I may have overdone this." As her words end a few beads of blood begin to drip from her nose. Her eyes rolling to the back of her head as she goes silent.

Preston's smile fades as he wraps his arms to the satyress' upper body. "Clover? Clover, wake up. Clover!"

- Part Three -

"Master Duscle, do you not think you have been down here long enough?"

The once dark-brown mane of Duscle has now become littered with new gray, his beard a bit stragglier from the lack of care. The once glorious red and black cloak too has become a dirt covered blanket like the *Únoff's* other clothing from the lengthy periods he has stayed in *HefterÁll*'s dank underground. Though like the call to him, it means nothing, his mind focused to his own task.

The young *Dẃoff* guard speak up again. "A few *Únoff* students have come to the castle seeking your-..."

"Quite!" Duscle finally turns to the guard as he snaps. His tattered mane sticks up in certain places but nevertheless the satyress' gaze does not share his crazed style. The satyress lowers his voice as he sighs. "Tell them I am busy, I will hold lecture again I just..." He rubs his hands together as he nods. "Guard, how long have you been posted here?"

The young, curly haired *Dẃoff* stutters as he answers. "S-since *Vón Dorñ* arrived?"

Duscle nods. "And in this time have you ever seen these?" The satyress points to the cluster of bright orange and yellow mushrooms with white spots growing at the base of Clamor's silent stone statue.

The almost pink skinned *Dwoff* shakes his head. "It was not there when first placed?"

Duscle nods. "Precisely." He now shifts his hand to the glowing stones above the statue. "My *Helió* stones are designed to stop all magic from the beast. Even the weak spells that seep from his stone."

The guard just stares to the small mushrooms as he speaks up. "Could they not have grown naturally?"

Duscle gives a slight laugh as he shakes his head. "Natural?! Even the seemingly mindless *Atémor* run rampant in the Capital... here I stand with a thinking *Dwoff* and I grow duller. Leave us! I must halt this beast's influences!"

The guard slowly turns from the room as he moves back to the magically created wall. The spell sends him back to the beginning of the altered pathway through the caverns, a sigh following his exit.

"Will not surface, will he?"

The younger guard shakes his head as he turns to his superior who sits next to the closed bunker door. "No."

"Ha! Let the tail-flicker starve." The older guard turns his attention back to his fingers as he continues to pick dirt from his nails. "I enjoy this post. We sit around and get paid for it."

The younger guard continues to loom over his superior as he adjusted the warming leather helmet he wears. "Should we alert Captain Pigřen?"

"No! Captain Pigřen needs not to worry about this. Tis nothing but an old *Únoff* lost his wits."

"Master Duscle states he needs to speak to the *Jartál*."

"Master?" The pig nosed man turns his snout to the young *Dwoff* as he picks himself up, leaving his spear to the ground. "Oi, I am your superior.

Refer to me as Master, not that tail-flicker. He thinks he is so smart, why is he looking at *Mushreeñ*?"

"Yes, sir. Sorry sir."

The older *Dẃoff* just smirks as he nods. "That be more like it. Now shut it, I am busy guarding here." A laugh rolls from the man as he plops down again.

Chapter 1

Wounds Heal Slowly

The town has slowly begun to simmer down since Clover fell the *Koá-Koé*. Still, the air hangs thick with fear and disbelief, the sounds of children crying can still sometimes be heard lofting with each passing breeze. Though none were hurt, the idea of such a monster near the sleepy town has drawn panic, even more so as word of the mine has begun to spread.

The wall Preston has found comfort in sitting against has provided a fair view of the town just up the dirt road to his right. However, its position from the main road has brought a slight feeling of loneliness to the man.

Of course, his thoughts are hardly to the town or himself. Though Preston has been told that this narrow sided, but rather lengthy all wood, two story building is the premier health-care center in *VéturVill* it does little to reassure him. Especially as he looks over the wilted flowers that attempt to brighten the dull building. Just beyond this shack of a hospital the fields sway with life, an unsettling contrast to the world as Preston see it.

Still, despite the man's doubt, he has remained hopeful and ever attentive to the comments of the would-be doctor.

The dull red door to Preston's right opens. Its sound bringing Preston up as he waits to see who it is.

"I have never trusted the *Únoff Héthtex*..." Elva continues as she motions to her wing which is now bound. "What sense does keeping the feathers from the air make?"

The *Flóff* woman's blonde hair has become tattered, a product of their fight from earlier, the colorful feathers have fallen from her ear and her armor lacks its clean look. All in all, Elva seems fair with merely a scrape to her wing.

Shifting her gaze Elva speaks up, her wings folding to her back. "Clover is resting. The *Héthtex* has said that her overuse of magic has led to a sort of sleep, nothing wakes her. But, he seems fairly confident he can break whatever hold her magic may have."

Preston takes his seat again, his hands folding as he replies. "Okay."

Elva squints her eyes a little as she speaks up. "You are not leaving?"

The man shakes his head as he speaks up. "I can leave in a little."

For a moment Elva is silent, but as she takes a step closer to Preston her voice comes back, albeit with a lower tone. "Preston, all must continue to fly, even when the winds knock our companions. You should accompany me back to the Town Hall."

Preston takes a breath, knowing how pointless the argument would be. "I can't leave yet."

Elva studies the man. "You are hurt?" She gestures to the red mark still around his neck and to the ripped clothing he still wears as she awaits a response.

Preston shakes his head. "I'm fine."

The words seem to annoy the woman, but her body language stays sincere as she places a hand to his shoulder. "Then share your strength with Reynard. I am sure he has not been informed of what has occurred."

Without another word Elva gives a little squeeze to his shoulder as she starts away. "I shall inform *Thrće* Lutin of what has happened."

As the avian woman begins to walk away her wings begin to spread. Sighting this, Preston speaks up. "Don't hurt yourself."

Elva shoots a smile as she responds. "The bandage is bound to me, my flaps shall not tear them."

As her words end she jumps into the air with a few quick flaps of her wings, and within a few moments the sound of her flight is gone. The silence comes back to Preston as he slowly turns to the dirt path leading back into town. With a sigh he stands and begins his journey.

- - -

(Later)

The walk-through town was a bit chaotic, the interesting inhabitants of *VéturVill* having begun to pour onto the town's main road. Bringing with them various stories and rumors of what and why something attacked the normally sleepy town. Preston's speed and desire to stay alone allowed him to navigate the street fairly well, despite the commotions. His pace has also allowed him to reach his destination a bit quicker than he actually wanted, and for the moment the man pauses at the door; just waiting for his mind to come up with the best way to explain the situation to Reynard.

However, after a few more moments of absent thinking the man instead pushes the normally unlocked door open. His timing is almost perfect as he notices the small orange and red furred fox-boy coming down from upstairs.

"Preston? What brings you by?" He yawns a little as he trails in. "Clover has not come back yet, she should be soon."

The words could not have been chosen more horribly for the man to follow as he moves to a seat on his left. "Yea... did you just wake up?"

Reynard nods. "Just a quick nap, Belle kept me busy." He blinks to Preston's attire as he smirks. "Did you and Elva spar again?"

"Something like that." Preston takes a breath. "Hey, Reynard... you should come sit down."

The fox-boy's ears begin to twitch at the sounds outside as he speaks up. "What's going on?"

Preston clears his throat as he nods. "Um, well-..."

"Reynard!"

The almost shrill voice causes Preston to jump as he turns to the door that has just swung open.

It takes a moment however to recognize the *Únoff* woman in the doorway. However, despite the windblown mane of the woman her name quickly comes to Reynard as he jumps from the stairs. "Bella? Are you well?"

The satyress feverishly attempts to get the normal curl back to her mane as she takes up an almost unbearable whiny tone. "Oh, yes I am just so tired from my quick trot." She blows her breath. "I feel as though I am going to collapse... could you bring me a drink, Reynard?"

With a quick nod the fox-boy leaps towards the kitchen as he nods. "Of course, just a moment!"

Bella waves her hand to the comment as she pauses the young lad. "Oh, take your time. It is embarrassing for you to see me this weary."

As Reynard leaves from the room Bella turns to Preston with a low whisper. "You say nothing to him, he is coming with me. He is far too young to worry."

Preston blinks almost surprised to Bella's acting just a moment ago. "What?"

The sudden burst of authority is quickly lost in Bella's eyes as she brings her hand to her mouth. "Ellette came, the sky is filled with the *Flóff* carrying the news. I cannot believe it..." Bella quickly comes from her drama as she turns her eyes back to Preston. "You have not told Reynard anything yes?"

"No, I-..."

"Good." Bella straightened her posture with a sigh as she shakes her head with a sad tone. "The poor dear will need a mare's touch, not a stallion's honesty."

As Reynard comes back into the room he holds the cup of water toward Bella. She takes the cup, brings it to her lips and takes a drink. Though she coughs a little as she looks the cup over. "I forgot Clover enjoys cloud water..." She quickly forces a smile as she passes the cup to Preston. "But of course, I feel much better, thank you Reynard."

The fox-boy just blinks a little confused as he nods. "No problem..."

Bella holds her smile as she turns to the door. "Reynard, Clover will be... occupied for a little, come with me tonight."

Reynard blinks to the comment, still obviously confused as he glances to Preston. Though, he does not turn the woman down as he nods. "Okay? Preston will you tell Clover if you are waiting?"

"Of course, he will." Bella's Southern Belle like voice holds strong as she nods to the door. "She knows I would properly thank you for your help. Now could you wait outside for a moment, I will be out soon. Do not stray from the door."

"Okay?" As the fox-boy leaves the room through the front door Bella follows after him. However, she closes the door and turns back to Preston with a slight bit of concern. "You shall be okay, yes? Reynard will wish to see you later."

The man nods as he speaks up. "I'm not going anywhere."

"Very well, I shall return with him *témont*." Bella gives a quick smile as she shakes her head. "Clover shall be well soon, she must be."

As the door closes Preston continues to sit in the silent room, all the while as the scent of books dominates his senses. However, the smell of the pages only helps to remind Preston of Clover's current situation. With the thoughts persisting, Preston finds security in his movements.; he stands, his walk hardly chasing the chatter away from his mind, even still this does not stop him as the man starts up the staircase.

The hall is fairly cold, and dark despite the late afternoon sun that surely hangs outside. The unwelcoming feeling of the upper hall does not deter Preston, as the man turns his attention to the closed door on the right.

The door's wood squeaks almost as if no one had been in the room since Preston last left. Even still, he presses on, his eyes coming to the folded blanket at the foot of the bed. The room itself feels sad, thanks to the closed drapes that hang in front of the window and the lack of personality that has always been absent from the room.

He lingers at the threshold, a faded shadow to a street in the evening's sun; though after a brief moment Preston steps inside. His walk bringing him to the edge of the bed as he merely sits down, his head coming to rest in his hands. His elbows digging into his thighs as he continues to rest, the room's bleak lighting only compounding his feelings.

Chapter 2

Paranoia

The day has turned slowly in the library, the streets have cleared and the noises outside now mimic the ear pounding silence in the house. The air is warm, and comfortable with the steady glow of Preston's green ball of magic floating above the bed Preston lays to.

Despite the emptiness of the library Preston has found comfort in it. Preston's original thoughts were to stay with Reynard tonight, mainly to make sure the fox-boy handles the situation alright. Of course, with Bella taking that role, Preston has been left to his thoughts, no faked sense of strength mustering for someone else's benefit.

The library has taken on the man's feelings it seems, its dark and silence self merely waiting for something more. The hundreds of books, all silent to their storied wisdoms. With nothing to distract the man, Preston has found himself simply watching the ball of magic floating above him, hypnotic as it is simple.

Yet, as the minutes turned to hours Preston has been left with little more than dry eyes. Within a moment more, Preston shifts his weight to the edge of the bed; the covers have remained undisturbed and the bed for the most part is neat.

He brings himself up as he strolls from the guest room he sat in for the better part of the day. His thoughts have carried the light ball of green magic behind him. Truthfully, Preston has never really learned how to control his magic once summoned, although the overflow of emotions that fills his mind seem to have influenced his abilities.

The magic illuminates the hall as Preston turns his attention to the stairs. It only takes a few seconds for the man to come to the bottom of them, his eyes now set to the door as he starts to it.

Preston has never had a key and from what Clover has said before a spell is supposed to guard the door. However, the man has never fully understood this and for the moment he hesitates before he starts outside. Though he still exits, the door closing behind him as he sighs and moves into the main street of *VéturVill*. No real sense of direction comes to him, nor does a desired time of arrival. Instead, Preston simply starts walking down the street, aimlessly.

The night's air is a bit cooler than the house, not by much but enough to be noticed. The sky is dull with the far-off flickers of stars and low shine of the broken moon rising in the distance. Preston has never enjoyed the night sky in this world, mostly because of the fear and confusion it stirs deep in his stomach. Yet, tonight the sky simply changes his uneasy thoughts instead of consuming them.

Preston has never before ventured into *VéturVill*'s streets at night, to his surprise he finds it fairly well lit, despite the night. Every so often a fire-lit lantern hangs from a house, not all of them are lit but the ones that are burn nicely.

The ball of light that follows behind the man also helps to guide his path into the lonely streets.

With a sigh Preston dips his hands into the pockets Bella sewed into his trousers. His right hand quickly takes hold to the item within. Preston does not bring his head down as he instead runs his fingertips to the cool feeling of amulet and broken wool chain.

Most of the day has involved the man's heart pounding a little more than normal, along with a feverish sweat, so it is unknown yet if the amulet's absences has begun to cause any changes. And with Clover and Nyota so far away it seems best that Preston keep his mind at ease. Yet even this thought does not keep the man from stroking the amulet, merely attempting to spark its dormant spell to ease him.

The houses around Preston all have their windows covered, and not a peep leaks through the wood. Even still, from somewhere around the road the sound of a wheel squeaking takes the man's attention; the faint noise is too low for the man to follow it, allowing his mind to wander once more.

His fingers have yet to stop caressing the amulet in his pocket, almost as if they were searching for something Preston's own mind cannot remember. The heavy beating in the man's chess and urges to yell and scream do not halt, but he does not act, merely letting the feelings stew as they have since Elva left him.

The lanterns to either side of Preston have begun to become more uniform, as most now seem to be lit. The added light to the street has allowed Preston to see a little farther, his sight turning to something down his path.

Two, what looks like *Dwoff* guards stand in the middle of the street. Preston of course does not know if they are the town's guards as it is too dark to actually see the insignia on their armor. However, they do both possess the same simple and curved wood bows he saw brandished earlier.

Preston's nighttime walk seems to come to an end as the guards meet him halfway. "Halt."

Preston does as the pig-man ask, his tired gaze meeting them as the guards readjust themselves to his cold stare.

"What be your business at this time of night?"

For a moment Preston studies the *Dwoffs* before him. It has always been a bit more difficult to tell the age of these pig-people, their skin, for the most part is pink, always carrying a baby-like smoothness to it when no beard is present. Though, age aside Preston glances to the weapons in their hold as he answers. "I'm just out for a walk."

The two guards look at each other for a moment, then back to Preston with a more skeptical look. "Have you been here all *déy*?"

Preston nods as he continues to study the dark forest green outfit with the yellow sash slung over their left shoulder.

"Well then you are aware of the attack on the town. *Jartál* Caféll has stated none are to wander the streets this night, for safety."

Preston nods again, tapping his sword on his side. "I think I'll be okay."

The *Dẃoff* on the left gives a light chuckle as his snout-like nose bounces a little. "Oh, so you are that confident, huh? Where you even there during the attack?"

Preston shrugs. "Would it matter? It's dead."

The other guard now speaks up as he waves his hand. "That may be, but you are to return to your home or we shall arrest you."

"Arrest me?" Preston chuckles. "I'm just walking around."

"Look." The guards shrugs. "The town be a bit scared right now, people do not want anyone mucking about, go home, will ya?"

Despite the casual and almost amicable tone and stance the guard holds, Preston does not back down. His temper flaring as his face grows hot. Luckily, before he can speak up a light catches his eyes from behind the guards.

Sighting his stare, both of the armored *Dẃoffs* turn around, the one on the right speaking up. "I see you have nothing, *GřavTrender*."

The much shorter *Dwoff* coming towards them merely chuckles. The short fur hat wearing *Dwoff* wheels a rather large cart behind him, the squeaky wheels of it coming to an end as the pig-man speaks up. "Hardly, I collected a few, though the rest were meat, I do not collect meat."

"Show some respect! Those were people." The two guards straighten a little at the comment as the other replies. "Return to your home or-..."

"Yes, yes, Kven. I do know the rules." The short *Dwoff* continues to mutter something to himself as he starts past where Preston stands. The two guards behind him shake their heads yet funnily enough they are the ones that move the quickest away.

However, the *Dwoff's* green eyes do catch to Preston as he drags his cart to halt. His voice is a bit lower as he speaks up. "Guards stopped you as well?"

Preston nods his eyes turning to the covered cart as he swallows. "Yea."

The short pig-man squints as he moves his hand to swing the lantern attached to the cart towards Preston. "Ah! It is the library's *brivtó*."

Preston just stares to the short man as he nods.

"Hmm." He moves the light from Preston's face as he turns back to the path before them. "How is Miss Vines? Rumor has it she fell ill after the fight?"

The *Dwoff's* voice is dry, perhaps not intentional but the tone does keep Preston from answering for a moment. "She'll be fine."

The *Dwoff* simply nods as he sighs. "I should hope... I have never enjoyed making *Únoff cáskte*, far too many rules for the *passmórtit*." The *Dwoff* stops his comment as he forces an awkward smile. "But of course, you would not want to hear that..." He glances back to the guards as he nods. "Enjoy your walk."

Without another word the *Dwoff* pulls to his cart, the squeaky wheels chiming into the town once more as he starts away.

Despite the comment Preston lingers, his eyes holding to the covered cart until it moves to far into the night. With it gone, Preston's eyes turn to where the library sits just up the road.

The pace is a bit slower, but he comes to the door once more, his hand to the knob as he half expect the library to be locked. To his surprise, the door opens and starts inside, though he presses his back to the door as he closes it.

The house is still, just as he left it, and despite this fact, he slumps to the door. Though it makes no sense, Preston short walk yielded no difference, and this fact only further plunges Preston's depression.

His hands tremble for a moment, though he pulls forth the amulet from his pocket as he sparks his magic to it.

At first nothing happens but the glow of Preston's magic, yet as he tightens his hand a soothing feeling rushes to him. The wave of coolness forces Preston to bite his bottom lip as he slams his head to the wood of the door behind him, his eyes widening to the dark of the room as he takes a few deep breaths.

With a slight shutter, Preston loosens his grip to the amulet, allowing to to fall into his lap as he stares at the ceiling, the swirling magic now taking over. With another shaky blow his breath he begins to ease himself up, his right hand collecting the amulet as he drops it to his pocket.

His walk is a bit wobbly, but he makes his way up the stairs as he sets his sights to his old room.

Moving inside, Preston pulls the covers back as he slowly comes into the bed. Despite the sudden tiredness in his muscles he cannot find the ability to simply close his eyes and rest. Instead, Preston moves a hand behind his head as he stares at the ceiling above once more. His free hand dipping again into his pocket as he pulls out the amulet piece.

Chapter 3

Before the Calm

The room is quiet, with only the steady sound of Preston's breathing filling the air. The town outside has begun to come alive with the rising of the sun, however the noises and voices do little to stir Preston from his slumber. Although the man's rest is not solid, he desperately attempts to cling to it, his mind forcing the world outside to stay at bay just a moment more.

Sadly, the ability to stay in his oblivious sleep comes to an end as the sound of someone knocking on the door downstairs finally wakes the man. With a deep sigh Preston raises his head from the pillow, for a moment his mind skips placing the room and he looks to his left where the digital clock would be. Yet, nothing but the wood of the house greets his view and Preston quickly remembers as to where he is.

The returned knowledge of his surroundings is regrettable as he forces himself from the comfort of the familiar bed. Preston ignores putting his boots on and barely fixes his tan colored pants and still slightly dirty top from yesterday as he comes downstairs.

The knocking at the door continues even as Preston brings his hand to unlock the door. "Yes?"

The sight of the avian woman at the door does not surprise Preston, as he merely loosens up.

Elva's armor is shiny, her colorful feathers have been replaced above her ear, and her skin is clean. For a moment she looks as she did every other day, though Preston is unable to take the lie her appearance yields as he looks to her stern face.

The avian woman crosses her arms as she looks the man over. "You do not own this house; how can you greet it?"

Preston takes a step back into the room as he allows Elva to step inside before he closes the door. "Bella took Reynard, so I didn't get a chance to talk to him... I wanted to be here for when he came back."

Elva has not uncrossed her arms as she continues to study the man. "Reynard was not here and yet you continued to linger. Why?"

Preston shrugs, his apathetic tone holding. "I just told you why."

The man's quick answer brings a response to Elva as she cocks her left eyebrow. "You would stay here instead of flying free in the sky?"

Preston bites a little to his cheek before he nods. "I don't have wings, Elva."

"You would have been honored at the camp, Preston."

With a sigh Preston starts to stretch his right arm a little. "Why? I didn't do anything but yell for help."

Elva nods to the words as she pulls forth the dagger she gave the man yesterday. "This dagger was stained with the blood of our foe, while you did not slay it, you had a role in its death..." Elva moves the dagger back to her belt. "You are not a warrior, nor would the camp have greeted you as one, but you fought, and that would have been recognized."

Her comment brings a quick chuckle from the man as he rubs his hands through his hair. "Well Elva, I didn't really see yesterday as a good day for celebration maybe I'll-..."

Preston's words are quickly brought to a halt as Elva forces the man to the ground, sweeping his legs as she tackles him. Elva's wings have sprawled out as she holds the man down. Her muscles ripple a little through her tan skin as she speaks up. "Your sorrow is disruptive, like a *yiftiñ* guiding a darkened cloud you see little beyond it. Dry your eyes with wind Preston, not mist!"

Preston quickly responds, his own hands to Elva's arms as he tightly wraps his finger to the woman. Though he attempts it, Elva proves too strong to escape from, instead, his actions turn to words as he yells. "I can't just push everything down! I can't just ignore everything!"

The avian's hard face yields no sympathy as the pointy eared woman simply shakes her head, and presses Preston down to the ground further, which loosens the man's grip on her arms. "Pathetic... I have killed creatures who have begged less with a dagger in them."

Preston pushes to the woman, which either by his straighten or her own desire finally forces Elva off him. As the man begins to stand again, he speaks up, although he does not face the woman behind him. "I should have done more; don't you understand that? I didn't do anything! I stood there; I did what I do every time! I stand and do nothing." He runs a hand to his face as he shakes his head. "Oh... Matt I should have-..."

"Stop!" Elva has quickly come to her feet as she slowly folds her wings to her back. "Clover is a capable fighter; she knew what she was doing." Her words draw Preston's eyes back though as she takes notice to the tears in his eyes she straightens up, a look of disgust crossing her face as she trails on. "If you continue to water I will beat you."

Preston just bites to his lip as he replies, the serious look to Elva's face drawing him from his emotions just long enough to reply. "I'm tired of feeling guilty."

"You are guilty, and you should feel as such."

The answer draws a stare of disbelief though Preston does not rage at the comment, his depression only furthering as he looks her over.

Elva however does not bat an eye to stare as she continues. "The *Flóff* call this, *Fro'Taski*. It means forward thrown; it is a term to describe warriors that wish to fight head on. You do not lack the courage you lack the skill needed." Elva nods. "You need training, and you need to fight."

Preston shakes his head. "I don't need training-..."

"Preston."

"No! I don't need training and I don't need to fight, I want to stop getting in fights, why is that so-..."

Elva again speaks up a hand coming to Preston's top as she pulls him closer. "And yet you find yourself in them!" Elva quickly loosens her hand. "You always will, so long as you choose to remain by Clover's side you will find fights. Now ask yourself, will you stand or will you do something next time?"

Preston merely falls silent to the comment, his mouth hanging open for a moment until he looks away, his right hand digging into his pocket. A slight tingle running through Preston's back as he swallows. "Have you been to see her today?"

Elva hesitates but answers as she shakes her head. "I pasted the building on my sweep. Bella and Reynard were traveling back into town, though they say Clover remains sleeping."

Preston nods as he turns his eyes a little to the ground.

Elva does not wait for a response as she speaks through the man's silence. "I am to report to the Town Hall for *Alphé* Kassie. I also am here to inform you that Lutin is angered by your lateness."

The man just gives a slight smirk as he shakes his head. "Who said I was going back to the camp?"

The avian woman narrows her eyes. "I do not beg and my tolerance for time steadily flies, Preston. Return to the camp, or stay and face what happens to those who desert."

With a nod Elva moves back to the door. "I shall come by once I am finished, best that you are not here." Without a word more she leaves.

- - -

A little later

The sun now begins to poke up over the houses of *VéturVill* as Preston continues down the main road. Despite yesterday's encounter with the *Koá-Koé* the people of the town have moved on with their lives, and surprisingly no one Preston passes glances to the sky. Yet, something has changed in this predominantly *Dŵoff* farming and trade village, there are more leather armored guards traveling the streets.

The sight of these young and mostly unseasoned guards however does not really bring a feeling of security to the man. Instead, the thoughts of how the guards acted yesterday during the attack continues to replay in his mind. As a result, the man finds himself running his right hand over the hilt of the sword on his waist every so often. The man's uneasy expression does get a few looks, but then again Preston has not had the opportunity to change his clothing so the tear in his shirt may be the reason.

Despite the slightly more crowded streets, Preston finds his destination quickly coming to his left. The marketplace is bustling with the yells of bookkeepers and the chatter of haggling. The guards seem to have multiplied from the sheer mass of people however they remain like ghost only being seen for a moment.

Preston finds his way through the mobs of shoppers by clinging to the shops that box the market square in. Luckily for Preston, Bella's boutique comes to him without too much hassle.

It only takes a few moments for Preston to near the store, surprisingly the outside is fairly empty, and Preston finds his way in rather smoothly. As he opens and then closes the door the small bell above the door chimes out, and a voice from behind the counter's red curtain calls in. "One moment dear!"

Preston speaks up as he looks around the shop. "Take your time, Bella."

The curtain quickly flies open as the familiar, curvy body of the satyress strides into the room. "Oh, Preston!" Her welcoming and upbeat voice falters a little as she looks back to the curtain. "Reynard is still asleep upstairs. I would rather not wake the poor dear."

Preston gives a little smile as he nods. "It's fine." His eyes look over the woman's mane, it is curled but looks to have been done rather quickly. "How is he?"

Bella gives a light sigh as she shakes her head. "I have never seen him so upset, if I had not known him before I would think he were *lóftor vestá*. We have just returned from seeing Clover... he still does not want to talk."

Preston nods as he takes notice to Bella's quickly lowering cheerfulness. With a glance to the shop Preston attempts to change the subject a little. "Well it looks a little busy out there, do you want some help around here?"

Bella turns her eyes to the window in the front of the shop as she shakes her head. "It seems everyone is buying food and supplies for a war." She shakes her head as she continues. "There will be no need for my specialty, especially with *Jartál's* decree for more guards. It seems everyone wishes to take up arms." With a slight sigh she ends her thoughts. "...but, you need not worry about me. My sister is still here, I am sure she will help if needed. Of course, she did gallop off with Elva's friend earlier." She cocks her head, her hand tightening under her chin as she trails on. "It was for the best though, she said something to Reynard that upset him. The poor dear has yet to tell me what."

It quickly becomes clear that Bella has not really held a conversation in a while as she brings her hand to her chin in thought. "Hmm... no matter." Her eyes turn back to Preston as she nods. "Have you gone to see Clover?"

"No, I wanted to come here."

Bella shakes her head as she brings her voice to an almost whisper. "I spoke with the *Héthtex*... can you believe no potion can wake her from the sleep? It is almost as if-..."

"*Preston?*"

The low almost dismal sounding voice takes center stage in the discussion as both Bella and Preston turn to the young *fróx*. The orange fur under his eyes looks matted from where he was obviously crying, and his fur overall looks ragged. The normally cute fox-boy is a shadow of his former self, the sight of this brings Preston's voice up rather quickly however, as he steps towards him with a smile. "Hey buddy, you okay?"

Reynard's ears lay down to his head as he speaks up. "Ellette said I was a cub... she said that a *fróx* my age should be able to deal with something like this she said-..."

Bella chimes in, a hand coming to Reynard's shoulder as she spurs him from the words. "Bite your tongue, that girl is a fool, we have every right to be upset."

The words do little to Reynard as his head drops to the ground. "I am a cub..."

Bella gives a slight groan as she lowers herself to Reynard's level. "You are a very grown up *fróx*, Reynard, you are very kind and sweet. Qualities most stallions would envy." Bella brings her hand to raise Reynard's chin a little as she continues. "And your fur is far too exquisite to dirty with sadness, dear."

The comment brings a smile to Preston's face as he watches Bella slowly winning over the young fox-boy. Preston has always believed Bella's looks and more uptight attitude has left her somewhat cold, however, it has quickly become clear that despite Bella's bumptious ways towards fashion and cleanliness she still holds some down to earth qualities as well as a knack for people in need.

Reynard gives a simple nod as he sniffles a little. "Okay..." The fox-boy turns his eyes to Preston as he speaks up. "Are you still leaving soon, Preston?"

The man gives a slight smile as he speaks up. "I'll be checking on you every chance I get, I'll just be at the camp, don't you worry."

"Okay."

With a nod Preston lowers himself. "But enough about that, come here."

Sighting the man's open arms Reynard dart forward, both now embracing one another Reynard shutters a little. Preston rubs a hand to his head as he nods. "I'm sorry, I'm so, so sorry."

Reynard continues to tremble, though he pushes himself from the man as he wipes to his eyes. "Ellette said you fought it, is that true?"

Preston cocks a smile as he shrugs. "W-well sort of." He shakes his head. "But Clover did everything else, she's strong, you know that, she's be back to herself in no time."

Bella gives a little nudge to Reynard as she stands. "You should get some rest, we can go and check on Clover a little later if you want."

"Okay." Reynard slowly begins himself from Preston, the look on his face suggests he wants to stay, though he listens well enough as Bella motions for him to continue on. With him out of the room Bella brings her hand to her head.

"Perhaps Gwendy can cheer him up. She has a way with everyone." The satyress brings her eyes to Preston as she looks to be steadying her thoughts. "Your clothing is rags, dear."

The comment brings a laugh to Preston as he nods and looks himself over. "Yeah, I need to change when I get back."

Bella's expression does not change as she replies. "The dreadful camp?"

Preston shrugs. "My things are there." Preston shrugs. "Elva said if I didn't go back they'd label me as a deserter."

"Oh?!" Bella's sweet tone shifts a little as she lowers her head to the man. "If you happen across Elva, please send her my way. It seems both she and Ellette have forgotten manners beyond their camp."

"No problem."

Bella takes a deep breath as she looks to the spools of fabric near the wall behind her. "I suppose I should get to work. Previous orders still must be filled, even with these events."

Preston shifts in his stance his eyes coming to where Reynard ventured off to. "Are you sure I can't help around here? I... I don't want to leave him."

Bella nods as she speaks up, her eyes pinning to the emotion in Preston's face. "Clover was never one to show her emotions, Reynard, I think struggles with that too... though I fear you may draw too much from the poor dear." She nods, obviously struggling to find the right words. "Stop by as much as you can, but-..."

"I get it." Preston swallows his thoughts as he nods. "Thanks, for-for everything."

Bella shrugs. "Clover has done right by me, there is no need to thank me, dear." She shifts her eyes to the man as she nods. "Take care, Preston."

With another simple nod Preston turns back to the door and starts outside. The marketplace's chatter keeps his thoughts from his mind as he instead mindlessly looks around the medieval flea market. Of course, as he closes the door he shutters, his hand dipping into his pocket in search of the amulet as he struggles to suppress his feelings. Though he feels wrong in leaving Reynard he knows Bella is right, even the spell he triggered before leaving the library now wanes at the mere sight of Reynard, something he could never admit.

Chapter 4

Fields of Envy

 The sweet scent of wildflowers has steadily begun to increase around the fields of *VéturVill*, and thanks to the night in the stuffy library the fresh aroma now hits Preston with its full uplifting effects. The warmth of the sun also helps add to the man's continued trek out of town. Normally, wishful thoughts of having a car or at least a bike fill Preston's mind when he has to go somewhere, however the silent and bright world of green around him has begun to clear his mind.

 The town sits a few good hills behind Preston, and the camp a fair distance away. The chatter of the ever-growing blades of grass have continued to keep the man company as he simply follows through the path with deep soothing breaths. Naturally, the clouds around the camp are few, with only one or two of the masses hanging in the sky. How the clouds are able to be manipulated have never made much sense to the man, but every once in a while, the wind does mix up the work due to the fluffs of water vapor.

 Still, most of the almost pure white wisp of color that hang to the blue canvas are smooth and unnatural. It has never really bothered Preston much before, but then again, the man has never really given the clouds' shapes much thought.

And it seems as if today will not be much different, as a familiar sight comes into view from behind a few higher up clouds. The brown winged and smaller than average *Flóff* soaring above is unmistakable, especially seeing as how there is only one young *Flóff* in *VéturVill*, at least that Preston is aware of.

Sure enough, the figure above begins to descend at a rather quick pace, and before long comes within earshot. "Preston!"

Ellette swoops down just above the man's head as she lands to the path a bit before him. Before she can continue Preston forces a smile and speaks up. "How'd you know it was me?"

The girl straightens her posture as she begins to walk beside the man. "Your hair makes you an easy target." Her upbeat tone falters a little as she cocks her head a bit to the right. "Are your winds tethered?"

"I'll be fine." Within seconds the normally energetic bird-girl speaks up, her typically tomboyish tone returning as she nods.

"A few in camp were upset that you stayed out." Ellette shrugs. "But many more talked of *Pexřá* Elva's kill." The bird-girl turns an eye to the man as she nods. "Would you tell me about it later?"

"Not today." Preston's quick answer brings a slight puff to Ellette's cheeks though she shrugs it off as she replies.

"Fine." She spreads her wings. "I suppose I should get back to my post. Camp is on alert because of the attack."

Preston just nods to the comment as he speaks up. "Good thing you already talked with Bella's sister than."

Ellette pauses her jump back into the sky as she simply shakes her head. "We were all told to carry the *Jartál's* message."

"It's not a problem, I won't tell Elva." Preston turns an eye to the girl beside him. "Were you nice to Rey?"

Ellette blinks to the comment, her wings falling a bit as she nods. "He was crying." Ellette shrug, a look of uneasiness coming from her as she trails on. "I have never seen someone in camp cry... so I called him a cub."

"Okay."

The simple answer draws Ellette's gaze as she puffs out her chest a little. "Tears do not honor the fallen, Preston."

"She's not dead." Preston stops as he turns to the girl. "And even if she was that doesn't help."

Ellette stares a little wide-eyed to the man, her wings setting out to her side as she stays silent.

Preston takes a breath however as he shakes his head. "Not everything Elva tells you is right."

A faint smile comes to Ellette, though before Preston can speak up the girl chimes in, her words saving herself from Preston's rant. "Juna told me it was wrong." She stammers a little, Preston taking notice to the bird-girl's first lack of words. Though, she does find them as she holds her head up. "I shall continue my patrol, Preston."

Within a second Ellette brings herself up and away from Preston, the sounds of her wings getting further and further from the man. The fields' natural sounds take hold again as he turns away unsure of how successful their conversation was.

However, as the fair-sized wood wall surrounding the camp comes ever closer the man's thoughts drift from the world around him.

It only takes a few moments for Preston to come to the closed gate and as he does, he calls out. "Gatekeeper?"

Within seconds the familiar avian woman that normally mans the gate rises above it. "Preston."

The brown haired *Flóff's* name comes quickly to Preston's mind, as he nods. "Good morning, Elwine."

The woman gives a slight smile as she speaks up. "Do not allow *Alphé* Kassie to hear you still wishing fair mornings; morning has long passed."

Preston simply nods to the comment as he replies. "Will do."

Elwine's figure again disappears as she descends back behind the gate. However, as the gate begins to open Preston pushes his way inside.

Elwine calls from where she now begins to close the gate. "Lutin wishes to see you."

The man gives a quick glance to the forge that only sits a mere jog from the entrance as he takes a deep breath. "Yeah, I guess I can't really sneak past him."

Preston turns back to the woman in front of him as he gives a simple nod goodbye. However, he halts his voice for the moment as he notices Elwine's eyes locked to the obvious tearing in his clothing.

Elwine holds a slight smile as she speaks up. "So Elva's tale was true? You and her vanquished a *Koá-Koé* and fought the other before it attacked?"

With a shrug Preston speaks up. "I hardly did anything." A slight laugh comes from the man. "But I was the one who noticed there were two of 'em."

The spotted brown wings Elwine had to her back now flair a little as she smiles to the man's comment. "Our *Pexřá* did not scout before her attack?"

Preston waves his hand to the comment. "Can't see much in a cave, she was too focused on the attack."

"...And what would you know of attack?!"

The deeply masculine voice quickly takes hold of the conversation as both Elwine and Preston turn to the brawny mass that strides towards them.

Lutin's expression, like normal, is dull. "Do you attempt to gloat on another's feat, boy?"

Preston squints to the comment as he shakes his head. "No I wasn't."

Lutin cocks an eyebrow to the comment as he crosses his arms over the heavy tool belt wrapped around him. "Oh? Then I suppose it was just your loudmouth, I hope you were not planning on sneaking away again, you owe me work, boy."

Preston motions to the tear on the leather armor from Clover's spell brought the amulet out. "Yeah, does that mean I can get better armor?"

Lutin's eyes widen a little more as he uncrosses his arms. "How did you ruin a set of armor so neatly made?" Lutin's disbelief quickly shifts to anger as he glares to Preston. "I fastened that myself, how does a *Koá-Koé* tear it without killing you?"

Preston hesitates for a moment, but he replies all the same. "Magic."

"Ugh, *Mŕad'*." Lutin shakes his head as he shifts to Elwine. "He is more stubborn than Stysen." Lutin trails on as he quickly turns to Preston. "Get to the forge, the *Jartál* has ordered new arrows for the guard."

Preston gives a simple sigh. "Right."

As the man walks past the muscular, dark skinned *Flóff* a light slap hits Preston's back. "This reminds me. Who gave you leave last night?"

Elwine watches for a few moments as Preston and Lutin start their short trip towards the forge, however as their voices gets a bit too harder to hear she turns back to her post.

Lutin continues to chatter on, every breath shaking his head. "...You wish to live with *Flóffs* but you continue to share the laziness of a *Dẃoff*!"

As the forge comes within steps Preston turns to the light brown apron hanging on the rack, all the while as Lutin trails on. "...you all are, either you are stubborn, lazy, or just *bafte*ñ." He shakes his head. "I should have stayed in *Flúry Fasá*."

Preston removes his torn shirt, looking over his armor as he speaks up. "Why'd you leave?"

The dark *Flóff* squints to Preston as he begins to poke at something in the forge. "Because, my words were whispers on the wind. Glory is more important to most than simply fighting another *déy*. I grew tired of seeing my comrades coming back injured or worse." Lutin pauses as he looks the man over. "You have just had your first brush with combat, and to no surprise you ruined my armor."

Preston just gives a little smirk as he undoes his armor, quickly placing it to the anvil in from him as he puts his shirt back on. "Where'd you want this?"

Lutin nods to the workbench as he continues. "I never fix broken *lehtó*, I shall make you a new set." Lutin uses the tongs to pull a bright red-orange bar of metal from the forge as he moves to the anvil. "As long as you remember your place in this camp."

Preston turns to the fire as he checks its height. "What working the forge?"

A slight chuckle comes from Lutin as he begins to strike the metal with his hammer. "You do not work the forge; I work the forge. You, merely clean it."

"Mmm... then why did you need me yesterday?"

Lutin continues to hammer away at the metal as he speaks up. "You are normally fair at direction, and you do not dismiss this work as so many in this camp have."

Preston squints a little as he straightens his posture. "Whoa, was that a compliment?"

The words twitch Lutin's wings as the dark *Flóff* gives a rather sharp glare to the man. "A compliment? I see nothing cleaned nor started, boy!"

Preston just smirks to the comment as he moves about his normal routine. However Preston stops as he turns his eyes to full box of ore near the furnace. "How'd you get this?"

Lutin pauses his next strike as he turns to Preston, though he looks back to his work as he nods. "They had the shipment, just never sent it out." Lutin bangs his hammer down again as he nods. "Stay to your work. Keeps your mind clear."

The sound of the hammer and roar of the fire takes hold in the forge as Preston fixes his gloves and begins to take a few pieces of ore from the box. However, as the absence of Lutin's voice continues Preston speaks up. "Did you want to know why I didn't come back yesterday?"

Lutin does not stall, though his voice lightens as he replies. "No, focus on your work. The past is the past, let it rest."

Chapter 5

Evanescent

The night sky glows with a faint grey like color, despite the absence of the bright moon. The night came quick, with Preston being lost in his work. However, the suddenness of it along with the same sudden loss of time Preston seems to have since the attack is a bit unnerving. While nothing has outwardly changed, the sobering reality of it is that Preston became mindless, merely following orders until Lutin said it was time to stop. While great to pass the time, it nevertheless brought no real feeling of satisfaction, especially as Preston found himself staring up into the sky, just the same as he had last night with nothing new to show for it.

Sure, his hands ache a little and his hair is a bit darker from the lengthy amount of time spent at the forge, but the change of clothing and chatter of people around him have done little to revive the man's spirit.

Even the question Preston has found himself answering have been little more than tedious moments of repeating what he just said. All the questions revolving around what Elva must have told the camp before. Preston did however find it humorous that he was asked to sit near the fire with everyone else, when most days he is not normally welcomed. Naturally, with Elva gone though, Preston followed his typical routine of getting whatever soupy or quick to eat dinner concocted from the pot and then simply returning to a makeshift seat away from the group.

In truth, most of the camp never has really had contact with Preston aside from the forge, and those who do talk to the man never seem to have a problem with him. Aside from Stysen, but Preston has learned simply to avoid the cocky *Flóff*. Yet, one side of Preston does wish to return to the fire and rub elbows with Stysen, if not just for the sake of taking center stage from him for a night. Still, the thought only graced Preston's mind for a moment as he continues to stare through the breaks in the clouds and floating lanterns above him.

"Ugh... Tra'vers made this stew."

The young voice takes Preston's attention as he watches the *Flóff* girl coming over and sitting down on the ground to his left. The same thick brown and orange stew that Preston has resting on the box in front of him jiggles in the bowl Ellette tries to steady in her lap.

Preston waits for the girl to catch his eyes and as does, Ellette talks, her gaze quickly shifting from the man as runs her spoon to the stew. "You did not tell Elva."

Preston thinks over the comment for a moment before giving a slight sigh. "Elva's not here."

Ellette cocks her head to the comment, her eyes still to the bowl in her lap as she nods. "Will you tell Elva?"

Looking away Preston speaks up, a slight shake in his head to the question. "No."

The answer draws Ellette's attention as she slurps to her spoon. "Why not?"

"Because I'm not an ass?" Preston shrugs as he turns back to the bird-girl. "Because I'm not going to get you in trouble, just because."

Ellette tightened her gaze to the man, the spoon in her hand coming to her lips as she sucks to it. "But I did not follow *Pexřá* Elva's command?"

Preston squints to the droplets of stew forming on Ellette's chin, though she hardly seems to care how slowly she looks as her gaze stays pinned to Preston. "You said you were just carrying news, right?"

Ellette nods. "I did not have to go to Bella's."

"Okay do you want me to tell her?" Preston gives a slight chuckle. "I can do that if you want."

"No." Ellette shifts her gaze, a faint sigh coming from her as she speaks up. "I just do not understand why."

Preston again chuckles to the comment as he crosses his arms. "I said why."

For a moment their conversation ends, Ellette slurping to the hot stew in her lap, though she does not stay silent for long as she turns back to Preston. "You are not going to force me into your bed with the threat of telling, are you?"

"What the-... no!" Preston turns to the bird-girl in a bit of disbelief as he speaks up. "Is it too hard to accept that I didn't want to hurt a friend?"

Ellette puffs her cheeks out as she takes a quick sip of soup. "I will stab you if you lie."

"I'm not lying." Preston huffs as he shakes his head. "And don't you remember our deal? I don't want to hear you say stuff like that."

Ellette playful laughs to the comment, rocking a little from where she sits. "What male does not like such comments? Swords in sheaths, everyone! The thrust of cloudy water! The thrust of cloudy water!"

Preston stands from his seat, quickly prompting Ellette to grow quiet as she looks up to him. Though her faded smile does not halt Preston's tone as he stares down to her. "I'm not sitting here if you're gonna talk like that."

"Fine." Ellette shuts her mouth as she forces the spoon to her lips, her body tightening to the bowl in her lap.

Preston lingers over her for a moment, though he slowly begins to sit down as he places his bowl back to the table, his eyes turning to the sky above him. Neither say a word, merely the sounds of Ellette slurping and faint muttering to the wind.

Yet as she huffs again Preston chimes in. "Don't like the stew?"

Ellette blows a bit of hair from her face as she begins to stir her bowl. "It tastes worse than *Cawlf* meat."

Preston just smiles as he points back to the group around the fire. "Why don't you go get something to sit on?"

"*Pfff*, you do not need a table to eat." Ellette turns back to her bowl in disgust as she continues. "Besides, this creation should not be enjoyed in comfort. Have you tried it?"

Preston looks back to the slush in the bowl as he shakes his head. "Nope."

"What have you been doing that?" Ellette shakes her head. "Sitting in a fog?"

"I've just been thinking."

Ellette gives a slight groan to the pause, though as she awaits another comment, she grows impatient. "What have you been thinking about?"

Preston shrugs. "The sky."

The comment seems to take Ellette's attention as she nods. "At least it is something I understand... what about?"

Preston simply shrugs as he speaks up. "Nothing really, just watching it."

"Watching?" Ellette turns her head to the sky as she spoons a little of the stew into her mouth. The spoon plops from her mouth with a rather unladylike sound as she continues. "I do not see why the sky is so interesting to stare at. Unless you are thinking about flying." She points the spoon to the nearest lantern as she continues. "Oh, I hear that Lutin is going to add a bit of color to the lantern's glass. That shall at least make the sky a bit brighter."

Preston just nods to the comment as he instead continues to stare at the sky.

His silence however prompts Ellette to speak up again. "Did Lutin provide you armor yet?"

"He said he would have something soon." Preston takes his attention from the sky and to his bowl as he stirs the stew a little.

Ellette nods as she takes a quick sip from her bowl before talking. "Well, *Alphé* Kassie is gone for the night and *Pexřá* Elva is sure to accompany her. So it would be up to Lutin to punish you for not having armor."

Preston just laughs as he takes the first spoonful of stew to his mouth. "He already punished me for today." As his words end he dips the spoon to his lips, the absence of any real smell does little to halt the horrible bitter tasting liquid that pours into the man's mouth. Unmistakably, there are some familiar vegetables, but the vast majority of Preston's taste sense is overloaded by the sheer bitterness of the liquid to care.

The look on the man's face prompts Ellette to smirk. "Tra'vers is no cook."

Preston shakes his head as he speaks up. "Yeah, no kidding. It needs some salt and pepper for it to even be tolerable."

Ellette merely nods to the comment as she takes another sip from her own bowl. Her mouth is still full as she brings her voice back. "Needs more meat." As she swallows she brushes her hand past her mouth before continuing. "So, what brings you so far from the fire?"

Preston shrugs as he looks to the girl. "I never sit with them."

The *Flöff* girl merely rolls her eyes as she speaks up. "I sat by the fire with Elva, the story was quite well received."

Preston nods. "So why are you here?"

Ellette shrugs. "Stysen does not want me there..." She trails on, her face half buried to her bowl. "And you are here."

Preston just smirks to the comment as he turns back to eating his food.

Slowly, Ellette moves the bowl from her face as she sets it aside, her arms coming behind her as she stretches. "I apologize for your cub friend."

Preston chews a little to the stew in his mouth as he shakes his head. "No, you don't apologize for him crying, you apologize for what you said."

"So that is why you are so short?"

Preston shrugs, his eyes staying pinned to the girl. "Maybe, do you understand why?"

Ellette shifts a bit uneasy, her gaze turning around the camp as she nods. "Because he is a friend?"

"So, what do you apologize for?"

The bird-girl takes a deep breath. "I apologize for speaking, now can I ask a favor?"

A laugh comes from Preston as he rolls his eyes. "Not good enough."

"What?" Ellette shakes her head. "I have said it, what more do you need?"

"Mean it." Preston nods. "Say it again."

"I apologize."

"That's good... for now." He sighs. "So, what's this favor?"

Ellette nods. "I want to write."

"Okay?" Preston chuckles. "So write?"

Her tone falling a bit, Ellette speaks up. "I do not know how."

Preston pauses for a moment as he looks to the completely serious and almost proud face Ellette wears. "Don't you think you need a better teacher? You've seen me write."

Ellette nods as she speaks up. "I know. But you already help me read, I thought you would help further." She trails on rather quickly. "Of course, if you are unable to help I-..."

"Deal, but if you say anything else to Reynard-..."

Ellette shakes her head. "I will not!"

"Fine." Preston sighs. "Well we can start with your name, some basic stuff." Preston rubs to his chin as he nods. "What are you trying to do? You know, with writing?"

"Juna will be returning to her parents soon. We have agreed to write letters." Ellette scoffs a little to Preston. "And I know my name, all *yiftiñ* learn basic *Flóff* writing... but it is not the same as New-Tongue."

"I guess I can do that-..."

A smile flashes to the girl's face, but only for a moment as she brings her voice over Preston's. "You will not read our letters."

"What?" Preston shrugs. "How can I help you write them?"

"I still have the books, I can make a letter off their spelling, I merely need to know if my spelling looks well enough and of the word's meaning." Ellette nods. "It should be simple."

"Alright and when does she leave?" Preston takes a sip of his stew as he awaits a response.

"She is to depart in the next *wek*." Ellette's answer does not stop her words as she trails on a bit impatient. "When do we start?"

Preston gives a deep clearing of the throat, mainly to get the stew down faster as he nods. "We can start it tomorrow." The man pauses for a moment before he continues. "Reynard would enjoy helping too. You can also apologize to him."

"But I have done so to you?!"

Preston nods. "Yes, you have. But Rey is who you said it to. If you want me, then you will do it."

Ellette hesitates to answer, but as she turns her head back to the bowl she speaks up. "I suppose. But none else shall know, or I will challenge you to a spare. I would kill you, do you understand?"

The comment sparks a slight laugh to the man that he fails to hide. His snicker prompts Ellette to chime in again as she watches him. "Why you laugh?"

Preston shakes his head as he waves his hand. "No, I think this stew is just starting to boil my insides."

A light smile comes to Ellette's face as she nods. "Hmm..."

Preston stirs the stew once more as she sighs. "So, Elva will be gone most of the night?"

"Yes. She will be escorting *Alphé* Kassie until relieved."

The man gives a slight overdone stretch as he sighs. "Well, no sense in waiting for her." Preston takes the bowl and pours it to the dirt as he motions for Ellette to take his makeshift box seat as he stands. "I'm turning in for the night."

Ellette brings herself from the ground with the help of her wings as she holds the bowl steady in her grip. "Sleep? So early?"

Preston gives a little smile as he looks around the walled in camp. "I doubt I would be allowed to go for a walk."

Ellette blows the comment off as a joke as she takes Preston's seat. "Walking is a harsh punishment."

The man simply just smiles as he takes a deep breath. "Maybe. Good night Ellette."

"Wait."

At Ellette's words Preston stops, though the girl seems rather surprised her command worked, as a result she pauses before speaking up. "You do not leave as punishment, yes?"

Straightening up a bit Preston shakes his head. "No, just tired."

Ellette blinks to the comment. "You are not mad? And you do not wish to talk? Do not all *Únoff* wish to speak?"

"Maybe." Preston nods. "But I'm tired. We can start tomorrow, when I'm feeling more like myself."

The girl merely nods to the friendly comment as she turns back to the bowl in front of her. The sounds of the camp continue to ring through the night, but as Preston nears his tent he begins to ignore the chatter behind him. As the tent's flap comes within reach Preston eagerly steps inside. The orange glow pouring through the tent's walls give a rather warm feeling to the simple inside dwelling. However, as Preston moves to the edge of the bed he sparks a quick spell to his hand. Before the annoying creaking of the frame can even dissipate in the tent Preston's green ball of light takes hold.

For a moment Preston just watches the ball of light hanging in the center of the room, but as he soon finds his attention shifting. Preston leans to his right a little as he dips his hand into his pocket, the amulet is quickly taken in hand as he pulls it out. The amulet is dull and cold and even as Preston brings it to his lap and begins to move a thumb over it. Even still, the man continues to stare into the lackluster magic amulet before he simply places it beside him on the bed.

With the amulet now beside him Preston moves his hands to his boots. Although snug to his feet, the boots have not caused any pain and have instead been surprisingly comfortable. Still, the feeling of having his feet completely free brings a sense of relief to the man as he kicks them a little ways from the bed he now lays to.

Preston takes the amulet to hand as he begins to work his way under the hard blanket. With a few outbursts from the bed's frame and a little bit of effort Preston lazily finds himself under the cover as he now stares to the tent's ceiling. The simple pillow is a far cry from the comfort he had at the library last night, but the chatter outside is a bit more enjoyable than the silence from yesterday. The voices outside however are not loud enough to stop Preston from relaxing as the man slowly finds himself lowering his gaze at the ceiling. A sense of emptiness washing over him, today, like many days is closing quickly, hardly a footnote in a life, yet for all Preston's desires to do more, he stays down. His mind set adrift in the ocean of bliss the amulet now draws forth, his fingers stroking it out as he remains.

Chapter 6

Capital Matters

 The early morning sun has found its way over the *ÉverMoar's* tree line, its golden light only further enchanting the already quaint fountain and sitting area in front of the Three's Meeting Hall. The air is fresh, but warm with a hint of forest pine as it lofts ever so gently up the hill to the *Únoff* castle. The banners that drape down from the dome like exterior of the meeting hall add a bit of color to the simple stone made structure, however the light that surrounds it does give a rather heavily hue to the building.

 "General Elden."

 The words barely sway the *Únoff's* head as he listens to the soldier now coming up behind him.

 "Princess Sóltina nears the castle's doors."

 Elden gives a simple nod as he keeps his upright posture and armored hands folded behind his back. "Our surveying of the area has found no threats. Tell her it is safe to venture to the Meeting Hall."

 The guard gives a quick bow as he starts back towards the castle with a fair pace to his trot. As the sound of hooves begin to grow distinct Elden turns to face the stone pathway leading to the castle. The sun's glow has struck the normally grey stone in such a way that the castle itself seems to have a shine, although still dull the excellent lighting does prompt Elden to give a slight smile as he turns his head back to the meeting hall's door. The two guards posted outside immediately straighten their stance as Elden speaks up.

"It seems extra bright... Pethon, how does my armor look? Stone Hooves insisted I shined it, though I feel as though I may have overdone it."

The guard on the right of the door replies, never once loosening his stance out of respect and duty. "The *Sivý* shines like fresh clouds, and your *Ord'* mimics a revived *Helió* stone, General Elden."

Elden gives a slight smile to the comment as he looks his own regal armor over. "Fine words." As the comment ends Elden catches a bright glow exiting the castle's doors. The tall, angelic and elegant white dressed woman makes short work of the pathway to where Elden stands, despite the few guards that travel alongside her.

As she comes within earshot of Elden she slows her pace and speaks up. Her voice mimics her aura as its low, sweet tone takes the satyr's attention. "Was securing of the castle's grounds necessary?"

Elden gives a proper bow before he continues. "Princess, security cannot be overlooked. Especially when *Flóff* view it so highly." His eyes turn to the gold and gem encrusted crown atop Sóltina's head as he continues. "And I see you too take precautions in such meetings."

Sóltina gives a heartfelt smile to the comment as she nods. "Svle Nyota and his company exhausted quite a lot of time to recreate an element of such harmony, I would not see it go to waste." Her smile holds as she gives a little nod to Elden. "And I believe we can both agree that lasting arguments among the Three are frivolous, should they arise, the crown will see them extinguished."

"Yes Princess." Elden breaks his hands apart as he holds his right arm to the door. "They await your arrival."

The woman starts towards the door as the guards behind her break away and post up outside. The two guards at the door make quick work of opening it as the Princess and then Elden step inside.

Sóltina slows her pace as she allows Elden to join her side. "I trust the construction at the field did not discomfort any?"

Elden shakes his head as he speaks up. "Actually no, Commander Fea'cile greatly admired the craftsmanship shown thus far."

As Sóltina begins to pass by both the *Dẃoff* and *Flóff* guards that line the interior walls of the hall she begins to grow silent. However, as the end of the hallway comes into view the sound of trumpets signal her arrival.

Despite the loud announcement the crowd of spectators that gather for the Three's meetings only give smiles and wide-eyed stares of glee to the all-white and almost glowing winged woman. The room however is quickly taken by a voice as Sóltina bows to the two people already seated at the round table in the center of the room. "*Plestá déy*, Chancellor Clay and to you Commander Fea'cile."

The slightly rounder and fancy dressed *Dẃoff* near the center of the table nods as he adjusted the scrolls in front of him. "Good *déy*, Princess."

The light grey feathered and older faced avian man clad in the traditional dark and white stormy armor however stays silent as he watches the woman move to her seat across the table from him.

Elden has found his spot in front of the *Únoff* banner as he looks around the room. The colorful banners are all but hidden in the hall, as guards from all three leaders stand before their respective insignias.

Sóltina finds her seat as she removes the crown from her head and places it to the table. As she does the avian man directly across from her finally speaks up. The deep and somewhat raspy voice echoing into the walls. "It is good to have such clear skies for these meetings. I trust you are well adjusted to your role as both Célntal keeper and Princess?"

Sóltina nods to the comment. "Yes, I admit my sister's departure has left a burden on me, but until new keepers are found I fervidly accept my duties to both the *Únoff* kingdom and the Célntals."

Commander Fea'cile nods to the Princess' comment with a smile as he relaxes a little in his own seat. "I admire your zeal, and I assure you, I shall relay your words to Emperor Gust. However, our benevolent Emperor still wishes me to ask something of you."

The *Flóff* clears his throat as he settles his grey colored wings to his back, all the while as he pulls the first scroll to his sight. "Emperor Gust wishes to know without a doubt that you are actively looking for a new Keeper. He also wishes to see proof of this come the next *Hig-Roth* season." Fea'cile continues as he squints to the bottom of the scroll. "He insists that it is for your own benefit as the *Hig-Roth* season will require your full attention during the *déy*."

Sóltina gives a low nod as she brings her voice up slowly behind Fea'cile's words. "Commander, you may thank Emperor Gust for his concern. You may also inform him that I and my advisors have been actively searching for new Keepers. Our findings will accompany you on your venture back home, rest assured." She gives a slight smile as she brings her words to a halt for a moment. "Now, what matters of the Three do we have to discuss?"

"U-uh..." Chancellor Clay's unsure noise takes both Sóltina and Fea'cile's attention as they watch the plump pig-nosed man spread a scroll out in front of him. "The request to unify the banners with the requirements specified in our last meeting are soon to follow... u-unless there are any more changes that is."

Clay gives a short turn of the head to Fea'cile as the armored *Flóff* begins to speak up. "Yes, well Emperor Gust agrees with this new sign of unity under one banner. Although, he does propose that all capital cities within the Three be exempt from using the new banner." Fea'cile nods to his own words as he trails on. "It is a sign of pride you see Princess, it should be a choice."

Sóltina gives a simple smirk to the comment as she nods. "I merely proposed a unified banner to which Artésque can show to the other lands. If Emperor Gust agrees with the exception of keeping our own bloc I find no problem. Tell Emperor Gust he is free to fly anything in his hold, though distant lands should see us as one, not three."

"Understood." Fea'cile turns his attention to one of the *Flóff* guards behind him as he flags him over with a flick of his wing. As the winged guard starts towards Commander Fea'cile the grey colored *Flóff* stamps the paper. "Fly this to the Emperor."

The exchange is quick and neat as Fea'cile places the insignia stamp back to the blue ink pad next to his scroll and paper pile. "I am sure the Emperor will be pleased." Fea'cile nods to the pig-man on his left as he goes silent.

Chancellor Clay nods back as he moves the paper he read to his left and pulls another scroll open in front of him. "The *Dẃoff* inhabitants near the *Dýnar* boundaries say that the land had begun to grow dry as the beginning of the *Lor-Roth* season continues, and request rain schedules to be longer."

Commander Fea'cile nods to the comment as he speaks up. "The clouds are thin their... though with the season, I suppose a few more shapers can be spared from the capital."

Chancellor Clay blinks a little surprised by the comment, though he nonetheless nods as he holds his hand to Commander Fea'cile. "I yield the table to you Commander Hercinia-I-mean Commander Fea'cile, yes."

The fumbling forces a slight smirk to the *Flóff* though he says nothing of it as he pulls from his own stack of papers. "Ah, yes, the weather patrol of *VéturVill* have reported an increase in security for the town. The *Jartál* Caféll seems to have asked for this request, though she has assured our flyer that all is well."

For the first time in many meetings Elden begins to listen in, his ears perking up to the exchange at the table. However, he bites his tongue for the moment as Chancellor Clay speaks up. "O-oh? I have not received any news regarding why. I would not wish to act without proper *Dẃoff* papers, you understand."

Commander Fea'cile nods as he moves the paper aside. "Yes, well the *Jartál* expresses no problems with the *Flóff* patrols or denizens. But, as it is your hold, I yield this matter to you, Chancellor. Next order."

At the comment Elden shifts his hooves to the stone floor, which despite the large room takes Sóltina's attention. The woman raises her hand as she speaks up. "I understand this matter does not concern the *Únoff* provinces, but I do wish to inquire what prompted the *Jartál's* request. After all, my new project will be connecting to the town and I would not wish to put any venturing to or fro in danger."

Commander Fea'cile nods as he moves the paper back in front of him. "Hmm, this order was merely a spoken relay. No details are illustrated other than the request, Princess."

Sóltina gives a slow nod to the comment as she speaks up again. "The request does not say why more security is needed?"

Commander Fea'cile is silent for a moment before he nods. "These orders were received just before we set out, it is a *Dẃoff* matter, I merely took them to inform Chancellor Clay."

A faint wiggle of happiness comes from the *Dẃoff* as he attempts to sit up in his chair. "And a very earned thank you, I may say."

"Of course." Sóltina holds her hand to Fea'cile as she continues. "Proceed with your orders."

Commander Fea'cile turns back to his pile as he shakes his head. "The *Flóff* have no urgent decrees or request. Though a consensus among the holds is for there to be less noise."

A slight laugh rolls through the onlookers, which prompts Commander Fea'cile to nod as he glances to those in the stands. "Merely a comment... as such I yield to you, Princess."

"Oh." Sóltina gives a little smile as she motions to the table in front of her. The few scrolls that do sit before her have no urgency to them, however the Princess does speak up. "I have received no urgent request or news from the *Únoff* provinces." She holds her hand to Chancellor Clay as she continues. "Though an agreement among the Lords of Trade has been reached, fare on travel shall be lowered for the coming *mořos*."

"Ah." Chancellor Clay's eyes widen as he raises his hand. "This reminds me." The pig-man quickly darts his hands to the pile of scrolls in front of him as he speaks up. "I did receive a request from *Passvórtall* regarding the expeditions into the *Oválll*... here." Chancellor Clay pauses as he looks to the Princess. "May I continue?"

Sóltina gives a little smile to the comment as she adjusts the crown she placed on the table. "The *Únoff* have no major concerns. Please, continue."

"Yes, *Jartál* Glortón wishes to know if *Passvórtall* will be receiving compensation for access of the *Passvórtall* entrance into the *Oválll*. The *Jartál* wishes to benefit the city with the *Ord*."

Sóltina pauses for a moment before she replies. "I understand the *Oválll* was before my time, but I still represent the *Únoff*. I believe they should be able to retrieve these old spells and tombs from the *Márjx Gréftor* free of charge. After all, it was an *Únoff* expedition lead by Svle Nyota that halted a possible *Atémor* overtaking of the city."

Chancellor Clay nods to the comment as he moves the paper. "Yes, I suppose I agree. How is the Castle's Mage?"

Sóltina gives a little smile as she speaks up. "He grows old, as we all do."

- - -

(A few hours later)

The meeting hall has slowly begun to dispense as Elden stands facing the onlookers that now exit the building. Behind him Commander Fea'cile and his entourage of guards that also stand lookout as the commander and Princess Sóltina finish their goodbyes.

Despite the few hours of talking the sun above has moved mere inches from where Sóltina brought it earlier. The lengthy morning however has not seemed to deter the city outside of the castle from continuing its day.

Elden's attention to the surroundings however is dropped as a voice takes his attention. "...and clear skies to you as well, General Elden."

The voice quickly prompts the armored General to give a little bow as he turns to the *Flóff* Commander. "Thank you Commander Fea'cile."

The *Flóff* gives a little chuckle to the comment as he turns back to Sóltina with a nod. Within a moment however the entirety of the *Flóff* that encompassed the Princess and General are in the air with a gust. As they start their ascent into the clouds Elden comes near the Princess. "Do you wish to venture anywhere else, Princess?"

Sóltina is silent as she stares away from where Elden stands. Yet, before the satyr speaks up again, she chimes in. "The Capital's school does look to be coming along quite nicely and the land was cleared fast was it not?"

Elden barely gives the direction a glance as he nods. "Yes, it was, Nyota still insists its creation is a bit extravagant."

"Hmm..." Sóltina turns back to Elden as she taps to check how the crown atop her head sits. "I admire your patience, General." The woman holds her smile as she speaks up. "As I have been told you put family before most matters, a very admirable quality." The Princess cocks her head for a moment as she continues. "I do hope you understand I need your watchful eyes here as contents of the *Márjx Gréftor* are brought in. We cannot afford anything too dangerous to be misplaced."

Elden gives a simple nod as he speaks up. "Yes Princess."

Sóltina turns her gaze to the sky for a moment as she takes a deep breath. "Though if you wish to take a leave the moment after, I shall not postpone it."

Elden nods. "Thank you."

"I also do not require to watch over me in the castle, see to it that you send a letter to your sister." Sóltina gives a gentle smile. "We shall talk later."

Chapter 7

Smithy

"No, no, no! What are these weak strikes? Are you a *Cáfty* cub?!"

The hammer is quickly taken from Preston's hands as he is pushed back from the anvil. An annoyed sigh rings up from him as he now watches the *Flóff* beside the anvil. "You must hit it from the side, the arrow needs to be folded."

Preston shakes his head as he points to the orangey-red metal still on the spacing block attached to the anvil. "But I was doing that."

Lutin squints to the man with a look of disbelief as he shakes his head. "No, you were striking it too slow. It must be worked quickly with a mighty gust, not a simple breeze. You erode the arrow with small hits."

Preston crosses his arms as he takes another deep breath. "I was doing that, I just don't want to swing too hard and hit myself."

"Fear." Lutin wiggles the hammer to the man as he continues. "That is your problem... watch *Preiśty*."

The comment draws a simple roll of the eyes Preston merely watches the *Flóff*. With a few quick and hard slams of the hammer the metal that has rapidly begun to cool starts to take shape. Although it does not look like a traditional arrowhead the open shaft in the metal of the pointed cylinder looks to be about the right size for the shafts of wood it needs to attach to. "Ah, see, this is proper."

Lutin takes the arrow in his gloved hand as he looks over the cooling piece of metal. "Do you believe you can fasten this to the shaft?"

Preston shrugs as he speaks up. "I just take the other metal thing and hammer it through the wood and this metal thing."

The comment brings a sigh to the dark skinned *Flöff* as he places the hammer and arrowhead to the anvil. He takes his gloves off as he beckons Preston to come closer with his hand. "Preston... come."

The request is a bit awkward, but Preston comes a little closer to the avian man. As he Lutin quickly moves his hand behind the man's head, planting a firm but not violent slap to Preston.

Although not painful the sound does prompt Preston to back away. "What was that for?"

Lutin takes his gloves from the anvil as he responds a bit more annoyed. "You never listen. I said you must heat the metal again before you can hammer the strip between the two and it can only be done once you score it. Now get a warmed arrowhead from the forge and bring it to me with what I need."

Preston shakes his head to the comment as he takes the few steps necessary to reach the forge. "You know, maybe no one works with you because of your attitude Lutin."

"Is that so *Preišty*. I suppose you think you are always a fresh cloud?" Lutin shakes his head as he moves to the large wood container of arrow shafts.

Preston takes the tongs from the side of the forge as he plucks one of the recently placed arrowheads from the low fire. "Alright, here."

Lutin nods as he beckons the man back to the anvil. "Here is the shaft. Show me that you are able to fasten the arrow yourself."

With a sigh Preston takes the wood and moves to the unoccupied anvil next to Lutin. Despite Preston's lack of attention to him the dark avian still pulls out a small, sharp piece of metal as he holds it to him. "Your fastener."

Preston takes the metal piece and simply puts it in his pocket as he attempts to ignore the avian-smith. "Yea, yea, yea... I got it." Preston pulls the small ice pick like tool from his own apron as he begins to score the thin side of the hot metal like Lutin showed him earlier. After a few good scraps Preston moves the arrowhead over the wooden shafts tip. The man's position is a bit awkward and he uses his legs to help steady the wood as he takes the metal fastener from his apron. Lutin passes the hammer to the man as he cocks a smile to the strange position Preston still stands in.

"Line the fastener up to the middle, if you hit it on the wrong side you will shatter the-..."

"I know, it's like putting a nail in wood." Preston lines the fastener up as best he can in the heavy gloves as he takes the hammer in his other hand.

"Use the smaller tongs to hold it or you will smash your hand Pr-..."

"Actually, you know what." Preston pulls his glove from his hand as he again moves the fastener to the scored spot. The arrow is hot, but he quickly puts his plan into action as his green magic steadies the metal against the arrow. With a quick but gentle strike from the hammer the fastener breaks through the thin metal of the heated arrow and the wood before reaching the other side without breaking it.

Preston gives a cocky smirk to the *Flóff,* however Lutin quickly speaks up as he motions with his hand to turn the arrow. "Do not smile at me, boy. You must hammer in the other side."

A sigh escapes Preston as he turns the shaft over and begins to gently hammer in the other side of the fastener. The process only takes a few seconds before he takes the mostly completed arrow in hand. "Alright, now it just needs the steadying piece."

Lutin just gives a quick one ha laugh to the comment as he moves to the forge to retrieve the other hammer and undoubtedly to start the process of creating another arrow. "Good, you learned. Now clean."

Preston pulls the gloves from his hands as he carries the arrow over to the crate next to the work bench. Like the hundreds of other times he has carried the uncompleted arrows that Lutin makes he places it in the wooden crate next to the workbench. However, this time he speaks up as he puts his gloves back to the apron's pockets. "Hey, the box is full. Do you want me to tie the feathers?"

Lutin turns to the man with a smirk as he speaks up. "If it is full then, yes. It should be simple enough for you." A slight chuckle rolls from the *Flóff* as he continues. "Ensure you do it correctly, just because a *Dẃoff* archer cannot aim is no an excuse for poor craft."

Preston nods as he pulls the simple wooden chair to the workbench to sit down. As he takes the first arrow, some string and a feather to the workbench's surface he speaks up. "Not all of them are bad."

"Oh?" Lutin cocks a smile. "And where have you seen a good one?"

Preston beings to fasten the feather to the shaft as he replies. "A mercenary from *Passvórtall*."

Lutin turns an eye to the man as he pauses his work for the moment. "Mercenary? What business did you have with mercenaries?"

Preston gives a light laugh as he speaks up. "Long story."

Lutin squints to the comment but does not ask another question as he turns back to his work. The absence of the *Flóff's* gaze does however prompt Preston back to his own work, despite how tedious it is. However, just as Preston begins on the next arrow something takes his attention.

Stysen and his retinue have returned to camp, which is strange as it is far too early for them to be back.

Of course, Preston does little than watch them as their path starts towards the forge. His eyes lock with Stysen as the dark-red haired avian shoots a cocky smile back to the man he draws near. As the group passes by Preston, Stysen speaks up. "Carry on *Únoff*, this will not concern you." Stysen's eyes turn to Lutin as he continues. "*Thŕće* Lutin..."

The group takes Preston's attention further as Stysen's voice continues. "...your fine weaponry will be squandered by the *slothéñ Dẃoff* guard. As you are camp overseer at the moment, we have a request for you to fulfill, one that will remedy such a problem."

- - -

(Much later)

The air is rapid with a slight chill that most would find unpleasant, yet for Elva the rush of sound past her ears, the whipping of her hair and the air under her wings only brings the sense of freedom and joy to mind. Which, for the better part of her time away from the camp has been absent. Elva has always taken her duties seriously, especially when around Kassie, however, flying between *Pegpolis* and *VéturVill* for the better part of two days has left the avian woman a bit exhausted. Still, the slight laceration on her wing has prompted Elva to prove to herself her own strength, albeit at the cost of perhaps overdoing it. Yet, despite the slight ache in her wings she continues strong.

The glow of the camp sits in contrast to the nighttime hue of the rolling fields, its gray boulders and darkened fields of green now dull to the evening's light. Elva's attention to the nearing camp however is drawn away as her approach slows.

The wind rushing past her ears halts for a moment, which allows her pointed ears a moment to listen beyond her own flaps. Despite the noise, Elva merely calls out. "Night-watch, your approach is careless and your speed gives you away."

No reply comes to Elva. This fact however only makes the *Flóff* hold her position in the sky as she scans her surroundings. There are only a few clouds in the area around the camp, as it allows spotters to see any oncoming threats. However, there is a mass of the fluffy like vapor that does sit to Elva's right that cannot be seen through.

Elva is silent as she merely watches the mass of clouds' organic movements. The sound of wings has not yet dissipated as the cloud begins to spread a little.

"Night-watch, your attack is slow." Elva crosses her arms as she continues to hold her position in the air.

The clouds have quickly begun to spread forward, almost as a cage as it now begins to encase Elva within the center. The ground and sky above her within moments are filled by the cloud and the sign of the surrounding fields are now absent.

Elva continues to watch for a few moments with a slight smile as she speaks up. "Ellette, your attempt at holding me is amusing." As her words end she pulls her wings back as she gives a quick and powerful flap. The cloud around her quickly is spun away in all directions as it begins to simmer as if it were turned to steam.

To Elva's surprise however the manipulator, that now hoovers just before her is not the young avian Elva had thought.

The sandy haired and ocean blue winged *Flóff* gives a slight bow as he speaks up. "My apologizes *Pexřá* Elva. My deception is merely a *Jáff*." The avian man motions to the clouds with his right hand, his left tucked behind his back for a moment as he continues. "It is hard here. Near the *Nagisa* the waters create many clouds."

Elva nods to the comment as she speaks up. "Perhaps a quicker attack, Umiko. Night-watch is an important task."

The *Flóff* gives another bow as he speaks up. "Yes, of course."

Elva uncrosses her arms as she turns her attention back to the camp. However, as she begins to move away the avian man speaks up. "Oh, *Pexřá*. Do you not wish to retrieve your sword?"

The comment prompts Elva to tap to her sheath only to find the sword she carried now missing. "Y-yes..."

Umiko nods as he moves his hand from behind his back to reveal Elva's sword. "You seem wary *Pexřá*, it is unwise to fly when in pain."

Elva takes the sword as she sheaths it. "Hmm, carrying on, Night-watch."

Umiko brings his hands together as he gives another slight bow. "Yes, *Pexřá*."

At the comment Elva starts back towards the camp. Her pace picks back up and within moments she finds herself passing by the main gate. The gatekeeper on duty makes a step towards her as she lands but she waves the guard off.

As normal the large fire has been light near the center of the camp, however the group around it seems to be a bit more rowdy than normal. Especially seeing as how it only seems to be a handful of members around the fire, yet Elva can hear their voices from the front posture of the camp. Her wings tighten behind her back as her stance straightens.

The few that see her approach nearing the fire immediately straighten their own relaxed postures. Their actions, however, do little to stop Stysen's jabbering. "...I say we leave the town defense to dirty *Dẃoff*, all we are required to do is provide the rain, not-..."

"Stysen."

Elva's voice does stop Stysen's slight rambling, but instead of getting the submissive reaction Elva expected, Stysen speaks up. "Ah, our great *Pexřá* returns." Stysen gives a slight bow as he continues. "Where is *Alphé Kassie?*"

Elva's overbearing posture holds as she places her hands to her hips. "Our *Alphé* remains in *Pegpolis* until word from the *Dŵoff* leadership is sent."

Stysen gives a light laugh as he holds his arms to the other *Flóff* sitting around the fire. "You see comrades, our wings are bound to the master of filth and mud. Tell us *Pexřá*, why does the *Jartál* hold so little power? Do the *Dŵoff* not even trust their own stewards?"

"All matters of guardianship and *millo'tróff* must be answered by Chancellor Clay. It is unnatural for any *Dŵoff* settlement to garrison any more fighter than another." Elva's words are brought to a halt as Stysen waves his hand. A surprising action to say the least.

"In other words, comrades. The *Dŵoff* are weak, and they wish to keep it as such. It is no wonder they side with those who are hooved. They fear our strength, our pride-..."

Elva squints to the avian man's flexed wings as she notices the other *Flóff* around her nodding or at least fixing their eyes to Stysen. "What is your wile Stysen? You wish to stir the winds in our camp?" Elva brings her hand to the hilt of her sword as she continues. "Because I shall not allow tumoral with *Alphé* Kassie away."

Stysen cocks his head to the woman as he lowers his arms. The crackle of the fire, for the moment is the only sound as Stysen shakes his head. "We merely wish to know why we are bound to this *Jartál*. No other attacks have come, and we are not allowed to send our own into the forest. We are trapped in the town until another force of security is allotted." Stysen points to the members of the camp around him as he speaks up. "We are adept hunters and worthy *Skréets*. If this were a *Flóff* settlement the forest would have been searched and all threats dealt with."

"What do you purpose than, Stysen?"

A smirk comes to the dark-red haired man as he nods to the few members around him. "We wish to seek out any threats, not wait for another." He brings his right hand up as he points to something in the camp. "This discussion has been settled already *Pexřá*. Those who wished their wings caked in mud sit there. We, however, are *dámeni*, like our winged brothers of latter *Oválll*, we desire the *Fra'ha*." Stysen lowers his hand as Elva turns to look at the area lit by the green ball of magic. A few eyes are directed towards the fire were Elva stands, but even those who are not facing her can still be recognized.

Stysen's voice is brought back as he lowers his head. "*Pexřá*, you have returned, we bow to your direction. But would you not allow us to act as those before would have?"

Elva turns back to the avian man standing beside the fire as she looks him over. His hair and dark wings are amplified by the fire's glow, giving Stysen an ominous look to him. Not that the battle-hardened Elva is discouraged by it, however she does pick her tone carefully as she replies. "The Treaty of The Three is what we are all bound to in Artésque, says the *Flóff* wings of old *Oválll*, all tribes are required to help another when needed." Her words slowly begin to drop Stysen's smile to more of a face of anger or perhaps disappointment. Despite this, Elva continues. "However, we *Flóff* are filled with duty and dignity to a degree none of the land dwellers could understand. As your *Pexřá* I allow your request, so long as your hunt stays well into the *ÉverMoar* and out of *Dẃoff* domain."

Her words spark a quick muttering to the six other *Flóff* around the fire, but Elva keeps her eyes to Stysen as he takes a few steps towards her. His expression has dropped to a more skeptical face though he nods all the same. "Would you venture with us, *Pexřá*?"

Elva is silent for the moment before she speaks up. "Your determination leads me to believe your *Fra'ha* begins at first light. I have returned and must stay within the camp until *Alphé* Kassie's arrival."

Stysen nods as he quickly points to Elva. "Comrades, a cheer for our fair *Pexřá*!"

The loud cheering echoes a little to the camp as Elva takes note to the familiar faces at the fire. However, as Stysen starts back to his spot Elva slinks from the spotlight. Stysen voice is high with joy as his toothy smile rears itself at every breath, the plans for their hunt are quick to spew from his mouth as Elva continues away from the fire.

Her approach to the makeshift table of boxes is not met as the avian woman speaks up to the darker skinned man sitting to Preston's right. "*Thrće* Lutin, you have failed to keep camp in order."

Elva stops her walk near the side of the table as she looks to the other faces. Preston sits silent with his hands cupped on the table, Elwine shyly holds her face from Elva and Ellette sits with her arms crossed, slumped into the cloud she brought down.

Lutin does not raise his head from the cup in his hand as his deep voice comes up. "I work the forge, *Pexřá*." He takes a sip of his drink. "My time of rabble has passed."

Elva is quick to respond as she shakes her head. "Age is hardly an excuse for inaction and dishonor, *Thrće*."

Lutin shakes his head as he points to the fire. "That *yiftiñ* is too reckless, his stories have grown more boisterous every time he retells them. He yearns for new tales, something no words can quell."

"It was your duty to keep the camp in order, Lutin." Elva halts her voice for the moment as she changes her words. "Why is Stysen acting this way?"

Lutin puts his cup to the table of boxes as he turns an eye to Elva. "The *Jartál's* request for help has been thought of as weak. You yourself must understand this, after all you have prided yourself in arguing for *Flóffs* to control rain rights since this settlement was allowed a *Jartál*."

Elva shrugs to the comment. "The *Dẃoff Jartál* understands nothing of our sway over the weather. We manipulate it, not control it as *Únoff* magic. Though I fail to see the point of this current you yield, Lutin."

Lutin nods as he speaks up. "Yes, but you fight against it." A slight smile comes to Lutin's face as he shakes his head. "I warned you as I did *Alphé* Kassie when I was awarded *Thrće*. I desire only to work my forge, matters not regarding a sword or armor I wish no part in. You have a young *Flóff* aspiring for something far beyond the docile fields of *VéturVill*."

Elva cocks her head. "You denied Stysen's request before I arrived?"

"Yes."

Elva turns back to face the fire as she speaks up. "Then he has disregarded your command and deserves to be punished for-..."

"He challenged me."

The comment quickly takes Elva's attention as she turns back to the dark *Flóff*. Lutin raises his right wing as he points to the ragged feathers. "I accepted but refused to fight. He bested me and struck me down." Lutin motions to Preston as he puts his tattered wing to his back. "I feel as though Stysen wished to prove something to everyone else. Although, to my surprise this one rose up and disarmed him."

Elva is silent for a moment as she simply looks to the blond-haired man across from her. The timid nature of his posture does not speak for the amount of bravery needed to face Stysen, and the fact that Elva cannot picture such a fight let alone see Preston unscaded yields Lutin's story a rather hard tale to swallow. "When did this happen?"

Ellette speaks up as she cuts in before Lutin. "Earlier in the *déy*. I was on scout until Umiko informed me that he was appointed."

Elwine now chimes in as her slightly lower than normal voice starts up. "I was in camp when Preston ended the challenge. Stysen claimed to be *Thrée*, none challenged him so he began replacing posts."

Lutin nods as he speaks up. "Our camp is small Elva. merely fourteen, six of which Stysen holds sway over, the others do not care or wish not to face him. Those who are not keen on the lad have retreated to their bed for the night. We chose to stay out until you or *Alphé* Kassie returned." Lutin squints as he continues. "I assume Stysen stayed silent about his new title?"

Elva nods. "This is the first I have heard." She turns again to the fire at the base of the watchtower, however the group around it does not meet her gaze.

Lutin stands from his seat as he speaks up. "It is best now to wait for the winds of time, *Pexřá*. Rejecting your word now would only cause turmoil. You are head of camp until *Alphé* returns, simply allow Stysen and his group their hunt."

No answer comes from Elva as she continues to study the small band of *Flóff* around the fire. Her lack of words does not stall Lutin further as the *Flóff* speaks up. "I shall be retiring to bed. *Mŕad'sci*, return my mug to the forge before you retire."

The comment brings a slight smile to the man, but Preston holds his laugh back as he watches the brawny blacksmith starting towards his tent. All the while unable to take his eyes from the tattered feathers of his injured wing.

Ellette is the first to speak up as she looks to Elva. "*Pexřá?*"

The avian woman slowly turns back to the three onlookers still residing at the table as she speaks up. "I shall bring Stysen's new position to Kassie's attention. If none challenged it and Lutin failed to secure it, it is rightful Stysen's." Elva's demeanor begins to lighten a little, despite her posture and tone as she speaks up again. "Though I shall see that your posts are returned at first light."

"Thank you, *Pexřá* Elva." Elwine continues as she gives a slight smile. "Stysen wished for me to scout the *ÉverMoar*, although I have no problem with it I-I prefer the camp."

Elva gives a simple nod to the comment as she speaks up. "Elwine, could you please inform the other members of the camp that I have returned?"

"Of course." Elwine stands as she collects her things from the box table.

As she begins away from the group Elva turns her attention to the young girl still at the table. "Ellette, I believe you should seek your bed for the night."

The girl is a little surprised by the comment and actually brings her own voice up as she looks between her and Preston. "I do not get to hear tales of your venture?"

For the first time tonight Elva gives a slight smile as she shakes her head. "*Témont*, I am a little fatigued at the moment."

Ellette hesitates but she nods as she stands with a hushed sigh. "Very well, another night…" The cloud she sat to begins to slowly rise, for a moment Preston looks to make sure it will not hit one of the floating lanterns. Noticing that it will not, he begins to stand.

However, Elva shoots him an eye that holds him where he stands. As Ellette moves from ear shoot Elva speaks up. "You used magic in camp?"

Her tone brings a slight chuckle to Preston as the man shrugs. "Yeah, I'm not going to lie to you. I did." He points to the ball of dissipating magic above the table as he continues. "I did that too."

Elva looks the man over as she nods. "I ask because if you disarmed Stysen with magic, embarrassing him, it may draw a rebuttal."

Preston shrugs. "I don't care, he could've hurt Lutin."

The comment prompts Elva to look to the ground for a moment before she speaks up. "I had no knowledge of your fondness to Lutin?"

"Doesn't matter, he didn't want to fight."

Elva nods. "An action that drew a proper challenge for Stysen."

"Don't care." Preston just gives a little snicker to the comment as he trails on. "I get that you agree with it, but I want you to know that's crazy. He disrespected an order; doesn't that count against his claim?"

"Lutin's loss of rank is punishment enough by *Flóff* code." Elva crosses her arms as she speaks up. "Have you ventured into town?"

"No, I stayed to help Lutin afterwards." Preston shrugs. "Why does that matter?"

Elva continues to hold a dull tone as she cocks her head. "You have not had contact with Reynard, Bella or any involvement with Clover?"

Preston shrugs to the comment as he shakes his head. "N-not today, why?"

"What prompted you to act, Preston?" Elva's face is solid as she silently awaits an answer.

"What prompted me to act? I wasn't going to stand by and watch someone almost get killed."

A faint smirk comes to Elva's face at the man's more animated reaction to her comments. Though she hides it well enough as she speaks up. "I was not here. Nor do I have a way of knowing what exactly happened. Instead, I rely on accounts of what happened. Do not take offence to my questions."

Preston nods as he points to the tents along the backside of the camp. "If you don't like my answer go ask someone else."

Elva squints to the words. "You are defensive, why?"

Elva's comment is short, this along with her posture prompts Preston to sigh with a bit of annoyance as he sucks to his teeth for a moment. "I guess I'm just surprised that you can stand here and question me, heck I was surprised you wanted to blame Lutin before asking what happened."

"You are angry with me? Yes?" Elva continues to hold her stance as she watches Preston's reactions.

Preston squints to the comment as he speaks up. "What does that have to do with anything?"

Elva shakes her head as she brings her voice back. "My question, Preston. Answer it. Do not fly in circles."

"I'm not angry, I just don't understand how everyone in this camp can just let things like that happen. You all sit around and talk about honor and glory but yet pushing someone on the ground and trying to kill them over a disagreement is fine? How does that make sense?"

Preston's words do little to Elva as the avian woman again speaks up. "Does the *Flöff* way of life anger you?"

Preston shakes his head in confusion as he throws his hands up. "What? What does that have to do with this?"

Elva shoots a cocky smile to the man as if she has proved a point as she speaks up once more. "You felt required to act in another's quarrel, Preston. Lutin accepted his challenger, it did not extend to you."

The words bring a new reaction to Preston as he now stares to the avian woman before him with a bit of true anger. Her back tingles and his hands feel warm as he speaks up. "So, what, I should have just let something happen?"

Elva takes a step closer to the man as she uncrosses her arms. Her approach does not prompt Preston to back down, which forces Elva to halt a few steps before the man as she motions to his top. "You wear no armor?"

Preston gives a slight glance to himself as he shrugs. "Lutin didn't have enough time to fasten it, obviously."

Elva nods as she motions with her hand again. "Pull your top down."

The strange request brings a confused response from Preston as he continues to hold his irritation to the conversation at bay. "Why would I do that?"

Elva brings her hand to lip of man's shirt as she tugs it and stares at the man's bare chest. Preston is quick to break away from her as he speaks up. "What are you doing?"

"You do not wear your amulet. Why?"

Preston shrugs the comment off as he fixes his shirt. "Because it broke."

Elva nods. "When did it break?"

"A little bit ago." Preston laughs. "It's fine."

Elva's wings twitch a little as she glares to the man. "How long, Preston?"

Preston shrugs again as he speaks up. "When I got into town."

"What was it for, and do not lie to me, Preston." Elva's tone and overall demeanor for the question is rather daunting. Despite Preston's irritation and general desire not to tell her Preston relents, though it takes the man a few seconds to muster the words.

"It was to help control some stuff."

Elva's face stays hard as she cocks her head. "Control what?"

Preston gives a light laugh as he backs away a little. "My magic. Nyota gave it to me a while back."

Elva studies the man's body language for a moment before she speaks up. "Have the amulet fixed."

Preston squints to the comment as he shrugs. "Just because of today? You don't even know what happened?"

"I do not. But I do know it is strange for you to act so boldly." Elva nods. "And I know that amulet is more than to control magic, Preston."

A slight laugh comes from the man as he nods. "I can't be bold?" The man takes a step towards the avian warrioress before him as he holds a smile. "There's a lot of stuff you don't know about me Elva."

The comment does little to the avian woman as she speaks up. "I know how my campmates act, Preston."

Preston gives a light chuckle as he nods. "Well obviously you don't know everything." The man gives a little bow as he points to the line of tents. "Now can I go to sleep?"

Elva's eyes widen as she speaks up. "I have not dismissed you nor have I ended this conversation."

Preston gives another little smile as he playfully bows again. "Oh! You know what, you're right, you're right. My apologizes, *Pexřá*."

Elva is slow to bring her voice back but as she does she speaks up. "You are to refrain from using magic in the presence of others until you have your amulet fixed."

Preston gives an overzealous nod of the head as he answered. "I'll go see Bella tomorrow." He turns back as he trails on. "By the way, next time you see them, how about you try to show some compassion, or does that word not exist?"

The man's sarcastic tone brings its own bit of annoyance to Elva as she replies. "Do not speak of compassion, you avoided Reynard with this."

"Hey don't-..."

Elva speaks up, firm, and cold. "Fix the amulet, Preston."

No response comes to the woman, though Elva merely gives a sigh as she watches the man starting towards the row of tents. Her mind however does begin to shift gears as she starts to plan for Kassie's possible arrival tomorrow.

Chapter 8

Lasso

"...How do you stay in here?"

The words are soothing, although slightly faint as they loft through the early morning light that soaks through the tent's tan canvas walls. Despite the obvious question, Preston halts his voice as he continues to stare to the woman beside him. The bed is warm, and the sheets like silk against his body, despite the deeper portions of his mind telling him otherwise.

A faint smile cuts across the satyress' face, as Clover shifts her green eyes to Preston's. Her tan skinned face glows in the light, a fact that holds Preston's sight as he merely stares to her lovingly. "You are quiet, Preston."

The man shrugs to the question as his hand now begins to run through the brown hair of the woman beside him. "I don't remember you coming in."

A slight giggle rolls through Clover as she nods and brings her own hand to halt Preston's tussling. "You were asleep, you would not recall it."

Preston gives a little sigh as he nods. "Yeah, that's right... what did you ask before?"

The smile stays to Clover's face as she brings her sweet, low tone back to the room. "I had asked why you stay here."

"You mean like in bed? We can get up-..."

"No." Clover shifts her hand from Preston's as she adjusts herself to her side a little better. "Why do you stay in the camp?"

Preston shrugs. "I don't really have anywhere to go."

"Oh, but you do. You can accompany me." Clover's smile fades a little as she focuses her light lime green eyes to Preston's. "You could stay with me."

For a moment Preston remains silent, but he brings his voice up again as he squints to the woman. A slight bit of joy takes to his voice despite his confusion. "I thought you wanted me to stop distracting you?"

Clover shifts her gaze a little as she tilts her head away from Preston's gaze, but only enough to be noticeable not alter her sight. "Distractions are worthwhile. Besides, I need you to do something, Preston."

The man shifts his position in the bed to get a better look at the satyress beside him as he speaks up. "Yeah, what's that?"

With a rather quick motion Clover brings her hand to Preston's body. In particular, where the scar from the stab wound sits just under the fabric of his shirt. The woman's force is a bit harsh, but Preston ignores it as merely her attempting to push herself up from the bed as she does now.

Clover's hand that sits pressed up against Preston's body begins to feel warm as a light green glow comes to it. "You need to go outside."

Preston squints to the comment. "Oh yea? Why's that?" As his words end a shadow crosses the tent, a low, unmistakable growl taking Preston's attention.

Yet, the satyress beside him remains calm, even wrapping her arms around the man as she feels him tense up. "There is nothing to fear, protect your queen, Preston." The flap of the tent begins to open, the animalistic growling only growing louder as Preston stares, paralyzed to his fear.

Though, the world around him is quickly rushed away, a sharp intake of air coming to Preston as he jerks up in bed. Though he at first is calm, his heart begins to pound, his eyes rocking as if he were swaying to boat upon the ocean.

Preston fights back the sickening feeling of his senses as he tightened his hold to the simple bed, his head still swaying. Yet, as a moment passes, he regains his mind, and quickly moves a hand to cover his eyes to the sunlight now pouring forth from the tent's walls. In a swift motion, he feet plant to the simple rug floor as he now begins to go through his normal morning routines. With a few good stretches, a fairly loud yawn and several rubbings of his eyes later Preston finds himself already moving to the chest where he stores his clothes.

The chatter of voices and sounds of people walking about outside are absent, meaning two things. One, it is early, which judging from the light pouring in from the tent Preston knows is not true. Or two, Preston has woken up late, a first for him since he joined the camp. Realizing this, Preston's motions are quick, as he pulls out his pants and begins to put them on however he halts his motions as his eyes focus into the dull colored amulet that sits beside the bed.

For a moment, Preston questions how it fell to the ground, but not truly remembering where he placed it the night before stops his thought. Instead, Elva's comment from the previous night plays through the man's head.

Preston closes the chest before him as he turns his attention to the boots and amulet beside the bed. As he sits down to put the boots on he continues to stare at the dull amulet below. A rather convince voice in the back of his head reassuring him to the pointlessness of the amulet. Without much fight, and hardly a second though he bends down and collects the amulet.

His sights now turn to the front of the tent as he once more opens the chest to retrieve his toothbrush, paste, and to place the amulet back to the wooden box before closing it again.

With his early morning items now in hand and properly clothed Preston sets out into the camp. However, as he does this he takes notice to the emptiness around him, he also looks to the position of the sun. Noticing this, Preston starts his pace up a little more as he focuses in on the forge across the way.

As Preston can see the forge is not running, but Lutin is near it most likely clearing it for later use.

"Hey, sorry I'm late!"

The comment goes unheeded for a few moments as Preston nears the forge. Lutin turns his back to the dull furnace and instead faces the man now rushing to his side. "You are not late."

"Okay... where is everyone then?" Preston looks around the camp as he waits for an answer.

"Some have chosen to join the *Fra'ha* Stysen now leads. Others, have chosen to take their duties a bit more seriously." A sigh runs through Lutin as he continues. "Others are needed for *Alphé* Kassie so that she may fully understand Stysen's new title."

The comment takes Preston back for a moment as the man gives a simple laugh. "You're kidding me right? He attacked you for no reason, and you rejected the fight."

"No." Lutin shakes his head as he crosses his arms. His hurt wing still hangs a little lower than the other, but he has postured himself to make it less obvious. "I accepted the fight and choose not to commit. I have rightly lost."

Preston adjust the items in his hands as he shakes his head. "I'll let Kassie know what really happened I'll-..."

Lutin's normal tone, which Preston has always associated to that of a large dog barking an order now starts up as the *Flóff* stares the man down.

"You have nothing to say in this matter. You interfered, something any *Flóff* should be punished for."

Preston gives a little scoff to the comment as he brushes it off. "What? I committed a crime by saving you?"

"To some of the older flock you would have. You have overstepped your boundaries and dishonored a dual. For this you would be punished-..."

Preston now interrupts the avian man, which catches Lutin off guard for a moment as he listens. "This is crazy. I swear my life is on repeat every damn day... look a crime is theft or murder; me stepping in is not."

Lutin squints to the comment as he shakes his head. "Theft is something only the lowest of *Flóff* do, as it makes them worse than the *Dwoff*. Murder, however, is only a crime when unfair or shameful."

Preston just laughs to the comment as he sighs. "Good to know, I'll just challenge someone to a duel and kill them."

Lutin's face stays hard and unamused as he speaks. "It is no *jáff*. Petty quarrels are still as sullying as any true crime. *Flóff* law is not rigid as the *Únoff*, though it will still be enforced when broken. I tell you this so that you may not claim ignorance." Lutin waves the man off. "Now boy, I have no need for you."

"Oh?" Preston looks around the camp as he continues. "Someone else going to make the arrows and clean this place?"

"I await my punishment. Go about your *déy*, Preston."

The use of the man's name brings a sobering thought to Preston's head as he shifts a little in his stance. "Punishment? What do you mean?"

A slight smirk comes to Lutin's face as he speaks up. "Do not show worry for me. I have had my fair share of it. Now off with you."

Preston stays silent, though he crosses his arms as he glances away. "Well, I hope it's nothing too bad. Otherwise you'll take it out on me tomorrow."

Lutin gives no smirk to the comment, but Preston still feels as though the avian man understood the jokey comment. Still, Preston and Lutin's friendship has never been one of talking, and as a moment passes with nothing more to say Preston turns from the forge.

Though the thought of Lutin being punished do not sit well within Preston, he nevertheless pushes them to the back of his mind. Instead, thoughts of making it to the bathroom and finding something to eat now hold the center of Preston's focus. A bit self-centered, though perhaps a very *Flóff* thing to think about.

- - -

(Later)

A slight yawn rolls through Preston as the man continues to stare to the dirt path before him, it's length just barely visible through his squinting eyes. The morning's warmth pats to Preston's back, similar to a friend's warm hand gently placed against him. Still, the pleasant weather does little to bring the man from the daze currently hanging within his mind. The strange dream does not reverberate in his thoughts, but the meager breakfast and tedious walk into town does. The somewhat more cynical and reserved feelings within Preston making the amazing and vibrate colors of Artésque's fields nothing more than a background to be ignored, a footnote to page that he gives little more than a glance to.

The fresh, rich mountain air simply passes in and out of Preston's body without even the slightest bit of acknowledgement. Each step brings another cycle of air to the man's lunges, yet each step also brings another irritating reminder to how far Preston must walk to return to the camp later.

In truth, the walk has always bothered Preston, but normally he would have someone to complain to. Luckily, the lack of complaining has allowed for Preston to maintain his own speed; which has led to the town's outer streets to come a bit quicker.

Like always the early morning vendors have begun to roll into the main street, each carrying with them their unique expressions to the world around them. From the distance Preston still has between himself and the town he can only see a few large *yáppy* pulled carts. Their hairy faced and pig nosed *Dwoff* masters ushering the six-legged beast ever onward.

The main road through the town still is rather docile though; Preston quickly picks his speed up as he nears the end of the dirt and grass filled pathway to the more traveled and trampled down road.

The trek through the town begins almost automatic as Preston's mind focuses in on the prerecorded path. There really is no way to get lost on the town's outer reaches, seeing as how the main street is pretty much the only street. But, the market's almost round-about set up is a bit confusing with the few side streets and clutter of venders. The chatter of the townsfolk can be heard every so often, naturally though Preston tunes out the normal greetings most everyone gives each other; half because they are uninteresting and half because they are never directed towards him. Instead, a simple glance will be thrown Preston's way, mainly due to his strange appearance or perhaps to his height, which at least in this world, is rather alien.

As usually, it takes about ten or so minutes to finally reach the market square. Unlike normal, Preston has arrived as the various peddlers begin to set up shop; the buildings lining the outer edges of the market are all dark with windows and doors closed. Most serve as house and business for the residence so it makes sense that these would be the last to open; the man's pace does slow a bit as he turns to the familiar two-story house a little further down on the right.

Preston's head stays straight, in the hopes that no one attempts to sell him something like most days. To his surprise, no one attempts to make a sell.

The windows are all closed, so too is the door of Bella's shop, sighting this Preston knocks.

It takes a moment but eventually the door is opened, and the familiar satyress meets Preston's gaze. "Oh, Preston. You need not knock, I have the same spell on the door Clover does."

The man gives a little smirk to the comment as he waits for Bella to take a step back into the room before he starts in. As she does, he speaks up. "Well I didn't want to be rude."

Bella shrugs as she motions for Preston to close the door. "Company is always expected for me."

As Preston closes the door behind him he begins to take notice to Bella's comment. Despite the early morning visit her mane is neat and her long elegant sundress is on and ready for the day.

Before Preston could give a comment, the woman speaks up as she squints her eyes. "You are rather early..." She cocks her head a little as she brings a finger to her lips in thought. "You also must remember to remove that hair around your face, that camp has rules about it, yes?"

Preston nods as he rubs his hand to the stubble already growing on his face. "Yeah, I needed to do it." The man's voice lowers a little as his initial scan of the room does not reveal the young fox-boy anywhere. "How was Reynard yesterday?"

Bella gives a slight shake of the head as she speaks up in a slightly lower voice. "He was fine, but I do believe our visiting of Clover will be more spaced out."

"Why?" Preston shrugs, a bit uneasy to the comment as he continues. "What's wrong? Did something happen?"

Bella gives a little sigh as she speaks up. "The head *Héthtex* has given us a bit of bad news." A faint and faked laugh rolls through Bella as she explains. "He has grown worried at Clover's current state, it seems his previous attempts have continued to yield nothing. She sleeps, never once eating. Magic can only do so much dear, to survive on it is... well it is not the best diet."

Preston remains silent for a moment as his face stays cold. However, he slowly brings his voice up as he nods. "S-so what now?"

The satyress sighs again. "Reynard and I were instructed to contact Clover's family in the next *wek* if she does not wake. When Reynard is ready, we shall be venturing to the library to retrieve Clover's mailing list. In case we must write the letter." Bella's tone quickly picks up as she looks the man's face over. "Oh, do cheer up. Sorrow will make no matters better."

Preston just gives a forced smirk to the comment as he holds his thoughts at bay. "Yeah."

Bella initially jumps on Preston's tone as she strengthens her posture, which is more humorous than anything, seeing as how Preston still stands tall. "I have things around the shop that needs doing, I can work a smile out of you."

The comment, for a split second brings a true to life smile to Preston's face as he speaks up. "I take it that's why Reynard is doing so well."

The woman nods. "You would be surprised how much joy a completed task can bring." Bella halts her words as she squints to the man. "I had thought you helped at the camp in the mornings? Forging, yes?"

Bella runs her eyes over the man as she continues. "You do a very fine job of cleaning yourself."

"I didn't have to help today."

A very feminine giggle rolls from Bella as she rolls her hand. "Oh? No doubt a *Flóff* pride issue, yes?"

Preston shakes his head as he speaks up. "No... there was a little confrontation yesterday. I was let off today until we see what happens."

Bella's much needed smile fades as she eyes the man. "Confrontation? You do not mean with swords do you, dear?"

Preston gives a shrug. "A few."

The rather nonchalant answer sparks a quick reaction to Bella as her normally sweet, and soft Southern Belle tone is spiked up to an almost bossy chime. She throws a hand to Preston's right arm, but her hit is so soft Preston ignores it. Even still, she does point a finger into Preston's chest as she stares up to the man's eyes with a rather demanding gaze. "Refrain from these dangerous things, Preston, I do not wish to go through another foolish friend hurting themselves." Bella gives a rather hard sigh as she shakes her head. "Reckless." She shakes her head a little more, a hand returning to her face. "My word, I sound like Clover." Bella's quick snap comes to an end as she continues to shake her head, all the while lightly touching and pulling to her mane.

Preston remains still, his mind pinned to the fact that Bella called him a friend. Regardless, he speaks up, as he looks the woman's expression over. "It wasn't a fair fight. I just stepped in for a moment, no big deal."

The satyress slowly brings her spike in emotions to her control as she nods. "Do what you must dear, just keep in mind those who could be hurt by it."

The comment both stuns and mystifies the man as he stands in the room with his mouth almost slightly a gasped. Preston does find his words however as he watches Bella trotting towards the red curtain behind the counter. "I don't have anyone here who would care."

Bella halts by the curtain as she looks back to the man. "Believe what you wish dear." Her normal voice comes back as she calls to the room above her. "Reynard, we should be leaving soon."

A faint reply of "Okay" echoes from above, and as it does Bella starts back around the counter. "I assume you shall be joining us this?"

Preston just gives a simple nod as he speaks up. "Yeah, I will."

Bella continues to turn her eyes around Preston's figure as she replies. "Have you fixed your clothing from the other *déy*?"

"No."

"Hmm... figures the *Flóff* camp would not have anyone suited to fix such fine wear." Bella nods as she continues. "Do bring it by whenever you get a chance, that and anything else needing repair."

Preston just nods to the comment as he rubs a hand to his chest. "I can't think of anything that needs to be fixed, but thank you."

Chapter 9

Messenger

The light noise of people exchanging stories rings around Preston's head as he buries his mouth to the cup in his hand. The day was hot, not truly scolding but enough to make the already fresh water's taste even better, despite the fact it is near the same temperature as the world around him.

Of course, Preston's concentration to his food and drink are brought to an abrupt halt as a thud slams into the makeshift table he always sets up. The sudden jolt to the table forces Preston to spill a bit of his water as he quickly places it back to the table to see who caused the commotion. However, he takes notice to the fair-sized sword and sheath now resting on the table before he looks to its undeniable owner.

"Where is your sword, Preston? Do you feel empowered after the other *déy's* acts?"

The man does not shift his gaze as he scoots the bowl of half eaten dinner to where he placed his cup. "No." His words do little to halt the steel enclosed *Flóff* as she continues to loosen her array of weapons stashed to her waist.

Elva looks to the barrels acting as seats around the table as she continues her dull almost commanding stare. "Expecting company?"

Preston just shrugs to the comment as he pulls the lip of his shirt up a little to his neck. "Well... you're here."

Elva moves to take her seat across from the man as she speaks up. "Where is your sword?"

With a slight clearing of the throat Preston nods. "How was your day Elva? Mine was pretty good, got to see where Clover is withering away, all the magic in the world not able to do a damn thing about it." He nods. "Oh, Reynard came along, you ever try to confront someone even though you have no idea what's going on yourself? It's not fun. But yea, let's talk about my sword."

Elva shakes her head. "With Lutin in the *Alphé's* claws you did nothing but find time to visit your slumbering mare. A rather tiresome trip, happy I avoided it."

"Wow." Preston crosses his arms as he shrugs. "Either you had a bad day or you're looking for an argument."

Elva replies, unchanged to the comment. "Pity you take offence to my comment. Such proximity to Bella's false ebullience has eroded the thicker skin you have begun to *Flóff*."

The comment sparks a slight bit of confusion to Preston as he speaks up. "I've begun to *Flóff*?"

"I would have thought Clover's braggart of *Nervál* would have led her to explain these words to you." Elva relaxes a little, rolling her arm as she trails on. "Perhaps she was not as brilliant as I thought."

Preston just laughs to the comment as he glances away, though he keeps from his growing anger as he takes the bait. "So, what all three mean something? What's the other two?"

"Hmm..." Elva looks over Preston's confusion and slightly ruffled expression with a bit of amusement as she speaks up. "I see why Clover halted on such *ová'El* teachings; your expression of intrigue is rather amusing." The normally reserved and to the point warrioress begins to trail on through her smirk, something that wins starts to win Preston over as he listens. "The Three's labels all have various meanings. *Nervál* compared to New-Tongue is rather small, with most words falling under the meanings of others. *Flóff*, in how I have used it means to commence a change or a start of something new. Much as how our tribe guides the winds. Or as the *Únoff* believe, creates the weather."

Preston nods as he slowly breaks away from his crossed arms. "So, what, you're saying my skin is starting to thicken?"

"*Hmpf*, a mere scratch on your arm bleed far too long for-..."

"Yeah so metaphorically, my skin is starting to get thick." Preston shakes his head. "I've been trying to confront everyone; I'm doing what you should be doing for Reynard and Bella."

Elva's smirk is quickly dissolved from her face as she loses the upper hand of knowledge. The strange word used by Preston instead inspires Elva to speak over the man as she takes the conversation back. "I do not wish to hear of your *Nervál* Preston, so I wish not to have you explain what is a metaphor, though I hear your words. Answer this, does my ignoring of duty help stir Clover? No, does yielding a shoulder for Reynard or Bella solve anything? No, it is best to focus on something else, allow those who can help time to do so without your gaze."

A slight laugh comes from Preston as he nods. "Alright I won't explain a metaphor and you won't give me a straight answer... what do the other two mean?"

The avian woman's voice picks up a bit more as she starts. "The *Únoff*, in most ways, means to interpret, control, or feel. The *Dẁoff*, to listen or work what no other will."

Preston nods as he slowly brings his voice up. "The words seem like stereotypes. Just something to describe them?"

"And yet it does so well, all *Únoff* are arrogant, they interpret how they wish, they control what they will, and they feel far too much."

Preston shakes his head. "You can't just use a word or even a few words to describe a whole group of people."

"Some believe it." Elva smirks. "At least by the *Únoff* old-tongue. We had our own before the two land dwellers forced a common tongue to our ways. The ferocity at which the *Únoff* believed in the Three sharing a common tongue is what led to the first war in *Ováłll*. They believed their will to be soft and gentle, as if we were a feather atop the water just waiting to reach the shores." Elva's gaze shifts a little away from Preston in thought before coming back to the man. "...the *Flóff* were no feather, but a strong wing that flapped against the breeze."

Although not able to truly follow the story in its entirety, Preston does stay charmed to Elva's hinted excitement and lengthy voice. "What happened?"

Elva's wings poke a little from her back as she continues. "The first great *Fra'ha* began and ended with none at ultimate power. *Únoff* magic was strange and new, *Dẃoff* numbers large and savagely thrown at both. The sky was what kept most from the fray, but there was nothing to stop the grips of magic once spotted."

Preston shakes his head as he speaks up. "Go on."

Elva smirks to the comment as she nods. Her armor has a glow from the moon and the fire in the distance behind her adds to the brightness of her eyes. Her story continues as Preston sits quietly. "There have been three *Fra'ha*. The first led to the land of *Ováłll* nearly becoming a wasteland or *Wréch'Tré'von* as the *Dẃoff* called it. The rains were halted as my tribe attempted to cease the fighting through its control. The bright *Célntal* was kept from the land, which made the clouds we lived in cold and unbearable. The *Únoff* faired well in the beginning, thanks to their abilities over the land's powers. Our elite raiders ensured it was not for long. The fighting lasted a few *moŕos* until most were starving or dying of cold. The land itself began to crack due to the *Únoff*'s manipulations. Eventually, the Three came to an agreement that the ways of the land must be restored. The second great *Fra'ha* was soon to follow however."

Elva gives a look to Preston as she trials on. "I pass no ill to my tribe, although most accept it was our elders that caused the second fray. With no treaties the *Flóffs* of old choose not to heed the need of a common tongue shared by the *Únoff* and *Dẃoff*, thus all attempts to replenish the land's forests, rivers and lakes were slowed as the barriers of tongue presented themselves. It was at this time the small dominion of Grifón near the *Ováll* gained power. As the *Únoff* and *Dẃoff* gave *Ord'* to the Grifón in order for them to deliver messages in our tongue." Elva pasues. "Need I go on?"

Preston nods. "I've never heard it, go on."

"Very well. The wealth the Grifón acquired allowed them to become powerful, and thus a war ensued over territory within the clouds." Elva nods as she halts her words for a moment. "The Grifón were not as fit for battle as we, and the *Fra'ha* was short lived. However, the *Únoff* using the air of supporting their new ally beckoned us to stop, or else war would break out once more. None listened, and fooled by easy conquests within the sky, another great battle grew inevitable. The *Dẃoff*, with their numbers lowered were forced to join their land dwelling comrades, despite their previous skirmish in the first great *Fra'ha*. None of the Three wished to see the same damages as before, and thus the fighting was long, tiring, and yielding little but pointless death."

Elva lowers her head a bit as she continues. "The last, I have experience with. The time after the first and second great *Fra'ha* had made the *Flóff* understand the importance of accepting a common tongue. With the threat of the Grifón at the borders, a treaty was signed. Which allowed the common tongue to spread while at the same time allowing the Three to maintain their own lands. This of course did little to affect the *Flóff* spread in the sky as conquest to the Grifón was swift. It did however lead the *Únoff* to conquer most of the rebellious *Dẃoff*. This expansion forced more and more arguments over borders and the rules of each. Bolstered by *céla*, the quick defeats of the Grifón, and dishonored by the other Emperor's failings, war grew to be a focus for us." Elva is silent for a moment as she sits to the makeshift seat.

"At the time I was a young *Skréét*. Most *Flóff* did not join in on the fighting, however, I, like a few groups of *Flóff*, were pulled down into the war as the *Únoff* and *Dẃoff* skirmishes grew close to our settlements above." Again, Elva hesitates as she continues. "The fighting was effortless, a graying cloud would strike fear into the *Dẃoff* and the sight of *Lit'Ten* halted *Únoff* concentration, stopping their spells. However, battle is not without loss. It was the first encounter I have ever had with the new magic, what *they* call *Diśtro Márjx*. Spells so furiously devastating it could turn tornados. My first, and only *yiftiñ* was struck by such a spell..."

The words send a rush of heat through Preston's face as his mouth opens a bit in shock as he looks the avian warrioress' complete lack of emotion. Preston slowly brings his voice over Elva's as he adjusts himself to the box he sits on. The wood of the makeshift table is uncomfortable, but he leans over it as he speaks in a whispered tone. "You had a kid?"

Elva cocks her head a little to one side as she shifts her eyes a bit downward. "Once..." The avian woman shifts her eyes a bit to the books next to Preston as she nods. "Should would have been Ellette's age by now."

Preston sags a bit in his posture, his shoulders dropping from the feelings Elva's words have brought forth. "I'm sorry. I don't know what it's like... but, I know enough about loss to know how you must feel."

"It is a terrible pain." Elva sits up. "Though I did not tell you such a story for your sympathy, all have seen some type of hardship, you cannot let them define you. Regret, sorrow, even dwelling thoughts keep you from what you must do, that is why you-..."

"You can't just suppress that, right?" Preston shakes his head. "You don't just forget about it, do you?"

"No. It is unchangeable, like the turning of the tide my thoughts come back to it. But I do not allow my mind to become clouded." Elva takes a breath, her sure face installing some sincerity to her words. "I understand you react more desirably to the *Únoff's* display of emotion. I wish for you to heed me. *Alphé* Kassie has decided to not take action against you, but she has issued a warning that another conflict will end your stay in our camp.

Do with that information as you wish, simply understand you must control your emotions, all actions, no matter your state of mind, are your own."

Preston thinks over the comment for a moment as he slowly folds his hands together in his lap. "Yeah..." Preston continues to bob his head for a moment as he trails on. "I want you to know that I saw it in your face. You're not over what happened, I honestly think that you've just been told too many times to push it down. I don't know how much good talking does, but back home I paid a guy a lot of money to listen to me talk for a few hours." He shrugs. "I'll do it for free if you ever want to talk again."

Elva gives a simple smirk to the comment. "If your skills with a blade were as adept as your persistence at talking you may actually make a fine warrior, Preston."

"Probably not..." Preston shifts his eyes to the campfire well behind Elva as he continues. "Ellette won't be back from watch for a bit longer. You want to talk about anything?"

Elva's smile fades a little as she speaks up. "I have said what I desired to."

"Mhm." Preston nods. "You know, I could never see you as a motherly figure."

The comment forces Elva to squint her eyes as she replies. "Oh?"

"Yea." Preston laughs. "And I can't even imagine the kinda guy you went for. Did you let him beat you at something or did someone really win?"

"You are asking about the father of my *yiftiñ*? What strange breeze would lead you to this?"

Preston shrugs. "Well I never knew any of this before, and I got the feeling neither Clover, Bella, or Reynard know anything either. It just makes me want to know more."

"Hmm... my mate was nothing more than an average *Skréét*, most likely he has not progressed. Not because he lacks potential but because his stature would not allow it. I felt pity on him when he challenged me. I went easy, and allowed my guard to be broken." She nods. "I was confident in my youth, and allowed him to pick his challenge. The challenge was to scout at first light-..."

Preston interrupts the story as he laughs a little. "And of course you accepted because you were the best scout ever trained."

Elva quickly takes the reigns of the story again as she continues. "A comment not too far off from how I felt, yes. It was out in the forest however when I saw the speed he possessed. It was quite interesting, as if he were a blur against the sky. Most males prefer strength over speed, I saw that with my fortitude and his legerity our offspring would be quite the warrior."

Preston nods as he waits for Elva's voice to come to an end. "W-was he um..."

"Killed in the fighting?"

"Yeah."

Elva shakes her head. "No, he was reassigned a few *weks* after our mating."

The nonchalant answer sparks a slight laugh to the man as he speaks up. "Well did you ever see him again?"

Elva squints to the question as she shakes her head. "Why would I?"

"Well..." Preston laughs again. "Because you shared a kid?"

"As a male he did his part, it is uncommon for a male to raise a *yiftiñ*. Not that it is improper, as I was raised by my father, though it is strange." Elva glances away for a moment, checking something far off in the camp as she trails on. "The concept of a unit around a child is abnormal, though I still carry my father's dagger, I believe I was his favorite."

Preston chuckles. "And you have more family? Who else?"

Elva shrugs. "Several half-brothers and half-sisters, my mother died not soon after my birth."

Preston nods to the comment as he speaks up. "Your dad must be proud of what you've done."

Elva cocks a smile as she nods. "His name shall once more be embellished when word reaches him of our encounter with the *Koá-Koé*."

The smile to Elva's face brings Preston's own ego out as he points a finger to her. "Yeah, want to thank me for-..."

The man's comment is cut short as a young, almost tomboyish voice chimes in. "Ugh, this smells worse than *Dẃoffs* at the market..."

Both Elva and Preston turn their attention to the young *Flóff* now sitting to the makeshift table. The conversation Preston and Elva held seems to quickly fall as a distant memory, Elva's normal, and somewhat commanding voice chiming out to the bird-girl. "I see you lingered on your post Ellette. I trust it was to ensure a safe camp for the night, yes?"

The young girl's cheeks seem to blush a little, however the typical yellowish tint of the thick *Flóff* skin makes it a bit unnoticeable. She brushes her hair which looks to be slightly flattened rather than windblown. "Of course, *Pexřá* Elva. I only wish to ensure my duties are completed in full." At the end of her remark she quickly changes the subject. "Has any news come of Lutin?"

Elva holds her eyes a little skeptical to the girl before answering the question. "He nor Preston are to receive punishment." As the two *Flóffs* begin their own conversation Preston turns his gaze back to the fire behind Elva. His mind merely settling in for the night.

Chapter 10

Medicine Man

The metallic clang of the hammer striking the heated metal continues to ripple through Preston's hand, each time he brings it down to meet it. The heat that radiates off the ever-cooling metal simply mixes with the ever growing warmth of the morning.

Preston's swing to his right arm comes to an end as he speaks up a bit winded. "Damn, I'm dying..."

"Do so more quietly."

Lutin's quick comment draws a smirk from Preston as he blows his breath and glances to the sky. "Is it spring or summer?"

Before an answer comes a stiff hand greets his shoulder as Lutin nears his side. "The metal grows cold, Preston. I did not allow you to do this so that you could talk."

The comment quickly kick starts the motions again as Preston continues to shape the metal. His voice, however, begins to chime out after every hit, much to Lutin's dismay. "I... just... wanted... to know?"

Lutin stands with his back to the forge and his arms crossed as he looks over the man's ever fading proper posture, he told him to keep. "How do you grow weak this soon?"

Preston drops the hammer into his tool pouch as he pulls the dark metal tongs from their holder. "Because it's hot!" The now flattened piece of metal Preston has worked on for so long is finally scooped up and placed into the water filled barrel next to the anvil.

The steam shoots high above the forge as Lutin comes closer to the barrel. "Raise it."

Preston follows the order as he brings the graphite colored metal from the water.

Lutin studies the thick, flat piece for a few moments before he brings his own pair of tongs to free it from Preston's. "Hmmm.... not the worst. A strong flyer could use this in their wing armor."

A slight laugh comes from Preston as he places the still dripping pair of tongs back to their slit in his tool belt. "Why do we make these? Even Stysen didn't use wing-armor when they went searching the forest."

Lutin puffs his chest, similar and quite fitting to how a penguin would just before squawking as he speaks up. "My armor is among the finest. I do not just forge for the camp, *Mŕad'*."

Preston just nods to the comment as he moves to the forge to pump more air into the smelting coals. "Yea, yea, yea, the great Lutin's armor emporium."

The dark *Flóff* merely squints at the words as he moves to one of the open crates sitting on the ground beside the forge. "Continuing speaking nonsense, Preston. See if I do not act."

Preston just cocks a slight smile to the comment as he watches the *Flóff* turn. It has been two weeks since the Lutin and Stysen conflict, yet the older blacksmith has yet to really flex his wings as much as he would.

Furthermore, Preston has noticed a slight bit of hesitation in how Lutin use to act towards him. Although, it is not just Lutin who has begun treating the man differently. Even Elva now shows some degree of satisfaction, or at least respect for the man's work ethic; at least, this is what Preston has taken away from Elva's slightly more open conversations. Of course, their talks that now last a few minutes more may simply be a result of Clover's unchanged condition. Perhaps a simple comforting.

As the forge's flames begin to spark back to life Preston's thought shifts from camp life, he lives throughout most of the days. The man's hands shift from feeding the forge to adjusting his tool belt as his thoughts continue. It has been weeks since Clover was last awake, and Bella's sure tone about the *Héthtex̀ Márjx's* magic keeping her safe has begun to falter, even when reassuring Reynard.

It has already been agreed that come the end of this week they would send a letter alerting Clover's family if she did not wake. Yet, the idea of Clover slowly dying in the bed has plagued Preston's dreams since they agreed. With all that Clover has done, and all that Preston has continued to learn of her it seems almost insane that she could go out like this. Though, with every passing day, this terrible idea goes more likely, a sickening reminder to just how fleeting each day truly is.

Still, as the tool belt tightens around Preston's waist the man begins to shift. The sweat on his brow comes to the man's attention now as he takes a deep sigh. "We should put some clouds over the camp."

Lutin finishes whatever he was doing with the create as he turns back. "The heat is good, look even your complexion has begun to glow healthy."

Preston removes his left hand from the thick blacksmith gloves as he wipes the sweat from his forehead. "Yea great, sun cancer."

Lutin squints to the comment as he speaks up. "*Drágeff*, at least that I have known enjoy the heat of *Hig-Roth*. Although, it does not surprise me that a *Drágeff* who cuts their tail and fillets their scales would be a bit peculiar."

Preston just nods to the comment with a smile as he puts his hand back to his glove. "Yeah, the cutting of the tail was always the hardest."

Lutin shows a bit of disgust as he moves to the heavy crate of ores. "The *Flóff* finds the cutting of wings to be the worst punishment known. As it removes our identity as a *Flóff*. You do not feel the same?"

"Whoa?" Preston chuckles. "You know that might be the first real question you've ever asked me."

"Keep squawking at it and it shall be the last."

"Alright, alright." Preston chuckles again. "But no, I don't feel any different without my um... my tail."

"Mhm." Lutin clears his throat as he wipes his face. "Well it is a great dishonor to us, in fact, the last *Dé-flok* was of the traitor Hercinia."

Preston cocks his head as he tries to hold his thoughts back about the name. "So he's still alive?"

Lutin gives a hearty laugh as he begins to sift through the ore crate. "Death would be too easy."

"What because he raised a blade to the Emperor? I would think you would want a traitor like that killed."

"You are not a traitor for raising your blade." Lutin nods. "You are only a traitor if you fail."

The draws a laugh from Preston as he shakes his head, stepping away from his work as he fully focuses on the dark avian. "Wait, wait, you're saying that doesn't make you a traitor?"

Lutin cocks an eye to Preston as he speaks up. "Do you not know how Emperor Gust came to power?"

"No?" Preston nods. "How did he?"

"Heat the forge and I shall say."

Following the comment Preston moves to the bellows he convince Lutin to add once his wing was hurt, though a bit crude and heavy Preston starts to heat the forge as Lutin speaks up. "Tymon Gust served under Ha-Taski, the *Flóff* who seized control after The Emperor of Great Disgrace failed during the great *Fra'ha*. Gust became Commander of the *Flúry Fasá* under the Emperor Ha-Taski, and remained as such until the third great *whaá*. It was Tymon Gust, and his trusted advisor Hercinia who rose up against Ha-Taski, stopping him from unleashing the power of *Léux*."

Preston squints to the comment. "Gust killed the Emperor before him?"

"Defeat breeds doubt, all positions can be challenged with enough backing, it is our code, it keeps the strong and smart at front." Lutin cocks a smile. "I fought with Tymon Gust during that time, a great leader, hardly what he is now in the clouds."

"You agree with Hercinia then?"

Without hesitation Lutin shakes his head, almost angered by Preston's quick assumption. "Hercinia is a traitor, a *tát* who attempted to fall the one man who sought peace. Though what makes Hercinia worthy of *Dé-flok* is who he held company with, the beast."

Preston swallows, a laugh coming from Lutin as the dark avian nods. "Ah, see that is a name even you have heard." Lutin chuckles a bit more as he crosses his arms. "Morybe-Serbellá, the would-be *Gértdestá* of *Únoff* secrets. It is that alliance that makes death too good for Hercinia."

"How do you know he wasn't forced?"

The comment seems to force Lutin from his confidence as he shakes his head confused. "Forced? No, no, a will such as Hercinia's could not be, it was his will that brought him to challenge the Emperor."

Preston shakes his head, a faint smile coming to his face. "Clamor is more than capable."

"Serbellá is evil, the worst of corruption, but those who fall to it are of weak stock." Lutin stalls his words as he brings out a heavy looking piece of iron. "Look to the last *Únoff* princess who fell, it was greed that stirred the beast, Hercinina had pride."

"Pride can be enough."

Again Lutin shakes his head with a faint laugh. "Perhaps for the late Princess it was, but not for the *Flóff*."

At the comment Preston straightens up, his hands tighten to the bellows in his hold. "Princess Clarity is the Queen of Artésque, to which all beings shall obey."

The strangeness of the comment coupled with Preston less than normal tone draws Lutin's gaze as the dark avian speaks up. "Preston?"

The man stutters a little as he gives a little laugh, quickly stepping aside from the forge as he talks. "I-I uh think I remember a story or something about that."

Lutin gives a slight smirk to the comment as he places the ore to the forge. "No one ruler shall preside over this land. Not even the *devún* are so apt. Look to what has already passed with the Wúna's betrayal... It is only a matter of tides turning for Sóltina's downfall. No *devún* can reside on this plane for so long, I merely hope she leaves before such power is shifted."

Preston blows his breath as he shakes his hands out, his focus coming back to the forge. "So, then what? Let the *Flóff* empire grow?"

Lutin shakes his head as he shoots Preston an eye. "I do not believe us so bold. We would merely leave the *Dŵoff* and *Únoff* to fight for the land. We only require a grower of food."

"What about the treaty? I thought it states if one attacks the other shall fight the aggressor?"

Lutin gives a sigh of annoyance as he quickly speaks up. "I do not reside in *Pegpolis*, the treaty is a guideline to stop war between the Three. If one's *poliś* falters and none are rightfully the leader, they are nothing more than that of the *Cáftys, fróx, Drágeff,* any other *Fárwift, or Artnervál* beings. They would lose their worthiness to speak at the meeting of the Three and would instead answer to the *Jartál* of their area."

Preston nods to the comment as he looks to the iron in the forge. "They would no longer be recognized... I get it."

Lutin shakes his head as he turns a faint glare to the man. "Your winded breaths should be used to fan flames, Preston." He eyes the forge's fire as he nods. "Actually, step aside, this is after all a *Flóff* forge."

"No, just let me heat the fire it won't make a difference-..."

"Hush boy!" Lutin moves Preston aside, his wings sprawling out as he beings a few hard, and obviously painful flaps of his wings. While Preston cannot deny there is some degree of magic to a *Flóff's* wings, he does disagree with Lutin's assertions that it makes better metal. Though, not wishing a fight Preston says nothing.

With a faint roll of his eyes Preston moves away, other routine actions of his job calling to him. As he does this, he begins to look around the camp. Most of the other residents are out now with their various tasks of moving clouds, or patrolling the town like Stysen and his gang of bellicose friends or merely carrying new. The tower towards the middle of the camp is maned, but the *Flóff* stationed there is not someone Preston readily remembers the name too. Elva has already left and Kassie remains in her tent, meaning anyone on post right now is doing nothing but their job, just in case the *Alphé* comes out.

Still, not everything is normal as a voice rings out from where the gatekeeper would be; today as most days, it is Elwine, and she does not sound all too happy as Preston turns towards the gate. "Halt! You must wait until you have been identified!"

Lutin has remained engrossed to his work allowing Preston the moment to stay distracted at the commotion now taking place. However, it is short lived as Ellette lands behind the gate and nears Elwine. Her pace however does not stop as she continues towards the forge. "Of course, gatekeeper, but this shall only take a moment!"

Elwine seems to accept the comment, though she does not look pleased about as she watches the bird-girl continuing on.

As the young *Flóff* girl's quick pace nears Preston he speaks up. "Hey, everything-..."

"You need to leave for Bella's, an *Únoff* is there and he has brought guards, stating that Bella and Reynard have been illegally intercepting mail and will be charged."

Preston's eyes widen as he speaks up. "What? W-well what can I do?"

"Elva is not around, and Kassie would not concern herself with these matters. You may know something about it and can help *bafteñ*!"

Again, the man just shakes his head as he looks on to the young girl a bit bewildered. "I don't know any-..."

"*Mŕad'* do not argue!"

Lutin now turns from the forge as he comes to where Preston and Ellette stand. "What is the commotion? Ellette, you should be at your post, and Preston why have you not brought me more fire stone?"

"I'll get more coal in a-..."

Ellette chimes in, her cheeks puffy as she attempts not to yell to the older avian. "Preston needs to attend a matter in town."

Lutin squints to the girl before him as he crosses his arms. His large figure now stands powerfully as he speaks up in his slow, deep tone. "Oh? And why should I allow his task to end so early?"

Ellette does not back down as she speaks up. "An unjust arrest is taking place; Preston may be able to clear it."

Lutin stays quiet for a moment as he studies the girl's face. However, he does eventually turn to Preston as he speaks up, a sigh and faint roll of the eyes exiting him. "You have blown spirit into this *Flóff,* Preston. I know she has never listened before, but attitude should always be held at bay when discussing matters with an elder." With a groan Lutin continues. "I suppose I will allow you to venture into town, seeing as how Ellette has come to take over your task."

Ellette's expression turns as she quickly speaks up. "I wear armor, it is unfit for the forge."

Lutin just smiles as he nods to the tents on the other side of the camp. "You must retrieve lighter armor than. Even Preston wears it under his clothing... as disrespectful as it is to my work." The *Flóff* nods again as he speaks to Preston. "Remove your apron and venture into town, I am no longer allowed to sanction for new leave, but I see it as two *Flóff* managing the other's task... Preston must have hurt himself in the forge and Ellette has come to aid her comrade."

Ellette gives a light sigh as she swiftly gets behind Preston and pushes him along, just barely giving him enough time to properly hand off his apron to Lutin. "Go, I do not wish to be here all *déy*!"

Lutin just smiles as he looks over the girl. "Perhaps the work will make you more respectful, Ellette. Now, go change."

Preston starts towards the gate as he attempts to think through what he needs to do. Elwine responds with a simple nod as she begins to open one of the wood doors, as it opens Preston gives a little smile and starts outside. However, the long journey ahead of him weighs to his mind as he begins to jog.

Chapter 11

Resistance

    The light jog Preston has maintained since he left the camp has not yet made him winded, but it has made a few beads of sweat roll from his hairline to his face, a rather unfortunate mix of coal and sweat now stinging his eyes. The fields of nothing but grass that have been baked by the rising sun have left the pathway into town a bit more humid, that and the beating sun above has made the trail rather unpleasant. Still, the fact that the world around the man is actually unpleasant is rather surprising, seeing as how all who live in it claim so much control over it.

    Bella's house is perhaps six or seven minutes from where Preston currently is, however this can change depending on how crowded the town's main street is. The last leg of the trip is quick to pass Preston as he dips down and then back up from the hilly path one last time. The outer road of the town, albeit not paved at least allows Preston to move a little faster. But, as the man reaches the town's outer banks he slows his jog, mainly to ward off any unwanted stares.

    Despite the slower speed Preston still weaves his way through the crowds, wagons, and, animals traversing the main road. After a few minutes of this Preston reaches the marketplace. Which, to his surprise is fairly empty of vendors, at least on one side. However, it is not because of a lack of people in the market, instead it is due to the two rather large, and rather regal looking carriages. The unmistakable banner of the Únoactroff

Capital proudly sits to the flags, although this is not what made Preston place the carriages so quickly. Instead, it was the combination of the large, all white unicorns pulling them and the sight of the *Únoff* guards that have only ever been seen in the Capital.

Seeing an armored *Únoff* is actually surprising, not because they look fearsome but rather because of the light leather and iron like armor they wield. Being around *Flóffs* and their insistence on full-metal armor all day makes the *Únoff* equipment seem like nothing. Two out of three guards also carry spears rather than swords, something the camp has none of.

Preston's stare and unwavering path towards the carriages do not go unnoticed forever though as a voice calls out.

"Halt, official *Únoff* matter, no *gók-tós*."

The voice takes Preston's attention as he turns to the three *Únoff* near Bella's shop. One of the guards, now that Preston has a better view of them, has a bit more visible metal to his armor, but not much and only around his chest. He also wields a *Gloftór* to his right hand, that glows with a faint bit of magic at the ready. The sight of the magic brings Preston to a stop as he speaks up.

"I may have knowledge to clear the names of Bella and Reynard."

The *Gloftór* wielding *Únoff* lightens his posture as he shakes his head. "Captain Elden has not finished his interrogation. You must appear at the Capital's court if summoned."

Preston squints to the comment a little annoyed as he shakes his head. "But I know what happened to Clover Vine, his sister. I was with her when she brought the *Koá-Koé* down."

The *Únoff* in the center of the group cocks his head as he speaks up. "State your name?"

"Preston."

The guard speaks up. "Last name?"

Preston nods. "Armor?"

The three *Únoffs* give each other a quick glance as they begin to act a little more watchful. The two lightly armored guards now tighten their hands to their spears, not that Preston takes much notice to it as he listens.

"You are to wait here, Preston."

As the *Únoff* in the center turns around he opens the door to the shop and walks in. The other two *Únoffs* quickly close in between each other, which also blocks Preston's view of the inside of the shop.

A few passersby glance towards the commotion at the one side of the market square, but none seem to stop and stare. Most, in fact, seem to ignore the scene entirely. Preston's attention however is quickly taken back to the door as the sound of voices begin to ring out. The door opens, however, the figure that leads outside is not the guard that went in before. Instead, the more ostentatious shine of silver and gold trim flash to Preston's eyes, the bearer of this fine armor is none other than Clover's brother, who Preston quickly attempts to talk to.

Yet, before Preston can bring his voice up a feminine wine continues from behind him. "...This is absurd! I cannot be dragged out of my shop! It will ruin my name! Ruin it!"

Bella's whole demeanor has changed since Preston last saw her. No one actually drags her from the shop, nor does anyone push her, seeing as how Reynard follows behind Elden with little more than walk. Though, her persistent complaining continues even after the guard that retrieved Elden exits the building.

Elden holds his gaze to Preston as he looks the man over. The guard finally bringing Bella's voice down as he speaks up in a rather demanding tone, most likely an effect of hearing Bella's complaining. "Quiet, if the charges are false you have nothing to worry about."

As the guard's voice comes down Elden's starts up. "You were with my sister?"

Preston nods. "Yeah." Preston nods. "Look you know who I am let's just-..."

Elden raises his hand, halting Preston's voice as he takes a deep breath. He moves his hands to his hips, the hilt of his sword now just fingertips away, something Preston quickly notices. "Then you willingly place yourself and all others around you in danger. Seize him!"

The guard closes to Preston rapidly and advances, spear tip pointed at Preston.

"Whoa, whoa, whoa!" Preston backs away just a little as he speaks up. "What for?"

Elden is quick to respond as he takes a step forward. "The amulet Nyota fashioned for you is absent from your neck. *Atémor* influence has corrupted your mind, I hold you accountable for my sister's agony." Before Preston can rebuttal Elden turns to Bella and Reynard. "And Bella Gems, for not responding to a letter from the Capital I hear by sanction you to appear before the *Jartál* for due punishment."

"Elden she-..."

"Quiet, Reynard... I am sending you home to mother, do not fight me on this." Elden sighs again as he looks away.

Bella stands in a silent shock, Reynard and Preston however speak up. Preston is quickly silenced however as the guard before him brings him to the ground in a flash of magic. Reynard though goes unopposed as he moves to Elden's sight. "This is wrong. You cannot punish Bella or Preston for Clover's choice."

The comment does not seem to sit well with the regal dressed satyr as he points to where Preston is now being bound to the ground by magic. "You do not know this *fárwift*, it was poisoned by the powers of corruption.

Despite my wishes Clover and Nyota sought it to be stayed from my blade. It no longer wears the amulet created for its own safety. It is now corrupted and will be dealt with properly."

"But-..."

Elden squints to Reynard's continued banter as he holds his hand to the fox-boy. "Bella Gems is to be handled by the town's *Jartál*, a very fair decree for withholding information about my sister and for ignoring a letter of urgency from the Capital."

Bella tightens and forces a small smile as she just stands silently. Preston has stopped his struggling as he now just stares to Reynard and Elden's exchange. The magic he is bound in is strong, but at the same time a strange calming effect has washed over the man's body. Leaving his mind and muscles relaxed, despite the fact he knows he is being arrested or perhaps worse. The two guards have now come to Preston's side, but they await orders it seems.

"...Reynard, you should find yourself lucky. Mother and father will be happy to see you. Now come, we have a long journey."

Elden nods to the guards who now bring Preston up, not with their hands but with the magic that still binds his arms and legs.

Reynard however does not give up as he speaks up once more. "It was Clover's fault; we only wish to see her recover. I shall not be leaving."

The boyish rant seems to break Elden's patience as the satyr holds his hand to the carriage. "Do not contest me again, you are to come with me!"

"No!" Reynard holds a paw towards Elden as he continues. "You do not even wish to see your sister, that is your choice. I however am not leaving, will you arrest me, Elden? Under what charge?"

Elden's expression turns to anger as he straightens his posture. Noticing this Bella tugs to Reynard's shoulder in an attempt to silence him, but the fox-boy shrugs it off as Elden speaks up. "My sister lies asleep for nearly a *moŕo*, if what you are saying is true then she is dead. I do not wish to court death. Now get in the carriage, Reynard!"

"What of Preston?! You would see him unfairly punished?"

Reynard's voice may not be strong, but his words pack a punch as Elden again allows his emotions to get the better of him. The guards around Preston watch a little surprised to the captain of the guard's raised tone now only growing louder. "It is a beast! I have seen it with my own eyes. I hold it responsible for Clover's wellbeing." Elden turns his gaze to the man still bound by magic as he shakes his head. "You no longer have Nyota's protection, creature."

"You claim him to be sick with *Atémor desatá*?" Reynard continues. "Prove it!"

The guards still restraining Preston begin to look the man over out of the corner of their eyes, and Preston can feel the slight loosening of the magic around his body. He can still not speak, but the feeling of the magic loosening brings an expression of encouragement to the man's face as he stares to the orange and red furred fox-boy now defending him.

Elden stands in shock as he simply gawks to Reynard. His silence only prompts the fox-boy to continue as he takes a step forward. "Preston has been within the *Flöff* camp since Clover fell ill. Not once has the *Flöffs* reported strange behavior, ask!"

The more prestigious looking guard comes in front of Preston as he speaks up. "General Elden, we can check if the creature has indeed stayed within the camp... if there have been no instances of violence than..."

"That will not be needed." The guards still restraining Preston seem a bit confused, but they still hold the man to their magic as Elden continues. "Reynard... my brother. You claim that this creature here is not to blame?"

Reynard nods. "Yes."

"You wish proof?"

Reynard again nods. "Yes!"

"Fine." Elden straightens his head. "Clover has slept for a *moŕo*, all indication of an *Atémor* sickness starts with slumber, it is the Aeróbeth *desatá*. You would defend this creature, and yet you do not even know it is he to blame."

Reynard blinks to the comment, his eyes shifting to Preston with nothing else to say.

Elden does not relent as he turns to his guards. "If my sister does not show any signs of *Atémor* scarring or magic I shall release Preston." As his comment ends he pulls out two silver colored bracelets that he walks over to Preston with. "If she does, we kill this beast, my justice."

Elden places the bracelets to Preston's hands, which quickly tighten around the man's wrist. The magic that restrained him however is dropped, although, the feeling of being held down still lingers.

Elden turns back to Reynard and Bella as he speaks up. "Reynard, you shall ride with us, and you shall watch what your words bring."

The comment is cruel, even for Elden as he starts towards the carriage with nary a hint of comfort for Reynard.

Bella gives an uncertain glance to the orange furred fox-boy next to her as she slowly brings her voice up. "C-Clover would want me to accompany Reynard. I do not wish to leave him now."

The sudden disobedience in Bella leaves Elden a little taken back. Yet, he nods as he speaks up. "You shall ride with my sergeant."

As Elden's command ends the two guards with spears move to take their spots at the driving seats of the carriages. Elden's sergeant escorts Bella to the carriage as Reynard and Preston are both ushered into theirs. All the while, under the watchful eye of the decorative armor clad *Únoff*.

It takes a moment for Preston and Reynard to settle, the fox-boy has chosen the seat beside Preston, much to Elden's obvious disapproval. As Elden settles into the carriage it begins to move. The cabin's coloring and upholstery is rather elegant with silver, blue, and gold colored trims and fabrics. Although, Preston nor Reynard truly pay much attention to it as the carriages begin the short but rocky journey down the main road.

- - -

A Short Ride Later.

The presence of the unicorn pulled carriages has not gone unnoticed in town; though unlike Preston would have thought, no one truly gawks to the out of place regal transport. But, everyone does move from its path, so much so that Preston has noticed even the side roads becoming crowded. However, not everyone of the town's inhabitants have abandoned the streets. In fact, every *Únoff* the carriage passes seems to bring a sense of pride, seeing as how almost every *Únoff* that is passed stops in their trail just to give a slight smile to the carriage.

Preston of course only guesses if the onlookers have such fleeting gazes, as the only window open is the one to Reynard's left, and it hardly yield much to see from where Preston sits. There is a closed window to Preston's right, but the cold gaze Elden has set to the man has stopped all thoughts about opening.

The outskirts of town do draw near though, as Preston continues to look out to the fields that now take the landscape outside of the window. Within a few moments Preston can even see the path he takes to get to the *Flóff* camp, not that the man really concerns himself with it at the moment.

It takes a few minutes to reach the outer banks of the town, and as they do the drive of the carriage speaks up from outside. "We near the *Héthtex*'s building."

Elden moves his head to the window nearest him as he calls back. "Good." He settles himself back to his seat as he looks between Preston and Reynard. "How does she look?"

The comment is carried on a low tone, a complete one-eighty from Elden's overbearing and almost heartless speech just a few moments ago. Despite this, Reynard answers, even giving a look of sympathy as he does. "She looks to be sleeping." Reynard's own low and almost solemn tone trails on he continues. "The magic they used helps maintain her appearance."

Elden does not respond to the comment, merely glancing away for a moment before turning back to Preston with a cold stare. The carriage comes to a halt a few minutes.

The carriage door is brought open as the spear wielding guard posts up outside. "Captain Elden, do you wish for us to accompany you?"

Reynard moves down from the carriage's cabin as Elden speaks up. "No, tell the other driver to wait outside as well. It is a place of healing; we do not wish to crowd the hallways."

The *Unoff* steps aside. "Yes, sir."

Elden takes a breath. "Bring me an amulet of finding as well." At the words the guard moves back towards his carriage, allowing Elden a moment to turn back to Preston. "Outside."

Preston does not hesitate to the comment as he begins to move towards the door, which proves to be a bit difficult with his hands still bound to the magical braces behind his back.

As Preston makes it outside Elden follows behind. He turns to the other carriage as Bella just now exits with the other guard behind her. "Sergeant, you shall accompany us inside, though you wait at the door." Elden turns to the other guard now coming to him, a box in his hand.

Sighting this Elden takes hold of the box, opening it as he pulls forth an amulet similar to the one Nyota gave Preston before. Though unlike the amulet Preston owns, it glows, a bright green as Elden holds a stern face to Reynard. "Look here, the amulet glows."

The guards around them seem to pick their heads up, their eyes falling to Preston as Elden too looks to the blond man. "You carry the *desatá*, Preston. You cannot deny it."

Even before the words Preston's shoulders have slumped, his eyes pinned to the amulet as he now rethinks Clover's reasons for falling ill. The thought of him not only being the cause but also not realizing it sooner only furthers the pit in his stomach. Yet the magic of his bindings, much like his own amulet keep his mind from fully realizing this.

Bella stands shocked, clearly not knowing any of this beforehand, though her eyes do not linger to Preston for long as Reynard steps towards Elden's display. He moves a paw to the amulet as he speaks up. "That does not mean Clover is."

While warming to see Reynard come to his defense once more, Preston speaks up, forcing his words past the bindings as he beckons the fox-boy. "Reynard, you should go home."

"No." Elden lowers the amulet as he shakes his head. "He needs to see this."

The armored *Únoff* behind Bella nods as he starts towards the dull red door of the hospital. Reynard and Bella draw closer together as they follow after the sergeant. Elden and Preston take the lead.

The sergeant immediately moves to open the dull, red door as the group moves inside.

Overall, the building is bright with a low, almost sweet melody of glowing balls of light cream or orange magic throughout its halls. The initial feeling the building gives from outside is rather unsettling; at least from Preston's point of view, as the idea of a hospital, doctor, or healer working out of an all wood building just seems strange. Back home, the hospitals were always state of the art, and the buildings themselves seemed to mimic how prestigious it was to be a doctor. Of course, no one is excited to visit a hospital, but at least the outside and inside of the building would lead anyone to feel they were in good hands. Here, however, the medical system seems almost penurious. Still, as different as the world is, some things that do stay the same always catch Preston by surprise. And, despite the fact that this is not the first time the man has ever visited the hospital, the sight of the reception desk to his left still seems strange.

The *Únoff* behind the dark wood counter stands from her seat as she speaks up. "Hello? Do the guards require care in the *Jartál's* hold?" The woman wears a long red and white robe that covers the majority of her horse legs; her hair is pinned up to a ponytail and her tail is tucked away somewhere beneath her robes.

Elden shakes his head as he speaks up. "I am Elden Vines, Captain of the Princess' guard and General to the *Únoff millo'tróff*. I have been told my sister is here."

The woman for a moment just stares to Elden and the rest of the group as she speaks up. "Who are you here to see?"

Bella now speaks up as she takes notice to the woman's obvious confusion. "We are here for Clover Vines."

The moment Bella's voice comes down Elden speaks up again, this time a bit more commanding as well as a bit more rushed. "I also wish to see the head *Héthtex*."

"Oh, well I apologize, but if you are not injured or sick I must ask you to leave. The head *Héthtex* Radisia is about to perform a cleansing spell, he may not be disturbed."

Elden cocks his head up a little as he places his hands to his sides. "If he has not started his spell he shall come forth. I request his presence."

The comment brings a swift change to the woman's face, not real anger or confusion but more of a look of annoyance mixed with a bit of arrogance. "You may not disturb a *Héthtex* spell, even if you are Elden of the Capital guard, without a warrant from the Capital you must wait."

Elden stands silent for a moment before he nods to his guard. "Sergeant, please stand post here and ensure no one disturbs the spell."

"Yes sir."

Elden starts down the long hallway in front of the group as his guard post up on the wall he passes. The woman quickly speaks up as she follows after him. "What are you doing? We have patients here."

"Correct, so please point me to my sister's room and kindly instruct the head *Héthtex* to meet us there."

"You cannot-..."

The *Únoff* sergeant to her right speaks up as he nods. "Please do not disturb the building. Failure to cooperate will result in arrest."

Much to the woman's reaction, Bella, Reynard, and Preston stand in amazement to Elden and his guard's choreographed plan. However, the idea of Elden, the supposed Captain of the Capital guard using such shady tactics to get what he wants is a bit unnerving, especially for Preston as Elden beckons him to follow.

The *Únoff* woman at the cusp of the hallways finally bends to Elden's will as she speaks up. "Eighth door to right, near the end of the hallway before the stairs." She holds a glare to Elden as she speaks up. "You *Distro Márjx* followers have always been arrogant."

Elden gives a little smile as he nods and allows the woman to go before him. "I studied in *Álter Márjx, jé Éordiarx álter méi.*"

The woman turns her head from Elden as she starts down the hall. The lack of a reaction from the woman has made Preston question what was said, but the time to think about it is quick and brief as he is moved along with Reynard and Bella.

The hall is lined with a dull red carpet, the glowing balls of light that hover to the ceiling dilute the color a bit, but it is still visible. The dark wood of the building is simple, with no interesting carving or anything to it, but there are pieces that look to be scrapped or flaked off. The rooms that Preston pass are all closed, and a brass label sits to each one with the corresponding number to the room. Ultimately, the hall is quiet aside from the footsteps of the group.

The woman leading the group down the hall comes to a stop at one of the last doors as she speaks up, this time in a slightly quieter voice. "You are welcome to go in. I shall retrieve *Héthtex* Radisia."

Elden gives a nod as he stares at the closed door on his right. The woman continues down the hall as she starts towards the staircase hidden just a little out of sight. Bella and Reynard move to the door, however, they do not go inside. Instead, they wait and turn back to where Preston and Elden still stand.

It has been a few weeks since Preston last came to the hospital, but even when he did, it was not to actually visit Clover, rather it was to comfort Reynard. Though unlike the satyr beside him, Preston moves forward despite not knowing what awaits him. Elden takes a sluggish hoof forward, allowing all others before him as his shifty eyes slowly lead him in.

The room is simple. The dark wood of the room brings the focus to the single bed in the center of the room. A window with the curtains half drawn sits to the other side, the light of the outside adequately lights the room for Preston as he looks it over as long as he can. Near the bed sits a simple nightstand, a few wilting wildflowers, most likely collected from outside sit in a murky vase next to the bed. The flowers have taken a brownish mustard color as they lay just barely above the vase's glass. The covers are a simple gray and brown, but they do look rather comforting.

Preston's eyes are slow to move, but they do finally turn up to the body, seemingly sleeping in the bed.

Clover's mane has grown out since the event, or at the very least the lack of her brushing it has caused the ends to split and curl. Giving the illusion of a much thicker and more unmanaged mane style. Despite the fact that it has only been near a month, her skin's once tan color has become light, almost signifying some type of sickness as the unnatural change in her hue sits on display for Preston.

The silence in the room is heavy. Reynard and Bella stand closest to the door with Elden and Preston nearest to the bed. The satyr next to Preston has lost his hard, military persona, as he stares to his younger sister's slowly rising and falling chest.

"Look at you..." Elden drops to a knee as he takes Clover's cooler hand to his.

Bella loosens her lips as she speaks up. "Clover is clearly not-..."

"A moment, please." Elden sighs as he shakes his head, his brief second alone broken by Bella's words. Sighting Elden's expression of pain, Preston takes a step aside, though Elden stands all the same as he glances to Preston and then to Reynard. His left-hand fidgeting with the low glowing amulet as he speaks up. "Step away, Preston. I wish for Reynard to see the amulet's magic as fair."

Following the order Preston steps away, Elden glancing back to Reynard as he speaks up. "Are you sure you wish to see this?"

The fox-boy swallows, though he defiantly raises his head as he nods. "Yes."

The sight of Reynard's nod only draws another sigh from Elden as he glances to Preston, though for once the look of anger or disgust does not greet his eyes, instead it is merely a look of sadness, though to what Preston cannot tell. Without a word Elden jets forth the amulet, holding over Clover as his eyes stay pinned to Preston's expression.

However, a collective sigh of relief comes from room as Preston breaks out in a slight chuckle, a tear coming to his eyes as he notices the amulet's dull glow.

Reynard is the first to speak as he steps forward. "Look! Look there! The amulet does not brighten! You are wrong, Elden! You are wrong!!"

A faint smile comes to Elden's face as he draws the amulet back, realizing its glow only stays to Preston's presence. Of course, as Reynard's continued scream echoes into the hallway Elden turns to him.

Unfortunately, Elden's response goes unheard as a new voice comes to the room. "What audacity is this that you believe my work for other patients can be stopped for just one!" The healers turns to Reynard as he wags a finger to him. "And you must be quiet, people are resting! Who are you? Say your names!"

Both Elden and Preston turn to the middle-aged, dark haired satyr now coming into the room. His body is mostly hidden away under the long white and red robe he wears, but the distinctive sound of hooves on wood and the rounded ears on his head give his *Unoff* appearance away. "To what droit am I bound to appear before you in my place of healing?"

Elden cocks his head a little to the right as he straightens his posture. "This patient you so carelessly leave to perish is both my sister and apprentice of Head Mage, Svle Nyota."

The doctor seems unimpressed as he continues just to stare at Elden with disdain. "Only patients closest to moribund warrant my immediate attention. She is both stable and unable to be freed from her slumber. I do not stay near one patient-..."

Elden cuts the doctor off as he speaks up. "You have done all that you can do? You swear by this?"

The doctor once more squints his eyes a little surprised to Elden as he chimes in. "Listen hear, colt. I shall not be spurred by a member of the Capital's guard. I know my rights and I abided by the laws. Your sister has and will continue to receive the best care I or any in the nearest settlement can offer. I advise it unwise to move her to the Capital if that be your next threat, shifting her from the bed while my spell keeps her breathing will be a grave mistake, mark my words!"

Elden is quick to speak up as he shifts a little. "My sister is unable to draw breath?"

The stallion at the door lightens up a little, though his arms cross as he holds on to his annoyance. "Her breath has been very shallow, I felt it unwise to allow her to continue in such a way without aid." The doctor shakes his head as he speaks up. "Have you come here just to question my actions and that of my staff? You have a guard posted in my entrance. For what? To intimidate?"

Elden shakes his head as he speaks up. "No... it seems I have come to wish my sister farewell." His words end the doctor's hard gaze as Elden now turns back to the bed where Clover lies. Without a glance to anyone in the room Elden moves to Clover's side and scoops her left hand to his as he talks. "I am sorry Clover... I have failed as a guard and a brother." He lingers a little over the bed before he turns back to the doorway. Without even a nod to Preston, Bella, or Reynard he speaks up. "Your magic only last for so long *Héthtex*. I shall return when it is time."

Reynard's eyes widen to the comment as the fox-boy moves in front of Elden. "What are those words? You act as if you accept Clover is dead?"

Visibly Elden grinds his teeth, a bit of sweat perhaps pooling to his armor as he tugs to it. "Clover's will faded some time ago, her breathing is a falsehood."

The doctor moves a little more into the room as he halts Elden's exit. "That is not true, you let your emotions cloud my words."

Elden turns to Radisia in anger. "Untrue, you said it yourself, you thought it unwise to leave her to her own facility. Your magic will fade, and so too my sister." He straightens up. "I came here for justice not to watch her fade."

"There is something I have held off from trying..." He motions to Bella and Reynard as he continues. "Miss Vines' friends have been informed on this, but only kin could ask it."

Elden squints to the comment. "Ask what?"

"It is a thing of last resort." Bella glances to both Elden and Preston as she continues. "Not something either of you need to hold the knowledge of."

Elden again squints to the words, his gaze coming to Preston and then to Reynard as he speaks up. "We are kin, Reynard, am I not important enough to heralded at my sister's wellbeing?"

Radisia steps in for the fox-boy and for Bella as he speaks up, his words carry a faint bit of calming as he does. "Miss Vines seems to be stuck between two spells. I had surmised early on that breaking this would cause whatever part of her mind that still holds onto this magic to be damaged. I would not know the severity. However, perhaps attempting to break these spells is what may be needed. There is a chance, that I may be able to wake her. Her time runs thin as you have even acknowledged." He pauses for a moment as he continues. "The hope is that she would return healthy, though a considerable risk is placed as I do not know the spell."

Bella chimes in as the doctor stops. "This is why we have held off on a letter Elden. It was not time, Clover is-..."

"My sister is a taciturn to her family, I know it. Worry is her fear for us." Elden's face seems to lighten a little as he nods. "But this, this may yet save my sister?"

Radisia nods slowly. "Yes, but if it fails, I would struggle to keep her stable."

Preston listens in on the conversation, almost biting his tongue as he glances between the doctor and Elden's continuing enthusiasm to the news, unable to speak through the magic at his back.

Elden hesitates as he answers. "Aside from this, what other options?"

The doctor takes a deep breath as he looks over to the bed where Clover lays. "We can wait, and hope that her magic falters and that she can bring herself from whatever spell she is under."

Elden's posture and tone do not return to their normal upbeat and sure position. Yet, he still speaks up. "I have always known my sister as strong. She can make it through the spell breaking. If she put a spell or spells over herself, she would have made it necessary. Your magic will not change it, it would be too advanced, I am sure of it."

The doctor holds his stern face as he cocks his head. "You wish for me to attempt the spell?"

"Yes." Elden's confidence is absent to his voice, but his eyes show an uncanny degree of faith.

"Elden?!" Reynard's call draws a quick response from Elden.

"Reynard I am the eldest, father would have her moved." Elden cocks an eye back to the doctor. "This is impossible?"

Radisia glances between Reynard and the armored satyr before him as he struggles to answer. "With her breathing I would not see how you could? A carriage would cause too much stress."

"There." Elden nods. "There is no other option Reynard."

The fox-boy again speaks up. "We wait! She will come back to us!"

Bella moves to the boy's side as she attempts to hush him, though Elden merely turns to the doctor as he nods. "I request this spell be performed."

A sigh rolls from Radisia. "Very well, I shall retrieve what I need in a moment."

Elden is quick to speak up as he looks back to his sister. "Now? You would do the spell now?"

"Yes, her magic showed no sign of altering this morning." Radisia glances to Bella and Reynard as he trails on. "This decision would have been needed to be made soon anyways. Give me a moment."

Elden follows the doctor into the hall as he shakes his head. "I have fought in countless battles near our land's boards, I have slept many nights thinking I would not see my wife again, but I have never stood idle. If this were me, I would have had the healer end my suffering, but it is not... as such, I cannot watch a member of my family pass before my eyes if your spell fails."

For a moment the doctor is silent, but he nods as he turns back to the door. "I have already contacted other *Héthtex*, as far as any know, this is the best solution other than waiting."

Elden steps back. "Has it ever worked?"

"A colleague of mine used a method like this to halt a misused sleeping spell. It was successful. Because of Miss Vines' state, I believe it may work." He moves a hand to Elden as he continues. "Waiting, though painful, at least allows time... you still have some left, but I can perform this spell if you wish?"

Reynard chimes in. "How do you know your spell will not make it worse?"

A friendly smile comes to Radisia as he shakes his head. "Young *fróx* I have been trained in *Héthtex Márjx*. My spells are not just a raw transition of thoughts and emotions into this world, there are steps used to ensure no corruption. I assure you, even if I fail, my spell shall not alter her... and I am confident I could stable her again if needed." The doctor once more looks to Elden as he talks. "Do you wish for me to continue?"

Again, Elden is silent, however he finds his voice as he nods. "Yes, I do not believe my sister's magic, as strong as it is, will falter before her body does." His voice waivers as he rushes something more. "But I cannot stay... I will not be here to watch my decision fail, I could not bear it." The comment brings a bit of anger to Preston as he watches the armored satyr exit into the hall. The fact that he can call others to action and not see the action through burns a little to Preston, however his mind quickly focuses back to the doctor.

"Once I start the spell you must leave the room, but you are welcome to stay until I start."

Bella nods as she speaks up. "Thank you, Radisia."

The doctor nods as he moves into the hallway. With him gone Preston moves into the hallway, quickly turning his eyes to where Elden paces, his hand rubbing a rash into his chin. Sighting Preston, Elden's magic takes hold, allowing the bracelets to his hands to be freed. "I suppose I should offer a-..."

Elden's words are cut off as Preston moves his hands to Elden's armor, his strength coupled with his surprise pushing the armored satyr, an action which quickly draws Bella and Reynard into the hallway as well as the sergeant at the entrance way. Elden waves his guard off as Preston speaks up, a fire in his breath and in his gaze. "You're a coward, do you know that? A spineless fucking coward."

The words do little to Elden as he only grows more calm to Preston's anger, a rather impressive traits he did not show earlier. "I am no caitiff, and I do not expect you to understand my actions." Elden squints to the man still holding him against the wall as he nods. "Can a beast like you even fathom the care I have for my family? All that I have done to ensure Clover's wellbeing?"

"Let me tell you something." Preston licks his lips as he nods, a fierce gaze settling to Elden. Sighting this Bella usher Reynard from the door, an act that takes a moment more than she expected, though she moves him all the same as Preston speaks up. "Reynard needs you, and after what you've done you owe it to him. But beyond that, understand this you pompous prick, if this doesn't work and you leave, I'll make sure your regret that decision, for her and Reynard"

A faint smirk comes to Elden's face as he nods back. "And when my decision saves my sister, and you have returned to the Capital for your departure, I will accept your groveling." Elden breaks away from Preston's hold as he continues their staring match. "I know my sister, she is strong, stronger than I, and far beyond you. She will prevail, of this I am sure."

Preston nods his head. "And yet you still turn tail, you don't control what happens, no matter how much you believe it."

Preston's comment finally shatters Elden's smirk as the shorter *Únoff* swallows hard and turns away, saying nothing in response. Preston now stands in total disbelief to the stallion as he trots away. Even still, Preston buries this hatred as he turns back to the doorway.

The fear to the fox-boy's face is evident, and it quickly brings Preston's voice up, though he finds the words hard to say as they mimic Elden's sentiment. "Don't worry, Clover will be fine."

Reynard's expression does not change to the comment as he speaks up. "Why would Elden leave?"

Bella waves the question on as she peers out into the hall. "Do not worry about that dear, you must think positive. Have Clover on your mind, Reynard."

Preston follows her quick glance into the hall, and from this he watches as Elden and his guard exit the building. The sight of this only boils Preston's blood further as he watches the door close behind him, not even a glance back from Elden.

Chapter 12

Faith

The process Radisia started has taken a little over fifteen minutes to set-up, and while it appears to be nothing major, the knowledge of its outcomes has weight heavy to Preston's mind. Even the simple set-up, coupled with Radisia's own confidence has done little to sway the fact that Clover either wakes or seemingly dies in a few weeks.

A fact that Preston has a hard time accepting, especially with Elden now gone.

Preston, Bella, and Reynard have been asked to stand either in the doorway or in the far side of the room. Naturally, no one chose the hallway.

Radisia continues the process as he places another, dull *Kélf* stone in Clover's left hand. The same as he did for her right hand.

As he takes a step back he speaks up. "If this spell works I should be able to force her magic into the stones, from there I can better study what befell her." Radisia nods. "Are you sure you wish to stay?"

For a moment everyone just looks between the other, but eventually a common nod is shared, and Bella sheepishly speaks up. "Yes, we shall stay."

"Very well, refrain from any magic as I commence the spell."

As Radisia's hands begin to take on a low blue almost purple glow the room falls silent. Reynard stands in front of Bella as he fixes his eyes to the bed Clover lays in. The satyress he stands in front of now looks to the bed with a bit of tension now etched into her face, but Bella still brings her hands to Reynard's shoulders as she squeezes him a little.

Preston on the other hand has no comfort as he just attempts to understand Radisia's method. Though Preston possess a novice understanding of magic he finds himself only watching Radisia motions with an even increasing look of confusion and angst.

The healer continues to walk around Clover, his hands lightly glowing and the sound of his magic radiating from his person. Each time he stops walking he gently pokes or prods to Clover's body, which for a moment makes the magical chime in the room a bit quieter. As he finishes his touching of Clover's arms or legs he takes a pinch of what looks like off greenish-white powder from his pocket and places it to where he just touched. The process also requires Radisia to speak, but the mumbles are too faint for Preston to properly make out. Overall the scene on display is primitive, and Preston expects at any moment a leech or two to placed on Clover's skin. Of course, he remains silent, as he merely watches, his hands tighten as he rubs them together.

Radisia continues to walk around Clover for a few more moments until he stops at her left hand. He brings her hand into his grasp as his magic begins to glow brighter. Clover's hand, which is now clutched begins to glow, this time with a light red color, as the stone in her palm begins to light up.

The sight of this brings everyone's heads a bit closer, the first hopefully gaze setting to their faces since the spell started.

The middle-aged satyr quickly moves to the other side of the bed as he takes Clover's right hand into his. The stone in Clover's left now looks to be pulsating as Radisia attempts to do this same process, his cherry colored magic prompting her.

To Preston's surprise, suspense does not take hold of the situation. The stone quickly takes on a mix of Clover's normal magic with a few swirls of what looks like dark green or almost black running through it. However, as the stone begins to glow a sharp intake of air can be heard from the bed as Clover's legs begin to squirm.

"Clover!" Reynard is almost in a fit of tears as Bella holds him back, an ambivalent smile now crosses her face as she too looks to hold her emotions. Preston however merely glances to the door as he walks into the hallway, an action which draws shock from Bella. Though she says nothing as she turns back to the events before her.

Radisia throws his hands up to Reynard as he speaks up. "Stay, the spell could come back if she is startled." The satyr takes hold of Clover's arms with what looks to be a firm but gentle hold as he talks to her. "Miss Vines, Miss Vines do you know where you are?"

Reynard stands to his tips of his paws as he tries to look over the *Únoff* bending in front of Clover.

A weak and panting voice creeps to the room as Clover's legs begin to stop moving. "I-I was taken to the *Héthtex*."

"Do you know how long you have been asleep?"

Clover's hands open and the stones fall to the bed as her weak voice comes back to her. "P-perhaps a *déy*?"

"Miss Vines..." Radisia's voice is cool and calm as he continues. "... you have been very strong, and you will feel a little weak for some time. Although you have rested, you must rest longer."

Clover pants a bit more, her attention to the face blocking the rest of the room. "H-how long was I-..."

"Time is not important, what is important is your healing." Radisia turns back to the group pressed to the wall as he nods. As he moves from the bed he takes the two stones from Clover's side.

Reynard is the first to dash over to Clover's bedside as he reaches for Clover's right hand. "Clover! Clover?!"

Clover attempts to sit up but finds herself to weak too as she smiles to Reynard. "Reynard..."

The sight of the fox-boy's face peering to her brings a bit of strength to Clover though not enough to comfort her friend's crying as she instead resorts to words. "T-there is no need to cry... it has only been a *déy*."

Bella glances to Radisia for a moment but the satyr shakes his head as he turns away from the dark stone in his right hand. The gesture brings Bella forward as she comes behind Reynard. "You need to rest Clover, we are just happy to finally see you awake, dear."

Clover gives a slight smile as she brings her head down to her pillow. "No, no, a *déy*'s rest was all I needed after that spell... is everyone well?"

"Of course, of course." Bella glances to the open hallway behind her as she bends her head to Reynard. "Comfort her, I shall be back in a moment."

Nearly instantly Reynard begins to talk, his child-like glee almost prompting him to crawl onto the bed, though he stays firmly in place as Bella trots way. Radisia continues his studying of the stones, though Bella pays him little mind as she moves into the hallway, her eyes casting down to where Preston now sits against the wall.

No tears greet her as the man merely looks up, an almost appealing lack of emotion in his face and indeed his face as he nods. "I should be getting back soon."

Bella's eyes widen and she moves away from the door, her voice coming as a whisper as she rolls her hand for the man to stand. "Whatever do you mean? Stand, come and greet your friend, our friend?"

Preston glances to the door as he chuckles. "More your friend than mine, I'm sure she-..."

"I do not know what game you play, Preston." Bella shakes her head. "Her own brother walked away, stand and greet her." She shakes her head some more. "Why it is almost as if you stayed to comfort Reynard, it is a morbid thing that you do not celebrate."

With a blow of the breath Preston stands, a nod coming as his only answer as he starts back into the room, Bella trailing behind him.

Coming in and despite the weak voice Clover wields still manages to call the man's name rather well as her eyes greet the new face. "Preston?"

Clover's eyes, which were once were a bright and soothing bastion for Preston to become lost in are now dull, though still blue, the shimmer to them has somewhat been lost. Even still, a faint sense of caring draws the man closer as he cocks a smile. "How are you feeling?"

Clover's eyes begin to work their way over Preston, her passive smile slowly draining away as her always clever mind begins to pick out the changes to Preston. She begins to blink a little more curiously. "Y-you look different?"

Preston cannot hide the fact that his skin is a bit tanner, nor can he explain away the workouts he has received with the *Flöffs*. Luckily, before he can speak up Bella chimes in. "You must be weary from the spell, you have simply forgotten... yes *Héthtex*?"

Bella's comment that now is directed to Radisia does not immediately stir the doctor as he just barely peals his gaze from the darkened stone in his hand. "Oh, yes, yes. Your mind needs time to recover." He smiles to everyone as he speaks up. "*Témont* you all should be able to visit longer, let us give Miss Vines some-..."

"How long have I been out?"

The raspy tone despite its quiet, is able to break the conversation as Clover now awaits an answer, a demanding face coming to her.

Radisia merely smirks to the expression as he drops the stones to his pockets. "Near a *mořo*, Miss Vines."

Clover's pale face turns almost ghost white at the answer. However, Radisia quickly continues. "You should however feel very relieved." A more appropriate smile comes to the doctor's face as he trails on. "Your protection spell may not have been needed, but all mares are different in these matters." Radisia holds up the now pinkish-red stone to the bed as he continues. "Needless to say, we broke through them and your foal seems to be fine, any longer would have proven dangerous for the both of you."

The room is silent, even Reynard's sniffles halt as everyone's eyes lock to Radisia and the stone he now slowly puts down.

Clover's mouth hangs open as her raspy voice crackles through her. "W-what did you say?"

Radisia's arms fall to his sides as he looks between everyone's expressions. "I said that your protection spell seems to have work. Both you and your foal are fine."

Clover pushes herself up which causes Preston and Bella to reach for her but Clover quickly reject their help. "I-I am not carrying a foal."

A laugh comes to Radisia as he joins the confusion in the room. "Yes, you are. Why else would you have used such an advanced protection spell? Two layers, why else?"

"No, no." Clover brings her tired right arm up as she points to the doctor. "M-my spell merely lingered, that is all that happened. W-why did you take so long to break it?"

Radisia shrugs. "I had deduced your spell was to keep you from harm, though I had not understood this second, underlying spell."

"I did not cast it." Clover shakes her head. "It is a mistake."

Bella chimes in as she nods. "Dear, you have-..."

"No." Clover's head snaps to her friend at the comment as she now pants harder and brings her hand to her chest. "I-I have never..." Her words halt for a moment as she does a quick glance to Preston. However, her mind quickly takes to another thought as she begins to push herself from the bed. Her action immediately prompts everyone to tell her no and take a step towards her, but she leans back to the bed as she speaks up. "I am fine, I need to go home."

Radisia shakes his head as he speaks up. "Absolutely not! You must remain here until I clear you."

Bella speaks up as she nods. "Yes dear, this may just be a mistake, nothing to worry about. You need to rest."

Clover shakes her head as she stumbles to her hooves, Reynard moves from her, though Preston jumps forward, his arms wrapping to the dead weight that now comes to his hold. Clover must have lost thirty pounds or perhaps more as her meager frame now greets Preston's arms.

The shock of this is not lost to Preston's face, and although Clover would never admit it she needs the support as she breaks away from Preston's tighter hold, merely resting an arm to his as she struggles to stand. "Where is my clothing?" Clover gestures to the patient gown she has on as she looks to Radisia. "I would rather not leave like this."

The doctor shakes his head as he speaks up. "You must remain here!"

Bella brings a hand to her face, her expression as frazzled as her hair as she speaks up. "Please Clover sit down think of the foal."

"I am not carrying a foal!" Clover's words are fierce as she trails on. "A fact I shall prove once I am home."

Radisia shakes his head as he stomps his right hoof. "I shall not have a patient of mind leave and die before I release them!"

Clover nods her head as she speaks up. "You have done a remarkable job of caring for me, I will make sure you and your assistants are well paid.

But I am not staying." At the end of her comment she begins to trot towards the hall, breaking away from Preston's support as she does.

Radisia just watches in silent astonishment as Bella and Reynard follow after her, though it is Preston who stops her as he wraps his arms around Clover and physically brings her back into the room.

Clover's hooves kicked to the ground and her eyes widen as she looks down to the man now bringing her back in. "What are you doing?"

"You're staying, Clover." Preston brings her back to the bed with ease, the woman's strength proving no problem in her current state.

Of course, just as Clover's flank comes back to the bed she forces herself up again, an angered expression crossing her face as she stares up to the man.

Her mane is wild, and although her display of annoyance to the situation is noted, Preston does not back down as he merely stares back. Luckily, Bella and Reynard come to Clover's side as the satyress leads the conversation. "Clover, this is ridiculous. You cannot go home yet dear, you are too weak."

Reynard follow the comment as he speaks up. "Clover, please. You need to rest."

"N-no, I must get home. He is wrong, and I can prove it." Clover pants a little, the feeling of being surrounded seeming breaking her down as her will to stand fails and she comes back to the bed.

Radisia stands in the hall with a nurse beside him just watching the ordeal unfold. Though Bella draws Clover's gaze from the hall as she pats a hand to her friend. "Clover, we have been worried about you, we will not let you do this."

Clover sniffles, pushing away her friend's gesture as she draws her own hands to her head. "I-I am not with a foal... I cannot be..."

Bella is forced away, her jaw biting shut as she looks for someone else to speak up. Though Preston merely stands dumbfounded and Reynard as clueless as a child. "Clover you must rest, please, you are hysterical..."

The words do nothing for Clover, her rambling teetering on the verge of a total meltdown as she continues to shake her head to the idea. Finally, Preston moves, squatting down in front of the satyress. He brings a hand to Clover's chin as he speaks up. Never one for motivational speeches, Preston speaks plainly. "We're not letting you leave, so what do you need from the library?"

Swallowing her pride and indeed her emotions Clover relents. "Fine..." Her gaze sets to Reynard as she speaks up. "Reynard, bring me every book, every scroll, anything you can find on... on gravidity from the library?"

Without hesitation Reynard nods. At the nod Preston stands, though Clover does not bring her head up as her gaze stays pinned to the floor. With Clover silent, the group moves out of the room, all now attempting to digest what has just happened in their own ways.

Though once they clear the door Radisia speaks up. "Thickness must gallop in the family." Radisia continue. "After a night's rest and a well-prepared meal I should have her ready to leave in the morning. I doubt she will let us keep her much longer, and I cannot turn her request down if she can walk out."

Bella now speaks up a little frustrated. "This spell must be wrong; Clover cannot be carrying a foal. I know most of the stallions in town... friends of course." The comment goes well past Reynard who accepts it as Bella turns back to the doctor. "Clover, she is far more content in her library. Are you truly certain in your words?"

Radisia takes a deep breath as he speaks up. "The stones do not normally have mistakes, and why else would a mare of such age use such a protective spell if not for this?"

Bella sighs as she nods. "Very well, when can we see her?"

Radisia clears his throat as he continues. "She has requested a few books as I hear, you may bring these. But, no other visitors and you may not stay for too long. I shall inform her of this. Now, if you excuse me." As Radisia's comment ends he turns back to the hall as he begins to trot the corridor.

Bella rubs her forehead as she speaks up. "Reynard, would you be a dear and wait outside for me? I need to clear my head."

"Alright, Bella."

Reynard moves to Preston as he gives a little smile. "Clover is better."

Preston copies the smile as he bends down and gives the fox-boy a little hug. "I know buddy." The exchange lasts a few moments before Reynard goes outside.

Once the little *fróx* is gone, Bella turns her gaze to Preston. "Perhaps you should have left." She gives a faint laugh as she shakes her head.

Preston just smirks to the comment, his hands dipping into his pockets as he looks to the ground for a moment. "I should talk with-..."

"No! No, no, not now. *Témont* if you need to talk, do so after she has rested." Bella holds her hand to Preston as she shakes her head. "I do not need to know what about." With a sigh Bella rubs her forehead. "I merely hope Reynard has no questions for me."

Preston speaks up as he shrugs. "I can stay with him at the library tonight if-..."

"No... I suppose these matters need a mare's mind." Bella takes a deep breath as she looks up to the ceiling. Preston takes notice to her frustration as he speaks up. "Your really are a good friend Bella, I'm sure Clover appreciates everything you've done."

"Oh, Preston... I am sure she does." Bella crosses her arms. "Clover is a bit grinding sometimes, she believes she needs to be, though if you get past that, she is a good friend." Bella cocks her head to the man as she continues. "And I hope you are not galloping off dear, Reynard is certainly not carrying all those books from the library, and my arms are much too frail to carry so many."

"Alright." Preston gives a little smile as he feels his mind starting to build up with everything that has just happened.

With one more sigh Bella straightens her posture. "Well, we have much to do. I still must return and clean my store, after what those uncouth guards did in their search. Come along, dear."

Preston nods as he follows Bella back out into the street, Reynard comes to their side as they begin the journey back to town. Preston's eyes however fall to the wheel marks left over from where Elden's carriages were.

Chapter 13

Twilight

The sky is a dim orange, with wisps of pink and light cream colors mixed throughout. The greens of the fields are dark and the dirt of the path is only visible because of this contrast. Light breezes every so often run through the fields, but mostly the twilight has been calm.

Preston's arms hang to his sides as he just enjoys the idea of not having to carry anymore books or help move stuff for Bella. Ellette is sure to be crossed at the man for not returning to the camp sooner, though in truth, Preston has far larger things to think about than the bird-girl's wrath.

The days have all run together so much lately that every day normally just feels like a tv show, one where no matter where you start paying attention, it always seems to be the same thing. A loop, lines in a play repeated and practiced until perfection. Yet, today has definitely left a different impression on Preston's mind. The idea of Clover being pregnant is almost mind-boggling, there is hardly any doubt that Preston has been the only person with Clover, but still the idea of it is absolutely frightening. Not only due to Preston own fright of fatherhood, but of fear of Elden, and beyond that simple biology.

Clover is no human, the idea of having a kid with her almost sickens Preston at the thought of what monster may be born. Worst still, are the thoughts Clover must be going through only with her books. All this combined only further adds to Preston's already guilt stricken mind.

Though even beyond this, the simple fact that he was unable to sit down and merely talk it out with Clover has chewed away at Preston since he left. The day has become a cocktail of problems with the ice of emotions now begin to melt and overflow the glass.

"Preston!"

The calm twilight is finally broken as a tomboyish voice rings out. Sure enough, the familiar *Flöff* lands next to the man and begins to follow after him. "You left your post all *déy*! My feathers are stained with smoke! You had better solved Bella's issue, you had better great my ears with a wonderful story!"

"She's fine."

Ellette cocks her head as her excitable voice slowly calms down. "Fine? Are you well?"

Preston just nods as he replies. "Yea, I just got a few things on my mind."

"What did the Capital guards want with Bella? That is who they were, yes? I saw the flags on their carriages." Ellette shakes her head. "*Múck'd Únoff*, they had no reason for such a display."

Again, the man just nods. "Yea, they were from the Capital. It was Clover's brother, just trying to figure out what happened to her."

A slight scoff comes from Ellette. "This is why the *Únoff* need better laws, to detain a citizen for questioning is clouded judgement."

Preston shrugs. "Clover's brother just wanted to know what happened to his sister."

Ellette again just blows the comment off as she shakes her head. "I think I have a sister in *Féllcreed,* does that give me the right to detain any I wish to?"

"No." Preston shakes his head. "But wouldn't you want to know if your sister was hurt?"

Ellette quickly shakes her head to the comment. "All wish to know a kin's status. Even I get letters from my parents, though I would not trade my time here to search for them!"

Although it is no shock to Preston to hear Ellette talk about how unimportant it is for her to be around her parents, the comments still carry weight. "Don't you think your parents worry about you when you don't send letters?"

"Mmmm..." Ellette cocks her head again as she continues. "Well, I do not like writing, and you are supposed to be helping." She shrugs. "My reports are just to ensure I am alive and that their coin has not gone to waste."

"I can help with the letters later." Preston nods. "Clover is awake now."

Ellette's face brightens as she takes herself a few inches from the ground in excitement. "That is great news! You will have more time to help write!"

"She's still not better yet... and to be honest, I hope she stays out of the library."

Ellette seems to ignore the comment as she speaks up. "I will go ahead and alert the gatekeeper. *Pexřá* Elva will want to know and when you are done, if you are not tired, we can work on my letters."

Preston squints a little as he cocks his head to the girl. "You don't listen well do you? I said I got a lot on my mind."

"*Pff,* you did not even work the forge. How can your mind be heavy?"

Preston shakes his head. "I have a few things I need to think about. Tomorrow I'll help you."

Preston's comment slows Ellette's wings, but the girl speaks up as she reluctantly nods. "Fine, but if you need a break from Lutin just say you are ill. That is how I get shorter patrols sometimes."

With a nod Preston watches the *Flóff* girl start up her wings as she cuts through the quiet night's air with a few quick and hard flaps towards the entrance of the camp. Preston's own pace starts a bit quicker as the camp grows ever nearer.

It only takes a few moments for Preston to get to the camp's opened wooden gates, with a little nod from the gatekeeper Preston steps in. Overhead, Ellette flies back into the field to continue her assignment. As Preston continues into camp, a familiar voice barks to him.

"Luck turns with the tides, Preston..."

Elva is quick to come to Preston as she directs him to walk on the outer edges of the camp. The campfire and ever persistent members of it have formed near the center of the courtyard, but Preston does not meet anyone's eyes as Elva comes to his left. "...you had better have a good reason for not venturing back to camp."

"Clover is awake." The smile and almost saddened eyes Preston now directed to Elva are greeted only by her solid almost more questioning expression as she replies.

"You were permitted at Clover's bedside for this long?"

The question brings a sharp stab to Preston's side as he shakes his head. "Elva, Clover woke up. Do you not even care?"

"Of course, the news of Clover's recovery is enjoyable, but this only excuses half of your absence. You have responsibility to-..."

"You're kidding right? This is a joke right? Look, I get that things are different here, but there is no way in Hell I am going to believe being gone for something like this is inexcusable-..."

"Lower your tone, Preston, you have no authority over me."

Preston gives a simple chuckle. "I'm not one of you. Throw me in jail, make me fight I don't care, I went to visit someone I care about, I went to visit your friend, Elva."

"I do not disregard this fact Preston. I am asking what your excuse is, where have you been?"

With a huff Preston answer. "I've been with Bella and Reynard since Clover woke up. I wanted to get my mind off a few things."

Elva's demeanor stays the same as she just takes the comment. "You left from the *Héthtex* to be with Bella and Reynard for the better part of your duty... why?"

Preston takes a deep breath. "Is this just because I was gone? I've been gone before."

The warrioress does not halt her questions at the man's voice as she speaks up again. "I am asking for my report."

"I went to see Clover." Preston begins to motion the events with his hands, not that his gestures help his story though he continues all the same. "She is up now, not that it seems you care. After that-..."

Elva's voice cuts through Preston's as she speaks up once more. "Do not throw words into-..."

"After that, I went with Bella and Reynard." Preston shrugs. "I can write it down."

Elva gently puts her head a little to the side as she stares down the man in front of her. "How is Clover? I have what I need, and you seem so eager to speak of something. How is my friend, Preston, tell me?"

Preston's breathing slows for a second as he attempts to figure out Elva's emotionless expression. "You're done now? Now we can talk like real friends?"

"You may refer to our affinity however you wish, Preston." Elva crosses her arms. "Speak."

"Alright." Preston darts his eyes toward the center of the camp, mainly just to see if any gawkers have turned to where he and Elva stand. Whether it be their general lack of interest in him or their military upbringing, none look their direction. This in mind, Preston's voice starts up in a fairly low tone. "Clover's up, but the doctor or healer, whatever you want to call him, he said that she's..." With a deep breath Preston pushes the words out. "That she's uh pregnant."

The reaction Preston halfheartedly expected is not found on Elva's face, instead the avian woman merely holds her crossed arms to the cold metal armor on her chest in thought. Because of this, Preston speaks back up again. "You know? Like with a foal or-or something, yea?"

"*Hmpf...*" Elva shakes her head a little as she continues. "Undoubtedly, Svle Nyota instructed Clover to watch over you. I find it ignoble that she found such a distasteful means of enjoyment, just because you are here does not mean her task was complete." Elva continues as her eyes tighten a little in thought. "Still, I must say, I am not too shocked at the news; *Únoffs* are so fascinated with their counterparts it only makes sense she would try something for her own gain. Or as *they* so typically call it, *shéo.*"

Preston just bobs his head, eyes to the dirt ground as he rubs to his chin. "Yea yea, yea... Elva, I think it might be my fault."

"Of course." Elva nods. "Without her assigned task she looked for another form of...."

"No." Preston shifts a little uncomfortable to his feet as he trails on. "I mean, I think it might be my doing."

For once a true to life look of expression graces Elva's avian face, her thick brown eyebrows raising and her pointed chin cocking as she speaks up to the comment. "You? You have bedded Clover?"

A rush of heat goes through Preston's face as clears his throat. "Yea."

"Impossible." Elva shakes her head, her hands drifting to her hips. "Clover is no simple mare, and while I claim to be no expert on *Únoff* attraction I must call into question your statement."

Preston's eyes widen and a laugh shoots from the man as he speaks up. "You're kidding right? You don't believe me?"

Elva squints her eyes as she nods. "*Flóff* matting is based off gains. No true *Flóff* would be swayed without a display of worth in their suiter. Although I respect your heart, you have nothing else to offer a suiter, Preston."

"R-really? Why would I lie about this?" Preston laughs. "I'm freaking out here and this is what you have to offer? I'm going to have a little monster running around in a few months! Who knows what it's going to look like!"

"Do not speak ill of your brood." Elva backs off a little, taking a breath as she nods. "If you do speak truthfully you would accept it. Clover's foal, if it is indeed your spawn, would not be allowed without either your or her own desire. *Cróff* births are the produce of magic, I feel Clover wasted that spell on you if this is how you act." Elva's wings adjust as she continues. "You truly do not lie?"

Preston is silent for a moment as he lets the words sink in. "What did that mean, *crofft* or *corfft* what-what does that mean?"

Elva's patience seems to wear thin as she replies. "A crossed birth. How could Clover carry your foal and not speak of this?"

"Well... she didn't seem to know she was. We didn't get to talk about it, she fell asleep when we got back."

The avian woman slowly loosens her stern hold to her hips as she cocks her head a little. "You are not an *Únoff*, no *Cróff* birth can be random, even between two beings of *Márjx* one must still prompt a spell."

Preston's heart slows for a moment as he pushes his voice forward. "So... you're saying she wanted this and just forgot?! How? Why?! That doesn't make any sense?"

"I do not know." Elva shrugs a little to the comment. "Your height is an enjoyable feature though hardly one for bedding, you boast no sizable muscles, your stance is poor, your chest is that of a mare's, and you whine."

"Thanks, I knew I would enjoy this." Preston shakes his head, a hand rubbing to his neck again as he sighs.

Elva merely cocks an eye to the sarcasm. "I do not have the answers you want Preston." Elva tights her arms to her chest again. "Perhaps the healer was mistaken."

"Yea." Preston chuckles, a wash of relief to the words as he nods. "C-Clover seems to think that."

"There you have it." Elva nods. "If she rejects this notion than she did not perform the necessary spell, you lack the ability, so your tryst was meaningless."

"Yea, yea, you're right." Preston blows his breath, his arms tightening as he looks away, his mind latching to the previous comment with glee.

Sighting the man's more relaxed posture Elva speaks up. "Preston, if you and Clover do indeed have a *yiftiñ*, do not ever say what you have said here." Elva nods. "Enjoy all moments, as clouds form very quickly in this world, and you will not know loss until it is too dark."

The body language in Elva's posture suggests her departure, but before she can follow through with her desire to leave, Preston speaks up one last time. His own thoughts pushed aside as he looks the woman over, now realizing how foolish his words must have sounded. "Why did you never have another kid?"

Elva is silent for a moment as she looks Preston over with a slightly skeptical eye. "Though feathers grow, a torn wing may never fly."

The words turn heavy to Preston's heart as he quickly speaks up. "I-I'm sorry."

A sharp breath comes to Elva as she nods. "Personal matters are my own accord, Preston." Elva continues to hold steady as she continues. "You have my permission to visit Clover *témont*. However, Lutin as well as I, will expect you to be in line soon."

Preston just gives a little laugh as he watches Elva walk away. As she leaves ear shot, he rubs to his neck and sighs. "Soon…" With a loud exhale of pure mental exhaustion Preston sets his eyes to the tent he has called home.

Chapter 14

Simplicity

Despite the fact that the surrounding landscape around the camp is mainly nothing more than tall grass, with a few rocks and boulders, the sounds of birds chirping early in the morning have begun to become more common. At first, Preston had thought it was one of the *Flöffs* in the camp doing it, but the idea of asking someone if they chirp like a bird has struck Preston as perhaps an insulting or racist comment; seeing as how they are in fact bird people. And so, because of this, most days Preston just tries to ignore the birds, mainly so no questions about whether or not the *Flöff* chirp or sing pop into mind throughout the day.

Yet, unlike normal, the birds have been successful in waking Preston, and now the man just sits quietly in the dark tent as he listens to the noises outside. The sun has not even begun to poke through the mountains nor has any of the normal commotions of outside started. Which, as far as Preston is concerned, suggest that he is the first person to wake up. This however, is no achievement as the man just sleeplessly stares to the dark tan coloring of the tent.

It is moments like these that make Preston regret fighting with Clover and leaving the library. The single cover and pillow are both inadequate in keeping comfortable and warm when laying in the almost straw thin bed. Most nights Preston must cross his legs to even stay fully under the blanket, which normally just causes a leg or foot to fall asleep and not himself.

Yet, today is obviously starting off differently, as Preston now rolls himself from the bed. The rug covered ground is cold, and the chill immediately makes Preston focus to the chest on the ground containing his normal day's wear. The small tent allows Preston to reach with relative ease, but as he opens it his train of thought stops for a moment.

Preston bends down as he reaches for the crystal gem sitting atop his clothing. "Why are you here..." The small light cream-colored stone is cold, but as Preston brings it from the chest it begins to warm. The color too bringing to take on a deep, cream hue. Preston continued to stare at the stone, almost lost in thought as his mind starts to drift. The stone is and will always be ready for him to leave. Clover has said it is just a clear mind and a well thought out image of where he wants to go that left. The idea of going back and leaving everything else behind begins to take over in Preston's mind, as he runs his fingers across the stone. Clover would be fine, is the thought that keeps popping into mind, the images of her parent's big house, huge fields of grapes and the idea of how well known she is to Sóltina are all surely beneficial, no matter her condition.

The man's hand tightens around the stone as he begins to bob his head in thought. Clover does not really need Preston around, and there is surely no way she actually carried a foal. Even still, she will be married off all the same, leaving Preston alone in the camp, as he finds himself now.

Preston turns his attention to his dull surroundings as he bites to his fingertips. The unmistakable taste of coal hits his tongue, but he does not stop as he begins to think out loud. "Why shouldn't I leave? There's nothing for me here, I can back now, no one would know..." As the thoughts begin to grow, the stone in Preston's hand begins to turn warm, and eventually an unpleasant hot.

However, before Preston can even put the stone down, it slips through his hand. The fever in his hand is gone and for a split-second Preston had thought he had lost it, yet as he bends down he finds it laying atop the clothing still in the chest just beside him. Though, he is unable to pick it up again, he cannot.

"What the Hell?"

The stone sits just a little embedded into his folded clothing that still resides in the chest. But, no matter how Preston grabs for it his fingers slip off or seemingly go straight through it. Out of frustration, Preston takes the chest up in pours the contents to the ground. The stone falls within view and he once more bends down to pick it up. The warmth of the stone is not felt, and instead Preston's fingertips brush against the rug's trampled and worn out surface.

"What the Hell?!"

Preston falls to his knees now attempting to scoop the stone, but his hands pass through it as if it were not there. "I-I want it! I want to go home! I don't want this! Please!!"

- - -

The quiet words and tensing in Preston's arms abruptly end the dream as his eyes now pin to the golden morning sun, coloring the top of his tent. Refusing to believe the dream, Preston jumps from the bed and starts to the chest. However, as he quickly slams the lid back his eyes are only met with the sight of his clothes.

"W-what?" His hands dart into the fabric as he destroys the neatly folded clothing in an attempt to see the bottom of the chest. As the wood of the bottom of the chest greets his eyes he stops. For a moment a feeling of dread comes to Preston as he finally accepts the dream as nothing more than a dream, yet, he does not scream or burst into tears. Instead, his mind focuses on one thing. Clover still has the stone, and unless she moved it, he knows where it is. With this in mind, Preston takes a deep breath and begins to clear the mess he has just made room. Though in doing this he glances to the amulet poking out just under some clothing. See it, Preston sighs again, his hand coming to it. Unlike the dream, the amulet happily greets him, it is cold, much like the dream, as he strokes it the spell within it awakens. As he has done several times before, he clenches his hand, his magic prompting the spell to his body as he lets out a pleasant groan. He slumps to the bed, his head coming to lay on the itchy covers as he stares up to the tent, the magic swirling in his mind. Feeling the happy buzz now washing over him a smile crosses his face, his arms growing limp as he lets the amulet fall to the wayside.

"Huhh..." With another blow of his breath Preston chuckles, patting the amulet beside him as he leans forward. His eyes wash over the various garments that still need to be stowed away, though the dopey smile holds strong as he lazily goes through the motions. All the while, his mind is set adrift, not a thought to the man as he moves about the room with ease.

Chapter 15

Homecoming

The morning routine was quicker than normal, which for Preston was good. Not only because it helps the day go faster, but also because he was able to avoid Lutin. Strangely, even though the camp has never felt very welcoming, Lutin has gained Preston's respect, and knowing that he will be working the forge alone does bother Preston a little. Mostly due to Preston's own self-destined failing of it. Yet, this and all other thoughts of his obligations to the camp or anyone in *VéturVill* have been pushed aside, his mind focusing on a different goal for the day. A real sense of relief greets Preston with every step he takes away from the camp. The idea that Preston can escape everything that has happened in the last few months is a great feeling. One that has only been spurred on by the amulet Preston has deep into his pocket.

Why not all moments have been miserable, the small sense of belonging that Clover gave to the man ended when Preston walked out well over a month ago. The fact is Clover falling ill was the only reason he even stayed, as the sense of guilt and the fear for Reynard was simply too great to ignore. However, with those issues now remedied a weight seems to be lifted from the man's mind, a belief he fervently holds as he strokes the amulet.

The sky is a bit cloudy than normal, however, it is earlier than the other days Preston has set out. Perhaps the schedule calls for rain today, not that Preston would know, as the camp always stays dry. But the winds are gentle enough and the rain is fairly refreshing rather than bothersome, the roads of course turn a bit muddy, but with whether bound by a time frame, it never gets out of hand, and something Preston could easily avoid. It is a bit strange to see how everyone acts when it rains, instead of people running to shelter it almost seems embraced. Come to think of it, Preston cannot even recall an umbrella ever insight. Then again, perhaps one has yet to be invented.

Preston's walk slows a little as he looks around the barren fields just on the outskirts of town. The breeze is still, no bugs buzz around, and no one else walking the trail leading to the *Flóff* camp. Preston stands on a hill, behind him the camp he left, and before him just a little ways away, the main road into *VéturVill*. The area looks like a painting, almost a perfect paradise of tranquility if not for what Preston knows of this world. Even still, tall, blue and white shaded mountains sit far off in the distance behind the camp, the other side of *VéturVill* is not visible from where Preston is, but he can still picture the dark, green forest of the *ÉverMoar*. The fields around him are mostly a light, green, most of the wildflowers seeming dying out since their last blooming. At night, the fields look dry and tired, but now, the fields look buoyant and bright, a life to them that Preston for once can agree with.

The fresh air is pleasant and the view, albeit plain is still enjoyable. After a few moments Preston begins to continue his original journey. Judging by how far he has already walked and how far away the town's main road is, it should take another ten or so minutes for the medieval hospital to come into view. Yet, even with this in mind Preston's thoughts still linger to the stone Clover still has hidden in the library.

- - -

A little later

The venture into town has neared its end as Preston sets his eyes to the hospital building just down the road. It only takes a few moments to reach the dull red wood door of it, and as Preston does, the sound of voices from within meet his ears. With a bit of hesitation, Preston pokes his head inside.

Truthfully, the sight that greets Preston's eyes is not all too surprising. The cause of the commotion is none other than, Clover seemingly arguing with the doctor, and the nurses stand in the hall, all brandishing such annoyed looks that even the most seasoned in customer service would have flinch.

"...Miss Vines, I insist you keep your voice down there are still other patients here."

Clover pulls the three books from Radisia. Which is actually fairly entertaining, seeing as how she already has a few books in her other hand, now she just looks to be performing a balancing act. Clover's mane is more brushed than the other day and her clothing is no longer the normal hospital gown, but her face and indeed her body still look worn and lacking its normal luster.

"And I will be, once I am gone."

Radisia takes back one of the books as he shakes his head. "You may still be feeling weak later, it is not wise to leave."

Clover snatches the book from the doctor through the use of her magic as she nods. "I thank you for everything you have done, but I must get back home."

Once more Radisia continues his protest as he shakes his head. "Miss Vines you must consider the health of your foal as well as-..."

"Oh look." Clover cuts Radisia off mid-breath as she moves to Preston. "I have someone to carry my belongs. No need to worry about stress on my body." Before Preston can truly agree with the obviously unavoidable request made by Clover the books drop to his hold. Her items are really not all too heavy, but seeing as how carrying books or any manual labor for instance has started to become a norm, Preston does not pay it much mind.

"Thank you again for your services. I hope you all wish me good health so that I will never have to return." Clover starts immediately towards the door with Preston behind her as her last words ring to the room.

"But…"

Without a moment of hesitation Clover opens the door and starts out into the street, Preston gives a slight nod to the doctor and nurse still inside as he dips out after Clover.

A sharp sigh comes from Clover as she rubs her forehead. *"Lóvo baf*te*ñ."*

Preston slowly comes to Clover's side as he cocks his head a little. "Frustrated?"

Another sigh rolls from Clover as she speaks up. "Very. What sort of learned *Héthteẋ* would dare say I carry a foal without proper inquiry? Nothing has been asked of me. Not any changes in magic, diet, sickness, nothing. Instead, accusations were made, based on nothing but a stone's color." Clover's normal brisk pace starts with a slightly more anger-based drive as she moves towards town.

Her comments however beg Preston to ask as he attempts to understand her. "So we agree you're not?"

A slightly overzealous laugh escapes from Clover as she shakes her head. The know-it-all tone of before quickly takes over her weaker sounding voice as she turns her soft blue eyes to Preston. "You are not an *Únoff*. It is that simple. And I am no *noṡton* when it comes to spells, I would never cast such a spell."

"But you know a spell?" Preston's speed finally matches the satyress beside him as he awaits an answer.

Clover gives a little chuckle as she nods. "Of course, I am a student of *Álter Márjx*, spells that would change any living or nonliving thing are naturally studied."

Preston just slowly nods to the comment as he speaks up a little more. "And you, you know getting sick and feeling a little weak, the few changes in your magic that's nothing, right?"

The comments quickly wash away the empowered smirk that has adorned Clover's face since they left Radisia; and as the smirk leaves her face, her voice starts up a little more vexed. "Circumstance, Preston, nothing more than unconnected events." She chuckles her head held high and her eyes closing. "Besides for there to be any issue we would have needed to-to…"

Preston blinks to the stuttering as he cocks an eye, his own doubts starting to come back at Clover's less than quick words. "Slept together?"

Clover's ear flicks to the word, her eyes darting the empty street as she replies in a hushed tone. "Not-not just that, several other things, along-along with the spell, which I NEVER would have used." Clover nods. "Besides, no mare can claim such fertility of one attempt."

A forced chuckle rolls from Preston as he nods awkwardly replies. "Um, I mean one?"

Quickly Clover waves the comment off. "There is no count, why would there be a count?" A laugh escapes Clover as she nods to the man. "You are not so conceded, are you?"

A faint laugh rolls from Preston as he shakes his head, attempting to brush the woman's words off with a joke. "Oh no, no, don't sweat it, you could have just said it wasn't enjoyable. I'm used to not getting a call back."

Clover's head lowers a bit as she notices the border buildings of the town just up the road, the sight of other people growing closer also force her to lower her voice as she glances a little to Preston. "We… we have talked about this. I enjoyed the experience, but did we not both agree it was a mistake, Preston?"

"N-no I was making a joke." Preston cocks a smile, the reminder of Clover's favorite word drawing a bit of a sting in the man's mind. "And don't worry, I get that they were a mistake."

"It, not they." Clover shakes her head. "We shall talk about this later."

"Ha, what's there to talk about?" Preston adjusts the books in his hold as he shakes his head. "I'm just here to carry your stuff and make sure you don't fall."

"Yes, of course." Clover nods. "There is nothing to discuss." The comment draws both Clover and Preston to lock eyes, though both merely pull away as Preston speaks up.

"So, you woke up good?" Preston clears his throat. "No problems sleeping?"

"No, I was fine." Clover folds her hands as she lowers her head, though she keeps the small talk alive as she replies. "Have you fared well? No issues?"

"Fine, fine." Preston takes a breath as he looks over the road laid out before them. "Been busy."

Clover cocks a smile to the comment as she nods. "Yes, I see you have found color."

"Meh, just getting use to the sun." Preston cocks a smile. "You could use some."

Though the comment was lighthearted, Clover's fall a bit as she glances to her pale hands. "I suppose I do."

Preston's smirk is lost, though he says nothing more as he merely focuses on the road.

The small, one lane street quickly becomes more congested with the addition of other people, carts, and the normal bustle of the day. Due to this, Clover moves a little closer to Preston as she directs him towards the market. "We should thank Bella for everything she has done for Reynard." Clover slowly pulls Preston from his pace as she nods. "Let us all get back to the library and then... we can talk more."

Preston quickly shakes his head as he stops, forcing Clover to halt her trot. "Hey it's like I said, I'll drop this stuff off and if Rey is going to be with you we can just get back to normal, I'll head back to the camp."

Clover's ear flicks a little to the comment as she cocks an eye to Preston. "You still stay with Elva?"

"Where else would I stay? When you got hurt I didn't really have anyone." Preston shrugs as he shifts the books in his hold. "It's been okay, like I said, I keep busy."

A slightly confused look comes to Clover as she shakes her head. "You would have been welcomed in the library; I do trust you Preston."

A sigh rolls from Preston as he shakes his head. "I wouldn't have felt welcomed."

"Would not have felt welcomed?" Clover shakes her head once more as she prods at Preston with her words. "How is that?"

The comment adds a little bit of irritation to Preston's voice, but he holds it off quite well as he talks. "How much do you remember?"

Clover is silent for a moment as her ears flatten a little to the back of her head, although a bit hard to see with the way her mane is at the moment, Preston takes notice. "To be quite honest Preston, I cannot recall everything that has happened." Clover stops her voice as she scrunches her face up for a moment in thought. "Did, did you come to see me while I was asleep?"

Preston straightens to the comment, a sincere nod following his breath. "Any day I could get out, yea."

Clover just nods to the comment, her lips quivering to say more, though she says nothing as she starts her tort up towards the market. Though as Preston joins her, she nods. "I cannot recall everything that has happened, but if I have hurt you Preston, I wish for you to know I did not mean it. Your company was... enjoyable." A slight laugh comes from the satyress as she nudges the man. "You were far better to look after than the time Master Nyota asked me to watch after Wispy for a *mořo*."

Preston smiles a little to the comment as he looks down to the woman. "I'm better than a cold-blooded reptile... neat."

The slight smile on Clover's face holds but her natural questioning attitude takes hold as she speaks up. "I hope Master Nyota is okay..."

The simple grin to Preston's face fades as he nods. "I'm sure he's fine, let's focus on you for a bit." Preston just shakes his head as he turns away from Clover and back to the market square that they now reach the outer edges of.

Although the conversation does not end, Clover holds her questions as she instead focuses on directing Preston to Bella's shop, almost as if she has forgotten Preston knows where it is. It only takes a few moments to reach Bella's store, and as they do Clover knocks to it.

Before the door even opens a soft, but perfectly audible Southern Belle tone rings from inside as the door slowly opens. "I am sorry but we are clo-... Clover!?" Bella practically jumps from the house as she looks her friend over, one hand darts to Clover's side almost as if she were trying to stop her from falling. "Are you well? Have you walked all this way?" Her eyes dart to Preston as Bella's dainty voice turns to a bossier tone. "You let her walk all this way? She should be resting?"

Clover quickly steps in as she speaks up. "It is okay Bella, I wanted to-..."

"No, no, no, dear, you must still be resting. There is no telling what prolonged spells can do to you."

"I am sure that-..."

"Clover?"

The boyish voice takes center stage in the conversation as Reynard quickly darts to the satyress with a hug. Clover bends down to meet his hug as the two embrace for a few long seconds. Reynard's tone begins to crack a little as he speaks up. "I was so worried about you..."

The tender moment forces Bella to shoot Preston an apologetic glance that he quickly nods. Clover and Reynard's conversation still hangs to their attention however as the woman speaks up. "I am okay, Reynard. I have dealt with far worse things than sleep."

Reynard's eyes are held tightly shut as he nods. "B-but you never woke up for so long..."

"I know. But it is okay now, Reynard. I feel much better."

Bella chimes in as she ushers to Clover. "Dear come inside, you do not want *gók-tós* from the market."

Clover and Reynard break the hug as Clover speaks up again. "Oh Bella, you have done so much for me already, do you not want to get back to normal?"

Bella holds her hand to Clover. "Normal will come in time, let us relax with some warm *Léle* and then we can attempt normal."

Reluctantly, Clover nods and gives a friendly smile as she replies. "Thank you, Bella."

"No thanks are necessary." Bella's smile is radiant as she moves aside to let Clover and Reynard inside. As they move inside Preston follows in behind them.

As normal, the store front part of Bella's house is kept neat and tidy, with the bright fabric rolls in the far right of the corner near a long standing mirror and the pre-made outfits. The decorative plants, and tables that are scattered around the room are easy to avoid; Bella moves to the large, what Preston has always known as the checkout counter as she goes behind it and lifts the long red curtain with her magic.

"I do apologize for the mess, I was just about to open the storefront, we have not cleaned up dishes back here."

Clover just gives a little smile as she shakes her head. "It is fine, Bella."

Preston, Reynard, and Clover all move into the back room which serves as a kitchen, fitting room, and storeroom all in one, a bit cramped, but the table nearest to the kitchen is the only thing that is needed, not the space.

"Well still, clutter is the first step to a disorganized life." Bella moves past her guest as she uses her magic to clear the two plates and cups from the light brown almost oak table. Despite the fact that she rarely uses her magic, the items float softly through the air and stack nicely in the kitchen's sink on the far-left side of the room. As she finishes the clean up her arms come out to the table. "Sit, sit, I do not want you to feel faint, Clover."

Clover and Reynard follow the welcome as they take their seats, but Preston hesitates as he looks for a clear table to place Clover's books down to. Yet, every small table has a plant with a little decorative white doily under it and moving it to the ground might annoy Bella. Luckily however, as he searches for a place Bella speaks up. "Oh, Preston you can just set those books on the crafting table just by the fabric dear. But, do be sure not to crease the material dear."

Preston nods to the comment as he moves to the one uncluttered area in the room. The mini trash can next to the workbench and chair is caked in strips of colored fabric, and the table itself is littered with metal pins, strange looking scissors, and the fabric itself. But, Preston does find a free spot eventually. As he does, he turns back to the conversation going on behind him.

Bella stands in the kitchen surely making tea like drink she promised. Yet, Bella still holds her friendly tone as she speaks up. "So, if you do not mind my prying, were you released or did you simple walk out, dear?"

The comment brings a slight smile to Preston's face as he takes the seat across from Clover.

"Your question is not prying Bella, I assume I will have to answer a few questions like this." Clover nods. "But, I did leave on my own accord."

"Oh..." Bella for a moment looks to bite her lip before she talks, but her own normal chattiness brings her voice back up. "D-did you feel well?"

Clover nods to the comment, despite the fact that Bella has her back towards the table as she talks. "Yes, sleeping more will not allow me to get better, it would only make me feel weaker."

"Well yes, it is always helpful to get back to normal. But dear, you do understand that they are only trying to help, yes?" Bella cocks an eye to her friend.

Clover merely sighs to the glance as she nods. "Are you suggesting I go back?"

"Ha, ha, ha, oh well no, of course. That is if you truly believe you should not." Bella shoots a smile back to Clover as she continues. "I just want to make sure you are... thinking it all over, is all."

Before Clover can chime in Preston speaks up. "I think she's made her mind up."

Another slight chuckle comes from Bella as she turns back to the table with a teapot and five white ceramic cups. Her magic quickly brings the cups and four coasters to the table as she places them neatly in front of everyone. "I do not doubt your decision Clover. You do look... better." Her voice drifts a little as she clears her throat. "And I am sure Reynard and Preston are happy to see you up."

Clover is silent for a few seconds as she glances to Reynard with an almost saddened expression, she quickly darts back to Bella as she talks in a lower voice. "T-thank you for what you have done with Reynard. I do not know how I can repay such kindness."

"Oh, it was nothing." Bella gives a loving, almost mother like smile to Reynard as she speaks up. "It was very nice having my little friend around so much."

Reynard finally breaks a smile through his sad face as he nods.

Bella turns her attention back to the teapot in her magic as she hovers it to her hand. However, as she touches the bottom of it, she quickly speaks up. "Perhaps when you begin feeling better you could help me with a few spells. I cannot ever seem to get this tea warm enough." Her eyes shift to Preston as she floats the teapot closer to Preston. "Would you be a dear and warm this?"

The comment for a moment strikes Preston as odd, but he speaks up all the same. "Uh... how?"

"Well, just use your magic of course. I find it best to warm it just a little more with magic before it is poured."

Preston gives a little laugh as he just shrugs. "Yea, of course." The man straightens his posture to the chair as he brings a hand up toward the pot, his eyes take on an almost overly concentrated stare as he takes the pot into his magic. With Bella no longer holding it, she takes her seat and begins to say something to Clover.

However, the satyress just nods to her friend's words as she focuses in on Preston's magical hold over the pot. Within a few moments the pot begins to screech as steam pours out from the spout. The sound takes Bella's attention as she motions to take it from Preston's hold. As she stands back up to pour the drink into each cup, Clover's voice comes out. "You did not even ask how?"

Preston gives a little laugh as he speaks up. "Well Lutin has me light the forge sometimes so I figured the same kinda principles apply. Pretty much, I was just hoping it didn't explode over me."

Clover cocks her head a little as she shrugs. "Forge?"

Bella now chimes in as she pours the last drink in front of her. "Oh, yes. Preston works with the *Flóff* in the forge. Not the cleanest of things." Bella gives a little smile as she wags a finger to Preston. "And I have warned him that my clothing is not to get too much smoke."

The small talk from Bella is again ignored a bit by Clover as she speaks up. "Did Elva assign you this?"

Preston shakes his head. "No, not really. And it's not all bad, Lutin is tough but he is not a bad guy."

Once more Bella chimes in as she gives a little laugh. "And it must be good for you. I have had to fit his clothing twice this *mořo*, and your darkening complexion..." Bella holds her eyes to Preston as she gives a friendly smile. "...is very becoming on you with that bright mane."

Preston just gives a little laugh as he wraps his hands to the warm cup in front of him.

Bella continues the chat as she turns now to Clover, her hand extending to the lip of Clover's top as she pulls a little to it. "I do hope you realize you must come in and let me fit your clothing as well, dear."

Clover backs away from Bella's hand a little as she gives a simple laugh. "Yes, of course. But only if you are not busy."

"I am never busy for a friend." Bella brings the cup to her mouth as she takes a sip. Her eyes light up a little as she turns back to Preston. "Oh, this is very good. Perhaps I need to have you around more often, Preston."

The comment just brings a smirk to the man as he shrugs. "As long as you don't have me sew again I'll help." The comment brings another laugh to Bella as the satyress now looks to Reynard across the table. Preston however continues to look over Clover as he notices her beginning to fidget a little in her chair, her eyes continuing to dart down to what Bella pointed out. Clover has never been close to heavy; in fact, she was always quite petite. Although not fragile looking, as she always carried herself with a bit of power in her step. Yet, the month has taken its toll, her whole body looks to have had its life sucked out of it. Literally in how she looks and perhaps now in the way she carries herself. In truth, Preston has never really known Clover's age, but her outward appearance now more closely resembles a young maybe eighteen or nineteen-year-old. Atop this, her eyes look tired and her mane is dull, perhaps the only color she truly maintains is her eyes, though even they have lost some gloss.

Knowing that his stare has lasted a little longer than it should Preston takes a sip of his drink. Clover across from him does the same, still not aware of his stare. Though as the man's eyes linger it does not stay as a stare. Perhaps it is the bland food he gets at camp or maybe it is in fact this weird tea, but a sweet almost gingerbread cookie taste strikes Preston's tongue. The taste quickly stunning the man as he becomes lost to it, though not for long as he turns to Bella. "This tea is really good."

Bella nods, but holds a bit of confusion as she takes herself from the conversation with Reynard. "What did you call it, dear?"

"Oh, sorry." Preston gives a little laugh as he gestured the cup towards her. "This would be called tea where I'm from. And really, I wouldn't have been caught dead drinking this, 'cuz it's healthy for you."

The confusion on Bella's face is masked a little by her smile, but the sight of it forces Preston to explain further. "I'm saying that it's really good, it's like eating a fresh gingerbread or something, it's just good."

Bella pauses for a moment before she just nods with a smile. "Oh, yes. Well I am very pleased to hear you enjoy it." Her sight quickly changes to Clover as she speaks up. "Clover?"

The satyress quickly gives a friendly response as she nods. "Yes, it is quite nice."

Reynard now chimes in as he nods. "It is good, Bella."

The comments seem to bring an even more positive tone from the already friendly Southern Belle as she speaks up. "Well I do blend it myself,

Gwendy helped with the idea, but I shall take the credit. Oh! That reminds me, I am sure she will want to see you Clover."

Clover gives a respectful nod as she speaks up. "Yes, but I do really wish to return to the library. Perhaps, meet with the *Jartál* after I get settled."

"Well Clover, the project is nearly done, from what I have heard. And I am sure your work can wait, yes?"

Clover nods, her hands clenching and unclenching rather quickly as she fidgets. "I would never rush anything. I just wish to show *Jartál* Caféll that I am well."

Bella nods as she takes another sip of her drink for a moment. "Understandable." Bella's smile drifts a little as she studies Clover's mostly still full cup, which to her is a surprise seeing as how Preston has almost downed his and Reynard is close behind already. "Dear, did you eat already?"

For a moment Clover hesitates, but she does speak up as she nods. "I will when I get home."

The comment draws Preston's attention, but Bella chimes in before he can. "W-well dear I am sure you will need to go to the market. Here, let me get you something so-..."

"Actually, I forgot, I ate before I left." Clover nods, her head coming up as she attempts a fake smile.

Bella bites a little to her lip as she drifts her head between Preston and Clover before her own inability to hold off from a conversation takes over yet again. "Dear... you do realize you have to eat a little more with a... with the possibility of a foal, yes?"

Clover glances away, her left hand finally stopping its movement as she nods. "Bella, although I trust that Radisia graduated from his studies, I do question such a bold claim, based solely off a rock."

A short laugh comes from Bella as she places her cup down to the wood coaster. "I of course agree with you, but until you are sure you should-..."

Clover nods quick as she replies. "Yes, yes. I have done my own research into the matter." Clover now takes a sip of her drink as she nods to the books on the other side of the room.

Bella hardly glances to the books as she attempts a warm smile. "I am sure you have. But there should be no problem in precautions, yes?"

Clover is silent for a moment at the suggestion of being wrong. Although not hurt or angered outwardly, it is almost an expression of sadness hidden under her blank pause.

Her lack of response forces Bella to turn back to Preston as she speaks up. "Preston, do you not have anything to say about the matter?"

Preston shrugs slowly as he speaks up. "We'll talk about it."

Bella's eyes widen a little as she gives an almost surprised laugh. "Y-you have not already?"

Clover is still silent as her eyes fall a little to the table. "Is it so hard to imagine someone not enjoying your terrible brew, Bella?"

Preston slowly places his cup to the table, a dumbfounded look to his face at Clover's comment. Reynard too stares in shock, unsure of what to say.

Clover however brings her head up, hardly a care to her expression as she stares to her friend. With no response Bella clears her throat, pushes her hair a little from her face as she speaks up. "Well... I do believe you two should head to the library."

Preston squints to the comment as he watches Bella stand up with her cup now floating beside her. Clover softens to the movement as she watches her friend leave from the table. "You wish for us to leave?"

Bella's stance has taken on an almost preppy tone as she speaks. "Well yes. Reynard and I will have one more night together and you two will talk about a few things."

Clover glances to Reynard, the fox-boy looks a little confused, but he remains silent as Clover again speaks up. "Bella, you have already done so much for me. You do not need to-..."

"No." Bella chances a smile though she cannot fake it as she nods. "There is no problem, my customers enjoy Reynard's courtesy so there is no problem on the shop front and with my sister gone it is nice to have company at night."

Her tone is strong, but Clover continues to protest as she speaks up. "Bella, there is nothing to talk about. I need to visit with *Jartál* Caféll before the *déy* is out anyways."

Bella turns a cocked eye to Clover as she speaks up. "I do believe you said soon, not that soon. If anything, you should be resting after your walk home."

"The library is but a short trot from here, Bella." Clover scoffs. "What is this protest?"

Bella holds her strong tone as she speaks up, her tone downright terrifying as Preston and Reynard merely sit to the edge of their seat. "Well, sometimes you can be wrong Clover, you should accept all possibilities for now."

Preston's eyes raise a little as he watches Clover staring to her friend in silence. Though for the moment, Clover's lack of words may be the best thing for their friendship.

Clover turns her attention to Reynard as she speaks up. "Reynard, do you really wish to stay? Do you not want to go back to normal?"

The trump card is quickly spotted as Bella sneaks a shake of the head towards Reynard as Clover's attention is held.

Reynard shifts his eyes between the two satyresses as he finally speaks up. "I... I think you should have more time to rest, Clover."

Once more Clover is caught silent, but her hushed words only last a moment as she swallows her pride. "Well... that is only if Preston is able to. *Flóff* rules are very difficult to follow."

Preston gives a little laugh as he speaks up. "As long as I can get back before night fall Elva won't say anything."

Bella takes the opportunity to chime in as she nods. "It is settled then, off you go."

Clover stands from the table as she moves to collect her items from the table on the other side of the room. "Very well." She gets halfway across the room before she just uses her magic to teleport the books to her arms. "Come along, Preston."

As Bella watches her friend moving quickly towards the curtain she chimes in. "D-do be careful, dear."

Chapter 16

Rounding Home base

It has been about ten or so minutes since Preston and Clover were asked to leave Bella's house. Clover's magic that once carried the books beside her is no longer present, and instead she carries them as normal. Refusing Preston's offer at every moment. Perhaps not out of anger but just to prove that she is actually fine despite what everyone may think. Overall though, the short walk to the library that now is mere feet away has not brought any doubt to Preston's mind. Although he may not agree with Clover wanting to leave the hospital, he does trust what she says, a fact and a thought that is further supported whenever he brushes a finger to the amulet hidden in his pocket.

Of course, Bella's suggestion to talk has dwelled on Preston's mind since they started out. Even if he is confident, Clover will defy logic do what she wishes.

The town is as normal, lively, but small, neither too crowded nor too bare for its one main street road. However, with the library so close Preston's thoughts do begin to drift away from the world around him and instead to the light brown haired satyress in front of him.

Clover moves to the door as she tries to open it, although she is unable as she finds it locked. "You locked it?"

The comment brings a quick remark from Preston as he nods. "Why wouldn't we? You were gone for so long."

Clover takes a quick sigh as she nods. "The spell on the door would have kept anyone out, but I suppose if it grew weak at least it was locked... do you or Reynard have the key?"

"Uh... Reynard has it."

"Well, Reynard should be with us, but you decided to lay camp with Bella." She sighs. "I do have a way in though." Clover adjust the books in her hold as her left hand takes on a light blue glow, the knob to the door takes on the same magical hue as the sound of a lock clicking comes to Preston's ears.

Clover is the first to step inside, but as she does she lets out a quick cough. The reason for her cough is quick to come to Preston as the strong odor of books strike his nose. "Yeah it was like this the last few times we came here."

"That is because the adhesive that binds the books needs to have fresh air more than a few times a *mořo*." Clover shakes her head as she moves her attention to the table. "Now where were these books pulled from? Once we have them put up, we can open the library for anyone to return books."

"Actually Clover, me and Reynard have been doing that." Preston shrugs. "Figure it would be one less thing for you to do when you woke up."

"Hmmm, I have to admit I am a little surprised." Clover's attention now comes to the bookshelves as she begins to search every row one book at a time.

The methodical process only lasts a few moments for Clover as Preston moves to the table and takes the books. "Why is that surprising?" He walks just a little past Clover to place the books back in the open slots he saw when he came in.

Noticing the books being put away Clover still checks to see if the order is correct, however seeing that they are she replies. "Well, I just would think having new rules to follow and being away would make it too difficult. And I have never enjoyed leaving Reynard to do it, as it is not his responsibility."

"It wasn't that hard." He shrugs. "A few people were pissed about not being able to check out another book. But you know, we did talk about opening back up soon." Preston looks back to the door as he continues. "I don't remember where we put the open sign though."

"I shall find it once I get clean." Just as Clover finishes her comment, she starts her trot to the stairs.

A sigh rolls from Preston as he rubs to the back of his neck, his walk bringing him to the last open slot in the shelves. "Clover, don't you think we should talk?"

A slight laugh comes from Clover as she stops just shy of the first stair. "A quick bath will not stop us from talking."

Preston hesitates as the words mow over in his head, but he still brings his voice up once more, this time just a little lower. "You're not just going to ignore this?"

Clover's eyes roll a little as she turns more to face the man. "Preston, did you agree with Bella because you actually feel as if we need to discuss something?"

"W-well yeah." Preston shrugs as he continues. "We haven't really talked about anyt-..."

"Look Preston..." Clover crosses her arms, her hips swaying a bit annoyed as she explains herself. "...Bella's emotions have led her astray. She is a good friend, but she has had her own obstetrical encounters with stallions that have led her to the way she is acting. So, Preston, I do not think we need to talk. No matter what any say, there is no way I could be carrying your foal, you lack the knowledge of the spell and I would never." Clover gives a little sigh as she continues. "Does this make you feel better?"

Preston turns his head to the ground for a moment in thought before he slowly shakes his head. "Clover, you read the books last night. What did you find?"

The question brings a bit of annoyance to Clover's tone now as she quickly replies. "It does not matter what I have found in the text. The process cannot start without the first step, Preston!"

The tone forces Preston to go into defense mode as he holds his hands to his chest. "Hey, look I don't like the idea any more than you do. I just want to be sure."

Clover's left ear twitches to the comment as she lowers her gaze a little to a more serious look. "Believe me Preston, I would not want it any more than you do."

Preston nods as he speaks up, a bit drafted and bit angry at himself for his sudden outburst. "So… you really don't think you are?"

With a calming breath Clover scoffs. "You have nothing to worry about Preston. Now I will take a quick bath get clean and then we can talk about something else."

"Alright Clover." With a simple smile Preston nods his head, which prompts Clover to head up stairs.

The sound of her hooves clapping to the hardwood floor rings throughout the house for a few minutes as she goes to her room to pick out something else to wear. However, Preston's mindless wandering around downstairs comes to an end as he hears the distinct sound of the magically tied pipes pouring water into the tube upstairs.

Without hesitation Preston starts up, his mind set to the contents under Clover's bed. The door to the bathroom is closed and although Preston has no reason to hide, he nevertheless sneaks past it, covered by the noise of the bath. Like a poorly dressed ninja Preston makes his way into Clover's room.

The room looks completely undisturbed and the door has been left open, two things Preston makes a note of as he kneels down next to Clover's bed. To his surprise, the chest is pulled a bit more to the edge, though he hardly cares as he pulls it out further.

With a quick flick of the lock Clover never seems to use, Preston opens the chest. The few books, her personal journal and a smaller box sit to. Sighting it, Preston smirks knowing all too well the stone is not in it. As Preston pushes the old books aside the stone catches his eyes. Its lackluster hue fooling any would-be thief.

The dull color almost brings a bit of fear to Preston that the stone has run out of power, yet as he brings his hand closer to it, it begins to shine. Preston takes the stone from the chest as he repositions everything and scoots it back under the bed.

His hand is warm from the stone, and its light and the unmistakable chime of magic begins to take over the room from his own increasing emotions. The fear of being caught and questioned, the anxiety of going through with his plan, the guilt of wanting to leave, and finally, the idea of what could have been if he stayed.

Preston quickly moves from the room though and down the hall well past where Clover undoubtedly still is. A hot sweat has begun to pool on Preston's neck as he finds himself in the bottom floor of the library. A room full of books used to inspire, entertain, and inform could not guide Preston in his next action. Instead, he slowly unclenched his hand and just stares to the stone, almost waiting for himself to wake up like last night.

"It's no big deal... heck, just a few weeks ago I was training just to go home. My whole time spent here has been attempting to go home!" His words are stops as he feels a shortness of breath creeping up his chest. "W-what's wrong with me? Nyota has given up so much, I have given up so much, all for the possibility to go home. So why the Hell am I even hesitating." The stone continues to almost block out the shine of the sun in the room as Preston just stares to it, a heavy sigh rolls from Preston as he feels his muscles starting to loosen. "You can do this, Nyota said it would work, Clover is confident, and I've been working for this. J-just focus… come on, there's a lot of people that need to know what happened to Matt and Damien, come on, do it for them!" Preston clenches his eyes tight as he feels the surge of warmth through his body now rushing to his hands. The stone now feels like a hot coal as he continues to try and remember something from home.

His breath turns to panting as he shakes his head. "Come on, imagine your room, that's easy… what a bed, window, desk, computer, come on… just picture it, you know what it looks like." The moments of struggling turn to frustration as every image in Preston's mind begins to grow more and more hazy. "Come on! Come on! The baseball field! Broken down, old, street near it, come on anything! I can see it I got it! Come on, work damn it!"

The tightness of his muscles does little to help him focus, but he pushes forward on the strongest memory, the last time he and Damien practiced baseball. However, as the sound of Preston's magic continues to grow louder to the man's ears, the image of the field begins to become harder to picture. Preston's breathing begins to become a bit more shaky as he realizes his failing spell.

As the man's eyes open a rage fills his actions as he quickly throws the stone in his hand across the room. The magical chime and glow that surrounded the stone quickly chased away as a loud thud rings to the room instead. Unlike a normal thrown object, the stone does not bounce, instead the one simple thud is the only sound that rings to the house.

Preston runs a hand to his forehead as he feels the heat of his body culminating in his brow. Yet, another sound takes Preston's attention as he begins to hear Clover's movements upstairs. Preston quickly moves to pick up the stone and place it into one of his pockets. A little bulge sits to his side where the stone is. Still, the possibility that Clover will notice in her current state is pretty slim, a thought that helps Preston calm down.

With a few sighs Preston catches his breath and begins to cool. However, his mind now burns with the desire to ask Clover why the stone did not work, yet, with everything that has happened, telling Clover that he tried to leave in secret may not be the best idea.

The sounds of Clover's hooves now on the wood grow more frequent as Clover undoubtedly begins into the hallway upstairs. Without even thinking about it, Preston's right hand moves over his pocket, almost as if he were hiding it as he moves to meet Clover at the end of the stairs.

Clover's face still has the same thin, and paler complexion as before. But, the satyress' light brown hair now has a more lively bounce to it, and the sight of her normal darker earth colored brown and dark green clothing does make her look a little healthier, or at the very least, more comfortable.

As she comes down the stairs Clover squints to where Preston stands. "You did not wait by standing the whole time, did you?"

Preston shrugs the question off as he replies. "Naw, I uh, heard you coming down the stairs and I didn't want you to fall or anything. You might be weak from the bath."

Clover cocks a slight smirk to the comment as she speaks up. "I know my limits, I may be a little tired, but that does not mean I am not thinking."

"Never would question you, Happy-Hooves."

Clover stops in her trot as she looks to be thinking over the comment. "You have not called me that in a while, yes?"

"Uh, well probably not. But, you know, kinda hard to say anything to you last month." Preston just cocks a smile, tapping into his pocket as he looks away.

"Hmm..." Clover looks around the library as she slowly brings her voice out. "Do I open the library or do I venture to the *Jartál*."

A slight laugh comes from Preston as he speaks up. "If you are feeling that much better why don't we just do more practice for Nyota?"

Clover's ear flicks to the comment as she quickly turns back to him. "Practice for Nyota? Oh! You mean for your spell, yes?"

"Yea." Preston shrugs. "Been awhile, maybe I've forgotten some stuff. Yea?"

Clover taps her hand to her mouth as she nods. "I do hope I can remember where I have placed his stone... I believe I have it-..."

"I have it." Without a moment of hesitation Preston quickly pulls the stone from his pocket as he stumbles through a lie. "I kept it when you fell asleep. You said it was important, so I didn't want anything to happen to it."

For a moment Clover looks a little skeptical at the comment, but as she looks over the stone she nods. "Y-yes. I believe I remember that." She continues to study the stone as she cocks her head a little to the left. "When I was... away, did you ever try to use it? The stone will just amplify your spell, all you need is to focus on a powerful thought and it will work."

Preston shakes his head as he speaks up. "No, I want more practice. Maybe, a better way of explaining how I use it, you know?"

Clover shrugs a little to the comment as she replies. "For a spell of that magnitude it is all about your thoughts and emotions, the stronger your desire the stronger your spell. Any matter, I do hope you will agree with me. While I may feel better, I do believe I should perhaps stay away from training, just for the *déy*."

Preston nods as he speaks up. "Fair enough." He moves the stone back to his pocket as he gives a silent disappointed sigh.

"Preston, perhaps you should allow me to take the stone."

The man is quick to shake his head to the comment as he plays it off. "It's alright Clover, I haven't lost it yet."

Clover gives a quick smile as she nods. "Yes, I suppose that is true." The smile fades almost as soon as it appears to her face as she continues. "Are you sure?"

Preston nods as he pats his pocket. "I've had it this whole time, Clover."

"Hmm..." Clover turns her eyes to the door as she speaks up. "Well, then I do believe it is time I seek out *Jartál* Caféll. I am sure a lot has changed since I fell ill. Do you wish to come with me?"

Preston shrugs. "Not sure if I could talk you out of it so sure... not going to eat anything?"

Clover gives a little laugh as she waves her hand to the comment. "I will need to stop by the market after our visit with *Jartál* Caféll. I had planned to retrieve Reynard from Bella after our trip, this way she can be satisfied with us having the proper amount of time to talk." Clover's tone changes a little as she looks to Preston. "You do agree we have talked, yes?"

A faint chuckle rolls from Preston. "Sure." He nods. "But, that's the whole other side of town? You sure you don't want to eat something sooner?"

Clover gives a little bow as she speaks up. "You have my word, Preston, I shall eat once Reynard is home. Now come." At the end of her breath she starts towards the door and waits for Preston to follow after her.

With little hesitation Preston moves past the satyress beside him as he stands to the edge of the street. Clover's hands take on a light blue glow as she most likely puts some spell to the door though she does not explain why.

Sighting it, Preston speaks up, merely attempting some small talk. "I've always wondered, Did Nyota teach you that or no?"

Clover looks away from the door as she finishes her spell. "Actually, the spell I use is a *Dújarx*."

A quick look of confusion crosses Preston face as he shakes his head. "What's that mean?"

The know it all tone comes through Clover rather fluently as she nods her head. "It is a spell of two schools of *Márjx*. An *Álter* spell to change the material within the lock, and a *Eñchar* spells to reverse it at a hand I deem safe. The spell will not allow any holding malicious thoughts within the library."

Preston thinks the explanation over for a moment before shaking his head. "But why not just lock it? How do you know it will work every time?"

Clover just rolls her eyes to the question as she starts towards the road. "A lock is easily picked or altered; the second part of my spell stops any magical attempts while the first part negates any picking."

"But if someone wanted into the house, they could just smash the window."

Though Preston's comment carries some logic, Clover shakes her head, a laugh rolling from her. "Someone would see the window? Just do not worry about it Preston it is just a-..."

"Clover!"

The hyper and almost shrieking feminine voice quickly steals Clover's attention, as well as a few others to the street, as both Preston and Clover turn to its source. The happily jogging cat-woman holds a toothy smile as she continues to talk even before she is the proper conversation's distance away. "Oh! Thank the *Shánbá*, you have awoken Clover!"

As normal the bright colors of Gwendy's clothing almost make the light reddish-orange furred *Cáftys* look to be dressed as a clown. However, despite the conflicting colors of her fur with the brighter colors of her clothing, she does pull it off rather well, perhaps only because of her bubbly personality.

"Gwendy, hello. I was going to stop by when I went to-..."

"No, no, no!" The cat-woman quickly cuts Clover off as she continues. "You must still be very weak, Gwendy wanted to bring you some of your favorite *BlekBúrry cúffys* to help you get well!" Gwendy brings the covered basket more into view in front of her as she holds it out to Clover. "Gwendy will come back for the *braskó* later. Go on, try one, try one!"

Clover hesitates for a moment before she takes the basket from Gwendy. "Uh, thank you Gwendy. But you really did not have to-..."

Once more the hyper cat shakes her head as she speaks up. "Gwendy wanted to, and do not worry about telling Gwendy anything, Bella already has informed Gwendy of everything!" With a smile still to Gwendy's whiskered face she bends down a little to Clover's stomach as she continues to speak. "Gwendy hopes you enjoy the *Cúffys*, little one."

The action, albeit a bit strange does have a sweet notice to it. However, Clover quickly reacts by turning herself from Gwendy as she looks now toward the door. "I suppose I should get these inside before we head out."

Gwendy cocks her head a little as she speaks up. "Where would you be going?" Gwendy continues. "You should be lying about! When one of ours bears cubs we pamper them, treat them better than the Princess herself, it is the only way to ensure a healthy little one after all." She giggles as he rolls a hand to Preston. "Gwendy does not have to worry about that though, Gwendy can have more fun, as her farm yields none, ha-ha!" The giddy tone does not halt as she trails on. "So where are you going?"

The comment stops Clover just short of finishing her spell on the door as she draws a blank. "Uh...."

Noticing the stutter Preston speaks up as he looks to the cat eyed woman before him. "Just walking around for a few minutes. You know, trying to clear our heads."

Gwendy holds her smile as her high-pitched tone continues. "Gwendy knows! Have you tried warm *Cawlf* milk? Oooh, it works wonders on the mind."

Clover gives a friendly laugh as she nods. "We may have to. But we were just about to head out and-..."

"*Plestá déy!*" Gwendy gives a little bow as she laughs. "Gwendy knows you are busy Clover. Stop by the shop when you get a moment of rest." The cat-woman's attention turns to Preston as she smiles. "*Plestá déy*, to you as well tall-one!"

With a friendly exchange, Gwendy turns back towards the road she came up as she begins to happily walk away. As she gets out of earshot Clover sighs and speaks up in a low voice. "I am surprised she did not ask to join us."

The door opens as Clover trots back inside, the basket firmly in her grasp. However, as she moves insisted Preston moves to the door's threshold as he talks. "You're lucky she didn't hear you. It was a nice thing she did."

Clover places the basket to the center of the table as she nods. "I do not doubt the thought and it was very nice of her. However, I do not need gifts to feel welcomed. Furthermore, now I will feel obligated to do something for her. I suppose both her and Bella must be running low on *Kélf* stones..."

"I'm sure they would be happy with you just talking to them."

A slight smile comes to Clover's face as she nods. "Gwendy is happy with any conversation; the problem is leaving. Bella would only wish to inform me of what everyone else has done while I was asleep." Clover rubs a hand to her forehead as she takes a deep breath.

However, as she begins to near the door Preston stops her. "Try a cupcake thing Clover. You need to eat something."

A slight laugh comes to Clover as she moves back to the basket. "Yes, of course, a *Cúffy*, that should fill me."

Preston shrugs as he speaks up. "Just eat it and we'll head out."

Chapter 17

Capital Training

As normal, the walk from the library to the town hall has been quiet. Few workers have been seen coming from the direction and unlike the past couple of weeks. In truth, the last time Preston saw the train area it was mostly done; the feat was both utterly surprising and at the same time, not unexpected. Especially seeing as how the *télpréith* Clover created was able to continue working without her tending to it. A show of her everlasting power ever on display. As the thoughts about how far the project has come begin to circle inside Preston's mind, he turns to the satyress walking just a few steps before him. "Hey, dumb question. Do you know how far the train tracks have gotten?"

Clover shakes her head as she speaks up. "How would I? None at the *Héthtex* clinic talked of it."

A slight laugh rolls through Preston as he nods. "Oh, so you'll be surprised."

The comment continues to hold Clover's attention as she looks to the yellow-hay topped roof of the town hall just up the road. The train tracks are still not insight yet but as they grow near the work area they come into view.

Unlike conventional work areas the workers never put up any fences or signs warning people to stay out of the area, instead it was always quite the opposite. The town, as well as the workers have always thought the project was a joke, seeing as how no one truly understands what is being built. The workers enjoy the money, and the town enjoys the laugh at seeing the pointless tracks. Yet, as the Town Hall comes within distance Clover trots past it and instead moves to look over the mostly completed train station.

Preston follows after her as he looks the area over. The road that use to lead out of town is still visible, but the large pavilion like construction that covers it as well as the tracks where the ticket building is still being built out of stone now dwarfs its importance. Not that the road had much use after the mine's attack.

The forest has been pushed back and the metal and wooden tracks shine to the sun light. The sound of hammers striking wood and the sight of *Dwoff* workers as far as the eye can see still suggest the project is not finished, but as Clover looks the area over, she speaks up. "How does it look Preston?"

One side of the area is nothing but stacked logs and cut trees, the other nearest the *télpréith* is littered with large wood crates most likely housing the material needed for the tracks. Yet, the tracks themselves look mostly done, at least in the direction towards the Capital as far as Preston can see. "Yeah, looks good. How far will the tracks go?"

Clover studies the area before her as she speaks up. "*HefterÁll* is the closest city to the Capital. From what I remember, the plan is to connect *HefterÁll*, *VéturVill*, and the Capital. Later Princess Sóltina wishes to connect *BalláVill*, *GráfUall*, and *Passvórtall*. Although, those three would be the hardest to connect *BalláVill* is far too close to the sea, *GráfUall's* lands are sandy and would surely be too shifting for these tracks and you know as well as I do that *Passvórtall* is too mountainous. And with the *ÉverMoar* so thick I see no way for this train to connect any city but this and the Capital." She sighs. "Of course, Dif refused to work unless the outer settlements were included before these, so I do not know what agreements have been forged while I rested."

A slight laugh comes from Preston as he shrugs. "Bridges could solve some of the problems, and tracks can go on sand. They have them in the desert where I'm from."

Clover rolls her eyes as she turns back to the town hall. "What bridge could hold such weight?"

"You'd be surprised."

Clover holds a friendly demeanor to the comment, but as Preston ends she speaks up. "I have always thought *Passvórtall's* bridge was nice, do you know of a longer one?"

"Oh yea, plenty." Preston bites to his lip as the name escapes him. "But... I can't think of its name."

"Hm." Clover nods. "Perhaps you need your own rest, Preston."

Before the man can contest the comment Clover's attention is turned to the guard now coming forth from the Town Hall's door. "Are you here to speak with *Jartál* Caféll. If not, do not stand near construction."

"Actually, I am." Clover gives a simple bow. "Clove Vines here to see the *Jartál*."

The name seems to draw a bit confusion to the *Dẁoff*, though in his stupor Preston merely looks him over. The Guard is clad in a dark, leather armor top, with gold and black colored wool sleeves coming out underneath where the armor's protection ends at his shoulders. He wields a heavy looking spear that he has sitting to the ground, his lower body is covered as his top in leather with the same gold and black colored wool where the leather armor ends. "Clover Vine?" The guards look Clover over a little skeptical as he continues. "Thought you was ill?"

Clover's left ear flicks to the comment as she reluctantly nods. "It was no *desatá*, it was a mishap with my magic when I killed the *Koá-Koé* that was attacking the town. I am sure you were at your post that day."

The guard's face goes straight as he stands a little more proper. "Y-yes. Welcome back Miss Vines." He motions for the duo to follow him back to the Town Hall.

With a nod, Clover starts into the bright yellowish light of the rounded building. Preston follows in behind her as he gives his own little nod to the guard.

As the door closes behind them Preston moves to Clover's side as he speaks up. "A little cranky?"

Clover raises an eyebrow to the man as she replies. "It was not a sickness. It was an unforeseen mishap."

Preston turns his head to the upper levels of the round building as he nods. "Mhm."

Clover looks around the building as she notices the plethora of armed *Dẃoffs* in the building. In truth, most are young, and truthfully not in the best physical condition weight wise to be considered a strong guard of the *Jartál*. Yet, despite their appearance and general, less than unserious look to them the sight of them does spark a thought to Clover as she shakes her head. "Perhaps we will head to the stairs and ask the guards to inform her of our presence."

"Makes sense." Preston waits for Clover to take the lead, as she does, he follows behind her. The banners hanging from the top floor now all show the insignia of the Capital, with only the hold's insignia near the bottom of it. The color of the banners however being white and gold do match with the bright room's shine however.

It only takes a few seconds for Clover and Preston to go up to the second level. But as they reach the guards at the bottom of the second stairs they stop, the guards quickly assume their roles, albeit with a slightly unprofessional tone. "Oi, what be your business?"

"Clover Vines, here to speak with *Jartál* Caféll."

The pig nosed, and hairy faced *Dẃoffs* squint to Clover for a moment before the taller one on the right snaps his fingers. "Vines! You killed the *Koá-Koé*!"

The other guard quickly speaks up as he nods his head. "The *Jartál* is having the *GřavTrender* clean the *Koá-Koé* head, it will be mounted in the hall. First trophy of the *VéturVill* guard that is not *Mostrér* pelt."

A smirk comes to Clover's head as she nods. "Oh?"

The guard continues as he nods. "It was the first attack *VéturVill* has had since the *Wóvátor* was powered by that *Únoff maná*."

Clover nods as she replies. "You mean the repellent spell."

"Aye." A slight laugh rolls between the two *Dẃoffs* as they speak up. "You wished to see the *Jartál*, yes? We will inform her." As the comment ends the guard on the left starts up the stairs behind him.

As he leaves the taller guard still in front of Clover and Preston continues to talk. "You looked over the Capital's project, right?"

"Yes."

The guard nods as his smile holds. "You tricked the Princess into it right? The *Ord'* the *Jartál* has received has been used all over town, guard ranks have bolstered quite a bit." A snort comes from the pig-man as he continues. "*Brivtó* to you."

Clover gives a friendly chuckle. "The train will work."

The guard leans forward a little. "Is it true that this whole idea was a *Dẃoff*'s in *HefterÁll*?"

Clover pauses for a moment before nodding. "Yes. I believe it was a steam engine he was working on that lead him to-..."

Another snorting laugh comes from the man as he nods. "What a *joás*."

The sight of the pig-man jiggling a little brings a little smile to Preston's face as he just nods to the *Dẃoff*'s laugh.

Clover however seems unamused to the laughter as she turns her attention to the top of the stairs where the other guard now returns.

"Miss Vines, *Jartál* Caféll will see you."

Clover gives a friendly little nod to the guard as she moves past him and upstairs. Preston follows behind her as he too nods to the guard.

The stairs only take a few moments to traverse as Clover sets her sights to Caféll's room. Clover's magic takes over the right door of the double doors as she opens it. The scent of pine trees strikes Preston's nose, despite the view of the long oak table being the first thing Preston notices in the bright light of the window at the back of the room. However, the man's sight is quickly changed as the familiar autumn haired, pig nosed, creamy white skinned *Dẃoff*. Caféll's red, almost bark colored robes blend in a little with the wall behind her, but the unmistakable jewels to her hands suggest her nobility, along with the softer voice that meets Clover and Preston's ears. "Clover Vines!"

Despite the fact that Caféll stands up behind her desk she does not move to greet Clover. Sure it would make sense for a ruler of a city to not openly go and hug anyone who returns to the Town Hall, but the fact that *Jartál* Caféll is more of a mayor rather than a king or queen as the other cities would suggest a more friendly display than just standing up. Then again, the fact that Caféll does not have a throne for herself like the other hold masters has always been something Preston has questioned.

Caféll's voice continues. "I had heard of your accident, and I cannot tell you how thrilled I am to see you better. Please take a seat."

Clover nods to the comment as she takes a seat across the table from the middle aged *Dẃoff*. "Thank you for your concern *Jartál*."

Caféll waits for Preston to take the seat next to Clover before she herself sits. This however, does not stop her from talking as she holds a finger up. "I must say, I am surprised you have come back so quickly. From what I have heard around town you have only been awake for perhaps a *déy*, yes?"

"Yes."

"Hm..." Caféll nods as she adjusts a few papers that sit next to her. "Were you able to speak with Elden? Your brother ventured into town looking for you."

Clover shakes her head as she speaks up. "I understand he left before I woke."

"Oh, then you will need to send a letter to him. He made it very clear to me and my assistant that he had not been informed of your status." Caféll gives a little laugh as she takes on a confused squint. "Which... I did not understand. I informed the Princess of our attack and of your wellbeing. She made it seem as if she would pass the information on."

Clover thinks the comment over a little before she nods. "I am sure she held the news from my brother for good reason. Perhaps she was awaiting more news."

Caféll nods as she continues. "I do have a few letters from the Capital, we held them in case they were important." The woman slides a few unopened letters from the stack of papers next to her to Clover as she continues. "One is from the Princess which I found peculiar, the other is from a Svle Nyota and the last one seemed to be a payment from the Capital for your services. It will be delivered from our purse *témont*, now that you can claim it you see." A smile comes to Caféll's face as she nods. "You will be happy to hear how well the project has come."

For a moment the comment goes unheeded as Clover looks over the two letters, however she focuses in on Nyota's letter as she rubs her hand to the red wax seal that covers it. However, she quickly comes back to the conversation at hand as she speaks up. "Yes, how has the *télpréith* been? Has anyone charged it?"

A slight laugh comes from Caféll as she speaks up. "Your spell was expertly crafted, the Princess did send someone to check it but they saw no problems with your work."

Clover's eyes widen a little as she nods. "W-well, how far has the project come?"

"You should be delighted to know that the um... tracks as it were, have reached just pass *Féllcreed*. Of course, the workers did get some help from the local *Flóff* populace. They were reluctant to help an *Únoff* and *Dẃoff* project, but the idea of having us further away from their cloud seemed to give them a gentle push to help. From the Princess's reports even the *Flóff Pegpolis* have agreed to aid in the future through the *ÉverMoar* towards *HefterÁll*." Another light laugh comes from the woman as she continues. "Of course, that information is only known to a select few as Princess Sóltina and Emperor Gust have not completed their arrangements."

Clover sits in silence as she slowly takes it all in.

Her lack of a response, however, does little to deter the talkative leader of *VéturVill*. "I have even been asked to seek court with the *Jartál* of *Passvórtall* in the coming *moŕos*. My position in *pĺiht* will be ensured once the citizens of *VéturVill* hear I have secured more trade routes." A light sigh comes from Caféll as she slowly comes back to the people before her. "Overall, there is nothing to report... did you need something?"

"May I see the planned map, I do not recall where I have placed mine."

Caféll nods as she speaks up. "I shall have my cartographer make you a copy. Although..." Caféll leans forward a little more as she speaks up. "Are you not done with your obligations?"

Clover blinks in silence to the comment as she slowly nods. "I-I was asked to oversee the project-..."

"But you have! Your plans were very thorough, and I have ensured everyone has followed them." Caféll holds her posture in her chair as she waves her hand. "I dare say you have done your part... u-unless you desire to handle more of the trivial speeches to the workers and merchants in town."

Clover shakes her head as she gives a friendly smile. "No, I am not looking to spread my name."

"Oh." Caféll clears her throat as she shrugs. "I do not blame you; the work is rather tedious. But I do so enjoy working for the betterment of this fair town." A laugh rolls through the pig-nosed woman as she trails on. "So, is there anything else you desire, Miss Vines?"

With a slow shake of the head Clover speaks up. "Just the map, if I have any concerns I will come see you."

"Very well, Miss Vine. *Plestá déy.*"

Clover nods to the comment as she takes the letter from the table and stands. Preston follows her lead with his own nod, but Caféll seems to not notice as she moves the stack of papers in front of her again. As Clover leads the trot outside of the room she removes the seal on the first letter and begins to read it for Preston to hear.

"Dear Clover, I have no doubt that you shall wake within the *mořo*, as such, I hope you take the proper time to get well. It has been *wek* since I last heard of your condition, I am sure that the healers in your town have been doing everything in their power to ensure your wellbeing. As such, I have decided to keep some information from your kin, Elden and Cherisa's presences at my side has become paramount in my own sister's absence. I hope you will forgive this, and I sincerely hope this letter will grace your eyes soon. If it does, I desire for you to know how thankful I am of what you have done for *VéturVill* and for Artésque. I look forward to seeing you again, sincerely, Sóltina."

Preston merely shakes his head. "When did she write that? Elden rolled in here saying he knew nothing."

Clover shakes her head as she turns the letter over. "It has no date."

"That's bull-crap, she can't just keep stuff like that."

The comment seems to hold no weight to Clover as she brushes it off. "The Princess has her reasons..."

Though the words bring a surprised expression to Preston he nevertheless holds his hand out for the letter as Clover hands it to him and begins to unseal Nyota's. Unlike other, Clover studies the words a bit more carefully as she remains silent. However, after a few minutes she speaks up. "Nyota's letter makes no sense?"

Preston looks over the letter as he replies. "Well what does it say?"

Clover shakes her head as she holds the letter to Preston's sight. "Look, it begins in *nervál*, then the words are spelled as if he were writing new-tongue. Master Nyota has never struggled with the words...." She shakes her head. "This date too? Why would he not come visit before this letter?"

"Well... maybe he's been busy. What does it say?"

Clover takes the letter back to her as she studies it. For a moment she shakes her head as she struggles to read it. "I believe he was asking how we were. But, it also looks as if he were saying something about the Capital. Perhaps the Capital's school has neared completion?" Clover pauses for a moment as she slowly continues. "I must venture to the Capital... Elden would enjoy it more than a letter and I clearly need to see Master Nyota."

Preston shrugs a little, the letter in his hand falling to his side as he speaks up. "Well you'll be out of the library so you won't stress over reorganizing everything."

The comment draws a flick of the ear from Clover as she turns an eye to the man. "You are being rather supportive?"

Preston merely chuckles, his free hand dug into his pocket as he strokes to the amulet hidden within it. "No sense in arguing, I don't win."

"Yes..." Clover folds the letters as she gives a little laugh. "Of course, Reynard may say something... I suppose I can wait; a letter should precede my arrival anyways." As her comment ends she starts towards the staircase, however she only goes a few steps before she turns back to Preston, who has just begun to follow after her. "Still nothing to say to this?"

"Well, do you want the truth?"

"Yes." Clover nods. "Why would I not?"

"Okay." Preston clears his throat, his hand coming from his pocket as he speaks up. "Elden acted crazy when he came here, I get that you need to see him, and I know I can't stop you from seeing Nyota... I just... I don't like it. I don't like that Sóltina knew, I don't like any of it." He nods. "I'd show Elden that letter, make him apologize to Bella, and definitely to Reynard."

Clover shrugs. "I agree."

A chuckle rolls from Preston. "Not so confident, what are you happy Elden didn't know?"

"You will not be allowed from your camp, correct?" Clover's decision to ignore the comment draws a smirk from Preston, though as he eases his hand back to his pocket he nods.

"I think it depends on when, Clover. I have a job to do at the camp, and I don't get to leave unless I get permission. Heck, without Elva letting me I wouldn't have been able to see you today."

"Oh, yes, of course." Clover nods her head a little as she looks the man over. "I understand *Flóff* rules to be fairly harsh." The woman's head falls a bit as she knocks her left hand to the simple wood railing of the stairs. "Why would you go through so much just to come visit me sleep?"

Preston pauses as he chews a little to his cheek. "Truth?"

Clover squints to the comment. "Of course?"

"I-I felt guilty, Clover." Preston shrugs, a freeing feeling coming to his chest as he speaks up plainly.

"Guilty?" Clover shakes her head as she comes to the stairs Preston stopped at, her tired eyes casting over the man. "But why?"

"It's our fault that thing woke up, and it's not like I could just leave Reynard alone?" Preston holds his voice down, but he still checks behind him a little to ensure no one is listening as he continues. "It felt good being there, feeling like I helped."

The soft blue eyes Clover had pinned to Preston's face turn away as Clover's shoulders straighten. "You owe me no debt, Preston, it was unnecessary."

A slight laugh comes to the man as he wipes his right thumb across his nose with a snort. "You know, I really hate this."

Clover's left ear flicks to the comment as she draws her gaze back, though Preston continues his apathetic complaint. "I hate trying to guess what you're saying."

Clover shrugs. "What are you talking about?"

"Oh my..." Preston passes the letter in his hand to Clover as he nods, a smile to his face as he begins to move past the satyress.

The letter drops to Clover's side as she swings back to the man now starting down the stairs, with a bit of speed Clover comes to Preston's side. "Where are you going?"

A laugh rolls from Preston as he nods. "I'm going for a walk, I'll see you back at the library."

"Preston, I do not understand you-..."

Preston turns around, his voice spiking up, though not truly a yell. "I know, I know you don't understand. I don't care, just-..."

The spikes in Preston's voice has sparked a low green glow to the man's hands, something Clover quickly takes notice to as she steps closer to the man. She moves her right hand to his arm as she glances around the building. "Preston, please calm down. We are surrounded by guards."

A laugh rolls from Preston as he looks around the room. "Ooooh, yea, yea." He continues his giddy chuckle as he nods. "I know, be quiet, just stay quiet."

His voice echoes to the circular building; and it is as if everyone in the room has come to the conversation as Clover attempts once more to hush the man. However, it is not the words that bring Preston's voice down, instead it is Clover's touch. Her hand comes to Preston's face as she studies the man's eyes.

The determination in Clover's face mixed with the gentle touch brings a pause to Preston, a bit of labored breathing now taking hold as he looks the woman over. However, her hands move to his chest as presses to the armor under his shirt. "You... you do not wear your-..." Distracted, Clover's right hoof slips a little to the step, but Preston quickly shoots his hand to catch her. A bit embarrassed, Clover regains her balance as she moves down the stairs a little more from Preston. Her voice holds to a low but still frightened almost aggravated tone as she speaks up. "H-how long, Preston? How long have you not been wearing it?"

"Oh like it matters." Preston shakes his head as he replies. "It broke when-..."

"Broke? Preston that amulet is to stop you from-..." Clover shuts her lips tight as she looks the man over.

The sudden tightening of her lips does not spur Preston forward, instead, and very calmly Preston nods. "To stop what, Clover?"

Clover's lips loosen as she nods, a sure tone coming to her words. "It stops nothing, it is merely to help."

"I'm fine." Preston gestures to himself. "Bit of sweat on my neck, hands shake a little, I bite my nails like normal, but I'm fine, everyday, I'm fine."

"Preston, that is not the point. No one knows how an *Atémor* acts. No one knows how to reverse it. The sickness is a transformation, the more raw magic, the more unstable emotions you carry, the more you hurt yourself."

"You said before I didn't need the amulet." Preston again gestures to himself. "I've not changed and I've been a wreck since you got hurt." He chuckles, a bit surprised that he could admit it so easily, even still he pushes on. "But guess what? I'm fine, I don't need to wear it."

"And how do you deal with your emotions?" Clover shakes her head. "I remember how you would act, you cannot have just-..."

"Fine, fine." Preston pulls the amulet from his pocket as he speaks up, a bit vexed to the continued questioning. "So I get a bit upset? I use this. I get a bit sad? I use this. I can't sleep? I use this! Getting the picture?"

Clover lowers her head as she speaks up. "Preston, please. Your voice. Come home with me, we can talk about this there."

"No, no listen." Preston clenches his hand as he points to Clover, his tight fist to the amulet. "I question why I'm still here every day, and when it gets to me, when I think about it too long, do you know what I do?" Without a comment he sparks his magic, though the spell takes a second to spark in the dull glow of the amulet Preston pulls it all the same, a deep sigh rolling from him as he feels its effects.

Clover however pushes the man's hand down as she strikes a more disappointed tone. "The amulet was to help maintain a healthy balance, not to bury your emotions, Preston."

A dopey smile comes to Preston as he sluggishly puts the amulet to his pocket.

The lack of a response however brings Clover forward as he moves into his sight. "Do you hear me?"

A calm reply comes to Preston as he nods. "I can't go back with you, Clover. If I don't go back to camp I'll get kicked out."

"Preston asking you to leave was a mistake, I enjoyed your company, and I see now you cannot be left alone. I am sorry."

Clover's words, albeit, strong and empowered by her locked gaze are not shared with the rest of her body language. The confidence in her shoulders is absent, and her stance is even wobbly, a simple breeze looks to be able to knock her, and for some reason this holds to Preston's mind he speaks up. "I can't forget what you said before, that you're scared of me, Clover. You get angry with me, we fight, and we never talk... I want to go with you, but it's just going to cause problems." He shrugs, his tone rather nonchalant thanks to the spell still swirling within him. "I still care about you, and I don't know why. I can't keep doing this, Damien and Matt's parents have the right to know what's happened. I can't deny them that just because I have feelings for you. I can't deny them that just because I'm scared of accepting I lived. Nothing is going to change here, first day up and all you want to do is run around, you want to solve some problem instead of just relax, and I don't get it. I don't want to do that." He shakes his head. "I probably shouldn't be saying any of this, but the amulet works pretty quick now, ha-ha. B-besides Clover, you have a life here. I've been passed around for months now, I've not done anything for anyone. I sleep, eat, and survive off the people around me, that's not living."

The words echo to the building and Clover's eyes lower, same as her ears as she stands in silence. Her stance quickly suggests to Preston that she is in fact sad, however, at the moment, nothing Preston has said was untrue. This in mind, Preston cannot bring himself to flat out comfort the woman before him, though he cannot walk away all the same. "Clover I just-..."

"Is everything alright?"

The sound of the guard's voice as he now comes up the stairs sparks Clover's head back up as she replies with a smile. "Oh, yes. We were just about to leave."

The guard nods to the comment as he begins the slow descent of the stairs. As he does Clover turns her gaze back to Preston, her eyes are a bit red, but her voice stays calm as she nods. "I understand, Preston." The smile to her face holds as she looks a little to the ground. "You no longer have to feel guilty, and you have no obligated to stay. You were a task assigned to me, my responsibility to you is to ensure you are well. So please, come with me to the Capital, Nyota can fix the amulet and you can return to the camp. Afterwards, we will continue your training and you will be home before next *wek*. You do not have much left to learn, and a *déy* or two venture to the Capital with me will not have you removed from camp. I will see to it."

Preston just nods to the comment as he clears his throat. "Fine."

Clover gives a little smile as she nods. "Good." Clover passes a simple smile as she nods. "You can go to the camp now, your whole reason for being allowed out was because Elva believed I was carrying a foal."

The comment brings a slight smirk to Preston's face as he nods. "I-I guess it's kinda silly to think that. Actually, it's crazy, wh-what would it even look like, you know? Some monster?"

Catching to the smirk on the man's face Clover responds. "Most *Cróffs* take after their mothers in appearance, though we do not even need to discuss this." Clover rolls her hand. "It is a foolish notion."

Preston just nods to the comments as he fiddles in his pocket. "Yea... so, one more trip?"

Clover nods. "I shall send for you late *témont*, Preston."

"Alright." With a sigh Preston speaks up. "You heading home?"

"No." Clover waves her hand once more to the man. "I will talk with the *Jartál* once more and then I shall retrieve Reynard. Head to camp, Preston, I shall be fine."

"Good." Preston gives a simple sigh, his hand still resting to the amulet in his pocket. He knows leaving is the wrong thing to do, especially with everything Clover has been through. But the simple truth is that he does not care, the amulet's numbing effects clearly taking over and clouding his judgment. There is no magic word to stop Clover from who she is, and there are no special incantations to bring back the joy Preston once had at being at her side. Merely half an afternoon later and Preston has found himself eyeing the door. Yet, as he lingers, he speaks up. "No, let me go with you, Bella won't believe it if you're alone."

Reluctant, though open to the comment, Clover nods. "Okay."

Chapter 18

Step One

Reynard needed no convincing of Preston's leave once Bella was assured of their lie. Yet, that fact hardly weighs to Preston's mind as he walks away from town. Unlike the normal fifteen or so minute walk to the hospital Preston has grown use to, the much lengthier almost twenty or so minute walk has started to wear Preston down. Despite the medieval footwear, the man's heels and feet are perfectly fine, the expertly crafted and magically enriched boots doing well throughout the venture home. Unfortunately, it is the man's thighs and legs that burn from the trek.

However, with a long sigh Preston pushes forward, as each step brings him closer to the camp's gate.

Interestingly, and despite how close Preston has gotten, whoever the scout is in the fields around the camp has done a poor job watching out for people approaching the camp. As Preston now nears the gate with still no greeting. Of course, Ellette has let him pass by without a greeting on some occasions, though Preston is unsure if she was on duty today.

It takes perhaps a minute more for Preston to reach the gate, yet again to his surprise, no one greets him with the customary, "halt, who goes there" speech. However, one thing that does greet Preston's ears is a commotion beyond the gate. The wood is tightly fastened so he is unable to see through any cracks, but the voices are one of two things, yells or cheers. Both of which can be equally as terrifying as Preston has learned.

With no response from the gatekeeper Preston bangs to the gate, his hand dipping to his sword as he does. "Hey?! Anyone in there?"

For a moment nothing happens, yet as another second passes a *Flóff* appears from above the gate. The unmistakable coloring of the avian-man is quickly recognized as Umiko speaks up. "Ah, *preiśty*, why not just fly over?"

"Funny." Preston moves his hand from his waist as he nods. "What's going on?"

Umiko looks back to something in camp as he continues. "Fleet-fra challenged Elwine, not a very fair fight. But she rejected his advances." He trails on. "Their spar now plays as an enjoyment for us."

Preston squints to the comment as he shakes his head. Fleet-fra is a prick, that much Preston has learned about Stysen's right hand lacky. Of course, like everyone else in the camp, he is well versed when it comes to fighting, and boasts a physique that keeps Preston from speaking his mind. Luckily, their exchanges have always been brief; though the idea of Elwine forced into a fight with him is not something that sits well with Preston.

Elwine of course is trained, and her well-toned and well-kept armament would suggest this fact. Though, Preston has never seen her fight, let alone leave her normal post at the gate. "Why would she accept?"

Umiko holds a smile as he continues. "As I said, she was challenged."

Preston shakes his head. "Open the gate."

"Hmmm...." Umiko sinks below the gate, and for a second Preston thinks he has just gone back to watching the fight, however as the gate begins to move Preston holds his tongue.

With the gate open Preston's eyes turn to the gathering near the watchtower in the center of camp. "Our fair *Pexřá* seemed not to enjoy the spare, though Stysen supported the challenge."

"I'm sure you didn't say anything?"

A smirk comes to Umiko's face as he shrugs. "A stream I choose not to drink from, yes."

Preston moves closer to the group with Umiko beside him, however the cheering, and sounds of swords clashing draw them in closer. The ever-animated wings of the onlookers surrounding the tight circle however yield little for Preston to see though.

Umiko however finds no problem with this as he brings himself from the ground, a smile set to his face.

It takes a moment, but Preston finds a slit in the crowd, and from what Preston can see, Elwine looks exhausted. Her hair is to her face, her shoulders and indeed her wings are slumped, yet she stands ready despite her expression. Fleet-fra, on the other hand, holds a cocky smile, a sword in one hand as he circles Elwine. There is no telling how long the fight has gone on, but judging by the way Fleet-fra is handling himself, he is the cause of the prolonged fight.

Yet, as Fleet-fra comes forward he disarms Elwine, knocking her to the ground as he does. The moment this happens the *Flóffs* Preston stand behind jump in excitement, prompting Preston to take a few steps back as he avoids the happily flapping wings.

The showboating that most likely has continued throughout the fight trails on as Fleet-fra flexes a little, his wings flapping to the cheers.

Despite his spotlight, Stysen's voice starts up from where he stands on the opposite side of the circle. "Now, now. Do not cheer for Fleet-fra, instead, weep for Elwine's display. For she is what happens when we grow *slothéñ*, a fate we all face when we shy from duties and training."

The comments draw a nod from Fleet-fra, and also bring the cheers down as the group surrounding this fight now cast their eyes to where Elwine struggles to stand.

As Stysen's voice starts back up again Preston begins to move along the outskirts of the crowd to find a better position. "...My fellow campmates, *Alphé* Kassie again leaves us to deal with matters beyond our flock, why does she not tend to the weak in her own camp? Instead, our laws of *Fra'ha* are a *jáff*! I say-..."

"*Thrće* Stysen!" The familiar, commanding tone is unmistakably Elva's, and as Preston finds a spot to view into the circle he watches as Elva moves inward. "Your comrade has clearly won his challenge. Sedition is not what was wagered."

The two *Flóffs* to Preston's sides give the man a look and just barely make room for him, but their side-eying yield no reaction from the man as he watches Stysen's cocky attitude shine brighter than his overly polished steel armor. "Mighty *Pexřá*, *dámeni* Elva, *Koá-Koé* slayer of *VéturVill*. Do not command me to silence. This challenge was forfeit the moment it began." Stysen gestures to Fleet-fra as he trails on. "This is what we should all strive to be, a warrior, something you yourself should know. Why, we have all heard the tales, the battle of *Rark-Kié*, where you cut through the lines of Grifón as none other. Speak now, who would you have at your back if such a battle was fought again? Elwine?"

Elva crosses her arms as she stands firm. "Stysen, you preen my wings with such titles though you still do not heed my command at silence." Elva nods. "You are so apt at showing weakness in our camp, why then do you not challenge me? Show us what strength looks like."

Stysen looks around the circle as he smiles. "I claim no strength over yours, *Pexřá*." He nods. "Though I would never shy from pushing myself, what would you wager?"

Elva nods. "I would wager a feather of my *Quétzal*."

At the comment Stysen gives a bow. "You humble me." He raises, a smile casting to the crowd around him. "But what male could reject such an offer? A *Quétzal* feather? A request all my own?"

The circle gives a little laugh as the predominantly male group begins to nod their heads. At their laughter Elva steps forth. "Come now, show us strength."

A slight laugh comes from Stysen as he looks to where Elwine still sits on the ground. Her face is set to the ground as her shoulders shrink a little to the feeling of Stysen's gaze. "Oh I shall."

Elva's smirk fades from her face as she pulls her sword from its sheath, the bright and sharpened edge drawing silence from the crowd as they realize Elva's keen blade.

Without a second of hesitation Stysen follows, bringing his own sword to his hand as the circle widens.

Elva takes her pose, her wings flaring, and her sword pointed to Stysen, yet as she stares the avian-man down she drops her sword. "Begin."

The sight of the sword on the ground makes Stysen a bit jittery, however, his second guessing does little to stop his charge toward Elva, his sword sharply pointed to the avian-woman. The speed at which he dashes forward is amazing, his wings giving his charge a bit of power as dirt is kicked up behind. Yet, the woman merely jumps to the side, her own bust of dust now following her, but her wings quickly shoot forward. Shooting the dust to Stysen's face, followed by a quick and harsh fist to his throat and back of the head.

Stysen falls flat to the floor gasping for air as blood begins to pour from his nose with every heavy cough he gives. One motion is all the fight took, though Elva does not boast nor does she cheer to the crowd as she strides to where Stysen struggles.

Nothing rings out from the awestruck circle of warriors as Elva speaks up. "Anything else you wish to say?"

Stysen just replies with a cough as he still heaves to the ground, though to his credit he never once let go of his sword, at least until he heard Elva's voice beside him.

Without a change in tone Elva turns to the circle as she nods to Stysen. "Be sure that he gets rest." As Elva turns to help Elwine up, Stysen's raspy voice chimes in, though not with his voice as he instead claps from where he kneels.

For a moment, the crowd just blinks to Stysen's clap, yet Fleet-fra as well as a few other members of Stysen's group began to follow suit, their own claps ringing to the camp. Stysen smiles, spitting some blood to the ground as he forces his raspy voice to the onlookers. "Gaze upon her, an example of what we should all strive for." Stysen slowly pushes himself up, collecting his sword as he bows. "Thank you, for such a display."

The circle that gathered now begins to break up, though not without a few nods to Stysen as he disappears within his mob of followers. Though even with Stysen's comments, many more nod to Elva as they step past her and move to their normal posts.

As the crowd begins to split up, Preston sets his eyes to where Elva and Elwine walk. With a quicker speed to his step Preston comes just behind the two avian-women as he speaks up. "You alright, Elwine?"

The man's voice takes the woman's attention as Elwine turns to Preston. Though she holds her head in shame as she nods. "Dirt cakes my wings, Walker... though my wounds will heal."

"You held your stance well, Fleet-fra simply has more experience in sparring, Elwine."

Elva's comment yields no difference in Elwine's expression as she replies. "Your words are easy, *Pexřá*, you fell Stysen in one motion."

"Stysen is a fair fighter, but untamed and foolish. His arrogance forced his loss." Elva nods. "That says more than losing from lack of skill."

Elwine gives a slow nod as she speaks up. "Perhaps so." She glances back to where Stysen and his group stand as she shrinks a little. "I must return to them, Fleet-fra will wish to claim his reward."

The comment draws a bit of shock and disgust to Preston's face as he glances back to the group of avians. However before he can speak up Elva chimes in. "Be sure you both return to your post quickly, off with you."

A nod comes from Elwine as she steps away, her eyes never once greeting Preston or Elva. Though as she steps away Preston speaks up. "That's sick, you're not going to say anything?"

Elva turns an eye to the man as she speaks up, a rather unyielding tone coming from her. "Elwine lost, I have no say in their actions."

"She doesn't fight, Elva!"

With a dismissive nod Elva's full attention turns to Preston. "You are not within *VéturVill*, Preston. I suggest you turn your thoughts now, less I turn my temper to you as I have with Stysen." Elva nods. "Speak of Clover, if nothing else to say."

A chuckle rolls from Preston but he crosses his arms all the same. "Unbelievable." A sigh rolls through Preston as he glances back to Stysen's group, though he still fumes his slight fear of Elva's warth keeps him from pushing the issue. "At least you got a good shot in on Stysen, did it feel good?"

Elva crosses her arms, though she loosens a little. "It will remind him of my rank. Something I may soon do with you."

"Any time you want some Feathers." Preston sighs, a smirk holding to his face. "Well if you want some good news, it turns out I'm not going to be a dad."

Elva nods. "I had my doubts at your bedding of Clover... it is no surprise."

"No." Preston shakes his head. "It turns out she not pregnant. Bad news, I will be gone for a day or two-...but! Before you get upset, Clover says she will have an excuse for me to give to Kassie."

"*Alphé* Kassie, Preston, and it had better be a reason, not an excuse." Elva looks the man over as she trails on. "Clover does not truly carry a foal? Even Ellette reported it from Bella."

Preston cocks an eye to the name. "Ellette?"

"Yes." Elva nods. "I had her follow you. Just to ensure the truth of your whereabouts."

"Okay? Obvious question." Preston shrugs. "Why would I lie to you about where I'm going, I know like four people in town and I have no money?"

"You did not lie, so it does not matter." Elva's response is quick, something that takes a bit of steam from Preston as the man sighs.

"Fine." With a groan Preston nods. "What all did she hear us talk about?"

"We have nothing further to discuss, Preston." Elva drops her arms as she trails on. "And as far as your request to leave, *Alphé* Kassie has once more been summoned to *Pegpolis*. It seems the *Jartál's* plans for having Féllcreed aid in her project has caused ripples within the camps. Some of them feel as though the Capital's project should never have been planned under a *Flóff* city, and many are displeased with the idea of it staying."

Preston shrugs to the comment as he speaks up. "What does that have to do with her?"

"*Alphé* Kassie has knowledge of what is planned, and also has approvals from both *VéturVill* and *Pegpolis*. Still, some are not settled; the hope is that those *Flóff* in Féllcreed that feel besieged will not retaliate in violence, once they see the Emperor's approval and better understand the plans."

A slight laugh comes from Preston as he nods. "So, more and more Stysens are popping up, huh?"

Elva's serious look does not alter as she continues. "Many *Flóff* view the new Princess as a strong and fair leader. Yet, with every turning tide another views her status as a *devún* as a threat."

Preston's smile fades a little in the presence of Elva's more serious look as he attempts to continue the conversation. "And having me around is still safe?"

Elva takes a deep breath as she nods. "It is good for the camp to deal with something other than themselves... and your work at the forge has helped, at least from what I hear."

"Happy to continue as a guinea pig." Preston chuckles, his arms crossing at his chest as he trails on. "But seriously, why keep me around?"

"Potential, you lack skill not courage, and you often find yourself in situations where such skills would be useful." Elva looks the man over for a moment. "Your attitude is your undoing, though I aim to break that."

"Hm." Preston nods. "You know, I think that's the nicest thing you've ever said."

"Do not expect more." Elva waves her hand. "Now seek Lutin, he may benefit from your early return."

Not wanting to try any more of Elva's patience Preston nods as he starts towards the other side of the camp. The area where the fighting took place now looks just as every other inch of the camp. Yet, as Preston walks past were Stysen laid the blood that came from him can still be seen in the dirt. Something that brings a bit of a smirk to Preston's face.

The camp's residents have all but vanished back to their patrol posts, or other various jobs within the camp and its surrounding area. Funny though, as Preston nears the other side of the camp Lutin seems to be hard at work already. Which, brings the thought to Preston's mind that he may have walked right past the dark skinned *Flóff* when he came in earlier.

As Preston nears the forge Lutin begins to pull his heavy gloves from his hands, his wings too fall to his back, obviously as he looks to take a break. Catching his eyes Preston speaks up. "Hey Lutin, how was-..."

"The forge needs to be cleaned, there are two orders of short swords with hand guards. Do not hammer them too flat they are training swords for *Mivtón*. After that, clean the forge again. I will be taking my leave for a moment, boy."

As Lutin moves pass Preston he presses the gloves to his tunic. Preston takes them to hand as he watches the blacksmith walk off into camp. "Nice to see you too Lutin. Don't worry, nothing can go wrong."

Without even missing a step Lutin continues as he calls back. "Better not mess my tools up you *přink, baft*eñ."

Preston just nods to the comment as he turns back to the forge's dying fire. "Yep, yep, whatever you say."

Chapter 19

Can't Skip the Small Stuff

A sharp and finally relaxing sigh rolls from Preston's dry lips as he tugs to the small, itchy tan blanket he now attempts to use to cover himself. The beds at the camp have never been a rejuvenating experience and in fact, the thought has often passed through Preston's mind that if his back hurts so much when he wakes up the idea of sleeping on these beds with wings must be ten times worse. The idea of one day everyone in the camp having a more comfortable bed starts to bring a slight smirk to Preston's face as he attempts to picture everyone with a good night's sleep. Undoubtedly, Elva might be a bit more open to talking and Stysen might finally cure his desire for violence. Of course, the thoughts are nothing more than fantasy, but it helps to keep the smile on Preston's face all the same.

Preston's breathing begins to get quieter as he finally adjust the blanket over his body and starts to drift into his thoughts. No matter how Preston positions the pillow his head lays on, it always seems to push the majority of cushion around his head, rather than underneath it. Not the most uncomfortable of head positions, but something Preston has gotten used to.

A slow breath comes from Preston as his mind continues to drift into its inevitable sleep. However, a quick and forceful jolt in the open space right next to his head, springs the man back to the waking world. Although, unlike normal, with a scream as he falls out of bed at the sight of a blade stabbed into the pillow just inches from his head.

Preston's eyes dart to were his attacker still stands, yet, as he places his assailant he speaks out. "Ellette?! W-what the Hell was-..."

Despite the teenage frame of the young *Flóff* girl she still holds a rather powerful angry look to her as she cuts Preston off. "You had given me your word, Preston. Is your word quickly changed like the tides?"

Preston waves his right hand quickly to the comment as he begins to stand up. "D-don't do the weather metaphors right now; why did you stab my pillow? You could have killed me."

Ellette rolls her eyes. "I was nowhere near your head, Preston."

The man wags a finger to the girl, almost as a father scolding their child, yet without any of the desired effect. "It's dark! You could've hit me!"

Ellette cocks her head to the comment as she gives a little laugh. She points to the ball of magic floating above the bed as she reaches for her knife still buried in the pillow. "Not with that thing."

Preston shrugs off the green glow that coats the tent's walls, bed, and pretty much everything else the man can see. "That's not the point."

"Hmmm." Ellette sheaths her sword as she talks over the man. "Why did you break your word? If you never desired to help you should not have offered. It would not have hurt."

The teenage, avian girl does a masterful job of getting her point across despite her wording as she attempts to look away and act like Preston's absence did not bother her. However, the more childish attempt at hiding her disappointment proves more effective as Preston gives a sigh of defeat. "Okay, I'm sorry. Lutin obviously didn't like the fact that I was gone again so he had me working right when I got back. And once Elva told him I would be gone the next two days he made me do the rest of his work. I have no problem helping you like I had no problem doing what Lutin wanted. I just got tired is all."

Ellette's power stance is dropped as the girl's wings slump a little from her back to her sides. "You will be gone *témont* as well?"

Preston nods. "Well yea, Clover woke up you know, and she wants me to go with her to the Capital." Preston gives a little shrug as he continues. "I'm not allowed to just leave the camp whenever, so Clover had the *Jartál* request that I deliver this month's weather report thingy. At least that's what Elva said." He shakes his head. "I guess Clover's been busy."

A simple nod comes from the avian girl as she speaks up. "I understand you have other tasks more important than mine. I suppose wanting to write as an *Únoff* is fairly foolish. My parents did not send me off to be a *Skréét* for no reason after all."

"Come on Ellette, you don't have to guilt trip me. It's just been a bad few days." Preston shrugs. "I will help."

"There is no guilt."

As Ellette moves back to the tent's entrance Preston moves towards her. "Hey, hey. It's okay, I can help. When is Bella's sister expecting a letter?"

Slowly Ellette speaks up from the question. "Well, Juna has never received letters from a *Flóff*. Our way of delivering them is much faster."

Preston nods as he gives a little smile. "Well prefect! Then we can knock it out tonight and when I get back she should just be sending one, right? You've been practicing what I showed you, right?"

With another moment of hesitation Ellette nods. "Knock it out? Finish the letter you mean?"

"Don't worry, I won't teach you any phrases like that." Preston bites his bottom lip a little as he nods. "Um, what do you have in mind? I don't really know how to spell any... well you know, your language."

Ellette nods as she brings her voice back. "No, I want to use New-Tongue." Her voice drops a little as she lowers her head. "Y-you will keep your word about not speaking of this? Yes?"

Preston shrugs. "Yeah, why wouldn't I?"

A slight smile comes to Ellette's face as she nods. "Alright. Then put your boots on, the ground is cold." With a new skip to her steps. As the avian girl's words finally click in the man's head his own friendly smile is dropped, as the thought of returning to the cold outside now takes his mind's attention.

Preston rubs his neck with his right hand as he turns his attention to the boots near the chest of his clothing. Although his nightwear is not fit for a lengthy stay outside, the glow from the camp's fire is still fairly bright, which at least means the full night's chill will not be greeting him. With a low yawn, Preston sits to the edge of the bed as he puts his shoes on for the second time today.

- - -

Elsewhere

The day has finally come to an end, though just because the sun settles beyond the sleepy town does not mean all within it rest. A fact Reynard now knows as he continues to follow after the satyress before him. It was a bit strange for Preston not to accompany the woman on her return to the library though Clover made quick work of any questions.

Clover and Preston made sure to stop by the library before retrieving Reynard, stashing away anything the *Jartál* gave her before Bella could see. Though, after leaving the woman, Clover found herself unable to keep her plans for the coming days from Reynard.

While the fox-boy did contest it, he nevertheless gave in, though a return to normal did not take place as Clover expected. Still, the day went on without a problem, and as the duo reaches the library just up the road Clover speaks up, her magic sparking up over hold of the small bag of groceries she has floating beside her. "Can you set this to the kitchen, Reynard?"

Glancing to the bag the fox-boy speaks up. "Okay."

"Thank you." Clover is first to the door as she holds it open. "Do not worry about putting it away, I will cook something soon."

Reynard moves inside of the darkened library, Clover's magic popping to the room as she lights it up. Sighting her spell however Reynard finds his voice. "Clover, are you sure you should be doing so much? Are you not tired?"

With a smile Clover replies, though her cheerful tone does little to hide the bags under her eyes as she speaks up. "I am fine, Reynard, it was merely sleep. I am happy to be walking." She closes the door as she waves her companion on. "Now go on, I shall be upstairs in a moment."

Reynard again nods to the comment, his eyes setting to the half wall on his left. Clover however turns her attention to the stairs as she starts up them, Reynard is gone from sight though Clover does not rush as her eyes fall to the bathroom on her left.

The sound of her hooves echoes to the hallway, though she finds herself on the tiled floor within seconds, her eyes to the folded towels she used earlier. Yet, as Clover steps towards them she catches a glimpse of herself in the mirror on her left. If not for the fact the Clover were the only one in the room she may have mistaken the sunken in face for that of another's. Sighting, Clover lingers before her reflection, her gaze widened to worn out features on display. For a moment she is caught in the trenches of her face, held down by the heavy bags under her eyes, though she pushes past it as she once more refocuses to the folded towels she used before.

Stepping aside she collects them, though it is not simply to ready them for a wash, instead her hand dips under them as she takes hold to the cold metal hidden within it. She draws out the dagger as she looks it over, no emotion to her face as her reflection once more greets her in the shine of the blade now.

Easing the dagger back to where it was hidden, she sighs, turning back to the hallway. Her trot comes to her, her eyes setting to her room as she moves to it, her hand continuing to fiddle with the dagger she hides. Reynard is downstairs, this she is sure of, though she nonetheless moves into her room, the dagger still hidden to her towels.

Kneeling down to the bed, she draws out the box underneath, and with a quick few motions she places her dagger back to its box. Afterwards she pushing it under the bed, and collects her towels, her trot drawing her back into the hallway, a dark thought pushed aside for a moment more.

Chapter 20

Winding Road

The bags and lack of color under Preston's eyes are a lasting reminder to the commitment the man had for Ellette's letter. Though a fulfilling night, the fact that Preston was only privy to read but certain parts of the letter definitely lengthened the process. Furthermore, the idea of what Preston thought a letter's length would be, was thrown out when Ellette handed him the thesis paper she seemingly had been working on for days.

Yet, despite Preston's own desire for sleep, he did not pick a fight when Clover and Reynard came to the camp. Half because he knew he would not win and half because of the looks the other campmates gave him upon their arrival. Aside from Lutin and Elwine, most at the camp still seem to distrust outsiders, Preston included in this sentiment. Though none clearly state it so plainly, as Preston guesses, out of some respect to his status as a campmate. Even still, the looks were passed to Clover and Reynard.

For the most part, Preston does not care about what everyone else thinks, although, with Stysen's call to fighting Preston has noticed the looks more often. Mostly the stares have just bought a feeling of awkwardness, perhaps a faint expression of "why are you here", though it was not something Preston wanted to test with Reynard nearby. Especially as the scrutinizing gazes begun to make Preston feel uneasy. Luckily, he was able to leave with no problem. Amazing how one fight and one day can bring such a drastic change, even with Elva's dominance of Stysen, his words seemed to have an impact. Though like most things, Preston merely pushes it aside, focusing on something else at hand.

A new thought comes to Preston's mind as he continues to look over the soft rolling hills of *VéturVill's* outskirts. Though it is not the wonderful world that takes Preston's eyes, instead it is the fresh cuts into the ground just off the road. There the recently laid wood and metal strips of the newly designed train system greet him. Preston's mind drifts from the camp to the rails he finally notices as he sits up a little more in his seat. "Wow, they really have the rails this far out?"

Preston's eyes glance to where the brown legged satyress sits across from him. However, as he notices her, she puts a finger to her mouth and nods to the fox-boy snoozing beside her. Noticing her gesture Preston falls silent.

Though, to Preston's surprise Clover puts the book in her hand to her lap as she whispers. "It has been a combined effort from what I understand. All Three seem to have contributed something." A slight smile comes from Clover as she nods. "Even if they do not understand its importance."

Preston gives his own smile as he replies. "Yeah, I can see that."

Clover gives a little glance to Reynard as she continues. "So... how are you feeling, Preston?"

The comment actually takes Preston by surprise, though he answers all the same. Of course, his fidgeting draws Clover's gaze as she watches the man pull his hand from his right pocket. "I'm fine, how have you been feeling?"

The satyress gives a quick shrug, however it could be just a normal jiggle from the slightly bumpy ride as far as Preston knows. "Fine, nothing to complain of." Clover leans forward a little more as she continues. "Are you sure you feel yourself?"

The fact that their first conversation has already devolved into questions forces a slight roll of the eyes in Preston, though he maintains a cordial attitude, thanks to spell he sparked before he left. Preston flashes a wide smile as he leans forward. His lean puts Clover back to her seat as she continues her friendly disposition to the man's answer. "I stayed up late helping Ellette with a letter to Bella's sister." His hands go to the bags under his eyes as he continues. "Tired, Clover. I'm not turning into a monster."

Clover's left ear flicks as she quickly speaks up. "Turning? I-I never said anything about that."

A slight nod comes from Preston as he speaks up. "I know, I'm just reading between the lines." He pats his pocket. "I got what I need, and I'm sure you know that." Preston leans back to the seat though he finds himself compelled to ask something, a bit of sincerity taking over his normally sarcasm. "You sure you're up for this?"

"Of course." Clover adjust the book in her lap as she trails on. "It is my duty to check up on Master Nyota... and I cannot hide away from family forever."

Preston turns his head to the world outside as he replies. "Yeah."

As Preston's comment rings to the cabin the conversation dies down as the sound of the wheels on the dirt road begin to take center stage. However, the silence only lasts a few moments before Clover speaks up once more. "How are you treated at the camp?"

"Mhmm..." Preston looks back to Clover as he tries to act nonchalant. "It's fine, like I've said... still hate the beds."

A slight laugh comes from Clover which prompts Preston to stop as he smiles to the woman. "That's funny?"

Clover waves a hand to the comment as she nods. "Traveling with Master Nyota you find yourself in very interesting sleeping arrangements."

Preston follows with a laugh as he speaks up. "You know, it's actually not the worst thing."

"Oh?"

"Call me crazy but if they can move clouds they can make them warm." Preston chuckles. "Just saying, I'm getting tired of cold showers."

Clover holds her smile, however Preston sees the little glimmer in her eye as he crosses his arms. "Well, I know that look... you're going to correct me about something, huh?"

"W-what? No, no." Clover waves her hand as she tightens her grip to the book in her lap. "The *Flöff* have certain powers over how the weather is crafted around Artésque. So there is nothing wrong with saying they influence how clouds move as well as its temperature."

Preston holds his smile to the woman across from him as he nods. "Well... that's my worst experience at camp."

"Hm... have you tried to cook anything for them?"

Another light laugh comes from Preston as he shakes his head. "No, I think they like stews and dry bread too much. And anyways, I would just make them sick, like I got you sick."

Clover's smile fades a little as she lowers her head a little to the left. "Well, perhaps when we return you could cook something. Just to be sure."

"No. Not unless you find some loophole in the camp's rules that says I can be a chef at night. Besides, I'll be gone soon enough." The quiet laugh is only half shared with Clover as the satyress attempts to play along. However, before she can speak up the fox-boy beside her is finally stirred from his nap. "Have we arrived?"

The boyish voice takes the attention of both Preston and Clover as she speaks up. "No, we woke you. Go back to your rest." As her comment ends Clover begins to open her book, with one last glance to Preston. Preston on the other hand looks to the bags beside him and then to the window on his right.

- - -

(A Few Hours Later)

The ride from *VéturVill* has always been a tiresome venture, not just because of the lack of sights, but also because of how uncomfortable the cabin's seats get after about three hours. Luckily though, the beefy draft horse like animal that pulls the carriage decided to go a little faster this time, which made the trip almost a whole hour shorter. Still, the carriage has yet to enter the hillside city that is the Capital, however as Preston continues to hold his head just a little outside of the window the sight of the city continues to grow near.

As the man takes himself back into the cabin a yawning voice greets his ears. "How much further?"

Preston shrugs as he speaks up. "A mile or two."

Reynard's still sleepy haze holds as he just stares blankly to the man for a moment before he turns to Clover. "How much further?"

Clover does not bat an eye away from the book she has almost finished as she speaks up. "A brisk gallop, I am sure."

Reynard yawns again as he sits up in his seat next to Clover's side. "The *Flóff* should allow us to use their chariots for long trips."

"The flying ones?" Preston crosses his arms as he gives a little laugh. "There ain't no way on Earth I'm getting back on one of those." The man's comment is quickly followed as he attempts to restate his worlds. "Err, any way on Artésque I'm... uh or..."

"*Éordiarx*, Preston."

"What?"

Clover shifts her gaze just above the book's pages as she nods to the man. "*Éordiarx*, that is the Célntal Stoná you are attempting to use in your comment."

Preston squints to the comment as he attempts to repeat the word. "*E-or-de-arc*? What's that?"

"The Célntal Stoná."

"Stoná? I thought that meant peace?"

To Preston's surprise it is not Clover who quickly corrects him, instead the fox-boy still waking up now speaks. "Stoná does mean peace, but it is also a place. Just as how *Éordiarx* is where *Ovállll* and Artésque are."

Preston closes his eyes for a moment as he sighs in thought. "So, that's the planet and that's like the continents on it?"

Reynard just stares at the man in a confused silence, but Clover quickly nods with a short. "Mhmm." As she flips the page in her book.

The noise from Clover however takes Reynard's attention as he speaks up. "There are other Célntal Stonás?"

Preston gives a little laugh as he speaks up. "Well, sure. Where do you think I came from?"

Reynard blinks to the comment as he speaks up. "I thought you were from the *Dýnar*?"

"Preston is from a different land, Reynard. Well past the *Dýnar* or the *Fárwift*."

"But..." Reynard taps his paw to his snout as he continues slowly through his words. "How do you know New Tongue? The *devún* taught it, and Wúna and Sóltina never left Artésque?"

Clover again is quick to speak up as she nods. "The spells they used to help everyone learn and teach New Tongue reached very far, Reynard."

Preston brings his own hand to his chin as he nods. "Y-yea..."

For a moment Reynard is silent, but he pushes past his questions as he takes a deep breath. "Maybe we can talk about it when I wake up more."

Preston just laughs a little as he shakes his head. "Well if talking is just from a spell no wonder you guys have trouble understanding me."

Clover gets a slight smile to her face as she nudges the fox-boy next to her. "*Néat sléfto.*"

Reynard gives a little groan as he speaks up. "But Clover you woke me up so early."

A smile crosses to the satyress' face as she nudges him again. "*Nervál,* Reynard. *Étrome méi fon.*"

Reynard follows the smile as he nods. "Preston *baýýo, baýýo ó neófto.*"

The name takes Preston's attention as he cocks a little smirk to the conversation. "What about me?"

Clover closes her book as both she and Reynard look between the man and each other in a silent confusion. The stares last a few moments until Clover lowers her mouth to Reynard's left ear. "*Yeófto,* Preston?"

Reynard shakes his head as he replied to the strange comment. "*Néat.*"

Preston shrugs to the comment as he leans back to his seat. "Yeah, sure, neat, neat, neat. I have no idea what you two are talking about."

The slight annoyance to Preston's voice brings a smile to Clover's face as she nudges Reynard and makes a whining motion with her hands. "*Baýýo, baýýo.*"

Reynard holds his own smile as he turns back to Preston for some type of response.

Preston nods as he slowly catches on to their joke. "Oh yea? Cómo estás? Estoy bien."

Clover cocks her head to the comment as she replies. "What does that mean?"

The man shrugs as he speaks up. "Don't know, guess you and me will both be confused."

The fox-boy now chimes in as he holds his smile. "You get upset easily, Preston."

"No I don't." Preston crosses his arms as he continues to shake his head.

The smile to Clover's face holds as she looks the man over. "Do you wish to know what we said? It was hardly a conversation."

The man hesitates for a moment, but as a thought comes to his mind he smirks. "Nope, because I'm not telling you what I said. It could be a voodoo curse for all you know."

Clover squints again to the comment, her facial expression only adds fuel to Preston as he holds a finger to her. "Bothers you, huh?"

The satyress simply shakes her head as she gently opens her book and places it to her lap. However, the snickering to her right halts her as she cocks an eye to the fox-boy. Sighting her stare Reynard speaks up with a laugh. "You want to know."

"I do not care." Clover shifts her gaze between Reynard and Preston as she attempts to adjust herself in the seat. "I have no interest in it. It does not concern me."

Preston nods to Reynard as he attempts to copy the words he heard before. "*Bayo-bayo,* Reynard."

Before Preston can get the last laugh the driver's voice comes to the cabin. "Mrs Vines, we have reached the castle's grounds."

The conversation is put on halt as Clover calls back through the open window beside her. "Thank you." As her comment ends she reaches for the bag next to Preston. Ultimately, Preston hands it to her but Clover pays the gesture no mind as she begins to put her book into her satchel. "Alright, a quick visit with Master Nyota and Princess Sóltina and we will be back on the road to *VéturVill*."

A slight groan comes from Reynard as the fox-boy stretches. "I am starting to regret this trip."

Slight smile passes to Clover's face, but it quickly fades as she turns to Preston. "You do have your letter from the *Flóff* yes?"

Preston nods. "Yes, and I know I need to give it to a Chancellor Clay."

Clover shakes her head as her magic sparks to her hands. The bag she allotted to Preston now floats to her as she shakes her head. "You cannot give the letter to him, you must give it to his assistant."

Clover opens the bag as she studies its contents, for a brief moment Preston wonders why she would be going through his stuff but before he can even voice his question, the letter is pulled from its contents. "Clover, I can take a letter to the guy."

"Yes, yes. I do not doubt that you would make a good courier Preston, but you do not know where he would be, so we shall deliver it together."

Preston takes his bag from the woman as he nods. "Okay?" As the man's comment ends the driver calls back and the carriage comes to a halt. "We have arrived Miss Vines."

At the voice Clover moves to the door and down the steps of the carriage, Reynard follows behind as Clover continues outside. Once out of the way Preston now moves from the carriage, carrying both his bag and the bag Reynard forgot to grab. However, he is stopped as he comes outside. His sight sets to the meeting hall and the fountain outside of it. "Huh, has that always been there?"

Clover has moved to the front of the carriage which prompts Preston to move after her as he continues to talk. "Hey, you see the waiting area outside the meeting place?"

His gaze is still set to the hall as Clover replies. "Look here, Preston."

The comment takes Preston's attention as he turns to the direction both Reynard and Clover look. The man takes a bit of a double take however as he looks over the once cluttered field next to the castle. A dull white stone now spreads from the castle's entrance down the hill to Nyota's tower. The tall grasses have been cleared or seemingly mowed down despite, at least to Preston's knowledge of the technology to do so. Still, these thoughts are kept from the man's mind as he continues to look across the field. "How did they lay the stone so quick?"

As the man continues to scan the area he does a second double take as he looks over the skeleton of a structure starting to form just a little past the Castle. The stone columns and basic walls as well as the wood scaffolding that currently host the workers does not provide a definite shape to the building, but the idea that so much has been completed in just months takes Preston by awe.

"Quite a feat for *Dwoff* workers is it not?"

The deep voice takes the group's attention as they now turn to three guards walking from the castle's great doors. The larger figure in the center quickly is recognized as Clover nods. "Very, much so Stone Hooves."

"General Stone Hooves, child."

Clover turns more to the stallion as she continues. "General?"

"Yes, it seems that Princess Sóltina has finally recognized my worth and has since prompted me to my rightful rank." The proud aura radiating off the satyr is matched only by the pompous military stance he holds.

However, the locked hands behind his back finally break as he waves his hand towards the carriage. "Now, Miss Vines, instruct your driver to move. We are expecting two other carriages for our guests."

Clover only has to look back to the driver before the *Dẃoff* man starts the horse pulled carriage out of the way and more towards the once rolling fields of grass and stone. However, Clover herself does not start the trek across the newly laid stone as she speaks up. "Who does the Princess hold court with?"

For a moment Stone Hooves stares at Clover in silence, but his words break through his lips as he nods. "The Princess is to hold court with the *Coñjro Á Diśtro Márjx* headmasters. I had assumed you were here to fill in for Mage Nyota... if you are not, why are you here?"

The now solely focused gaze of Stone Hooves' bushy eyebrows brings a bit of discomfort to Preston and Reynard as they shift a little under the stallion's watch. "Master Nyota is not here? Where has he gone?"

Stone Hooves shakes his head as he speaks up. "First answer my question. If you are not a part of this gathering, why should I not place you three under arrest for disturbance of court?"

Clover straightens her stance but before she can speak up the door of the castle opens, the sound of it takes Stone Hooves' full attention as he and the two guards beside him take a proper, lined up stance parallel to the door.

Now leaving the building are two long robe wearing *Únoffs* followed by what Preston can only assume would be their assistant, seeing as how both match the color scheme of the older *Únoff* they follow and both seemly have been forced to carry their master's belongings. The *Únoff* more to the right is dressed in an orange, red, and gold colored robe, although definitely older the dark spots under the satyr's eyes and overall sunken in face makes the stallion look almost like a walking skeleton. The short white hair and lack of a beard also do not do any justice to the almost colorless man.

The other older *Únoff* more to the left is dressed in a dark blue, purple, and white lined robe. Unlike the other master beside him, at least this *Únoff* looks livelier, although he is considerably shorter and has a slight hunch to his back. Adding to the more alive aura of this individual is the almost dopey smile he holds as he blindly stares off into the distance.

Stone Hooves quickly speaks up. "My apologies Master Nuri and Master Mér your carriages have not arrived."

The *Únoff* dressed in red puts his hands into the opposite arms of his robe as he folds his hands. "Very well…"

The other master turns his gaze to Clover as he brings a finger up. "I know this one…"

Clover gives a little bow as she speaks up. "Hello, Master Mér, I am Svle Nyota's assistant."

The short *Únoff* nods as he speaks up. "Clover Vines, that you are."

"I do hope my master's absence did not dispute your meeting with the Princess." Clover raises from her bow.

"Oh no. Master Nuri and I have been summoned for a different reason as the fair Princess says." A pause comes to the *Únoff* as he smacks his cracked lips in thought, even as he does this however, he continues to shuffle closer to Clover. As he nears however Preston notices something strange about the old satyr, his eyes are a milky white and do not even remotely seem to be set to Clover. The old *Únoff*'s voice comes back to him as his smile grows. "We have been asked to construct Gr'óll for each city in Artésque."

Clover squints to the comment as she speaks up. "Gr'óll?"

Stone Hooves looks on with a look that would surely silence the old satyr if he saw it, but as it is, Master Mér continues on, both in his words and his shuffle forward. His continued movements has prompted the younger *Únoff* dressed in a similar color scheme to move after the old master. The boy looks perhaps no older than late teens but as he nears the old *Únoff* a fairly deep voice comes from him. "Master Mér you can stop your trot now."

A smile comes to Mér's face as he waves in the general direction of Clover. "Ah, well, as I understand it your Master as well as Master Duscle shall be heading the construction of a new *Márjx Gréftor* near the castle! Splendid news as I hear the old masters in the *Oválll* have disappeared."

The words bring a response from the thin satyr still close to the castle. The raspy tone carries over the conversation as Mér's voice is put down. "That is because they were all killed. Now, Master Mér I do believe you should exercise some discretion in our meeting. Although I trust Svle Nyota's apprentice I would not continue further with the contents of our meeting in such an open environment."

Stone Hooves nods to the comment as he quickly speaks up. "Very well put Master Nuri. Perhaps you would feel more comfortable in the castle Miss Vines and... company."

Clover nods as she starts towards the castle. "Quite right. Princess Sóltina is surely free, I believe I shall meet with her for a moment."

Stone Hooves quickly shakes his head as he speaks up. "There is no open court mage Vines."

"Yes, but Master Nyota is out, and I am acting head mage of the Capital. I do wish to know where my Master's task has sent him." She turns back to Preston and Reynard as she continues. "Come along." As Preston and Reynard begin to move forward Clover turns to Master Mér as she takes hold of the old master's hands. "Take care, Master Mér."

The old *Únoff* nods with a simple smile as his assistant guides him back to where Stone Hooves and the other guards are. Despite the look on Stone Hooves' face the large stallion stands silent as he watches the group move closer to the castle doors. Master Nuri and his stone-faced appearance beside him continue to stare down the trail leading away from the castle as they impatiently await their carriage.

For a moment the guard at the door hesitates at opening the door, but after a brief glance to Stone Hooves he opens the door and the group moves inside. A few guards and other *Únoffs* are within the castle's main entrance, but Clover pays them no mind as she directs her attention to the corridor leading to the throne room. Of course, it is not just the look of determination that halts anyone from questioning Clover, Reynard, or Preston, as far as anyone inside is concerned, Stone Hooves would never let a threat into the castle without dying first.

With that said however, after a few minutes of navigating the castle's interior, the group is finally stopped just outside the closed throne room. The two guards stationed outside the doors speak up as Clover stops in front of them. "There is no open court."

Clover nods, her trot coming to a halt. "Could you please inform Princess Sóltina that Clover Vines is here."

The guards look at each other before they turn back to Clover. "Miss Vine, we know who you are. But the court is still closed, Stone Hooves' orders."

Clover nods once more as she speaks up. "Could you please inform Princess Sóltina."

Another moment of silence passes before the guard on the right turns around and moves through the door, ensuring they close it behind him. Not a second later he returns and holds the door open. Near the back of the room stands the unmistakable ruler of the *Únoffs*, as normal standing beside the empty throne, clad in her whitish gold looking clothing with her bright wings firmly to her back. Her voice greets the group as she nods. "I was beginning to think Stone Hooves might have actually stopped your venture, as it has been quite some time since a guard informed me of a *VéturVill* carriage nearing the castle."

Sóltina gives a little nod to the guards behind Clover, the nod prompts the guards to close the door as Clover moves a little closer to the angelic being. "Princess Sóltina, if I may speak my mind…"

The princess gives a simple nod as she continues. "I would expect nothing but the truth from Svle Nyota's pupil."

Clover nods, but the vigor she had while walking through the castle and talking back to Stone Hooves is lost as she holds her voice down a little. "Very well, I believe your judgment in promoting Stone Hooves is perhaps mistaken. I also feel obligated to inform you that the creation of the *Diśtro Márjx* Gr'óll has been forbidden since the first great war of the Three."

Sóltina nods as she moves closer to the group. The smile to her face is both warm and kind, albeit with a hint of surprise. "A whole *moř̌o* of sleep and you are more alert than most advisors allotted to me... Stone Hooves is a frightful choice in General, I agree, Clover. I am also well aware of the first war's treaty."

Preston and Reynard stay silent, mainly in shock of how blunt Clover was in calling the Princess out though their surprise only furthers as they blink to how open the Princess actually was in her response.

"B-but why..."

"Why promote Stone Hooves?" Sóltina nods as she begins to pace a little around the room. "Although a bit more controlling than others, Stone Hooves is very loyal to the *Únoff* laws. Of course, having such a controlling guard even under your brother's watch has created a few problems. So, I have but one option, to send him to a place where strong order is needed. I believe you have meet with *Jartál* Glortón, yes? I believe that having someone of Stone Hooves' traits around would perhaps clean up some of the *Jartál's* less than desirable acts. Furthermore, the *Atémor* were last seen there, mostly likely returning to the *Ovállĺ*, and I know having so many *Únoff* troops in a *Dẃoff* hold can only be allowed so long. With Stone Hooves in Glortón's court I at least know I have a General of my court who will actively report any changes in the area, no matter how small. Thus, a promotion and a relocation will take place soon."

Sóltina continues for a moment as she nods. "Your brother was sent to secure Stone Hooves' position. I expect him to return quickly, though I understand he stopped in *VéturVill*." The princess's voice gets a little softer as she looks over the young satyress before her. "It is good to know you are well."

"T-thank you Princess..." Clover shifts a little. "But why do you insist on creating Gr'óll?"

A slight laugh comes to Sóltina as she continues. "The treaty's arrangements have already been overruled. It states that no *Binderstró* types of *Márjx* can be used in times of war or for the purpose of war. It does not say the creation of a *Gr'óll* for peacekeeping is forbidden." Sóltina holds the smile to her face as she brings a finger up to halt Clover's impending comment. "And as I have said to your master, this was not my immediate decision. It was first decided by the Lords of Trade, I had no knowledge of *Gr'óll* creation until a request came to me."

"But Princess, surely you understand that having the golems means that in times of war they could be used. This would undoubtedly cause problems with the *Flóff*."

"As I thought." Sóltina continues. "But, the towns under *Dẃoff* keep are not suited for any major threat. As an example, *VéturVill*. I have reached an agreement with the Three, as well as the Lords of Trade. If these constructs are to be crafted there would only be allowed two in each hold, four within larger cities. They would only be allowed near the public if the hold's guard decided and each Gr'óll is to be bound only to their hold's *Jartál*. *Únoff* settlements do not require this level of protection, so to please the *Flóff* none shall have any. Furthermore, with the addition of these creations to the ranks of *Dẃoff* holds it lessens the dependency on *Flóff* patrols to act, which has always been an issue for the *Flóff*."

Despite the explanation Clover remains silent though, the same soft tone Sóltina has held only pauses for a moment before she continues. "As I understand it, very few still can recall the spells needed to create these *Gr'óll*, so I have asked the *Coñjro Márjx* headmaster to construct it, the *Diśtro Márjx* to teach them and finally, *Álter Márjx* to control them."

"B-but this is a creation only ever used by the highest of *Coñjro Márjx* or *Diśtro Márjx*, why would you ask for Master Nyota's help?" Clover shrugs. "Our spells have nothing to do with creation nor destruction."

"Yes, but *Álter Márjx* can create a controlling stone, a type of controlling device that would allow each *Jartál* to use the creations without magic."

"Without magic? B-but why?"

Sóltina holds her soft smile as she nods to Clover's question. "The biggest fear is for these creations to become tools of war. If they are only controlled with magic, who then other than the *Únoff* could use them? A device to control them keeps the fear of magic from the Three."

Clover squints to the comment. "You would put the benefit of the Three before values of the *Únoffs*?"

Sóltina pauses for a moment as she lets the comment sink in. Though she speaks up in a calm, well thought out reply all the same. "Are we not all of Artésque now? Protection as a whole is what matters, not of one. If tradition stops a greatness of action, it is not worthy of recognition."

Clover gives a little smirk to the comment as she nods. "Master Nyota must have been very persuasive."

The Princess turns back to the throne as she replies. "I found myself having to take a seat for his lecture. Although, it was worth it."

Taking a step closer, Clover nods. "Where is Master Nyota?"

The cheerful tone of the conversation turns as Sóltina stays silent with her back to the group. The silence prompts Preston and Reynard to grow more anxious as they await Clover to ask again. "Princess?"

The smile that once graced the angelic woman's face is gone as she turns. "*HefterÁll*, which, I fear, is where I must ask you and your company to venture."

Clover cocks her head a bit taken aback by Sóltina's sudden change in expression. "Why? Has something happened?"

"It seems Master Duscle has begun to act strangely. I feared that somehow Clamor has a part in it. The *Jartál* of course assures me that nothing is amiss. However, when I requested both Duscle and Nyota to discuss the plans for the school outside he did not come. Fearing he may have fallen ill I have asked Nyota to check on him. Your Master also insisted that I send him and not anyone else." Sóltina gives a slight sigh as she continues. "I do not wish to ask for your help, but with your brother gone I have no one else to send but Stone Hooves or an advisor of mine. While Stone Hooves would be ideal for a problem, if he does not meet one, he would create one. If however there was a problem and I had sent an advisor, they would be powerless to help solve it."

"No." Preston speaks up to the Princess' breath. "Why can't you go?"

Clover quickly reacts to Preston's intrusion to Sóltina's speech as she turns to him. "Preston! Now is not the time to-..."

"No, it is fine, Clover." Sóltina nods to Preston as she speaks up. "If I knew that Clamor had somehow escaped I would never send anyone other than myself. But, Nyota reports no problems, and I cannot just leave my post as Princess. I may not be an *Únoff*, but I honor what is expected of me in my actions, and to venture into such a place would stir opinions."

Preston shakes his head though he says nothing as he instead turns to the door, walking out as his hand dips into his pocket. The sight of the man's walk draws Reynard's gaze, though the door to the throne room quickly closes without a comment more from Preston.

Clover however merely nods, a confidence in her tone despite Preston's display. "Princess I would be happy to go, I wish to see Master Nyota anyways. Although, Preston does need to deliver a letter to Chancellor Clay before we depart."

The comment sparks a slight smile to Sóltina as she extends her hand. "I have a meeting with the *Dwoff* Chancellor later. It would be the least your Princess could do."

The hand prompts Clover to retrieves the letter from her satchel as she gives it to the Princess. However, as they exchange a little goodbye the doors to the throne room open, Stone Hooves leading the assault inside.

"Forgive me Princess I had not known they came within the throne-..."

"Ah, General Stone Hooves. Would you be so kind as to escort my guests to their carriage, I have a task for them and would hate it if they got held back by guards asking questions."

"A-a task, Princess?" Stone Hooves shakes his head. "I saw their companion in the hallway... did they not disturb your peace?"

A simple laugh comes from Sóltina as she replies. "Clover and her companions could never disturb my peace."

Stone Hooves stands a little bewildered as he nods. "Y-yes my Princess." Still trying to hold his confusion at bay he steps aside from the doors as he holds his arm out. "I will escort you through the castle Miss Vines."

A slight smirk comes to Clover's face as she moves past the man and into the hall. Reynard following after her as Stone Hooves looks back to the Princess. "Um... sorry for any interruption, Princess." Stone Hooves and the two guards that were stationed by the door take a few steps back as they close the throne room off and turn their attention to the group before them. Preston leans against the wall, a dopey expression to his face as he just smirks to the sight of swords around him, his own hand dipping to the blade he has around his waist.

Clover gives an eye to Preston's expression, though she nods all the same as she turns to Stone Hooves' trot as she speaks up. "We shall need a fresh carriage, I am sure you can oblige, General."

Chapter 21

Thicket

The venture into the forest and towards *HefterAll* has commenced, despite the protest Preston gave. In truth, it was too late when Preston finally came to his senses, his sarcasm to the whole affair was evident, though he never out right attempted to stop the venture. Though the spell he prompted was quick to end, a sobering reminder to how weak his amulet has gotten, or perhaps a side effect of how often he has used it.

Then again, it may have been the fact that they were all crammed back into the carriage after such a lengthy trip. Sure, *HefterAll* is close, but even the half an hour trip is still nerve wracking; and now that Preston has the slight urge to pee it makes it all the worse. But, as the forest slowly starts to grow thin outside the window, and the slight incline of *HefterAll's* outskirts are felt to the carriage Preston finally relents. The silent protest has failed, especially seeing as how both Clover and Reynard never even really paid attention to the fact that the man has been silent.

Knowing that the inevitable cannot be changed Preston sighs and speaks up. "So?"

Clover peaks her eyes just above her book as she replies. "Yes?"

Preston nods as he throws his hands up a little. "So, what's the plan? What are we doing?"

The comment prompts Clover's eyes back to her book as she speaks up. "We are here just to ensure Master Nyota is safe. He has not asked for help, so we are to assume nothing."

Reynard now turns back from the window as his fox ears poke up to the conversation.

Preston just cups his hands to his lap, all the while as he leans to the wood back of his seat. "Alright, what happens if we get to the city and it's overrun with those *things*."

"There will be no *Atémor*. There have been no sightings of them since Princess Clarity retreat into the *Oválll*."

"Mhmm..."

Clover pauses for a moment, but the satyress brings her voice back as she shakes her head. "Simply because you do not wish to believe something does not mean we have to."

Preston bobs his head a little in thought at the comment before he responds. "Belief that there are *Atémor* or belief that this is stupid?"

Clover gives a little sigh as she flips a page in her book. "Both."

"Clover..." The boyish voice draws the woman from her book as she looks to where Reynard points out the window. Preston follows the gathered eyes as he too notices the rows of grapevines to the outskirts of the city. "...will we see Eadric and Clematis?"

"No, our task will keep us far too busy for any trips... Although, I do wonder how far that *Dwoff* inventor has come on the Princess's plans. Perhaps, we can ask when we reach the *Jartál*."

Preston continues to look over the perfectly keep rows of plants as he speaks up. "I have a question... and this has always bothered me... why does it seem every city has a castle, but *VéturVill* doesn't?"

Clover squints a little to the question as she slightly cocks her head to the right. "*VéturVill* is far too small for such a structure. Perhaps, as the town grows a new outpost will be constructed for the *Jartál*, but that is up to the *Dẃoff* leaders."

"So…" Preston nods. "Pretty much everywhere I've been is a *Dẃoff* place, right? So, what does an *Únoff* city look like?"

"Well, the *Jartál* is not the only power in each city. *HefterÁll* may have a *Dẃoff Jartál*, but most of the city is that of *Únoff* or *Dẃoff* crafters and merchants. The Lords of Trade have more say in bigger cities than the *Jartál*, as their job is to report to the hold's ruler."

Preston slowly brings his right hand to his mouth as he chews to his nails, or at least what remains. "So… they can make decisions?"

Clover nods as she quickly corrects the man. "If it were an *Únoff* hold." Clover squints to the man. "Why the sudden questions?"

"I don't know." A sigh rolls from Preston. "I've been sitting her in silence too long, I'm bored." He nods to the woman. "So, what about that Master Yoda guy and Lord Tall Dude back at the castle? I know they're masters of something, but do they have as much say as like Nyota would?"

Clover blinks to the names. "Are you referring to Masters Nuri and Mér? They are the heads of their schools. They report to the Princess, but yes, they have power in their provinces just as Master Duscle holds respect amongst the *Jartál* of *HefterÁll*."

Preston nods as he leans a little forward. "Yeah, I had a question about the shorter one… his eyes were like, you know, different. Is his city like under some magical cloud that blocks the sun out or something or is it near a volcano?"

"Master Mér is the head of the *Coñjro Márjx*. Such dedication to his school's magic has left him blind, a fate many within it will face." Clover shakes her head. "Your comments are a bit rude, Preston."

Preston gives a little laugh as he shakes his head. "Why would they agree to that?"

With a sigh Clover is unable to stop herself from explaining. "*Coñjro Márjx* deals with harnessing thoughts and emotions to create. Because of how powerful the spell created can be, their influence must come from within. The *ocúlús* must be blinded, as most use this as their primary sense, they must see beyond."

Another slight laugh comes from Preston as he shakes his head. "I don't see how the eyes can be the only thing that could screw up a spell... and how did he know who you were? You didn't talk?"

Clover gives her own smile as she shakes her head. "That I do not know, perhaps he has found another way of knowing who is around."

Preston just shakes his head to the comment as he speaks up. "See now that make no sense, if he can see you, how does that not affect his spells?"

"Preston, I am not a student of *Coñjro Márjx*."

The quick comment brings a laugh to the man as he holds his hands up. "Alright, alright. I know you hate it when you don't have all the answers."

Clover gives a slight shake of the head as she turns her attention to the window on her left. As she opens the shutter, she pokes her head outside, however only for a moment as she brings her eyes back to Preston. "Well, Master Duscle's spell still stands around the city, do keep your thoughts clear, Preston. It would be a shame for you to be kept outside."

With a snarky smirk Preston shoots back a comment. "You're the one upset at not knowing stuff."

Reynard's voice quickly takes the conversation as he calls back into the cabin, his head hangs out the window like a dog, but the boyish voice quickly reminds Preston that the furred and tailed creature is no simple animal. "How did Master Duscle create such a spell? Clover your head hurt after working on one *télpréith*."

Clover ignores the question as she calls to her companion. "Reynard, perhaps you should take a seat, the magic is a bit loud in the ears and I do not want you hitting your head on the window."

"Oh." Reynard brings himself back to his seat, but the childish excitement does not leave the fox-boy, as evident with the position of his upright ears and eyes, still pinned to the window.

Preston cracks a slight smile to Reynard as he just stares out the window. Within moments the low chime of the magical barrier comes into ear shoot. And, within seconds of hearing it the faint screech of magic that chimes as the carriage passes through it fades.

Reynard flinches a little at the noise, but he does not complain as he begins to ask more about the spell. Having heard most of it before, Preston tunes the conversation out as he instead stares into the city moving past them.

The ride after this carries on rather smoothly, and with the icy silence between Clover and Preston at least broken, the man can sit in peace. Unlike *VéturVill*, the streets of *HefterÁll* have a fair amount of traffic, even with other carriages. Even still, the ride through the city only takes a little while longer as the castle's grounds come into view.

However, as the carriage comes closer to the bottom of the stairs to the castle a few guards as well as a fancy dressed *Dẃoff* await its stop. The pig-nosed man in the center of the two halberd wielding guards is dressed in a dark blue and gold trimmed robe that hangs just above the ground. The man's hair is short and slicked back, how Preston could not tell moving so quickly in the carriage, but as the sight of the *Dẃoff* is lost in the window Preston speaks up. "He looks fancy. Think he's for us?"

Clover has already begun to put her book to her satchel as she slowly shakes her head. "I would not see how. The Princess said she had not received any word from the *Jartál*." Her attention comes to the bag near Reynard as she speaks up. "Bring your bag Reynard, just in case we are here awhile."

The driver calls out as the carriage comes to a halt. "We have arrived, Miss. Vines."

Clover moves to the door as she quickly calls back to the driver, all the while moving into the courtyard.

Unlike the Capital, the courtyard to the castle is surrounded on all sides with the covered stone walkways, and although the area is incredibly open the structures bring an uneasy feeling to Preston the man cannot explain. The strange feeling aside, Preston waits for Reynard to move out of the carriage first before following after him. The sun has reached its afternoon high, but with the way time works here Preston is left unsure if it is truly still noon or not.

The group perhaps go two steps before the guards and robe wearing *Dẃoff* greet them. "I am sorry, but *Jartál* Dauth is not holding court. If you have any grievances, you may direct them to your local head of row."

Clover gives a little bow to the comment as she adjusts the strap on her satchel. "Oh no, we are not here for court. My name is Clover Vines, I am Master Nyota's assistant here to check on him."

The three *Dẃoffs* before Preston, Clover, and Reynard give a few glances to each other in silence. Their armor is a bit flashier than *VéturVill*, though after being around armor and swords for so long Preston merely smirks to the guards. His eyes instead to the spears they wield, which greatly go pass their heads, hardly a fitting weapon for the short, pig-nosed men. Even still, they wield it with a sense of duty, something that does prompt Preston to straighten up a bit. Reynard on the other simple yawns as Clover speaks up again. "Is something wrong?"

"No, no." The robe wearing man shakes his head with a smile as he continues. "We had just not assumed you would arrive so quickly; we had only sent a messenger *swóóp* a short while ago."

Clover's overall tone changes as her ears perk up. "Yes, what seems to be the problem? The Princess will be sending addition aid, but until then, I can assist. Where is Master Nyota?"

Reynard immediately stops his yawn as he too perks up, a bit of angst coming to the conversation and to Clover's sudden change in tone. Clover remains too focused to notice, though Preston moves a hand to the fox-boy as he passes a reassuring smile to the fox-boy.

The fancy *Dẃoff* rubs his hands together a little as he glances to the carriage. "Your banner is that of *VéturVill*. How could you have arrived so quickly?"

"We were at the castle already, the Princess had asked us to check on my Master, but while I am here, I wish to help." Clover glances to the guards as she nods. "It would be best to tell me."

"Hm..." Once more the *Dẃoff* fiddles with his hands before nodding. "Very well, but I hope you are aware, the *Jartál* has met with Master Nyota's assistant before. If you are lying, we will detain you."

Clover shrugs. "Very well."

Once more the slick haired *Dẃoff* speaks up as he takes a step towards the castle. "Do ask your driver to move and then follow me."

Clover turns back to the carriage, her eyes tactically avoiding Preston's now locked gaze. With a few steps she moves to the driver, however, her voice is not the first to be heard as the *Dẃoff* on the wooden seat speaks up with a faint laugh. "I suppose we will be here for the *déy*. I will send word to the castle when I find an inn." He rubs his back as he nods. "I believe removing myself from this seat would be a good idea."

Clover nods to the *Dẃoff* as she speaks up. "Thank you."

"Take care, Miss Vines."

As the satyress turns back to the group she gives a quick smile to Reynard and Preston. "It is a good thing most *VéturVill's* drivers know us." The light joke gets no reaction from Preston and Reynard just replies in a slightly confused smile, unsure of what is going on.

The lack of response does not take the peep from Clover's steps however, as she turns to follow the three *Dwoffs*. Preston squints to this, the confidence in Clover has returned, her shoulders now rise, and her head is on a swivel, her hands too tug to her satchel a bit anxiously. Though Preston says nothing as they follow the group into the castle.

Preston lags behind, but ultimately follows after the satyress, all the while looking around the castle for any signs of damage. His hand to Reynard's shoulder only parting for a second to adjust the sword on his waist.

Chapter 22

Bunker Down

The walk through the castle has been brisk with the guards leading them, however as they are led out of the cloister the group is stopped in silence. The garden area that is host to the bunker in which Clamor's statue sits has withered. The once blue-green grass has become nothing but dirt, the large once magnificent cherry tree that sits to the center of the area is now nothing but a dead spire now on display.

Noticing the stop, the fancy dressed *Dŵoff* speaks up. "Follow and stay to the path." The sense of urgency to his words draw a nod from the group.

Clover, Preston, and Reynard start after the others as they are led around the large tree's base. It only takes a few steps, and as they round it a new sight greets them. A few more guards stands in front of the closed bunker, but before anyone can truly survey the area they are pulled into a conversation.

"*Jartál* Dauth. This *Únoff* claims to be Mage Nyota's assistant. Do you know her?"

The fairly heavier set *Dŵoff* in the gold and silver trimmed robes turns to the voice as he gives a slight smile. However, the faintly gray bearded Santa like impersonator gives a low sigh as he speaks up. "Clover Vine. I had wondered when you may show." He turns his tired gaze to the *Dŵoff* in front of the new group as he continues. "Thank you Malfin, please return to your post. We cannot have any enter the castle until it is safe."

With a nod, Malfin and the two guards that escorted the group to the *Jartál* turn back and head into the castle. Without a moment's hesitation, Clover speaks up. "What has happened? Where is Master Nyota?"

The *Jartál* nods as he points to the bunker's door. "Your Master and a few of my guards are in the castle's sanctuary. He has been there for quite some time."

Clover starts forward but just as she does the *Jartál* speaks up again. "Watch your step! Be clear of the *mushreeñ*."

The words halt her trot as she looks to the dead ground around her, there are a few small orange mushroom bulbs that can be seen just breaking through the death around the courtyard. "The *mushreeñ*?"

"Yes, we have reason to believe that this is the work of Vón Dorñ, do not let the spores get on your hoof." Dauth turns his gaze to the *fróx* near Preston as he continues. "Both of you must watch your steps."

Clover moves back to Reynard and Preston, however before she can explain what her plan is a flash of light engulfs them and the group finds themselves next to Dauth. The quick sound of the teleportation spell forces every nervous guards' eyes to Clover's position, but as she speaks up the fear dies down. "If this is the work of Clamor why do you all stand here and not rush into help Master Nyota?"

The *Jartál* shakes his head as he speaks up. "Both I and your Master thought it best if someone stays up top." The *Dẃoff* raises his hand as he points firmly to the door. "I wish to uphold my responsibilities more than any, but the plan is to sabotage the entrance to the sanctuary and burn the garden."

"Sabotage? You would bury Master Nyota?" The shock to Clover's face quickly draws a reaction from the *Jartál* as he straightens his pose and firms his voice. "To halt Vón Dorñ's escape I would give my life. Last report we have received Master Duscle's spell is still active. This means the sanctuary still holds Vón Dorñ, if the spell holds the only way out is through the door, we will cave in the walls leading to it."

Clover points to the spots of orange growing around the garden as she speaks over the *Jartál*. "Look around, if this is truly Clamor's doing his power still spreads, no matter if the door is opened."

"Clover." the boyish voice quickly brings a halt to Clover's building display of power and control, though she does not turn to the source out of anger. Especially as she watches Reynard now tugging to his fur, his stance jittery at best. "Clover I want to go home."

Dauth's expression does not alter though he does glance to his guards before stepping in front of Clover with a whispered comment. "This no place for a child."

With a faint sigh Clover trots towards Reynard, coming to his level as she nods, though despite her confidence and charisma to the quickly unfolding situation, Reynard only grows more anxious. "Reynard if Master Nyota needs my help I will have to help."

The candid comment does little for Reynard as he pulls his fur a bit more. "I want to go home, Clover, please."

A faint bit of surprise comes to Clover's face, though Reynard has little experience with Clover's travels, this does mark the first time her words have had little effect over the normally submissive fox-boy.

Fiddling a little more to his pocket Preston catches the glances of the guards now turning to Reynard's display. Sighting this, Preston drops down, a hand coming to Reynard's shoulder as he nods. "Hey buddy, nothing's going on, look around, look, we have all these guards, and nothing's happened yet, let's just listen in, Nyota is just taking a bit longer to walk around down there, that's all."

"Yes." Clover glances back to the *Jartál* as she nods. "Master Nyota was not feeling well before, give me the key."

The words spark a response in Preston as the man speaks up. "What? Clover-..."

His comment is cut short as Clover's dominant tone spikes up. "I shall retrieve Master Nyota, that is all this issue is." She turns an eye to the *Jartál*. "There is no need to destroy the entrance, especially not while it is under a spell."

Dauth stands in silence as he continues to just stare down the woman before him. Though his lack of a response draws Clover's voice, this time, a bit softer. "Master Nyota and your guards could be hurt. Let me try."

"The path is riddled with *mushreeñ*, you will go *lóva* as the others did."

Though Reynard has tuned out the conversation, Preston has not, and at the comment he glances back to the mushrooms around them, tapping Reynard to step forward a little.

Clover however remains determined to get her way as she shakes her head. "I am Master Nyota's pupil, as such, in his absence I am acting Head Mage of Únoactroff until the Princess elects a new mage. You do not hold power over my request unless the Princess wills it. Now will you wait longer, or will you allow me to act?" Her hand still extends towards Dauth, her cold blue eyes still challenging the *Jartál's* gaze.

Finally, however, the *Dŵoff* gives in as he reaches into his robe and pulls the glowing stone out. "If you do not return before nightfall, we are carrying out Nyota's plan. He is your superior, alive or not."

Clover takes the key as she nods. "Good." Her trot starts up quick as she points to Preston and Reynard. "Stay here, I will be back in just a moment."

The fox-boy's mouth quivers as he watches the satyress move to open the door. Preston stands in silent disbelief to what he sees, all the while screaming in his head for Clover to stop. Yet, as the door opens and Clover takes her first hoof inside the man groans. He tosses the satchel around him to the ground, his hand dipping to his blade as he starts forward.

Preston does not dare look back to the fox-boy he just left as he hears *Jartál* Dauth's voice. "Guards, quickly close the door, we cannot have it open long."

Preston slides in, just behind Clover as the door seals behind him. Clover continues forward, despite the darkening path before her hooves, the only light leading her on from the low glow of the stone key in her hand. As the door closes completely Preston reaches out and grabs Clover's arm. The force he uses to stop her has her stumble back a little, With the entrance closed the only light in the room is from the key in Clover's hand. Hardly enough to see the path though enough to see her expression, which from the tightening muscles in Clover's arm must be somewhere between annoyed and angry or fearful and shocked. Perhaps the only emotions the woman seems to know in these last few months.

Within moments a ball of light blue magic sparks to the bunker as Clover tugs her arm from Preston's hand. "Do not tug me, what if I stepped on something?"

Preston's voice starts up in a rage as he shakes his head. "You were walking in the dark, Clover! What are you a fucking bat now?"

Clover pauses for a moment as she looks the man over. "Preston, you chose to come with me, I did not ask!" She brings her right hand up as she points to him. "If I put you down I shall; now be quiet, we do not know if Clamor is free."

Once more as Clover steps away Preston tugs to her arm. The action brings a groan from Clover as she again frees herself from his hold. Yet, despite her expression, her tone takes on a drastic change. "Preston... Nyota would do this for me, now leave or help."

Preston gives a shaky sigh as he nods. "Let me go first, I can kick the mushrooms out of the way at least." Without waiting for a response, Preston starts down the cave's narrow entrance, all the while ensuring he watches his footing. Despite the small buds outside of the bunker there are no signs of the mushrooms on the ground, however, a simple survey of the area would suggest that stone flooring would be too hard to grow through.

Clover's ball of light follows just behind the satyress as the two push on. Though a dense air clouds them as Preston frees his sword from his side. "You shouldn't have done that, I may understand how you act around this stuff but that doesn't make it any easier for Reynard."

"Preston we can discuss my lack of emotions later, right now we have to focus."

The confidence in Clover voice draws a slight chuckle from Preston, though he glances back to the woman behind him all the same. "Clover, if we end up not making it. I want you to know something."

The satyress does not take her eyes from the ground as she responds in a slight huff. "What, Preston?"

The man drags the comment on as he switches between intensively looking at the stone floor and his thoughts. His tone is kept down due to the echo off the walls but even still he pushes forward in his words. "Clover, I think you have a death wish, and I think you should get help."

Clover just nods to the comment as she responds. "I thank you for your concern. Now focus."

The man shakes his head with a little bit of a laugh as he speaks up. "Also, I've had to pee for like the last hour. Just want you to know that if I die, I'm going to be really pissed."

"Wonderful *fon*, Preston, and I know you deal with situations through laughter, but please?" Clover brings her head up from the ground as she moves the ball of light in front of Preston. The low chime is a bit annoying in the man's ear, but being able to see the path more clearly is a bit of a relief. However, the noise in his ears along with his racing mind do start to play tricks on the man's eyes as he watches for any movement in the dark.

After a few more minutes of the slow walk forward Preston finally spots something. "That split in the path is coming."

The man's voice brings Clover's eyes up as she taps Preston on the shoulder, her tap stops Preston's walk as the satyress takes the lead. "Yes the spell... what did Master Duscle say..." Clover taps to her mouth with her free hand as she looks over the glowing key in her hand. "The key unlocks the chamber... oh!" Clover turns back to the three paths before them as she smiles. "This is the other spell, we simply have to be sure of where we are going, we must walk as if we are supposed to be here, something a thief would not do."

"Um... like to what extent? Because I don't know where I'm going because I can't see, but I know I want to find Nyota so would this take me to him?"

The question flicks Clover's ear as she stutters for an answer. "W-well the spell was designed to stop intruders from reaching Clamor. So, we need to think about finding Clamor to find the chamber. Master Nyota surely would be there with Master Duscle."

"Gibberish." Preston shakes his head as he speaks up. "Try again, if the spell leads us to what we want than we need to think about Nyota, not Clamor."

Clover nods as she speaks up. "Yes, but the paths are all illusions, and all lead to one area, do you not remember what Master Duscle said before?"

"C-Clover, you have been asleep for a month. How do you know that you didn't dream this thing?"

"You do not trust me, Preston?" A smart-ass smile comes to Clover's face as she points to the paths. "This is a spell, the paths are not real, it was designed to mess with one's mind until they are lost. It is hardly a brisk walk down the path."

Preston nods as he shrugs. "I get that, but why would we think about Clamor if we are after Nyota, Clover?"

The comment again shuts the woman down. However, her silence is brought to an end as she extends her hand. "Together?"

With a sigh, Preston brings his hand to Clover's. He takes a deep breath as he readies himself. "I don't like this."

The satyress' trot starts up as she holds her eyes to the ground. "The rocks here are a little more broken, be careful where you walk, there could be something in the cracks."

The comment sparks an action in Preston as he breaks from Clover's hand and moves forward. "Let me go first then." As the man moves past the woman the path goes pitch black. For a quick second Preston's mind almost completely shuts at the sudden loss of sight, however as he focuses in on his breathing, he sparks his hands up in the one spell he has mastered. The greenish-blue ball of light that pops from the man's hands now floats just above him as he turns around. His heart drops as he sees nothing but an empty tunnel. With a swift one-eighty, he turns back the other way, still, nothing but an empty tunnel of rock meets his eyes. His heart races as the man's breathing begins to shudder. "C-Clover?"

"Clover?!"

No response comes to the man as he frantically runs back towards where the entrance of the cave should be. "W-what the Hell?! It was right here!" Preston snaps his head towards the other direction as he runs down the tunnel. The ball of light attempts to follow after the man but as his speed increases, he finds himself running into nothing but darkness. "Clover! Where are you?!"

The ball of chiming light slowly starts to come to the man's ears, but as paranoia begins to set in the chime of his magic begins to sound like voices. The fact that the annoying little ball of light is the only thing other than the rapid heartbeat in the man's chest that can be heard begins to almost instantly enrage the man further. Preston's face becomes hot and his hands begin to twitch as he runs his fingers through his hair. The idea of being lost in a spell and knowing that the entrance is going to be caved in draws a loud yell from the man as he slams his hand to the wall beside him. "Why! Why did I do this!?"

As his yell echoes through the cave a sharp pain runs through the man's hand. It is at this point he realizes that the force he hit the wall with has caused the hilt of his sword to dig into his hand, cutting the outer flesh of his hand just a little. Once more Preston calls out as he leans to the wall, all the while cradling his hand as a small amount of blood begins to seep out from the fresh wound. The throbbing in his hand is intense as he looks over the cut. "Damn it!" He looks over his sword as he trades it to his other hand.

However, the situation only gets worse as the blue-green ball of light he uses to stare at his cut begins to look almost orange on the blood.

The man quickly looks back to the wall to ensure he did not just slam his hand into a mushroom. But, as his eyes meet nothing but stone he calms down. The throbbing in his hand still runs through his body as he slowly begins to realize something. Preston takes a step back as he looks over the wall. "Wait a minute... how can a spell make me bleed?"

He moves back to the wall as he kicks at it, not hard enough to hurt him but hard enough to check the wall. He slowly moves to the right as he continues this action, sure enough, just a few feet away the rock feels different. Noticing this, Preston touches it. The warm feeling of the rock quickly brings Preston back to the left as he feels the cooler surface. Walking his hands across the rock he follows the cooler feeling. Strangely, he notices that the warming feeling comes back only a few feet in the other direction.

Knowing this Preston looks around him. "It's a spell, the hall is only so big... it teleports you... so how can it only be straight both ways?" As the man thinks the rocks over, he states to the wall in front of him. Slowly he reaches his hand to it. The warming feeling again meets his hand. Preston takes his hand from the wall as he looks around, however his thoughts only last a moment before he decides something crazy. Without a second thought he charges full speed at the wall, closing his eyes instinctively before hitting face first. Only, as the man stops, sure that he should have hit it he opens his eyes. Before him, is the three paths and the old hallway back to the entrance.

A feeling of relief washes over the man as he listens to the sound of the ball of light beside him. However, the moment is short lived as he notices Clover no longer around him.

Preston looks down the two side halls, knowing that he and Clover went into the center one together. For a moment, the thought of leaving graces his mind, but the idea is quickly suppressed as he takes his first step into the left tunnel. Like before, the path goes dark and the chime of the ball of light is lost. Although, unlike last time the man keeps his cool and pops the ball of light in front of him. Yet, this time the man is not alone in the cave.

Just a little down the path is the distinctive reflection of Preston's magic to armor. The sight of this prompts Preston forward. However, as he moves he notices something disturbing. There is more than one person in front of him. Horrified at the sight Preston stands in shock as he watches the hunched over *Dwoff* guard plunging his hands into the body of another guard on the ground.

The ball of light continues to chime beside Preston as he watches the cannibalistic act just a few feet away from him. The sounds of chewing following each sickening plunge back into the body. The slurping and sloping of the pig-man's mouth is what is most disturbing however, as the sounds of bones grinding to the *Dwoff's* teeth ring to Preston's ears he shutters.

Unfortunately, his lingering has not gone unnoticed as the guard's head now begins to raise to the light in the tunnel. Preston's heart pumps sporadically as he watches, almost in slow motion as the guard turns to face him. Blood coats the pig nose, and pink strips of meat hang from its mouth, the guard's chewing continuing as he stares towards him.

His dilated, black eyes are what Preston settles to however, at least until he notices the distinct orange colored buds sprouting on the *Dwoff's* head.

"*LAAHHHHH!!*"

The scream is almost deafening as the guard stands, a hobbled run now starting towards Preston. The man's eyes widen as he just stands there unable to move in fear, his mind comes back to him just in the nick of time as he presses himself to the wall, a fair slash of his sword as his reply.

If this were any duel Preston would surely have been cut down, his back opened by his opponent's weapon. Though the *Dwoff* yields nothing, save for the blood-stained nails on his hands, and because of this, Preston's spin maneuver seems to have worked flawlessly.

Sadly, though a wound has been stuck deep into the pig-man's neck, just above his armor, it does not fall. With a grunt, a squealing almost, it thrashes back around, Preston once more slashing to it. Though the curved blade merely slides off the armor as the *Dwoff* lunges. Within seconds Preston is tackled to the ground and now in a fist fight with the crazed *Dwoff*. Preston lets out his own scream as he holds the shorter man from his face, the *Dwoff* snapping his teeth as his arms flail wildly around Preston's head, just barely missing him and hitting the ground. The squeals let out are those of a pure nightmare, though what causes the most panic are the spores falling from the creature's head. Something Preston takes notice to as they begin to clump on his clothing, just below his neck.

Preston lets out one more yell as he attempts to push the manic guard from him. To his surprise, he is able to as a flash of green magic sends the *Dwoff* to his back on the ground just in front of Preston. Yet not for long as Preston can tell.

Luckily, he is the first to stand, as the *Dwoff* gets into a hunched position. Acting quickly, Preston's hands begin to glow as he balls his fist.

Once more, the deranged, yet determined guard charges, but this time Preston meets the *Dwoff* with a stiff right hand. A flash of fire popping to the *Dwoff*'s cheek as the smell of burnt flesh now fills the tunnel. Surprised that the spell has worked just as Preston wanted it to the man capitalizes on the downed *Dwoff*. His hands now coated in the magic as he brings his fist down, every punch landing with a small, fiery flash the, much to his delight.

No longer does fears hold, instead an unbridled rage fills Preston's entire being, each punch leading Preston further from a simple fight for survival. No, the rage is beyond such matters; an almost beast like yell bellows from Preston as he now mashes at the already dead *Dwoff* he has pinned to the ground. Every fist splatters blood to the man's clothing and every flash of fire highlights the carnage Preston lays out on the ground. A sea of red is all Preston can see, yet even this does not stop him as he renders the guard totally unrecognizable, the face now little more than a beaten in crater.

Yet, it all ends as a bolt of blue magic shoves Preston to the wall. The sudden jolt brings Preston to his senses as he sits to the stone, still shaking from the heat of magic that just struck him.

The attack or better yet attackers quickly come into view as a blue ball of light takes over the cave.

"That was not necessary, Clover!"

The familiar old voice is quickly followed by the sight of Nyota's bearded face coming into view. Clover follows behind him but her hands still glow with the blue hue of her magic. "Master, be careful."

"Bah! It is Preston." Nyota kneels beside the man as he removes his satchel. "Preston! Look at me."

The man follows the words as he sits quietly just catching his breath.

"Did you allow any of the spores into your body?"

Preston slowly shakes his head as his breathing comes under control. "N-no."

"Good, let me see your hand there."

Preston slowly brings his hand to Nyota as the old satyr pulls a bit of cloth from his bag. He begins to wrap it around Preston's wounded hand as he looks over where the bolt struck Preston's shirt. "Ah, just a jolt. You will be fine, my friend."

Realizing that it is in fact Preston covered in blood Clover's magic drops from her hands, she quickly rushes to Nytoa's side. "I-I thought you were another guard! How did you get here Preston? You disappeared?!"

Preston pushes himself from the ground with the help of Nytoa as he speaks up. "I-I figured out how to get out of the spell. The walls are fake in some spots and it will take you to the entrance."

Nyota gives a slight laugh as his raspy voice starts up. "Remarkable, when I had found Sagitta Duscle's spell no longer under his control I feared we were stuck here."

Preston glances over to the dead body still next to him as he feels himself getting sick, though he holds it down as he shakes, his hand dipping into his pocket as he falls back to the floor. Though he sparks his magic, the amulet does not respond, and Preston is left gazing to what he has done, no quick escape washing over him. Nyota rushes a hand to the man's back as he speaks up. "Preston, it is alright. No one blames you for defending yourself. Even I had-..."

"L-look at him..." Preston shakes his head. "Th-that's not defending myself."

Nyota gives a weak cough as he wags a finger to the man. "Keep your mind clear, Preston. We still have more to confront."

Preston shakes his head as he speaks up. "No, what? No! We need to get out of here, we need to leave."

Clover chimes in as she takes a step closer, however the blood on Preston's clothing forces her to take a step back as she tries to still sound convincing. "Preston, if Master Duscle is truly dead and Clamor has taken over his spell that means he is not yet powerful enough to leave. We must stop him before he regains his stre-..."

"No..." Nyota halts Clover's voice as the old mage speaks up. "Perhaps Preston is right. You have brought me the key Clover, give it to me. I shall confront Clamor alone. You two must return to the entrance. If I do not reach you within a reasonable amount of time to carry on with our plans. Clamor cannot be allowed to leave."

The satyress shakes her head as she speaks up. "Absolutely not Master, even if Clamor is weak, he is still dangerous. We can stop him, but you know only together."

"I may not be young, but I have my strength, Clover. Do not contest me, you and Preston shall return to the surface." Just as Nyota's words end the old satyr starts up in a coughing fit. Still, the old mage holds his posture as he waves Clover on. "Go!"

Clover remains stubborn, her posture unchanged as she speaks up. "You are sick, Master. Confronting Clamor alone is not something I will allow." Without another word Clover takes the key from her clothing and trots back towards where she and Nytoa came from.

The old mage glances back to Preston as he holds a hand to him. "If you are well enough to leave head back through the tunnel. If not, we shall return for you."

Preston shakes his head, his hand drawing from his pocket as he fumbles with the dormant amulet in his holds, though despite its lack of comfort, Preston nods. "I'm-I'm sticking it out till the end."

Nyota simply shakes his head as he adjusts his bag to his shoulder. "The both of you are fools!" With a sigh Nyota follows after Clover. "But, I suppose we all are." Without a word Nyota walks away.

Alone for a moment Preston struggles to stand, his eyes casting over the amulet as he slowly begins to draw some relief from its spell. Though what little it does is not enough to stop the shaking in Preston's body, especially as he moves to collect his sword. Despite this though, he trudged forward, a fool's road set out before him, yet one that he follows all the same. He drops the amulet to his pocket, though he does not remove his hand as he moves past the half devoured *Dwoff* on the ground.

Nyota has moved a considerable distance after Clover, and as Preston follows he begins to notice the faint purple glow at the end of the tunnel.

Within a few moments Preston, Nyota, and Clover stand at the threshold to Clamor's keep. The wall of magic makes it impossible for the three to see inside, a cloudy haze covering what lies beyond it. Though it is a bit reassuring, as it at least suggest some sort of containment.

As Preston stares to the magical barrier he speaks up one last time. "Are we sure this is the best idea?"

Nyota gives a sigh as he moves between where Clover and Preston stand. "Sagitta Duscle still lives, if not his spells would have collapsed." The bushy eyebrowed satyr continues to look between Preston and Clover as he trials on. "If Clamor has taken control of his mind it could mean he keeps these spells alive purely to allow him more time to regain his power. Even if Duscle lives, he will not survive for long without food and water. The hope I have is that we can stop Clamor before he is too powerful, with or without Duscle's aid." A light chuckle comes from the old satyr as he moves his bag from his shoulder and onto the ground. "Perhaps, with a little bit of luck, this is all a misunderstanding, and Sagitta Duscle is waiting just beyond this gate."

Preston just shakes his head to the comment as he takes a deep breath to steady his mind.

Clover holds the key just inches from the barrier as she speaks up, her tone is cold and straightforward. "Master?"

Nyota takes a deep breath as he closes his eyes for a moment. Yet, the second of preparation is quickly lost as the old stallion throws his hands to his sides, his fingers glowing with the bright hue of his magic. "Now Clover!"

Within seconds Clover brings the stone to the wall, the magical veil is dropped and she takes her hands up in her own defenses. Preston clenches hard to the sword as he glares into the room revealing itself to him. Yet, stunningly what is revealed is a brightly lit room, almost immediately all eyes shoot to the statue still sitting in the middle. The *Helió* stones designed to keep the beast's magic at bay still glowing as clear as the day Preston and Clover saw them. However, not everything in the room is the same as a quick scan reveals. The outer edges of the room are littered with mushroom spores, and what looks like a small lab has been created in the chamber.

"There!"

Nyota's comment takes the focus as he points to the corner directly across from the entrance. It takes a moment for Clover and Preston to recognize the dust covered robes, but as they do the full shape of Sagitta Duscle greets their eyes.

Nyota quickly moves into the room, his eyes still focused on the statute in the center. His voice starts up as a whisper as he moves closer to where the old mage slumps against the wall. "Sagitta Duscle? My friend, do you hear me?"

Clover and Preston advance, their own attention split between the fungus around the room, Clamor's statue, and Nyota's movements. "Master, this could be a trick."

Nyota's hands slowly begin to lose their glow as he nears Duscle. "My friend, do you hear me?"

Clover anxiously stares to her master's movements both her and Preston now change their sights to the old stallion as they near Nyota.

"Master Duscle, it is Svle Nyota."

A twitch in Duscle's face sparks Nyota to rush his hands to the downed *Únoff.* "My friend! Are you-..."

"YOU SHALL NOT TRICK ME!" The slumped over satyr lunges forward as a thunderous bolt of magic is sent forth. In a flash of light Nyota is sent across the room, landing hard to the rock flooring. Duscle's burst of energy is quickly lost as he stares horrified to the other two people in the room. His eyes lock with Clover's as he slumps back to the wall. "No, no, no, I-I thought..." The mage's hair is wild, and his beard is unmanaged, but the wide eyes he stares at Clover speak volumes as the older *Ünoff* begins to give a tired weep.

Preston stands in shock, unmoving, and unsure of what just happened.

Words however, are not lost to Clover as she turns to where Nyota was sent across the room "M-Master?" Her trot comes to her slowly, though in panic she rushes to her fallen elder, her emotions getting the best of her as she notices the burn into his cloak. "Master! Master Nyota?!"

Duscle now holds his hands over his eyes as he buries his face to the ground, pained weeps slowly drawing Preston from his bewilderment.

He merely shakes, his mind screaming for some sort of reprieve, perhaps that at any moment he will awake, perhaps that somehow Nyota will stand from his injury, perhaps that Clover, always the planner has something for this. Yet, as he moves to Clover's side he realizes just how impossible that is.

A deep gash has been carved into Nyota, the old mage slumps against the wall, his eyes open, his head hanging to one side. A look of total stupefaction forever on display. His dead gaze says it all, for he will never know what happened, the magic most likely killed him instantly, his fragile frame somewhat jagged in its posture.

Yet, as Person slowly brings himself to move towards Clover, this is not what is most gut turning. No, it is not the body or even the expression of confusion that pulls to Preston's heart. Instead, what plunges a madness in his mind is the suddenness, the lack of words, the lack of a final goodbye. Like a car speeding down the road, there is no moment of acceptance, there was no indication that his last step, his last words were forevermore his final. This, this alone is what shatters Preston as he stands near where Clover has knelt.

It is a rare sight to see Clover upset, yet she is, her hand placed to the old stallion's as she weeps, quietly. There is no scream, no begging or pleading, just the acceptance of reality.

Though as Clover lingers in the sadness that was so quickly thrust to her, she does attempt to stir the old man. However, after a few attempts it becomes clear, the once great Svle Nyota, mage to the Capital, is dead.

Despite Clover's tear-filled eyes she does not bellow, nor does she call out in anger toward Duscle. Instead, she sits in silence, staring to Nyota. Sadly, the moment of stillness is lost as both Clover and Preston are taken from their positions. The sudden feeling of weightlessness forces Preston to drop his sword as both Clover and Preston find themselves hovering above the ground where Nyota still lays. The unmistakable sound of magic chiming in their ears however nag at their heart strings as their puppet master reveals himself.

The stone statue is gone, and standing in its place is the one thing neither Preston nor Clover are prepared for.

The devilish, slender, claw handed, goat horned, lion eyed, chestnut red furred monstrosity, stands just smirking to the two puppets he now controls. Clamor's lips move slowly as he turns his gaze to where Nyota lays. "You have my sincerest apologies."

The goat legged creature shifts his eyes to where Duscle still sits, now with his mouth gasped to the beast before him. Clamor's tail swings behind his legs as he nods. "I did ask. But..." Clamor swings his head back to Clover and Preston as he cocks his neck. "The silly mage insisted on keeping his wits. I knew he would slip eventually. Look there Duscle, you may become the new Capital mage! Ha-ha!"

"You will not leave this place alive, Clamor!"

The fragile words of Duscle as the *Únoff* stands to his hooves barely make it through the glow of magic as he looks to ready himself for battle.

Clamor however simply nods as he speaks up. "Alive? Can you kill what was never truly born, Duscle?"

Duscle's eyes lock to Clamor as the *Únoff* barks back, this time his own words taking height. "You shall not talk your way through me beast!"

Clamor's smirk turns into a simple frown as one of his uneven arms raised to the *Únoff*. "I never intended to." With just a simple flick of Clamor's wrist Duscle's body is encased in a bright orange light. Yet, no screams are heard and as the flash ends nothing but a skeleton pouring forth, as it falls to the floor.

Clover merely closes her eyes to the sight, though Preston drinks it in, as he stares to the remains now crashing to the floor.

Clamor takes a deep breath turns a smile back to where Clover and Preston still hover in his magic. The smile in Clamor's goat shaped face flexes a little as his lion eyes widen. "Why, it feels fantastic to smile again. No, no, really. You have no idea how long I have been stuck in one pose. You know…" His clawed hands come to his neck as he begins to shift his head a little. "… I do believe my neck is a little stiff… one moment." A sickening sound comes from the beast as Clamor snaps his own neck, the slender figure of his body falls limp as Clover and Preston are dropped from his spell. Both stare speechless to what they just witnessed, yet, Clover wastes no time as she pushed Preston's shoulder. "Run!"

With another small jolt to Preston's shoulder the two start up in a mad gallop toward the entrance of the chamber. However, as both already knew, their ordeal was not over as indeed, Clamor poofs before them. The orange of his magic sparkles a little as his neck still hangs to one side, forcing the demented creature to shift his back a little to look Clover and Preston in the eyes. "Tell me, do your necks hurt as well?"

Without hesitation Clover sends a flash of magic toward Clamor; a wicked laugh starts up as bolt after bolt of magic make the creature stumble backwards, yet he never falls. Preston, turns his eyes back to the sword he dropped as he dashes over to it. Clover continuing her fruitless onslaught as Clamor's laughter echoes around the chamber.

The sword now in hand, Preston clutches it, his bandaged hand pressed against the hilt as he charges for Clamor. Clover's spells just narrowly miss the blond-haired man as he plunges the sword into Clamor's stomach. A pained yell escaping the beast as his laughter quickly fades, a swift swipe of his claw however follows as Preston is thrown back into the room, just behind Clover.

"Presto-..AH!"

Clover's words are stopped mid-breath as Clamor's clawed hand clenches to the young satyress' neck. The same sickening sound of bones popping ring through the chamber as Clamor's neck straightens out. The mad orange eyes of Clamor lock to Clover as he speaks up. "*Shhhh*, I wanted to talk. Have we not had enough death?"

Another laugh comes from Clamor as he drops the woman to her knees, however, unlike his last fit of laughter this one really seems to get the beast going as he bends down in a fit of coughing, all the while as he pulls the sword from his body. The wound quickly heals before Clover's eyes as Clamor brings his bloody right hand to his eyes to wipe away a tear. "Ah, truly laughter is the best medicine." The smile on Clamor's face stops as his eyes bulge a little from his face. "Wouldn't you agree?"

Clover, despite her heavy breath locks eyes with the beast before her as she speaks up. "Never."

Clamor's smile fades as his mouth stays open in a half smirked fashion. He slowly brings himself to his hands and knees, his head still pinned to Clover's gaze. Once more, his body contorts to fit his wishes as his goat like legs bend in ways never thought possible. "Ask, ask a question, please. Ask me anything you want. Ask for anything you want." Clamor's smile returns as he nods his head happily. "Go on. No really, DO IT!"

Clover turns her head as she speaks up. "Do you know where Preston is?"

"Well actually..."

Before Clamor's sentence can be completed Preston has gone through with his silent plan. The sword Clamor pulled from his body has once more pierced him, however this time Clamor's head has been cleared from his body. For a split-second Preston is surprised he was able to cut through Clamor's neck so quickly, but the thoughts are dashed as he pulls Clover to her hooves.

Just as Clover and Preston make it just a few feet out of the chamber, they find themselves bound. Seemingly out of nowhere a bright orange rope has wrapped itself around them and now pulls them back to where Clamor now stands. Their mouths are gagged by the ropes and their hands and legs encased as if the rope itself were a snake constricting to its prey.

The laughter from the beast seems almost doubled as Clamor turns around, revealing something both Clover and Preston now stare in utter silence to.

Two small heads now adorn the devilish body, both laughing just slightly out of sync. Yet, just as fast as they appeared the two heads slowly melt into one. Clamor once more stopping his manic cackle as he speaks. "Now, please? I have been wanting for a monologue for so long." The beast sighs as he nods. "There is only so much fun you can have alone." A faint laugh comes from Clamor as he nods. "But I understand now, hearing yourself talk really does wonders for your health, and-and telling someone what you want to do truly brings motivation." The words ends with a sigh as Clamor's smile slowly fades. "... I cannot remember what I wanted to say. Perhaps I left it on the ground somewhere. Ha ha ha! *Shhh, shhh*! No matter, no matter!"

Another deep breath comes from Clamor as he points to Clover and Preston. He slowly comes to where they are bound on the ground as he continues. "You see." Clamor wiggles his right claw a little as he continues to repeat himself. "You see... well, you see.... um... hold on." The other clawed hand takes hold of the shaking claw as he seemingly forces it down to his side. "I need messengers." Clamor snaps his fingers as the ropes quickly pull Clover and Preston apart, the muffled words of the two are hushed further as Clamor lays down on the ground beside him. His joy filled voice filling their ears, the stench of animal filling their noses. "I cannot just kill everyone around me. No, no, no, that would make me evil!" He quickly looks between the two people beside him as he nods. "Nyota was a tragedy! And look at how we have progressed, we hardly mourn it! But, but, but... my point is this. If I destroy everything around me, I am left with nothing." Clamor's smile fades as he nods. "I was created to protect. Killing was never evil, it-it was necessary. Yet, what fun would there be in making sense? And of course, this makes sense, a lovely chat of friends." He glances between Clover and Preston as he nods however, as no response comes, he trails on. "I am not evil, I merely wish to enjoy what I have, I wish to protect what is mine. And, of course, what is mine is me. Not justifying what happened earlier, Duscle had to go... but surely, you both wish to stay alive, yes?"

Clamor moves to his feet again as he folds his hands behind his back. "I mean, you both attacked me, I am protecting myself, as I intended to protect everyone. As I have always done." Clamor nods to Preston as he continues. "When a tornado devastates a town, no one runs into the next storm swinging a sword." Clamor's face turns cold as he turns to Clover. "I am not wicked, I am willing, I am not black-hearted, I am whole-hearted. I merely have a different perspective." He nods, his goat head turning to the ceiling as he stares to it. "Pounder this? If someone can see all? Understand all, and know all, is it not their fault when catastrophe lands in cluttered streets? If they do nothing, what then?"

Clamor straightens his posture as he brings one clawed hand beside him, as he stands in a proper posture, his head to the ceiling and his eyes closed. "Head Mage Nyota killed, Master Duscle dead, guards slaughtered and *Vón Dorñ* escaped... yet, the two of you come out unharmed. Is it mercy? Does not my action warrant praise? After all, what favor have you forged to survive such a calamity. Clamor for reason, suffer from guilt, though never once forget it." A smile graces Clamor's face as he looks to where Clover and Preston still lay bound to the ground. "Tell your Princess, say that disaster has a name, spin what story she wishes to share, though do not forget." He takes a breath. "Now, if you excuse me, an important event is coming, and I must ready it. I must lay the sod to which my kingdom will be placed. Ta, my friends."

Without another word Clamor's figure vanishes, the ropes that bound Preston and Clover falls limp and both of them sit up a little as they stare in silence to the other. However, as the silence of the cave continues both Preston and Clover dart to each other in an embrace. Preston's whole body trembles a little as he runs his hands through the dirt filled hair of the woman beside him. Clover's own hands clench into Preston's back as the always strong willed *Únoff* finally cracks. "N-Nyota..."

The whimper in Clover's voice almost sparks a fit of tears in Preston as he tightened his hold to the woman, all the while as he pulls her closer. "I know... I know..."

Clover's hands move from the man's back as she pushes to his stomach. "W-we cannot tell anyone about Clamor."

The words take Preston by surprise as the man shakes his head. "W-what are you saying?"

Clover's blue eyes shimmer from the light pouring out of Clamor's old chamber and a scrape has found its way to her face, both of which halt Preston's next questions as she continues. "There would be panic, that... that cannot happen. Only Princess Sóltina can know. M-Master Nyota died vanquishing Clamor, not by the hands of Sagitta Duscle."

Preston loosens his hold to the woman as he blinks to her words. "B-but that's a lie? What-what good does a lie do? What good does that do when he destroys a city, Clover?!"

Clover's lips quiver as she turns her eyes to the ground. "His goal is Sóltina, if he wishes a different message, there will be nothing left outside."

Preston shakes his head as he speaks up. "What if we're wrong?"

The satyress gives a little sniffle as she nods. "If we are wrong, then at least we hold off panic for a moment more." Clover's words go soft as she turns her eyes back to Preston. "W-will you not stand by me in this?"

The face of sorrow forces a lump in Preston's throat, but he does not turn away as he merely thinks.

CPSIA information can be obtained
at www.ICGtesting.com
Printed in the USA
BVHW030013270620
582308BV00001BA/3